ANTHONY TROLLOPE

Three Great Novels

ANTHONY TROLLOPE

Three Great Novels

The Warden

Barchester Towers

An Eye for an Eye

CARROLL & GRAF INC.
New York

This edition first published in Great Britain in 1994,
First Carroll & Graf edition 1994

Carroll & Graf Publishers, Inc.
260 Fifth Avenue
New York, NY 10001

A copy of the Cataloguing in Publication
Data is available from the Library of Congress.

Printed and bound by Firmin-Didot (France),
Group Herissey. No d'impression : 27423.

CONTENTS

INTRODUCTION

Anthony Trollope was a Londoner, born in 1815 (Waterloo year), the son of an unsuccessful barrister who became an equally unsuccessful farmer. Anthony's schooldays were by his own admission unhappy, and frequent changes of school as funds straitened cannot have helped. In 1834 his father's bankruptcy and exile to Belgium ended all prospect of a University education. His resourceful mother (with whom his dealings remained relatively cool) supported the younger members of the family by means of her pen, producing a brilliantly splenetic travel-book, *Domestic Manners of the Americans*, and, in quick succession, a series of combative, controversial novels. Anthony was turned loose to earn his living. After a brief spell as a teacher he entered the permanent Civil Service as a Post Office clerk at a salary of one hundred pounds a year. For a man whose later life was marked by conscientiousness and efficiency in everything he did, the beginnings of Trollope's official career were inauspicious. He quarrelled with his superior, Colonel Maberly, and departmental tradition maintains that he was once minuted as a 'very bad clerk'. It was only when he was posted to Ireland (to get him out of the way?) in 1841 that his stock began to rise. He married, started a family, moved to a large house in Essex, rose steadily in the Post Office and became its favourite ambassador on foreign Postal missions. Meanwhile literary ambitions began to surface, and he published two wholly creditable – if not particularly successful – novels with an Irish setting, *The Macdermots of Ballycloran* (1847) and *The Kellys and the O'Kellys* (1848). Only after the failure of an historical novel called *La Vendée* (1850) and a five-act play in blank verse entitled *The Noble Jilt* (no one would stage it!)

did he settle to the manner and material for which he is best known.

The Warden (1855) and *Barchester Towers* (1857), reprinted here, are the first two novels in a series of six set in Trollope's imaginary 'forty-first county' of Barsetshire – the others are *Dr Thorne* (1858), *Framley Parsonage* (1860), *The Small House at Allington* (1864) and *The Last Chronicle of Barset* (1867) (Trollope's own favourite among all his novels). In the early 1850s Trollope had temporarily left Ireland to conduct a professional survey of south-western England (the postal rounds needed rearranging in the wake of the introduction of the Penny Postal service). In the course of this job he visited Salisbury, and (as he tells us in his *Autobiography*) it was 'whilst wandering there on a midsummer evening round the purlieus of the cathedral' that he conceived *The Warden*. Both *The Warden* and its sequel, *Barchester Towers*, show how comfortably upholstered Anglican sinecures – the products of centuries of tasteful inertia – are subject to the burning-glass of 'New Men and New Measures'. In *The Warden* a radical local politician means to do away with the Wardenship of Hiram's Hospital – a nice little moneyspinner for a harmless old clergyman addicted to early Church Music. In *Barchester Towers* a whole tribe of brisk Evangelicals – dapper Bishop Proudie, overweening Mrs Proudie and time-serving Mr Slope – try to force-feed the 'High and Dry' clergy of Barchester with a diet of grandiloquent humility, judgmental sermons and 'Bishop's Barchester Young Men's Sabbath Evening Lectures'. Trollope handles both crises with exemplary (and customary) fairmindedness, neither sentimentalising the conservatives nor unfairly stigmatising the apostles of progress. Though he admits his own High Church sympathies, he assures us that the pushy Low Church chaplain Mr Slope is 'not in all things a bad man', that 'he believed in the religion which he taught.' The Bishop and his wife (perhaps his best-known comic creations) tug even more firmly at his heartstrings: he follows them through three subsequent novels and to the far end of their lives, admitting after he finally killed Mrs Proudie off in *The Last Chronicle*' that he spent much time 'in company with her ghost'.

It was while engaged in the writing of *Barchester Towers* that Trollope evolved the celebrated (and to some tastes distressingly mechanical) methods of composition that were to serve him until the end of his literary career, and which resulted in a 'pile' of sixty-five books (forty-seven of them novels) by the time of his death in 1882. He wrote at a constant rate of two hundred and fifty words every quarter of an hour. He paid a faithful Irish groom to wake him at five-thirty, put in a three-hour stint before going on to his day's labours at the Post Office, and recorded the progress of each book faithfully in a ledger, so that his conscience might be suitably pricked by any daily shortfall. He became adept at writing anywhere: on buses, trains, even in the cabins of ocean liners. He plumed himself on keeping deadlines, and confessed that there was for him 'no human bliss equal to twelve hours of work with only six hours in which to do it.' And after all this grind Trollope left behind him not an array of prolix potboilers, but, in the words of Gordon Ray, 'more novels of lasting value than any other writer in English.' Three of the most representative of these novels are combined in the present volume: to *The Warden* and *Barchester Towers* is added *An Eye for an Eye*, which Trollope wrote in 1870, but kept in a drawer until he cleared a space for it in his busy publishing schedule in 1879. He need not have been so modest. *An Eye for an Eye* is a story of towering maternal passion on the steepling Atlantic cliffs of County Clare: evidence that Trollope was not averse to exploring the byways of Victorian sexual irregularity, nor to a whiff of sensation in the Wilkie Collins style, and that what Henry James famously called his 'complete appreciation of the usual' included an interest in the most extraordinary states of mind.

Julian Thompson
Brackley, 1994

BOOK 1

The Warden

CHAPTER I

Hiram's Hospital

THE Rev. Septimus Harding was, a few years since, a beneficed clergyman residing in the cathedral town of —; let us call it Barchester. Were we to name Wells or Salisbury, Exeter, Hereford, or Gloucester, it might be presumed that something personal was intended; and as this tale will refer mainly to the cathedral dignitaries of the town in question, we are anxious that no personality may be suspected. Let us presume that Barchester is a quiet town in the west of England, more remarkable for the beauty of its cathedral and the antiquity of its monuments, than for any commercial prosperity; that the west end of Barchester is the cathedral close, and that the aristocracy of Barchester are the bishop, dean, and canons,[1] with their respective wives and daughters.

Early in life Mr Harding found himself located at Barchester. A fine voice and a taste for sacred music had decided the position in which he was to exercise his calling, and for many years he performed the easy but not highly paid duties of a minor canon. At the age of forty a small living in the close vicinity of the town increased both his work and his income, and at the age of fifty he became precentor of the cathedral.[2]

Mr Harding had married early in life, and was the father of two daughters. The eldest, Susan, was born soon after his marriage; the other, Eleanor, not till ten years later. At the time at which we introduce him to our readers he was living as precentor at Barchester with his youngest daughter, then twenty-four years of age; having been many years a widower, and having married his eldest daughter to a son of the bishop, a very short time before his installation to the office of precentor.

Scandal at Barchester affirmed that had it not been for the beauty of his daughter, Mr Harding would have remained a minor canon; but here probably Scandal lied, as she so often does: for even as a minor canon no one had been more popular among his reverend brethren in the close than Mr Harding; and Scandal, before she had reprobated Mr Harding for being made precentor by his friend the bishop, had loudly blamed the bishop for having so long omitted to do something for his friend Mr Harding. Be this as it may, Susan Harding, some twelve years since, had married the Rev. Dr Theophilus Grantly, son of the bishop, Archdeacon of Barchester, and rector of Plumstead Episcopi, and her father became, a few months later, precentor of Barchester Cathedral, that office being, as is not usual, in the bishop's gift.[3]

Now there are peculiar circumstances connected with the precentorship which must be explained. In the year 1434 there died at Barchester one John Hiram, who had made money in the town as a wool-stapler, and in his will he left the house in which he died and certain meadows and closes near the town, still called Hiram's Butts, and Hiram's Patch, for the support of twelve superannuated wool-carders,[4] all of whom should have been born and bred and spent their days in Barchester; he also appointed that an almshouse should be built for their abode, with a fitting residence for a warden, which warden was also to receive a certain sum annually out of the rents of the said butts and patches. He, moreover, willed, having had a soul alive to harmony, that the precentor of the cathedral should have the option of being also warden of the almshouses, if the bishop in each case approved.

From that day to this the charity had gone on and prospered – at least, the charity had gone on, and the estates had prospered. Wool-carding in Barchester there was no longer any; so the bishop, dean, and warden, who took it in turn to put in the old men, generally appointed some hangers-on of their own; worn-out gardeners, decrepit grave-diggers, or octogenarian sextons, who thankfully received a comfortable lodging and one shilling and fourpence a day, such being the stipend to which, under the will of John Hiram, they were declared to be entitled. Formerly, indeed – that is, till within some fifty years of the present time – they received but sixpence a day, and their breakfast and dinner was found them at a common table by the warden, such an arrangement being in stricter conformity with the absolute wording of old Hiram's will: but this was thought to be inconvenient, and to suit the tastes of neither warden nor bedesmen,[5] and the daily one shilling and fourpence was substituted with the

common consent of all parties, including the Bishop and the
Corporation of Barchester.

Such was the condition of Hiram's twelve old men when Mr
Harding was appointed warden; but if they may be considered as
well-to-do in the world according to their condition, the happy
warden was much more so. The patches and butts which, in John
Hiram's time, produced hay or fed cows, were now covered with
rows of houses; the value of the property had gradually increased
from year to year, and century to century, and was now presumed
by those who knew anything about it, to bring in a very nice
income; and by some who knew nothing about it, to have increased to an almost fabulous extent.

The property was farmed by a gentleman in Barchester, who
also acted as the bishop's steward – a man whose father and
grandfather had been stewards to the bishops of Barchester, and
farmers of John Hiram's estate. The Chadwicks had earned a good
name in Barchester; they had lived respected by bishops, deans,
canons, and precentors; they had been buried in the precincts of
the cathedral; they had never been known as griping, hard men,
but had always lived comfortably, maintained a good house, and
held a high position in Barchester society. The present Mr Chadwick was a worthy scion of a worthy stock, and the tenants living
on the butts and patches, as well as those on the wide episcopal
domains of the see,[6] were well pleased to have to do with so worthy
and liberal a steward.

For many, many years – records hardly tell how many, probably
from the time when Hiram's wishes had been first fully carried out
– the proceeds of the estate had been paid by the steward or farmer
to the warden, and by him divided among the bedesmen; after
which division he paid himself such sums as became his due.
Times had been when the poor warden got nothing but his bare
house, for the patches had been subject to floods, and the land of
Barchester butts was said to be unproductive; and in these hard
times, the warden was hardly able to make out the daily dole for
his twelve dependants. But by degrees things mended; the patches
were drained, and cottages began to rise upon the butts, and the
wardens, with fairness enough, repaid themselves for the evil days
gone by. In bad times the poor men had had their due, and

therefore in good times they could expect no more. In this manner the income of the warden had increased; the picturesque house attached to the hospital had been enlarged and adorned, and the office had become one of the most coveted of the snug clerical sinecures attached to our church. It was now wholly in the bishop's gift, and though the dean and chapter, in former days, made a stand on the subject, they had thought it more conducive to their honour to have a rich precentor appointed by the bishop, than a poor one appointed by themselves. The stipend of the precentor of Barchester was eighty pounds a year. The income arising from the wardenship of the hospital was eight hundred, besides the value of the house.

Murmurs, very slight murmurs, had been heard in Barchester – few indeed, and far between – that the proceeds of John Hiram's property had not been fairly divided: but they can hardly be said to have been of such a nature as to have caused uneasiness to anyone: still the thing had been whispered, and Mr Harding had heard it. Such was his character in Barchester, so universal was his popularity, that the very fact of his appointment would have quieted louder whispers than those which had been heard; but Mr Harding was an open-handed, just-minded man, and feeling that there might be truth in what had been said, he had, on his instalment, declared his intention of adding twopence a day to each man's pittance, making a sum of sixty-two pounds eleven shillings and fourpence,[7] which he was to pay out of his own pocket. In doing so, however, he distinctly and repeatedly observed to the men, that though he promised for himself, he could not promise for his successors, and that the extra twopence could only be looked on as a gift from himself, and not from the trust. The bedesmen, however, were most of them older than Mr Harding, and were quite satisfied with the security on which their extra income was based.

This munificence on the part of Mr Harding had not been unopposed. Mr Chadwick had mildly but seriously dissuaded him from it; and his strong-minded son-in-law, the archdeacon, the man of whom alone Mr Harding stood in awe, had urgently, nay, vehemently, opposed so impolitic a concession: but the warden had made known his intention to the hospital before the archdeacon had been able to interfere, and the deed was done.

Hiram's Hospital, as the retreat is called, is a picturesque build-ing enough, and shows the correct taste with which the ecclesiast-ical architects of those days were imbued. It stands on the banks of the little river which flows nearly round the cathedral close, being on the side furthest from the town. The London road crosses the river by a pretty one-arched bridge, and, looking from this bridge, the stranger will see the windows of the old men's rooms, each pair of windows separated by a small buttress. A broad gravel walk runs between the building and the river, which is always trim and cared for; and at the end of the walk, under the parapet of the approach to the bridge, is a large and well-worn seat, on which, in mild weather, three or four of Hiram's bedesmen are sure to be seen seated. Beyond this row of buttresses, and further from the bridge, and also further from the water which here suddenly bends, are the pretty oriel windows of Mr Harding's house, and his well-mown lawn. The entrance to the hospital is from the London road, and is made through a ponderous gateway under a heavy stone arch, unnecessary, one would suppose, at any time, for the protection of twelve old men, but greatly con-ducive to the good appearance of Hiram's charity. On passing through this portal, never closed to anyone from six a.m. till ten p.m., and never open afterwards, except on application to a huge, intricately hung, medieval bell, the handle of which no uninitiated intruder can possibly find, the six doors of the old men's abodes are seen, and beyond them is a slight iron screen, through which the more happy portion of the Barchester *élite* pass into the Elysium of Mr Harding's dwelling.[8]

Mr Harding is a small man, now verging on sixty years, but bearing few of the signs of age; his hair is rather grizzled, though not grey, his eye is very mild, but clear and bright, though the double glasses which are held swinging from his hand, unless when fixed upon his nose, show that time has told upon his sight: his hands are delicately white, and both hands and feet are small; he always wears a black frock-coat, black knee-breeches, and black gaiters, and somewhat scandalizes some of his more hyper-clerical brethren by a black neck-handkerchief.[9]

Mr Harding's warmest admirers cannot say that he was ever an

industrious man; the circumstances of his life have not called on
him to be so; and yet he can hardly be called an idler. Since his
appointment to his precentorship, he has published, with all possible additions of vellum, typography, and gilding, a collection of
our ancient church music, with some correct dissertations on
Purcell, Crotch, and Nares.[10] He has greatly improved the choir of
Barchester, which, under his dominion, now rivals that of any
cathedral in England. He has taken something more than his fair
share in the cathedral services, and has played the violoncello
daily to such audiences as he could collect, or, *faute de mieux*,[11] to
no audience at all.

We must mention one other peculiarity of Mr Harding. As we
have before stated, he has an income of eight hundred a year, and
has no family but his one daughter; and yet he is never quite at
ease in money matters. The vellum and gilding of *Harding's Church
Music* cost more than anyone knows, except the author, the
publisher, and the Rev. Theophilus Grantly, who allows none of
his father-in-law's extravagances to escape him. Then he is
generous to his daughter, for whose service he keeps a small
carriage and pair of ponies. He is, indeed, generous to all, but
especially to the twelve old men who are in a peculiar manner
under his care. No doubt with such an income Mr Harding should
be above the world, as the saying is; but at any rate, he is not above
Archdeacon Theophilus Grantly, for he is always more or less in
debt to his son-in-law, who has, to a certain extent, assumed the
arrangement of the precentor's pecuniary affairs.

CHAPTER 2

The Barchester Reformer

MR HARDING has been now precentor of Barchester for ten years; and, alas, the murmurs respecting the proceeds of Hiram's estate are again becoming audible. It is not that anyone begrudges to Mr Harding the income which he enjoys, and the comfortable place which so well becomes him; but such matters have begun to be talked of in various parts of England. Eager pushing politicians have asserted in the House of Commons, with very telling indignation, that the grasping priests of the Church of England are gorged with the wealth which the charity of former times has left for the solace of the aged, or the education of the young. The well-known case of the Hospital of St Cross[1] has even come before the law courts of the country, and the struggles of Mr Whiston,[2] at Rochester, have met with sympathy and support. Men are beginning to say that these things must be looked into.

Mr Harding, whose conscience in the matter is clear, and who has never felt that he had received a pound from Hiram's will to which he was not entitled, has naturally taken the part of the Church in talking over these matters with his friend, the bishop, and his son-in-law, the archdeacon. The archdeacon, indeed, Dr Grantly, has been somewhat loud in the matter: he is a personal friend of the dignitaries of the Rochester Chapter, and has written letters in the public press on the subject of that turbulent Dr Whiston, which, his admirers think, must well nigh set the question at rest. It is also known at Oxford that he is the author of the pamphlet signed 'Sacerdos'[3] on the subject of the Earl of Guildford and St Cross, in which it is so clearly argued that the manners of the present times do not admit of a literal adhesion to the very words of the founder's will, but that the interests of the church for which the founder was so deeply concerned are best consulted in enabling its bishops to reward those shining lights whose services have been most signally serviceable to Christianity. In answer to this, it is asserted that Henry de Blois, founder of St Cross, was not

greatly interested in the welfare of the reformed church, and that
the masters of St Cross, for many years past, cannot be called
shining lights in the service of Christianity; it is, however, stoutly
maintained, and no doubt felt, by all the archdeacon's friends, that
his logic is conclusive and has not, in fact, been answered.

With such a tower of strength to back both his arguments and
his conscience, it may be imagined that Mr Harding has never felt
any compunction as to receiving his quarterly sum of two
hundred pounds. Indeed, the subject has never presented itself to
his mind in that shape. He has talked not infrequently, and heard
very much about the wills of old founders and the incomes arising
from their estates, during the last year or two; he did even, at one
moment, feel a doubt (since expelled by his son-in-law's logic) as
to whether Lord Guildford was clearly entitled to receive so enormous an income as he does from the revenues of St Cross, but that
he himself was overpaid with his modest eight hundred pounds
– he who, out of that, voluntarily gave up sixty-two pounds eleven
shillings and fourpence a year to his twelve old neighbours; he
who, for the money, does his precentor's work as no precentor has
done it before, since Barchester Cathedral was built – such an idea
has never sullied his quiet, or disturbed his conscience.

Nevertheless, Mr Harding is becoming uneasy at the rumour
which he knows to prevail in Barchester on the subject. He is
aware that, at any rate, two of his old men have been heard to
say that if everyone had his own, they might each have their
hundred pounds a year, and live like gentlemen, instead of a
beggarly one shilling and sixpence a day; and that they had
slender cause to be thankful for a miserable dole of twopence,
when Mr Harding and Mr Chadwick, between them, ran away
with thousands of pounds which good old John Hiram never
intended for the like of them. It is the ingratitude of this which
stings Mr Harding. One of this discontented pair, Abel Handy, was
put into the hospital by himself; he had been a stonemason in
Barchester, and had broken his thigh by a fall from a scaffolding,
while employed about the cathedral; and Mr Harding had given
him the first vacancy in the hospital after the occurrence,
although Dr Grantly had been very anxious to put into it an
insufferable clerk of his at Plumstead Episcopi, who had lost all his

teeth, and whom the archdeacon hardly knew how to get rid of by other means. Dr Grantly has not forgotten to remind Mr Harding how well satisfied with his one and sixpence a day old Joe Mutters would have been, and how injudicious it was on the part of Mr Harding to allow a radical from the town to get into the concern. Probably Dr Grantly forgot, at the moment, that the charity was intended for broken-down journeymen of Barchester.

There is living at Barchester a young man, a surgeon, named John Bold, and both Mr Harding and Dr Grantly are well aware that to him is owing the pestilent rebellious feeling which has shown itself in the hospital; yes, and the renewal, too, of that disagreeable talk about Hiram's estates which is now again prevalent in Barchester. Nevertheless, Mr Harding and Mr Bold are acquainted with each other; we may say, are friends, considering the great disparity in their years. Dr Grantly, however, has a holy horror of the impious demagogue, as on one occasion he called Bold, when speaking of him to the precentor; and being a more prudent far-seeing man than Mr Harding, and possessed of a stronger head, he already perceives that this John Bold will work great trouble in Barchester. He considers that he is to be regarded as an enemy, and thinks that he should not be admitted into the camp on anything like friendly terms. As John Bold will occupy much of our attention, we must endeavour to explain who he is, and why he takes the part of John Hiram's bedesmen.

John Bold is a young surgeon, who passed many of his boyish years at Barchester. His father was a physician in the city of London, where he made a moderate fortune, which he invested in houses in that city. The Dragon of Wantly inn and posting-house belonged to him, also four shops in the High Street, and a moiety of the new row of genteel villas (so called in the advertisements), built outside the town just beyond Hiram's Hospital. To one of these Dr Bold retired to spend the evening of his life, and to die; and here his son John spent his holidays, and afterwards his Christmas vacation, when he went from school to study surgery in the London hospitals. Just as John Bold was entitled to write himself surgeon and apothecary, old Dr Bold died, leaving his Barchester property to his son, and a certain sum in the three per cents to his daughter Mary, who is some four or five years older than her brother.

John Bold determined to settle himself at Barchester, and look after his own property, as well as the bones and bodies of such of his neighbours as would call upon him for assistance in their troubles. He therefore put up a large brass plate with JOHN BOLD, SURGEON on it, to the great disgust of the nine practitioners who were already trying to get a living out of the bishop, dean, and canons; and began housekeeping with the aid of his sister. At this time he was not more than twenty-four years old; and though he has now been three years in Barchester, we have not heard that he has done much harm to the nine worthy practitioners. Indeed, their dread of him has died away; for in three years he has not taken three fees.

Nevertheless, John Bold is a clever man, and would, with practice, be a clever surgeon; but he has got quite into another line of life. Having enough to live on, he has not been forced to work for bread; he has declined to subject himself to what he calls the drudgery of the profession, by which, I believe, he means the general work of a practising surgeon, and has found other employment. He frequently binds up the bruises and sets the limbs of such of the poorer classes as profess his way of thinking – but this he does for love. Now I will not say that the archdeacon is strictly correct in stigmatizing John Bold as a demagogue, for I hardly know how extreme must be a man's opinions before he can be justly so called; but Bold is a strong reformer. His passion is the reform of all abuses; state abuses, church abuses, corporation abuses (he has got himself elected a town councillor of Barchester, and has so worried three consecutive mayors, that it became somewhat difficult to find a fourth), abuses in medical practice, and general abuses in the world at large. Bold is thoroughly sincere in his patriotic endeavours to mend mankind, and there is something to be admired in the energy with which he devotes himself to remedying evil and stopping injustice; but I fear that he is too much imbued with the idea that he has a special mission for reforming. It would be well if one so young had a little more diffidence himself, and more trust in the honest purposes of others – if he could be brought to believe that old customs need not necessarily be evil, and that changes may possibly be dangerous; but no, Bold has all the ardour, and all the self-assurance of a

Danton,[4] and hurls his anathemas against time-honoured practices with the violence of a French Jacobin.

No wonder that Dr Grantly should regard Bold as a firebrand, falling, as he has done, almost in the centre of the quiet ancient close of Barchester Cathedral. Dr Grantly would have him avoided as the plague; but the old doctor and Mr Harding were fast friends. Young Johnny Bold used to play as a boy on Mr Harding's lawn; he has many a time won the precentor's heart by listening with wrapt attention to his sacred strains; and since those days, to tell the truth at once, he has nearly won another heart within the same walls.

Eleanor Harding has not plighted her troth to John Bold, nor has she, perhaps, owned to herself how dear to her the young reformer is; but she cannot endure that anyone should speak harshly of him. She does not dare to defend him when her brother-in-law is so loud against him; for she, like her father, is somewhat afraid of Dr Grantly; but she is beginning greatly to dislike the archdeacon. She persuades her father that it would be both unjust and injudicious to banish his young friend because of his politics; she cares little to go to houses where she will not meet him, and, in fact, she is in love.

Nor is there any good reason why Eleanor Harding should not love John Bold. He has all those qualities which are likely to touch a girl's heart. He is brave, eager, and amusing; well-made and good-looking; young and enterprising; his character is in all respects good; he has sufficient income to support a wife; he is her father's friend; and, above all, he is in love with her: then why should not Eleanor Harding be attached to John Bold?

Dr Grantly, who has as many eyes as Argus,[5] and has long seen how the wind blows in that direction, thinks there are various strong reasons why this should not be so. He has not thought it wise as yet to speak to his father-in-law on the subject, for he knows how foolishly indulgent is Mr Harding in everything that concerns his daughter; but he has discussed the matter with his all-trusted helpmate, within that sacred recess formed by the clerical bedcurtains at Plumstead Episcopi.

How much sweet solace, how much valued counsel has our archdeacon received within that sainted enclosure! 'Tis there alone that he unbends, and comes down from his high church pedestal to the level of a mortal man. In the world Dr Grantly never lays aside that demeanour which so well becomes him. He has all the dignity of an ancient saint with the sleekness of a modern bishop; he is always the same; he is always the archdeacon; unlike Homer, he never nods. Even with his father-in-law, even with the bishop and dean, he maintains that sonorous tone and lofty deportment which strikes awe into the young hearts of Barchester, and absolutely cows the whole parish of Plumstead Episcopi. 'Tis only when he has exchanged that ever-new shovel hat[6] for a tasselled nightcap, and those shining black habiliments for his accustomed *robe de nuit*,[7] that Dr Grantly talks, and looks, and thinks like an ordinary man.

Many of us have often thought how severe a trial of faith must this be to the wives of our great church dignitaries. To us these men are personifications of St Paul: their very gait is a speaking sermon; their clean and sombre apparel exacts from us faith and submission, and the cardinal virtues seem to hover round their sacred hats. A dean or archbishop, in the garb of his order, is sure of our reverence, and a well-got-up bishop fills our very souls with awe. But how can this feeling be perpetuated in the bosoms of those who see the bishops without their aprons,[8] and the archdeacons even in a lower state of dishabille?[9]

Do we not all know some reverend, all but sacred, personage before whom our tongue ceases to be loud, and our step to be elastic? But were we once to see him stretch himself beneath the bedclothes, yawn widely, and bury his face upon his pillow, we could chatter before him as glibly as before a doctor or a lawyer. From some such cause, doubtless, it arose that our archdeacon listened to the counsels of his wife, though he considered himself entitled to give counsel to every other being whom he met.

'My dear,' he said, as he adjusted the copious folds of his nightcap, 'there was that John Bold at your father's again today. I must say your father is very imprudent.'

'He is imprudent – he always was,' replied Mrs Grantly, speaking from under the comfortable bedclothes. 'There's nothing new in that.'

'No, my dear, there's nothing new – I know that; but, at the present juncture of affairs, such imprudence is – is – I'll tell you what, my dear, if he does not take care what he's about, John Bold will be off with Eleanor.'

'I think he will, whether papa takes care or no; and why not?'

'Why not!' almost screamed the archdeacon, giving so rough a pull at his nightcap as almost to bring it over his nose; 'why not! – that pestilent, interfering upstart, John Bold – the most vulgar young person I ever met! Do you know that he is meddling with your father's affairs in a most uncalled for – most –' And being at a loss for an epithet sufficiently injurious, he finished his expressions of horror by muttering, 'Good heavens!' in a manner that had been found very efficacious in clerical meetings of the diocese. He must for the moment have forgotten where he was.

'As to his vulgarity, archdeacon,' (Mrs Grantly had never assumed a more familiar term than this in addressing her husband) 'I don't agree with you. Not that I like Mr Bold – he is a great deal too conceited for me; but then Eleanor does, and it would be the best thing in the world for papa if they were to marry. Bold would never trouble himself about Hiram's Hospital if he were papa's son-in-law.' And the lady turned herself round under the bedclothes, in a manner to which the doctor was well accustomed, and which told him, as plainly as words, that as far as she was concerned the subject was over for that night.

'Good heavens!' murmured the doctor again – he was evidently much put beside himself.

Dr Grantly is by no means a bad man; he is exactly the man which such an education as his was most likely to form; his intellect being sufficient for such a place in the world, but not sufficient to put him in advance of it. He performs with a rigid constancy such of the duties of a parish clergyman as are, to his thinking, above the sphere of his curate, but it is as an archdeacon that he shines.[10]

We believe, as a general rule, that either a bishop or his archdeacons have sinecures: where a bishop works, archdeacons have but little to do, and vice versa. In the diocese of Barchester the Archdeacon of Barchester does the work. In that capacity he is diligent, authoritative, and, as his friends particularly boast, judicious. His great fault is an overbearing assurance of the virtues and claims of his order, and his great foible is an equally strong confidence in the dignity of his own manner and the eloquence of his own words. He is a moral man, believing the precepts which he teaches, and believing also that he acts up to them; though we cannot say that he would give his coat to the man who took his cloak, or that he is prepared to forgive his brother even seven times.[11] He is severe enough in exacting his dues, considering that any laxity in this respect would endanger the security of the church; and, could he have his way, he would consign to darkness and perdition not only every individual reformer, but every committee and every commission that would even dare to ask a question respecting the appropriation of church revenues.

'They are church revenues: the laity admit it. Surely the Church is able to administer her own revenues.' 'Twas thus he was accustomed to argue, when the sacrilegious doings of Lord John Russell[12] and others were discussed either at Barchester or at Oxford.

It was no wonder that Dr Grantly did not like John Bold, and that his wife's suggestion that he should become closely connected with such a man dismayed him. To give him his due, the archdeacon never wanted courage; he was quite willing to meet his enemy on any field, and with any weapon. He had that belief in his own arguments that he felt sure of success, could he only be sure of a fair fight on the part of his adversary. He had no idea that John Bold could really prove that the income of the hospital was malappropriated; why, then, should peace be sought for on such base terms? What! bribe an unbelieving enemy of the Church with the sister-in-law of one dignitary, and the daughter of another – with a young lady whose connections with the diocese and chapter of Barchester were so close as to give her an undeniable claim to a husband endowed with some of its sacred wealth! When Dr Grantly talks of unbelieving enemies, he does not mean to imply want of belief in the doctrines of the Church, but an equally dangerous scepticism as to its purity in money matters.

Mrs Grantly is not usually deaf to the claims of the high order to which she belongs. She and her husband rarely disagree as to the tone with which the church should be defended; how singular, then, that in such a case as this she should be willing to succumb!

The archdeacon again murmurs 'Good heavens!' as he lays him-self beside her, but he does so in a voice audible only to himself, and he repeats it till sleep relieves him from deep thought.

Mr Harding himself has seen no reason why his daughter should not love John Bold. He has not been unobservant of her feelings, and perhaps his deepest regret at the part which he fears Bold is about to take regarding the hospital arises from a dread that he may be separated from his daughter, or that she may be separated from the man she loves. He has never spoken to Eleanor about her lover; he is the last man in the world to allude to such a subject unconsulted, even with his own daughter; and had he considered that he had ground to disapprove of Bold, he would have removed her, or forbidden him his house; but he saw no such ground. He would probably have preferred a second clerical son-in-law, for Mr Harding, also, is attached to his order; and, failing in that, he would at any rate have wished that so near a connec-tion should have thought alike with him on church matters. He would not, however, reject the man his daughter loved because he differed on such subjects with himself.

Hitherto Bold had taken no steps in the matter in any way annoying to Mr Harding personally. Some months since, after a severe battle, which cost him not a little, he gained a victory over a certain old turnpike woman in the neighbourhood, of whose charges another old woman had complained to him. He got the act of Parliament relating to the trust, found that his *protégée*[13] had been wrongly taxed, rode through the gate himself, paying the toll, then brought an action against the gate-keeper, and proved that all people coming up a certain by-lane, and going down a certain other by-lane, were toll-free. The fame of his success spread widely abroad, and he began to be looked on as the upholder of the rights of the poor of Barchester. Not long after this success, he heard from different quarters that Hiram's bedesmen were treated as paupers, whereas the property to which they were, in effect, heirs, was very large; and he was instigated by the lawyer whom he had employed in the case of the turnpike to call upon Mr Chadwick for a statement as to the funds of the estate.

Bold had often expressed his indignation at the malappropria-tion of church funds in general, in the hearing of his friend the precentor; but the conversation had never referred to anything at Barchester; and when Finney, the attorney, induced him to interfere with the affairs of the hospital, it was against Mr Chadwick that his efforts were to be directed. Bold soon found that if he interfered with Mr Chadwick as steward, he must also interfere with Mr Harding as warden; and though he regretted the situation in which this would place him, he was not the man to flinch from his undertaking from personal motives.

As soon as he had determined to take the matter in hand, he set about his work with his usual energy. He got a copy of John Hiram's will, of the wording of which he made himself perfectly master. He ascertained the extent of the property, and as nearly as he could the value of it; and made out a schedule of what he was informed was the present distribution of its income. Armed with these particulars, he called on Mr Chadwick, having given that gentleman notice of his visit; and asked him for a statement of the income and expenditure of the hospital for the last twenty-five years.

This was of course refused, Mr Chadwick alleging that he had no authority for making public the concerns of a property in managing which he was only a paid servant.

'And who is competent to give you that authority, Mr Chadwick?' asked Bold.

'Only those who employ me, Mr Bold,' said the steward.

'And who are those, Mr Chadwick?' demanded Bold.

Mr Chadwick begged to say that if these inquiries were made merely out of curiosity, he must decline answering them: if Mr Bold had any ulterior proceeding in view, perhaps it would be desirable that any necessary information should be sought for in a professional way by a professional man. Mr Chadwick's attorneys were Messrs Cox and Cummins, of Lincoln's Inn. Mr Bold took down the address of Cox and Cummins, remarked that the weather was cold for the time of the year, and wished Mr Chadwick good morning. Mr Chadwick said it was cold for June, and bowed him out.

He at once went to his lawyer, Finney. Now, Bold was not very fond of his attorney, but, as he said, he merely wanted a man who knew the forms of law, and who would do what he was told for his money. He had no idea of putting himself in the hands of a lawyer. He wanted law from a lawyer as he did a coat from a tailor, because he could not make it so well himself; and he thought Finney the fittest man in Barchester for his purpose. In one respect, at any rate, he was right: Finney was humility itself.

Finney advised an instant letter to Cox and Cummins, mindful of his six and eightpence.[14] 'Slap at them at once, Mr Bold; demand categorically and explicitly a full statement of the affairs of the hospital.'

'Suppose I were to see Mr Harding first,' suggested Bold.

'Yes, yes, by all means,' said the acquiescing Finney; 'though, perhaps, as Mr Harding is no man of business, it may lead – lead to some little difficulties; but perhaps you're right. Mr Bold, I don't think seeing Mr Harding can do any harm.' Finney saw from the expression of his client's face that he intended to have his own way.

CHAPTER 3

The Bishop of Barchester

BOLD at once repaired to the hospital. The day was now far advanced, but he knew that Mr Harding dined in the summer at four, that Eleanor was accustomed to drive in the evening, and that he might therefore probably find Mr Harding alone. It was between seven and eight when he reached the slight iron gate leading into the precentor's garden, and though, as Mr Chadwick observed, the day had been cold for June, the evening was mild, and soft, and sweet. The little gate was open. As he raised the latch he heard the notes of Mr Harding's violoncello from the far end of the garden, and, advancing before the house and across the lawn, he found him playing: and not without an audience. The musician was seated in a garden chair just within the summer-house, so as to allow the violoncello which he held between his knees to rest upon the dry stone flooring; before him stood a rough music desk, on which was open a page of that dear sacred book, that much-laboured and much-loved volume of church music, which had cost so many guineas; and around sat, and lay, and stood, and leaned, ten of the twelve old men who dwelt with him beneath old John Hiram's roof. The two reformers were not there. I will not say that in their hearts they were conscious of any wrong done or to be done to their mild warden, but latterly they had kept aloof from him, and his music was no longer to their taste.

It was amusing to see the positions, and eager listening faces of these well-to-do old men. I will not say that they all appreciated the music which they heard, but they were intent on appearing to do so; pleased at being where they were, they were determined, as far as in them lay, to give pleasure in return; and they were not unsuccessful. It gladdened the precentor's heart to think that the old bedesmen whom he loved so well admired the strains which were to him so full of almost ecstatic joy; and he used to boast that such was the air of the hospital, as to make it a precinct specially fit for the worship of St Cecilia.[1]

Immediately before him, on the extreme corner of the bench which ran round the summer-house, sat one old man, with his handkerchief smoothly lain upon his knees, who did enjoy the moment, or acted enjoyment well. He was one on whose large frame many years, for he was over eighty, had made small havoc – he was still an upright, burly, handsome figure, with an open, ponderous brow, round which clung a few, though very few, thin grey locks. The coarse black gown of the hospital, the breeches, and buckled shoes became him well; and as he sat with his hands folded on his staff, and his chin resting on his hands, he was such a listener as most musicians would be glad to welcome.

This man was certainly the pride of the hospital. It had always been the custom that one should be selected as being to some extent in authority over the others; and though Mr Bunce, for such was his name, and so he was always designated by his inferior brethren, had no greater emoluments than they, he had assumed, and well knew how to maintain, the dignity of his elevation. The precentor delighted to call him his sub-warden, and was not ashamed, occasionally, when no other guest was there, to bid him sit down by the same parlour fire, and drink the full glass of port which was placed near him. Bunce never went without the second glass, but no entreaty ever made him take a third.

'Well, well, Mr Harding; you're too good, much too good,' he'd always say, as the second glass was filled; but when that was drunk, and the half-hour over, Bunce stood erect, and with a benediction which his patron valued, retired to his own abode. He knew the world too well to risk the comfort of such halcyon moments, by prolonging them till they were disagreeable.

Mr Bunce, as may be imagined, was most strongly opposed to innovation. Not even Dr Grantly had a more holy horror of those who would interfere in the affairs of the hospital; he was every inch a churchman, and though he was not very fond of Dr Grantly personally, that arose from there not being room in the hospital for two people so much alike as the doctor and himself, rather than from any dissimilarity in feeling. Mr Bunce was inclined to think that the warden and himself could manage the hospital without further assistance; and that, though the bishop was the constitutional visitor,[2] and as such entitled to special reverence from all connected with John Hiram's will, John Hiram never intended that his affairs should be interfered with by an archdeacon.

At the present moment, however, these cares were off his mind, and he was looking at his warden as though he thought the music heavenly, and the musician hardly less so.

As Bold walked silently over the lawn, Mr Harding did not at first perceive him, and continued to draw his bow slowly across the plaintive wires; but he soon found from his audience that some stranger was there, and looking up, began to welcome his young friend with frank hospitality.

'Pray, Mr Harding; pray don't let me disturb you,' said Bold; 'you know how fond I am of sacred music.'

'Oh! it's nothing,' said the precentor, shutting up the book, and then opening it again as he saw the delightfully imploring look of his old friend Bunce. Oh, Bunce, Bunce, Bunce, I fear that after all thou art but a flatterer. 'Well, I'll just finish it then; it's a favourite little bit of Bishop's;[3] and then, Mr Bold, we'll have a stroll and a chat till Eleanor comes in and gives us tea.' And so Bold sat down on the soft turf to listen, or rather to think how, after such sweet harmony, he might best introduce a theme of so much discord, to disturb the peace of him who was so ready to welcome him kindly.

Bold thought that the performance was soon over, for he felt that he had a somewhat difficult task, and he almost regretted the final leave-taking of the last of the old men, slow as they were in going through their adieus.

Bold's heart was in his mouth, as the precentor made some ordinary but kind remark as to the friendliness of the visit.

'One evening call,' said he, 'is worth ten in the morning. It's all formality in the morning; real social talk never begins till after dinner. That's why I dine early, so as to get as much as I can of it.'

'Quite true, Mr Harding,' said the other; 'but I fear I've reversed the order of things, and I owe you much apology for troubling you on business at such an hour; but it is on business that I have called just now.'

Mr Harding looked blank and annoyed; there was something in the tone of the young man's voice which told him that the interview was intended to be disagreeable, and he shrank back at finding his kindly greeting so repulsed.

'I wish to speak to you about the hospital,' continued Bold.

'Well, well, anything I can tell you I shall be most happy –'

'It's about the accounts.'

'Then, my dear fellow, I can tell you nothing, for I'm as ignorant as a child. All I know is that they pay me £800 a year. Go to Chadwick, he knows all about the accounts; and now tell me, will poor Mary Jones ever get the use of her limb again?'

'Well, I think she will, if she's careful; but, Mr Harding, I hope you won't object to discuss with me what I have to say about the hospital.'

Mr Harding gave a deep, long-drawn sigh. He did object, very strongly object, to discuss any such subject with John Bold; but he had not the business tact of Mr Chadwick, and did not know how to relieve himself from the coming evil; he sighed sadly, but made no answer.

'I have the greatest regard for you, Mr Harding,' continued Bold; 'the truest respect, the most sincere –'

'Thank ye, thank ye, Mr Bold,' interjaculated the precentor somewhat impatiently; 'I'm much obliged, but never mind that; I'm as likely to be in the wrong as another man – quite as likely.'

'But, Mr Harding, I must express what I feel, lest you should think there is personal enmity in what I'm going to do.'

'Personal enmity! Going to do! Why you're not going to cut my throat, nor put me into the Ecclesiastical Court –'

Bold tried to laugh, but he couldn't. He was quite in earnest, and determined in his course, and couldn't make a joke of it. He walked on awhile in silence before he recommenced his attack, during which Mr Harding, who had still the bow in his hand, played rapidly on an imaginary violoncello. 'I fear there is reason to think that John Hiram's will is not carried out to the letter, Mr Harding,' said the young man at last; 'and I have been asked to see into it.'

'Very well, I've no objection on earth; and now we need not say another word about it.'

'Only one word more, Mr Harding. Chadwick has referred me to Cox and Cummins, and I think it my duty to apply to them for some statement about the hospital. In what I do I may appear to be interfering with you, and I hope you will forgive me for doing so.'

'Mr Bold,' said the other, stopping, and speaking with some solemnity, 'if you act justly, say nothing in this matter but the truth, and use no unfair weapons in carrying out your purposes, I shall have nothing to forgive. I presume you think I am not entitled to the income I receive from the hospital, and that others are entitled to it. Whatever some may do, I shall never attribute to you base motives because you hold an opinion opposed to my own, and adverse to my interests: pray do what you consider to be your duty; I can give you no assistance, neither will I offer you any obstacle. Let me, however, suggest to you, that you can in no wise forward your views nor I mine, by any discussion between us. Here comes Eleanor and the ponies, and we'll go in to tea.'

Bold, however, felt that he could not sit down at ease with Mr Harding and his daughter after what had passed, and therefore excused himself with much awkward apology; and merely raising his hat and bowing as he passed Eleanor and the pony-chair,[4] left her in disappointed amazement at his departure.

Mr Harding's demeanour certainly impressed Bold with a full conviction that the warden felt that he stood on strong grounds, and almost made him think that he was about to interfere without due warrant in the private affairs of a just and honourable man; but Mr Harding himself was anything but satisfied with his own view of the case.

In the first place, he wished for Eleanor's sake to think well of Bold and to like him, and yet he could not but feel disgusted at the arrogance of his conduct. What right had he to say that John Hiram's will was not fairly carried out? But then the question would arise within his heart: Was that will fairly acted on? Did John Hiram mean that the warden of his hospital should receive considerably more out of the legacy than all the twelve old men together for whose behoof the hospital was built? Could it be possible that John Bold was right, and that the reverend warden of the hospital had been for the last ten years and more the unjust recipient of an income legally and equitably belonging to others? What if it should be proved before the light of day that he, whose life had been so happy, so quiet, so respected, had absorbed £8,000, to which he had no title, and which he could never repay? I do not say that he feared that such was really the case; but the first shade of doubt now fell across his mind, and from this evening, for many a long, long day, our good, kind, loving warden was neither happy nor at ease.

Thoughts of this kind, these first moments of much misery, oppressed Mr Harding as he sat sipping his tea, absent and ill at ease. Poor Eleanor felt that all was not right, but her ideas as to the cause of the evening's discomfort did not go beyond her lover, and his sudden and uncivil departure: she thought there must have been some quarrel between Bold and her father, and she was half angry with both, though she did not attempt to explain to herself why she was so.

Mr Harding thought long and deeply over these things, both before he went to bed, and after it, as he lay awake, questioning within himself the validity of his claim to the income which he enjoyed. It seemed clear at any rate that, however unfortunate he might be at having been placed in such a position, no one could say that he ought either to have refused the appointment first, or to have rejected the income afterwards. All the world – meaning the ecclesiastical world as confined to the English Church – knew that the wardenship of the Barchester Hospital was a snug sinecure, but no one had ever been blamed for accepting it. To how much blame, however, would he have been open had he rejected it! How mad would he have been thought had he declared, when the situation was vacant and offered to him, that he had scruples as to receiving £800 a year from John Hiram's property, and that he had rather some stranger should possess it! How would Dr Grantly have shaken his wise head, and have consulted with his friends in the close as to some decent retreat for the coming insanity of the poor minor canon! If he was right in accepting the place, it was clear to him also that he would be wrong in rejecting any part of the income attached to it. The patronage was a valuable appanage[s] of the bishopric; and surely it would not be his duty to lessen the value of that preferment which had been bestowed on himself; surely he was bound to stand by his order.

But somehow these arguments, though they seemed logical,

were not satisfactory. Was John Hiram's will fairly carried out? that was the true question: and if not, was it not his especial duty to see that this was done – his especial duty, whatever injury it might do to his order – however ill such duty might be received by his patron and his friends? At the idea of his friends, his mind turned unhappily to his son-in-law: he knew well how strongly he would be supported by Dr Grantly, if he could bring himself to put his case into the archdeacon's hands, and to allow him to fight the battle; but he knew also that he would find no sympathy there for his doubts, no friendly feeling, no inward comfort. Dr Grantly would be ready enough to take up his cudgel against all comers on behalf of the church militant, but he would do so on the distasteful ground of the Church's infallibility. Such a contest would give no comfort to Mr Harding's doubts; he was not so anxious to prove himself right, as to be so.

I have said before that Dr Grantly was the working man of the diocese, and that his father the bishop was somewhat inclined to an idle life: so it was; but the bishop, though he had never been an active man, was one whose qualities had rendered him dear to all who knew him. He was the very opposite to his son; he was a bland and a kind old man, opposed by every feeling to authoritative demonstrations and episcopal ostentation. It was perhaps well for him, in his situation, that his son had early in life been able to do that which he could not well do when he was younger, and which he could not have done at all now that he was over seventy. The bishop knew how to entertain the clergy of his diocese, to talk easy smalltalk with the rectors' wives, and put curates at their ease; but it required the strong hand of the archdeacon to deal with such as were refractory either in their doctrines or their lives.

The bishop and Mr Harding loved each other warmly. They had grown old together, and had together spent many, many years in clerical pursuits and clerical conversation. When one of them was a bishop and the other only a minor canon they were even then much together; but since their children had married, and Mr Harding had become warden and precentor, they were all in all to each other. I will not say that they managed the diocese between them, but they spent much time in discussing the man who did, and in forming little plans to mitigate his wrath against church delinquents, and soften his aspirations for church dominion.

Mr Harding determined to open his mind, and confess his doubts to his old friend; and to him he went on the morning after John Bold's uncourteous visit.

Up to this period no rumour of these cruel proceedings against the hospital had reached the bishop's ears. He had doubtless heard that men existed who questioned his right to present to a sinecure of £800 a year, as he had heard from time to time of some special immorality or disgraceful disturbance in the usually decent and quiet city of Barchester: but all he did, and all he was called on to do on such occasions, was to shake his head, and to beg his son, the great dictator, to see that no harm happened to the church.

It was a long story that Mr Harding had to tell before he made the bishop comprehend his own view of the case; but we need not follow him through the tale. At first the bishop counselled but one step, recommended but one remedy, had but one medicine in his whole pharmacopoeia strong enough to touch so grave a disorder – he prescribed the archdeacon. 'Refer him to the archdeacon,' he repeated, as Mr Harding spoke of Bold and his visit. 'The archdeacon will set you quite right about that,' he kindly said, when his friend spoke with hesitation of the justness of his cause. 'No man has got up all that so well as the archdeacon'; but the dose, though large, failed to quiet the patient; indeed it almost produced nausea.

'But, bishop,' said he, 'did you ever read John Hiram's will?'

The bishop thought probably he had, thirty-five years ago, when first instituted to his see, but could not state positively: however, he very well knew that he had the absolute right to present to the wardenship, and that the income of the warden had been regularly settled.

'But, bishop, the question is, who has the power to settle it? If, as this young man says, the will provides that the proceeds of the property are to be divided into shares, who has the power to alter these provisions?' The bishop had an indistinct idea that they altered themselves by the lapse of years; that a kind of ecclesiastical statute of limitation barred the rights of the twelve bedesmen to any increase of income arising from the increased value of property. He said something about tradition; more of the many learned men who by their practice had confirmed the present

arrangement; then went at some length into the propriety of
maintaining the due difference in rank and income between
a beneficed clergyman, and certain poor old men who were
dependent on charity; and concluded his argument by another
reference to the archdeacon.

The precentor sat thoughtfully gazing at the fire, and listening
to the good-natured reasoning of his friend. What the bishop said
had a sort of comfort in it, but it was not a sustaining comfort. It
made Mr Harding feel that many others – indeed, all others of his
own order – would think him right; but it failed to prove to him
that he truly was so.

'Bishop,' said he, at last, after both had sat silent for a while, 'I
should deceive you and myself too, if I did not tell you that I am
very unhappy about this. Suppose that I cannot bring myself to
agree with Dr Grantly! – that I find, after inquiry, that the young
man is right, and that I am wrong – what then?'

The two men were sitting near each other – so near, that the
bishop was able to lay his hand upon the other's knee, and he did
so with a gentle pressure. Mr Harding well knew what that
pressure meant. The bishop had no further argument to adduce;
he could not fight for the cause as his son would do; he could not
prove all the precentor's doubts to be groundless; but he could
sympathize with his friend, and he did so; and Mr Harding felt that
he had received that for which he came. There was another period
of silence, after which the bishop asked with a degree of irritable
energy, very unusual with him, whether this 'pestilent intruder'
(meaning John Bold) had any friends in Barchester.

Mr Harding had fully made up his mind to tell the bishop
everything; to speak of his daughter's love, as well as his own
troubles; to talk of John Bold in his double capacity of future son-
in-law and present enemy; and though he felt it to be sufficiently
disagreeable, now was his time to do it.

'He is very intimate at my own house, bishop.' The bishop
stared; he was not so far gone in orthodoxy and church-militancy
as his son, but still he could not bring himself to understand how
so declared an enemy of the establishment could be admitted on
terms of intimacy into the house, not only of so firm a pillar as Mr
Harding, but one so much injured as the warden of the hospital.

'Indeed, I like Mr Bold much, personally,' continued the disinterested victim; 'and to tell you the "truth"' – he hesitated as he brought out the dreadful tidings – 'I have sometimes thought it not improbable that he would be my second son-in-law.' The bishop did not whistle; we believe that they lose the power of doing so on being consecrated; and that in these days one might as easily meet a corrupt judge as a whistling bishop; but he looked as though he would have done so, but for his apron.

What a brother-in-law for the archdeacon! what an alliance for Barchester Close! what a connection for even the episcopal palace! The bishop, in his simple mind, felt no doubt that John Bold, had he so much power, would shut up all cathedrals, and probably all parish churches; distribute all tithes among Methodists, Baptists, and other savage tribes; utterly annihilate the sacred bench, and make shovel hats and lawn sleeves as illegal as cowls, sandals, and sackcloth!⁶ Here was a nice man to be initiated into the comfortable arcana of ecclesiastical snuggeries; one who doubted the integrity of parsons, and probably disbelieved the Trinity!

Mr Harding saw what an effect his communication had made, and almost repented the openness of his disclosure; he, however, did what he could to moderate the grief of his friend and patron. 'I did not say that there is any engagement between them. Had there been, Eleanor would have told me: I know her well enough to be assured that she would have done so; but I see that they are fond of each other; and as a man and a father, I have had no objection to urge against their intimacy.'

'But, Harding,' said the bishop, 'how are you to oppose him, if he is your son-in-law?'

'I don't mean to oppose him; it is he who opposes me: if anything is to be done in defence, I suppose Chadwick will do it. I suppose –'

'Oh, the archdeacon will see to that: were the young man twice his brother-in-law, the archdeacon will never be deterred from doing what he feels to be right.'

Mr Harding reminded the bishop that the archdeacon and the reformer were not yet brothers, and very probably never would be; exacted from him a promise that Eleanor's name should not be mentioned in any discussion between the father bishop and son archdeacon respecting the hospital; and then took his departure, leaving his poor old friend bewildered, amazed, and confounded.

CHAPTER 4

Hiram's Bedesmen

THE parties most interested in the movement which is about to set Barchester by the ears were not the foremost to discuss the merit of the question, as is often the case; but when the bishop, the archdeacon, the warden, the steward, and Messrs Cox and Cummins, were all busy with the matter, each in his own way, it is not to be supposed that Hiram's bedesmen themselves were altogether passive spectators. Finney, the attorney, had been among them, asking sly questions, and raising immoderate hopes, creating a party hostile to the warden, and establishing a corps in the enemy's camp, as he figuratively calls it to himself. Poor old men; whoever may be righted or wronged by this inquiry, they at any rate will assuredly be only injured; to them it can only be an unmixed evil. How can their lot be improved? all their wants are supplied; every comfort is administered; they have warm houses, good clothes, plentiful diet, and rest after a life of labour; and above all, that treasure so inestimable in declining years, a true and kind friend to listen to their sorrows, watch over their sickness, and administer comfort as regards this world, and the world to come!

John Bold sometimes thinks of this, when he is talking loudly of the rights of the bedesmen, whom he has taken under his protection; but he quiets the suggestion within his breast with the high-sounding name of justice – 'fiat justitia ruat cœlum'.[1] These old men should, by rights, have one hundred pounds a year instead of one shilling and sixpence a day, and the warden should have two hundred or three hundred pounds instead of eight hundred pounds. What is unjust must be wrong; what is wrong should be righted; and if he declined the task, who else would do it?

'Each one of you is clearly entitled to one hundred pounds a year by common law': such had been the important whisper made by Finney into the ears of Abel Handy, and by him retailed to his eleven brethren.

Too much must not be expected from the flesh and blood even of John Hiram's bedesmen, and the positive promise of one hundred a year to each of the twelve old men had its way with most of them. The great Bunce was not to be wiled away, and was upheld in his orthodoxy by two adherents. Abel Handy, who was the leader of the aspirants after wealth, had, alas, a stronger following. No less than five of the twelve soon believed that his views were just, making with their leader a moiety of the hospital. The other three, volatile unstable minds, vacillated between the two chieftains, now led away by the hope of gold, now anxious to propitiate the powers that still existed.

It had been proposed to address a petition to the bishop as visitor, praying his lordship to see justice done to the legal recipients of John Hiram's Charity, and to send copies of this petition and of the reply it would elicit to all the leading London papers, and thereby to obtain notoriety for the subject. This it was thought would pave the way for ulterior legal proceedings. It would have been a great thing to have had the signatures and marks of all the twelve injured legatees; but this was impossible: Bunce would have cut his hand off sooner than have signed it. It was then suggested by Finney that if even eleven could be induced to sanction the document, the one obstinate recusant might have been represented as unfit to judge on such a question – in fact, as being *non compos mentis*[2] – and the petition would have been taken as representing the feeling of the men. But this could not be done: Bunce's friends were as firm as himself, and as yet only six crosses adorned the document. It was the more provoking, as Bunce himself could write his name legibly, and one of those three doubting souls had for years boasted of like power, and possessed, indeed, a Bible, in which he was proud to show his name written by himself some thirty years ago – 'Job Skulpit'; but it was thought that Job Skulpit, having forgotten his scholarship, on that account recoiled from the petition, and that the other doubters would follow as he led them. A petition signed by half the hospital would have but a poor effect.

It was in Skulpit's room that the petition was now lying, waiting such additional signatures as Abel Handy, by his eloquence, could obtain for it. The six marks it bore were duly attested, thus:

    his   his   his

Abel +Handy, Greg^y +Moody, Mathew +Spriggs,

   mark   mark   mark

etc., and places were duly designated in pencil for those brethren who were now expected to join: for Skulpit alone was left a spot on which his genuine signature might be written in fair clerk-like style. Handy had brought in the document, and spread it out on the small deal table, and was now standing by it persuasive and eager. Moody had followed with an inkhorn, carefully left behind by Finney; and Spriggs bore aloft, as though it were a sword, a well-worn ink-black pen, which from time to time he endeavoured to thrust into Skulpit's unwilling hand.

With the learned man were his two abettors in indecision, William Gazy and Jonathan Crumple. If ever the petition were to be forwarded, now was the time, so said Mr Finney; and great was the anxiety on the part of those whose one hundred pounds a year, as they believed, mainly depended on the document in question.

'To be kept out of all that money,' as the avaricious Moody had muttered to his friend Handy, 'by an old fool saying that he can write his own name like his betters.'

'Well Job,' said Handy, trying to impart to his own sour, ill-omened visage a smile of approbation, in which he greatly failed; 'so you're ready now, Mr Finney says; here's the place, d'ye see' – and he put his huge brown finger down on the dirty paper – 'name or mark, it's all one. Come along, old boy; if so be we're to have the spending of this money, why the sooner the better – that's my maxim.'

'To be sure,' said Moody; 'we a'n't none of us so young: we can't stay waiting for old Catgut no longer.'

It was thus these miscreants named our excellent friend: the nickname he could easily have forgiven, but the allusion to the divine source of all his melodious joy would have irritated even him. Let us hope he never knew the insult.

'Only think, old Billy Gazy,' said Spriggs, who rejoiced in greater youth than his brethren, but having fallen into a fire when drunk, had had one eye burnt out, one cheek burnt through, and one arm nearly burnt off, and who, therefore, in regard to personal appearance, was not the most prepossessing of men; 'a hundred a year, and all to spend: only think, old Billy Gazy'; and he gave a hideous grin that showed off his misfortunes to their full extent.

Old Billy Gazy was not alive to much enthusiasm – even these golden prospects did not arouse him to do more than rub his poor old bleared eyes with the cuff of his bedesman's gown, and gently mutter, 'he didn't know, not he; he didn't know.'

'But you'd know, Jonathan,' continued Spriggs, turning to the other friend of Skulpit's, who was sitting on a stool by the table, gazing vacantly at the petition. Jonathan Crumple was a meek, mild man, who had known better days; his means had been wasted by bad children, who had made his life wretched till he had been received into the hospital, of which he had not long been a member. Since that day he had known neither sorrow nor trouble, and this attempt to fill him with new hopes was, indeed, a cruelty.

'A hundred a year's a nice thing, for sartain, neighbour Spriggs,' said he: 'I once had nigh to that myself, but it didn't do me no good.' And he gave a low sigh, as he thought of the children of his own loins who had robbed him.

'And shall have again, Joe,' said Handy; 'and will have someone to keep it right and tight for you this time.'

Crumple sighed again – he had learned the impotency of worldly wealth, and would have been satisfied, if left untempted, to have remained happy with one and sixpence a day.

'Come, Skulpit,' repeated Handy, getting impatient, 'you're not going to go along with old Bunce in helping that parson to rob us all. Take the pen, man, and right yourself. Well,' he added, seeing that Skulpit still doubted, 'to see a man as is afraid to stand by hisself, is, to my thinking, the meanest thing as is.'

'Sink them all for parsons, says I,' growled Moody; 'hungry beggars, as never thinks their bellies full till they have robbed all and every thing.'

'Who's to harm you, man?' argued Spriggs: 'let them look never so black at you, they can't get you put out when you're once in – no, not old Catgut, with Calves to help him!' I am sorry to say the archdeacon himself was designated by this scurrilous allusion to his nether person.

'A hundred a year to win, and nothing to lose,' continued

Handy, 'my eyes! – Well, how a man's to doubt about sich a bit of cheese as that passes me – but some men is timorous – some men is born with no pluck in them – some men is cowed at the very first sight of a gentleman's coat and waistcoat.'

Oh, Mr Harding, if you had but taken the archdeacon's advice in that disputed case, when Joe Mutters was this ungrateful demagogue's rival candidate!

'Afraid of a parson,' growled Moody, with a look of ineffable scorn; 'I tell ye what I'd be afraid of – I'd be afraid of not getting nothing from 'em but just what I could take by might and right – that's the most I'd be afraid on of any parson of 'em all.'

'But,' said Skulpit, apologetically, 'Mr Harding's not so bad – he did give us twopence a day, didn't he now?'

'Twopence a day!' exclaimed Spriggs with scorn, opening awfully the red cavern of his lost eye.

'Twopence a day!' muttered Moody with a curse; 'sink his twopence!'

'Twopence a day!' exclaimed Handy; 'and I'm to go, hat in hand, and thank a chap for twopence a day, when he owes me a hundred pounds a year; no, thank ye; that may do for you, but it won't for me. Come, I say, Skulpit, are you a going to put your mark to this here paper, or are you not?'

Skulpit looked round in wretched indecision to his two friends. 'What d'ye think, Billy Gazy?' said he.

But Billy Gazy couldn't think: he made a noise like the bleating of an old sheep, which was intended to express the agony of his doubt, and again muttered that 'he didn't know'.

'Take hold, you old cripple,' said Handy, thrusting the pen into poor Billy's hand: 'there, so – ugh! you old fool, you've been and smeared it all – there – that'll do for you – that's as good as the best name as ever was written': and a big blotch of ink was presumed to represent Billy Gazy's acquiescence.

'Now Jonathan,' said Handy, turning to Crumple.

'A hundred a year's a nice thing, for sartain,' again argued Crumple. 'Well, neighbour Skulpit, how's it to be?'

'Oh, please yourself,' said Skulpit; 'please yourself, and you'll please me.'

The pen was thrust into Crumple's hand, and a faint, wandering, meaningless sign was made, betokening such sanction and authority as Jonathan Crumple was able to convey.

'Come, Job,' said Handy, softened by success, 'don't let 'em have to say that old Bunce has a man like you under his thumb – a man that always holds his head in the hospital as high as Bunce himself, though you're never axed to drink wine, and sneak, and tell lies about your betters, as he does.'

Skulpit held the pen, and made little flourishes with it in the air, but still hesitated.

'And if you'll be said by me,' continued Handy, 'you'll not write your name to it at all, but just put your mark like the others' – the cloud began to clear from Skulpit's brow – 'we all know you can do it if you like, but maybe you wouldn't like to seem uppish, you know.'

'Well, the mark would be best,' said Skulpit: 'one name and the rest marks wouldn't look well, would it?'

'The worst in the world,' said Handy; 'there – there': and stooping over the petition, the learned clerk made a huge cross on the place left for his signature.

'That's the game,' said Handy, triumphantly pocketing the petition; 'we're all in a boat now, that is, the nine of us; and as for old Bunce, and his cronies, they may –' But as he was hobbling off to the door, with a crutch on one side and a stick on the other, he was met by Bunce himself.

'Well, Handy, and what may old Bunce do?' said the grey-haired, upright senior.

Handy muttered something, and was departing; but he was stopped in the doorway by the huge frame of the newcomer.

'You've been doing no good here, Abel Handy,' said he, ''tis plain to see that; and 'tisn't much good, I'm thinking, you ever do.'

'I mind my own business, Master Bunce,' muttered the other, 'and do you do the same. It a'n't nothing to you what I does – and your spying and poking here won't do no good nor yet no harm.'

'I suppose then, Job,' continued Bunce, not noticing his opponent, 'if the truth must out, you've stuck your name to that petition of theirs at last.'

Skulpit looked as though he were about to sink into nothing with shame.

'What is it to you what he signs?' said Handy. 'I suppose if we all wants to ax for our own, we needn't ax leave of you first, Mr Bunce, big a man as you are: and as to your sneaking in here, into Job's room when he's busy, and where you're not wanted –'

'I've knowed Job Skulpit, man and boy, sixty years,' said Bunce, looking at the man of whom he spoke, 'and that's ever since the day he was born. I knowed the mother that bore him, when she and I were little wee things, picking daisies together in the close yonder; and I've lived under the same roof with him more nor ten years; and after that I may come into his room without axing leave, and yet no sneaking neither.'

'So you can, Mr Bunce,' said Skulpit; 'so you can, any hour, day or night.'

'And I'm free also to tell him my mind,' continued Bunce, looking at the one man and addressing the other; 'and I tell him now that he's done a foolish and a wrong thing: he's turned his back upon one who is his best friend; and is playing the game of others, who care nothing for him, whether he be poor or rich, well or ill, alive or dead. A hundred a year? Are the lot of you soft enough to think that if a hundred a year be to be given, it's the likes of you that will get it?' – and he pointed to Billy Gazy, Spriggs, and Crumple. 'Did any of us ever do anything worth half the money? Was it to make gentlemen of us we were brought in here, when all the world turned against us, and we couldn't longer earn our daily bread? A'n't you all as rich in your ways as he in his?' – and the orator pointed to the side on which the warden lived. 'A'n't you getting all you hoped for, ay, and more than you hoped for? Wouldn't each of you have given the dearest limb of his body to secure that which now makes you so unthankful?'

'We wants what John Hiram left us,' said Handy; 'we wants what's ourn by law; it don't matter what we expected; what's ourn by law should be ourn, and by goles³ we'll have it.'

'Law!' said Bunce, with all the scorn he knew how to command – 'law! Did ye ever know a poor man yet was the better for law, or for a lawyer? Will Mr Finney ever be as good to you, Job, as that man has been? Will he see to you when you're sick, and comfort you when you're wretched? Will he –'

'No, nor give you port wine, old boy, on cold winter nights! he won't do that, will he?' asked Handy: and laughing at the severity of his own wit, he and his colleagues retired, carrying with them, however, the now powerful petition.

There is no help for spilt milk; and Mr Bunce could only retire to his own room, disgusted at the frailty of human nature – Job Skulpit scratched his head – Jonathan Crumple again remarked that 'for sartain, sure a hundred a year was very nice' – and Billy Gazy again rubbed his eyes, and lowly muttered that 'he didn't know'.

CHAPTER 5

Dr Grantly Visits the Hospital

THOUGH doubt and hesitation disturbed the rest of our poor warden, no such weakness perplexed the nobler breast of his son-in-law. As the indomitable cock preparing for the combat sharpens his spurs, shakes his feathers, and erects his comb, so did the archdeacon arrange his weapons for the coming war, without misgiving and without fear. That he was fully confident of the justice of his cause let no one doubt. Many a man can fight his battle with good courage, but with a doubting conscience; such was not the case with Dr Grantly. He did not believe in the Gospel with more assurance than he did in the sacred justice of all ecclesiastical revenues. When he put his shoulder to the wheel to defend the income of the present and future precentors of Barchester, he was animated by as strong a sense of a holy cause as that which gives courage to a missionary in Africa, or enables a sister of mercy to give up the pleasures of the world for the wards of a hospital. He was about to defend the holy of holies from the touch of the profane; to guard the citadel of his church from the most rampant of its enemies; to put on his good armour in the best of fights; and secure, if possible, the comforts of his creed for coming generations of ecclesiastical dignitaries. Such a work required no ordinary vigour; and the archdeacon was, therefore, extraordinarily vigorous: it demanded a buoyant courage, and a heart happy in its toil; and the archdeacon's heart was happy, and his courage was buoyant.

He knew that he would not be able to animate his father-in-law with feelings like his own, but this did not much disturb him. He preferred to bear the brunt of the battle alone, and did not doubt that the warden would resign himself into his hands with passive submission.

'Well, Mr Chadwick,' he said, walking into the steward's office a day or two after the signing of the petition as commemorated in the last chapter; 'anything from Cox and Cummins this morn-

ing?' Mr Chadwick handed him a letter, which he read, stroking
the tight-gaitered calf of his right leg as he did so. Messrs Cox and
Cummins merely said that they had as yet received no notice from
their adversaries; that they could recommend no preliminary
steps; but that should any proceeding really be taken by the
bedesmen, it would be expedient to consult that very eminent
Queen's Counsel, Sir Abraham Haphazard.

'I quite agree with them,' said Dr Grantly, refolding the letter.
'I perfectly agree with them. Haphazard is no doubt the best man;
a thorough churchman, a sound conservative, and in every
respect the best man we could get – he's in the house,[1] too, which
is a great thing.'

Mr Chadwick quite agreed.

'You remember how completely he put down that scoundrel
Horseman about the Bishop of Beverly's income;[2] how completely
he set them all adrift in the earl's case.' Since the question of St
Cross had been mooted by the public, one noble lord had become
'the earl', par excellence, in the doctor's estimation. 'How he silenced
that fellow at Rochester.[3] Of course we must have Haphazard; and
I'll tell you what, Mr Chadwick, we must take care to be in time,
or the other party will forestall us.'

With all his admiration for Sir Abraham, the doctor seemed to
think it not impossible that that great man might be induced to
lend his gigantic powers to the side of the Church's enemies.

Having settled this point to his satisfaction, the doctor stepped
down to the hospital, to learn how matters were going on there;
and as he walked across the hallowed close, and looked up at the
ravens who cawed with a peculiar reverence as he wended his
way, he thought with increased acerbity of those whose impiety
would venture to disturb the goodly grace of cathedral institutions.

And who has not felt the same? We believe that Mr Horseman
himself would relent, and the spirit of Sir Benjamin Hall give way,[4]
were those great reformers to allow themselves to stroll by moonlight round the towers of some of our ancient churches. Who
would not feel charity for a prebendary, when walking the quiet
length of that long aisle at Winchester, looking at those decent
houses, that trim grassplat, and feeling, as one must, the solemn,

orderly comfort of the spot! Who could be hard upon a dean while wandering round the sweet close of Hereford, and owning that in that precinct, tone and colour, design and form, solemn tower and storied window, are all in unison, and all perfect! Who could lie basking in the cloisters of Salisbury, and gaze on Jewel's library,[5] and that unequalled spire, without feeling that bishops should sometimes be rich.

The tone of our archdeacon's mind must not astonish us; it has been the growth of centuries of Church ascendancy; and though some fungi now disfigure the tree, though there be much dead wood, for how much good fruit have not we to be thankful? Who, without remorse, can batter down the dead branches of an old oak, now useless, but, ah! still so beautiful, or drag out the fragments of the ancient forest, without feeling that they sheltered the younger plants, to which they are now summoned to give way in a tone so peremptory and so harsh?

The archdeacon, with all his virtues, was not a man of delicate feeling; and after having made his morning salutations in the warden's drawing-room, he did not scruple to commence an attack on 'pestilent' John Bold in the presence of Miss Harding, though he rightly guessed that that lady was not indifferent to the name of his enemy.

'Nelly, my dear, fetch me my spectacles from the back room,' said her father, anxious to save both her blushes and her feelings.

Eleanor brought the spectacles, while her father was trying, in ambiguous phrases, to explain to her too-practical brother-in-law that it might be as well not to say anything about Bold before her, and then retreated. Nothing had been explained to her about Bold and the hospital; but, with a woman's instinct, she knew that things were going wrong.

'We must soon be doing something,' commenced the archdeacon, wiping his brows with a large, bright-coloured handkerchief, for he had felt busy, and had walked quick, and it was a broiling summer's day. 'Of course you have heard of the petition?'

Mr Harding owned, somewhat unwillingly, that he had heard of it.

'Well,' – the archdeacon looked for some expression of opinion, but none coming, he continued – 'We must be doing something, you know; we mustn't allow these people to cut the ground from under us while we sit looking on.' The archdeacon, who was a practical man, allowed himself the use of everyday expressive modes of speech when among his closest intimates, though no one could soar into a more intricate labyrinth of refined phraseology when the Church was the subject, and his lower brethren were his auditors.

The warden still looked mutely in his face, making the slightest possible passes with an imaginary fiddle-bow, and stopping, as he did so, sundry imaginary strings with the fingers of his other hand. 'Twas his constant consolation in conversational troubles. While these vexed him sorely, the passes would be short and slow, and the upper hand would not be seen to work; nay the strings on which it operated would sometimes lie concealed in the musician's pocket, and the instrument on which he played would be beneath his chair; but as his spirit warmed to the subject – as his trusting heart, looking to the bottom of that which vexed him, would see its clear way out – he would rise to a higher melody, sweep the unseen strings with a bolder hand, and swiftly fingering the cords from his neck, down along his waistcoat, and up again to his very ear, create an ecstatic strain of perfect music, audible to himself and to St Cecilia, and not without effect.

'I quite agree with Cox and Cummins,' continued the arch-deacon: 'they say we must secure Sir Abraham Haphazard. I shall not have the slightest fear in leaving the case in Sir Abraham's hands.'

The warden played the slowest and saddest of tunes: it was but a dirge on one string.

'I think Sir Abraham will not be long in letting Master Bold know what he's about. I fancy I hear Sir Abraham cross-questioning him at the Common Pleas.'

The warden thought of his income being thus discussed, his modest life, his daily habits, and his easy work; and nothing issued from that single cord, but a low wail of sorrow. 'I suppose they've sent this petition up to my father.' The warden didn't know; he imagined they would do so this very day.

'What I can't understand is, how you let them do it, with such a command as you have in the place, or should have with such a man as Bunce; I cannot understand why you let them do it.'

'Do what?' asked the warden.

'Why, listen to this fellow Bold, and that other low pettifogger, Finney – and get up this petition too: why didn't you tell Bunce to destroy the petition?'

'That would have been hardly wise,' said the warden.

'Wise – yes, it would have been very wise if they'd done it among themselves. I must go up to the palace and answer it now, I suppose; it's a very short answer they'll get, I can tell you.'

'But why shouldn't they petition, doctor?'

'Why shouldn't they!' responded the archdeacon, in a loud brazen voice, as though all the men in the hospital were expected to hear him through the walls; 'why shouldn't they? I'll let them know why they shouldn't: by the by, warden, I'd like to say a few words to them all together.'

The warden's mind misgave him, and even for a moment he forgot to play. He by no means wished to delegate to his son-in-law his place and authority of warden; he had expressly determined not to interfere in any step which the men might wish to take in the matter under dispute; he was most anxious neither to accuse them nor to defend himself. All these things he was aware the archdeacon would do in his behalf, and that not in the mildest manner; and yet he knew not how to refuse the permission requested.

'I'd so much sooner remain quiet in the matter,' said he, in an apologetic voice.

'Quiet!' said the archdeacon, still speaking with his brazen trumpet; 'do you wish to be ruined in quiet?'

'Why, if I am to be ruined, certainly.'

'Nonsense, warden; I tell you something must be done – we must act; just let me ring the bell, and send the men word that I'll speak to them in the quad.'

Mr Harding knew not how to resist, and the disagreeable order was given. The quad, as it was familiarly called, was a small quadrangle, open on one side to the river, and surrounded on the others by the high wall of Mr Harding's garden, by one gable end of Mr Harding's house, and by the end of the row of buildings which formed the residences of the bedesmen. It was flagged all round, and the centre was stoned; small stone gutters ran from the four corners of the square to a grating in the centre; and attached to the end of Mr Harding's house was a conduit with four cocks covered over from the weather, at which the old men got their water, and very generally performed their morning toilet. It was a quiet, sombre place, shaded over by the trees of the warden's garden. On the side towards the river, there stood a row of stone seats, on which the old men would sit and gaze at the little fish, as they flitted by in the running stream. On the other side of the river was a rich, green meadow, running up to and joining the deanery, and as little open to the public as the garden of the dean itself. Nothing, therefore, could be more private than the quad of the hospital; and it was there that the archdeacon determined to convey to them his sense of their refractory proceedings.

The servant soon brought in word that the men were assembled in the quad, and the archdeacon, big with his purpose, rose to address them.

'Well, warden, of course you're coming,' said he, seeing that Mr Harding did not prepare to follow him.

'I wish you'd excuse me,' said Mr Harding.

'For heaven's sake, don't let us have division in the camp,' replied the archdeacon: 'let us have a long pull and a strong pull, but above all a pull altogether; come, warden, come; don't be afraid of your duty.'

Mr Harding was afraid; he was afraid that he was being led to do that which was not his duty: he was not, however, strong enough to resist, so he got up and followed his son-in-law.

The old men were assembled in groups in the quadrangle – eleven of them at least, for poor old Johnny Bell was bedridden, and couldn't come; he had, however, put his mark to the petition, as one of Handy's earliest followers. 'Tis true he could not move from the bed where he lay; 'tis true he had no friend on earth, but those whom the hospital contained; and of those the warden and his daughter were the most constant and most appreciated; 'tis true that everything was administered to him which his failing body could require, or which his faint appetite could enjoy; but still his dull eye had glistened for a moment at the idea of possessing a hundred pounds a year 'to his own cheek', as Abel Handy had eloquently expressed it; and poor old Johnny Bell had greedily put his mark to the petition.

When the two clergymen appeared, they all uncovered their heads. Handy was slow to do it, and hesitated; but the black coat and waistcoat, of which he had spoken so irreverently in Skulpit's room, had its effect even on him, and he too doffed his hat. Bunce, advancing before the others, bowed lowly to the archdeacon, and with affectionate reverence expressed his wish, that the warden and Miss Eleanor were quite well; 'and the doctor's lady,' he added, turning to the archdeacon, 'and the children at Plumstead, and my lord'; and having made his speech, he also retired among the others, and took his place with the rest upon the stone benches.

As the archdeacon stood up to make his speech, erect in the middle of that little square, he looked like an ecclesiastical statue placed there, as a fitting impersonation of the church militant here on earth; his shovel hat, large, new, and well pronounced, a churchman's hat in every inch, declared the profession as plainly as does the Quaker's broad brim; his heavy eyebrows, large open eyes, and full mouth and chin expressed the solidity of his order; the broad chest, amply covered with fine cloth, told how well-to-do was its estate; one hand ensconced within his pocket evinced the practical hold which our mother Church keeps on her temporal possessions; and the other, loose for action, was ready to fight if need be in her defence; and below these the decorous breeches, and neat black gaiters showing so admirably that well-turned leg, betokened the decency, the outward beauty and grace of our church establishment.

'Now my men,' he began, when he had settled himself well in his position; 'I want to say a few words to you. Your good friend, the warden here, and myself, and my lord the bishop, on whose behalf I wish to speak to you, would all be very sorry, very sorry indeed, that you should have any just ground of complaint. Any just ground of complaint on your part would be removed at once by the warden, or by his lordship, or by me on his behalf, without the necessity of any petition on your part.' Here the orator stopped for a moment, expecting that some little murmurs of applause would show that the weakest of the men were beginning to give way; but no such murmurs came. Bunce, himself, even sat with closed lips, mute and unsatisfactory. 'Without the necessity of any petition at all,' he repeated. 'I'm told you have addressed a petition to my lord.' He paused for a reply from the men, and after a while Handy plucked up courage, and said, 'Yes, we has.'

'You have addressed a petition to my lord, in which, as I am informed, you express an opinion that you do not receive from Hiram's estate all that is your due.' Here most of the men expressed their assent. 'Now what is it you ask for? what is it you want that you haven't got here? what is it –'

'A hundred a year,' muttered old Moody, with a voice as if it came out of the ground.

'A hundred a year!' ejaculated the archdeacon militant, defying the impudence of these claimants with one hand stretched out and closed, while with the other he tightly grasped, and secured within his breeches pocket, that symbol of the Church's wealth which his own loose half-crowns not unaptly represented. 'A hundred a year! Why, my men, you must be mad; and you talk about John Hiram's will! When John Hiram built a hospital for worn-out old men, worn-out old labouring men, infirm old men past their work, cripples, blind, bedridden, and such like, do you think he meant to make gentlemen of them? Do you think John Hiram intended to give a hundred a year to old single men, who earned perhaps two shillings or half a crown a day for themselves and families in the best of their time? No, my men, I'll tell you what John Hiram meant; he meant that twelve poor old worn-out labourers, men who could no longer support themselves, who had no friends to support them, who must starve and perish miserably if not pro-tected by the hand of charity; he meant that twelve such men as these should come in here in their poverty and wretchedness, and find within these walls shelter and food before their death, and a little leisure to make their peace with God. That was what John Hiram meant: you have not read John Hiram's will, and I doubt whether those wicked men who are advising you have done so. I have; I know what his will was; and I tell you that that was his will, and that that was his intention.'

Not a sound came from the eleven bedesmen, as they sat listen-ing to what, according to the archdeacon, was their intended estate. They grimly stared upon his burly figure, but did not then express, by word or sign, the anger and disgust to which such language was sure to give rise.

'Now let me ask you,' he continued, 'do you think you are worse off than John Hiram intended to make you? Have you not shelter, and food, and leisure? Have you not much more? Have you not every indulgence which you are capable of enjoying? Have you not twice better food, twice a better bed, ten times more money in your pocket than you were ever able to earn for yourselves before you were lucky enough to get into this place? And now you send a petition to the bishop, asking for a hundred pounds a year! I tell you what, my friends; you are deluded, and made fools of by wicked men who are acting for their own ends. You will never get a hundred pence a year more than what you have now: it is very possible that you may get less; it is very possible that my lord the bishop, and your warden may make changes –'

'No, no, no,' interrupted Mr Harding, who had been listening with indescribable misery to the tirade of his son-in-law; 'no, my friends. I want no changes – at least no changes that shall make you worse off than you now are, as long as you and I live together.'

'God bless you, Mr Harding,' said Bunce; and 'God bless you, Mr Harding, God bless you sir, we know you was always our friend' was exclaimed by enough of the men to make it appear that the sentiment was general.

The archdeacon had been interrupted in his speech before he had quite finished it; but he felt that he could not recommence with dignity after this little ebullition, and he led the way back into the garden, followed by his father-in-law.

'Well,' said he, as soon as he found himself within the cool retreat of the warden's garden; 'I think I spoke to them plainly.' And he wiped the perspiration from his brow; for making a speech under a broiling midday sun in summer, in a full suit of thick black cloth, is warm work.

'Yes, you were plain enough,' replied the warden, in a tone which did not express approbation.

'And that's everything,' said the other, who was clearly well satisfied with himself; 'that's everything: with those sort of people one must be plain, or one will not be understood. Now, I think they did understand me – I think they knew what I meant.'

The warden agreed. He certainly thought they had understood to the full what had been said to them.

'They know pretty well what they have to expect from us; they know how we shall meet any refractory spirit on their part; they know that we are not afraid of them. And now I'll just step into Chadwick's, and tell him what I've done; and then I'll go up to the palace, and answer this petition of theirs.'

The warden's mind was very full – full nearly to overcharging itself; and had it done so – had he allowed himself to speak the thoughts which were working within him, he would indeed have astonished the archdeacon by the reprobation he would have expressed as to the proceeding of which he had been so unwilling a witness. But different feelings kept him silent; he was as yet afraid of differing from his son-in-law – he was anxious beyond measure to avoid even a semblance of rupture with any of his order, and was painfully fearful of having to come to an open quarrel with any person on any subject. His life had hitherto been so quiet, so free from strife; his little early troubles had required nothing but passive fortitude; his subsequent prosperity had never forced upon him any active cares – had never brought him into disagreeable contact with anyone. He felt that he would give almost anything – much more than he knew he ought to do – to relieve himself from the storm which he feared was coming. It was so hard that the pleasant waters of his little stream should be disturbed and muddied by rough hands; that his quiet paths should be made a battlefield; that the unobtrusive corner of the world which had been allotted to him, as though by Providence, should be invaded and desecrated, and all within it made miserable and unsound.

Money he had none to give; the knack of putting guineas together had never belonged to him; but how willingly, with what a foolish easiness, with what happy alacrity, would he have abandoned the half of his income for all time to come, could he by so doing have quietly dispelled the clouds that were gathering over him – could he have thus compromised the matter between the reformer and the conservative, between his possible son-in-law, Bold, and his positive son-in-law, the archdeacon.

And this compromise would not have been made from any prudential motive of saving what would yet remain, for Mr Harding still felt little doubt but he should be left for life in quiet possession of the good things he had, if he chose to retain them. No; he would have done so from the sheer love of quiet, and from a horror of being made the subject of public talk. He had very often been moved to pity – to that inward weeping of the heart for others' woes; but none had he ever pitied more than that old lord, whose almost fabulous wealth, drawn from his church preferments, had become the subject of so much opprobrium, of such public scorn; that wretched clerical octogenarian Croesus,[6] whom men would not allow to die in peace – whom all the world united to decry and to abhor.

Was he to suffer such a fate? Was his humble name to be bandied in men's mouths, as the gormandizer of the resources of the poor, as of one who had filched from the charity of other ages wealth which had been intended to relieve the old and the infirm? Was he to be gibbeted in the press, to become a byword for oppression, to be named as an example of the greed of the English church? Should it ever be said that he had robbed those old men, whom he so truly and so tenderly loved in his heart of hearts? As he slowly paced, hour after hour, under those noble lime trees, turning these sad thoughts within him, he became all but fixed in his resolve that some great step must be taken to relieve him from the risk of so terrible a fate.

In the meanwhile, the archdeacon, with contented mind and unruffled spirit, went about his business. He said a word or two to Mr Chadwick, and then finding, as he expected, the petition lying in his father's library, he wrote a short answer to the men, in which he told them that they had no evils to redress, but rather great mercies for which to be thankful; and having seen the bishop sign it, he got into his brougham[7] and returned home to Mrs Grantly, and Plumstead Episcopi.

CHAPTER 6

The Warden's Tea Party

AFTER much painful doubting, on one thing only could Mr
Harding resolve. He determined that at any rate he would take no
offence, and that he would make this question no cause of quarrel
either with Bold or with the bedesmen. In furtherance of this
resolution, he himself wrote a note to Mr Bold, the same afternoon,
inviting him to meet a few friends and hear some music on an
evening named in the next week. Had not this little party been
promised to Eleanor, in his present state of mind he would probably
have avoided such gaiety; but the promise had been given, the
invitations were to be written, and when Eleanor consulted her
father on the subject, she was not ill pleased to hear him say, 'Oh,
I was thinking of Bold, so I took it into my head to write to him
myself, but you must write to his sister.'

Mary Bold was older than her brother, and, at the time of our
story, was just over thirty. She was not an unattractive young
woman, though by no means beautiful. Her great merit was the
kindliness of her disposition. She was not very clever, nor very
animated, nor had she apparently the energy of her brother; but
she was guided by a high principle of right and wrong; her temper
was sweet, and her faults were fewer in number than her virtues.
Those who casually met Mary Bold thought little of her; but those
who knew her well loved her well, and the longer they knew her
the more they loved her. Among those who were fondest of her
was Eleanor Harding, and though Eleanor had never openly talked
to her of her brother, each understood the other's feelings about
him. The brother and sister were sitting together when the two
notes were brought in.

'How odd,' said Mary, 'that they should send two notes.
Well, if Mr Harding becomes fashionable, the world is going to
change.'

Her brother understood immediately the nature and intention
of the peace-offering; but it was not so easy for him to behave well

in the matter as it was for Mr Harding. It is much less difficult for the sufferer to be generous than for the oppressor. John Bold felt that he could not go to the warden's party: he never loved Eleanor better than he did now; he had never so strongly felt how anxious he was to make her his wife as now, when so many obstacles to his doing so appeared in view. Yet here was her father himself, as it were clearing away those very obstacles, and still he felt that he could not go to the house any more as an open friend.

As he sat thinking of these things with the note in his hand, his sister was waiting for his decision.

'Well,' said she, 'I suppose we must write separate answers, and both say we shall be very happy.'

'You'll go, of course, Mary,' said he; to which she readily assented. 'I cannot,' he continued, looking serious and gloomy; 'I wish I could, with all my heart.'

'And why not, John?' said she. She had as yet heard nothing of the new-found abuse which her brother was about to reform; at least, nothing which connected it with her brother's name.

He sat thinking for a while till he determined that it would be best to tell her at once what it was that he was about: it must be done sooner or later.

'I fear I cannot go to Mr Harding's house any more as a friend, just at present.'

'Oh, John! Why not? Ah, you've quarrelled with Eleanor!'

'No, indeed,' said he; 'I've no quarrel with her as yet.'

'What is it, John?' said she, looking at him with an anxious, loving face, for she knew well how much of his heart was there in that house which he said he could no longer enter.

'Why,' said he at last, 'I've taken up the case of these twelve old men of Hiram's Hospital, and of course that brings me into contact with Mr Harding. I may have to oppose him, interfere with him, perhaps injure him.'

Mary looked at him steadily for some time before she committed herself to reply, and then merely asked him what he meant to do for the old men.

'Why, it's a long story, and I don't know that I can make you understand it. John Hiram made a will, and left his property in charity for certain poor old men, and the proceeds, instead of going to the benefit of these men, goes chiefly into the pocket of the warden, and the bishop's steward.'

'And you mean to take away from Mr Harding his share of it?'

'I don't know what I mean yet. I mean to inquire about it. I mean to see who is entitled to this property. I mean to see, if I can, that justice be done to the poor of the city of Barchester generally, who are, in fact, the legatees under the will. I mean, in short, to put the matter right, if I can.'

'And why are you to do this, John?'

'You might ask the same question of anybody else,' said he; 'and according to that, the duty of righting these poor men would belong to nobody. If we are to act on that principle, the weak are never to be protected, injustice is never to be opposed, and no one is to struggle for the poor!' And Bold began to comfort himself in the warmth of his own virtue.

'But is there no one to do this but you, who have known Mr Harding so long? Surely, John, as a friend, as a young friend, so much younger than Mr Harding –'

'That's woman's logic, all over, Mary. What has age to do with it? Another man might plead that he was too old; and as to his friendship, if the thing itself be right, private motives should never be allowed to interfere. Because I esteem Mr Harding, is that a reason that I should neglect a duty which I owe to these old men? or should I give up a work which my conscience tells me is a good one, because I regret the loss of his society?'

'And Eleanor, John?' said the sister, looking timidly into her brother's face.

'Eleanor, that is, Miss Harding, if she thinks fit – that is, if her father – or rather, if she – or, indeed, he – if they find it necessary – but there is no necessity now to talk about Eleanor Harding; but this I will say, that if she has the kind of spirit for which I give her credit, she will not condemn me for doing what I think to be a duty.' And Bold consoled himself with the consolation of a Roman.[1]

Mary sat silent for a while, till at last her brother reminded her that the notes must be answered, and she got up, and placed her desk before her, took out her pen and her paper, wrote on it slowly –

Pakenham Villas, Tuesday morning

MY DEAR ELEANOR,

   I –

and then stopped, and looked at her brother.

'Well, Mary, why don't you write it?'

'Oh, John,' said she, 'dear John, pray think better of this.'

'Think better of what?' said he.

'Of this about the hospital – of all this about Mr Harding – of what you say about those old men. Nothing can call upon you – no duty can require you to set yourself against your oldest, your best friend. Oh, John, think of Eleanor; you'll break her heart and your own.'

'Nonsense, Mary; Miss Harding's heart is as safe as yours.'

'Pray, pray, for my sake, John, give it up. You know how dearly you love her.' And she came and knelt before him on the rug. 'Pray give it up. You are going to make yourself, and her, and her father miserable: you are going to make us all miserable. And for what? For a dream of justice. You will never make those twelve men happier than they now are.'

'You don't understand it, my dear girl,' said he, smoothing her hair with his hand.

'I do understand it, John. I understand that this is a chimera – a dream that you have got. I know well that no duty can require you to do this mad – this suicidal thing. I know you love Eleanor Harding with all your heart, and I tell you now that she loves you as well. If there was a plain, a positive duty before you, I would be the last to bid you neglect it for any woman's love; but this – oh, think again, before you do anything to make it necessary that you and Mr Harding should be at variance.' He did not answer, as she knelt there, leaning on his knees, but by his face she thought that he was inclined to yield. 'At any rate let me say that you will go to this party. At any rate do not break with them while your mind is in doubt.' And she got up, hoping to conclude her note in the way she desired.

'My mind is not in doubt,' at last he said, rising; 'I could never respect myself again, were I to give way now because Eleanor Harding is beautiful. I do love her: I would give a hand to hear her tell me what you have said, speaking on her behalf; but I cannot for her sake go back from the task which I have commenced. I hope she may hereafter acknowledge and respect my motives, but I cannot now go as a guest to her father's house.' And the Barchester Brutus[2] went out to fortify his own resolution by meditations on his own virtue.

Poor Mary Bold sat down, and sadly finished her note, saying that she would herself attend the party, but that her brother was unavoidably prevented from doing so. I fear that she did not admire as she should have done the self-devotion of his singular virtue.

The party went off as such parties do: there were fat old ladies in fine silk dresses, and slim young ladies in gauzy muslin frocks; old gentlemen stood up with their backs to the empty fireplace, looking by no means so comfortable as they would have done in their own armchairs at home; and young gentlemen, rather stiff about the neck, clustered near the door, not as yet sufficiently in courage to attack the muslin frocks, who awaited the battle, drawn up in a semicircular array. The warden endeavoured to induce a charge, but failed signally, not having the tact of a general: his daughter did what she could to comfort the forces under her command, who took in refreshing rations of cake and tea, and patiently looked for the coming engagement: but she herself, Eleanor, had no spirit for the work; the only enemy whose lance she cared to encounter was not there, and she and others were somewhat dull.

Loud above all voices was heard the clear sonorous tones of the archdeacon as he dilated to brother parsons of the danger of the Church, of the fearful rumours of mad reforms even at Oxford,[3] and of the damnable heresies of Dr Whiston.

Soon, however, sweeter sounds began timidly to make themselves audible. Little movements were made in a quarter, notable for round stools and music stands. Wax candles were arranged in sconces, big books were brought from hidden recesses, and the work of the evening commenced.

How often were those pegs twisted and retwisted before our friend found that he had twisted them enough; how many discordant scrapes gave promise of the coming harmony! How much the muslin fluttered and crumpled before Eleanor and another nymph were duly seated at the piano; how closely did that tall Apollo[4] pack himself against the wall, with his flute, long as himself, extending high over the heads of his pretty neighbours; into how small a corner crept that round and florid little minor canon, and there with skill amazing found room to tune his accustomed fiddle!

And now the crash begins: away they go in full flow of harmony together – up hill and down dale – now louder and louder, then lower and lower: now loud, as though stirring the battle; then low, as though mourning the slain. In all, through all, and above all, is heard the violoncello. Ah, not for nothing were those pegs so twisted and retwisted – listen, listen! Now alone that saddest of instruments tells its touching tale. Silent, and in awe, stand fiddle, flute, and piano, to hear the sorrows of their wailing brother. 'Tis but for a moment: before the melancholy of those low notes has been fully realized, again comes the full force of all the band – down go the pedals, away rush twenty fingers scouring over the bass notes with all the impetus of passion. Apollo blows till his stiff neckcloth is no better than a rope, and the minor canon works both arms till he falls in a syncope of exhaustion against the wall.

How comes it that now, when all should be silent, when courtesy, if not taste, should make men listen – how is it at this moment the black-coated corps leave their retreat and begin skirmishing? One by one they creep forth, and fire off little guns timidly, and without precision. Ah, my men, efforts such as these will take no cities, even though the enemy should be never so open to assault. At length a more deadly artillery is brought to bear; slowly, but with effect, the advance is made; the muslin ranks are broken, and fall into confusion; the formidable array of chairs gives way; the battle is no longer between opposing regiments, but hand to hand, and foot to foot with single combatants, as in the glorious days of old, when fighting was really noble. In corners, and under the shadow of curtains, behind sofas and half hidden by doors, in retiring windows, and sheltered by hanging tapestry, are blows given and returned, fatal, incurable, dealing death.

Apart from this another combat arises, more sober and more serious. The archdeacon is engaged against two prebendaries,[5] a pursy full-blown rector assisting him, in all the perils and all the enjoyments of short whist.[6] With solemn energy do they watch the shuffled pack, and, all-expectant, eye the coming trump. With what anxious nicety do they arrange their cards, jealous of each other's eyes! Why is that lean doctor so slow – cadaverous man with hollow jaw and sunken eye, ill beseeming the richness of his mother church! Ah, why so slow, thou meagre doctor? See how the archdeacon, speechless in his agony, deposits on the board his cards, and looks to heaven or to the ceiling for support. Hark, how he sighs, as with thumbs in his waistcoat pocket he seems to signify that the end of such torment is not yet even nigh at hand! Vain is the hope, if hope there be, to disturb that meagre doctor. With care precise he places every card, weighs well the value of each mighty ace, each guarded king, and comfort-giving queen; speculates on knave and ten, counts all his suits, and sets his price upon the whole. At length a card is led, and quick three others fall upon the board. The little doctor leads again, while with lustrous eye his partner absorbs the trick. Now thrice has this been done – thrice has constant fortune favoured the brace of prebendaries, ere the archdeacon rouses himself to the battle: but at the fourth assault he pins to the earth a prostrate king, laying low his crown and sceptre, bushy beard, and lowering brow, with a poor deuce.

'As David did Goliath,' says the archdeacon, pushing over the four cards to his partner. And then a trump is led, then another trump; then, a king – and then an ace – and then a long ten, which brings down from the meagre doctor his only remaining tower of strength – his cherished queen of trumps.

'What, no second club?' says the archdeacon to his partner.

'Only one club,' mutters from his inmost stomach the pursy rector, who sits there red-faced, silent, impervious, careful, a safe but not a brilliant ally.

But the archdeacon cares not for many clubs, or for none. He dashes out his remaining cards with a speed most annoying to his antagonists, pushes over to them some four cards as their allotted portion, shoves the remainder across the table to the red-faced rector: calls out 'two by cards and two by honours, and the odd trick last time', marks a treble under the candlestick,[7] and has dealt round the second pack before the meagre doctor has calculated his losses.

And so went off the warden's party, and men and women arranging shawls and shoes declared how pleasant it had been; and Mrs Goodenough, the red-faced rector's wife, pressing the warden's hand, declared she had never enjoyed herself better; which showed how little pleasure she allowed herself in this world, as she had sat the whole evening through in the same chair without occupation, not speaking, and unspoken to. And Matilda Johnson, when she allowed young Dickson of the bank to fasten her cloak round her neck, thought that two hundred pounds a year and a little cottage would really do for happiness; besides he was sure to be manager some day. And Apollo, folding his flute into his pocket, felt that he had acquitted himself with honour; and the archdeacon pleasantly jingled his gains; but the meagre doctor went off without much audible speech, muttering ever and anon as he went 'three and thirty points', 'three and thirty points!'[*]

And so they all were gone, and Mr Harding was left alone with his daughter.

What had passed between Eleanor Harding and Mary Bold need not be told. It is indeed a matter of thankfulness that neither the historian nor the novelist hears all that is said by their heroes or heroines, or how would three volumes or twenty suffice! In the present case so little of this sort have I overheard, that I live in hopes of finishing my work within 300 pages, and of completing that pleasant task – a novel in one volume; but something had passed between them, and as the warden blew out the wax candles, and put his instrument into its case, his daughter stood sad and thoughtful by the empty fireplace, determined to speak to her father, but irresolute as to what she would say.

'Well, Eleanor,' said he, 'are you for bed?'

'Yes,' said she, moving, 'I suppose so; but, papa – Mr Bold was not here tonight: do you know why not?'

'He was asked; I wrote to him myself,' said the warden.

'But do you know why he did not come, papa?'

'Well, Eleanor, I could guess; but it's no use guessing at such things, my dear. What makes you look so earnest about it?'

'Oh papa, do tell me,' she exclaimed, throwing her arms round him, and looking into his face; 'what is it he is going to do? What is it all about? Is there any – any – any –' she didn't well know what word to use – 'any danger?'

'Danger, my dear, what sort of danger?'

'Danger to you, danger of trouble, and of loss, and of – Oh papa, why haven't you told me of all this before?'

Mr Harding was not the man to judge harshly of anyone, much less of the daughter whom he now loved better than any living creature; but still he did judge her wrongly at this moment. He knew that she loved John Bold; he fully sympathized in her affection; day after day he thought more of the matter, and, with the tender care of a loving father, tried to arrange in his own mind how matters might be so managed that his daughter's heart should not be made the sacrifice to the dispute which was likely to exist between him and Bold. Now, when she spoke to him for the first time on the subject, it was natural that he should think more of her than of himself, and that he should imagine that her own cares, and not his, were troubling her.

He stood silent before her awhile, as she gazed up into his face, and then kissing her forehead he placed her on the sofa.

'Tell me, Nelly,' he said (he only called her Nelly in his kindest, softest, sweetest moods, and yet all his moods were kind and sweet), 'tell me, Nelly, do you like Mr Bold – much?'

She was quite taken aback by the question. I will not say that she had forgotten herself and her own love in thinking about John Bold, and while conversing with Mary: she certainly had not done so. She had been sick at heart to think that a man of whom she could not but own to herself that she loved him, of whose regard she had been so proud, that such a man should turn against her father to ruin him. She had felt her vanity hurt, that his affection for her had not kept him from such a course; had he really cared for her, he would not have risked her love by such an outrage; but her main fear had been for her father, and when she spoke of danger, it was of danger to him and not to herself.

She was taken aback by the question altogether: 'Do I like him, papa?'

'Yes, Nelly, do you like him? Why shouldn't you like him; but that's a poor word – do you love him?' She sat still in his arms without answering him. She certainly had not prepared herself for an avowal of affection, intending, as she had done, to abuse John Bold herself, and to hear her father do so also. 'Come, my love,' said he, 'let us make a clean breast of it: do you tell me what concerns yourself, and I will tell you what concerns me and the hospital.'

And then, without waiting for an answer, he described to her, as he best could, the accusation that was made about Hiram's will; the claims which the old men put forward; what he considered the strength and what the weakness of his own position; the course which Bold had taken, and that which he presumed he was about to take; and then by degrees, without further question, he presumed on the fact of Eleanor's love, and spoke of that love as a feeling which he could in no way disapprove: he apologized for Bold, excused what he was doing; nay praised him for his energy and intentions: made much of his good qualities, and harped on none of his foibles; then, reminding his daughter how late it was, and comforting her with much assurance which he hardly felt himself, he sent her to her room, with flowing eyes and a full heart.

When Mr Harding met his daughter at breakfast the next morning, there was no further discussion on the matter, nor was the subject mentioned between them for some days. Soon after the party Mary Bold called at the hospital, but there were various persons in the drawing-room at the time, and she therefore said nothing about her brother. On the day following, John Bold met Miss Harding in one of the quiet sombre shaded walks of the close: he was most anxious to see her, but unwilling to call at the warden's house, and had in truth waylaid her in her private haunts.

'My sister tells me,' said he, abruptly hurrying on with his premeditated speech, 'my sister tells me that you had a delightful party the other evening. I was so sorry I could not be there.'

'We were all sorry,' said Eleanor, with dignified composure.

'I believe, Miss Harding, you understood why, at this moment –' And Bold hesitated, muttered, stopped, commenced his explanation again, and again broke down.

Eleanor would not help him in the least.

'I think my sister explained to you, Miss Harding?'

'Pray don't apologize, Mr Bold; my father will, I am sure, always be glad to see you, if you like to come to the house now as formerly; nothing has occurred to alter his feelings; of your own views you are, of course, the best judge.'

'Your father is all that is kind and generous; he always was so, but you, Miss Harding, yourself – I hope you will not judge me harshly, because –'

'Mr Bold,' said she, 'you may be sure of one thing; I shall always judge my father to be right, and those who oppose him I shall judge to be wrong. If those who do not know him oppose him, I shall have charity enough to believe that they are wrong, through error of judgement; but should I see him attacked by those who ought to know him, and to love him, and revere him, of such I shall be constrained to form a different opinion.' And then curtseying low she sailed on, leaving her lover in anything but a happy state of mind.

CHAPTER 7

The Jupiter

THOUGH Eleanor Harding rode off from John Bold on a high horse, it must not be supposed that her heart was so elate as her demeanour. In the first place, she had a natural repugnance to losing her lover; and in the next, she was not quite so sure that she was in the right as she pretended to be. Her father had told her, and that now repeatedly, that Bold was doing nothing unjust or ungenerous, and why then should she rebuke him, and throw him off, when she felt herself so ill able to bear his loss? – but such is human nature, and young-lady-nature especially. As she walked off from him beneath the shady elms of the close, her look, her tone, every motion and gesture of her body, belied her heart; she would have given the world to have taken him by the hand, to have reasoned with him, persuaded him, cajoled him, coaxed him out of his project; to have overcome him with all her female artillery, and to have redeemed her father at the cost of herself; but pride would not let her do this, and she left him without a look of love or a word of kindness.

Had Bold been judging of another lover and of another lady he might have understood all this as well as we do; but in matters of love men do not see clearly in their own affairs. They say that faint heart never won fair lady; and it is amazing to me how fair ladies are won, so faint are often men's hearts! Were it not for the kindness of their nature, that seeing the weakness of our courage they will occasionally descend from their impregnable fortresses, and themselves aid us in effecting their own defeat, too often would they escape unconquered if not unscathed, and free of body if not of heart.

Poor Bold crept off quite crestfallen; he felt that as regarded Eleanor Harding his fate was sealed, unless he could consent to give up a task to which he had pledged himself, and which indeed it would not be easy for him to give up. Lawyers were engaged, and the question had to a certain extent been taken up by the public; besides, how could a high-spirited girl like Eleanor Harding really learn to love a man for neglecting a duty which he assumed! Could she allow her affection to be purchased at the cost of his own self-respect?

As regarded the issue of his attempt at reformation in the hospital, Bold had no reason hitherto to be discontented with his success. All Barchester was by the ears about it. The bishop, the archdeacon, the warden, the steward, and several other clerical allies, had daily meetings, discussing their tactics, and preparing for the great attack. Sir Abraham Haphazard had been consulted, but his opinion was not yet received: copies of Hiram's will, copies of wardens' journals, copies of leases, copies of accounts, copies of everything that could be copied, and of some that could not, had been sent to him; and the case was assuming most creditable dimensions. But above all, it had been mentioned in the daily *Jupiter*.[1] That all-powerful organ of the press in one of its leading thunderbolts launched at St Cross, had thus re-marked:

Another case, of smaller dimensions indeed, but of similar import, is now likely to come under public notice. We are informed that the warden or master of an old almshouse attached to Barchester Cathedral is in receipt of twenty-five times the annual income appointed for him by the will of the founder, while the sum yearly expended on the absolute purposes of the charity has always remained fixed. In other words, the legatees under the founder's will have received no advantage from the increase in the value of the property during the last four centuries, such increase having been absorbed by the so-called warden. It is impossible to conceive a case of greater injustice. It is no answer to say that some six or nine or twelve old men receive as much of the goods of this world as such old men require. On what foundation, moral or divine, traditional or legal, is grounded the warden's claim to the large income he receives for doing nothing? The contentment of these almsmen, if content they be, can give him no title to this wealth! Does he ever ask himself, when he stretches wide his clerical palm to receive the pay of some dozen of the working clergy, for what service he is so remunerated? Does his conscience ever entertain the question of his right to such subsidies? Or is it possible that the subject never so presents itself to his mind; that he has received for many years, and intends, should God spare him, to receive for years to come, these fruits of the industrious piety of past ages, indifferent as to any right on his own part, or of any injustice to others! We must express an opinion that nowhere but in the Church of England, and only there among its priests, could such a state of moral indifference be found.

I must for the present leave my readers to imagine the state of Mr Harding's mind after reading the above article. They say that forty thousand copies of the *Jupiter* are daily sold, and that each copy is read by five persons at the least. Two hundred thousand readers then would hear this accusation against him; two hundred thousand hearts would swell with indignation at the griping injustice, the barefaced robbery of the warden of Barchester Hospital! And how was he to answer this? How was he to open his inmost heart to this multitude, to these thousands, the educated, the polished, the picked men of his own country; how show them that he was no robber, no avaricious lazy priest scrambling for gold, but a retiring humble-spirited man who had innocently taken what had innocently been offered to him?

'Write to the *Jupiter*,' suggested the bishop.

'Yes,' said the archdeacon, more worldly wise than his father, 'yes, and be smothered with ridicule; tossed over and over again with scorn; shaken this way and that, as a rat in the mouth of a practised terrier. You will leave out some word or letter in your answer, and the ignorance of the cathedral clergy will be harped upon; you will make some small mistake, which will be a falsehood, or some admission, which will be self-condemnation; you will find yourself to have been vulgar, ill-tempered, irreverend, and illiterate, and the chances are ten to one but that being a clergyman you will have been guilty of blasphemy! A man may have the best of causes, the best of talents, and the best of tempers; he may write as well as Addison,[2] or as strongly as Junius;[3] but even with all this he cannot successfully answer, when attacked by the *Jupiter*. In such matters it is omnipotent. What the Czar is in Russia, or the mob in America, that the *Jupiter* is in England. Answer such an article! No, warden; whatever you do, don't do that. We were to look for this sort of thing you know; but we need not draw down on our heads more of it than is necessary.'

The article in the *Jupiter*, while it so greatly harassed our poor warden, was an immense triumph to some of the opposite party.

Sorry as Bold was to see Mr Harding attacked so personally, it still gave him a feeling of elation to find his cause taken up by so powerful an advocate: and as to Finney, the attorney, he was beside himself. What! to be engaged in the same cause and on the same side with the *Jupiter*; to have the views he had recommended seconded, and furthered, and battled for by the *Jupiter*! Perhaps to have his own name mentioned as that of the learned gentleman whose efforts had been so successful on behalf of the poor of Barchester! He might be examined before committees of the House of Commons, with heaven knows how much a day for his personal expenses – he might be engaged for years on such a suit! There was no end to the glorious golden dreams which this leader in the *Jupiter* produced in the soaring mind of Finney.

And the old bedesmen, they also heard of this article, and had a glimmering, indistinct idea of the marvellous advocate which had now taken up their cause. Abel Handy limped hither and thither through the rooms, repeating all that he understood to have been printed, with some additions of his own which he thought should have been added. He told them how the *Jupiter* had declared that their warden was no better than a robber, and that what the *Jupiter* said was acknowledged by the world to be true. How the *Jupiter* had affirmed that each one of them – 'each one of us, Jonathan Crumple, think of that' – had a clear right to a hundred a year; and that if the *Jupiter* had said so, it was better than a decision of the Lord Chancellor; and then he carried about the paper, supplied by Mr Finney, which, though none of them could read it, still afforded in its very touch and aspect positive corroboration of what was told them, and Jonathan Crumple pondered deeply over his returning wealth; and Job Skulpit saw how right he had been in signing the petition, and said so many scores of times; and Spriggs leered fearfully with his one eye; and Moody, as he more nearly approached the coming golden age, hated more deeply than ever those who still kept possession of what he so coveted. Even Billy Gazy and poor bedridden Bell became active and uneasy, and the great Bunce stood apart with lowering brow, with deep grief seated in his heart, for he perceived that evil days were coming.

It had been decided, the archdeacon advising, that no remonstrance, explanation, or defence should be addressed from the Barchester conclave to the editor of the *Jupiter*, but hitherto that was the only decision to which they had come.

Sir Abraham Haphazard was deeply engaged in preparing a bill for the mortification of papists, to be called the 'Convent Custody Bill',[4] the purport of which was to enable any protestant clergyman over fifty years of age to search any nun whom he suspected of being in possession of treasonable papers or jesuitical symbols: and as there were to be a hundred and thirty-seven clauses in the bill, each clause containing a separate thorn for the side of the papist, and as it was known the bill would be fought inch by inch by fifty maddened Irishmen, the due construction and adequate dovetailing of it did consume much of Sir Abraham's time. The bill had all its desired effect. Of course it never passed into law; but it so completely divided the ranks of the Irish members, who had bound themselves together to force on the ministry a bill for compelling all men to drink Irish whiskey, and all women to wear Irish poplins, that for the remainder of the session the Great Poplin and Whiskey League was utterly harmless.

Thus it happened that Sir Abraham's opinion was not at once forthcoming, and the uncertainty, the expectation, and suffering of the folk of Barchester was maintained at a high pitch.

CHAPTER 8

Plumstead Episcopi

THE reader must now be requested to visit the rectory of Plumstead Episcopi; and as it is as yet still early morning, to ascend again with us into the bedroom of the archdeacon. The mistress of the mansion was at her toilet; on which we will not dwell with profane eyes, but proceed into a small inner room, where the doctor dressed and kept his boots and sermons; and here we will take our stand, premising that the door of the room was so open as to admit of a conversation between our reverend Adam and his valued Eve.

'It's all your own fault, archdeacon,' said the latter; 'I told you from the beginning how it would end, and papa has no one to thank but you.'

'Good gracious, my dear,' said the doctor, appearing at the door of his dressing-room, with his face and head enveloped in the rough towel which he was violently using; 'how can you say so? I am doing my very best.'

'I wish you had never done so much,' said the lady, interrupting him; 'if you'd just have let John Bold come and go there, as he and papa liked, he and Eleanor would have been married by this time, and we should not have heard one word about all this affair.'

'But, my dear —'

'Oh, it's all very well, archdeacon, and of course you're right; I don't for a moment think you'll ever admit that you could be wrong; but the fact is, you've brought this young man down upon papa by huffing him as you have done.'

'But, my love —'

'And all because you didn't like John Bold for a brother-in-law. How is she ever to do better? papa hasn't got a shilling; and though Eleanor is well enough, she has not at all a taking style of beauty. I'm sure I don't know how she's to do better than marry John Bold, or as well indeed,' added the anxious sister, giving the last twist to her last shoestring.

Dr Grantly felt keenly the injustice of this attack; but what could he say? He certainly had huffed John Bold; he certainly had objected to him as a brother-in-law, and a very few months ago the very idea had excited his wrath: but now matters were changed; John Bold had shown his power, and, though he was as odious as ever to the archdeacon, power is always respected, and the reverend dignitary began to think that such an alliance might not have been imprudent. Nevertheless, his motto was still 'no surrender'; he would still fight it out; he still believed confidently in Oxford, in the bench of bishops,[1] in Sir Abraham Haphazard, and in himself; and it was only when alone with his wife that doubts of defeat ever beset him. He once more tried to communicate this confidence to Mrs Grantly, and for the twentieth time began to tell her of Sir Abraham.

'Oh, Sir Abraham!' said she, collecting all her house keys into her basket before she descended; 'Sir Abraham won't get Eleanor a husband; Sir Abraham won't get papa another income when he has been worreted[2] out of the hospital. Mark what I tell you, archdeacon: while you and Sir Abraham are fighting, papa will lose his preferment; and what will you do then with him and Eleanor on your hands? besides, who's to pay Sir Abraham? I suppose he won't take the case up for nothing?' And so the lady descended to family worship among her children and servants, the pattern of a good and prudent wife.

Dr Grantly was blessed with a happy, thriving family. There were, first, three boys, now at home from school for the holidays. They were called, respectively, Charles James, Henry, and Samuel. The two younger (there were five in all) were girls; the elder, Florinda, bore the name of the Archbishop of York's wife, whose godchild she was; and the younger had been christened Grizzel, after a sister of the Archbishop of Canterbury. The boys were all clever, and gave good promise of being well able to meet the cares and trials of the world; and yet they were not alike in their dispositions, and each had his individual character, and each his separate admirers among the doctor's friends.

Charles James[3] was an exact and careful boy; he never committed himself; he well knew how much was expected from the eldest son of the Archdeacon of Barchester, and was therefore mindful not to mix too freely with other boys. He had not the great talents of his younger brothers, but he exceeded them in judgement and propriety of demeanour; his fault, if he had one, was an over-attention to words instead of things; there was a thought too much finesse about him, and, as even his father sometimes told him, he was too fond of a compromise.

The second was the archdeacon's favourite son, and Henry[4] was indeed a brilliant boy. The versatility of his genius was surprising, and the visitors at Plumstead Episcopi were often amazed at the marvellous manner in which he would, when called on, adapt his capacity to apparently most uncongenial pursuits. He appeared once before a large circle as Luther the reformer, and delighted them with the perfect manner in which he assumed the character; and within three days he again astonished them by acting the part of a Capuchin friar to the very life.[5] For this last exploit his father gave him a golden guinea, and his brothers said the reward had been promised beforehand in the event of the performance being successful. He was also sent on a tour into Devonshire; a treat which the lad was most anxious of enjoying. His father's friends there, however, did not appreciate his talents, and sad accounts were sent home of the perversity of his nature. He was a most courageous lad, game to the backbone. It was soon known, both at home, where he lived, and within some miles of Barchester Cathedral, and also at Westminster, where he was at school, that young Henry could box well and would never own himself beat; other boys would fight while they had a leg to stand on, but he would fight with no leg at all. Those backing him would sometimes think him crushed by the weight of blows and faint with loss of blood, and his friends would endeavour to withdraw him from the contest; but no, Henry never gave in, was never weary of the battle. The ring was the only element in which he seemed to enjoy himself; and while other boys were happy in the number of their friends, he rejoiced most in the multitude of his foes.

His relations could not but admire his pluck, but they sometimes were forced to regret that he was inclined to be a bully; and those not so partial to him as his father was observed with pain that, though he could fawn to the masters and the archdeacon's friends, he was imperious and masterful to the servants and the poor.

But perhaps Samuel was the general favourite; and dear little Soapy,⁶ as he was familiarly called, was as engaging a child as ever fond mother petted. He was soft and gentle in his manners, and attractive in his speech; the tone of his voice was melody, and every action was a grace; unlike his brothers, he was courteous to all, he was affable to the lowly, and meek even to the very scullery maid. He was a boy of great promise, minding his books and delighting the hearts of his masters. His brothers, however, were not particularly fond of him; they would complain to their mother that Soapy's civility all meant something; they thought that his voice was too often listened to at Plumstead Episcopi, and evidently feared that, as he grew up, he would have more weight in the house than either of them; there was, therefore, a sort of agreement among them to put young Soapy down. This, however, was not so easy to be done; Samuel, though young, was sharp; he could not assume the stiff decorum of Charles James, nor could he fight like Henry; but he was a perfect master of his own weapons, and contrived, in the teeth of both of them, to hold the place which he had assumed. Henry declared that he was a false, cunning creature; and Charles James, though he always spoke of him as his dear brother Samuel, was not slow to say a word against him when opportunity offered. To speak the truth, Samuel was a cunning boy, and those even who loved him best could not but own that for one so young he was too adroit in choosing his words, and too skilled in modulating his voice.

The two little girls Florinda and Grizzel were nice little girls enough, but they did not possess the strong sterling qualities of their brothers; their voices were not often heard at Plumstead Episcopi; they were bashful and timid by nature, slow to speak before company even when asked to do so; and though they looked very nice in their clean white muslin frocks and pink sashes, they were but little noticed by the archdeacon's visitors.

Whatever of submissive humility may have appeared in the gait and visage of the archdeacon during his colloquy with his wife in the sanctum of their dressing-rooms was dispelled as he entered his breakfast-parlour with erect head and powerful step. In the presence of a third person he assumed the lord and master; and that wise and talented lady too well knew the man to whom her

lot for life was bound, to stretch her authority beyond the point
at which it would be borne. Strangers at Plumstead Episcopi,
when they saw the imperious brow with which he commanded
silence from the large circle of visitors, children, and servants who
came together in the morning to hear him read the word of God,
and watched how meekly that wife seated herself behind her
basket of keys with a little girl on each side, as she caught that
commanding glance; strangers, I say, seeing this, could little guess
that some fifteen minutes since she had stoutly held her ground
against him, hardly allowing him to open his mouth in his own
defence. But such is the tact and talent of women!

And now let us observe the well-furnished breakfast-parlour at
Plumstead Episcopi, and the comfortable air of all the belongings
of the rectory. Comfortable they certainly were, but neither
gorgeous nor even grand; indeed, considering the money that had
been spent there, the eye and taste might have been better served;
there was an air of heaviness about the rooms which might have
been avoided without any sacrifice of propriety; colours might
have been better chosen and lights more perfectly diffused: but
perhaps in doing so the thorough clerical aspect of the whole
might have been somewhat marred; at any rate, it was not without ample consideration that those thick, dark, costly carpets were
put down; those embossed, but sombre papers hung up; those
heavy curtains draped so as to half exclude the light of the sun:
nor were these old-fashioned chairs, bought at a price far exceeding that now given for more modern goods, without a purpose.
The breakfast-service on the table was equally costly and equally
plain; the apparent object had been to spend money without
obtaining brilliancy or splendour. The urn was of thick and solid
silver, as were also the teapot, coffeepot, cream-ewer, and sugar-
bowl; the cups were old, dim dragon china, worth about a pound
a piece, but very despicable in the eyes of the uninitiated. The silver
forks were so heavy as to be disagreeable to the hand, and the
breadbasket was of a weight really formidable to any but robust
persons. The tea consumed was the very best, the coffee the very
blackest, the cream the very thickest; there was dry toast and
buttered toast, muffins and crumpets; hot bread and cold bread,
white bread and brown bread, home-made bread and bakers'

bread, wheaten bread and oaten bread, and if there be other breads than these, they were there; there were eggs in napkins, and crispy bits of bacon under silver covers; and there were little fishes in a little box, and devilled kidneys frizzling on a hot-water dish; which, by the by, were placed closely contiguous to the plate of the worthy archdeacon himself. Over and above this, on a snow-white napkin, spread upon the sideboard, was a huge ham and a huge sirloin; the latter having laden the dinner-table on the previous evening. Such was the ordinary fare at Plumstead Episcopi.

And yet I have never found the rectory a pleasant house. The fact that man shall not live by bread alone seemed to be somewhat forgotten; and noble as was the appearance of the host, and sweet and good-natured as was the face of the hostess, talented as were the children, and excellent as were the viands and the wines, in spite of these attractions, I generally found the rectory somewhat dull. After breakfast the archdeacon would retire, of course to his clerical pursuits. Mrs Grantly, I presume, inspected her kitchen, though she had a first-rate housekeeper, with sixty pounds a year; and attended to the lessons of Florinda and Grizzel, though she had an excellent governess with thirty pounds a year: but at any rate she disappeared: and I never could make companions of the boys. Charles James, though he always looked as though there was something in him, never seemed to have much to say; and what he did say he would always unsay the next minute. He told me once, that he considered cricket, on the whole, to be a gentleman-like game for boys, provided they would play without running about; and that fives, also, was a seemly game, so that those who played it never heated themselves. Henry once quarrelled with me for taking his sister Grizzel's part, in a contest between them as to the best mode of using a watering-pot for the garden flowers; and from that day to this he has not spoken to me, though he speaks at me often enough. For half an hour or so I certainly did like Sammy's gentle speeches; but one gets tired of honey, and I found that he preferred the more admiring listeners whom he met in the kitchen-garden and back precincts of the establishment; besides, I think I once caught Sammy fibbing.

On the whole, therefore, I found the rectory a dull house, though it must be admitted that everything there was of the very best.

After breakfast, on the morning of which we are writing, the archdeacon, as usual, retired to his study, intimating that he was going to be very busy, but that he would see Mr Chadwick if he called. On entering this sacred room he carefully opened the paper case on which he was wont to compose his favourite sermons, and spread on it a fair sheet of paper, and one partly written on; he then placed his inkstand, looked at his pen, and folded his blotting paper; having done so, he got up again from his seat, stood with his back to the fireplace, and yawned comfortably, stretching out vastly his huge arms, and opening his burly chest. He then walked across the room and locked the door; and having so prepared himself, he threw himself into his easy chair, took from a secret drawer beneath his table a volume of Rabelais, and began to amuse himself with the witty mischief of Panurge;[7] and so passed the archdeacon's morning on that day.

He was left undisturbed at his studies for an hour or two, when a knock came to the door, and Mr Chadwick was announced. Rabelais retired into the secret drawer, the easy chair seemed knowingly to betake itself off, and when the archdeacon quickly undid his bolt, he was discovered by the steward working, as usual, for that church of which he was so useful a pillar. Mr Chadwick had just come from London, and was, therefore, known to be the bearer of important news.

'We've got Sir Abraham's opinion at last,' said Mr Chadwick, as he seated himself.

'Well, well, well!' exclaimed the archdeacon impatiently.

'Oh, it's as long as my arm,' said the other; 'it can't be told in a word, but you can read it'; and he handed him a copy, in heaven knows how many spun-out folios, of the opinion which the attorney-general[8] had managed to cram on the back and sides of the case as originally submitted to him.

'The upshot is,' said Chadwick, 'that there's a screw loose in their case, and we had better do nothing. They are proceeding against Mr Harding and myself, and Sir Abraham holds that, under the wording of the will and subsequent arrangements legally sanctioned, Mr Harding and I are only paid servants. The defendants should have been either the Corporation of Barchester, or possibly the chapter or your father.'

'W—hoo!' said the archdeacon; 'so Master Bold is on a wrong scent, is he?'

'That's Sir Abraham's opinion; but any scent almost would be a wrong scent. Sir Abraham thinks that if they'd taken the corporation, or the chapter, we could have baffled them. The bishop, he thinks, would be the surest shot; but even there we could plead that the bishop is only visitor, and that he has never made himself a consenting party to the performance of other duties.'

'That's quite clear,' said the archdeacon.

'Not quite so clear,' said the other. 'You see the will says, "My lord, the bishop, being graciously pleased to see that due justice be done." Now, it may be a question whether, in accepting and administering the patronage, your father has not accepted also the other duties assigned. It is doubtful, however; but even if they hit that nail – and they are far off from that yet – the point is so nice, as Sir Abraham says, that you would force them into fifteen thousand pounds' cost before they could bring it to an issue! and where's that sum of money to come from?'

The archdeacon rubbed his hands with delight; he had never doubted the justice of his case, but he had begun to have some dread of unjust success on the part of his enemies. It was delightful to him thus to hear that their cause was surrounded with such rocks and shoals; such causes of shipwreck unseen by the landsman's eye, but visible enough to the keen eyes of practical law mariners. How wrong his wife was to wish that Bold should marry Eleanor! Bold! why, if he should be ass enough to persevere, he would be a beggar before he knew whom he was at law with!

'That's excellent, Chadwick – that's excellent! I told you Sir Abraham was the man for us'; and he put down on the table the copy of the opinion, and patted it fondly.

'Don't you let that be seen, though, archdeacon.'

'Who? – I! – not for worlds,' said the doctor.

'People will talk, you know, archdeacon.'

'Of course, of course,' said the doctor.

'Because, if that gets abroad, it would teach them how to fight their own battle.'

'Quite true,' said the doctor.

'No one here in Barchester ought to see that but you and I, archdeacon.'

'No, no, certainly no one else,' said the archdeacon, pleased with the closeness of the confidence; 'no one else shall.'

'Mrs Grantly is very interested in the matter, I know,' said Mr Chadwick.

Did the archdeacon wink, or did he not? I am inclined to think he did not quite wink; but that without such, perhaps, unseemly gesture he communicated to Mr Chadwick, with the corner of his eye, intimation that, deep as was Mrs Grantly's interest in the matter, it should not procure for her a perusal of that document; and at the same time he partly opened the small drawer, above spoken of, deposited the paper on the volume of Rabelais, and showed to Mr Chadwick the nature of the key which guarded these hidden treasures. The careful steward then expressed himself contented. Ah! vain man! he could fasten up his Rabelais, and other things secret, with all the skill of Bramah or of Chubb;° but where could he fasten up the key which solved these mechanical mysteries? It is probable to us that the contents of no drawer in that house were unknown to its mistress, and we think, moreover, that she was entitled to all such knowledge.

'But,' said Mr Chadwick, 'we must, of course, tell your father and Mr Harding so much of Sir Abraham's opinion as will satisfy them that the matter is doing well.'

'Oh, certainly – yes, of course,' said the doctor.

'You had better let them know that Sir Abraham is of opinion that there is no case at any rate against Mr Harding; and that as the action is worded at present, it must fall to the ground; they must be nonsuited if they carry it on; you had better tell Mr Harding that Sir Abraham is clearly of opinion that he is only a servant, and as such, not liable – or if you like it, I'll see Mr Harding myself.'

'Oh, I must see him tomorrow, and my father too, and I'll explain to them exactly so much – you won't go before lunch, Mr Chadwick: well, if you will, you must, for I know your time is precious;' and he shook hands with the diocesan steward, and bowed him out.

And the archdeacon had again recourse to his drawer, and twice read through the essence of Sir Abraham Haphazard's law-enlightened and law-bewildered brains. It was very clear that to Sir Abraham the justice of the old men's claim or the justice of Mr

Harding's defence were ideas that had never presented themselves. A legal victory over an opposing party was the service for which Sir Abraham was, as he imagined, to be paid; and that he, according to his lights, had diligently laboured to achieve, and with probable hope of success. Of the intense desire which Mr Harding felt to be assured on fit authority that he was wronging no man, that he was entitled in true equity to his income, that he might sleep at night without pangs of conscience, that he was no robber, no spoiler of the poor; that he and all the world might be openly convinced that he was not the man which the *Jupiter* had described him to be; of such longings on the part of Mr Harding, Sir Abraham was entirely ignorant; nor, indeed, could it be looked on as part of his business to gratify such desires. Such was not the system on which his battles were fought, and victories gained. Success was his object, and he was generally successful. He conquered his enemies by their weakness rather than by his own strength, and it had been found almost impossible to make up a case in which Sir Abraham, as an antagonist, would not find a flaw.

The archdeacon was delighted with the closeness of the reasoning. To do him justice, it was not a selfish triumph that he desired; he would personally lose nothing by defeat, or at least what he might lose did not actuate him; but neither was it love of justice which made him so anxious, nor even mainly solicitude for his father-in-law. He was fighting a part of a never-ending battle against a never-conquered foe – that of the Church against its enemies.

He knew Mr Harding could not pay all the expense of these doings; for these long opinions of Sir Abraham's, these causes to be pleaded, these speeches to be made, these various courts through which the case was, he presumed, to be dragged. He knew that he and his father must at least bear the heavier portion of this tremendous cost; but to do the archdeacon justice, he did not recoil from this. He was a man fond of obtaining money, greedy of a large income, but open-handed enough in expending it, and it was a triumph to him to foresee the success of this measure, although he might be called on to pay so dearly for it himself.

CHAPTER 9

The Conference

ON the following morning the archdeacon was with his father betimes, and a note was sent down to the warden begging his attendance at the palace. Dr Grantly, as he cogitated on the matter, leaning back in his brougham as he journeyed into Barchester, felt that it would be difficult to communicate his own satisfaction either to his father or his father-in-law. He wanted success on his own side and discomfiture on that of his enemies. The bishop wanted peace on the subject; a settled peace if possible, but peace at any rate till the short remainder of his own days had spun itself out; but Mr Harding required, not only success and peace, but he also demanded that he might stand justified before the world.

The bishop, however, was comparatively easy to deal with; and before the arrival of the other, the dutiful son had persuaded his father that all was going on well, and then the warden arrived.

It was Mr Harding's wont, whenever he spent a morning at the palace, to seat himself immediately at the bishop's elbow, the bishop occupying a huge armchair fitted up with candlesticks, a reading table, a drawer, and other paraphernalia, the position of which chair was never moved, summer or winter; and when, as was very usual, the archdeacon was there also, he confronted the two elders, who thus were enabled to fight the battle against him together; and together submit to defeat, for such was their constant fate.

Our warden now took his accustomed place, having greeted his son-in-law as he entered, and then affectionately inquired after his friend's health. There was a gentleness about the bishop to which the soft womanly affection of Mr Harding particularly endeared itself, and it was quaint to see how the two mild old priests pressed each other's hands, and smiled and made little signs of love.

'Sir Abraham's opinion has come at last,' began the arch-

deacon. Mr Harding had heard so much, and was most anxious
to know the result.

'It is quite favourable,' said the bishop, pressing his friend's arm.
'I am so glad.'

Mr Harding looked at the mighty bearer of the important news
for confirmation of these glad tidings.

'Yes,' said the archdeacon, 'Sir Abraham has given most minute
attention to the case; indeed, I knew he would – most minute
attention, and his opinion is – and as to his opinion on such a
subject being correct, no one who knows Sir Abraham's character
can doubt – his opinion is, that they haven't got a leg to stand on.'

'But as how, archdeacon?'

'Why, in the first place – but you're no lawyer, warden, and I
doubt you won't understand it; the gist of the matter is this: under
Hiram's will two paid guardians have been selected for the hospital; the law will say two paid servants, and you and I won't
quarrel with the name.'

'At any rate I will not if I am one of the servants,' said Mr
Harding. 'A rose you know –'

'Yes, yes,' said the archdeacon, impatient of poetry at such a
time. 'Well, two paid servants, we'll say; one to look after the men,
and the other to look after the money. You and Chadwick are these
two servants, and whether either of you be paid too much, or too
little, more or less in fact than the founder willed, it's as clear as
daylight that no one can fall foul of either of you for receiving an
allotted stipend.'

'That does seem clear,' said the bishop, who had winced visibly
under the words servants and stipend, which, however, appeared
to have caused no uneasiness to the archdeacon.

'Quite clear,' said he, 'and very satisfactory. In point of fact, it
being necessary to select such servants for the use of the hospital,
the pay to be given to them must depend on the rate of pay for
such services, according to their market value at the period in
question; and those who manage the hospital must be the only
judges of this.'

'And who does manage the hospital?' asked the warden.

'Oh, let them find that out; that's another question; the action
is brought against you and Chadwick, and that's your defence,

and a perfect and full defence it is. Now that I think very satisfactory.'

'Well,' said the bishop, looking inquiringly up into his friend's face, who sat silent awhile, and apparently not so well satisfied.

'And conclusive,' continued the archdeacon; 'if they press it to a jury, which they won't do, no twelve men in England will take five minutes to decide against them.'

'But according to that,' said Mr Harding, 'I might as well have sixteen hundred a year as eight, if the managers choose to allot it to me; and as I am one of the managers, if not the chief manager, myself, that can hardly be a just arrangement.'

'Oh, well, all that's nothing to the question; the question is, whether this intruding fellow, and a lot of cheating attorneys and pestilent dissenters, are to interfere with an arrangement which everyone knows is essentially just and serviceable to the Church. Pray don't let us be splitting hairs, and that amongst ourselves, or there'll never be an end of the cause or the cost.'

Mr Harding again sat silent for a while, during which the bishop once and again pressed his arm, and looked in his face to see if he could catch a gleam of a contented and eased mind; but there was no such gleam, and the poor warden continued playing sad dirges on invisible stringed instruments in all manner of positions: he was ruminating in his mind on this opinion of Sir Abraham, looking to it wearily and earnestly for satisfaction, but finding none. At last he said, 'Did you see the opinion, archdeacon?'

The archdeacon said he had not – that was to say, he had – that was, he had not seen the opinion itself; he had seen what had been called a copy, but he could not say whether of a whole or part; nor could he say that what he had seen were the *ipsissima verba*[1] of the great man himself; but what he had seen contained exactly the decision which he had announced, and which he again declared to be to his mind extremely satisfactory.

'I should like to see the opinion,' said the warden; 'that is, a copy of it.'

'Well, I suppose you can if you make a point of it; but I don't see the use myself; of course it is essential that the purport of it should not be known, and it is therefore unadvisable to multiply copies.'

'Why should it not be known?' asked the warden.

'What a question for a man to ask!' said the archdeacon, throwing up his hands in token of his surprise; 'but it is like you – a child is not more innocent than you are in matters of business. Can't you see that if we tell them that no action will lie against you, but that one may possibly lie against some other person or persons, that we shall be putting weapons into their hands, and be teaching them how to cut our own throats?'

The warden again sat silent, and the bishop again looked at him wistfully: 'The only thing we have now to do,' continued the archdeacon, 'is to remain quiet, hold our peace, and let them play their own game as they please.'

'We are not to make known then,' said the warden, 'that we have consulted the attorney-general, and that we are advised by him that the founder's will is fully and fairly carried out.'

'God bless my soul!' said the archdeacon, 'how odd it is that you will not see that all we are to do is to do nothing: why should we say anything about the founder's will? We are in possession; and we know that they are not in a position to put us out: surely that is enough for the present.'

Mr Harding rose from his seat and paced thoughtfully up and down the library, the bishop the while watching him painfully at every turn, and the archdeacon continuing to pour forth his convictions that the affair was in a state to satisfy any prudent mind.

'And the *Jupiter*?' said the warden, stopping suddenly.

'Oh! the *Jupiter*,' answered the other. 'The *Jupiter* can break no bones. You must bear with that; there is much of course which it is our bounden duty to bear; it cannot be all roses for us here,' and the archdeacon looked exceedingly moral; 'besides the matter is too trivial, of too little general interest to be mentioned again in the *Jupiter*, unless we stir up the subject': and the archdeacon again looked exceedingly knowing and worldly wise.

The warden continued his walk; the hard and stinging words of that newspaper article, each one of which had thrust a thorn as it were into his inmost soul, were fresh in his memory: he had read it more than once, word by word, and what was worse, he fancied it was as well known to everyone as to himself. Was he to be looked on as the unjust griping priest he had been there described? Was he to be pointed at as the consumer of the bread of the poor, and to be allowed no means of refuting such charges, of clearing his begrimed name, of standing innocent in the world, as hitherto he had stood? Was he to bear all this, to receive as usual his now hated income, and be known as one of those greedy priests who by their rapacity have brought disgrace on their church? and why? Why should he bear all this? why should he die, for he felt that he could not live, under such a weight of obloquy? As he paced up and down the room he resolved in his misery and enthusiasm that he could with pleasure, if he were allowed, give up his place, abandon his pleasant home, leave the hospital, and live poorly, happily, and with an unsullied name, on the small remainder of his means.

He was a man somewhat shy of speaking of himself, even before those who knew him best, and whom he loved the most; but at last it burst forth from him, and with a somewhat jerking eloquence he declared that he could not, would not, bear this misery any longer.

'If it can be proved,' said he at last, 'that I have a just and honest right to this, as God well knows I always deemed I had; if this salary or stipend be really my due, I am not less anxious than another to retain it. I have the well-being of my child to look to. I am too old to miss without some pain the comforts to which I have been used; and I am, as others are, anxious to prove to the world that I have been right, and to uphold the place I have held; but I cannot do it at such a cost as this. I cannot bear this. Could you tell me to do so?' And he appealed, almost in tears, to the bishop, who had left his chair, and was now leaning on the warden's arm as he stood on the further side of the table facing the archdeacon. 'Could you tell me to sit there at ease, indifferent, and satisfied, while such things as these are said loudly of me in the world?'

The bishop could feel for him and sympathize with him, but he could not advise him, he could only say, 'No, no, you shall be asked to do nothing that is painful; you shall do just what your heart tells you to be right; you shall do whatever you think best yourself. Theophilus, don't advise him, pray don't advise the warden to do anything which is painful.'

But the archdeacon, though he could not sympathize, could advise; and he saw that the time had come when it behoved him to do so in a somewhat peremptory manner.

'Why, my lord,' he said speaking to his father: and when he called his father 'my lord', the good old bishop shook in his shoes, for he knew that an evil time was coming. 'Why, my lord, there are two ways of giving advice; there is advice that may be good for the present day; and there is advice that may be good for days to come: now I cannot bring myself to give the former, if it be incompatible with the other.'

'No, no, no, I suppose not,' said the bishop, reseating himself, and shading his face with his hands. Mr Harding sat down with his back to the further wall, playing to himself some air fitted for so calamitous an occasion, and the archdeacon said out his say standing, with his back to the empty fireplace.

'It is not to be supposed, but that much pain will spring out of this unnecessarily raised question. We must all have foreseen that, and the matter has in no wise gone on worse than we expected; but it will be weak, yes, and wicked also, to abandon the cause and own ourselves wrong, because the inquiry is painful. It is not only ourselves we have to look to: to a certain extent the interest of the Church is in our keeping. Should it be found that one after another of those who hold preferment abandoned it whenever it might be attacked, is it not plain that such attacks would be renewed till nothing was left us? and that if so deserted, the Church of England must fall to the ground altogether? If this be true of many, it is true of one. Were you, accused as you now are, to throw up the wardenship, and to relinquish the preferment which is your property, with the vain object of proving yourself disinterested, you would fail in that object, you would inflict a desperate blow on your brother clergymen, you would encourage every cantankerous dissenter in England to make a similar charge against some source of clerical revenue, and you would do your best to dishearten those who are most anxious to defend you and uphold your position. I can fancy nothing more weak, or more wrong. It is not that you think that there is any justice in these charges, or that you doubt your own right to the wardenship: you are convinced of your own honesty, and yet would yield to them through cowardice.'

'Cowardice!' said the bishop, expostulating. Mr Harding sat unmoved, gazing on his son-in-law.

'Well, would it not be cowardice? would he not do so because he is afraid to endure the evil things which will be falsely spoken of him? Would that not be cowardice? And now let us see the extent of the evil which you dread. The *Jupiter* publishes an article which a great many, no doubt, will read; but of those who understand the subject how many will believe the *Jupiter*? Everyone knows what its object is; it has taken up the case against Lord Guildford and against the Dean of Rochester, and that against half a dozen bishops;[2] and does not everyone know that it would take up any case of the kind, right or wrong, false or true, with known justice or known injustice, if by doing so it could further its own views? Does not all the world know this of the *Jupiter*? Who that really knows you will think the worse of you for what the *Jupiter* says? And why care for those who do not know you? I will say nothing of your own comfort, but I do say that you could not be justified in throwing up, in a fit of passion, for such it would be, the only maintenance that Eleanor has; and if you did so, if you really did vacate the wardenship, and submit to ruin, what would that profit you? If you have no future right to the income, you have had no past right to it; and the very fact of your abandoning your position, would create a demand for repayment of that which you have already received and spent.'

The poor warden groaned as he sat perfectly still, looking up at the hard-hearted orator who thus tormented him, and the bishop echoed the sound faintly from behind his hands; but the archdeacon cared little for such signs of weakness, and completed his exhortation.

'But let us suppose the office to be left vacant, and that your own troubles concerning it were over; would that satisfy you? Are your only aspirations in the matter confined to yourself and family? I know they are not. I know you are as anxious as any of us for the church to which we belong; and what a grievous blow would such an act of apostasy give her! You owe it to the church of which you are a member and a minister, to bear with this affliction, however severe it may be: you owe it to my father, who instituted you, to support his rights: you owe it to those who preceded you to assert the legality of their position: you owe it to those who are to come after you, to maintain uninjured for them that which you received uninjured from others; and you owe to us all the unflinching assistance of perfect brotherhood in this matter, so that upholding one another we may support our great cause without blushing and without disgrace.'

And so the archdeacon ceased, and stood self-satisfied, watching the effect of his spoken wisdom.

The warden felt himself, to a certain extent, stifled; he would have given the world to get himself out into the open air without speaking to, or noticing those who were in the room with him; but this was impossible. He could not leave without saying something, and he felt himself confounded by the archdeacon's eloquence. There was a heavy, unfeeling, unanswerable truth in what he had said; there was so much practical, but odious common sense in it, that he neither knew how to assent or to differ. If it were necessary for him to suffer, he felt that he could endure without complaint and without cowardice, providing that he was self-satisfied of the justice of his own cause. What he could not endure was that he should be accused by others, and not acquitted by himself. Doubting, as he had begun to doubt, the justice of his own position in the hospital, he knew that his own self-confidence would not be restored because Mr Bold had been in error as to some legal form; nor could he be satisfied to escape, because, through some legal fiction, he who received the greatest benefit from the hospital might be considered only as one of its servants.

The archdeacon's speech had silenced him – stupefied him – annihilated him; anything but satisfied him. With the bishop it fared not much better. He did not discern clearly how things were, but he saw enough to know that a battle was to be prepared for; a battle that would destroy his few remaining comforts, and bring him with sorrow to the grave.

The warden still sat, and still looked at the archdeacon, till his thoughts fixed themselves wholly on the means of escape from his present position, and he felt like a bird fascinated by gazing on a snake.

'I hope you agree with me,' said the archdeacon at last, breaking the dread silence; 'my lord, I hope *you* agree with me.'

Oh what a sigh the bishop gave! 'My lord, I hope you agree with me,' again repeated the merciless tyrant.

'Yes, I suppose so,' groaned the poor old man, slowly.

'And you, warden?'

Mr Harding was now stirred to action – he must speak and move, so he got up and took one turn before he answered.

'Do not press me for an answer just at present; I will do nothing lightly in the matter, and of whatever I do I will give you and the bishop notice.' And so without another word he took his leave, escaping quickly through the palace hall, and down the lofty steps, nor did he breathe freely till he found himself alone under the huge elms of the silent close. Here he walked long and slowly, thinking on his case with a troubled air, and trying in vain to confute the archdeacon's argument. He then went home, resolved to bear it all – ignominy, suspense, disgrace, self-doubt, and heart-burning – and to do as those would have him, who he still believed were most fit and most able to counsel him aright.

CHAPTER 10

Tribulation

MR HARDING was a sadder man than he had ever yet been when he returned to his own house. He had been wretched enough on that well-remembered morning when he was forced to expose before his son-in-law the publisher's account for ushering into the world his dear book of sacred music; when after making such payments as he could do unassisted, he found that he was a debtor of more than three hundred pounds: but his sufferings then were as nothing to his present misery – then he had done wrong, and he knew it, and was able to resolve that he would not sin in like manner again; but now he could make no resolution, and comfort himself by no promises of firmness. He had been forced to think that his lot had placed him in a false position, and he was about to maintain that position against the opinion of the world and against his own convictions.

He had read with pity, amounting almost to horror, the strictures which had appeared from time to time against the Earl of Guildford as master of St Cross, and the invectives that had been heaped on rich diocesan dignitaries and overgrown sinecure pluralists. In judging of them, he judged leniently; the whole bias of his profession had taught him to think that they were more sinned against than sinning, and that the animosity with which they had been pursued was venomous and unjust; but he had not the less regarded their plight as most miserable. His hair had stood on end and his flesh had crept as he read the things which had been written; he had wondered how men could live under such a load of disgrace; how they could face their fellow-creatures while their names were bandied about so injuriously and so publicly – and now this lot was to be his – he, that shy retiring man, who had so comforted himself in the hidden obscurity of his lot, who had so enjoyed the unassuming warmth of his own little corner, he was now to be dragged forth into the glaring day, and gibbeted before ferocious multitudes. He entered his own house a crestfallen, humiliated man, without a hope of overcoming the wretchedness which affected him.

He wandered into the drawing-room where was his daughter; but he could not speak to her now, so he left it, and went into the book-room. He was not quick enough to escape Eleanor's glance, or to prevent her from seeing that he was disturbed; and in a little while she followed him. She found him seated in his accustomed chair, with no book open before him, no pen ready in his hand, no ill-shapen notes of blotted music lying before him as was usual, none of those hospital accounts with which he was so precise and yet so unmethodical: he was doing nothing, thinking of nothing, looking at nothing; he was merely suffering.

'Leave me Eleanor, my dear,' he said, 'leave me my darling for a few minutes, for I am busy.'

Eleanor saw well how it was, but she did leave him, and glided silently back to her drawing-room. When he had sat awhile, thus alone and unoccupied, he got up to walk again – he could make more of his thoughts walking than sitting, and was creeping out into his garden, when he met Bunce on the threshold.

'Well, Bunce,' said he, in a tone that for him was sharp, 'what is it? do you want me?'

'I was only coming to ask after your reverence,' said the old bedesman, touching his hat; 'and to inquire about the news from London,' he added after a pause.

The warden winced, and put his hand to his forehead and felt bewildered.

'Attorney Finney has been there this morning,' continued Bunce, 'and by his looks I guess he is not so well pleased as he once was, and it has got abroad somehow that the archdeacon has had down great news from London, and Handy and Moody are both as black as devils; and I hope,' said the man, trying to assume a cheery tone, 'that things are looking up, and that there'll be an end soon to all this stuff which bothers your reverence so sorely.'

'Well, I wish there may be, Bunce.'

'But about the news, your reverence?' said the old man, almost whispering.

Mr Harding walked on, and shook his head impatiently. Poor Bunce little knew how he was tormenting his patron.

'If there was anything to cheer you, I should be so glad to know it,' said he, with a tone of affection which the warden in all his misery could not resist.

He stopped, and took both the old man's hands in his. 'My friend,' said he, 'my dear old friend, there is nothing: there is no news to cheer me – God's will be done': and two small hot tears broke away from his eyes and stole down his furrowed cheeks.

'Then God's will be done,' said the other solemnly, 'but they told me that there was good news from London, and I came to wish your reverence joy; but God's will be done'; and so the warden again walked on, and the bedesman looking wistfully after him, and receiving no encouragement to follow, returned sadly to his own abode.

For a couple of hours the warden remained thus in the garden, now walking, now standing motionless on the turf, and then, as his legs got weary, sitting unconsciously on the garden seats, and then walking again. And Eleanor, hidden behind the muslin curtains of the window, watched him through the trees as he now came in sight, and then again was concealed by the turnings of the walk; and thus the time passed away till five, when the warden crept back to the house and prepared for dinner.

It was but a sorry meal. The demure parlourmaid, as she handed the dishes and changed the plates, saw that all was not right, and was more demure than ever: neither father nor daughter could eat, and the hateful food was soon cleared away, and the bottle of port placed upon the table.

'Would you like Bunce to come in, papa?' said Eleanor, thinking that the company of the old man might lighten his sorrow.

'No, my dear, thank you, not today; but are not you going out, Eleanor, this lovely afternoon? don't stay in for me, my dear.'

'I thought you seemed so sad, papa.'

'Sad,' said he, irritated; 'well, people must all have their share of sadness here; I am not more exempt than another: but kiss me, dearest, and go now; I will, if possible, be more sociable when you return.'

And Eleanor was again banished from her father's sorrow. Ah! her desire now was not to find him happy, but to be allowed to share his sorrows; not to force him to be sociable, but to persuade him to be trustful.

She put on her bonnet as desired, and went up to Mary Bold; this was now her daily haunt, for John Bold was up in London among lawyers and church reformers, diving deep into other questions than that of the wardenship of Barchester; supplying information to one member of parliament, and dining with another; subscribing to funds for the abolition of clerical incomes, and seconding at that great national meeting at the Crown and Anchor a resolution to the effect that no clergyman of the Church of England, be he who he might, should have more than a thousand a year, and none less than two hundred and fifty. His speech on this occasion was short, for fifteen had to speak, and the room was hired for two hours only, at the expiration of which the Quakers and Mr Cobden were to make use of it for an appeal to the public in aid of the Emperor of Russia;[1] but it was sharp and effective: at least he was told so by a companion with whom he now lived much, and on whom he greatly depended – one Tom Towers,[2] a very leading genius, and supposed to have high employment on the staff of the *Jupiter*.

So Eleanor, as was now her wont, went up to Mary Bold, and Mary listened kindly while the daughter spoke much of her father, and, perhaps kinder still, found a listener in Eleanor while she spoke about her brother. In the meantime the warden sat alone, leaning on the arm of his chair; he had poured out a glass of wine, but had done so merely from habit, for he left it untouched: there he sat gazing at the open window, and thinking, if he can be said to have thought, of the happiness of his past life. All manner of past delights came before his mind, which at the time he had enjoyed without considering them; his easy days, his absence of all kind of hard work, his pleasant shady home, those twelve old neighbours whose welfare till now had been the source of so much pleasant care, the excellence of his children, the friendship of the dear old bishop, the solemn grandeur of those vaulted aisles, through which he loved to hear his own voice pealing; and then that friend of friends, that choice ally that had never deserted him, that eloquent companion that would always, when asked, discourse such pleasant music, that violoncello of his – ah, how happy he had been! but it was over now; his easy days and absence of work had been the crime which brought on him his tribulation; his shady home was pleasant no longer; maybe it was no longer his; the old neighbours, whose welfare had been so desired by him, were his enemies; his daughter was as wretched as himself, and even the bishop was made miserable by his position. He could never again lift up his voice boldly as he had hitherto done among his brethren, for he felt that he was disgraced; and he feared even to touch his bow, for he knew how grievous a sound of wailing, how piteous a lamentation, it would produce.

He was still sitting in the same chair and the same posture, having hardly moved a limb for two hours, when Eleanor came back to tea, and succeeded in bringing him with her into the drawing-room.

The tea seemed as comfortless as the dinner, though the warden, who had hitherto eaten nothing all day, devoured the plateful of bread and butter, unconscious of what he was doing.

Eleanor had made up her mind to force him to talk to her, but she hardly knew how to commence: she must wait till the urn was gone, till the servant would no longer be coming in and out.

At last everything was gone, and the drawing-room door was permanently closed; then Eleanor, getting up and going round to her father, put her arm round his neck, and said, 'Papa, won't you tell me what it is?'

'What what is, my dear?'

'This new sorrow that torments you; I know you are unhappy, papa.'

'New sorrow! it's no new sorrow, my dear, we have all our cares sometimes,' and he tried to smile, but it was a ghastly failure; 'but I shouldn't be so dull a companion; come, we'll have some music.'

'No papa, not tonight – it would only trouble you tonight': and she sat upon his knee, as she sometimes would in their gayest moods, and with her arm round his neck, she said, 'Papa, I will not leave you till you talk to me; oh, if you only knew how much good it would do to you, to tell me of it all.'

The father kissed his daughter, and pressed her to his heart; but still he said nothing: it was so hard to him to speak of his own sorrows; he was so shy a man even with his own child.

'Oh, papa, do tell me what it is; I know it is about the hospital, and what they are doing up in London, and what that cruel newspaper has said; but if there be such cause for sorrow, let us be sorrowful together; we are all in all to each other now: dear, dear papa, do speak to me.'

Mr Harding could not well speak now, for the warm tears were running down his cheeks like rain in May, but he held his child close to his heart, and squeezed her hand as a lover might, and she kissed his forehead and his wet cheeks, and lay upon his bosom, and comforted him as a woman only can do.

'My own child,' he said, as soon as his tears would let him speak; 'my own, own child, why should you too be unhappy before it is necessary: it may come to that, that we must leave this place, but till that time comes, why should your young days be clouded?'

'And is that all, papa? If that be all, let us leave it, and have light hearts elsewhere: if that be all, let us go. Oh, papa, you and I could be happy if we had only bread to eat, so long as our hearts were light.'

And Eleanor's face was lighted up with enthusiasm as she told her father how he might banish all his care; and a gleam of joy shot across his brow as this idea of escape again presented itself, and he again fancied for a moment that he could spurn away from him the income which the world envied him; that he could give the lie to that wielder of the tomahawk who had dared to write such things of him in the *Jupiter*. That he could leave Sir Abraham, and the archdeacon, and Bold, and the rest of them with their lawsuit among them, and wipe his hands altogether of so sorrow-stirring a concern. Ah, what happiness might there be in the distance, with Eleanor and him in some small cottage, and nothing left of their former grandeur but their music! Yes, they would walk forth with their music books, and their instruments, and shaking the dust from off their feet as they went, leave the ungrateful place. Never did a poor clergyman sigh for a warm benefice more anxiously than our warden did now to be rid of his.

'Give it up, papa,' she said again, jumping from his knees and standing on her feet before him, looking boldly into his face; 'give it up, papa.'

Oh, it was sad to see how that momentary gleam of joy passed away; how the look of hope was dispersed from that sorrowful face, as the remembrance of the archdeacon came back upon our poor warden, and he reflected that he could not stir from his now hated post. He was as a man bound with iron, fettered with adamant: he was in no repect a free agent; he had no choice. 'Give it up!' Oh, if he only could: what an easy way that were out of all his troubles!

'Papa, don't doubt about it,' she continued, thinking that his hesitation arose from his unwillingness to abandon so comfortable a home; 'is it on my account that you would stay here? Do you think that I cannot be happy without a pony-carriage and a fine drawing-room? Papa, I never can be happy here, as long as there is a question as to your honour in staying here; but I could be gay as the day is long in the smallest tiny little cottage, if I could see you come in and go out with a light heart. Oh! papa, your face tells so much; though you won't speak to me with your voice, I know how it is with you every time I look at you.'

How he pressed her to his heart again with almost a spasmodic pressure! how he kissed her as the tears fell like rain from his old eyes! how he blessed her, and called her by a hundred soft sweet names which now came new to his lips! how he chid himself for ever having been unhappy with such a treasure in his house, such a jewel on his bosom, with so sweet a flower in the choice garden of his heart! And then the floodgates of his tongue were loosed, and, at length, with unsparing detail of circumstances, he told her all that he wished, and all that he could not do. He repeated those arguments of the archdeacon, not agreeing in their truth, but explaining his inability to escape from them; how it had been declared to him that he was bound to remain where he was by the interests of his order, by gratitude to the bishop, by the wishes of his friends, by a sense of duty, which, though he could not understand it, he was fain to acknowledge. He told her how he had been accused of cowardice, and though he was not a man to make much of such a charge before the world, now in the full candour of his heart he explained to her that such an accusation was grievous to him; that he did think it would be unmanly to desert his post, merely to escape his present sufferings, and that, therefore, he must bear as best he might the misery which was prepared for him.

And did she find these details tedious? Oh, no – she encouraged him to dilate on every feeling he expressed, till he laid bare the inmost corners of his heart to her. They spoke together of the archdeacon, as two children might of a stern, unpopular, but still respected schoolmaster, and of the bishop as a parent kind as kind could be, but powerless against an omnipotent pedagogue.

And then, when they had discussed all this, when the father had told all to the child, she could not be less confiding than he had been; and as John Bold's name was mentioned between them, she owned how well she had learned to love him – 'had loved him once,' she said, 'but she would not, could not do so now – no, even had her troth been plighted to him, she would have taken it back again – had she sworn to love him as his wife, she would have discarded him and not felt herself forsworn, when he proved himself the enemy of her father.'

But the warden declared that Bold was no enemy of his, and encouraged her love; and gently rebuked, as he kissed her, the stern resolve she had made to cast him off; and then he spoke to her of happier days when their trials would all be over; and declared that her young heart should not be torn asunder to please either priest or prelate, dean or archdeacon. No, not if all Oxford were to convocate together,[3] and agree as to the necessity of the sacrifice.

And so they greatly comforted each other – and in what sorrow will not such mutual confidence give consolation! – and with a last expression of tender love they parted, and went comparatively happy to their rooms.

CHAPTER II

Iphigenia

WHEN Eleanor laid her head on her pillow that night, her mind was anxiously intent on some plan by which she might extricate her father from his misery; and, in her warm-hearted enthusiasm, self-sacrifice was decided on as the means to be adopted. Was not so good an Agamemnon worthy of an Iphigenia?[1] She would herself personally implore John Bold to desist from his undertaking; she would explain to him her father's sorrows, the cruel misery of his position; she would tell him how her father would die if he were thus dragged before the public and exposed to such unmerited ignominy; she would appeal to his old friendship, to his generosity, to his manliness, to his mercy; if need were she would kneel to him for the favour she would ask; but before she did this, the idea of love must be banished. There must be no bargain in the matter. To his mercy, to his generosity, she could appeal; but as a pure maiden, hitherto even unsolicited, she could not appeal to his love, nor under such circumstances could she allow him to do so. Of course when so provoked, he would declare his passion; that was to be expected; there had been enough between them to make such a fact sure; but it was equally certain that he must be rejected. She could not be understood as saying, Make my father free and I am the reward. There would be no sacrifice in that – not so had Jephthah's daughter saved her father[2] – not so could she show to that kindest, dearest of parents how much she was able to bear for his good. No; to one resolve must her whole soul be bound; and so resolving, she felt that she could make her great request to Bold with as much self-assured confidence as she could have done to his grandfather.

And now I own I have fears for my heroine: not as to the upshot of her mission – not in the least as to that; as to the full success of her generous scheme, and the ultimate result of such a project, no one conversant with human nature and novels can have a doubt; but as to the amount of sympathy she may receive from those of her own sex. Girls below twenty and old ladies above sixty will do her justice; for in the female heart the soft springs of sweet romance reopen after many years, and again gush out with waters pure as in earlier days, and greatly refresh the path that leads downwards to the grave. But I fear that the majority of those between these two eras will not approve of Eleanor's plan. I fear that unmarried ladies of thirty-five will declare that there can be no probability of so absurd a project being carried through; that young women on their knees before their lovers are sure to get kissed, and that they would not put themselves in such a position did they not expect it; that Eleanor is going to Bold only because circumstances prevent Bold from coming to her; that she is certainly a little fool, or a little schemer, but that in all probability she is thinking a good deal more about herself than her father.

Dear ladies, you are right as to your appreciation of the circumstances, but very wrong as to Miss Harding's character. Miss Harding was much younger than you are, and could not, therefore, know, as you may do, to what dangers such an encounter might expose her. She may get kissed; I think it very probable that she will; but I give my solemn word and positive assurance, that the remotest idea of such a catastrophe never occurred to her, as she made the great resolve now alluded to.

And then she slept; and then she rose refreshed, and met her father with her kindest embrace and most loving smiles; and on the whole their breakfast was by no means so triste[3] as had been their dinner the day before; and then, making some excuse to her father for so soon leaving him, she started on the commencement of her operations.

She knew that John Bold was in London, and that, therefore, the scene itself could not be enacted today; but she also knew that he was soon to be home, probably on the next day, and it was necessary that some little plan for meeting him should be concerted with his sister Mary. When she got up to the house, she went as usual into the morning sitting-room, and was startled by perceiving, by a stick, a greatcoat, and sundry parcels which were lying about, that Bold must already have returned.

'John has come back so suddenly,' said Mary, coming into the room; 'he has been travelling all night.'

'Then I'll come up again some other time,' said Eleanor, about to beat a retreat in her sudden dismay.

'He's out now, and will be for the next two hours,' said the other; 'he's with that horrid Finney; he only came to see him, and he returns by the mail-train tonight.'

Returns by the mail-train tonight, thought Eleanor to herself, as she strove to screw up her courage – away again tonight – then it must be now or never; and she again sat down, having risen to go.

She wished the ordeal could have been postponed: she had fully made up her mind to do the deed, but she had not made up her mind to do it this very day; and now she felt ill at ease, astray, and in difficulty.

'Mary,' she began, 'I must see your brother before he goes back.'

'Oh yes, of course,' said the other; 'I know he'll be delighted to see you'; and she tried to treat it as a matter of course, but she was not the less surprised; for Mary and Eleanor had daily talked over John Bold and his conduct, and his love, and Mary would insist on calling Eleanor her sister, and would scold her for not calling Bold by his christian name; and Eleanor would half confess her love, but like a modest maiden would protest against such familiarities even with the name of her lover: and so they talked hour after hour, and Mary Bold, who was much the elder, looked forward with happy confidence to the day when Eleanor would not be ashamed to call her her sister. She was, however, fully sure that just at present Eleanor would be much more likely to avoid her brother than to seek him.

'Mary, I must see your brother, now, today, and beg from him a great favour,' and she spoke with a solemn air, not at all usual to her; and then she went on, and opened to her friend all her plan, her well-weighed scheme for saving her father from a sorrow which would, she said, if it lasted, bring him to his grave. 'But Mary,' she continued, 'you must now, you know, cease any joking about me and Mr Bold; you must now say no more about that; I am not ashamed to beg this favour from your brother, but when I have done so, there can never be anything further between us'; and this she said with a staid and solemn air, quite worthy of Jephthah's daughter or of Iphigenia either.

It was quite clear that Mary Bold did not follow the argument: that Eleanor Harding should appeal, on behalf of her father, to Bold's better feelings, seemed to Mary quite natural; it seemed quite natural that he should relent, overcome by such filial tears, and by so much beauty; but, to her thinking, it was at any rate equally natural that, having relented, John should put his arm round his mistress's waist, and say, 'Now having settled that, let us be man and wife, and all will end happily!' Why his good nature should not be rewarded, when such reward would operate to the disadvantage of none, Mary, who had more sense than romance, could not understand; and she said as much.

Eleanor, however, was firm, and made quite an eloquent speech to support her own view of the question: she could not condescend, she said, to ask such a favour on any other terms than those proposed. Mary might, perhaps, think her high-flown, but she had her own ideas, and she could not submit to sacrifice her self-respect.

'But I am sure you love him – don't you?' pleaded Mary; 'and I am sure he loves you better than anything in the world.'

Eleanor was going to make another speech, but a tear came to each eye, and she could not; so she pretended to blow her nose, and walked to the window, and made a little inward call on her own courage, and finding herself somewhat sustained, said sententiously, 'Mary, this is nonsense.'

'But you do love him,' said Mary, who had followed her friend to the window, and now spoke with her arms close wound round the other's waist. 'You do love him with all your heart – you know you do; I defy you to deny it.'

'I –' commenced Eleanor, turning sharply round to refute the charge; but the intended falsehood stuck in her throat, and never came to utterance. She could not deny her love, so she took plentifully to tears, and leant upon her friend's bosom and sobbed there, and protested that, love or no love, it would make no difference in her resolve, and called Mary, a thousand times, the most cruel of girls, and swore her to secrecy by a hundred oaths, and ended by declaring that the girl who could betray her friend's love, even to a brother, would be as black a traitor as a soldier in a garrison who should open the city gates to the enemy. While they were yet discussing the matter, Bold returned, and Eleanor was forced into sudden action: she had either to accomplish or abandon her plan; and having slipped into her friend's bedroom, as the gentleman closed the hall door, she washed the marks of tears from her eyes, and resolved within herself to go through with it. 'Tell him I am here,' said she, 'and coming in; and mind, whatever you do, don't leave us.' So Mary informed her brother, with a somewhat sombre air, that Miss Harding was in the next room, and was coming to speak to him.

Eleanor was certainly thinking more of her father than herself, as she arranged her hair before the glass, and removed the traces of sorrow from her face, and yet I should be untrue if I said that she was not anxious to appear well before her lover: why else was she so sedulous with that stubborn curl that would rebel against her hand, and smooth so eagerly her ruffled ribands? why else did she damp her eyes to dispel the redness, and bite her pretty lips to bring back the colour? Of course she was anxious to look her best, for she was but a mortal angel after all. But had she been immortal, had she flitted back to the sitting-room on a cherub's wings, she could not have had a more faithful heart, or a truer wish to save her father at any cost to herself.

John Bold had not met her since the day when she left him in dudgeon in the cathedral close. Since that his whole time had been occupied in promoting the cause against her father, and not unsuccessfully. He had often thought of her, and turned over in his mind a hundred schemes for showing her how disinterested was his love. He would write to her and beseech her not to allow the performance of a public duty to injure him in her estimation; he would write to Mr Harding, explain all his views, and boldly claim the warden's daughter, urging that the untoward circumstances between them need be no bar to their ancient friendship, or to a closer tie; he would throw himself on his knees before his mistress; he would wait and marry the daughter when the father had lost his home and his income; he would give up the lawsuit and go to Australia, with her of course, leaving the *Jupiter* and Mr Finney to complete the case between them. Sometimes as he woke in the morning fevered and impatient, he would blow out his brains and have done with all his cares – but this idea was generally consequent on an imprudent supper enjoyed in company with Tom Towers.

How beautiful Eleanor appeared to him as she slowly walked into the room! Not for nothing had all those little cares been taken. Though her sister, the archdeacon's wife, had spoken slightingly of her charms, Eleanor was very beautiful when seen aright. Hers was not one of those impassive faces which have the beauty of a marble bust; finely chiselled features, perfect in every line, true to the rules of symmetry, as lovely to a stranger as to a friend, unvarying unless in sickness, or as age affects them. She had no startling brilliancy of beauty, no pearly whiteness, no radiant carnation: she had not the majestic contour that rivets attention, demands instant wonder, and then disappoints by the coldness of its charms. You might pass Eleanor Harding in the street without notice, but you could hardly pass an evening with her and not lose your heart.

She had never appeared more lovely to her lover than she now did. Her face was animated though it was serious, and her full, dark, lustrous eyes shone with anxious energy; her hand trembled as she took his, and she could hardly pronounce his name, when she addressed him. Bold wished with all his heart that the Australian scheme was in the act of realization, and that he and Eleanor were away together, never to hear further of the lawsuit.

He began to talk, asked after her health – said something about London being very stupid, and more about Barchester being very pleasant: declared the weather to be very hot, and then inquired after Mr Harding.

'My father is not very well,' said Eleanor.

John Bold was very sorry, so sorry: he hoped it was nothing serious, and put on the unmeaningly solemn face, which people usually use on such occasions.

'I especially want to speak to you about my father, Mr Bold; indeed, I am now here on purpose to do so. Papa is very unhappy, very unhappy indeed, about this affair of the hospital: you would pity him, Mr Bold, if you could see how wretched it has made him.'

'Oh Miss Harding!'

'Indeed you would – anyone would pity him: but a friend, an old friend as you are – indeed you would. He is an altered man;

his cheerfulness has all gone, and his sweet temper, and his kind happy tone of voice; you would hardly know him if you saw him, Mr Bold, he is so much altered; and – and – if this goes on, he will die.' Here Eleanor had recourse to her handkerchief, and so also had her auditors; but she plucked up her courage and went on with her tale. 'He will break his heart, and die. I am sure, Mr Bold, it was not you who wrote those cruel things in the newspaper –'

John Bold eagerly protested that it was not, but his heart smote him as to his intimate alliance with Tom Towers.

'No, I am sure it was not; and papa has not for a moment thought so; you would not be so cruel – but it has nearly killed him. Papa cannot bear to think that people should so speak of him, and that everybody should hear him so spoken of – they have called him avaricious, and dishonest, and they say he is robbing the old men, and taking the money of the hospital for nothing.'

'I have never said so, Miss Harding. I –'

'No,' continued Eleanor, interrupting him, for she was now in the full floodtide of her eloquence; 'no, I am sure you have not, but others have said so; and if this goes on, if such things are written again, it will kill papa. Oh! Mr Bold, if you only knew the state he is in! Now papa does not care much about money.'

Both her auditors, brother and sister, assented to this, and declared on their own knowledge that no man lived less addicted to filthy lucre than the warden.

'Oh! it's so kind of you to say so, Mary, and of you too, Mr Bold. I couldn't bear that people should think unjustly of papa. Do you know he would give up the hospital altogether, only he cannot. The archdeacon says it would be cowardly, and that he would be deserting his order, and injuring the Church. Whatever may happen, papa will not do that: he would leave the place tomorrow willingly, and give up his house, and the income and all, if the archdeacon –' Eleanor was going to say 'would let him', but she stopped herself before she had compromised her father's dignity; and giving a long sigh, she added – 'Oh, I do so wish he would.'

'No one who knows Mr Harding personally accuses him for a moment,' said Bold.

'It is he that has to bear the punishment; it is he that suffers,' said Eleanor; 'and what for? what has he done wrong? how has he deserved this persecution? he that never had an unkind thought in his life, he that never said an unkind word!' and here she broke down, and the violence of her sobs stopped her utterance.

Bold, for the fifth or sixth time, declared that neither he nor any of his friends imputed any blame personally to Mr Harding.

'Then why should he be persecuted?' ejaculated Eleanor through her tears, forgetting in her eagerness that her intention had been to humble herself as a suppliant before John Bold – 'why should he be made so wretched? Oh! Mr Bold' – and she turned towards him as though the kneeling scene were about to be commenced – 'oh! Mr Bold, why did you begin all this? you whom we all so – so – valued!'

To speak the truth, the reformer's punishment was certainly come upon him, for his present plight was not enviable; he had nothing for it but to excuse himself by platitudes about public duty, which it is by no means worthwhile to repeat, and to reiterate his eulogy on Mr Harding's character. His position was certainly a cruel one: had any gentleman called upon him on behalf of Mr Harding he could of course have declined to enter upon the subject; but how could he do so with a beautiful girl, with the daughter of the man whom he had injured, with his own love?

In the meantime Eleanor recollected herself, and again summoned up her energies.

'Mr Bold,' said she, 'I have come here to implore you to abandon this proceeding.'

He stood up from his seat, and looked beyond measure distressed.

'To implore you to abandon it, to implore you to spare my father, to spare either his life or his reason, for one or the other will pay the forfeit if this goes on. I know how much I am asking, and how little right I have to ask anything; but I think you will listen to me as it is for my father. Oh, Mr Bold, pray, pray do this for us – pray do not drive to distraction a man who has loved you so well.'

She did not absolutely kneel to him, but she followed him as he moved from his chair, and laid her soft hands imploringly upon his arm. Ah! at any other time how exquisitely valuable would have been that touch! but now he was distraught, dumbfounded, and unmanned. What could he say to that sweet suppliant; how explain to her that the matter now was probably beyond his control; how tell her that he could not quell the storm which he had raised?

'Surely, surely, John, you cannot refuse her,' said his sister.

'I would give her my soul,' said he, 'if it would serve her.'

'Oh, Mr Bold,' said Eleanor, 'do not speak so; I ask nothing for myself; and what I ask for my father, it cannot harm you to grant.'

'I would give her my soul, if it would serve her,' said Bold, still addressing his sister; 'everything I have is hers, if she will accept it; my house, my heart, my all; every hope of my breast is centred in her: her smiles are sweeter to me than the sun, and when I see her in sorrow as she now is, every nerve in my body suffers. No man can love better than I love her.'

'No, no, no,' ejaculated Eleanor, 'there can be no talk of love between us; will you protect my father from the evil you have brought upon him?'

'Oh, Eleanor, I will do anything; let me tell you how I love you!'

'No, no, no,' she almost screamed; 'this is unmanly of you, Mr Bold. Will you, will you, will you leave my father to die in peace in his quiet home?' and seizing him by his arm and hand, she followed him across the room towards the door. 'I will not leave you till you promise me; I'll cling to you in the street; I'll kneel to you before all the people. You shall promise me this, you shall promise me this, you shall –' And she clung to him with fixed tenacity, and reiterated her resolve with hysterical passion.

'Speak to her, John; answer her,' said Mary, bewildered by the unexpected vehemence of Eleanor's manner; 'you cannot have the cruelty to refuse her.'

'Promise me, promise me,' said Eleanor; 'say that my father is safe – one word will do. I know how true you are; say one word, and I will let you go.'

She still held him, and looked eagerly into his face, with her hair dishevelled, and her eyes all bloodshot. She had no thought now of herself, no care now for her appearance, and yet he thought he had never seen her half so lovely; he was amazed at the intensity of her beauty, and could hardly believe that it was she whom he had dared to love. 'Promise me,' said she; 'I will not leave you till you have promised me.'

'I will.' said he at length, 'I do – all I can do, I will do.'

'Then may God Almighty bless you for ever and ever!' said Eleanor; and falling on her knees with her face on Mary's lap, she wept and sobbed like a child: her strength had carried her through her allotted task, but now it was well nigh exhausted.

In a while she was partly recovered, and got up to go, and would have gone, had not Bold made her understand that it was necessary for him to explain to her how far it was in his power to put an end to the proceedings which had been taken against Mr Harding. Had he spoken on any other subject, she would have vanished, but on that she was bound to hear him; and now the danger of her position commenced. While she had an active part to play, while she clung to him as a suppliant, it was easy enough for her to reject his proferred love, and cast from her his caressing words; but now – now that he had yielded, and was talking to her calmly and kindly as to her father's welfare, it was hard enough for her to do so. Then Mary Bold assisted her, but now she was quite on her brother's side. Mary said but little, but every word she did say gave some direct and deadly blow. The first thing she did was to make room for her brother between herself and Eleanor on the sofa: as the sofa was full large for three, Eleanor could not resent this, nor could she show suspicion by taking another seat; but she felt it to be a most unkind proceeding. And then Mary would talk as though they three were joined in some close peculiar bond together; as though they were in future always to wish together, contrive together, and act together; and Eleanor could not gainsay this; she could not make another speech, and say, 'Mr Bold and I are mere strangers, Mary, and are always to remain so!'

He explained to her that, though undoubtedly the proceeding against the hospital had commenced solely with himself, many others were now interested in the matter, some of whom were much more influential than himself: that it was to him alone, however, that the lawyers looked for instruction as to their doings, and, more important still. for the payment of their bills; and he promised that he would at once give them notice that it was his intention to abandon the cause. He thought, he said, that it was not probable that any active steps would be taken after he had seceded from the matter, though it was possible that some passing allusion might still be made to the hospital in the daily *Jupiter*. He promised, however, that he would use his best influence to prevent any further personal allusion being made to Mr Harding. He then suggested that he would on that afternoon ride over himself to Dr Grantly, and inform him of his altered intentions on the subject, and with this view, he postponed his immediate return to London.

This was all very pleasant, and Eleanor did enjoy a sort of triumph in the feeling that she had attained the object for which she had sought this interivew; but still the part of Iphigenia was to be played out. The gods had heard her prayer, granted her request, and were they not to have their promised sacrifice? Eleanor was not a girl to defraud them wilfully; so, as soon as she decently could, she got up for her bonnet.

'Are you going so soon?' said Bold, who half an hour since would have given a hundred pounds that he was in London, and she still at Barchester.

'Oh yes!' said she. 'I am so much obliged to you; papa will feel this to be so kind' (she did not quite appreciate all her father's feelings); 'of course I must tell him, and I will say that you will see the archdeacon.'

'But may I not say one word for myself?' said Bold.

'I'll fetch you your bonnet, Eleanor,' said Mary, in the act of leaving the room.

'Mary, Mary,' said she, getting up and catching her by her dress, 'don't go, I'll get my bonnet myself'; but Mary, the traitress, stood fast by the door, and permitted no such retreat. Poor Iphigenia!

And with a volley of impassioned love, John Bold poured forth the feelings of his heart, swearing, as men do, some truths and many falsehoods; and Eleanor repeated with every shade of vehemence the 'No, no, no' which had had a short time since so much effect; but now, alas! its strength was gone. Let her be never so vehement, her vehemence was not respected; all her 'No, no, noes' were met with counter asseverations, and at last were overpowered. The ground was cut from under her on every side: she was pressed to say whether her father would object; whether she herself had any aversion (aversion! God help her, poor girl! the word nearly made her jump into his arms); any other preference (this she loudly disclaimed); whether it was impossible that she should love him (Eleanor could not say that it was impossible): and so at last, all her defences demolished, all her maiden barriers swept away, she capitulated, or rather marched out with the honours of war, vanquished evidently, palpably vanquished, but still not reduced to the necessity of confessing it.

And so the altar on the shore of the modern Aulis reeked with no sacrifice.

CHAPTER 12

Mr Bold's Visit to Plumstead

WHETHER or no the ill-natured prediction made by certain ladies in the beginning of the last chapter, was or was not carried out to the letter, I am not in a position to state; Eleanor, however, certainly did feel herself to have been baffled, as she returned home with all her news to her father. Certainly she had been victorious, certainly she had achieved her object, certainly she was not unhappy, and yet she did not feel herself triumphant. Everything would run smooth now. Eleanor was not at all addicted to the Lydian school of romance;[1] she by no means objected to her lover because he came in at the door under the name of Absolute, instead of pulling her out of a window under the name of Beverley; and yet she felt that she had been imposed upon, and could hardly think of Mary Bold with sisterly charity. 'I did think I could have trusted Mary,' she said to herself over and over again. 'Oh that she should have dared to keep me in the room when I tried to get out!' Eleanor, however, felt that the game was up, and that she had now nothing further to do but to add to the budget of news which was prepared for her father, that John Bold was her accepted lover.

We will, however, now leave her on her way, and go with John Bold to Plumstead Episcopi, merely premising that Eleanor on reaching home will not find things so smooth as she fondly expected; two messengers had come, one to her father, and the other to the archdeacon, and each of them much opposed to her quiet mode of solving all their difficulties; the one in the shape of a number of the *Jupiter*; and the other in that of a further opinion from Sir Abraham Haphazard.

John Bold got on his horse and rode off to Plumstead Episcopi; not briskly and with eager spur, as men do ride when self-satisfied with their own intentions, but slowly, modestly, thoughtfully, and somewhat in dread of the coming interview. Now and again he would recur to the scene which was just over, support himself by the remembrance of the silence that gives consent, and exult as a happy lover; but even this feeling was not without a shade of remorse. Had he not shown himself childishly weak thus to yield up the resolve of many hours of thought to the tears of a pretty girl? How was he to meet his lawyer? How was he to back out of a matter in which his name was already so publicly concerned? What, oh what! was he to say to Tom Towers? While meditating these painful things he reached the lodge leading up to the arch-deacon's glebe,[2] and for the first time in his life found himself within the sacred precincts.

All the doctor's children were together on the slope of the lawn close to the road, as Bold rode up to the hall door. They were there holding high debate on matters evidently of deep interest at Plum-stead Episcopi, and the voices of the boys had been heard before the lodge gate was closed.

Florinda and Grizzel, frightened at the sight of so well-known an enemy to the family, fled on the first appearance of the horse-man, and ran in terror to their mother's arms; not for them was it, tender branches, to resent injuries, or as members of a church militant to put on armour against its enemies: but the boys stood their ground like heroes, and boldly demanded the business of the intruder.

'Do you want to see anybody here, sir?' said Henry, with a defiant eye and a hostile tone, which plainly said that at any rate no one there wanted to see the person so addressed; and as he spoke he brandished aloft his garden water-pot, holding it by the spout, ready for the braining of anyone.

'Henry,' said Charles James slowly, and with a certain dignity of diction, 'Mr Bold of course would not have come without wanting to see someone; if Mr Bold has a proper ground for wanting to see some person here, of course he has a right to come.'

But Samuel stepped lightly up to the horse's head, and offered his services. 'Oh, Mr Bold,' said he, 'papa, I'm sure, will be glad to see you; I suppose you want to see papa. Shall I hold your horse for you? Oh, what a very pretty horse!' and he turned his head and winked funnily at his brothers; 'papa has heard such good news about the old hospital today. We know you'll be glad to hear it, because you're such a friend of grandpapa Harding, and so much in love with aunt Nelly!'

'How d'ye do, lads?' said Bold, dismounting; 'I want to see your father if he's at home.'

'Lads!' said Henry, turning on his heel and addressing himself to his brother, but loud enough to be heard by Bold; 'lads, indeed! if we're lads, what does he call himself?'

Charles James condescended to say nothing further, but cocked his hat with much precision, and left the visitor to the care of his youngest brother.

Samuel stayed till the servant came, chatting and patting the horse; but as soon as Bold had disappeared through the front door, he stuck a switch under the animal's tail to make him kick, if possible.

The church reformer soon found himself *tête à tête* with the archdeacon in that same room, in that sanctum sanctorum[3] of the rectory, to which we have already been introduced. As he entered he heard the click of a certain patent lock, but it struck him with no surprise: the worthy clergyman was no doubt hiding from eyes profane his last much-studied sermon, for the archdeacon, though he preached but seldom, was famous for his sermons. No room, Bold thought, could have been more becoming for a dignitary of the church; each wall was loaded with theology; over each separate bookcase was printed in small gold letters the names of those great divines whose works were ranged beneath: beginning from the early fathers in due chronological order, there were to be found the precious labours of the chosen servants of the church down to the last pamphlet written in opposition to the consecration of Dr Hampden;[4] and raised above this were to be seen the busts of the greatest among the great: Chrysostom, St Augustine, Thomas à Becket, Cardinal Wolsey, Archbishop Laud, and Dr Philpotts.[5]

Every appliance that could make study pleasant and give ease to the over-toiled brain was there: chairs made to relieve each limb and muscle; reading-desks and writing-desks to suit every attitude; lamps and candles mechanically contrived to throw their light on any favoured spot, as the student might desire; a shoal of newspapers to amuse the few leisure moments which might be stolen from the labours of the day; and then from the window a view right through a bosky vista along which ran a broad green

path from the rectory to the church, at the end of which the
tawny-tinted fine old tower was seen with all its variegated pinnacles and parapets. Few parish churches in England are in better
repair, or better worth keeping so, than that at Plumstead Episcopi;
and yet it is built in a faulty style: the body of the church is low
– so low that the nearly flat leaden roof would be visible from the
churchyard, were it not for the carved parapet with which it is
surrounded. It is cruciform, though the transepts are irregular,
one being larger than the other; and the tower is much too high
in proportion to the church: but the colour of the building is
perfect; it is that rich yellow grey which one finds nowhere but
in the south and west of England, and which is so strong a
characteristic of most of our old houses of Tudor architecture. The
stonework also is beautiful; the mullions of the windows and the
thick tracery of the Gothic workmanship is as rich as fancy can
desire; and though in gazing on such a structure, one knows by
rule that the old priests who built it, built it wrong, one cannot
bring oneself to wish that they should have made it other than it
is.

When Bold was ushered into the book-room, he found its owner
standing with his back to the empty fireplace ready to receive him,
and he could not but perceive that that expansive brow was elated
with triumph, and that those full heavy lips bore more prominently than usual an appearance of arrogant success.

'Well, Mr Bold,' said he – 'well, what can I do for you? Very
happy, I can assure you, to do anything for such a friend of my
father-in-law.'

'I hope you'll excuse my calling, Dr Grantly.'

'Certainly, certainly,' said the archdeacon; 'I can assure you, no
apology is necessary from Mr Bold; only let me know what I can
do for him.'

Dr Grantly was standing himself, and he did not ask Bold to sit,
and therefore he had to tell his tale standing, leaning on the table,
with his hat in his hand. He did, however, manage to tell it; and
as the archdeacon never once interrupted him, or even encouraged
him by a single word, he was not long in coming to the end of it.

'And so, Mr Bold, I'm to understand, I believe, that you are
desirous of abandoning this attack upon Mr Harding.'

'Oh, Dr Grantly, there has been no attack, I can assure you –'

'Well, well, we won't quarrel about words; I should call it an attack – most men would so call an endeavour to take away from a man every shilling of income that he has to live upon; but it shan't be an attack, if you don't like it; you wish to abandon this – this little game of backgammon you've begun to play.'

'I intend to put an end to the legal proceedings which I have commenced.'

'I understand,' said the archdeacon. 'You've already had enough of it; well, I can't say that I am surprised; carrying on a losing lawsuit where one has nothing to gain, but everything to pay, is not pleasant.'

Bold turned very red in the face. 'You misinterpret my motives,' said he; 'but, however, that is of little consequence. I did not come to trouble you with my motives, but to tell you a matter of fact. Good morning, Dr Grantly.'

'One moment – one moment,' said the other. 'I don't exactly appreciate the taste which induced you to make any personal communication to me on the subject; but I dare say I'm wrong, I dare say your judgement is the better of the two; but as you have done me the honour – as you have, as it were, forced me into a certain amount of conversation on a subject which had better, perhaps, have been left to our lawyers, you will excuse me if I ask you to hear my reply to your communication.'

'I am in no hurry, Dr Grantly.'

'Well, I am, Mr Bold; my time is not exactly leisure time, and, therefore, if you please, we'll go to the point at once – you're going to abandon this lawsuit?' – and he paused for a reply.

'Yes, Dr Grantly, I am.'

'Having exposed a gentleman who was one of your father's warmest friends to all the ignominy and insolence which the press could heap upon his name; having somewhat ostentatiously declared that it was your duty as a man of high public virtue to protect those poor old fools whom you have humbugged there at the hospital, you now find that the game costs more than it's worth, and so you make up your mind to have done with it. A prudent resolution, Mr Bold; but it is a pity you should have been so long coming to it. Has it struck you that we may not now choose to give over? that we may find it necessary to punish the injury you have done to us? Are you aware, sir, that we have gone to enormous expense to resist this iniquitous attempt of yours?'

Bold's face was now furiously red, and he nearly crushed his hat between his hands; but he said nothing.

'We have found it necessary to employ the best advice that money could procure. Are you aware, sir, what may be the probable cost of securing the services of the attorney-general?'

'Not in the least, Dr Grantly.'

'I dare say not, sir. When you recklessly put this affair into the hands of your friend Mr Finney, whose six and eightpences and thirteen and fourpences may, probably, not amount to a large sum, you were indifferent as to the cost and suffering which such a proceeding might entail on others; but are you aware, sir, that these crushing costs must now come out of your own pocket?'

'Any demand of such a nature which Mr Harding's lawyer may have to make, will doubtless be made to my lawyer.'

'"Mr Harding's lawyer and my lawyer"! Did you come here merely to refer me to the lawyers? Upon my word I think the honour of your visit might have been spared! And now, sir, I'll tell you what my opinion is – my opinion is, that we shall not allow you to withdraw this matter from the courts.'

'You can do as you please, Dr Grantly; good morning.'

'Hear me out, sir,' said the archdeacon; 'I have here in my hands the last opinion given in this matter by Sir Abraham Haphazard. I dare say you have already heard of this – I dare say it has had something to do with your visit here today.'

'I know nothing whatever of Sir Abraham Haphazard or his opinion.'

'Be that as it may, here it is; he declares most explicitly that under no phasis[6] of the affair whatever have you a leg to stand upon; that Mr Harding is as safe in his hospital as I am here in my rectory; that a more futile attempt to destroy a man was never made, than this which you have made to ruin Mr Harding. Here,' and he slapped the paper on the table, 'I have this opinion from the very first lawyer in the land; and under these circumstances you expect me to make you a low bow for your kind offer to release Mr Harding from the toils of your net! Sir, your net is not strong

enough to hold him; sir, your net has fallen to pieces, and you
knew that well enough before I told you – and now, sir, I'll wish
you good morning, for I'm busy.'

Bold was now choking with passion; he had let the archdeacon
run on, because he knew not with what words to interrupt him;
but now that he had been so defied and insulted, he could not leave
the room without some reply.

'Dr Grantly,' he commenced.

'I have nothing further to say or to hear,' said the archdeacon;
'I'll do myself the honour to order your horse:' and he rang the
bell.

'I came here, Dr Grantly, with the warmest, kindest feelings –'

'Oh, of course you did; nobody doubts it.'

'With the kindest feelings – and they have been most grossly
outraged by your treatment.'

'Of course they have – I have not chosen to see my father-in-
law ruined; what an outrage that has been to your feelings!'

'The time will come, Dr Grantly, when you will understand why
I called upon you today.'

'No doubt, no doubt. Is Mr Bold's horse there? That's right, open
the front door – good morning, Mr Bold'; and the doctor stalked
into his own drawing-room, closing the door behind him, and
making it quite impossible that John Bold should speak another
word.

As he got on his horse, which he was fain to do feeling like a
dog turned out of a kitchen, he was again greeted by little Sammy.

'Good-bye, Mr Bold; I hope we may have the pleasure of seeing
you again before long; I am sure papa will always be glad to see
you.'

That was certainly the bitterest moment in John Bold's life; not
even the remembrance of his successful love could comfort him;
nay, when he thought of Eleanor, he felt that it was that very
love which had brought him to such a pass. That he should have
been so insulted, and be unable to reply! That he should have
given up so much to the request of a girl, and then have had his
motives so misunderstood! That he should have made so gross a
mistake as this visit of his to the archdeacon's! He bit the top of
his whip, till he penetrated the horn of which it was made: he

struck the poor animal in his anger, and then was doubly angry with himself at his futile passion. He had been so completely checkmated, so palpably overcome! and what was he to do? He could not continue his action after pledging himself to abandon it; nor was there any revenge in that – it was the very step to which his enemy had endeavoured to goad him!

He threw the reins to the servant who came to take his horse, and rushed upstairs into his drawing-room, where his sister Mary was sitting.

'If there be a devil,' said he, 'a real devil here on earth, it is Dr Grantly.' He vouchsafed her no further intelligence, but again seizing his hat, he rushed out, and took his departure for London without another word to anyone.

CHAPTER 13

The Warden's Decision

THE meeting between Eleanor and her father was not so stormy as that described in the last chapter, but it was hardly more successful. On her return from Bold's house, she found her father in a strange state. He was not sorrowful and silent as he had been on that memorable day when his son-in-law lectured him as to all that he owed to his order; nor was he in his usual quiet mood. When Eleanor reached the hospital, he was walking quickly to and fro upon the lawn, and she soon saw that he was much excited.

'I am going to London, my dear,' he said as soon as he saw her.

'London, papa!'

'Yes, my dear, to London; I will have this matter settled some way: there are some things, Eleanor, which I cannot bear.'

'Oh, papa, what is it?' said she, leading him by the arm into the house – 'I had such good news for you, and now you make me fear I am too late'; and then, before he could let her know what had caused this sudden resolve, or could point to the fatal paper which lay on the table, she told him that the lawsuit was over, that Bold had commissioned her to assure her father in his name that it would be abandoned, that there was no further cause for misery, that the whole matter might be looked on as though it had never been discussed. She did not tell him with what determined vehemence she had obtained this concession in his favour, nor did she mention the price she was to pay for it.

The warden did not express himself peculiarly gratified at this intelligence, and Eleanor, though she had not worked for thanks, and was by no means disposed to magnify her own good offices, felt hurt at the manner in which her news was received.

'Mr Bold can act as he thinks proper, my love,' said he: 'if Mr Bold thinks that he has been wrong, of course he will discontinue what he is doing; but that cannot change my purpose.'

'Oh, papa!' she exclaimed, all but crying with vexation – 'I thought you would have been so happy – I thought all would have been right now.'

'Mr Bold,' continued he, 'has set great people to work; so great that I doubt they are now beyond his control. Read that, my dear': and the warden, doubling up a number of the *Jupiter*, pointed to the peculiar article which she was to read. It was to the last of the three leaders, which are generally furnished daily for the support of the nation, that Mr Harding directed her attention. It dealt some heavy blows on various clerical delinquents; on families who had received their tens of thousands yearly for doing nothing; on men who, as the article stated, rolled in wealth which they had neither earned nor inherited, and which was in fact stolen from the poorer clergy. It named some sons of bishops, and grandsons of arch-bishops; men great in their way, who had redeemed their disgrace in the eyes of many by the enormity of their plunder; and then having disposed of these leviathans, it descended to Mr Harding.

We alluded some few weeks since to an instance of similar injustice, though in a more humble scale, in which the warden of an almshouse at Barchester has become possessed of the income of the greater part of the whole institution. Why an almshouse should have a warden we cannot pretend to explain, nor can we say what special need twelve old men can have for the services of a separate clergyman, seeing that they have twelve reserved seats for themselves in Barchester Cathedral. But be this as it may, let the gentleman call himself warden or precentor, or what he will, let him be never so scrupulous in exacting religious duties from his twelve dependants, or never so negligent as regards the services of the cathedral, it appears palpably clear that he can be entitled to no portion of the revenue of the hospital, excepting that which the founder set apart for him; and it is equally clear that the founder did not intend that three fifths of his charity should be so consumed.

The case is certainly a paltry one after the tens of thousands with which we have been dealing, for the warden's income is after all but a poor eight hundred a year: eight hundred a year is not magnificent preferment of itself, and the warden may, for anything we know, be worth much more to the church; but if so, let the church pay him out of funds justly at its own disposal.

We allude to the question of the Barchester almshouse at the present moment, because we understand that a plea has been set up which will be peculiarly revolting to the minds of English churchmen. An action has been taken against Mr Warden Harding, on behalf of the almsmen, by a gentleman acting solely on public grounds, and it is to be argued that Mr Harding takes nothing but what he receives as a servant of the hospital, and that he is not himself responsible for the amount of stipend given to him for his work. Such a plea would doubtless be fair, if anyone questioned the daily wages of a bricklayer employed on the building, or the fee of the charwoman who cleans it; but we cannot envy the feeling of a clergyman of the Church of England who could allow such an argument to be put into his mouth.

If this plea be put forward, we trust Mr Harding will be forced as a witness to state the nature of his employment; the amount of work that he does; the income which he receives, and the source from whence he obtained his appointment. We do not think he will receive much public sympathy to atone for the annoyance of such an examination.

As Eleanor read the article her face flushed with indignation, and when she had finished it, she almost feared to look up at her father.

'Well, my dear,' said he, 'what do you think of that – is it worth while to be a warden at that price?'

'Oh, papa – dear papa.'

'Mr Bold can't unwrite that my dear – Mr Bold can't say that that shan't be read by every clergyman at Oxford; nay, by every gentleman in the land'; and then he walked up and down the room, while Eleanor in mute despair followed him with her eyes – 'and I'll tell you what, my dear,' he continued, speaking now very calmly, and in a forced manner very unlike himself. 'Mr Bold can't dispute the truth of every word in that article you have just read – nor can I.' Eleanor stared at him, as though she scarcely understood the words he was speaking. 'Nor can I, Eleanor: that's the worst of all, or would be so if there were no remedy; I have thought much of all this since we were together last night'; and he came and sat beside her, and put his arm round her waist as he had done then. 'I have thought much of what the archdeacon has said, and of what this paper says; and I do believe I have no right to be here.'

'No right to be warden of the hospital, papa?'

'No right to be warden with eight hundred a year; no right to be warden with such a house as this; no right to spend in luxury money that was intended for charity. Mr Bold may do as he pleases about his suit, but I hope he will not abandon it for my sake.'

Poor Eleanor! this was hard upon her. Was it for this she had made her great resolve! For this that she had laid aside her quiet demeanour, and taken upon her the rants of a tragedy heroine! One may work and not for thanks, but yet feel hurt at not receiving them; and so it was with Eleanor: one may be disinterested in one's good actions, and yet feel discontented that they are not recognized. Charity may be given with the left hand so privily that the right hand does not know it, and yet the left hand may regret to feel that it has no immediate reward. Eleanor had had no wish to burden her father with a weight of obligation, and yet she had looked forward to much delight from the knowledge that she had freed him from his sorrows: now such hopes were entirely over; all that she had done was of no avail; she had humbled herself to Bold in vain; the evil was utterly beyond her power to cure!

She had thought also how gently she would whisper to her father all that her lover had said to her about herself, and how impossible she had found it to reject him: and then she had anticipated her father's kindly kiss and close embrace as he gave his sanction to her love. Alas, she could say nothing of this now. In speaking of Mr Bold, her father put him aside as one whose thoughts and sayings and acts could be of no moment. Gentle reader, did you ever feel yourself snubbed? Did you ever, when thinking much of your own importance, find yourself suddenly reduced to a nonentity? Such was Eleanor's feeling now.

'They shall not put forward this plea on my behalf,' continued the warden. 'Whatever may be the truth of the matter, that at any rate is not true; and the man who wrote that article is right in saying that such a plea is revolting to an honest mind. I will go up to London, my dear, and see these lawyers myself, and if no better excuse can be made for me than that, I and the hospital will part.'

'But the archdeacon, papa?'

'I can't help it, my dear; there are some things which a man cannot bear – I cannot bear that' – and he put his hand upon the newspaper.

'But will the archdeacon go with you?'

To tell the truth Mr Harding had made up his mind to steal a march upon the archdeacon. He was aware that he could take no steps without informing his dread son-in-law, but he had resolved that he would send out a note to Plumstead Episcopi detailing his plans, but that the messenger should not leave Barchester till he himself had started for London; so that he might be a day before the doctor, who, he had no doubt, would follow him. In that day, if he had luck, he might arrange it all; he might explain to Sir Abraham that he, as warden, would have nothing further to do with the defence about to be set up; he might send in his official resignation to his friend the bishop, and so make public the whole transaction that even the doctor would not be able to undo what he had done. He knew too well the doctor's strength and his own weakness to suppose he could do this, if they both reached London together; indeed, he would never be able to get to London if the doctor knew of his intended journey in time to prevent it.

'No, I think not,' said he; 'I think I shall start before the arch-deacon could be ready – I shall go early tomorrow morning.'

'That will be best, papa,' said Eleanor, showing that her father's ruse was appreciated.

'Why, yes, my love: the fact is, I wish to do all this before the archdeacon can – can interfere. There is a great deal of truth in all he says – he argues very well, and I can't always answer him; but there is an old saying, Nelly, "Everyone knows where his own shoe pinches!" He'll say that I want moral courage, and strength of character, and power of endurance, and it's all true; but I'm sure I ought not to remain here, if I have nothing better to put forward than a quibble: so, Nelly, we shall have to leave this pretty place.'

Eleanor's face brightened up, as she assured her father how cordially she agreed with him.

'True, my love,' said he, now again quite happy and at ease in his manner. 'What good to us is this place or all the money, if we are to be ill-spoken of?'

'Oh, papa, I am so glad.'

'My darling child. It did cost me a pang at first, Nelly, to think that you should lose your pretty drawing-room, and your ponies, and your garden: the garden will be the worst of all – but there is a garden at Crabtree, a very pretty garden.'

Crabtree Parva was the name of the small living which Mr

Harding had held as a minor canon, and which still belonged to him. It was only worth some eighty pounds a year, and a small house and glebe, all of which were now handed over to Mr Harding's curate; but it was to Crabtree glebe that Mr Harding thought of retiring. This parish must not be mistaken for that other living, Crabtree Canonicorum as it is called. Crabtree Canonicorum is a very nice thing; there are only two hundred parishioners; there are four hundred acres of glebe; and the great and small tithes,[1] which both go to the rector, are worth four hundred pounds a year more. Crabtree Canonicorum is in the gift of the dean and chapter, and is at this time possessed by the Honourable and Reverend Dr Vesey Stanhope, who also fills the prebendal stall[2] of Goosegorge in Barchester Chapter, and holds the united rectory of Eiderdown and Stogpingum, or Stoke Pinquium as it should be written. This is the same Dr Vesey Stanhope whose hospitable villa on the Lake of Como is well known to the *élite* of English travellers, and whose collection of Lombard butterflies is supposed to be unique.

'Yes,' said the warden musing, 'there is a very pretty garden at Crabtree, but I shall be sorry to disturb poor Smith.' Smith was the curate of Crabtree, a gentleman who was maintaining a wife and half a dozen children on the income arising from his profession.

Eleanor assured her father that as far as she was concerned, she could leave her house and her ponies without a single regret: she was only so happy that he was going – going where he would escape all this dreadful turmoil.

'But we will take the music, my dear.'

And so they went on planning their future happiness, and plotting how they would arrange it all without the interposition of the archdeacon, and at last they again became confidential, and then the warden did thank her for what she had done, and Eleanor, lying on her father's shoulder, did find an opportunity to tell her secret: and the father gave his blessing to his child, and said that the man whom she loved was honest, good, and kind-hearted, and right-thinking in the main – one who wanted only a good wife to put him quite upright – 'a man, my love,' he ended by saying, 'to whom I firmly believe that I can trust my treasure with safety.'

'But what will Dr Grantly say?'

'Well, my dear, it can't be helped – we shall be out at Crabtree then.'

And Eleanor ran upstairs to prepare her father's clothes for his journey; and the warden returned to his garden to make his last adieus to every tree, and shrub, and shady nook that he knew so well.

CHAPTER 14

Mount Olympus

WRETCHED in spirit, groaning under the feeling of insult, self-condemning, and ill-satisfied in every way, Bold returned to his London lodgings. Ill as he had fared in his interview with the archdeacon, he was not less under the necessity of carrying out his pledge to Eleanor; and he went about his ungracious task with a heavy heart.

The attorneys whom he had employed in London received his instructions with surprise and evident misgiving: however, they could only obey, and mutter something of their sorrow that such heavy costs should only fall upon their own employer – especially as nothing was wanting but perseverance to throw them on the opposite party. Bold left the office which he had latterly so much frequented, shaking the dust from off his feet; and before he was down the stairs, an edict had already gone forth for the preparation of the bill.

He next thought of the newspapers. The case had been taken up by more than one; and he was well aware that the keynote had been sounded by the *Jupiter*. He had been very intimate with Tom Towers, and had often discussed with him the affairs of the hospital. Bold could not say that the articles in that paper had been written at his own instigation; he did not even know as a fact that they had been written by his friend. Tom Towers had never said that such a view of the case, or such a side in the dispute, would be taken by the paper with which he was connected. Very discreet in such matters was Tom Towers, and altogether indisposed to talk loosely of the concerns of that mighty engine of which it was his high privilege to move in secret some portion. Nevertheless, Bold believed that to him were owing those dreadful words which had caused him such panic at Barchester – and he conceived himself bound to prevent their repetition. With this view he betook himself from the attorneys' to that laboratory where, with amazing chemistry, Tom Towers compounded thunderbolts for the destruction of all that is evil, and for the furtherance of all that is good, in this and other hemispheres.

Who has not heard of Mount Olympus[1] – that high abode of all the powers of type, that favoured seat of the great goddess Pica,[2] that wondrous habitation of gods and devils, from whence, with ceaseless hum of steam and never-ending flow of Castalian ink,[3] issue forth fifty thousand nightly edicts for the governance of a subject nation?

Velvet and gilding do not make a throne, nor gold and jewels a sceptre. It is a throne because the most exalted one sits there – and a sceptre because the most mighty one wields it. So it is with Mount Olympus. Should a stranger make his way thither at dull noonday, or during the sleepy hours of the silent afternoon, he would find no acknowledged temple of power and beauty, no fitting fane for the great Thunderer, no proud façades and pillared roofs to support the dignity of this greatest of earthly potentates. To the outward and uninitiated eye, Mount Olympus is a somewhat humble spot – undistinguished, unadorned – nay, almost mean. It stands alone, as it were, in a mighty city, close to the densest throng of men, but partaking neither of the noise nor the crowd; a small, secluded, dreary spot, tenanted, one would say, by quite unambitious people at the easiest rents. 'Is this Mount Olympus?' asks the unbelieving stranger. 'Is it from these small, dark, dingy buildings that those infallible laws proceed which cabinets are called upon to obey; by which bishops are to be guided, lords and commons controlled – judges instructed in law, generals in strategy, admirals in naval tactics, and orange-women in the management of their barrows?' 'Yes, my friend – from these walls. From here issue the only known infallible bulls[4] for the guidance of British souls and bodies. This little court is the Vatican of England. Here reigns a pope, self-nominated, self-consecrated – ay, and much stranger too – self-believing! – a pope whom, if you cannot believe him, I would advise you to disobey as silently as possible; a pope hitherto afraid of no Luther; a pope who manages his own inquisition, who punishes unbelievers as no most skilful inquisitor of Spain ever dreamt of doing – one who can excommunicate thoroughly, fearfully, radically; put you beyond the pale of men's charity; make you odious to your dearest friends, and turn you into a monster to be pointed at by the finger!'

Oh heavens! and this is Mount Olympus!

It is a fact amazing to ordinary mortals that the *Jupiter* is never wrong. With what endless care, with what unsparing labour, do we not strive to get together for our great national council the men most fitting to compose it. And how we fail! Parliament is always wrong: look at the *Jupiter*, and see how futile are their meetings, how vain their council, how needless all their trouble! With what pride do we regard our chief ministers, the great servants of state, the oligarchs of the nation on whose wisdom we lean, to whom we look for guidance in our difficulties! But what are they to the writers of the *Jupiter*? They hold council together and with anxious thought painfully elaborate their country's good; but when all is done, the *Jupiter* declares that all is nought. Why should we look to Lord John Russell – why should we regard Palmerston and Gladstone,[5] when Tom Towers without a struggle can put us right? Look at our generals, what faults they make; at our admirals, how inactive they are. What money, honesty, and science can do, is done; and yet how badly are our troops brought together, fed, conveyed, clothed, armed, and managed. The most excellent of our good men do their best to man our ships, with the assistance of all possible external appliances, but in vain. All, all is wrong – alas! alas! Tom Towers, and he alone, knows all about it. Why, oh why, ye earthly ministers, why have ye not followed more closely this heaven-sent messenger that is among us?

Were it not well for us in our ignorance that we confided all things to the *Jupiter*? Would it not be wise in us to abandon useless talking, idle thinking, and profitless labour? Away with majorities in the House of Commons, with verdicts from judicial bench given after much delay, with doubtful laws, and the fallible attempts of humanity! Does not the *Jupiter*, coming forth daily with fifty thousand impressions[6] full of unerring decision on every mortal subject, set all matters sufficiently at rest? Is not Tom Towers here, able to guide us and willing?

Yes indeed – able and willing to guide all men in all things, so long as he is obeyed as autocrat should be obeyed – with un-doubting submission: only let not ungrateful ministers seek other colleagues than those whom Tom Towers may approve; let church and state, law and physic, commerce and agriculture – the arts of war, and the arts of peace – all listen and obey, and all will be made perfect. Has not Tom Towers an all-seeing eye? From the diggings of Australia to those of California, right round the habitable globe, does he not know, watch, and chronicle the doings of everyone? From a bishopric in New Zealand to an unfortunate director of a north-west passage, is he not the only fit judge of capability? From the sewers of London to the Central Railway of India – from the palaces of St Petersburg to the cabins of Connaught, nothing can escape him. Britons have but to read, to obey, and be blessed. None but the fools doubt the wisdom of the *Jupiter*; none but the mad dispute its facts.

No established religion has ever been without its unbelievers, even in the country where it is the most firmly fixed; no creed has been without scoffers; no church has so prospered as to free itself entirely from dissent. There are those who doubt the *Jupiter*! They live and breathe the upper air walking here unscathed, though scorned – men, born of British mothers and nursed on English milk, who scruple not to say that Mount Olympus has its price, that Tom Towers can be bought for gold!

Such is Mount Olympus, the mouthpiece of all the wisdom of this great country. It may probably be said that no place in this nineteenth century is more worthy of notice. No treasury mandate armed with the signatures of all the government has half the power of one of those broadsheets, which fly forth from hence so abundantly, armed with no signature at all.

Some great man, some mighty peer – we'll say a noble duke – retires to rest feared and honoured by all his countrymen – fearless himself; if not a good man, at any rate a mighty man – too mighty to care much what men may say about his want of virtue. He rises in the morning degraded, mean, and miserable; an object of men's scorn, anxious only to retire as quickly as may be to some German obscurity, some unseen Italian privacy, or, indeed, anywhere out of sight. What has made this awful change? what has so afflicted him? An article has appeared in the *Jupiter*; some fifty lines of a narrow column have destroyed all his grace's equanimity, and banished him for ever from the world. No man knows who wrote the bitter words; the clubs talk confusedly of the matter, whispering to each other this and that name; while Tom Towers walks quietly along Pall Mall, with his coat buttoned close against the east wind, as though he were a mortal man, and not a god dispensing thunderbolts from Mount Olympus.

It was not to Mount Olympus that our friend Bold betook
himself. He had before now wandered round that lonely spot,
thinking how grand a thing it was to write articles for the *Jupiter*;
considering within himself whether by any stretch of the powers
within him he could ever come to such distinction; wondering
how Tom Towers would take any little humble offering of his
talents; calculating that Tom Towers himself must have once had
a beginning, have once doubted as to his own success. Towers
could not have been born a writer in the *Jupiter*. With such ideas,
half ambitious and half awe-struck, had Bold regarded the silent-
looking workshop of the gods; but he had never yet by word or
sign attempted to influence the slightest word of his unerring
friend. On such a course was he now intent; and not without
much inward palpitation did he betake himself to the quiet abode
of wisdom, where Tom Towers was to be found o' mornings inhaling ambrosia and sipping nectar in the shape of toast and tea.[7]

Not far removed from Mount Olympus, but somewhat nearer
to the blessed regions of the West, is the most favoured abode of
Themis.[8] Washed by the rich tide which now passes from the
towers of Caesar to Barry's halls of eloquence;[9] and again back,
with new offerings of a city's tribute, from the palaces of peers to
the mart of merchants, stand those quiet walls which Law has
delighted to honour by its presence. What a world within a world
is the Temple! how quiet are its 'entangled walks', as someone
lately has called them, and yet how close to the densest concourse
of humanity! how gravely respectable its sober alleys, though
removed but by a single step from the profanity of the Strand and
the low iniquity of Fleet Street! Old St Dunstan, with its bell-
smiting bludgeoners,[10] has been removed; the ancient shops with
their faces full of pleasant history are passing away one by one;
the bar itself is to go[11] – its doom has been pronounced by the
Jupiter; rumour tells us of some huge building that is to appear in
these latitudes dedicated to law,[12] subversive of the courts of Westminster, and antagonistic to the Rolls and Lincoln's Inn; but
nothing yet threatens the silent beauty of the Temple: it is the
medieval court of the metropolis.

Here, on the choicest spot of this choice ground, stands a lofty
row of chambers, looking obliquely upon the sullied Thames;
before the windows, the lawn of the Temple Gardens stretches

with that dim yet delicious verdure so refreshing to the eyes of Londoners. If doomed to live within the thickest of London smoke, you would surely say that that would be your chosen spot. Yes, you, you whom I now address, my dear, middle-aged bachelor friend, can nowhere be so well domiciled as here. No one here will ask whether you are out or at home; alone or with friends: here no Sabbatarian will investigate your Sundays, no censorious land-lady will scrutinize your empty bottle, no valetudinarian neigh-bour will complain of late hours. If you love books, to what place are books so suitable? The whole spot is redolent of typography. Would you worship the Paphian goddess,[13] the groves of Cyprus are not more taciturn than those of the Temple. Wit and wine are always here, and always together; the revels of the Temple are as those of polished Greece, where the wildest worshipper of Bacchus[14] never forgot the dignity of the god whom he adored. Where can retirement be so complete as here? where can you be so sure of all the pleasures of society?

It was here that Tom Towers lived, and cultivated with eminent success the tenth Muse who now governs the periodical press.[15] But let it not be supposed that his chambers were such, or so comfort-less, as are frequently the gaunt abodes of legal aspirants. Four chairs, a half-filled deal bookcase with hangings of dingy green baize, an old office table covered with dusty papers, which are not moved once in six months, and an older Pembroke brother with rickety legs, for all daily uses[16] – a despatcher for the preparation of lobsters and coffee, and an apparatus for the cooking of toast and mutton chops; such utensils and luxuries as these did not suffice for the well-being of Tom Towers. He indulged in four rooms on the first floor, each of which was furnished, if not with the splendour, with probably more than the comfort of Stafford House.[17] Every addition that science and art have lately made to the luxuries of modern life was to be found there. The room in which he usually sat was surrounded by bookshelves carefully filled; nor was there a volume there which was not entitled to its place in such a collection, both by its intrinsic worth and exterior splen-dour: a pretty portable set of steps in one corner of the room showed that those even on the higher shelves were intended for use. The chamber contained but two works of art – the one, an admirable bust of Sir Robert Peel, by Power,[18] declared the individual politics of our friend; and the other, a singularly long figure of a female devotee, by Millais,[19] told equally plainly the school of art to which he was addicted. This picture was not hung, as pictures usually are, against the wall; there was no inch of wall vacant for such a purpose: it had a stand or desk erected for its own accomodation; and there on her pedestal, framed and glazed, stood the devotional lady looking intently at a lily as no lady ever looked before.[20]

Our modern artists, whom we style Pre-Raphaelites, have delighted to go back, not only to the finish and peculiar manner, but also to the subjects of the early painters. It is impossible to give them too much praise for the elaborate perseverance with which they have equalled the minute perfections of the masters from whom they take their inspiration: nothing probably can exceed the painting of some of these latterday pictures. It is, however, singular into what faults they fall as regards their subjects: they are not quite content to take the old stock groups – a Sebastian with his arrows, a Lucia with her eyes in a dish, a Lorenzo with a gridiron, or the virgin with two children. But they are anything but happy in their change. As a rule, no figure should be drawn in a position which it is impossible to suppose any figure should maintain. The patient endurance of St Sebastian, the wild ecstasy of St John in the Wilderness, the maternal love of the virgin, are feelings naturally portrayed by a fixed posture; but the lady with the stiff back and bent neck, who looks at her flower, and is still looking from hour to hour, gives us an idea of pain without grace, and abstraction without a cause.

It was easy, from his rooms, to see that Tom Towers was a Sybarite,[21] though by no means an idle one. He was lingering over his last cup of tea, surrounded by an ocean of newspapers, through which he had been swimming, when John Bold's card was brought in by his tiger.[22] This tiger never knew that his master was at home, though he often knew that he was not, and thus Tom Towers was never invaded but by his own consent. On this occasion, after twisting the card twice in his fingers, he signified to his attendant imp that he was visible; and the inner door was unbolted, and our friend announced.

I have before said that he of the *Jupiter* and John Bold were
intimate. There was no very great difference in their ages, for
Towers was still considerably under forty; and when Bold had
been attending the London hospitals, Towers, who was not then
the great man that he had since become, had been much with him.
Then they had often discussed together the objects of their ambition and future prospects; then Tom Towers was struggling hard
to maintain himself, as a briefless barrister, by shorthand report-
ing for any of the papers that would engage him; then he had not
dared to dream of writing leaders for the *Jupiter*, or canvassing the
conduct of cabinet ministers. Things had altered since that time:
the briefless barrister was still briefless, but he now despised briefs:
could he have been sure of a judge's seat, he would hardly have
left his present career. It is true he wore no ermine, bore no
outward marks of a world's respect; but with what a load of
inward importance was he charged! It is true his name appeared
in no large capitals; on no wall was chalked up TOM TOWERS FOR
EVER – FREEDOM OF THE PRESS AND TOM TOWERS: but what
member of Parliament had half his power? It is true that in far-
off provinces men did not talk daily of Tom Towers, but they read
the *Jupiter*, and acknowledged that without the *Jupiter* life was not
worth having. This kind of hidden but still conscious glory suited
the nature of the man. He loved to sit silent in a corner of his club
and listen to the loud chattering of politicians, and to think how
they all were in his power – how he could smite the loudest of
them, were it worth his while to raise his pen for such a purpose.
He loved to watch the great men of whom he daily wrote, and
flatter himself that he was greater than any of them. Each of them
was responsible to his country, each of them must answer if
inquired into, each of them must endure abuse with good humour,
and insolence without anger. But to whom was he, Tom Towers,
responsible? No one could insult him; no one could inquire into
him. He could speak out withering words, and no one could
answer him: ministers courted him, though perhaps they knew
not his name; bishops feared him; judges doubted their own
verdicts unless he confirmed them; and generals, in their councils
of war, did not consider more deeply what the enemy would do,
than what the *Jupiter* would say. Tom Towers never boasted of the

Jupiter; he scarcely ever named the paper even to the most intimate of his friends; he did not even wish to be spoken of as connected with it; but he did not the less value his privileges, or think the less of his own importance. It is probable that Tom Towers considered himself the most powerful man in Europe; and so he walked on from day to day, studiously striving to look a man, but knowing within his breast that he was a god.

CHAPTER 15

Tom Towers, Dr Anticant, and Mr Sentiment

'Ah, Bold! how are you? You haven't breakfasted?'

'Oh yes, hours ago. And how are you?'

When one Esquimau meets another, do the two, as an invariable rule, ask after each other's health? is it inherent in all human nature to make this obliging inquiry? Did any reader of this tale ever meet any friend or acquaintance without asking some such question, and did anyone ever listen to the reply? Sometimes a studiously courteous questioner will show so much thought in the matter as to answer it himself, by declaring that had he looked at you he needn't have asked; meaning thereby to signify that you are an absolute personification of health: but such persons are only those who premeditate small effects.

'I suppose you're busy?' inquired Bold.

'Why, yes, rather; or I should say rather not: if I have a leisure hour in the day, this is it.'

'I want to ask you if you can oblige me in a certain matter.'

Towers understood in a moment, from the tone of his friend's voice, that the certain matter referred to the newspaper. He smiled, and nodded his head, but made no promise.

'You know this lawsuit that I've been engaged in?' said Bold.

Tom Towers intimated that he was aware of the action which was pending about the hospital.

'Well, I've abandoned it.'

Tom Towers merely raised his eyebrows, thrust his hands into his trousers' pockets, and waited for his friend to proceed.

'Yes, I've given it up. I needn't trouble you with all the history; but the fact is that the conduct of Mr Harding – Mr Harding is the –'

'Oh yes, the master of the place; the man who takes all the money and does nothing,' said Tom Towers, interrupting him.

'Well, I don't know about that; but his conduct in the matter has been so excellent, so little selfish, so open, that I cannot proceed in the matter to his detriment.' Bold's heart misgave him as to Eleanor as he said this; and yet he felt that what he said was not untrue. 'I think nothing should now be done till the wardenship be vacant.'

'And be again filled,' said Towers, 'as it certainly would, before anyone heard of the vacancy; and the same objection would again exist. It's an old story that of the vested rights of the incumbent; but suppose the incumbent has only a vested wrong, and that the poor of the town have a vested right, if they only knew how to get at it: is not that something the case here?'

Bold couldn't deny it, but thought it was one of those cases which required a good deal of management before any real good could be done. It was a pity that he had not considered this before he crept into the lion's mouth, in the shape of an attorney's office.

'It will cost you a good deal, I fear,' said Towers.

'A few hundreds,' said Bold – 'perhaps three hundred; I can't help that, and am prepared for it.'

'That's philosophical; it's quite refreshing to hear a man talking of his hundreds in so purely indifferent a manner. But I'm sorry you are giving the matter up; it injures a man to commence a thing of this kind, and not carry it through. Have you seen that?' and he threw a small pamphlet across the table, which was all but damp from the press.

Bold had not seen it nor heard of it; but he was well acquainted with the author of it – a gentleman whose pamphlets, condemnatory of all things in these modern days, had been a good deal talked about of late.

Dr Pessimist Anticant was a Scotchman,[1] who had passed a great portion of his early days in Germany; he had studied there with much effect, and had learnt to look with German subtlety into the root of things, and to examine for himself their intrinsic worth and worthlessness. No man ever resolved more bravely than he to accept as good nothing that was evil; to banish from him as evil nothing that was good. 'Tis a pity that he should not have recognized the fact that in this world no good is unalloyed, and that there is but little evil that has not in it some seed of what is goodly.

Returning from Germany, he had astonished the reading public by the vigour of his thoughts, put forth in the quaintest language. He cannot write English, said the critics. No matter, said the public; we can read what he does write, and that without yawning. And so Dr Pessimist Anticant became popular. Popularity spoilt him for all further real use, as it has done many another. While, with some diffidence, he confined his objurgations to the occasional follies or shortcomings of mankind; while he ridiculed the energy of the squire devoted to the slaughter of partridges, or the mistake of some noble patron who turned a poet into a gauger of beer-barrels, it was all well; we were glad to be told our faults and to look forward to the coming millennium, when all men, having sufficiently studied the works of Dr Anticant, would become truthful and energetic. But the doctor mistook the signs of the times and the minds of men, instituted himself censor of things in general, and began the great task of reprobating everything and everybody, without further promise of any millennium at all. This was not so well: and, to tell the truth, our author did not succeed in his undertaking. His theories were all beautiful, and the code of morals that he taught us certainly an improvement on the practices of the age. We all of us could, and many of us did, learn much from the doctor while he chose to remain vague, mysterious, and cloudy; but when he became practical, the charm was gone.

His allusion to the poet and the partridges was received very well.[2]

Oh, my poor brother (said he) slaughtered partridges a score of brace to each gun, and poets gauging ale-barrels, with sixty pounds a year, at Dumfries, are not the signs of a great era! perhaps of the smallest possible era yet written of. Whatever economies we pursue, political or other, let us see at once that this is the maddest of the uneconomic: partridges killed by our land magnates at, shall we say, a guinea a head, to be retailed in Leadenhall at one shilling and ninepence, with one poacher in limbo for every fifty birds! our poet, maker, creator, gauging ale, and that badly, with no leisure for making or creating, only a little leisure for drinking, and suchlike beer-barrel avocations! Truly, a cutting of blocks with fine razors while we scrape our chins so uncomfortably with rusty knives! Oh, my political economist, master of supply and demand, division of labour and high pressure – oh, my loud-speaking friend, tell me, if so much be in you, what is the demand for poets in these kingdoms of Queen Victoria, and what the vouchsafed supply?

This was all very well; this gave us some hope. We might do better with our next poet, when we got one; and though the partridges might not be abandoned, something could perhaps be done as to the poachers. We were unwilling, however, to take lessons in politics from so misty a professor; and when he came to tell us that the heroes of Westminster were naught, we began to think that he had written enough. His attack upon despatch boxes was not thought to have much in it; but as it is short, the doctor shall again be allowed to speak his sentiments:[3]

Could utmost ingenuity in the management of red tape avail anything to men lying gasping – we may say, all but dead; could despatch boxes with never-so-much velvet lining and Chubb's patent,[4] be of comfort to a people *in extremis*, I also, with so many others, would, with parched tongue, call on the name of Lord John Russell; or, my brother, at your advice, on Lord Aberdeen; or, my cousin, on Lord Derby,[5] at yours; being, with my parched tongue, indifferent in such matters. 'Tis all one. Oh, Derby! Oh, Gladstone! Oh, Palmerston! Oh, Lord John! Each comes running with serene face and despatch box. Vain physicians! though there were hosts of such, no despatch box will cure this disorder! What! are there other doctors' new names, disciples who have not burdened their souls with tape? Well, let us call again. Oh, Disraeli,[6] great oppositionist, man of the bitter brow! or, Oh, Molesworth,[7] great reformer, thou who promisest Utopia. They come; each with that serene face, and each – alas, me! alas, my country! – each with a despatch box!

Oh, the serenity of Downing Street!

My brothers, when hope was over on the battlefield, when no dimmest chance of victory remained, the ancient Roman could hide his face within his toga, and die gracefully. Can you and I do so now? If so, 'twere best for us; if not, oh my brothers, we must die disgracefully, for hope of life and victory I see none left to us in this world below. I for one cannot trust much to serene face and despatch box!

There might be truth in this, there might be depth of reasoning; but Englishmen did not see enough in the argument to induce them to withdraw their confidence from the present arrangements of the government, and Dr Anticant's monthly pamphlet on the decay of the world did not receive so much attention as his earlier works. He did not confine himself to politics in these publications, but roamed at large over all matters of public interest, and found everything bad. According to him nobody was true, and not only nobody, but nothing; a man could not take off his hat to a lady without telling a lie – the lady would lie again in smiling. The ruffles of the gentleman's shirt would be fraught with deceit, and the ladies' flounces full of falsehood. Was ever anything more severe than that attack of his on chip-bonnets, or the anathemas with which he endeavoured to dust the powder out of the bishops' wigs?

The pamphlet which Tom Towers now pushed across the table was entitled 'Modern Charity', and was written with the view of proving how much in the way of charity was done by our predecessors – how little by the present age; and it ended by a comparison between ancient and modern times, very little to the credit of the latter.[8]

'Look at this,' said Towers, getting up and turning over the pages of the pamphlet, and pointing to a passage near the end; 'your friend the warden, who is so little selfish, won't like that, I fear.' Bold read as follows:

Heavens, what a sight! Let us with eyes wide open see the godly man of four centuries since, the man of the dark ages: let us see how he does his god-like work, and, again, how the godly man of these latter days does his.

Shall we say that the former is one walking painfully through the world, regarding, as a prudent man, his worldly work, prospering in it as a diligent man will prosper, but always with an eye to that better treasure to which thieves do not creep in?[9] Is there not much nobility in that old man, as, leaning on his oaken staff, he walks down the high street of his native town, and receives from all courteous salutation and acknowledgement of his worth? A noble old man, my august inhabitants of Belgrave Square and suchlike vicinity[10] – a very noble old man, though employed no better than in the wholesale carding of wool.

This carding of wool, however, did in those days bring with it much profit, so that our ancient friend, when dying, was declared, in whatever slang then prevailed, to cut up exceeding well. For sons and daughters there was ample sustenance, with assistance of due industry; for friends and relatives some relief for grief at this great loss; for aged dependants comfort in declining years. This was much for one old man to get done in that dark fifteenth century. But this was not all: coming generations of poor wool-carders should bless the name of this rich one; and a hospital should be founded and endowed with his wealth for the feeding of such of the trade as could not, by diligent carding, any longer duly feed themselves.

'Twas thus that an old man in the fifteenth century did his god-like work to the best of his power, and not ignobly, as appears to me.

We will now take our godly man of latter days. He shall no longer be a wool-carder, for such are not now men of mark. We will suppose him to be one of the best of the good – one who has lacked no opportunities. Our old friend, was, after all, but illiterate; our modern friend shall be a man educated in all seemly knowledge; he shall, in short, be that blessed being – a clergyman of the Church of England!

And now, in what perfectest manner does he in this lower world get his god-like work done and put out of hand? Heavens! in the strangest of manners. Oh, my brother! in a manner not at all to be believed but by the most minute testimony of eyesight. He does it by the magnitude of his appetite – by the power of his gorge; his only occupation is to swallow the bread prepared with so much anxious care for these impoverished carders of wool – that, and to sing indifferently through his nose once in the week some psalm more or less long – the shorter the better, we should be inclined to say.

Oh, my civilized friends! – great Britons that never will be slaves, men advanced to infinite state of freedom and knowledge of good and evil – tell me, will you, what becoming monument you will erect to an highly educated clergyman of the Church of England?

Bold certainly thought that his friend would not like that: he could not conceive anything that he would like less than this. To what a world of toil and trouble had he, Bold, given rise by his indiscreet attack upon the hospital!

'You see,' said Towers, 'that this affair has been much talked of, and the public are with you. I am sorry you should give the matter up. Have you seen the first number of *The Almshouse?*'[11]

No; Bold had not seen *The Almshouse*. He had seen advertisements of Mr Popular Sentiment's new novel of that name, but had in no way connected it with Barchester Hospital, and had never thought a moment on the subject.

'It's a direct attack on the whole system,' said Towers. 'It'll go a long way to put down Rochester, and Barchester, and Dulwich,[12] and St Cross, and all such hotbeds of peculation. It's very clear that

Sentiment has been down to Barchester, and got up the whole story there; indeed, I thought he must have had it all from you. It's very well done, as you'll see: his first numbers always are.'

Bold declared that Mr Sentiment had got nothing from him, and that he was deeply grieved to find that the case had become so notorious.

'The fire has gone too far to be quenched,' said Towers; 'the building must go now; and as the timbers are all rotten, why, I should be inclined to say, the sooner the better. I expected to see you get some *éclat* in the matter.'[13]

This was all wormwood to Bold. He had done enough to make his friend the warden miserable for life, and had then backed out just when the success of his project was sufficient to make the question one of real interest. How weakly he had managed his business! He had already done the harm, and then stayed his hand when the good which he had in view was to be commenced. How delightful would it have been to have employed all his energy in such a cause – to have been backed by the *Jupiter*, and written up to by two of the most popular authors of the day! The idea opened a view into the very world in which he wished to live. To what might it not have given rise? what delightful intimacies – what public praise – to what Athenian banquets and rich flavour of Attic salt?[14]

This, however, was now past hope. He had pledged himself to abandon the cause; and could he have forgotten the pledge, he had gone too far to retreat. He was now, this moment, sitting in Tom Towers's room with the object of deprecating any further articles in the *Jupiter*, and, greatly as he disliked the job, his petition to that effect must be made.

'I couldn't continue it,' said he, 'because I found I was in the wrong.'

Tom Towers shrugged his shoulders. How could a successful man be in the wrong! 'In that case,' said he, 'of course you must abandon it.'

'And I called this morning to ask you also to abandon it,' said Bold.

'To ask me,' said Tom Towers with the most placid of smiles, and a consummate look of gentle surprise, as though Tom Towers was well aware that he of all men was the last to meddle in such matters.

'Yes,' said Bold, almost trembling with hesitation. 'The *Jupiter*, you know, has taken the matter up very strongly. Mr Harding has felt what it has said deeply; and I thought that if I could explain to you that he personally has not been to blame, these articles might be discontinued.'

How calmly impassive was Tom Towers's face, as this innocent little proposition was made! Had Bold addressed himself to the doorposts in Mount Olympus, they would have shown as much outward sign of assent or dissent. His quiescence was quite admirable; his discretion certainly more than human.

'My dear fellow,' said he, when Bold had quite done speaking, 'I really cannot answer for the *Jupiter*.'

'But if you saw that these articles were unjust, I think you would endeavour to put a stop to them: of course nobody doubts that you could, if you chose.'

'Nobody and everybody are always very kind, but unfortunately are generally very wrong.'

'Come, come, Towers,' said Bold, plucking up his courage, and remembering that for Eleanor's sake he was bound to make his best exertion; 'I have no doubt in my own mind but that you wrote the articles yourself; and very well written they were: it will be a great favour if you will in future abstain from any personal allusion to poor Harding.'

'My dear Bold,' said Tom Towers, 'I have a sincere regard for you. I have known you for many years, and value your friendship; I hope you will let me explain to you, without offence, that none who are connected with the public press can with propriety listen to interference.'

'Interference!' said Bold, 'I don't want to interfere.'

'Ah, but my dear fellow, you do; what else is it? You think that I am able to keep certain remarks out of a newspaper. Your information is probably incorrect, as most public gossip on such subjects is; but, at any rate, you think I have such power, and you ask me to use it: now that is interference.'

'Well, if you choose to call it so.'

'And now suppose for a moment that I had this power, and used

it as you wish: isn't it clear that it would be a great abuse? Certain
men are employed in writing for the public press; and if they are
induced either to write or to abstain from writing by private
motives, surely the public press would soon be of little value. Look
at the recognized worth of different newspapers, and see if it does
not mainly depend on the assurance which the public feel that
such a paper is, or is not, independent. You alluded to the *Jupiter*:
surely you cannot but see that the weight of the *Jupiter* is too great
to be moved by any private request, even though it should be made
to a much more influential person than myself: you've only to
think of this, and you'll see that I am right.'

The discretion of Tom Towers was boundless: there was no
contradicting what he said, no arguing against such propositions.
He took such high ground that there was no getting on it. 'The
public is defrauded,' said he, 'whenever private considerations are
allowed to have weight.' Quite true, thou greatest oracle of the
middle of the nineteenth century, thou sententious proclaimer of
the purity of the press – the public is defrauded when it is purposely
misled. Poor public! how often is it misled! against what a world
of fraud has it to contend!

Bold took his leave and got out of the room as quickly as he
could, inwardly denouncing his friend Tom Towers as a prig and
a humbug. 'I know he wrote those articles,' said Bold to himself;
'I know he got his information from me. He was ready enough to
take my word for gospel when it suited his own views, and to set
Mr Harding up before the public as an impostor on no other
testimony than my chance conversation; but when I offer him real
evidence opposed to his own views, he tells me that private
motives are detrimental to public justice! Confound his arrogance!
What is any public question but a conglomeration of private
interests? What is any newspaper article but an expression of the
views taken by one side? Truth! it takes an age to ascertain the
truth of any question! The idea of Tom Towers talking of public
motives and purity of purpose! Why, it wouldn't give him a
moment's uneasiness to change his politics tomorrow, if the paper
required it.'

Such were John Bold's inward exclamations as he made his way
out of the quiet labyrinth of the Temple; and yet there was no

position of worldly power so coveted in Bold's ambition as that held by the man of whom he was thinking. It was the impregnability of the place which made Bold so angry with the possessor of it, and it was the same quality which made it appear so desirable.

Passing into the Strand, he saw in a bookseller's window an announcement of the first number of *The Almshouse*; so he purchased a copy, and hurrying back to his lodgings, proceeded to ascertain what Mr Popular Sentiment had to say to the public on the subject which had lately occupied so much of his own attention.

In former times great objects were attained by great work. When evils were to be reformed, reformers set about their heavy task with grave decorum and laborious argument. An age was occupied in proving a grievance, and philosophical researches were printed in folio pages, which it took a life to write, and an eternity to read. We get on now with a lighter step, and quicker: ridicule is found to be more convincing than argument, imaginary agonies touch more than true sorrows, and monthly novels convince, when learned quartos fail to do so. If the world is to be set right, the work will be done by shilling numbers.[15]

Of all such reformers Mr Sentiment is the most powerful. It is incredible the number of evil practices he has put down: it is to be feared he will soon lack subjects, and that when he has made the working classes comfortable, and got bitter beer put into proper-sized pint bottles, there will be nothing further for him left to do. Mr Sentiment is certainly a very powerful man, and perhaps not the less so that his good poor people are so very good; his hard rich people so very hard; and the genuinely honest so very honest. Namby-pamby in these days is not thrown away if it be introduced in the proper quarters. Divine peeresses are no longer interesting, though possessed of every virtue; but a pattern peasant or an immaculate manufacturing hero may talk as much twaddle as one of Mrs Radcliffe's heroines,[16] and still be listened to. Perhaps, however, Mr Sentiment's great attraction is in his second-rate characters. If his heroes and heroines walk upon stilts, as heroes and heroines, I fear, ever must, their attendant satellites are as natural as though one met them in the street: they walk and talk like men and women, and live among our friends a rattling, lively life; yes, live, and will live till the names of their callings shall be forgotten in their own, and Bucket and Mrs Gamp will be the only words left to us to signify a detective police officer or a monthly nurse.[17]

The Almshouse opened with a scene in a clergyman's house. Every luxury to be purchased by wealth was described as being there: all the appearances of household indulgence generally found among the most self-indulgent of the rich were crowded into this abode. Here the reader was introduced to the demon of the book, the Mephistopheles[18] of the drama. What story was ever written without a demon? what novel, what history, what work of any sort, what world, would be perfect without existing principles both of good and evil? The demon of *The Almshouse* was the clerical owner of this comfortable abode. He was a man well stricken in years, but still strong to do evil: he was one who looked cruelly out of a hot, passionate, bloodshot eye; who had a huge red nose with a carbuncle, thick lips, and a great double, flabby chin, which swelled out into solid substance, like a turkey-cock's comb, when sudden anger inspired him: he had a hot, furrowed, low brow, from which a few grizzled hairs were not yet rubbed off by the friction of his handkerchief: he wore a loose unstarched white handkerchief, black loose ill-made clothes, and huge loose shoes, adapted to many corns and various bunions: his husky voice told tales of much daily port wine, and his language was not so decorous as became a clergyman. Such was the master of Mr Sentiment's *Almshouse*. He was a widower, but at present accompanied by two daughters, and a thin and somewhat insipid curate. One of the young ladies was devoted to her father and the fashionable world, and she of course was the favourite; the other was equally addicted to Puseyism and the curate.[19]

The second chapter of course introduced the reader to the more especial inmates of the hospital. Here were discovered eight old men; and it was given to be understood that four vacancies remained unfilled, through the perverse ill-nature of the clerical gentleman with the double chin. The state of these eight paupers was touchingly dreadful: sixpence-farthing a day had been sufficient for their diet when the almshouse was founded; and on sixpence-farthing a day were they still doomed to starve, though food was four times as dear, and money four times as plentiful. It was shocking to find how the conversation of these eight starved old men in their dormitory shamed that of the clergyman's family in his rich drawing-room. The absolute words they uttered were not perhaps spoken in the purest English, and it might be difficult to distinguish from their dialect to what part of the country they belonged; the beauty of the sentiment, however, amply atoned for the imperfection of the language; and it was really a pity that these eight old men could not be sent through the country as moral missionaries, instead of being immured and starved in that wretched almshouse.

Bold finished the number; and as he threw it aside, he thought that that at least had no direct appliance to Mr Harding, and that the absurdly strong colouring of the picture would disenable the work from doing either good or harm. He was wrong. The artist who paints for the million must use glaring colours, as no one knew better than Mr Sentiment when he described the inhabitants of his almshouse; and the radical reform which has now swept over such establishments has owed more to the twenty numbers of Mr Sentiment's novel, than to all the true complaints which have escaped from the public for the last half-century.

CHAPTER 16

A Long Day in London

THE warden had to make use of all his very moderate powers of intrigue to give his son-in-law the slip, and get out of Barchester without being stopped on his road. No schoolboy ever ran away from school with more precaution and more dread of detection; no convict, slipping down from a prison wall, ever feared to see the gaoler more entirely than Mr Harding did to see his son-in-law, as he drove up in the pony-carriage to the railway station on the morning of his escape to London.

The evening before he went, he wrote a note to the archdeacon, explaining that he should start on the morrow on his journey; that it was his intention to see the attorney-general if possible, and to decide on his future plans in accordance with what he heard from that gentleman; he excused himself for giving Dr Grantly no earlier notice by stating that his resolve was very sudden; and having entrusted this note to Eleanor, with the perfect, though not expressed, understanding that it was to be sent over to Plumstead Episcopi without haste, he took his departure.

He also prepared and carried with him a note for Sir Abraham Haphazard, in which he stated his name, explaining that he was the defendant in the case of 'The Queen on behalf of the Wool-carders of Barchester v. Trustees under the will of the late John Hiram', for so was the suit denominated, and begged the illustrious and learned gentleman to vouchsafe to him ten minutes' audience at any hour on the next day. Mr Harding calculated that for that one day he was safe; his son-in-law, he had no doubt, would arrive in town by an early train, but not early enough to reach the truant till he should have escaped from his hotel after breakfast; and could he thus manage to see the lawyer on that very day, the deed might be done before the archdeacon could interfere.

On his arrival in town the warden drove, as was his wont, to the Chapter Hotel and Coffee House, near St Paul's. His visits to London of late had not been frequent; but in those happy days

when *Harding's Church Music* was going through the press, he had
been often there; and as the publisher's house was in Paternoster
Row, and the printer's press in Fleet Street, the Chapter Hotel and
Coffee House had been convenient. It was a quiet, sombre, clerical
house, beseeming such a man as the warden, and thus he afterwards frequented it. Had he dared, he would on this occasion have
gone elsewhere to throw the archdeacon further off the scent; but
he did not know what violent steps his son-in-law might take for
his recovery if he were not found at his usual haunt, and he
deemed it not prudent to make himself the object of a hunt
through London.

Arrived at his inn, he ordered dinner, and went forth to the
attorney-general's chambers. There he learnt that Sir Abraham
was in Court, and would not probably return that day. He would
go direct from Court to the House; all appointments were, as a rule,
made at the chambers; the clerk could by no means promise an
interview for the next day; was able, on the other hand, to say that
such interview was, he thought, impossible; but that Sir Abraham
would certainly be at the House in the course of the night, when
an answer from himself might possibly be elicited.

To the House Mr Harding went, and left his note, not finding
Sir Abraham there. He added a most piteous entreaty that he
might be favoured with an answer that evening, for which he
would return. He then journeyed back sadly to the Chapter Coffee
House, digesting his great thoughts, as best he might, in a clattering omnibus, wedged in between a wet old lady and a journeyman
glazier, returning from his work with his tools in his lap. In
melancholy solitude he discussed his mutton chop and pint of port.
What is there in this world more melancholy than such a dinner?
A dinner, though alone, in a country hotel may be worthy of some
energy; the waiter, if you are known, will make much of you; the
landlord will make you a bow, and perhaps put the fish on the
table; if you ring you are attended to, and there is some life about
it. A dinner at a London eating-house is also lively enough, if it
have no other attraction. There is plenty of noise and stir about
it, and the rapid whirl of voices and rattle of dishes disperses
sadness. But a solitary dinner in an old, respectable, sombre, solid
London inn, where nothing makes any noise but the old waiter's

creaking shoes; where one plate slowly goes and another slowly comes without a sound; where the two or three guests would as soon think of knocking each other down as of speaking; where the servants whisper, and the whole household is disturbed if an order be given above the voice – what can be more melancholy than a mutton chop and a pint of port in such a place?

Having gone through this, Mr Harding got into another omnibus, and again returned to the House. Yes, Sir Abraham was there, and was that moment on his legs, fighting eagerly for the hundred and seventh clause of the Convent Custody Bill.[1] Mr Harding's note had been delivered to him; and if Mr Harding would wait some two or three hours, Sir Abraham could be asked whether there was any answer. The House was not full, and perhaps Mr Harding might get admittance into the Strangers' Gallery, which admission, with the help of five shillings, Mr Harding was able to effect.

This bill of Sir Abraham's had been read a second time and passed into committee. A hundred and six clauses had already been discussed, and had occupied only four mornings and five evening sittings: nine of the hundred and six clauses were passed, fifty-five were withdrawn by consent, fourteen had been altered so as to mean the reverse of the original proposition, eleven had been postponed for further consideration, and seventeen had been directly negatived. The hundred and seventh ordered the bodily searching of nuns for Jesuitical symbols by aged clergymen, and was considered to be the real mainstay of the whole bill. No intention had ever existed to pass such a law as that proposed, but the government did not intend to abandon it till their object was fully attained by the discussion of this clause. It was known that it would be insisted on with terrible vehemence by Protestant Irish members, and as vehemently denounced by the Roman Catholic; and it was justly considered that no further union between the parties would be possible after such a battle. The innocent Irish fell into the trap as they always do, and whiskey and poplins became a drug in the market.

A florid-faced gentleman with a nice head of hair, from the south of Ireland, had succeeded in catching the speaker's eye by the time that Mr Harding had got into the gallery, and was denouncing the proposed sacrilege, his whole face glowing with a fine theatrical frenzy.

'And is this a Christian country?' said he. (Loud cheers; counter cheers from the ministerial benches. 'Some doubt as to that,' from a voice below in the gangway.) 'No, it can be no Christian country, in which the head of the bar, the lagal adviser (loud laughter and cheers) – yes, I say the lagal adviser of the crown (great cheers and laughter) – can stand up in his seat in this House (prolonged cheers and laughter), and attempt to lagalize indacent assaults on the bodies of religious ladies.' (Deafening cheers and laughter, which were prolonged till the honourable member resumed his seat.)

When Mr Harding had listened to this and much more of the same kind for about three hours, he returned to the door of the House, and received back from the messenger his own note, with the following words scrawled in pencil on the back of it: 'Tomorrow, 10 p.m. – my chambers. A.H.'

He was so far successful – but 10 p.m.: what an hour Sir Abraham had named for a legal interview! Mr Harding felt perfectly sure that long before that Dr Grantly would be in London. Dr Grantly could not, however, know that this interview had been arranged, nor could he learn it unless he managed to get hold of Sir Abraham before that hour; and as this was very improbable, Mr Harding determined to start from his hotel early, merely leaving word that he should dine out, and unless luck were much against him, he might still escape the archdeacon till his return from the attorney-general's chambers.

He was at breakfast at nine, and for the twentieth time consulted his *Bradshaw*[2] to see at what earliest hour Dr Grantly could arrive from Barchester. As he examined the columns, he was nearly petrified by the reflection that perhaps the archdeacon might come up by the night mail-train! His heart sank within him at the horrid idea, and for a moment he felt himself dragged back to Barchester without accomplishing any portion of his object. Then he remembered that had Dr Grantly done so, he would have been in the hotel, looking for him long since.

'Waiter,' said he, timidly.

The waiter approached, creaking in his shoes, but voiceless.

'Did any gentleman – a clergyman, arrive here by the night mail-train?'

'No, sir, not one,' whispered the waiter, putting his mouth nearly close to the warden's ear.

Mr Harding was reassured.

'Waiter,' said he again, and the waiter again creaked up; 'if anyone calls for me, I am going to dine out, and shall return about eleven o'clock.'

The waiter nodded, but did not this time vouchsafe any reply; and Mr Harding, taking up his hat, proceeded out to pass a long day in the best way he could, somewhere out of sight of the archdeacon.

Bradshaw had told him twenty times that Dr Grantly could not be at Paddington station till 2 p.m., and our poor friend might therefore have trusted to the shelter of the hotel for some hours longer with perfect safety; but he was nervous. There was no knowing what steps the archdeacon might take for his apprehension: a message by electric telegraph might desire the landlord of the hotel to set a watch upon him; some letter might come which he might find himself unable to disobey; at any rate, he could not feel himself secure in any place at which the archdeacon could expect to find him; and at 10 a.m. he started forth to spend twelve hours in London.

Mr Harding had friends in town, had he chosen to seek them; but he felt that he was in no humour for ordinary calls, and he did not now wish to consult with anyone as to the great step which he had determined to take. As he had said to his daughter, no one knows where the shoe pinches but the wearer. There are some points on which no man can be contented to follow the advice of another – some subjects on which a man can consult his own conscience only. Our warden had made up his mind that it was good for him at any cost to get rid of this grievance; his daughter was the only person whose concurrence appeared necessary to him, and she did concur with him most heartily. Under such circumstances he would not, if he could help it, consult anyone further, till advice would be useless. Should the archdeacon catch him, indeed, there would be much advice, and much consultation of a kind not to be avoided; but he hoped better things; and as he felt that he could not now converse on indifferent subjects, he resolved to see no one till after his interview with the attorney-general.

He determined to take sanctuary in Westminster Abbey, so he again went thither in an omnibus, and finding that the doors were not open for morning service, he paid his twopence, and went in as a sightseer. It occurred to him that he had no definite place of rest for the day, and that he should be absolutely worn out before his interview if he attempted to walk about from 10 a.m. to 10 p.m., so he sat himself down on a stone step, and gazed up at the figure of William Pitt,[3] who looks as though he had just entered the church for the first time in his life, and was anything but pleased at finding himself there.

He had been sitting unmolested about twenty minutes, when the verger asked him whether he wouldn't like to walk round. Mr Harding didn't want to walk anywhere, and declined, merely observing that he was waiting for the morning service. The verger, seeing that he was a clergyman, told him that the doors of the choir were now open, and showed him into a seat. This was a great point gained; the archdeacon would certainly not come to morning service at Westminster Abbey, even though he were in London; and here the warden could rest quietly, and, when the time came, duly say his prayers.

He longed to get up from his seat, and examine the music-books of the choristers, and the copy of the litany from which the service was chanted, to see how far the little details at Westminster corresponded with those at Barchester, and whether he thought his own voice would fill the church well from the Westminster precentor's seat. There would, however, be impropriety in such meddling, and he sat perfectly still, looking up at the noble roof, and guarding against the coming fatigues of the day.

By degrees two or three people entered: the very same damp old woman who had nearly obliterated him in the omnibus, or some other just like her; a couple of young ladies, with their veils down, and gilt crosses conspicuous on their prayer-books; an old man on crutches; a party who were seeing the abbey, and thought they might as well hear the service for their twopence, as opportunity served; and a young woman with her prayer-book done up in her handkerchief, who rushed in late, and, in her hurried entry, tumbled over one of the forms, and made such a noise that everyone, even the officiating minor canon, was startled, and she herself was so frightened by the echo of her own catastrophe, that she was nearly thrown into fits by the panic.

Mr Harding was not much edified by the manner of the service. The minor canon in question hurried in, somewhat late, in a surplice not in the neatest order, and was followed by a dozen choristers, who were also not as trim as they might have been: they all jostled into their places with a quick hurried step, and the service was soon commenced. Soon commenced, and soon over, for there was no music, and time was not unnecessarily lost in the chanting. On the whole, Mr Harding was of opinion that things were managed better at Barchester, though even there he knew that there was room for improvement.

It appears to us a question whether any clergyman can go through our church service with decorum, morning after morning, in an immense building, surrounded by not more than a dozen listeners. The best actors cannot act well before empty benches, and though there is, of course, a higher motive in one case than the other, still even the best of clergymen cannot but be influenced by their audience; and to expect that a duty should be well done under such circumstances, would be to require from human nature more than human power.

When the two ladies with the gilt crosses, the old man with his crutch, and the still palpitating housemaid were going, Mr Harding found himself obliged to go too. The verger stood in his way, and looked at him and looked at the door, and so he went. But he returned again in a few minutes, and re-entered with another twopence. There was no other sanctuary so good for him.

As he walked slowly down the nave, and then up one aisle, and then again down the nave and up the other aisle, he tried to think gravely of the step he was about to take. He was going to give up eight hundred a year voluntarily; and doom himself to live for the rest of his life on about a hundred and fifty. He knew that he had hitherto failed to realize this fact as he ought to do. Could he maintain his own independence and support his daughter on a hundred and fifty pounds a year without being a burden on anyone? His son-in-law was rich, but nothing could induce him to lean on his son-in-law after acting, as he intended to do, in most direct opposition to his counsel. The bishop was rich, but he was about to throw away the bishop's best gift, and that in a manner to injure materially the patronage of the giver: he could neither expect nor accept anything further from the bishop. There would be not only no merit, but positive disgrace, in giving up his wardenship, if he were not prepared to meet the world without it. Yes, he must from this time forward bound all his human wishes for himself and his daughter to the poor extent of so limited an income. He knew he had not thought sufficiently of this, that he had been carried away by enthusiasm, and had hitherto not brought home to himself the full reality of his position.

He thought most about his daughter, naturally. It was true that she was engaged, and he knew enough of his proposed son-in-law to be sure that his own altered circumstances would make no obstacle to such a marriage; nay, he was sure that the very fact of his poverty would induce Bold more anxiously to press the matter; but he disliked counting on Bold in this emergency, brought on, as it had been, by his doing. He did not like saying to himself, Bold has turned me out of my house and income, and, therefore, he must relieve me of my daughter; he preferred reckoning on Eleanor as the companion of his poverty and exile – as the sharer of his small income.

Some modest provision for his daughter had been long since made. His life was insured for three thousand pounds, and this sum was to go to Eleanor. The archdeacon, for some years past, had paid the premium, and had secured himself by the immediate possession of a small property which was to have gone to Mrs Grantly after her father's death. This matter, therefore, had been out of the warden's hands long since, as, indeed, had all the business transactions of his family, and his anxiety was, therefore, confined to his own life income.

Yes. A hundred and fifty per annum was very small, but still it might suffice; but how was he to chant the litany at the cathedral on Sunday mornings, and get the service done at Crabtree Parva? True, Crabtree Church was not quite a mile and a half from the cathedral; but he could not be in two places at once! Crabtree was a small village, and afternoon service might suffice, but still this went against his conscience; it was not right that his parishioners should be robbed of any of their privileges on account of his poverty. He might, to be sure, make some arrangement for doing weekday service at the cathedral, but he had chanted the litany at Barchester so long, and had a conscious feeling that he did it so well, that he was unwilling to give up the duty.

Thinking of such things, turning over in his own mind together small desires and grave duties, but never hesitating for a moment as to the necessity of leaving the hospital, Mr Harding walked up and down the abbey, or sat still meditating on the same stone step, hour after hour. One verger went and another came, but they did not disturb him; every now and then they crept up and looked at him, but they did so with a reverential stare, and, on the whole, Mr Harding found his retreat well chosen. About four o'clock his comfort was disturbed by an enemy in the shape of hunger; it was necessary that he should dine, and it was clear that he could not dine in the abbey; so he left his sanctuary not willingly, and betook himself to the neighbourhood of the Strand to look for food.

His eyes had become so accustomed to the gloom of the church, that they were dazed when he got out into the full light of day, and he felt confused and ashamed of himself, as though people were staring at him. He hurried along, still in dread of the arch-deacon, till he came to Charing Cross, and then remembered that in one of his passages through the Strand he had seen the words CHOPS AND STEAKS on a placard in a shop window. He remembered the shop distinctly; it was next door to a trunk-seller's, and there was a cigar shop on the other side. He couldn't go to his hotel for dinner, which to him hitherto was the only known mode of dining in London at his own expense; and, therefore, he would get a steak at the shop in the Strand. Archdeacon Grantly would certainly not come to such a place for his dinner.

He found the house easily – just as he had observed it, between the trunks and the cigars. He was rather daunted by the huge quantity of fish which he saw in the window. There were barrels of oysters, hecatombs of lobsters, a few tremendous-looking crabs, and a tub full of pickled salmon; not, however, being aware of any connection between shellfish and iniquity, he entered, and modestly asked a slatternly woman, who was picking oysters out of a great watery reservoir, whether he could have a mutton chop and a potato.

The woman looked somewhat surprised, but answered in the affirmative, and a slipshod girl ushered him into a long back room, filled with boxes for the accommodation of parties, in one of which he took his seat. In a more miserably forlorn place he could not have found himself: the room smelt of fish, and sawdust, and stale tobacco smoke, with a slight taint of escaped gas; everything was rough, and dirty, and disreputable; the cloth which they put before him was abominable; the knives and forks were bruised, and hacked, and filthy; and everything was impregnated with fish. He had one comfort, however: he was quite alone; there was no one there to look on his dismay; nor was it probable that anyone would come to do so. It was a London supper-house.* About one o'clock at night the place would be lively enough, but at the present time his seclusion was as deep as it had been in the abbey.

In about half an hour the untidy girl, not yet dressed for her evening labours, brought him his chop and potatoes, and Mr Harding begged for a pint of sherry. He was impressed with an idea, which was generally prevalent a few years since, and is not yet wholly removed from the minds of men, that to order a dinner at any kind of inn, without also ordering a pint of wine for the benefit of the landlord, was a kind of fraud; not punishable, indeed, by law, but not the less abominable on that account. Mr Harding remembered his coming poverty, and would willingly have saved his half-crown, but he thought he had no alternative; and he was soon put in possession of some horrid mixture procured from the neighbouring public house.

His chop and potatoes, however, were eatable, and having got over as best he might the disgust created by the knives and forks, he contrived to swallow his dinner. He was not much disturbed: one young man, with pale face and watery fish-like eyes, wearing his hat ominously on one side, did come in and stare at him, and ask the girl, audibly enough, 'Who that old cock was'; but the annoyance went no further, and the warden was left seated on his wooden bench in peace, endeavouring to distinguish the different scents arising from lobsters, oysters, and salmon.

Unknowing as Mr Harding was in the ways of London, he felt that he had somehow selected an ineligible dining-house, and that he had better leave it. It was hardly five o'clock – how was he to pass the time till ten? Five miserable hours! He was already tired, and it was impossible that he should continue walking so long. He thought of getting into an omnibus, and going out to Fulham for the sake of coming back in another: this, however, would be weary work, and as he paid his bill to the woman in the shop, he asked her if there were any place near where he could get a cup of coffee. Though she did keep a shellfish supper-house, she was very civil, and directed him to the cigar divan⁵ on the other side of the street.

Mr Harding had not a much correcter notion of a cigar divan than he had of a London dinner-house, but he was desperately in want of rest, and went as he was directed. He thought he must have made some mistake when he found himself in a cigar shop, but the man behind the counter saw immediately that he was a stranger, and understood what he wanted. 'One shilling, sir – thank ye, sir – cigar, sir? – ticket for coffee, sir – you'll only have to call the waiter. Up those stairs, if you please, sir. Better take the cigar, sir – you can always give it to a friend you know. Well, sir, thank ye, sir – as you are so good, I'll smoke it myself.' And so Mr Harding ascended to the divan, with his ticket for coffee, but minus the cigar.

The place seemed much more suitable to his requirements than the room in which he had dined: there was, to be sure, a strong smell of tobacco, to which he was not accustomed; but after the shellfish, the tobacco did not seem disagreeable. There were quantities of books, and long rows of sofas. What on earth could be more luxurious than a sofa, a book, and a cup of coffee? An old waiter came up to him, with a couple of magazines and an evening paper. Was ever anything so civil? Would he have a cup of coffee, or would he prefer sherbet? Sherbet!⁶ Was he absolutely in an Eastern divan, with the slight addition of all the London periodicals? He had, however, an idea that sherbet should be drunk sitting cross-legged, and as he was not quite up to this, he ordered the coffee.

The coffee came, and was unexceptionable. Why, this divan was a paradise! The civil old waiter suggested to him a game of chess: though a chess-player he was not equal to this, so he declined, and, putting up his weary legs on the sofa, leisurely sipped his coffee, and turned over the pages of his *Blackwood.*' He might have been so engaged for about an hour, for the old waiter enticed him to a second cup of coffee, when a musical clock began to play. Mr Harding then closed his magazine, keeping his place with his finger, and lay, listening with closed eyes to the clock. Soon the clock seemed to turn into a violoncello, with piano accompaniments, and Mr Harding began to fancy the old waiter was the Bishop of Barchester; he was inexpressibly shocked that the bishop should have brought him his coffee with his own hands; then Dr Grantly came in, with a basket full of lobsters, which he would not be induced to leave downstairs in the kitchen; and then the warden couldn't quite understand why so many people would smoke in the bishop's drawing-room; and so he fell fast asleep, and his dreams wandered away to his accustomed stall in Barchester Cathedral, and the twelve old men he was so soon about to leave for ever.

He was fatigued, and slept soundly for some time. Some sudden stop in the musical clock woke him at length, and he jumped up with a start, surprised to find the room quite full; it had been nearly empty when his nap began. With nervous anxiety he pulled out his watch, and found that it was half-past nine. He seized his hat, and, hurrying downstairs, started at a rapid pace for Lincoln's Inn.

It still wanted twenty minutes to ten when the warden found himself at the bottom of Sir Abraham's stairs, so he walked leisurely up and down the quiet inn to cool himself. It was a beautiful evening at the end of August. He had recovered from his fatigue; his sleep and the coffee had refreshed him, and he was surprised to find that he was absolutely enjoying himself, when the inn clock struck ten. The sound was hardly over before he knocked at Sir Abraham's door, and was informed by the clerk who received him that the great man would be with him immediately.

CHAPTER 17

Sir Abraham Haphazard

MR HARDING was shown into a comfortable inner sitting-room, looking more like a gentleman's bookroom than a lawyer's chambers, and there waited for Sir Abraham. Nor was he kept waiting long: in ten or fifteen minutes he heard a clatter of voices speaking quickly in the passage, and then the attorney-general entered.

'Very sorry to keep you waiting, Mr Warden,' said Sir Abraham, shaking hands with him; 'and sorry, too, to name so disagreeable an hour; but your notice was short, and as you said today, I named the very earliest hour that was not disposed of.'

Mr Harding assured him that he was aware that it was he that should apologize.

Sir Abraham was a tall thin man, with hair prematurely grey, but bearing no other sign of age; he had a slight stoop, in his neck rather than his back, acquired by his constant habit of leaning forward as he addressed his various audiences. He might be fifty years old, and would have looked young for his age, had not constant work hardened his features, and given him the appearance of a machine with a mind. His face was full of intellect, but devoid of natural expression. You would say he was a man to use, and then have done with; a man to be sought for on great emergencies, but ill adapted for ordinary services; a man whom you would ask to defend your property, but to whom you would be sorry to confide your love. He was bright as a diamond, and as cutting, and also as unimpressionable. He knew everyone whom to know was an honour, but he was without a friend; he wanted none, however, and knew not the meaning of the word in other than its parliamentary sense. A friend! Had he not always been sufficient to himself, and now, at fifty, was it likely that he should trust another? He was married, indeed, and had children, but what time had he for the soft idleness of conjugal felicity? His working days or term-times were occupied from his time of rising to the late hour at which he went to rest, and even his vacations were more full of labour than the busiest days of other men. He never quarrelled with his wife, but he never talked to her – he never had time to talk, he was so taken up with speaking. She, poor lady, was not unhappy; she had all that money could give her, she would probably live to be a peeress, and she really thought Sir Abraham the best of husbands.

Sir Abraham was a man of wit, and sparkled among the brightest at the dinner-tables of political grandees; indeed, he always sparkled; whether in society, in the House of Commons, or the courts of law, coruscations flew from him; glittering sparkles, as from hot steel, but no heat; no cold heart was ever cheered by warmth from him, no unhappy soul ever dropped a portion of its burden at his door.

With him success alone was praiseworthy, and he knew none so successful as himself. No one had thrust him forward; no powerful friends had pushed him along on his road to power. No, he was attorney-general, and would, in all human probability, be Lord Chancellor[1] by sheer dint of his own industry and his own talent. Who else in all the world rose so high with so little help? A premier, indeed! Who had ever been premier without mighty friends? An archbishop! Yes, the son or grandson of a great noble, or else, probably, his tutor. But he, Sir Abraham, had had no mighty lord at his back; his father had been a country apothecary, his mother a farmer's daughter. Why should he respect any but himself? And so he glitters along through the world, the brightest among the bright; and when his glitter is gone, and he is gathered to his fathers, no eye will be dim with a tear, no heart will mourn for its lost friend.

'And so, Mr Warden,' said Sir Abraham, 'all our trouble about this lawsuit is at an end.'

Mr Harding said he hoped so, but he didn't at all understand what Sir Abraham meant. Sir Abraham, with all his sharpness, could not have looked into his heart and read his intentions.

'All over. You need trouble yourself no further about it; of course they must pay the costs, and the absolute expense to you and Dr Grantly will be trifling – that is, compared with what it might have been if it had been continued.'

'I fear I don't quite understand you, Sir Abraham.'

'Don't you know that their attorneys have noticed us that they have withdrawn the suit?'

Mr Harding explained to the lawyer that he knew nothing of this, although he had heard in a roundabout way that such an intention had been talked of; and he also at length succeeded in making Sir Abraham understand that even this did not satisfy him. The attorney-general stood up, put his hands into his breeches' pockets, and raised his eyebrows, as Mr Harding proceeded to detail the grievance from which he now wished to rid himself.

'I know I have no right to trouble you personally with this matter, but as it is of most vital importance to me, as all my happiness is concerned in it, I thought I might venture to seek your own advice.'

Sir Abraham bowed, and declared his clients were entitled to the best advice he could give them; particularly a client so respectable in every way as the Warden of Barchester Hospital.

'A spoken word, Sir Abraham, is often of more value than volumes of written advice. The truth is, I am ill satisfied with this matter as it stands at present. I do see – I cannot help seeing, that the affairs of the hospital are not arranged according to the will of the founder.'

'None of such institutions are, Mr Harding, nor can they be; the altered circumstances in which we live do not admit of it.'

'Quite true – that is quite true; but I can't see that those altered circumstances give me a right to eight hundred a year. I don't know whether I ever read John Hiram's will, but were I to read it now I could not understand it. What I want you, Sir Abraham, to tell me, is this – am I, as warden, legally and distinctly entitled to the proceeds of the property, after the due maintenance of the twelve bedesmen?'

Sir Abraham declared that he couldn't exactly say in so many words that Mr Harding was legally entitled to, etc., etc., etc., and ended in expressing a strong opinion that it would be madness to raise any further question on the matter, as the suit was to be – nay, was, abandoned.

Mr Harding, seated in his chair, began to play a slow tune on an imaginary violoncello.

'Nay, my dear sir,' continued the attorney-general, 'there is no further ground for any question; I don't see that you have the power of raising it.'

'I can resign,' said Mr Harding, slowly playing away with his right hand, as though the bow were beneath the chair in which he was sitting.

'What! throw it up altogether?' said the attorney-general, gazing with utter astonishment at his client.

'Did you see those articles in the *Jupiter?*' said Mr Harding, piteously, appealing to the sympathy of the lawyer.

Sir Abraham said he had seen them. This poor little clergyman, cowed into such an act of extreme weakness by a newspaper article, was to Sir Abraham so contemptible an object, that he hardly knew how to talk to him as to a rational being.

'Hadn't you better wait,' said he, 'till Dr Grantly is in town with you? Wouldn't it be better to postpone any serious step till you can consult with him?'

Mr Harding declared vehemently that he could not wait, and Sir Abraham began seriously to doubt his sanity.

'Of course,' said the latter, 'if you have private means sufficient for your wants, and if this –'

'I haven't a sixpence, Sir Abraham,' said the warden.

'God bless me! Why, Mr Harding, how do you mean to live?'

Mr Harding proceeded to explain to the man of law that he meant to keep his precentorship – that was eighty pounds a year; and, also, that he meant to fall back upon his own little living of Crabtree, which was another eighty pounds. That, to be sure, the duties of the two were hardly compatible; but perhaps he might effect an exchange. And then, recollecting that the attorney-general would hardly care to hear how the service of a cathedral church is divided among the minor canons, stopped short in his explanations.

Sir Abraham listened in pitying wonder. 'I really think, Mr Harding, you had better wait for the archdeacon. This is a most serious step: one for which, in my opinion, there is not the slightest necessity; and, as you have done me the honour of asking my advice, I must implore you to do nothing without the approval of your friends. A man is never the best judge of his own position.'

'A man is the best judge of what he feels himself. I'd sooner beg my bread till my death than read such another article as those two that have appeared, and feel, as I do, that the writer has truth on his side.'

'Have you not a daughter, Mr Harding – an unmarried daughter?'

'I have,' said he, now standing also, but still playing away on his fiddle with his hand behind his back. 'I have, Sir Abraham; and she and I are completely agreed on this subject.'

'Pray excuse me, Mr Harding, if what I say seems impertinent: but surely it is you that should be prudent on her behalf. She is young, and does not know the meaning of living on an income of a hundred and fifty pounds a year. On her account give up this idea. Believe me, it is sheer Quixotism.'[2]

The warden walked away to the window, and then back to his chair; and then, irresolute what to say, took another turn to the window. The attorney-general was really extremely patient, but he was beginning to think that the interview had been long enough.

'But if this income be not justly mine, what if she and I have both to beg?' said the warden at last, sharply, and in a voice so different from that he had hitherto used, that Sir Abraham was startled. 'If so, it would be better to beg.'

'My dear sir, nobody now questions its justness.'

'Yes, Sir Abraham, one does question it – the most important of all witnesses against me – I question it myself. My God knows whether or no I love my daughter; but I would sooner that she and I should both beg, than that she should live in comfort on money which is truly the property of the poor. It may seem strange to you, Sir Abraham, it is strange to myself, that I should have been ten years in that happy home, and not have thought of these things, till they were so roughly dinned into my ears. I cannot boast of my conscience, when it required the violence of a public newspaper to awaken it; but, now that it is awake, I must obey it. When I came here I did not know that the suit was withdrawn by Mr Bold, and my object was to beg you to abandon my defence. As there is no action, there can be no defence; but it is, at any rate, as well that you should know that, from tomorrow, I shall cease to be the warden of the hospital. My friends and I differ on this subject, Sir Abraham, and that adds much to my sorrow: but it cannot be helped.' And, as he finished what he had to say, he played up such a tune as never before had graced the chambers of any attorney-general. He was standing up, gallantly fronting Sir Abraham, and his right arm passed with bold and rapid sweeps before him, as though he were embracing some huge instrument, which allowed him to stand thus erect; and with the fingers of his left hand he stopped, with preternatural velocity, a multitude of strings, which ranged from the top of his collar to the bottom of the lappet of his coat. Sir Abraham listened and looked in wonder. As he had never before seen Mr Harding, the meaning of these wild gesticulations was lost upon him; but he perceived that the gentleman who had a few minutes since been so subdued as to be unable to speak without hesitation, was now impassioned – nay, almost violent.

'You'll sleep on this, Mr Harding, and tomorrow –'

'I have done more than sleep on it,' said the warden; 'I have laid awake upon it, and that night after night. I found I could not sleep upon it; now I hope to do so.'

The attorney-general had no answer to make to this; so he expressed a quiet hope that whatever settlement was finally made would be satisfactory; and Mr Harding withdrew, thanking the great man for his kind attention.

Mr Harding was sufficiently satisfied with the interview to feel a glow of comfort as he descended into the small old square of Lincoln's Inn. It was a calm, bright, beautiful night, and by the light of the moon, even the chapel of Lincoln's Inn, and the sombre row of chambers, which surround the quadrangle, looked well. He stood still a moment to collect his thoughts; and reflect on what he had done, and was about to do. He knew that the attorney-general regarded him as little better than a fool, but that he did not mind; he and the attorney-general had not much in common between them; he knew also that others, whom he did care about, would think so too; but Eleanor, he was sure, would exult in what he had done, and the bishop, he trusted, would sympathize with him.

In the meantime he had to meet the archdeacon, and so he

walked slowly down Chancery Lane and along Fleet Street, feeling
sure that his work for the night was not yet over. When he reached
the hotel he rang the bell quietly, and with a palpitating heart; he
almost longed to escape round the corner, and delay the coming
storm by a further walk round St Paul's Churchyard, but he heard
the slow creaking shoes of the old waiter approaching, and he
stood his ground manfully.

CHAPTER 18

The Warden is Very Obstinate

'DR GRANTLY is here, sir,' greeted his ears before the door was well open, 'and Mrs Grantly; they have a sitting-room above, and are waiting up for you.'

There was something in the tone of the man's voice which seemed to indicate that even he looked upon the warden as a runaway schoolboy, just recaptured by his guardian, and that he pitied the culprit, though he could not but be horrified at the crime.

The warden endeavoured to appear unconcerned, as he said, 'Oh, indeed! I'll go upstairs at once'; but he failed signally: there was, perhaps, a ray of comfort in the presence of his married daughter; that is to say, of comparative comfort, seeing that his son-in-law was there: but how much would he have preferred that they should both have been safe at Plumstead Episcopi! However, upstairs he went, the waiter slowly preceding him; and on the door being opened the archdeacon was discovered standing in the middle of the room, erect, indeed, as usual, but oh! how sorrowful! and on a dingy sofa behind him reclined his patient wife.

'Papa, I thought you were never coming back,' said the lady; 'it's twelve o'clock.'

'Yes, my dear,' said the warden. 'The attorney-general named ten for my meeting; to be sure ten is late, but what could I do, you know? Great men will have their own way.'

And he gave his daughter a kiss, and shook hands with the doctor, and again tried to look unconcerned.

'And you have absolutely been with the attorney-general?' asked the archdeacon.

Mr Harding signified that he had.

'Good heavens, how unfortunate!' And the archdeacon raised his huge hands in the manner in which his friends are so accustomed to see him express disapprobation and astonishment. 'What will Sir Abraham think of it? Did you not know that it is not customary for clients to go direct to their counsel?'

'Isn't it!' asked the warden, innocently. 'Well, at any rate, I've done it now. Sir Abraham didn't seem to think it so very strange.'

The archdeacon gave a sigh that would have moved a man-of-war.

'But, papa, what did you say to Sir Abraham?' asked the lady.

'I asked him, my dear, to explain John Hiram's will to me. He couldn't explain it in the only way which would have satisfied me, and so I resigned the wardenship.'

'Resigned it!' said the archdeacon, in a solemn voice, sad and low, but yet sufficiently audible; a sort of whisper that Macready[1] would have envied, and the galleries have applauded with a couple of rounds. 'Resigned it! Good heavens!' and the dignitary of the Church sank back horrified into a horse-hair armchair.

'At least I told Sir Abraham that I would resign; and of course I must now do so.'

'Not at all,' said the archdeacon, catching a ray of hope. 'Nothing that you say in such a way to your own counsel can be in any way binding on you; of course you were there to ask his advice. I'm sure, Sir Abraham did not advise any such step.'

Mr Harding could not say that he had.

'I am sure he disadvised you from it,' continued the reverend cross-examiner.

Mr Harding could not deny this.

'I'm sure Sir Abraham must have advised you to consult your friends.'

To this proposition also Mr Harding was obliged to assent.

'Then your threat of resignation amounts to nothing, and we are just where we were before.'

Mr Harding was now standing on the rug, moving uneasily from one foot to the other. He made no distinct answer to the archdeacon's last proposition, for his mind was chiefly engaged on thinking how he could escape to bed. That his resignation was a thing finally fixed on, a fact all but completed, was not in his mind a matter of any doubt; he knew his own weakness; he knew how prone he was to be led; but he was not weak enough to give way now, to go back from the position to which his conscience had driven him, after having purposely come to London to declare his determination: he did not in the least doubt his resolution, but he greatly doubted his power of defending it against his son-in-law.

'You must be very tired, Susan,' said he: 'wouldn't you like to go to bed?'

But Susan didn't want to go till her husband went – she had an idea that her papa might be bullied if she were away: she wasn't tired at all, or at least she said so.

The archdeacon was pacing the room, expressing, by certain noddles of his head, his opinion of the utter fatuity of his father-in-law.

'Why,' at last he said – and angels might have blushed at the rebuke expressed in his tone and emphasis – 'why did you go off from Barchester so suddenly? Why did you take such a step without giving us notice, after what had passed at the palace?'

The warden hung his head, and made no reply: he could not condescend to say that he had not intended to give his son-in-law the slip; and as he had not the courage to avow it, he said nothing.

'Papa has been too much for you,' said the lady.

The archdeacon took another turn, and again ejaculated, 'Good heavens!' this time in a very low whisper, but still audible.

'I think I'll go to bed,' said the warden, taking up a side candle.

'At any rate you'll promise me to take no further step without consultation,' said the archdeacon. Mr Harding made no answer, but slowly proceeded to light his candle. 'Of course,' continued the other, 'such a declaration as that you made to Sir Abraham means nothing. Come, warden, promise me this. The whole affair, you see, is already settled, and that with very little trouble or expense. Bold has been compelled to abandon his action, and all you have to do is to remain quiet at the hospital.' Mr Harding still made no reply, but looked meekly into his son-in-law's face. The archdeacon thought he knew his father-in-law, but he was mistaken; he thought that he had already talked over a vacillating man to resign his promise. 'Come,' said he, 'promise Susan to give up this idea of resigning the wardenship.'

The warden looked at his daughter, thinking probably at the moment that if Eleanor were contented with him, he need not so much regard his other child, and said, 'I am sure Susan will not ask me to break my word, or to do what I know to be wrong.'

'Papa,' said she, 'it would be madness in you to throw up your preferment. What are you to live on?'

'God, that feeds the young ravens,[2] will take care of me also,' said Mr Harding, with a smile, as though afraid of giving offence by making his reference to scripture too solemn.

'Pish!' said the archdeacon, turning away rapidly; 'if the ravens persisted in refusing the food prepared for them, they wouldn't be fed.' A clergyman generally dislikes to be met in argument by any scriptural quotation; he feels as affronted as a doctor does, when recommended by an old woman to take some favourite dose, or as a lawyer when an unprofessional man attempts to put him down by a quibble.

'I shall have the living of Crabtree,' modestly suggested the warden.

'Eighty pounds a year!' sneered the archdeacon.

'And the precentorship,' said the father-in-law.

'It goes with the wardenship,' said the son-in-law. Mr Harding was prepared to argue this point, and began to do so, but Dr Grantly stopped him. 'My dear warden,' said he, 'this is all nonsense. Eighty pounds or a hundred and sixty makes very little difference. You can't live on it – you can't ruin Eleanor's prospects for ever. In point of fact, you can't resign; the bishop wouldn't accept it; the whole thing is settled. What I now want to do is to prevent any inconvenient tittle-tattle – any more newspaper articles.'

'That's what I want, too,' said the warden.

'And to prevent that,' continued the other, 'we mustn't let any talk of resignation get abroad.'

'But I shall resign,' said the warden, very, very meekly.

'Good heavens! Susan, my dear, what can I say to him?'

'But, papa,' said Mrs Grantly, getting up, and putting her arm through that of her father, 'what is Eleanor to do if you throw away your income?'

A hot tear stood in each of the warden's eyes as he looked round upon his married daughter. Why should one sister who was so rich predict poverty for another? some such idea as this was on his mind, but he gave no utterance to it. Then he thought of the pelican feeding its young with blood from its own breast, but he gave no utterance to that either; and then of Eleanor waiting for him at home, waiting to congratulate him on the end of all his trouble.

'Think of Eleanor, papa,' said Mrs Grantly.

'I do think of her,' said her father.

'And you will not do this rash thing!' The lady was really moved beyond her usual calm composure.

'It can never be rash to do right,' said he. 'I shall certainly resign this wardenship.'

'Then, Mr Harding, there is nothing before you but ruin,' said the archdeacon, now moved beyond all endurance. 'Ruin both for you and Eleanor. How do you mean to pay the monstrous expenses of this action?'

Mrs Grantly suggested that, as the action was abandoned, the costs would not be heavy.

'Indeed they will, my dear,' continued he. 'One cannot have the attorney-general up at twelve o'clock at night for nothing – but of course your father has not thought of this.'

'I will sell my furniture,' said the warden.

'Furniture!' ejaculated the other, with a most powerful sneer.

'Come, archdeacon,' said the lady, 'we needn't mind that at present. You know you never expected papa to pay the costs.'

'Such absurdity is enough to provoke Job,'³ said the archdeacon, marching quickly up and down the room. 'Your father is like a child. Eight hundred pounds a year! – eight hundred and eighty with the house – with nothing to do. The very place for him. And to throw that up because some scoundrel writes an article in a newspaper! Well – I have done my duty. If he chooses to ruin his child I cannot help it'; and he stood still at the fireplace, and looked at himself in a dingy mirror which stood on the chimneypiece.

There was a pause for about a minute, and then the warden, finding that nothing else was coming, lighted his candle, and quietly said, 'Good night.'

'Good night, papa,' said the lady.

And so the warden retired; but, as he closed the door behind him, he heard the well-known ejaculation – slower, lower, more solemn, more ponderous than ever – 'Good heavens!'

CHAPTER 19

The Warden Resigns

THE party met the next morning at breakfast; and a very sombre affair it was – very unlike the breakfasts at Plumstead Episcopi.

There were three thin, small, dry bits of bacon, each an inch long, served up under a huge old plated cover; there were four three-cornered bits of dry toast, and four square bits of buttered toast; there was a loaf of bread, and some oily-looking butter; and on the sideboard there were the remains of a cold shoulder of mutton. The archdeacon, however, had not come up from his rectory to St Paul's Churchyard to enjoy himself, and therefore nothing was said of the scanty fare.

The guests were as sorry as the viands – hardly anything was said over the breakfast-table. The archdeacon munched his toast in ominous silence, turning over bitter thoughts in his deep mind. The warden tried to talk to his daughter, and she tried to answer him; but they both failed. There were no feelings at present in common between them. The warden was thinking only of getting back to Barchester, and calculating whether the archdeacon would expect him to wait for him; and Mrs Grantly was preparing herself for a grand attack which she was to make on her father, as agreed upon between herself and her husband during their curtain confabulation of that morning.

When the waiter had creaked out of the room with the last of the teacups, the archdeacon got up and went to the window, as though to admire the view. The room looked out on a narrow passage which runs from St Paul's Churchyard to Paternoster Row; and Dr Grantly patiently perused the names of the three shopkeepers whose doors were in view. The warden still kept his seat at the table, and examined the pattern of the tablecloth; and Mrs Grantly, seating herself on the sofa, began to knit.

After a while the warden pulled his *Bradshaw* out of his pocket, and began laboriously to consult it. There was a train for Barchester at 10 a.m. That was out of the question, for it was nearly

ten already. Another at 3 p.m.; another, the night mail-train, at
9 p.m. The three o'clock train would take him home to tea, and
would suit very well.

'My dear,' said he, 'I think I shall go back home at three o'clock
today. I shall get home at half-past eight. I don't think there's
anything to keep me in London.'

'The archdeacon and I return by the early train tomorrow,
papa; won't you wait and go back with us?'

'Why, Eleanor will expect me tonight; and I've so much to do;
and —'

'Much to do!' said the archdeacon *sotto voce*;[1] but the warden
heard him.

'You'd better wait for us, papa.'

'Thank ye, my dear! I think I'll go this afternoon.' The tamest
animal will turn when driven too hard, and even Mr Harding was
beginning to fight for his own way.

'I suppose you won't be back before three?' said the lady,
addressing her husband.

'I must leave this at two,' said the warden.

'Quite out of the question,' said the archdeacon, answering his
wife, and still reading the shopkeepers' names; 'I don't suppose I
shall be back till five.'

There was another long pause, during which Mr Harding continued to study his *Bradshaw*.

'I must go to Cox and Cummins,' said the archdeacon at last.

'Oh, to Cox and Cummins,' said the warden. It was quite a
matter of indifference to him where his son-in-law went. The
names of Cox and Cummins had now no interest in his ears. What
had he to do with Cox and Cummins further, having already had
his suit finally adjudicated upon in a court of conscience, a judgement without power of appeal fully registered, and the matter
settled so that all the lawyers in London could not disturb it. The
archdeacon could go to Cox and Cummins, could remain there all
day in anxious discussion; but what might be said there was no
longer matter of interest to him, who was so soon to lay aside the
name of Warden of Barchester Hospital.

The archdeacon took up his shining new clerical hat, and put
on his black new clerical gloves, and looked heavy, respectable,

decorous, and opulent, a decided clergyman of the Church of England, every inch of him. 'I suppose I shall see you at Barchester the day after tomorrow,' said he.

The warden supposed he would.

'I must once more beseech you to take no further steps till you see my father; if you owe me nothing,' and the archdeacon looked as though he thought a great deal were due to him, 'at least you owe so much to my father'; and, without waiting for a reply, Dr Grantly wended his way to Cox and Cummins.

Mrs Grantly waited till the last fall of her husband's foot was heard, as he turned out of the court into St Paul's Churchyard, and then commenced her task of talking her father over.

'Papa,' she began, 'this is a most serious business.'

'Indeed it is,' said the warden, ringing the bell.

'I greatly feel the distress of mind you must have endured.'

'I am sure you do, my dear'; and he ordered the waiter to bring him pen, ink, and paper.

'Are you going to write, papa?'

'Yes, my dear – I am going to write my resignation to the bishop.'

'Pray, pray, papa, put it off till our return – pray put it off till you have seen the bishop – dear papa! for my sake, for Eleanor's! –'

'It is for your sake and Eleanor's that I do this. I hope, at least, that my children may never have to be ashamed of their father.'

'How can you talk about shame, papa?' and she stopped while the waiter creaked in with the paper, and then slowly creaked out again; 'how can you talk about shame? you know what all your friends think about this question.'

The warden spread his paper on the table, placing it on the meagre blotting-book which the hotel afforded, and sat himself down to write.

'You won't refuse me one request, papa?' continued his daughter; 'you won't refuse to delay your letter for two short days? – two days can make no possible difference.'

'My dear,' said he naïvely, 'if I waited till I got to Barchester, I might, perhaps, be prevented.'

'But surely you would not wish to offend the bishop?' said she.

'God forbid! The bishop is not apt to take offence, and knows me

too well to take in bad part anything that I may be called on to
do.'

'But, papa –'

'Susan,' said he, 'my mind on this subject is made up; it is not
without much repugnance that I act in opposition to the advice
of such men as Sir Abraham Haphazard and the archdeacon; but
in this matter I can take no advice, I cannot alter the resolution
to which I have come.'

'But two days, papa –'

'No – nor can I delay it. You may add to my present unhappiness
by pressing me, but you cannot change my purpose; it will be a
comfort to me if you will let the matter rest'; and, dipping his pen
into the inkstand, he fixed his eyes intently on the paper.

There was something in his manner which taught his daughter
to perceive that he was in earnest; she had at one time ruled
supreme in her father's house, but she knew that there were
moments when, mild and meek as he was, he would have his way,
and the present was an occasion of the sort. She returned, therefore, to her knitting, and very shortly after left the room.

The warden was now at liberty to compose his letter, and, as
it was characteristic of the man, it shall be given at full length. The
official letter, which, when written, seemed to him to be too
formally cold to be sent alone to so dear a friend, was accompanied
by a private note: and both are here inserted.

The letter of resignation ran as follows:

> Chapter Hotel, St Paul's
> London, August, 18—

MY LORD BISHOP,

It is with the greatest pain that I feel myself constrained to resign into
your Lordship's hands the wardenship of the hospital at Barchester which
you so kindly conferred upon me, now nearly twelve years since.

I need not explain the circumstances which have made this step appear
necessary to me. You are aware that a question has arisen as to the right
of the warden to the income which has been allotted to the wardenship;
it has seemed to me that this right is not well made out, and I hesitate to
incur the risk of taking an income to which my legal claim appears
doubtful.

The office of precentor of the cathedral is, as your Lordship is aware,
joined to that of the warden; that is to say, the precentor has for many
years been the warden of the hospital; there is, however, nothing to make

the junction of the two offices necessary, and, unless you or the dean and chapter object to such an arrangement, I would wish to keep the precentorship. The income of this office will now be necessary to me; indeed, I do not know why I should be ashamed to say that I should have difficulty in supporting myself without it.

Your Lordship, and such others as you may please to consult on the matter, will at once see that my resignation of the wardenship need offer not the slightest bar to its occupation by another person. I am thought in the wrong by all those whom I have consulted in the matter; I have very little but an inward and an unguided conviction of my own to bring me to this step, and I shall, indeed, be hurt to find that any slur is thrown on the preferment which your kindness bestowed on me, by my resignation of it. I, at any rate for one, shall look on any successor whom you may appoint as enjoying a clerical situation of the highest respectability, and one to which your Lordship's nomination gives an indefeasible right.

I cannot finish this official letter without again thanking your Lordship for all your great kindness, and I beg to subscribe myself

Your Lordship's most obedient servant,

SEPTIMUS HARDING,

Warden of Barchester Hospital,

and Precentor of the cathedral.

He then wrote the following private note:

MY DEAR BISHOP,

I cannot send you the accompanying official letter without a warmer expression of thanks for all your kindness than would befit a document which may to a certain degree be made public. You, I know, will understand the feeling, and, perhaps, pity the weakness which makes me resign the hospital. I am not made of calibre strong enough to withstand public attack. Were I convinced that I stood on ground perfectly firm, that I was certainly justified in taking eight hundred a year under Hiram's will, I should feel bound by duty to retain the position, however unendurable might be the nature of the assault; but, as I do not feel this conviction, I cannot believe that you will think me wrong in what I am doing.

I had at one time an idea of keeping only some moderate portion of the income; perhaps three hundred a year, and of remitting the remainder to the trustees; but it occurred to me, and I think with reason, that by so doing I should place my successors in an invidious position, and greatly damage your patronage.

My dear friend, let me have a line from you to say that you do not blame me for what I am doing, and that the officiating vicar of Crabtree Parva will be the same to you as the warden of the hospital.

I am very anxious about the precentorship; the archdeacon thinks it must go with the wardenship; I think not, and that, having it, I cannot be ousted. I will, however, be guided by you and the dean. No other duty will suit me so well, or come so much within my power of adequate performance.

I thank you from my heart for the preferment which I am now giving up, and for all your kindness, and am, dear bishop, now as always,

Yours most sincerely,
SEPTIMUS HARDING

London, August, 18—

Having written these letters and made a copy of the former one for the benefit of the archdeacon, Mr Harding, whom we must now cease to call the warden, he having designated himself so for the last time, found that it was nearly two o'clock, and that he must prepare for his journey. Yes, from this time he never again admitted the name by which he had been so familiarly known, and in which, to tell the truth, he had rejoiced. The love of titles is common to all men, and a vicar or fellow is as pleased at becoming Mr Archdeacon or Mr Provost, as a lieutenant at getting his captaincy, or a city tallow-chandler in becoming Sir John on the occasion of a Queen's visit to a new bridge. But warden he was no longer, and the name of precentor, though the office was to him so dear, confers in itself no sufficient distinction; our friend, therefore, again became Mr Harding.

Mrs Grantly had gone out; he had, therefore, no one to delay him by further entreaties to postpone his journey; he had soon arranged his bag, and paid his bill, and, leaving a note for his daughter, in which he put the copy of his official letter, he got into a cab and drove away to the station with something of triumph in his heart.

Had he not cause for triumph? Had he not been supremely successful? Had he not for the first time in his life held his own purpose against that of his son-in-law, and manfully combated against great odds – against the archdeacon's wife as well as the archdeacon? Had he not gained a great victory, and was it not fit that he should step into his cab with triumph?

He had not told Eleanor when he would return, but she was on the look out for him by every train by which he could arrive, and the pony-carriage was at the Barchester station when the train drew up at the platform.

'My dear,' said he, sitting beside her, as she steered her little vessel to one side of the road to make room for the clattering omnibus as they passed from the station into the town; 'I hope you'll be able to feel a proper degree of respect for the vicar of Crabtree.'

'Dear papa,' said she, 'I am so glad.'

There was great comfort in returning home to that pleasant house, though he was to leave it so soon, and in discussing with his daughter all that he had done, and all that he had to do. It must take some time to get out of one house into another; the curate at Crabtree could not be abolished under six months, that is, unless other provision could be made for him; and then the furniture – the most of that must be sold to pay Sir Abraham Haphazard for sitting up till twelve at night. Mr Harding was strangely ignorant as to lawyers' bills; he had no idea, from twenty pounds to two thousand, as to the sum in which he was indebted for legal assistance. True, he had called in no lawyer himself; true, he had been no consenting party to the employment of either Cox and Cummins, or Sir Abraham; he had never been consulted on such matters – the archdeacon had managed all this himself, never for a moment suspecting that Mr Harding would take upon him to end the matter in a way of his own. Had the lawyers' bills been ten thousand pounds, Mr Harding could not have helped it; but he was not on that account disposed to dispute his own liability. The question never occurred to him; but it did occur to him that he had very little money at his banker's, that he could receive nothing further from the hospital, and that the sale of the furniture was his only resource.

'Not all, papa,' said Eleanor, pleadingly.

'Not quite all, my dear,' said he; 'that is, if we can help it. We must have a little at Crabtree – but it can only be a little; we must put a bold front on it, Nelly; it isn't easy to come down from affluence to poverty.'

And so they planned their future mode of life; the father taking comfort from the reflection that his daughter would soon be freed from it, and she resolving that her father would soon have in her own house a ready means of escape from the solitude of the Crabtree vicarage.

When the archdeacon left his wife and father-in-law at the Chapter Coffee House to go to Messrs Cox and Cummins, he had no very defined idea of what he had to do when he got there. Gentlemen when at law, or in any way engaged in matters requiring legal assistance, are very apt to go to their lawyers without much absolute necessity – gentlemen when doing so, are apt to describe such attendance as quite compulsory, and very disagreeable. The lawyers, on the other hand, do not at all see the necessity, though they quite agree as to the disagreeable nature of the visit – gentlemen when so engaged are usually somewhat gravelled[2] at finding nothing to say to their learned friends; they generally talk a little politics, a little weather, ask some few foolish questions about their suit, and then withdraw, having passed half an hour in a small, dingy waiting-room, in company with some junior assistant-clerk, and ten minutes with the members of the firm; the business is then over for which the gentleman has come up to London, probably a distance of a hundred and fifty miles. To be sure he goes to the play, and dines at his friend's club, and has a bachelor's liberty and bachelor's recreation for three or four days; and he could not probably plead the desire of such gratifications as a reason to his wife for a trip to London.

Married ladies, when your husbands find they are positively obliged to attend their legal advisers, the nature of the duty to be performed is generally of this description.

The archdeacon would not have dreamt of leaving London without going to Cox and Cummins; and yet he had nothing to say to them. The game was up; he plainly saw that Mr Harding in this matter was not to be moved; his only remaining business on this head was to pay the bill and have done with it: and I think it may be taken for granted, that whatever the cause may be that takes a gentleman to a lawyer's chambers, he never goes there to pay his bill.

Dr Grantly, however, in the eyes of Messrs Cox and Cummins represented the spiritualities of the diocese of Barchester, as Mr Chadwick did the temporalities, and was, therefore, too great a man to undergo the half-hour in the clerk's room. It will not be necessary that we should listen to the notes of sorrow in which the archdeacon bewailed to Mr Cox the weakness of his father-in-law, and the end of all their hopes of triumph; nor need we repeat the various exclamations of surprise with which the mournful intelligence was received. No tragedy occurred, though Mr Cox, a short and somewhat bull-necked man, was very near a fit of apoplexy when he first attempted to ejaculate that fatal word – resign!

Over and over again did Mr Cox attempt to enforce on the archdeacon the propriety of urging on Mr Warden the madness of the deed he was about to do.

'Eight hundred a year!' said Mr Cox.

'And nothing whatever to do!' said Mr Cummins, who had joined the conference.

'No private fortune, I believe,' said Mr Cox.

'Not a shilling,' said Mr Cummins, in a very low voice, shaking his head.

'I never heard of such a case in all my experience,' said Mr Cox.

'Eight hundred a year, and as nice a house as any gentleman could wish to hang up his hat in,' said Mr Cummins.

'And an unmarried daughter, I believe,' said Mr Cox, with much moral seriousness in his tone. The archdeacon only sighed as each separate wail was uttered, and shook his head, signifying that the fatuity of some people was past belief.

'I'll tell you what he might do,' said Mr Cummins, brightening up. 'I'll tell you how you might save it – let him exchange.'

'Exchange where?' said the archdeacon.

'Exchange for a living. There's Quiverful,[3] of Puddingdale; he has twelve children, and would be delighted to get the hospital. To be sure Puddingdale is only four hundred, but that would be saving something out of the fire: Mr Harding would have a curate, and still keep three hundred or three hundred and fifty.'

The archdeacon opened his ears and listened; he really thought the scheme might do.

'The newspapers,' continued Mr Cummins, 'might hammer away at Quiverful every day for the next six months without his minding them.'

The archdeacon took up his hat, and returned to his hotel, thinking the matter over deeply: at any rate he would sound Quiverful; a man with twelve children would do much to double his income.

CHAPTER 20

Farewell

ON the morning after Mr Harding's return home, he received a note from the bishop full of affection, condolence, and praise. 'Pray come to me at once,' wrote the bishop, 'that we may see what had better be done; as to the hospital, I will not say a word to dissuade you; but I don't like your going to Crabtree: at any rate, come to me at once.'

Mr Harding did go to him at once; and long and confidential was the consultation between the two old friends. There they sat together the whole long day plotting to get the better of the archdeacon, and to carry out little schemes of their own, which they knew would be opposed by the whole weight of his authority.

The bishop's first idea was that Mr Harding, if left to himself, would certainly starve – not in the figurative sense in which so many of our ladies and gentlemen do starve on incomes from one to five hundred a year; not that he would be starved as regarded dress-coats, port wine, and pocket-money; but that he would positively perish of inanition for want of bread.

'How is a man to live, when he gives up all his income?' said the bishop to himself. And then the good-natured little man began to consider how his friend might be best rescued from a death so horrid and painful.

His first proposition to Mr Harding was that they should live together at the palace. He, the bishop, positively assured Mr Harding that he wanted another resident chaplain: not a young, working chaplain, but a steady, middle-aged chaplain; one who would dine and drink a glass of wine with him, talk about the archdeacon, and poke the fire. The bishop did not positively name all these duties, but he gave Mr Harding to understand that such would be the nature of the service required.

It was not without much difficulty that Mr Harding made his friend see that this would not suit him; that he could not throw up the bishop's preferment, and then come and hang on at the bishop's table; that he could not allow people to say of him that it was an easy matter to abandon his own income, as he was able to sponge on that of another person. He succeeded, however, in explaining that the plan would not do, and then the bishop brought forward another which he had in his sleeve. He, the bishop, had in his will left certain moneys to Mr Harding's two daughters, imagining that Mr Harding would himself want no such assistance during his own lifetime. This legacy amounted to three thousand pounds each, duty free; and he now pressed it as a gift on his friend.

'The girls, you know,' said he, 'will have it just the same when you're gone – and they won't want it sooner – and as for the interest during my lifetime, it isn't worth talking about. I have more than enough.'

With much difficulty and heartfelt sorrow, Mr Harding refused also this offer. No; his wish was to support himself, however poorly – not to be supported on the charity of anyone. It was hard to make the bishop understand this; it was hard to make him comprehend that the only real favour he could confer was the continuation of his independent friendship; but at last even this was done. At any rate, thought the bishop, he will come and dine with me from time to time, and if he be absolutely starving I shall see it.

Touching the precentorship, the bishop was clearly of opinion that it could be held without the other situation – an opinion from which no one differed; and it was therefore soon settled among all the parties concerned, that Mr Harding should still be the precentor of the cathedral.

On the day following Mr Harding's return, the archdeacon reached Plumstead full of Mr Cummins's scheme regarding Puddingdale and Mr Quiverful. On the very next morning he drove over to Puddingdale, and obtained the full consent of the wretched clerical Priam who was endeavouring to feed his poor Hecuba and a dozen of Hectors[1] on the small proceeds of his ecclesiastical kingdom. Mr Quiverful had no doubts as to the legal rights of the warden; his conscience would be quite clear as to accepting the income; and as to the *Jupiter*, he begged to assure the archdeacon that he was quite indifferent to any emanations from the profane portion of the periodical press.

Having so far succeeded, he next sounded the bishop; but here he was astonished by most unexpected resistance. The bishop did not think it would do. 'Not do, why not?' and seeing that his father was not shaken, he repeated the question in a severer form: 'Why not do, my lord?'

His lordship looked very unhappy, and shuffled about in his chair, but still didn't give way; he thought Puddingdale wouldn't do for Mr Harding; it was too far from Barchester.

'Oh! of course he'll have a curate.'

The bishop also thought that Mr Quiverful wouldn't do for the hospital; such an exchange wouldn't look well at such a time; and, when pressed harder, he declared he didn't think Mr Harding would accept of Puddingdale under any circumstances.

'How is he to live?' demanded the archdeacon.

The bishop, with tears in his eyes, declared that he had not the slightest conception how life was to be sustained within him at all.

The archdeacon then left his father, and went down to the hospital; but Mr Harding wouldn't listen at all to the Puddingdale scheme. To his eyes it had no attraction; it savoured of simony,² and was likely to bring down upon him harder and more deserved strictures than any he had yet received: he positively declined to become vicar of Puddingdale under any circumstances.

The archdeacon waxed wroth, talked big, and looked bigger; he said something about dependence and beggary, spoke of the duty every man was under to earn his bread, made passing allusions to the follies of youth and waywardness of age, as though Mr Harding were afflicted by both, and ended by declaring that he had done. He felt that he had left no stone unturned to arrange matters on the best and easiest footing; that he had, in fact, so arranged them, that he had so managed that there was no further need of any anxiety in the matter. And how had he been paid? His advice had been systematically rejected; he had been not only slighted, but distrusted and avoided; he and his measures had been utterly thrown over, as had been Sir Abraham, who, he had reason to know, was much pained at what had occurred. He now found it was useless to interfere any further, and he should retire. If any further assistance were required from him, he would probably be called on, and should be again happy to come forward. And so he left the hospital, and has not since entered it from that day to this.

And here we must take leave of Archdeacon Grantly. We fear that he is represented in these pages as being worse than he is; but we have had to do with his foibles, and not with his virtues. We have seen only the weak side of the man, and have lacked the opportunity of bringing him forward on his strong ground. That he is a man somewhat too fond of his own way, and not sufficiently scrupulous in his manner of achieving it, his best friends cannot deny. That he is bigoted in favour, not so much of his doctrines as of his cloth, is also true: and it is true that the possession of a large income is a desire that sits near his heart. Nevertheless, the archdeacon is a gentleman and a man of conscience; he spends his money liberally, and does the work he has to do with the best of his ability; he improves the tone of society of those among whom he lives. His aspirations are of a healthy, if not of the highest, kind. Though never an austere man, he upholds propriety of conduct both by example and precept. He is generous to the poor, and hospitable to the rich; in matters of religion he is sincere, and yet no Pharisee;[3] he is in earnest, and yet no fanatic. On the whole, the Archdeacon of Barchester is a man doing more good than harm – a man to be furthered and supported, though perhaps also to be controlled; and it is matter of regret to us that the course of our narrative has required that we should see more of his weakness than his strength.

Mr Harding allowed himself no rest till everything was prepared for his departure from the hospital. It may be as well to mention that he was not driven to the stern necessity of selling all his furniture: he had been quite in earnest in his intention to do so, but it was soon made known to him that the claims of Messrs Cox and Cummins made no such step obligatory. The archdeacon had thought it wise to make use of the threat of the lawyer's bill, to frighten his father-in-law into compliance; but he had no intention to saddle Mr Harding with costs, which had been incurred by no means exclusively for his benefit. The amount of the bill was added to the diocesan account, and was, in fact, paid out of the bishop's pocket, without any consciousness on the part of his lordship. A great part of his furniture he did resolve to sell, having no other

means to dispose of it; and the ponies and carriage were transferred, by private contract, to the use of an old maiden lady in the
city.

For his present use Mr Harding took a lodging in Barchester,
and thither were conveyed such articles as he wanted for daily use
– his music, books, and instruments, his own armchair, and
Eleanor's pet sofa; her teapoy and his cellaret,⁴ and also the slender
but still sufficient contents of his wine-cellar. Mrs Grantly had
much wished that her sister would reside at Plumstead, till her
father's house at Crabtree should be ready for her; but Eleanor
herself strongly resisted this proposal. It was in vain urged upon
her that a lady in lodgings costs more than a gentleman; and that,
under her father's present circumstances, such an expense should
be avoided. Eleanor had not pressed her father to give up the
hospital, in order that she might live at Plumstead Rectory, and
he alone in his Barchester lodgings; nor did Eleanor think that she
would be treating a certain gentleman very fairly, if she betook
herself to the house which he would be the least desirous of
entering of any in the county. So she got a little bedroom for
herself behind the sitting-room, and just over the little back
parlour of the chemist, with whom they were to lodge. There was
somewhat of a savour of senna softened by peppermint about the
place; but, on the whole, the lodgings were clean and comfortable.

The day had been fixed for the migration of the ex-warden, and
all Barchester were in a state of excitement on the subject. Opinion
was much divided as to the propriety of Mr Harding's conduct. The
mercantile part of the community, the mayor and corporation,
and council, also most of the ladies, were loud in his praise.
Nothing could be more noble, nothing more generous, nothing
more upright. But the gentry were of a different way of thinking
– especially the lawyers and the clergymen. They said such
conduct was very weak and undignified; that Mr Harding evinced
a lamentable want of *esprit de corps*,⁵ as well as courage; and that
such an abdication must do much harm, and could do but little
good.

On the evening before he left, he summoned all the bedesmen
into his parlour to wish them good-bye. With Bunce he had been
in frequent communication since his return from London, and had

been at much pains to explain to the old man the cause of his resignation, without in any way prejudicing the position of his successor. The others, also, he had seen more or less frequently; and had heard from most of them separately some expression of regret at his departure; but he had postponed his farewell till the last evening.

He now bade the maid put wine and glasses on the table; and had the chairs arranged around the room; and sent Bunce to each of the men to request they would come and say farewell to their late warden. Soon the noise of aged scuffling feet was heard upon the gravel and in the little hall, and the eleven men who were enabled to leave their rooms were assembled.

'Come in, my friends, come in,' said the warden – he was still warden then. 'Come in, and sit down'; and he took the hand of Abel Handy, who was the nearest to him, and led the limping grumbler to a chair. The others followed slowly and bashfully: the infirm, the lame, and the blind; poor wretches! who had been so happy, had they but known it! Now their aged faces were covered with shame, and every kind word from their master was a coal of fire burning on their heads.

When first the news had reached them that Mr Harding was going to leave the hospital, it had been received with a kind of triumph – his departure was, as it were, a prelude to success. He had admitted his want of right to the money about which they were disputing; and as it did not belong to him, of course it did to them. The one hundred a year to each of them was actually becoming a reality; and Abel Handy was a hero, and Bunce a faint-hearted sycophant, worthy neither honour nor fellowship. But other tidings soon made their way into the old men's rooms. It was first notified to them that the income abandoned by Mr Harding would not come to them; and these accounts were confirmed by attorney Finney. They were then informed that Mr Harding's place would be at once filled by another. That the new warden could not be a kinder man they all knew; that he would be a less friendly one most suspected; and then came the bitter information that, from the moment of Mr Harding's departure, the twopence a day, his own peculiar gift, must of necessity be withdrawn.

And this was to be the end of all their mighty struggle – of their fight for their rights – of their petition, and their debates, and their hopes! They were to change the best of masters for a possible bad one, and to lose twopence a day each man! No; unfortunate as this was, it was not the worst, or nearly the worst, as will just now be seen.

'Sit down, sit down, my friends,' said the warden. 'I want to say a word to you, and to drink your healths, before I leave you. Come up here, Moody, here is a chair for you; come, Jonathan Crumple –' and by degrees he got the men to be seated. It was not surprising that they should hang back with faint hearts, having returned so much kindness with such deep ingratitude. Last of all of them came Bunce, and with sorrowful mien and slow step got into his accustomed seat near the fireplace.

When they were all in their places, Mr Harding rose to address them; and then finding himself not quite at home on his legs, he sat down again. 'My dear old friends,' said he, 'you all know that I am going to leave you.'

There was a sort of murmur ran round the room, intended, perhaps, to express regret at his departure; but it was but a murmur, and might have meant that or anything else.

'There has been lately some misunderstanding between us. You have thought, I believe, that you did not get all that you were entitled to, and that the funds of the hospital have not been properly disposed of. As for me, I cannot say what should be the disposition of these moneys, or how they should be managed, and I have therefore thought it best to go.'

'We never wanted to drive your reverence out of it,' said Handy.

'No, indeed, your reverence,' said Skulpit. 'We never thought it would come to this. When I signed the petition – that is, I didn't sign it, because –'

'Let his reverence speak, can't you?' said Moody.

'No,' continued Mr Harding; 'I am sure you did not wish to turn me out; but I thought it best to leave you. I am not a very good hand at a lawsuit, as you may all guess; and when it seemed necessary that our ordinary quiet mode of living should be disturbed, I thought it better to go. I am neither angry nor offended with any man in the hospital.'

Here Bunce uttered a kind of groan, very clearly expressive of disagreement.

'I am neither angry nor displeased with any man in the hospital,' repeated Mr Harding emphatically. 'If any man has been wrong – and I don't say any man has – he has erred through wrong advice. In this country all are entitled to look for their own rights, and you have done no more. As long as your interests and my interests were at variance, I could give you no counsel on this subject; but the connection between us has ceased; my income can no longer depend on your doings, and therefore, as I leave you, I venture to offer to you my advice.'

The men all declared that they would from henceforth be entirely guided by Mr Harding's opinion in their affairs.

'Some gentleman will probably take my place here very soon, and I strongly advise you to be prepared to receive him in a kindly spirit, and to raise no further question among yourselves as to the amount of his income. Were you to succeed in lessening what he has to receive, you would not increase your own allowance. The surplus would not go to you; your wants are adequately provided for, and your position could hardly be improved.'

'God bless your reverence, we knows it,' said Spriggs.

'It's all true, your reverence,' said Skulpit; 'we sees it all now.'

'Yes, Mr Harding,' said Bunce, opening his mouth for the first time; 'I believe they do understand it now, now that they've driven from under the same roof with them such a master as not one of them will ever know again – now that they're like to be in sore want of a friend.'

'Come, come, Bunce,' said Mr Harding, blowing his nose, and manoeuvring to wipe his eyes at the same time.

'Oh, as to that,' said Handy, 'we none of us never wanted to do Mr Harding no harm; if he's going now, it's not along of us; and I don't see for what Mr Bunce speaks up agen us that way.'

'You've ruined yourselves, and you've ruined me too, and that's why,' said Bunce.

'Nonsense, Bunce,' said Mr Harding; 'there's nobody ruined at all. I hope you'll let me leave you all friends, I hope you'll all drink a glass of wine in friendly feeling with me and with one another. You'll have a good friend, I don't doubt, in your new warden; and if ever you want any other, why after all I'm not going so far off but that I shall sometimes see you'; and then, having finished his speech, Mr Harding filled all the glasses, and himself handed each a glass to the men round him, and raising his own, said –

'God bless you all! you have my heartfelt wishes for your welfare. I hope you may live contented, and die trusting in the Lord Jesus Christ, and thankful to Almighty God for the good things he has given you. God bless you, my friends!' and Mr Harding drank his wine.

Another murmur, somewhat more articulate than the first, passed round the circle, and this time it was intended to imply a blessing on Mr Harding. It had, however, but little cordiality in it. Poor old men! how could they be cordial with their sore consciences and shamed faces? how could they bid God bless him with hearty voices and a true benison, knowing, as they did, that their vile cabal had driven him from his happy home, and sent him in his old age to seek shelter under a strange roof-tree? They did their best, however; they drank their wine, and withdrew.

As they left the hall door, Mr Harding shook hands with each of the men, and spoke a kind word to them about their individual cases and ailments; and so they departed, answering his questions in the fewest words, and retreated to their dens, a sorrowful repentant crew.

All but Bunce, who still remained to make his own farewell. 'There's poor old Bell,' said Mr Harding, 'I mustn't go without saying a word to him; come through with me, Bunce, and bring the wine with you'; and so they went through to the men's cottages, and found the old man propped up as usual in his bed.

'I've come to say good-bye to you, Bell,' said Mr Harding, speaking loud, for the old man was deaf.

'And are you going away, then, really?' asked Bell.

'Indeed I am, and I've brought you a glass of wine; so that we may part friends, as we lived, you know.'

The old man took the proffered glass in his shaking hands, and drank it eagerly. 'God bless you, Bell!' said Mr Harding; 'good-bye, my old friend.'

'And so you're really going?' the man again asked.

'Indeed I am, Bell.'

The poor old bedridden creature still kept Mr Harding's hand in his own, and the warden thought that he had met with something like warmth of feeling in the one of all his subjects from whom it was the least likely to be expected, for poor old Bell had nearly outlived all human feelings. 'And your reverence,' said he, and then he paused, while his old palsied head shook horribly, and his shrivelled cheeks sank lower within his jaws, and his glazy eye gleamed with a momentary light; 'and, your reverence, shall we get the hundred a year then?'

How gently did Mr Harding try to extinguish the false hope of money which had been so wretchedly raised to disturb the quiet of the dying man! One other week and his mortal coil would be shuffled off;[6] in one short week would God resume his soul, and set it apart for its irrevocable doom; seven more tedious days and nights of senseless inactivity, and all would be over for poor Bell in this world; and yet, with his last audible words, he was demanding his moneyed rights, and asserting himself to be the proper heir of John Hiram's bounty! Not on him, poor sinner as he was, be the load of such sin!

Mr Harding returned to his parlour, meditating with a sick heart on what he had seen, and Bunce with him. We will not describe the parting of these two good men, for good men they were. It was in vain that the late warden endeavoured to comfort the heart of the old bedesman; poor old Bunce felt that his days of comfort were gone. The hospital had to him been a happy home, but it could be so no longer. He had had honour there, and friendship; he had recognized his master, and been recognized; all his wants, both of soul and body, had been supplied, and he had been a happy man. He wept grievously as he parted from his friend, and the tears of an old man are bitter. 'It is all over for me in this world,' said he, as he gave the last squeeze to Mr Harding's hand; 'I have now to forgive those who have injured me – and to die.'

And so the old man went out, and then Mr Harding gave way to his grief, and he too wept aloud.

CHAPTER 21

Conclusion

OUR tale is now done, and it only remains to us to collect the scattered threads of our little story, and to tie them into a seemly knot. This will not be a work of labour, either to the author or to his readers; we have not to deal with many personages, or with stirring events, and were it not for the custom of the thing, we might leave it to the imagination of all concerned to conceive how affairs at Barchester arranged themselves.

On the morning after the day last alluded to, Mr Harding, at an early hour, walked out of the hospital, with his daughter under his arm, and sat down quietly to breakfast at his lodgings over the chemist's shop. There was no parade about his departure; no one, not even Bunce, was there to witness it: had he walked to the apothecary's thus early to get a piece of court plaster,[1] or a box of lozenges, he could not have done it with less appearance of an important movement. There was a tear in Eleanor's eye as she passed through the big gateway and over the bridge; but Mr Harding walked with an elastic step, and entered his new abode with a pleasant face.

'Now, my dear,' said he, 'you have everything ready, and you can make tea here just as nicely as in the parlour at the hospital.' So Eleanor took off her bonnet and made the tea. After this manner did the late Warden of Barchester Hospital accomplish his flitting, and change his residence.

It was not long before the archdeacon brought his father to discuss the subject of a new warden. Of course he looked upon the nomination as his own, and he had in his eye three or four fitting candidates, seeing that Mr Cummins's plan as to the living of Puddingdale could not be brought to bear. How can I describe the astonishment which confounded him, when his father declared that he would appoint no successor to Mr Harding? 'If we can get the matter set to rights, Mr Harding will return.' said the bishop;

'and if we cannot, it will be wrong to put any other gentleman into so cruel a position.'

It was in vain that the archdeacon argued and lectured, and even threatened; in vain he my-lorded his poor father in his sternest manner; in vain his 'good heavens!' were ejaculated in a tone that might have moved a whole synod, let alone one weak and aged bishop. Nothing would induce his father to fill up the vacancy caused by Mr Harding's retirement.

Even John Bold would have pitied the feelings with which the archdeacon returned to Plumstead: the Church was falling, nay, already in ruins; its dignitaries were yielding without a struggle before the blows of its antagonists; and one of its most respected bishops, his own father – the man considered by all the world as being in such matters under his, Dr Grantly's control – had positively resolved to capitulate, and own himself vanquished!

And how fared the hospital under this resolve of its visitor? Badly indeed. It is now some years since Mr Harding left it, and the warden's house is still tenantless. Old Bell has died, and Billy Gazy; the one-eyed Spriggs has drunk himself to death, and three others of the twelve have been gathered into the churchyard mould. Six have gone, and the six vacancies remain unfilled! Yes, six have died, with no kind friend to solace their last moments, with no wealthy neighbour to administer comforts and ease the stings of death. Mr Harding, indeed, did not desert them; from him they had such consolation as a dying man may receive from his Christian pastor; but it was the occasional kindness of a stranger which ministered to them, and not the constant presence of a master, a neighbour, and a friend.

Nor were those who remained better off than those who died. Dissensions rose among them, and contests for pre-eminence; and then they began to understand that soon one among them would be the last – some one wretched being would be alone there in that now comfortless hospital – the miserable relic of what had once been so good and comfortable.

The building of the hospital itself has not been allowed to go to ruins. Mr Chadwick, who still holds his stewardship, and pays the accruing rents into an account opened at a bank for the purpose, sees to that; but the whole place has become disordered and ugly.

The warden's garden is a wretched wilderness, the drive and paths are covered with weeds, the flowerbeds are bare, and the unshorn lawn is now a mass of long damp grass and unwholesome moss. The beauty of the place is gone; its attractions have withered. Alas! a very few years since it was the prettiest spot in Barchester, and now it is a disgrace to the city.

Mr Harding did not go out to Crabtree Parva. An arrangement was made which respected the homestead of Mr Smith and his happy family, and put Mr Harding into possession of a small living within the walls of the city. It is the smallest possible parish, containing a part of the Cathedral Close and a few old houses adjoining. The church is a singular little Gothic building, perched over a gateway, through which the Close is entered, and is approached by a flight of stone steps which leads down under the archway of the gate. It is no bigger than an ordinary room – perhaps twenty-seven feet long by eighteen wide – but still it is a perfect church.[2] It contains an old carved pulpit and reading-desk, a tiny altar under a window filled with dark old-coloured glass, a font, some half-dozen pews, and perhaps a dozen seats for the poor, and also a vestry. The roof is high-pitched, and of black old oak, and the three large beams which support it run down to the side walls, and terminate in grotesquely carved faces – two devils and an angel on one side, two angels and a devil on the other. Such is the church of St Cuthbert at Barchester, of which Mr Harding became rector, with a clear income of seventy-five pounds a year.

Here he performs afternoon service every Sunday, and administers the Sacrament once in every three months. His audience is not large; and, had they been so, he could not have accommodated them: but enough come to fill his six pews, and on the front seat of those devoted to the poor is always to be seen our old friend Mr Bunce, decently arrayed in his bedesman's gown.

Mr Harding is still precentor of Barchester; and it is very rarely the case that those who attend the Sunday morning service miss the gratification of hearing him chant the litany, as no other man in England can do it. He is neither a discontented nor an unhappy man; he still inhabits the lodgings to which he went on leaving the hospital, but he now has them to himself. Three months after that time Eleanor became Mrs Bold, and of course removed to her husband's house.

There were some difficulties to be got over on the occasion of her marriage. The archdeacon, who could not so soon overcome his grief, would not be persuaded to grace the ceremony with his presence, but he allowed his wife and children to be there. The marriage took place at the palace, and the bishop himself officiated. It was the last occasion on which he ever did so; and, though he still lives, it is not probable that he will ever do so again.

Not long after the marriage, perhaps six months, when Eleanor's bridal-honours were fading, and persons were beginning to call her Mrs Bold without twittering, the archdeacon consented to meet John Bold at a dinner-party, and since that time they have become almost friends. The archdeacon firmly believes that his brother-in-law was, as a bachelor, an infidel, an unbeliever in the great truths of our religion; but that matrimony has opened his eyes, as it has those of others. And Bold is equally inclined to think that time has softened the asperities of the archdeacon's character. Friends though they are, they do not often revert to the feud of the hospital.

Mr Harding, we say, is not an unhappy man; he keeps his lodgings, but they are of little use to him, except as being the one spot on earth which he calls his own. His time is spent chiefly at his daughter's or at the palace; he is never left alone, even should he wish to be so; and within a twelvemonth of Eleanor's marriage his determination to live at his own lodging had been so far broken through and abandoned, that he consented to have his violoncello permanently removed to his daughter's house.

Every other day a message is brought to him from the bishop. 'The bishop's compliments, and his lordship is not very well today, and he hopes Mr Harding will dine with him.' This bulletin as to the old man's health is a myth; for though he is over eighty he is never ill, and will probably die some day, as a spark goes out, gradually and without a struggle. Mr Harding does dine with him very often, which means going to the palace at three and remaining till ten; and whenever he does not the bishop whines, and says that the port wine is corked, and complains that nobody attends to him, and frets himself off to bed an hour before his time.

It was long before the people of Barchester forgot to call Mr Harding by his long well-known name of Warden. It had become so customary to say Mr Warden, that it was not easily dropped. 'No, no,' he always says when so addressed, 'not warden now, only precentor.'

THE END

BOOK 2

Barchester Towers

BARCHESTER TOWERS

CHAPTER I

WHO WILL BE THE NEW BISHOP ?

IN the latter days of July in the year 185—, a most important question was for ten days hourly asked in the cathedral city of Barchester, and answered every hour in various ways—Who was to be the new Bishop ?

The death of old Dr. Grantly, who had for many years filled that chair with meek authority, took place exactly as the ministry of Lord —— was going to give place to that of Lord ——. The illness of the good old man was long and lingering, and it became at last a matter of intense interest to those concerned whether the new appointment should be made by a conservative or liberal government.

It was pretty well understood that the out-going premier had made his selection, and that if the question rested with him, the mitre would descend on the head of Archdeacon Grantly, the old bishop's son. The archdeacon had long managed the affairs of the diocese ; and for some months previous to the demise of his father, rumour had confidently assigned to him the reversion of his father's honours.

Bishop Grantly died as he had lived, peaceably, slowly, without pain and without excitement. The breath ebbed from him almost imperceptibly, and for a month before his death, it was a question whether he were alive or dead.

A trying time was this for the archdeacon, for whom was designed the reversion of his father's see by those who then had the giving away of episcopal thrones. I would not be understood to say that the prime minister had in so many words promised the bishopric to Dr. Grantly. He was too discreet a man for that. There is a proverb with reference to the killing of cats, and those who know anything either of high or low government places, will

be well aware that a promise may be made without positive
words, and that an expectant may be put into the highest
state of encouragement, though the great man on whose
breath he hangs may have done no more than whisper
that ' Mr. So-and-so is certainly a rising man.'

Such a whisper had been made, and was known by those
who heard it to signify that the cures of the diocese of
Barchester should not be taken out of the hands of the
archdeacon.   The then prime minister was all in all at
Oxford, and had lately passed a night at the house of the
master of Lazarus.   Now the master of Lazarus—which
is, by the bye, in many respects the most comfortable,
as well as the richest college at Oxford,—was the archdeacon's most intimate friend and most trusted counsellor.
On the occasion of the prime minister's visit, Dr. Grantly
was of course present, and the meeting was very gracious.
On the following morning Dr. Gwynne, the master, told
the archdeacon that in his opinion the thing was settled.

At this time the bishop was quite on his last legs ; but
the ministry also were tottering.   Dr. Grantly returned
from Oxford happy and elated, to resume his place in the
palace, and to continue to perform for the father the last
duties of a son ; which, to give him his due, he performed
with more tender care than was to be expected from his
usual somewhat worldly manners.

A month since the physicians had named four weeks as
the outside period during which breath could be supported
within the body of the dying man.   At the end of the
month the physicians wondered, and named another
fortnight.   The old man lived on wine alone, but at the
end of the fortnight he still lived ; and the tidings of the
fall of the ministry became more frequent.   Sir Lamda
Mewnew and Sir Omicron Pie, the two great London
doctors, now came down for the fifth time, and declared,
shaking their learned heads, that another week of life
was impossible ; and as they sat down to lunch in the
episcopal dining-room, whispered to the archdeacon their
own private knowledge that the ministry must fall within
five days.   The son returned to his father's room, and
after administering with his own hands the sustaining
modicum of madeira, sat down by the bedside to calculate
his chances.

The ministry were to be out within five days : his father was to be dead within—No, he rejected that view of the subject. The ministry were to be out, and the diocese might probably be vacant at the same period. There was much doubt as to the names of the men who were to succeed to power, and a week must elapse before a Cabinet was formed. Would not vacancies be filled by the out-going men during this week ? Dr. Grantly had a kind of idea that such would be the case, but did not know ; and then he wondered at his own ignorance on such a question.

He tried to keep his mind away from the subject, but he could not. The race was so very close, and the stakes were so very high. He then looked at the dying man's impassive, placid face. There was no sign there of death or disease ; it was something thinner than of yore, somewhat grayer, and the deep lines of age more marked ; but, as far as he could judge, life might yet hang there for weeks to come. Sir Lamda Mewnew and Sir Omicron Pie had thrice been wrong, and might yet be wrong thrice again. The old bishop slept during twenty of the twenty-four hours, but during the short periods of his waking moments, he knew both his son and his dear old friend, Mr. Harding, the archdeacon's father-in-law, and would thank them tenderly for their care and love. Now he lay sleeping like a baby, resting easily on his back, his mouth just open, and his few gray hairs straggling from beneath his cap ; his breath was perfectly noiseless, and his thin, wan hand, which lay above the coverlid, never moved. Nothing could be easier than the old man's passage from this world to the next.

But by no means easy were the emotions of him who sat there watching. He knew it must be now or never. He was already over fifty, and there was little chance that his friends who were now leaving office would soon return to it. No probable British prime minister but he who was now in, he who was so soon to be out, would think of making a bishop of Dr. Grantly. Thus he thought long and sadly, in deep silence, and then gazed at that still living face, and then at last dared to ask himself whether he really longed for his father's death.

The effort was a salutary one, and the question was answered in a moment. The proud, wishful, worldly man,

sank on his knees by the bedside, and taking the bishop's
hand within his own, prayed eagerly that his sins might
be forgiven him.

His face was still buried in the clothes when the door
of the bed-room opened noiselessly, and Mr. Harding
entered with a velvet step. Mr. Harding's attendance
at that bedside had been nearly as constant as that of
the archdeacon, and his ingress and egress was as much
a matter of course as that of his son-in-law. He was
standing close beside the archdeacon before he was perceived, and would also have knelt in prayer had he not
feared that his doing so might have caused some sudden
start, and have disturbed the dying man. Dr. Grantly,
however, instantly perceived him, and rose from his knees.
As he did so Mr. Harding took both his hands, and pressed
them warmly. There was more fellowship between them
at that moment than there had ever been before, and it
so happened that after circumstances greatly preserved
the feeling. As they stood there pressing each other's
hands, the tears rolled freely down their cheeks.

'God bless you, my dears,'—said the bishop with
feeble voice as he woke—'God bless you—may God bless
you both, my dear children : ' and so he died.

There was no loud rattle in the throat, no dreadful
struggle, no palpable sign of death ; but the lower jaw
fell a little from its place, and the eyes, which had been
so constantly closed in sleep, now remained fixed and open.
Neither Mr. Harding nor Dr. Grantly knew that life was
gone, though both suspected it.

'I believe it's all over,' said Mr. Harding, still pressing
the other's hands. 'I think—nay, I hope it is.'

'I will ring the bell,' said the other, speaking all but in
a whisper. 'Mrs. Phillips should be here.'

Mrs Phillips, the nurse, was soon in the room, and
immediately, with practised hand, closed those staring
eyes.

'It's all over, Mrs. Phillips ? ' asked Mr. Harding.

'My lord's no more,' said Mrs. Phillips, turning round
and curtseying low with solemn face ; 'his lordship's gone
more like a sleeping babby than any that I ever saw.'

'It's a great relief, archdeacon,' said Mr. Harding,
'a great relief—dear, good, excellent old man. Oh that

our last moments may be as innocent and as peaceful
as his ! '

'Surely,' said Mrs. Phillips. 'The Lord be praised for all
his mercies ; but, for a meek, mild, gentle-spoken Christian,
his lordship was——' and Mrs. Phillips, with unaffected
but easy grief, put up her white apron to her flowing eyes.

'You cannot but rejoice that it is over,' said Mr. Harding,
still consoling his friend. The archdeacon's mind, however,
had already travelled from the death chamber to the
closet of the prime minister. He had brought himself to
pray for his father's life, but now that that life was done,
minutes were too precious to be lost. It was now useless
to dally with the fact of the bishop's death—useless to
lose perhaps everything for the pretence of a foolish
sentiment.

But how was he to act while his father-in-law stood
there holding his hand ? how, without appearing unfeeling,
was he to forget his father in the bishop—to overlook what
he had lost, and think only of what he might possibly
gain ?

'No ; I suppose not,' said he, at last, in answer to Mr.
Harding. 'We have all expected it so long.'

Mr. Harding took him by the arm and led him from the
room. 'We will see him again to-morrow morning,'
said he ; ' we had better leave the room now to the women.'
And so they went down stairs.

It was already evening and nearly dark. It was most
important that the prime minister should know that
night that the diocese was vacant. Everything might
depend on it ; and so, in answer to Mr. Harding's further
consolation, the archdeacon suggested that a telegraph
message should be immediately sent off to London. Mr.
Harding who had really been somewhat surprised to find
Dr. Grantly, as he thought, so much affected, was rather
taken aback ; but he made no objection. He knew that
the archdeacon had some hope of succeeding to his father's
place, though he by no means knew how highly raised that
hope had been.

'Yes,' said Dr. Grantly, collecting himself and shaking
off his weakness, ' we must send a message at once ; we
don't know what might be the consequence of delay.
Will you do it ? '

'I! oh yes; certainly: I'll do anything, only I don't know exactly what it is you want.'

Dr. Grantly sat down before a writing table, and taking pen and ink, wrote on a slip of paper as follows :—

'By Electric Telegraph.
'For the Earl of ——, Downing Street, or elsewhere.
' "The Bishop of Barchester is dead."
'Message sent by the Rev. Septimus Harding.'

'There,' said he, ' just take that to the telegraph office at the railway station, and give it in as it is; they'll probably make you copy it on to one of their own slips; that's all you'll have to do: then you'll have to pay them half-a-crown;' and the archdeacon put his hand in his pocket and pulled out the necessary sum.

Mr. Harding felt very much like an errand-boy, and also felt that he was called on to perform his duties as such at rather an unseemly time; but he said nothing, and took the slip of paper and the proffered coin.

'But you've put my name into it, archdeacon.'

'Yes,' said the other, ' there should be the name of some clergyman you know, and what name so proper as that of so old a friend as yourself ? The Earl won't look at the name, you may be sure of that; but my dear Mr. Harding, pray don't lose any time.'

Mr. Harding got as far as the library door on his way to the station, when he suddenly remembered the news with which he was fraught when he entered the poor bishop's bed-room. He had found the moment so inopportune for any mundane tidings, that he had repressed the words which were on his tongue, and immediately afterwards all recollection of the circumstance was for the time banished by the scene which had occurred.

'But, archdeacon,' said he, turning back, ' I forgot to tell you—The ministry are out.'

'Out!' ejaculated the archdeacon, in a tone which too plainly showed his anxiety and dismay, although under the circumstances of the moment he endeavoured to control himself : 'Out! who told you so ?'

Mr. Harding explained that news to this effect had come down by electric telegraph, and that the tidings had been left at the palace door by Mr. Chadwick.

The archdeacon sat silent for awhile meditating, and Mr. Harding stood looking at him. ' Never mind,' said the archdeacon at last ; ' send the message all the same. The news must be sent to some one, and there is at present no one else in a position to receive it. Do it at once, my dear friend ; you know I would not trouble you, were I in a state to do it myself. A few minutes' time is of the greatest importance.'

Mr. Harding went out and sent the message, and it may be as well that we should follow it to its destination. Within thirty minutes of its leaving Barchester it reached the Earl of —— in his inner library. What elaborate letters, what eloquent appeals, what indignant remon-strances, he might there have to frame, at such a moment, may be conceived, but not described ! How he was pre-paring his thunder for successful rivals, standing like a British peer with his back to the sea-coal fire, and his hands in his breeches pockets,—how his fine eye was lit up with anger, and his forehead gleamed with patriotism,—how he stamped his foot as he thought of his heavy associates,— how he all but swore as he remembered how much too clever one of them had been,—my creative readers may imagine. But was he so engaged ? No : history and truth compel me to deny it. He was sitting easily in a lounging chair, conning over a Newmarket list, and by his elbow on the table was lying open an uncut French novel on which he was engaged.

He opened the cover in which the message was enclosed, and having read it, he took his pen and wrote on the back of it—

> ' For the Earl of ——,
> ' With the Earl of ——'s compliments,'

and sent it off again on its journey.

Thus terminated our unfortunate friend's chance of possessing the glories of a bishopric.

The names of many divines were given in the papers as that of the bishop elect. ' The British Grandmother ' declared that Dr. Gwynne was to be the man, in compli-ment to the late ministry. This was a heavy blow to Dr. Grantly, but he was not doomed to see himself super-seded by his friend. ' The Anglican Devotee ' put forward confidently the claims of a great London preacher of austere doctrines ; and ' The Eastern Hemisphere,' an evening paper supposed to possess much official knowledge, declared in favour of an eminent naturalist, a gentleman most completely versed in the knowledge of rocks and minerals, but supposed by many to hold on religious subjects no special doctrines whatever. ' The Jupiter,' that daily paper, which, as we all know, is the only true source of infallibly correct information on all subjects, for a while was silent, but at last spoke out. The merits of all these candidates were discussed and somewhat irreverently disposed of, and then ' The Jupiter ' declared that Dr. Proudie was to be the man.

Dr. Proudie was the man. Just a month after the demise of the late bishop, Dr. Proudie kissed the Queen's hand as his successor elect.

We must beg to be allowed to draw a curtain over the sorrows of the archdeacon as he sat, sombre and sad at heart, in the study of his parsonage at Plumstead Episcopi. On the day subsequent to the despatch of the message he heard that the Earl of —— had consented to undertake the formation of a ministry, and from that moment he knew that his chance was over. Many will think that he was wicked to grieve for the loss of episcopal power, wicked to have coveted it, nay, wicked even to have thought about it, in the way and at the moments he had done so.

With such censures I cannot profess that I completely agree. The *nolo episcopari*, though still in use, is so directly at variance with the tendency of all human wishes, that it cannot be thought to express the true aspirations of rising priests in the Church of England. A lawyer does not sin in seeking to be a judge, or in compassing his wishes by all honest means. A young diplomate entertains a fair ambition when he looks forward to be the lord of a first-rate embassy ; and a poor novelist when he attempts to rival Dickens or rise above Fitzjeames, commits no fault, though he may be foolish. Sydney Smith truly said that in these recreant days we cannot expect to find the majesty of St. Paul beneath the cassock of a curate. If we look to our clergymen to be more than men, we shall probably teach ourselves to think that they are less, and can hardly hope to raise the character of the pastor by denying to him the right to entertain the aspirations of a man.

Our archdeacon was worldly—who among us is not so ? He was ambitious—who among us is ashamed to own that ' last infirmity of noble minds ! ' He was avaricious, my readers will say. No—it was for no love of lucre that he wished to be bishop of Barchester. He was his father's only child, and his father had left him great wealth. His preferment brought him in nearly three thousand a year. The bishopric, as cut down by the Ecclesiastical Commission, was only five. He would be a richer man as archdeacon than he could be as bishop. But he certainly did desire to play first fiddle ; he did desire to sit in full lawn sleeves among the peers of the realm ; and he did desire, if the truth must out, to be called ' My Lord ' by his reverend brethren.

His hopes, however, were they innocent or sinful, were not fated to be realised ; and Dr. Proudie was consecrated Bishop of Barchester.

CHAPTER II

HIRAM'S HOSPITAL ACCORDING TO ACT OF PARLIAMENT

IT is hardly necessary that I should here give to the public any lengthened biography of Mr. Harding, up to the period of the commencement of this tale. The public cannot have forgotten how ill that sensitive gentleman bore the attack that was made on him in the columns of the Jupiter, with reference to the income which he received as warden of Hiram's Hospital, in the city of Barchester. Nor can it yet be forgotten that a law-suit was instituted against him on the matter of that charity by Mr. John Bold, who afterwards married his, Mr. Harding's, younger and then only unmarried daughter. Under pressure of these attacks, Mr. Harding had resigned his wardenship, though strongly recommended to abstain from doing so, both by his friends and by his lawyers. He did, however, resign it, and betook himself manfully to the duties of the small parish of St. Cuthbert's, in the city, of which he was vicar, continuing also to perform

those of precentor of the cathedral, a situation of small
emolument which had hitherto been supposed to be joined,
as a matter of course, to the wardenship of the Hospital
above spoken of.

When he left the hospital from which he had been so
ruthlessly driven, and settled himself down in his own
modest manner in the High Street of Barchester, he had
not expected that others would make more fuss about
it than he was inclined to do himself ; and the extent
of his hope was, that the movement might have been made
in time to prevent any further paragraphs in the Jupiter.
His affairs, however, were not allowed to subside thus
quietly, and people were quite as much inclined to talk
about the disinterested sacrifice he had made, as they had
before been to upbraid him for his cupidity.

The most remarkable thing that occurred, was the
receipt of an autograph letter from the Archbishop of
Canterbury, in which the primate very warmly praised
his conduct, and begged to know what his intentions were
for the future. Mr. Harding replied that he intended
to be rector of St. Cuthbert's, in Barchester : and so that
matter dropped. Then the newspapers took up his case,
the Jupiter among the rest, and wafted his name in
eulogistic strains through every reading-room in the nation.
It was discovered also, that he was the author of that great
musical work, Harding's Church music,—and a new
edition was spoken of, though, I believe, never printed.
It is, however, certain that the work was introduced into
the Royal Chapel at St. James's, and that a long criticism
appeared in the Musical Scrutator, declaring that in no
previous work of the kind had so much research been
joined with such exalted musical ability, and asserting
that the name of Harding would henceforward be known
wherever the Arts were cultivated, or Religion valued.

This was high praise, and I will not deny that Mr.
Harding was gratified by such flattery ; for if Mr. Harding
was vain on any subject, it was on that of music. But here
the matter rested. The second edition, if printed, was
never purchased ; the copies which had been introduced
into the Royal Chapel disappeared again, and were laid
by in peace, with a load of similar literature. Mr. Towers,
of the Jupiter, and his brethren, occupied themselves

with other names, and the undying fame promised to our friend was clearly intended to be posthumous.

Mr. Harding had spent much of his time with his friend the bishop, much with his daughter Mrs. Bold, now, alas, a widow; and had almost daily visited the wretched remnant of his former subjects, the few surviving bedesmen now left at Hiram's Hospital. Six of them were still living. The number, according to old Hiram's will, should always have been twelve. But after the abdication of their warden, the bishop had appointed no successor to him, no new occupants of the charity had been nominated, and it appeared as though the hospital at Barchester would fall into abeyance, unless the powers that be should take some steps towards putting it once more into working order.

During the past five years, the powers that be had not overlooked Barchester Hospital, and sundry political doctors had taken the matter in hand. Shortly after Mr. Harding's resignation, the Jupiter had very clearly shown what ought to be done. In about half a column it had distributed the income, rebuilt the building, put an end to all bickerings, regenerated kindly feeling, provided for Mr. Harding, and placed the whole thing on a footing which could not but be satisfactory to the city and Bishop of Barchester, and to the nation at large. The wisdom of this scheme was testified by the number of letters which ' Common Sense,' ' Veritas,' and ' One that loves fair play ' sent to the Jupiter, all expressing admiration, and amplifying on the details given. It is singular enough that no adverse letter appeared at all, and, therefore, none of course was written.

But Cassandra was not believed, and even the wisdom of the Jupiter sometimes falls on deaf ears. Though other plans did not put themselves forward in the columns of the Jupiter, reformers of church charities were not slack to make known in various places their different nostrums for setting Hiram's Hospital on its feet again. A learned bishop took occasion, in the Upper House, to allude to the matter, intimating that he had communicated on the subject with his right reverend brother of Barchester. The radical member for Staleybridge had suggested that the funds should be alienated for the

education of the agricultural poor of the country, and he
amused the house by some anecdotes touching the superstition and habits of the agriculturists in question. A
political pamphleteer had produced a few dozen pages,
which he called ' Who are John Hiram's heirs ? ' intending
to give an infallible rule for the governance of all such
establishments ; and, at last, a member of the government
promised that in the next session a short bill should be
introduced for regulating · the affairs of Barchester, and
other kindred concerns.

The next session came, and, contrary to custom, the
bill came also. Men's minds were then intent on other
things. The first threatenings of a huge war hung heavily
over the nation, and the question as to Hiram's heirs did
not appear to interest very many people either in or out
of the house. The bill, however, was read and re-read,
and in some undistinguished manner passed through its
eleven stages without appeal or dissent. What would John
Hiram have said in the matter, could he have predicted
that some forty-five gentlemen would take on themselves
to make a law altering the whole purport of his will,
without in the least knowing at the moment of their
making it, what it was that they were doing ? It is however to be hoped that the under-secretary for the Home
Office knew, for to him had the matter been confided.

The bill, however, did pass, and at the time at which
this history is supposed to commence, it had been ordained
that there should be, as heretofore, twelve old men in
Barchester Hospital, each with 1s. 4d. a day ; that there
should also be twelve old women to be located in a house
to be built, each with 1s. 2d. a day ; that there should be
a matron, with a house and 70l. a year ; a steward with
150l. a year ; and latterly, a warden with 450l. a year,
who should have the spiritual guidance of both establishments, and the temporal guidance of that appertaining
to the male sex. The bishop, dean, and warden were,
as formerly, to appoint in turn the recipients of the charity,
and the bishop was to appoint the officers. There was
nothing said as to the wardenship being held by the
precentor of the cathedral, nor a word as to Mr. Harding's
right to the situation.

It was not, however, till some months after the death

of the old bishop, and almost immediately consequent on the installation of his successor, that notice was given that the reform was about to be carried out. The new law and the new bishop were among the earliest works of a new ministry, or rather of a ministry who, having for a while given place to their opponents, had then returned to power; and the death of Dr. Grantly occurred, as we have seen, exactly at the period of the change.

Poor Eleanor Bold! How well does that widow's cap become her, and the solemn gravity with which she devotes herself to her new duties. Poor Eleanor!

Poor Eleanor! I cannot say that with me John Bold was ever a favourite. I never thought him worthy of the wife he had won. But in her estimation he was most worthy. Hers was one of those feminine hearts which cling to a husband, not with idolatry, for worship can admit of no defect in its idol, but with the perfect tenacity of ivy. As the parasite plant will follow even the defects of the trunk which it embraces, so did Eleanor cling to and love the very faults of her husband. She had once declared that whatever her father did should in her eyes be right. She then transferred her allegiance, and became ever ready to defend the worst failings of her lord and master.

And John Bold was a man to be loved by a woman; he was himself affectionate, he was confiding and manly; and that arrogance of thought, unsustained by first-rate abilities, that attempt at being better than his neighbours which jarred so painfully on the feelings of his acquaintance, did not injure him in the estimation of his wife.

Could she even have admitted that he had a fault, his early death would have blotted out the memory of it. She wept as for the loss of the most perfect treasure with which mortal woman had ever been endowed; for weeks after he was gone the idea of future happiness in this world was hateful to her; consolation, as it is called, was insupportable, and tears and sleep were her only relief.

But God tempers the wind to the shorn lamb. She knew that she had within her the living source of other cares. She knew that there was to be created for her another subject of weal or woe, of unutterable joy or despairing sorrow, as God in his mercy might vouchsafe to her. At first this did but augment her grief! To be the mother

of a poor infant, orphaned before it was born, brought
forth to the sorrows of an ever desolate hearth, nurtured
amidst tears and wailing, and then turned adrift into
the world without the aid of a father's care! There was
at first no joy in this.

By degrees, however, her heart became anxious for
another object, and, before its birth, the stranger was
expected with all the eagerness of a longing mother. Just
eight months after the father's death a second John Bold
was born, and if the worship of one creature can be innocent
in another, let us hope that the adoration offered over the
cradle of the fatherless infant may not be imputed as a sin.

It will not be worth our while to define the character of
the child, or to point out in how far the faults of the father
were redeemed within that little breast by the virtues of
the mother. The baby, as a baby, was all that was delightful, and I cannot foresee that it will be necessary for us
to inquire into the facts of his after life. Our present
business at Barchester will not occupy us above a year
or two at the furthest, and I will leave it to some other
pen to produce, if necessary, the biography of John Bold
the Younger.

But, as a baby, this baby was all that could be desired.
This fact no one attempted to deny. 'Is he not delightful?'
she would say to her father, looking up into his face from
her knees, her lustrous eyes overflowing with soft tears,
her young face encircled by her close widow's cap and her
hands on each side of the cradle in which her treasure
was sleeping. The grandfather would gladly admit that
the treasure was delightful, and the uncle archdeacon
himself would agree, and Mrs. Grantly, Eleanor's sister,
would re-echo the word with true sisterly energy; and
Mary Bold —— but Mary Bold was a second worshipper
at the same shrine.

The baby was really delightful; he took his food with
a will, struck out his toes merrily whenever his legs were
uncovered, and did not have fits. These are supposed to
be the strongest points of baby perfection, and in all these
our baby excelled.

And thus the widow's deep grief was softened, and
a sweet balm was poured into the wound which she had
thought nothing but death could heal. How much kinder

is God to us than we are willing to be to ourselves ! At the loss of every dear face, at the last going of every well beloved one, we all doom ourselves to an eternity of sorrow, and look to waste ourselves away in an ever-running fountain of tears. How seldom does such grief endure ! how blessed is the goodness which forbids it to do so ! ' Let me ever remember my living friends, but forget them as soon as dead,' was the prayer of a wise man who understood the mercy of God. Few perhaps would have the courage to express such a wish, and yet to do so would only be to ask for that release from sorrow, which a kind Creator almost always extends to us.

I would not, however, have it imagined that Mrs. Bold forgot her husband. She daily thought of him with all conjugal love, and enshrined his memory in the innermost centre of her heart. But yet she was happy in her baby. It was so sweet to press the living toy to her breast, and feel that a human being existed who did owe, and was to owe everything to her ; whose daily food was drawn from herself ; whose little wants could all be satisfied by her ; whose little heart would first love her and her only ; whose infant tongue would make its first effort in calling her by the sweetest name a woman can hear. And so Eleanor's bosom became tranquil, and she set about her new duties eagerly and gratefully.

As regards the concerns of the world, John Bold had left his widow in prosperous circumstances. He had bequeathed to her all that he possessed, and that comprised an income much exceeding what she or her friends thought necessary for her. It amounted to nearly a thousand a year ; and when she reflected on its extent, her dearest hope was to hand it over, not only unimpaired but increased, to her husband's son, to her own darling, to the little man who now lay sleeping on her knee, happily ignorant of the cares which were to be accumulated in his behalf.

When John Bold died she earnestly implored her father to come and live with her, but this Mr. Harding declined, though for some weeks he remained with her as a visitor. He could not be prevailed upon to forego the possession of some small home of his own, and so remained in the lodgings he had first selected over a chemist's shop in the High Street of Barchester.

CHAPTER III

DR. AND MRS. PROUDIE

THIS narrative is supposed to commence immediately after the installation of Dr. Proudie. I will not describe the ceremony, as I do not precisely understand its nature. I am ignorant whether a bishop be chaired like a member of parliament, or carried in a gilt coach like a lord mayor, or sworn in like a justice of peace, or introduced like a peer to the upper house, or led between two brethren like a knight of the garter; but I do know that every thing was properly done, and that nothing fit or becoming to a young bishop was omitted on the occasion.

Dr. Proudie was not the man to allow anything to be omitted that might be becoming to his new dignity. He understood well the value of forms, and knew that the due observance of rank could not be maintained unless the exterior trappings belonging to it were held in proper esteem. He was a man born to move in high circles; at least so he thought himself, and circumstances had certainly sustained him in this view. He was the nephew of an Irish baron by his mother's side, and his wife was the niece of a Scotch earl. He had for years held some clerical office appertaining to courtly matters, which had enabled him to live in London, and to entrust his parish to his curate. He had been preacher to the royal beefeaters, curator of theological manuscripts in the Ecclesiastical Courts, chaplain to the Queen's yeomanry guard, and almoner to his Royal Highness the Prince of Rappe-Blankenburg.

His residence in the metropolis, rendered necessary by the duties thus entrusted to him, his high connections, and the peculiar talents and nature of the man, recommended him to persons in power; and Dr. Proudie became known as a useful and rising clergyman.

Some few years since, even within the memory of many who are not yet willing to call themselves old, a liberal clergyman was a person not frequently to be met. Sydney Smith was such, and was looked on as little better than an infidel; a few others also might be named, but they were ' raræ aves,' and were regarded with doubt and distrust by their brethren. No man was so surely a tory as a country rector—nowhere were the powers that be so cherished as at Oxford.

When, however, Dr. Whately was made an archbishop, and Dr. Hampden some years afterwards regius professor, many wise divines saw that a change was taking place in men's minds, and that more liberal ideas would henceforward be suitable to the priests as well as to the laity. Clergymen began to be heard of who had ceased to anathematise papists on the one hand, or vilify dissenters on the other. It appeared clear that high church principles, as they are called, were no longer to be surest claims to promotion with at any rate one section of statesmen, and Dr. Proudie was one among those who early in life adapted himself to the views held by the whigs on most theological and religious subjects. He bore with the idolatry of Rome, tolerated even the infidelity of Socinianism, and was hand and glove with the Presbyterian Synods of Scotland and Ulster.

Such a man at such a time was found to be useful, and Dr. Proudie's name began to appear in the newspapers. He was made one of a commission who went over to Ireland to arrange matters preparative to the working of the national board ; he became honorary secretary to another commission nominated to inquire into the revenues of cathedral chapters ; and had had something to do with both the regium donum and the Maynooth grant.

It must not on this account be taken as proved that Dr. Proudie was a man of great mental powers, or even of much capacity for business, for such qualities had not been required in him. In the arrangement of those church reforms with which he was connected, the ideas and original conception of the work to be done were generally furnished by the liberal statesmen of the day, and the labour of the details was borne by officials of a lower rank. It was, however, thought expedient that the name of some clergyman should appear in such matters, and as Dr. Proudie had become known as a tolerating divine, great use of this sort was made of his name. If he did not do much active good, he never did any harm ; he was amenable to those who were really in authority, and at the sittings of the various boards to which he belonged maintained a kind of dignity which had its value.

He was certainly possessed of sufficient tact to answer the purpose for which he was required without making himself troublesome ; but it must not therefore be surmised that he doubted his own power, or failed to believe that he could himself take a high part in high affairs when his own turn came. He was biding his time, and patiently looking forward to the days when he himself would sit authoritative at some board, and talk and direct, and rule the roast, while lesser stars sat round and obeyed, as he had so well accustomed himself to do.

His reward and his time had now come. He was selected for the vacant bishopric, and on the next vacancy which might occur in any diocese would take his place in the House of Lords, prepared to give not a silent vote in all matters concerning the weal of the church establishment. Toleration was to be the basis on which he was to fight his battles, and in the honest courage of his heart he thought no evil would come to him in encountering even such foes as his brethren of Exeter and Oxford.

Dr. Proudie was an ambitious man, and before he was well consecrated Bishop of Barchester, he had begun to look up to archiepiscopal splendour, and the glories of Lambeth, or at any rate of Bishopsthorpe. He was comparatively young, and had, as he fondly flattered himself, been selected as possessing such gifts, natural and acquired, as must be sure to recommend him to a yet higher notice, now that a higher sphere was opened to him. Dr. Proudie was, therefore, quite prepared to take a conspicuous part in all theological affairs appertaining to these realms ; and having such views, by no means intended to bury himself at Barchester as his predecessor had done. No : London should still be his ground : a comfortable mansion in a provincial city might be well enough for the dead months of the year. Indeed Dr. Proudie had always felt it necessary to his position to retire from London when other great and fashionable people did so ; but London should still be his fixed residence, and it was in London that he resolved to exercise that hospitality so peculiarly recommended to all bishops by St. Paul. How otherwise could he keep himself before

the world ? how else give to the government, in matters
theological, the full benefit of his weight and talents ?

This resolution was no doubt a salutary one as regarded
the world at large, but was not likely to make him popular
either with the clergy or people of Barchester. Dr. Grantly
had always lived there ; and in truth it was hard for a
bishop to be popular after Dr. Grantly. His income had
averaged 9000*l.* a year ; his successor was to be rigidly
limited to 5000*l.* He had but one child on whom to spend
his money ; Dr. Proudie had seven or eight. He had been
a man of few personal expenses, and they had been confined to the tastes of a moderate gentleman ; but Dr.
Proudie had to maintain a position in fashionable society,
and had that to do with comparatively small means.
Dr. Grantly had certainly kept his carriage, as became
a bishop ; but his carriage, horses, and coachman, though
they did very well for Barchester, would have been almost
ridiculous at Westminster. Mrs. Proudie determined
that her husband's equipage should not shame her, and
things on which Mrs. Proudie resolved, were generally
accomplished.

From all this it was likely to result that Dr. Proudie
would not spend much money at Barchester ; whereas
his predecessor had dealt with the tradesmen of the city
in a manner very much to their satisfaction. The Grantlys,
father and son, had spent their money like gentlemen ;
but it soon became whispered in Barchester that Dr.
Proudie was not unacquainted with those prudent devices
by which the utmost show of wealth is produced from
limited means.

In person Dr. Proudie is a good-looking man ; spruce
and dapper, and very tidy. He is somewhat below middle
height, being about five feet four ; but he makes up for
the inches which he wants by the dignity with which
he carries those which he has. It is no fault of his own
if he has not a commanding eye, for he studies hard to
assume it. His features are well formed, though perhaps the
sharpness of his nose may give to his face in the eyes of
some people an air of insignificance. If so, it is greatly
redeemed by his mouth and chin, of which he is justly proud.

Dr. Proudie may well be said to have been a fortunate
man, for he was not born to wealth, and he is now bishop

of Barchester; but nevertheless he has his cares. He has
a large family, of whom the three eldest are daughters,
now all grown up and fit for fashionable life; and he has
a wife. It is not my intention to breathe a word against
the character of Mrs. Proudie, but still I cannot think
that with all her virtues she adds much to her husband's
happiness. The truth is that in matters domestic she
rules supreme over her titular lord, and rules with a rod
of iron. Nor is this all. Things domestic Dr. Proudie
might have abandoned to her, if not voluntarily, yet
willingly. But Mrs. Proudie is not satisfied with such
home dominion, and stretches her power over all his
movements, and will not even abstain from things spiritual.
In fact, the bishop is henpecked.

The archdeacon's wife, in her happy home at Plumstead,
knows how to assume the full privileges of her rank, and
express her own mind in becoming tone and place. But
Mrs. Grantly's sway, if sway she has, is easy and beneficent.
She never shames her husband; before the world she
is a pattern of obedience; her voice is never loud, nor
her looks sharp: doubtless she values power, and has
not unsuccessfully striven to acquire it; but she knows
what should be the limits of a woman's rule.

Not so Mrs. Proudie. This lady is habitually authoritative to all, but to her poor husband she is despotic.
Successful as has been his career in the eyes of the world,
it would seem that in the eyes of his wife he is never right.
All hope of defending himself has long passed from him;
indeed he rarely even attempts self-justification; and
is aware that submission produces the nearest approach
to peace which his own house can ever attain.

Mrs. Proudie has not been able to sit at the boards and
committees to which her husband has been called by the
state; nor, as he often reflects, can she make her voice
heard in the House of Lords. It may be that she will
refuse to him permission to attend to this branch of a
bishop's duties; it may be that she will insist on his close
attendance to his own closet. He has never whispered
a word on the subject to living ears, but he has already
made his fixed resolve. Should such an attempt be made
he will rebel. Dogs have turned against their masters,
and even Neapolitans against their rulers, when oppression

has been too severe. And Dr. Proudie feels within himself that if the cord be drawn too tight, he also can muster courage and resist.

The state of vassalage in which our bishop has been kept by his wife has not tended to exalt his character in the eyes of his daughters, who assume in addressing their father too much of that authority which is not properly belonging, at any rate, to them. They are, on the whole, fine engaging young ladies. They are tall and robust like their mother, whose high cheek-bones, and——, we may say auburn hair, they all inherit. They think somewhat too much of their grand uncles, who have not hitherto returned the compliment by thinking much of them. But now that their father is a bishop, it is probable that family ties will be drawn closer. Considering their connection with the church, they entertain but few prejudices against the pleasures of the world; and have certainly not distressed their parents, as too many English girls have lately done, by any enthusiastic wish to devote themselves to the seclusion of a protestant nunnery. Dr. Proudie's sons are still at school.

One other marked peculiarity in the character of the bishop's wife must be mentioned. Though not averse to the society and manners of the world, she is in her own way a religious woman; and the form in which this tendency shows itself in her is by a strict observance of Sabbatarian rule. Dissipation and low dresses during the week are, under her control, atoned for by three services, an evening sermon read by herself, and a perfect abstinence from any cheering employment on the Sunday. Unfortunately for those under her roof to whom the dissipation and low dresses are not extended, her servants namely and her husband, the compensating strictness of the Sabbath includes all. Woe betide the recreant housemaid who is found to have been listening to the honey of a sweetheart in the Regent's park, instead of the soul-stirring evening discourse of Mr. Slope. Not only is she sent adrift, but she is so sent with a character which leaves her little hope of a decent place. Woe betide the six-foot hero who escorts Mrs. Proudie to her pew in red plush breeches, if he slips away to the neighbouring beer-shop, instead of falling into the back seat appropriated

to his use. Mrs. Proudie has the eyes of Argus for such
offenders. Occasional drunkenness in the week may be
overlooked, for six feet on low wages are hardly to be
procured if the morals are always kept at a high pitch;
but not even for grandeur or economy will Mrs. Proudie
forgive a desecration of the Sabbath.

In such matters Mrs. Proudie allows herself to be often
guided by that eloquent preacher, the Rev. Mr. Slope,
and as Dr. Proudie is guided by his wife, it necessarily
follows that the eminent man we have named has obtained
a good deal of control over Dr. Proudie in matters concerning religion. Mr. Slope's only preferment has hitherto
been that of reader and preacher in a London district
church: and on the consecration of his friend the new
bishop, he readily gave this up to undertake the onerous
but congenial duties of domestic chaplain to his lordship.

Mr. Slope, however, on his first introduction must not
be brought before the public at the tail of a chapter.

CHAPTER IV

THE BISHOP'S CHAPLAIN

Of the Rev. Mr. Slope's parentage I am not able to
say much. I have heard it asserted that he is lineally
descended from that eminent physician who assisted at
the birth of Mr. T. Shandy, and that in early years he
added an ' e ' to his name, for the sake of euphony, as
other great men have done before him. If this be so,
I presume he was christened Obadiah, for that is his name,
in commemoration of the conflict in which his ancestor
so distinguished himself. All my researches on the subject
have, however, failed in enabling me to fix the date on
which the family changed its religion.

He had been a sizar at Cambridge, and had there conducted himself at any rate successfully, for in due process
of time he was an M.A., having university pupils under
his care. From thence he was transferred to London,
and became preacher at a new district church built on
the confines of Baker Street. He was in this position
when congenial ideas on religious subjects recommended

him to Mrs. Proudie, and the intercourse had become close and confidential.

Having been thus familiarly thrown among the Misses Proudie, it was no more than natural that some softer feeling than friendship should be engendered. There have been some passages of love between him and the eldest hope, Olivia; but they have hitherto resulted in no favourable arrangement. In truth, Mr. Slope having made a declaration of affection, afterwards withdrew it on finding that the doctor had no immediate worldly funds with which to endow his child; and it may easily be conceived that Miss Proudie, after such an announcement on his part, was not readily disposed to receive any further show of affection. On the appointment of Dr. Proudie to the bishopric of Barchester, Mr. Slope's views were in truth somewhat altered. Bishops, even though they be poor, can provide for clerical children, and Mr. Slope began to regret that he had not been more disinterested. He no sooner heard the tidings of the doctor's elevation, than he recommenced his siege, not violently, indeed, but respectfully, and at a distance. Olivia Proudie, however, was a girl of spirit: she had the blood of two peers in her veins, and, better still, she had another lover on her books; so Mr. Slope sighed in vain; and the pair soon found it convenient to establish a mutual bond of inveterate hatred.

It may be thought singular that Mrs. Proudie's friendship for the young clergyman should remain firm after such an affair; but, to tell the truth, she had known nothing of it. Though very fond of Mr. Slope herself, she had never conceived the idea that either of her daughters would become so, and remembering their high birth and social advantages, expected for them matches of a different sort. Neither the gentleman nor the lady found it necessary to enlighten her. Olivia's two sisters had each known of the affair, so had all the servants, so had all the people living in the adjoining houses on either side; but Mrs. Proudie had been kept in the dark.

Mr. Slope soon comforted himself with the reflection, that as he had been selected as chaplain to the bishop, it would probably be in his power to get the good things in the bishop's gift, without troubling himself with the

bishop's daughter; and he found himself able to endure
the pangs of rejected love. As he sat himself down in the
railway carriage, confronting the bishop and Mrs. Proudie,
as they started on their first journey to Barchester, he
began to form in his own mind a plan of his future life.
He knew well his patron's strong points, but he knew
the weak ones as well. He understood correctly enough
to what attempts the new bishop's high spirit would soar,
and he rightly guessed that public life would better suit
the great man's taste, than the small details of diocesan
duty.

He, therefore, he, Mr. Slope, would in effect be bishop
of Barchester. Such was his resolve; and to give Mr.
Slope his due, he had both courage and spirit to bear him
out in his resolution. He knew that he should have a hard
battle to fight, for the power and patronage of the see
would be equally coveted by another great mind—Mrs.
Proudie would also choose to be bishop of Barchester.
Mr. Slope, however, flattered himself that he could out-
manoeuvre the lady. She must live much in London, while
he would always be on the spot. She would necessarily
remain ignorant of much, while he would know everything
belonging to the diocese. At first, doubtless, he must
flatter and cajole, perhaps yield, in some things; but he
did not doubt of ultimate triumph. If all other means
failed, he could join the bishop against his wife, inspire
courage into the unhappy man, lay an axe to the root of
the woman's power, and emancipate the husband.

Such were his thoughts as he sat looking at the sleeping
pair in the railway carriage, and Mr. Slope is not the man
to trouble himself with such thoughts for nothing. He
is possessed of more than average abilities, and is of good
courage. Though he can stoop to fawn, and stoop low indeed, if need be, he has still within him the power to assume
the tyrant; and with the power he has certainly the wish.
His acquirements are not of the highest order, but such
as they are they are completely under control, and he
knows the use of them. He is gifted with a certain kind
of pulpit eloquence, not likely indeed to be persuasive
with men, but powerful with the softer sex. In his sermons
he deals greatly in denunciations, excites the minds of
his weaker hearers with a not unpleasant terror, and leaves

an impression on their minds that all mankind are in a perilous state, and all womankind too, except those who attend regularly to the evening lectures in Baker Street. His looks and tones are extremely severe, so much so that one cannot but fancy that he regards the greater part of the world as being infinitely too bad for his care. As he walks through the streets, his very face denotes his horror of the world's wickedness; and there is always an anathema lurking in the corner of his eye.

In doctrine, he, like his patron, is tolerant of dissent, if so strict a mind can be called tolerant of anything. With Wesleyan-Methodists he has something in common, but his soul trembles in agony at the iniquities of the Puseyites. His aversion is carried to things outward as well as inward. His gall rises at a new church with a high pitched roof; a full-breasted black silk waistcoat is with him a symbol of Satan; and a profane jest-book would not, in his view, more foully desecrate the church seat of a Christian, than a book of prayer printed with red letters, and ornamented with a cross on the back. Most active clergymen have their hobby, and Sunday observances are his. Sunday, however, is a word which never pollutes his mouth—it is always ' the Sabbath.' The ' desecration of the Sabbath,' as he delights to call it, is to him meat and drink :—he thrives upon that as policemen do on the general evil habits of the community. It is the loved subject of all his evening discourses, the source of all his eloquence, the secret of all his power over the female heart. To him the revelation of God appears only in that one law given for Jewish observance. To him the mercies of our Saviour speak in vain, to him in vain has been preached that sermon which fell from divine lips on the mountain—' Blessed are the meek, for they shall inherit the earth '—' Blessed are the merciful, for they shall obtain mercy.' To him the New Testament is comparatively of little moment, for from it can he draw no fresh authority for that dominion which he loves to exercise over at least a seventh part of man's allotted time here below.

Mr. Slope is tall, and not ill made. His feet and hands are large, as has ever been the case with all his family, but he has a broad chest and wide shoulders to carry off these excrescences, and on the whole his figure is good. His countenance, however, is not specially prepossessing. His hair is lank, and of a dull pale reddish hue. It is always formed into three straight lumpy masses, each brushed with admirable precision, and cemented with much grease; two of them adhere closely to the sides of his face, and the other lies at right angles above them. He wears no whiskers, and is always punctiliously shaven. His face is nearly of the same colour as his hair, though perhaps a little redder: it is not unlike beef,—beef, however, one would say, of a bad quality. His forehead is capacious and high, but square and heavy, and unpleasantly shining. His mouth is large, though his lips are thin and bloodless; and his big, prominent, pale brown eyes inspire anything but confidence. His nose, however, is his redeeming feature: it is pronounced straight and well-formed; though I myself should have liked it better did it not possess a somewhat spongy, porous appearance, as though it had been cleverly formed out of a red coloured cork.

I never could endure to shake hands with Mr. Slope. A cold, clammy perspiration always exudes from him, the small drops are ever to be seen standing on his brow, and his friendly grasp is unpleasant.

Such is Mr. Slope—such is the man who has suddenly fallen into the midst of Barchester Close, and is destined there to assume the station which has heretofore been filled by the son of the late bishop. Think, oh, my meditative reader, what an associate we have here for those comfortable prebendaries, those gentlemanlike clerical doctors, those happy well-used well-fed minor canons, who have grown into existence at Barchester under the kindly wings of Bishop Grantly!

But not as a mere associate for these does Mr. Slope travel down to Barchester with the bishop and his wife. He intends to be, if not their master, at least the chief among them. He intends to lead, and to have followers; he intends to hold the purse strings of the diocese, and draw round him an obedient herd of his poor and hungry brethren.

And here we can hardly fail to draw a comparison between the archdeacon and our new private chaplain;

and despite the manifold faults of the former, one can
hardly fail to make it much to his advantage.

Both men are eager, much too eager, to support and
increase the power of their order. Both are anxious that
the world should be priest-governed, though they have
probably never confessed so much, even to themselves.
Both begrudge any other kind of dominion held by man
over man. Dr. Grantly, if he admits the Queen's supremacy in things spiritual, only admits it as being due to the
quasi priesthood conveyed in the consecrating qualities
of her coronation; and he regards things temporal as
being by their nature subject to those which are spiritual.
Mr. Slope's ideas of sacerdotal rule are of quite a different
class. He cares nothing, one way or the other, for the
Queen's supremacy; these to his ears are empty words,
meaning nothing. Forms he regards but little, and such
titular expressions as supremacy, consecration, ordination,
and the like, convey of themselves no significance to him.
Let him be supreme who can. The temporal king, judge,
or gaoler, can work but on the body. The spiritual master,
if he have the necessary gifts, and can duly use them,
has a wider field of empire. He works upon the soul.
If he can make himself be believed, he can be all powerful
over those who listen. If he be careful to meddle with
none who are too strong in intellect, or too weak in flesh,
he may indeed be supreme. And such was the ambition
of Mr. Slope.

Dr. Grantly interfered very little with the worldly
doings of those who were in any way subject to him.
I do not mean to say that he omitted to notice misconduct
among his clergy, immorality in his parish, or omissions
in his family; but he was not anxious to do so where the
necessity could be avoided. He was not troubled with
a propensity to be curious, and as long as those around him
were tainted with no heretical leaning towards dissent,
as long as they fully and freely admitted the efficacy of
Mother Church, he was willing that that mother should
be merciful and affectionate, prone to indulgence, and
unwilling to chastise. He himself enjoyed the good things
of this world, and liked to let it be known that he did so.
He cordially despised any brother rector who thought
harm of dinner-parties, or dreaded the dangers of a

moderate claret-jug; consequently dinner-parties and
claret-jugs were common in the diocese. He liked to
give laws and to be obeyed in them implicity, but he
endeavoured that his ordinances should be within the
compass of the man, and not unpalatable to the gentleman. He had ruled among his clerical neighbours now
for sundry years, and as he had maintained his power
without becoming unpopular, it may be presumed that
he had exercised some wisdom.

Of Mr. Slope's conduct much cannot be said, as his
grand career is yet to commence; but it may be premised
that his tastes will be very different from those of the
archdeacon. He conceives it to be his duty to know all
the private doings and desires of the flock entrusted to
his care. From the poorer classes he exacts an uncon-
ditional obedience to set rules of conduct, and if disobeyed
he has recourse, like his great ancestor, to the fulmina-
tions of an Ernulfus: ' Thou shalt be damned in thy
going in and in thy coming out—in thy eating and thy
drinking,' &c. &c. &c. With the rich, experience has
already taught him that a different line of action is
necessary. Men in the upper walks of life do not mind
being cursed, and the women, presuming that it be done
in delicate phrase, rather like it. But he has not, therefore,
given up so important a portion of believing Christians.
With the men, indeed, he is generally at variance; they
are hardened sinners, on whom the voice of the priestly
charmer too often falls in vain; but with the ladies, old
and young, firm and frail, devout and dissipated, he is,
as he conceives, all powerful. He can reprove faults with
so much flattery, and utter censure in so caressing a
manner, that the female heart, if it glow with a spark
of low church susceptibility, cannot withstand him. In
many houses he is thus an admired guest: the husbands,
for their wives' sake, are fain to admit him; and when
once admitted it is not easy to shake him off. He has,
however, a pawing, greasy way with him, which does
not endear him to those who do not value him for their
souls' sake, and he is not a man to make himself at once
popular in a large circle such as is now likely to surround
him at Barchester.

CHAPTER V

A MORNING VISIT

IT was known that Dr. Proudie would immediately have to reappoint to the wardenship of the hospital under the act of Parliament to which allusion has been made; but no one imagined that any choice was left to him—no one for a moment thought that he could appoint any other than Mr. Harding. Mr. Harding himself, when he heard how the matter had been settled, without troubling himself much on the subject, considered it as certain that he would go back to his pleasant house and garden. And though there would be much that was melancholy, nay, almost heartrending, in such a return, he still was glad that it was to be so. His daughter might probably be persuaded to return there with him. She had, indeed, all but promised to do so, though she still entertained an idea that that greatest of mortals, that important atom of humanity, that little god upon earth, Johnny Bold her baby, ought to have a house of his own over his head.

Such being the state of Mr. Harding's mind in the matter, he did not feel any peculiar personal interest in the appointment of Dr. Proudie to the bishopric. He, as well as others at Barchester, regretted that a man should be sent among them who, they were aware, was not of their way of thinking; but Mr. Harding himself was not a bigoted man on points of church doctrine, and he was quite prepared to welcome Dr. Proudie to Barchester in a graceful and becoming manner. He had nothing to seek and nothing to fear; he felt that it behoved him to be on good terms with his bishop, and he did not anticipate any obstacle that would prevent it.

In such a frame of mind he proceeded to pay his respects at the palace the second day after the arrival of the bishop and his chaplain. But he did not go alone. Dr. Grantly proposed to accompany him, and Mr. Harding was not sorry to have a companion, who would remove from his shoulders the burden of the conversation in such an interview. In the affair of the consecration Dr. Grantly had been introduced to the bishop, and Mr. Harding had also been there. He had, however, kept himself in the background, and he was now to be presented to the great man for the first time.

The archdeacon's feelings were of a much stronger nature. He was not exactly the man to overlook his own slighted claims, or to forgive the preference shown to another. Dr. Proudie was playing Venus to his Juno, and he was prepared to wage an internecine war against the owner of the wished-for apple, and all his satellites, private chaplains, and others.

Nevertheless, it behoved him also to conduct himself towards the intruder as an old archdeacon should conduct himself to an incoming bishop; and though he was well aware of all Dr. Proudie's abominable opinions as regarded dissenters, church reform, the hebdomadal council, and such like; though he disliked the man, and hated the doctrines, still he was prepared to show respect to the station of the bishop. So he and Mr. Harding called together at the palace.

His lordship was at home, and the two visitors were shown through the accustomed hall into the well-known room, where the good old bishop used to sit. The furniture had been bought at a valuation, and every chair and table, every bookshelf against the wall, and every square in the carpet, was as well known to each of them as their own bedrooms. Nevertheless they at once felt that they were strangers there. The furniture was for the most part the same, yet the place had been metamorphosed. A new sofa had been introduced, a horrid chintz affair, most unprelatical and almost irreligious: such a sofa as never yet stood in the study of any decent high church clergyman of the Church of England. The old curtains had also given away. They had, to be sure, become dingy, and that which had been originally a rich and goodly ruby had degenerated into a reddish brown. Mr. Harding, however, thought the old reddish brown much preferable to the gaudy buff-coloured trumpery moreen which Mrs. Proudie had deemed good enough for her husband's own room in the provincial city of Barchester.

Our friends found Dr. Proudie sitting on the old bishop's chair, looking very nice in his new apron; they found, too,

Mr. Slope standing on the hearthrug, persuasive and eager, just as the archdeacon used to stand; but on the sofa they also found Mrs. Proudie, an innovation for which a precedent might in vain be sought in all the annals of the Barchester bishopric!

There she was, however, and they could only make the best of her. The introductions were gone through in much form. The archdeacon shook hands with the bishop, and named Mr. Harding, who received such an amount of greeting as was due from a bishop to a precentor. His lordship then presented them to his lady wife; the archdeacon first, with archidiaconal honours, and then the precentor with diminished parade. After this Mr. Slope presented himself. The bishop, it is true, did mention his name, and so did Mrs. Proudie too, in a louder tone; but Mr. Slope took upon himself the chief burden of his own introduction. He had great pleasure in making himself acquainted with Dr. Grantly; he had heard much of the archdeacon's good works in that part of the diocese in which his duties as archdeacon had been exercised (thus purposely ignoring the archdeacon's hitherto unlimited dominion over the diocese at large). He was aware that his lordship depended greatly on the assistance which Dr. Grantly would be able to give him in that portion of his diocese. He then thrust out his hand, and grasping that of his new foe, bedewed it unmercifully. Dr. Grantly in return bowed, looked stiff, contracted his eyebrows, and wiped his hand with his pocket-handkerchief. Nothing abashed, Mr. Slope then noticed the precentor, and descended to the grade of the lower clergy. He gave him a squeeze of the hand, damp indeed, but affectionate, and was very glad to make the acquaintance of Mr. ——; oh yes, Mr. Harding; he had not exactly caught the name—'Precentor in the cathedral,' surmised Mr. Slope. Mr. Harding confessed that such was the humble sphere of his work. 'Some parish duty as well,' suggested Mr. Slope. Mr. Harding acknowledged the diminutive incumbency of St. Cuthbert's. Mr. Slope then left him alone, having condescended sufficiently, and joined the conversation among the higher powers.

There were four persons there, each of whom considered

himself the most important personage in the diocese ;
himself, indeed, or herself, as Mrs. Proudie was one of
them ; and with such a difference of opinion it was not
probable that they would get on pleasantly together.
The bishop himself actually wore the visible apron, and
trusted mainly to that—to that and his title, both being
facts which could not be overlooked.   The archdeacon
knew his subject, and really understood the business of
bishoping, which the others did not ; and this was his
strong ground.   Mrs. Proudie had her sex to back her,
and her habit of command, and was nothing daunted
by the high tone of Dr. Grantly's face and figure.   Mr.
Slope had only himself and his own courage and tact to
depend on, but he nevertheless was perfectly self-assured,
and did not doubt but that he should soon get the better
of weak men who trusted so much to externals, as both
bishop and archdeacon appeared to do.

‘ Do you reside in Barchester, Dr. Grantly ? ’ asked
the lady with her sweetest smile.

Dr. Grantly explained that he lived in his own parish
of Plumstead Episcopi, a few miles out of the city.   Whereupon the lady hoped that the distance was not too great
for country visiting, as she would be so glad to make the
acquaintance of Mrs. Grantly.   She would take the earliest
opportunity, after the arrival of her horses at Barchester ;
their horses were at present in London ; their horses were
not immediately coming down, as the bishop would be
obliged, in a few days, to return to town.   Dr. Grantly
was no doubt aware that the bishop was at present much
called upon by the ‘ University Improvement Committee : ’
indeed, the Committee could not well proceed without
him, as their final report had now to be drawn up.   The
bishop had also to prepare a scheme for the ‘ Manufacturing Towns Morning and Evening Sunday School Society,’
of which he was a patron, or president, or director, and
therefore the horses would not come down to Barchester
at present ; but whenever the horses did come down,
she would take the earliest opportunity of calling at
Plumstead Episcopi, providing the distance was not too
great for country visiting.

The archdeacon made his fifth bow : he had made one
at each mention of the horses ; and promised that Mrs.

Grantly would do herself the honour of calling at the palace on an early day. Mrs. Proudie declared that she would be delighted : she hadn't liked to ask, not being quite sure whether Mrs. Grantly had horses; besides, the distance might have been, &c. &c.

Dr. Grantly again bowed, but said nothing. He could have bought every individual possession of the whole family of the Proudies, and have restored them as a gift, without much feeling the loss ; and had kept a separate pair of horses for the exclusive use of his wife since the day of his marriage; whereas Mrs. Proudie had been hitherto jobbed about the streets of London at so much a month during the season ; and at other times had managed to walk, or hire a smart fly from the livery stables.

' Are the arrangements with reference to the Sabbath-day schools generally pretty good in your archdeaconry ? ' asked Mr. Slope.

' Sabbath-day schools ! ' repeated the archdeacon with an affectation of surprise. ' Upon my word, I can't tell ; it depends mainly on the parson's wife and daughters. There is none at Plumstead.'

This was almost a fib on the part of the Archdeacon, for Mrs. Grantly has a very nice school. To be sure it is not a Sunday school exclusively, and is not so designated ; but that exemplary lady always attends there an hour before church, and hears the children say their catechism, and sees that they are clean and tidy for church, with their hands washed, and their shoes tied ; and Grisel and Florinda, her daughters, carry thither a basket of large buns, baked on the Saturday afternoon, and distribute them to all the children not especially under disgrace, which buns are carried home after church with considerable content, and eaten hot at tea, being then split and toasted. The children of Plumstead would indeed open their eyes if they heard their venerated pastor declare that there was no Sunday school in his parish.

Mr. Slope merely opened his eyes wider, and slightly shrugged his shoulders. He was not, however, prepared to give up his darling project.

' I fear there is a great deal of Sabbath travelling here,' said he. ' On looking at the " Bradshaw," I see that there are three trains in and three out every Sabbath. Could nothing be done to induce the company to withdraw them ? Don't you think, Dr. Grantly, that a little energy might diminish the evil ? '

'Not being a director, I really can't say. But if you can withdraw the passengers, the company, I dare say, will withdraw the trains,' said the doctor. 'It's merely a question of dividends.'

'But surely, Dr. Grantly,' said the lady, 'surely we should look at it differently. You and I, for instance, in our position : surely we should do all that we can to control so grievous a sin. Don't you think so, Mr. Harding ? ' and she turned to the precentor, who was sitting mute and unhappy.

Mr. Harding thought that all porters and stokers, guards, breaksmen, and pointsmen ought to have an opportunity of going to church, and he hoped that they all had.

'But surely, surely,' continued Mrs. Proudie, 'surely that is not enough. Surely that will not secure such an observance of the Sabbath as we are taught to conceive is not only expedient but indispensable ; surely——'

Come what come might, Dr. Grantly was not to be forced into a dissertation on a point of doctrine with Mrs. Proudie, nor yet with Mr. Slope ; so without much ceremony he turned his back upon the sofa, and began to hope that Dr. Proudie had found that the palace repairs had been such as to meet his wishes.

'Yes, yes,' said his lordship ; upon the whole he thought so—upon the whole, he didn't know that there was much ground for complaint ; the architect, perhaps, might have ——but his double, Mr. Slope, who had sidled over to the bishop's chair, would not allow his lordship to finish his ambiguous speech.

'There is one point I would like to mention, Mr. Archdeacon. His lordship asked me to step through the premises, and I see that the stalls in the second stable are not perfect.'

'Why—there's standing there for a dozen horses,' said the archdeacon.

'Perhaps so,' said the other ; 'indeed, I've no doubt of it ; but visitors, you know, often require so much accommodation. There are so many of the bishop's relatives who always bring their own horses.'

Dr. Grantly promised that due provision for the relatives' horses should be made, as far at least as the extent of the original stable building would allow. He would himself communicate with the architect.

'And the coach-house, Dr. Grantly,' continued Mr. Slope; 'there is really hardly room for a second carriage in the large coach-house, and the smaller one, of course, holds only one.'

'And the gas,' chimed in the lady; 'there is no gas through the house, none whatever, but in the kitchen and passages. Surely the palace should have been fitted through with pipes for gas, and hot water too. There is no hot water laid on anywhere above the ground-floor; surely there should be the means of getting hot water in the bed-rooms without having it brought in jugs from the kitchen.'

The bishop had a decided opinion that there should be pipes for hot water. Hot water was very essential for the comfort of the palace. It was, indeed, a requisite in any decent gentleman's house.

Mr. Slope had remarked that the coping on the garden wall was in many places imperfect.

Mrs. Proudie had discovered a large hole, evidently the work of rats, in the servants' hall.

The bishop expressed an utter detestation of rats. There was nothing, he believed, in this world, that he so much hated as a rat.

Mr. Slope had, moreover, observed that the locks of the out-houses were very imperfect: he might specify the coal-cellar, and the wood-house.

Mrs. Proudie had also seen that those on the doors of the servants' bedrooms were in an equally bad condition; indeed the locks all through the house were old-fashioned and unserviceable.

The bishop thought that a great deal depended on a good lock, and quite as much on the key. He had observed that the fault very often lay with the key, especially if the wards were in any way twisted.

Mr. Slope was going on with his catalogue of grievances, when he was somewhat loudly interrupted by the arch-

deacon, who succeeded in explaining that the diocesan
architect, or rather his foreman, was the person to be
addressed on such subjects; and that he, Dr. Grantly,
had inquired as to the comfort of the palace, merely as
a point of compliment. He was sorry, however, that so
many things had been found amiss: and then he rose
from his chair to escape.

Mrs. Proudie, though she had contrived to lend her
assistance in recapitulating the palatial dilapidations,
had not on that account given up her hold of Mr. Harding,
nor ceased from her cross-examinations as to the iniquity of
Sabbatical amusements. Over and over again had she
thrown out her ' Surely, surely,' at Mr. Harding's devoted
head, and ill had that gentleman been able to parry the
attack.

He had never before found himself subjected to such
a nuisance. Ladies hitherto, when they had consulted
him on religious subjects, had listened to what he might
choose to say with some deference, and had differed, if
they differed, in silence. But Mrs. Proudie interrogated
him, and then lectured. ' Neither thou, nor thy son,
nor thy daughter, nor thy man servant, nor thy maid
servant,' said she, impressively, and more than once, as
though Mr. Harding had forgotten the words. She shook
her finger at him as she quoted the favourite law, as though
menacing him with punishment; and then called upon
him categorically to state whether he did not think that
travelling on the Sabbath was an abomination and a
desecration.

Mr. Harding had never been so hard pressed in his life.
He felt that he ought to rebuke the lady for presuming
so to talk to a gentleman and a clergyman many years
her senior; but he recoiled from the idea of scolding the
bishop's wife, in the bishop's presence, on his first visit
to the palace; moreover, to tell the truth, he was somewhat afraid of her. She, seeing him sit silent and absorbed,
by no means refrained from the attack.

' I hope, Mr. Harding,' said she, shaking her head
slowly and solemnly, ' I hope you will not leave me to
think that you approve of Sabbath travelling,' and she
looked a look of unutterable meaning into his eyes.

There was no standing this, for Mr. Slope was now

looking at him, and so was the bishop, and so was the
archdeacon, who had completed his adieux on that side
of the room. Mr. Harding therefore got up also, and
putting out his hand to Mrs. Proudie said : ' If you will
come to St. Cuthbert's some Sunday, I will preach you
a sermon on that subject.'

And so the archdeacon and the precentor took their
departure, bowing low to the lady, shaking hands with
the lord, and escaping from Mr. Slope in the best manner
each could. Mr. Harding was again maltreated ; but
Dr. Grantly swore deeply in the bottom of his heart,
that no earthly consideration should ever again induce
him to touch the paw of that impure and filthy animal.

And now, had I the pen of a mighty poet, would I sing
in epic verse the noble wrath of the archdeacon. The
palace steps descend to a broad gravel sweep, from whence
a small gate opens out into the street, very near the
covered gateway leading into the close. The road from
the palace door turns to the left, through the spacious
gardens, and terminates on the London-road, half a mile
from the cathedral.

Till they had both passed this small gate and entered
the close, neither of them spoke a word ; but the precentor
clearly saw from his companion's face that a tornado
was to be expected, nor was he himself inclined to stop
it. Though by nature far less irritable than the archdeacon, even he was angry : he even—that mild and
courteous man—was inclined to express himself in anything but courteous terms.

CHAPTER VI

WAR

' GOOD heavens ! '' exclaimed the archdeacon, as he
placed his foot on the gravel walk of the close, and raising
his hat with one hand, passed the other somewhat violently
over his now grizzled locks ; smoke issued forth from
the uplifted beaver as it were a cloud of wrath, and the
safety-valve of his anger opened, and emitted a visible
steam, preventing positive explosion and probable
apoplexy. ' Good heavens ! '—and the archdeacon

looked up to the gray pinnacles of the cathedral tower, making a mute appeal to that still living witness which had looked down on the doings of so many bishops of Barchester.

'I don't think I shall ever like that Mr. Slope,' said Mr. Harding.

'Like him!' roared the archdeacon, standing still for a moment to give more force to his voice; 'like him!' All the ravens of the close cawed their assent. The old bells of the tower, in chiming the hour, echoed the words; and the swallows flying out from their nests mutely expressed a similar opinion. Like Mr. Slope! Why no, it was not very probable that any Barchester-bred living thing should like Mr. Slope!

'Nor Mrs. Proudie either,' said Mr. Harding.

The archdeacon hereupon forgot himself. I will not follow his example, nor shock my readers by transcribing the term in which he expressed his feeling as to the lady who had been named. The ravens and the last lingering notes of the clock bells were less scrupulous, and repeated in corresponding echoes the very improper exclamation. The archdeacon again raised his hat, and another salutary escape of steam was effected.

There was a pause, during which the precentor tried to realise the fact that the wife of a bishop of Barchester had been thus designated, in the close of the cathedral, by the lips of its own archdeacon: but he could not do it.

'The bishop seems to be a quiet man enough,' suggested Mr. Harding, having acknowledged to himself his own failure.

'Idiot!' exclaimed the doctor, who for the nonce was not capable of more than such spasmodic attempts at utterance.

'Well, he did not seem very bright,' said Mr. Harding, 'and yet he has always had the reputation of a clever man. I suppose he's cautious and not inclined to express himself very freely.'

The new bishop of Barchester was already so contemptible a creature in Dr. Grantly's eyes, that he could not condescend to discuss his character. He was a puppet to be played by others; a mere wax doll, done up in an apron and a shovel hat, to be stuck on a throne or elsewhere,

and pulled about by wires as others chose. Dr. Grantly
did not choose to let himself down low enough to talk
about Dr. Proudie; but he saw that he would have to
talk about the other members of his household, the
coadjutor bishops, who had brought his lordship down,
as it were, in a box, and were about to handle the wires
as they willed. This in itself was a terrible vexation to
the archdeacon. Could he have ignored the chaplain,
and have fought the bishop, there would have been, at
any rate, nothing degrading in such a contest. Let the
Queen make whom she would bishop of Barchester;
a man, or even an ape, when once a bishop, would be a
respectable adversary, if he would but fight, himself.
But what was such a person as Dr. Grantly to do, when
such another person as Mr. Slope was put forward as his
antagonist?

If he, our archdeacon, refused the combat, Mr. Slope
would walk triumphant over the field, and have the
diocese of Barchester under his heel.

If, on the other hand, the archdeacon accepted as his
enemy the man whom the new puppet bishop put before
him as such, he would have to talk about Mr. Slope, and
write about Mr. Slope, and in all matters treat with Mr.
Slope, as a being standing, in some degree, on ground
similar to his own. He would have to meet Mr. Slope;
to——Bah! the idea was sickening. He could not bring
himself to have to do with Mr. Slope.

'He is the most thoroughly bestial creature that ever
I set my eyes upon,' said the archdeacon.

'Who—the bishop?' asked the other, innocently.

'Bishop! no—I'm not talking about the bishop. How
on earth such a creature got ordained!—they'll ordain
anybody now, I know; but he's been in the church these
ten years; and they used to be a little careful ten years ago.'

'Oh! you mean Mr. Slope.'

'Did you ever see any animal less like a gentleman?'
asked Dr. Grantly.

'I can't say I felt myself much disposed to like him.'

'Like him!' again shouted the doctor, and the assenting
ravens again cawed an echo; 'of course, you don't like
him: it's not a question of liking. But what are we to
do with him?'

'Do with him ?' asked Mr. Harding.

'Yes—what are we to do with him ? How are we to treat him ? There he is, and there he'll stay. He has put his foot in that palace, and he will never take it out again till he's driven. How are we to get rid of him ?'

'I don't suppose he can do us much harm.'

'Not do harm !—Well, I think you'll find yourself of a different opinion before a month is gone. What would you say now, if he got himself put into the hospital ? Would that be harm ?'

Mr. Harding mused awhile, and then said he didn't think the new bishop would put Mr. Slope into the hospital.

'If he doesn't put him there, he'll put him somewhere else where he'll be as bad. I tell you that that man, to all intents and purposes, will be Bishop of Barchester ;' and again Dr. Grantly raised his hat, and rubbed his hand thoughtfully and sadly over his head.

'Impudent scoundrel !' he continued after a while. 'To dare to cross-examine me about the Sunday schools in the diocese, and Sunday travelling too : I never in my life met his equal for sheer impudence. Why, he must have thought we were two candidates for ordination !'

'I declare I thought Mrs. Proudie was the worst of the two,' said Mr. Harding.

'When a woman is impertinent, one must only put up with it, and keep out of her way in future ; but I am not inclined to put up with Mr. Slope. "Sabbath travelling !"' and the doctor attempted to imitate the peculiar drawl of the man he so much disliked : '"Sabbath travelling !" Those are the sort of men who will ruin the Church of England, and make the profession of a clergyman disreputable. It is not the dissenters or the papists that we should fear, but the set of canting, low-bred hypocrites who are wriggling their way in among us : men who have no fixed principle, no standard ideas of religion or doctrine, but who take up some popular cry, as this fellow has done about "Sabbath travelling."'

Dr. Grantly did not again repeat the question aloud, but he did so constantly to himself, 'What were they to do with Mr. Slope ?' How was he openly, before the world, to show that he utterly disapproved of and abhorred such a man ?

Hitherto Barchester had escaped the taint of any extreme rigour of church doctrine. The clergymen of the city and neighbourhood, though very well inclined to promote high-church principles, privileges, and prerogatives, had never committed themselves to tendencies, which are somewhat too loosely called Puseyite practices. They all preached in their black gowns, as their fathers had done before them; they wore ordinary black cloth waistcoats; they had no candles on their altars, either lighted or unlighted; they made no private genuflexions, and were contented to confine themselves to such ceremonial observances as had been in vogue for the last hundred years. The services were decently and demurely read in their parish churches, chanting was confined to the cathedral, and the science of intoning was unknown. One young man who had come direct from Oxford as a curate to Plumstead had, after the lapse of two or three Sundays, made a faint attempt, much to the bewilderment of the poorer part of the congregation. Dr. Grantly had not been present on the occasion; but Mrs. Grantly, who had her own opinion on the subject, immediately after the service expressed a hope that the young gentleman had not been taken ill, and offered to send him all kinds of condiments supposed to be good for a sore throat. After that there had been no more intoning at Plumstead Episcopi.

But now the archdeacon began to meditate on some strong measures of absolute opposition. Dr. Proudie and his crew were of the lowest possible order of Church of England clergymen, and therefore it behoved him, Dr. Grantly, to be of the very highest. Dr. Proudie would abolish all forms and ceremonies, and therefore Dr. Grantly felt the sudden necessity of multiplying them. Dr. Proudie would consent to deprive the church of all collective authority and rule, and therefore Dr. Grantly would stand up for the full power of convocation, and the renewal of all its ancient privileges.

It was true that he could not himself intone the service, but he could procure the co-operation of any number of gentlemanlike curates well trained in the mystery of doing so. He would not willingly alter his own fashion of dress, but he could people Barchester with young clergymen dressed in the longest frocks, and in the highest-breasted silk waistcoats. He certainly was not prepared to cross himself, or to advocate the real presence ; but, without going this length, there were various observances, by adopting which he could plainly show his antipathy to such men as Dr. Proudie and Mr. Slope.

All these things passed through his mind as he paced up and down the close with Mr. Harding. War, war, internecine war was in his heart. He felt that, as regarded himself and Mr. Slope, one of the two must be annihilated as far as the city of Barchester was concerned ; and he did not intend to give way until there was not left to him an inch of ground on which he could stand. He still flattered himself that he could make Barchester too hot to hold Mr. Slope, and he had no weakness of spirit to prevent his bringing about such a consummation if it were in his power.

'I suppose Susan must call at the palace,' said Mr. Harding.

'Yes, she shall call there ; but it shall be once and once only. I dare say "the horses" won't find it convenient to come out to Plumstead very soon, and when that once is done the matter may drop.'

'I don't suppose Eleanor need call. I don't think Eleanor would get on at all well with Mrs. Proudie.'

'Not the least necessity in life,' replied the archdeacon, not without the reflection that a ceremony which was necessary for his wife, might not be at all binding on the widow of John Bold. 'Not the slighest reason on earth why she should do so, if she doesn't like it. For myself, I don't think that any decent young woman should be subjected to the nuisance of being in the same room with that man.'

And so the two clergymen parted, Mr. Harding going to his daughter's house, and the archdeacon seeking the seclusion of his brougham.

The new inhabitants of the palace did not express any higher opinion of their visitors than their visitors had expressed of them. Though they did not use quite such strong language as Dr. Grantly had done, they felt as much personal aversion, and were quite as well aware as he was that there would be a battle to be fought, and that there was hardly room for Proudieism in Barchester as long as Grantlyism was predominant.

Indeed, it may be doubted whether Mr. Slope had not already within his breast a better prepared system of strategy, a more accurately-defined line of hostile conduct than the archdeacon. Dr. Grantly was going to fight because he found that he hated the man. Mr. Slope had predetermined to hate the man, because he foresaw the necessity of fighting him. When he had first reviewed the *carte du pays*, previous to his entry into Barchester, the idea had occurred to him of conciliating the archdeacon, of cajoling and flattering him into submission, and of obtaining the upper hand by cunning instead of courage. A little inquiry, however, sufficed to convince him that all his cunning would fail to win over such a man as Dr. Grantly to such a mode of action as that to be adopted by Mr. Slope ; and then he determined to fall back upon his courage. He at once saw that open battle against Dr. Grantly and all Dr. Grantly's adherents was a necessity of his position, and he deliberately planned the most expedient methods of giving offence.

Soon after his arrival the bishop had intimated to the dean that, with the permission of the canon then in residence, his chaplain would preach in the cathedral on the next Sunday. The canon in residence happened to be the Hon. and Rev. Dr. Vesey Stanhope, who at this time was very busy on the shores of the Lake of Como, adding to that unique collection of butterflies for which he is so famous. Or, rather, he would have been in residence but for the butterflies and other such summer-day considerations ; and the vicar-choral, who was to take his place in the pulpit, by no means objected to having his work done for him by Mr. Slope.

Mr. Slope accordingly preached, and if a preacher can have satisfaction in being listened to, Mr. Slope ought to have been gratified. I have reason to think that he was gratified, and that he left the pulpit with the conviction that he had done what he intended to do when he entered it.

On this occasion the new bishop took his seat for the first time in the throne allotted to him. New scarlet cushions and drapery had been prepared, with new gilt binding and new fringe. The old carved oak-wood of the throne, ascending with its numerous grotesque pinnacles half-way up to the roof of the choir, had been washed, and dusted, and rubbed, and it all looked very smart. Ah ! how often sitting there, in happy early days, on those lowly benches in front of the altar, have I whiled away the tedium of a sermon in considering how best I might thread my way up amidst those wooden towers, and climb safely to the topmost pinnacle !

All Barchester went to hear Mr. Slope ; either for that or to gaze at the new bishop. All the best bonnets of the city were there, and moreover all the best glossy clerical hats. Not a stall but had its fitting occupant ; for though some of the prebendaries might be away in Italy or elsewhere, their places were filled by brethren, who flocked into Barchester on the occasion. The dean was there, a heavy old man, now too old, indeed, to attend frequently in his place ; and so was the archdeacon. So also were the chancellor, the treasurer, the precentor, sundry canons and minor canons, and every lay member of the choir, prepared to sing the new bishop in with due melody and harmonious expression of sacred welcome.

The service was certainly very well performed. Such was always the case at Barchester, as the musical education of the choir had been good, and the voices had been carefully selected. The psalms were beautifully chanted ; the Te Deum was magnificently sung ; and the litany was given in a manner, which is still to be found at Barchester, but, if my taste be correct, is to be found nowhere else. The litany in Barchester cathedral has long been the special task to which Mr. Harding's skill and voice have been devoted. Crowded audiences generally make good performers, and though Mr. Harding was not aware of any extraordinary exertion on his part, yet probably he rather exceeded his usual mark. Others were doing their best, and it was natural that he should emulate his brethren. So the service went on, and at last Mr. Slope got into the pulpit.

He chose for his text a verse from the precepts addressed by St. Paul to Timothy, as to the conduct necessary in a spiritual pastor and guide, and it was immediately evident that the good clergy of Barchester were to have a lesson.

'Study to show thyself approved unto God, a workman that needeth not to be ashamed, rightly dividing the word of truth.' These were the words of his text, and with such a subject in such a place, it may be supposed that such a preacher would be listened to by such an audience. He was listened to with breathless attention, and not without considerable surprise. Whatever opinion of Mr. Slope might have been held in Barchester before he commenced his discourse, none of his hearers, when it was over, could mistake him either for a fool or a coward.

It would not be becoming were I to travestie a sermon, or even to repeat the language of it in the pages of a novel. In endeavouring to depict the characters of the persons of whom I write, I am to a certain extent forced to speak of sacred things. I trust, however, that I shall not be thought to scoff at the pulpit, though some may imagine that I do not feel all the reverence that is due to the cloth. I may question the infallibility of the teachers, but I hope that I shall not therefore be accused of doubt as to the thing to be taught.

Mr. Slope, in commencing his sermon, showed no slight tact in his ambiguous manner of hinting that, humble as he was himself, he stood there as the mouthpiece of the illustrious divine who sat opposite to him; and having premised so much, he gave forth a very accurate definition of the conduct which that prelate would rejoice to see in the clergymen now brought under his jurisdiction. It is only necessary to say, that the peculiar points insisted upon were exactly those which were most distasteful to the clergy of the diocese, and most averse to their practice and opinions; and that all those peculiar habits and privileges which have always been dear to high-church priests, to that party which is now scandalously called the high-and-dry church, were ridiculed, abused, and anathematised. Now, the clergymen of the diocese of Barchester are all of the high-and-dry church.

Having thus, according to his own opinion, explained how a clergyman should show himself approved unto God, as a workman that needeth not to be ashamed, he went on to explain how the word of truth should be divided; and here he took a rather narrow view of the question, and fetched his arguments from afar. His

object was to express his abomination of all ceremonious
modes of utterance, to cry down any religious feeling
which might be excited, not by the sense, but by the
sound of words, and in fact to insult cathedral practices.
Had St. Paul spoken of rightly pronouncing instead of
rightly dividing the word of truth, this part of his sermon
would have been more to the purpose; but the preacher's
immediate object was to preach Mr. Slope's doctrine,
and not St. Paul's, and he contrived to give the necessary
twist to the text with some skill.

He could not exactly say, preaching from a cathedral
pulpit, that chanting should be abandoned in cathedral
services. By such an assertion, he would have overshot
his mark and rendered himself absurd, to the delight of
his hearers. He could, however, and did, allude with
heavy denunciations to the practice of intoning in parish
churches, although the practice was all but unknown in
the diocese; and from thence he came round to the undue
preponderance, which he asserted, music had over meaning
in the beautiful service which they had just heard. He
was aware, he said, that the practices of our ancestors
could not be abandoned at a moment's notice; the feelings
of the aged would be outraged, and the minds of respectable men would be shocked. There were many, he was
aware, of not sufficient calibre of thought to perceive,
of not sufficient education to know, that a mode of service,
which was effective when outward ceremonies were of
more moment than inward feelings, had become all but
barbarous at a time when inward conviction was everything, when each word of the minister's lips should fall
intelligibly into the listener's heart. Formerly the
religion of the multitude had been an affair of the imagination: now, in these latter days, it had become necessary
that a Christian should have a reason for his faith—should
not only believe, but digest—not only hear, but understand. The words of our morning service, how beautiful,
how apposite, how intelligible they were, when read with
simple and distinct decorum! but how much of the
meaning of the words was lost when they were produced
with all the meretricious charms of melody! &c. &c.

Here was a sermon to be preached before Mr. Archdeacon Grantly, Mr. Precentor Harding, and the rest of

them! before a whole dean and chapter assembled in
their own cathedral! before men who had grown old in
the exercise of their peculiar services, with a full conviction of their excellence for all intended purposes! This
too from such a man, a clerical *parvenu*, a man without
a cure, a mere chaplain, an intruder among them; a
fellow raked up, so said Dr. Grantly, from the gutters of
Marylebone! They had to sit through it! None of them,
not even Dr. Grantly, could close his ears, nor leave the
house of God during the hours of service. They were
under an obligation of listening, and that too, without
any immediate power of reply.

There is, perhaps, no greater hardship at present
inflicted on mankind in civilised and free countries, than
the necessity of listening to sermons. No one but a
preaching clergyman has, in these realms, the power
of compelling an audience to sit silent, and be tormented.
No one but a preaching clergyman can revel in platitudes,
truisms, and untruisms, and yet receive, as his undisputed
privilege, the same respectful demeanour as though words
of impassioned eloquence, or persuasive logic, fell from
his lips. Let a professor of law or physic find his place
in a lecture-room, and there pour forth jejune words and
useless empty phrases, and he will pour them forth to
empty benches. Let a barrister attempt to talk without
talking well, and he will talk but seldom. A judge's charge
need be listened to per force by none but the jury, prisoner,
and gaoler. A member of Parliament can be coughed
down or counted out. Town-councillors can be tabooed.
But no one can rid himself of the preaching clergyman.
He is the bore of the age, the old man whom we Sindbads
cannot shake off, the nightmare that disturbs our Sunday's
rest, the incubus that overloads our religion and makes
God's service distasteful. We are not forced into church!
No: but we desire more than that. We desire not to
be forced to stay away. We desire, nay, we are resolute,
to enjoy the comfort of public worship; but we desire
also that we may do so without an amount of tedium
which ordinary human nature cannot endure with patience;
that we may be able to leave the house of God, without
that anxious longing for escape, which is the common
consequence of common sermons.

With what complacency will a young parson deduce false conclusions from misunderstood texts, and then threaten us with all the penalties of Hades if we neglect to comply with the injunctions he has given us! Yes, my too self-confident juvenile friend, I do believe in those mysteries, which are so common in your mouth; I do believe in the unadulterated word which you hold there in your hand; but you must pardon me if, in some things, I doubt your interpretation. The bible is good, the prayer-book is good, nay, you yourself would be acceptable, if you would read to me some portion of those time-honoured discourses which our great divines have elaborated in the full maturity of their powers. But you must excuse me, my insufficient young lecturer, if I yawn over your imperfect sentences, your repeated phrases, your false pathos, your drawlings and denouncings, your humming and hawing, your oh-ing and ah-ing, your black gloves and your white handkerchief. To me, it all means nothing; and hours are too precious to be so wasted——if one could only avoid it.

And here I must make a protest against the pretence, so often put forward by the working clergy, that they are overburdened by the multitude of sermons to be preached. We are all too fond of our own voices, and a preacher is encouraged in the vanity of making his heard by the privilege of a compelled audience. His sermon is the pleasant morsel of his life, his delicious moment of self-exaltation. 'I have preached nine sermons this week,' said a young friend to me the other day, with hand languidly raised to his brow, the picture of an over-burdened martyr. 'Nine this week, seven last week, four the week before. I have preached twenty-three sermons this month. It is really too much.' 'Too much, indeed,' said I, shuddering; 'too much for the strength of any one.' 'Yes,' he answered meekly, 'indeed it is; I am beginning to feel it painfully.' 'Would,' said I, 'you could feel it—would that you could be made to feel it.' But he never guessed that my heart was wrung for the poor listeners.

There was, at any rate, no tedium felt in listening to Mr. Slope on the occasion in question. His subject came too home to his audience to be dull; and, to tell the truth,

Mr. Slope had the gift of using words forcibly. He was heard through his thirty minutes of eloquence with mute attention and open ears; but with angry eyes, which glared round from one enraged parson to another, with wide-spread nostrils from which already burst forth fumes of indignation, and with many shufflings of the feet and uneasy motions of the body, which betokened minds disturbed, and hearts not at peace with all the world.

At last the bishop, who, of all the congregation, had been most surprised, and whose hair almost stood on end with terror, gave the blessing in a manner not at all equal to that in which he had long been practising it in his own study, and the congregation was free to go their way.

CHAPTER VII

THE DEAN AND CHAPTER TAKE COUNSEL

ALL Barchester was in a tumult. Dr. Grantly could hardly get himself out of the cathedral porch before he exploded in his wrath. The old dean betook himself silently to his deanery, afraid to speak; and there sat, half stupefied, pondering many things in vain. Mr. Harding crept forth solitary and unhappy; and, slowly passing beneath the elms of the close, could scarcely bring himself to believe that the words which he had heard had proceeded from the pulpit of Barchester cathedral. Was he again to be disturbed? was his whole life to be shown up as a useless sham a second time? would he have to abdicate his precentorship, as he had his wardenship, and to give up chanting, as he had given up his twelve old bedesmen? And what if he did! Some other Jupiter, some other Mr. Slope, would come and turn him out of St. Cuthbert's. Surely he could not have been wrong all his life in chanting the litany as he had done! He began, however, to have his doubts. Doubting himself was Mr. Harding's weakness. It is not, however, the usual fault of his order.

Yes! all Barchester was in a tumult. It was not only the clergy who were affected. The laity also had listened to Mr. Slope's new doctrine, all with surprise, some with indignation, and some with a mixed feeling, in which dislike of the preacher was not so strongly blended. The old bishop and his chaplains, the dean and his canons and minor canons, the old choir, and especially Mr. Harding who was at the head of it, had all been popular in Barchester. They had spent their money and done good; the poor had not been ground down; the clergy in society had neither been overbearing nor austere; and the whole repute of the city was due to its ecclesiastical importance. Yet there were those who had heard Mr. Slope with satisfaction.

It is so pleasant to receive a fillip of excitement when suffering from the dull routine of every-day life! The anthems and Te Deums were in themselves delightful, but they had been heard so often! Mr. Slope was certainly not delightful, but he was new, and, moreover, clever. They had long thought it slow, so said now many of the Barchesterians, to go on as they had done in their old humdrum way, giving ear to none of the religious changes which were moving the world without. People in advance of the age now had new ideas, and it was quite time that Barchester should go in advance. Mr. Slope might be right. Sunday certainly had not been strictly kept in Barchester, except as regarded the cathedral services. Indeed the two hours between services had long been appropriated to morning calls and hot luncheons. Then Sunday schools! really more ought to have been done as to Sunday schools; Sabbath-day schools Mr. Slope had called them. The late bishop had really not thought of Sunday schools as he should have done. (These people probably did not reflect that catechisms and collects are quite as hard work to the young mind as book-keeping is to the elderly; and that quite as little feeling of worship enters into the one task as the other.) And then, as regarded that great question of musical services, there might be much to be said on Mr. Slope's side of the question. It certainly was the fact, that people went to the cathedral to hear the music, &c. &c.

And so a party absolutely formed itself in Barchester on Mr. Slope's side of the question! This consisted, among the upper classes, chiefly of ladies. No man— that is, no gentleman—could possibly be attracted by

Mr. Slope, or consent to sit at the feet of so abhorrent a Gamaliel. Ladies are sometimes less nice in their appreciation of physical disqualification; and, provided that a man speak to them well, they will listen, though he speak from a mouth never so deformed and hideous. Wilkes was most fortunate as a lover; and the damp, sandy-haired, saucer-eyed, red-fisted Mr. Slope was powerful only over the female breast.

There were, however, one or two of the neighbouring clergy who thought it not quite safe to neglect the baskets in which for the nonce were stored the loaves and fishes of the diocese of Barchester. They, and they only, came to call on Mr. Slope after his performance in the cathedral pulpit. Among these Mr. Quiverful, the rector of Pudding-dale, whose wife still continued to present him from year to year with fresh pledges of her love, and so to increase his cares and, it is to be hoped, his happiness equally. Who can wonder that a gentleman, with fourteen living children and a bare income of 400*l.* a year, should look after the loaves and fishes, even when they are under the thumb of a Mr. Slope?

Very soon after the Sunday on which the sermon was preached, the leading clergy of the neighbourhood held high debate together as to how Mr. Slope should be put down. In the first place he should never again preach from the pulpit of Barchester cathedral. This was Dr. Grantly's earliest dictum; and they all agreed, providing only that they had the power to exclude him. Dr. Grantly declared that the power rested with the dean and chapter, observing that no clergyman out of the chapter had a claim to preach there, saving only the bishop himself. To this the dean assented, but alleged that contests on such a subject would be unseemly; to which rejoined a meagre little doctor, one of the cathedral prebendaries, that the contest must be all on the side of Mr. Slope if every prebendary were always there ready to take his own place in the pulpit. Cunning little meagre doctor, whom it suits well to live in his own cosy house within Barchester close, and who is well content to have his little fling at Dr. Vesey Stanhope and other absentees, whose Italian villas, or enticing London homes, are more tempting than cathedral stalls and residences!

To this answered the burly chancellor, a man rather silent indeed, but very sensible, that absent prebendaries had their vicars, and that in such case the vicar's right to the pulpit was the same as that of the higher order. To which the dean assented, groaning deeply at these truths. Thereupon, however, the meagre doctor remarked that they would be in the hands of their minor canons, one of whom might at any hour betray his trust. Whereon was heard from the burly chancellor an ejaculation sounding somewhat like ' Pooh, pooh, pooh ! ' but it might be that the worthy man was but blowing out the heavy breath from his windpipe. Why silence him at all ? suggested Mr. Harding. Let them not be ashamed to hear what any man might have to preach to them, unless he preached false doctrine ; in which case, let the bishop silence him. So spoke our friend ; vainly ; for human ends must be attained by human means. But the dean saw a ray of hope out of those purblind old eyes of his. Yes, let them tell the bishop how distasteful to them was this Mr. Slope : a new bishop just come to his seat could not wish to insult his clergy while the gloss was yet fresh on his first apron.

Then up rose Dr. Grantly ; and, having thus collected the scattered wisdom of his associates, spoke forth with words of deep authority. When I say up rose the archdeacon, I speak of the inner man, which then sprang up to more immediate action, for the doctor had, bodily, been standing all along with his back to the dean's empty fire-grate, and the tails of his frock coat supported over his two arms. His hands were in his breeches pockets.

' It is quite clear that this man must not be allowed to preach again in this cathedral. We all see that, except our dear friend here, the milk of whose nature runs so softly, that he would not have the heart to refuse the Pope the loan of his pulpit, if the Pope would come and ask it. We must not, however, allow the man to preach again here. It is not because his opinion on church matters may be different from ours—with that one would not quarrel. It is because he has purposely insulted us. When he went up into the pulpit last Sunday, his studied object was to give offence to men who had grown old in reverence of those things of which he dared to speak so slightingly. What! to come here a stranger, a young, unknown, and unfriended stranger, and tell us, in the name of the bishop his master, that we are ignorant of our duties, old-fashioned, and useless! I don't know whether most to admire his courage or his impudence! And one thing I will tell you: that sermon originated solely with the man himself. The bishop was no more a party to it than was the dean here. You all know how grieved I am to see a bishop in this diocese holding the latitudinarian ideas by which Dr. Proudie has made himself conspicuous. You all know how greatly I should distrust the opinion of such a man. But in this matter I hold him to be blameless. I believe Dr. Proudie has lived too long among gentlemen to be guilty, or to instigate another to be guilty, of so gross an outrage. No! that man uttered what was untrue when he hinted that he was speaking as the mouthpiece of the bishop. It suited his ambitious views at once to throw down the gauntlet to us—at once to defy us here in the quiet of our own religious duties—here within the walls of our own loved cathedral —here where we have for so many years exercised our ministry without schism and with good repute. Such an attack upon us, coming from such a quarter, is abominable.'

'Abominable,' groaned the dean. 'Abominable,' muttered the meagre doctor. 'Abominable,' re-echoed the chancellor, uttering the sound from the bottom of his deep chest. 'I really think it was,' said Mr. Harding.

'Most abominable and most unjustifiable,' continued the archdeacon. 'But, Mr. Dean, thank God, that pulpit is still our own: your own, I should say. That pulpit belongs solely to the dean and chapter of Barchester Cathedral, and, as yet, Mr. Slope is no part of that chapter. You, Mr. Dean, have suggested that we should appeal to the bishop to abstain from forcing this man on us; but what if the bishop allow himself to be ruled by his chaplain? In my opinion, the matter is in our own hands. Mr. Slope cannot preach there without permission asked and obtained, and let that permission be invariably refused. Let all participation in the ministry of the cathedral service be refused to him. Then, if the bishop choose to interfere, we shall know what answer to make to the bishop My

friend here has suggested that this man may again find
his way into the pulpit by undertaking the duty of some
of your minor canons; but I am sure that we may fully
trust to these gentlemen to support us, when it is known
that the dean objects to any such transfer.'

'Of course you may,' said the chancellor.

There was much more discussion among the learned
conclave, all of which, of course, ended in obedience to
the archdeacon's commands. They had too long been
accustomed to his rule to shake it off so soon; and in
this particular case they had none of them a wish to abet
the man whom he was so anxious to put down.

Such a meeting as that we have just recorded is not
held in such a city as Barchester unknown and untold
of. Not only was the fact of the meeting talked of in
every respectable house, including the palace, but the
very speeches of the dean, the archdeacon, and chancellor
were repeated; not without many additions and imaginary circumstances, according to the tastes and opinions
of the relaters.

All, however, agreed in saying that Mr. Slope was to
be debarred from opening his mouth in the cathedral of
Barchester; many believed that the vergers were to be
ordered to refuse him even the accommodation of a seat;
and some of the most far-going advocates for strong
measures, declared that his sermon was looked upon as
an indictable offence, and that proceedings were to be
taken against him for brawling.

The party who were inclined to defend him—the
enthusiastically religious young ladies, and the middle-
aged spinsters desirous of a move—of course took up his
defence the more warmly on account of this attack. If
they could not hear Mr. Slope in the cathedral, they would
hear him elsewhere; they would leave the dull dean, the
dull old prebendaries, and the scarcely less dull young
minor canons, to preach to each other; they would work
slippers and cushions, and hem bands for Mr. Slope, make
him a happy martyr, and stick him up in some new Sion
or Bethesda, and put the cathedral quite out of fashion.

Dr. and Mrs. Proudie at once returned to London.
They thought it expedient not to have to encounter any
personal application from the dean and chapter respecting

the sermon, till the violence of the storm had expended itself; but they left Mr. Slope behind them nothing daunted, and he went about his work zealously, flattering such as would listen to his flattery, whispering religious twaddle into the ears of foolish women, ingratiating himself with the few clergy who would receive him, visiting the houses of the poor, inquiring into all people, prying into everything, and searching with his minutest eye into all palatial dilapidations. He did not, however, make any immediate attempt to preach again in the cathedral.

And so all Barchester was by the ears.

CHAPTER VIII

THE EX-WARDEN REJOICES IN HIS PROBABLE RETURN TO THE HOSPITAL

AMONG the ladies in Barchester who have hitherto acknowledged Mr. Slope as their spiritual director, must not be reckoned either the widow Bold, or her sister-in-law. On the first outbreak of the wrath of the denizens of the close, none had been more animated against the intruder than these two ladies. And this was natural. Who could be so proud of the musical distinction of their own cathedral as the favourite daughter of the precentor? Who would be so likely to resent an insult offered to the old choir? And in such matters Miss Bold and her sister-in-law had but one opinion.

This wrath, however, has in some degree been mitigated, and I regret to say that these ladies allowed Mr. Slope to be his own apologist. About a fortnight after the sermon had been preached, they were both of them not a little surprised by hearing Mr. Slope announced, as the page in buttons opened Mrs. Bold's drawing-room door. Indeed, what living man could, by a mere morning visit, have surprised them more? Here was the great enemy of all that was good in Barchester coming into their own drawing-room, and they had no strong arm, no ready tongue, near at hand for their protection. The widow snatched her baby out of its cradle into her lap, and Mary

Bold stood up ready to die manfully in that baby's behalf, should, under any circumstances, such a sacrifice become necessary.

In this manner was Mr. Slope received. But when he left, he was allowed by each lady to take her hand, and to make his adieux as gentlemen do who have been graciously entertained! Yes; he shook hands with them, and was curtseyed out courteously, the buttoned page opening the door, as he would have done for the best canon of them all. He had touched the baby's little hand and blessed him with a fervid blessing; he had spoken to the widow of her early sorrows, and Eleanor's silent tears had not rebuked him; he had told Mary Bold that her devotion would be rewarded, and Mary Bold had heard the praise without disgust. And how had he done all this? how had he so quickly turned aversion into, at any rate, acquaintance? how had he overcome the enmity with which these ladies had been ready to receive him, and made his peace with them so easily?

My readers will guess from what I have written that I myself do not like Mr. Slope; but I am constrained to admit that he is a man of parts. He knows how to say a soft word in the proper place; he knows how to adapt his flattery to the ears of his hearers; he knows the wiles of the serpent, and he uses them. Could Mr. Slope have adapted his manners to men as well as to women, could he ever have learnt the ways of a gentleman, he might have risen to great things.

He commenced his acquaintance with Eleanor by praising her father. He had, he said, become aware that he had unfortunately offended the feelings of a man of whom he could not speak too highly; he would not now allude to a subject which was probably too serious for drawing-room conversation, but he would say, that it had been very far from him to utter a word in disparagement of a man, of whom all the world, at least the clerical world, spoke so highly as it did of Mr. Harding. And so he went on, unsaying a great deal of his sermon, expressing his highest admiration for the precentor's musical talents, eulogising the father and the daughter and the sister-in-law, speaking in that low silky whisper which he always had specially prepared for feminine ears, and, ultimately, gaining his object. When he left, he expressed a hope that he might again be allowed to call; and though Eleanor gave no verbal assent to this, she did not express dissent: and so Mr. Slope's right to visit at the widow's house was established.

The day after this visit Eleanor told her father of it, and expressed an opinion that Mr. Slope was not quite so black as he had been painted. Mr. Harding opened his eyes rather wider than usual when he heard what had occurred, but he said little; he could not agree in any praise of Mr. Slope,. and it was not his practice to say much evil of any one. He did not, however, like the visit, and simple-minded as he was, he felt sure that Mr. Slope had some deeper motive than the mere pleasure of making soft speeches to two ladies.

Mr. Harding, however, had come to see his daughter with other purpose than that of speaking either good or evil of Mr. Slope. He had come to tell her that the place of warden in Hiram's hospital was again to be filled up, and that in all probability he would once more return to his old home and his twelve bedesmen.

'But,' said, he, laughing, 'I shall be greatly shorn of my ancient glory.'

'Why so, papa?'

'This new act of parliament, that is to put us all on our feet again,' continued he, 'settles my income at four hundred and fifty pounds per annum.'

'Four hundred and fifty,' said she, 'instead of eight hundred! Well; that is rather shabby. But still, papa, you'll have the dear old house and the garden?'

'My dear,' said he, 'it's worth twice the money;' and as he spoke he showed a jaunty kind of satisfaction in his tone and manner, and in the quick, pleasant way in which he paced Eleanor's drawing-room. 'It's worth twice the money. I shall have the house and the garden, and a larger income than I can possibly want.'

'At any rate, you'll have no extravagant daughter to provide for;' and as she spoke, the young widow put her arm within his, and made him sit on the sofa beside her; 'at any rate you'll not have that expense.'

'No, my dear; and I shall be rather lonely without her; but we won't think of that now. As regards income I shall have plenty for all I want. I shall have my old house; and I don't mind owning now that I have felt sometimes the inconvenience of living in a lodging. Lodgings are very nice for young men, but at my time of life there is a want of——I hardly know what to call it, perhaps not respectability——'

'Oh, papa! I'm sure there's been nothing like that. Nobody has thought it; nobody in all Barchester has been more respected than you have been since you took those rooms in High Street. Nobody! Not the dean in his deanery, or the archdeacon out at Plumstead.'

'The archdeacon would not be much obliged to you if he heard you,' said he, smiling somewhat at the exclusive manner in which his daughter confined her illustration to the church dignitaries of the chapter of Barchester; 'but at any rate I shall be glad to get back to the old house. Since I heard that it was all settled, I have begun to fancy that I can't be comfortable without my two sitting-rooms.'

'Come and stay with me, papa, till it is settled—there's a dear papa.'

'Thank ye, Nelly. But no; I won't do that. It would make two movings. I shall be very glad to get back to my old men again. Alas! alas! There have six of them gone in these few last years. Six out of twelve! And the others I fear have had but a sorry life of it there. Poor Bunce, poor old Bunce!'

Bunce was one of the surviving recipients of Hiram's charity; an old man, now over ninety, who had long been a favourite of Mr. Harding's.

'How happy old Bunce will be,' said Mrs. Bold, clapping her soft hands softly. 'How happy they all will be to have you back again. You may be sure there will soon be friendship among them again when you are there.'

'But,' said he, half laughing, 'I am to have new troubles, which will be terrible to me. There are to be twelve old women, and a matron. How shall I manage twelve women and a matron!'

'The matron will manage the women of course.'

'And who'll manage the matron?' said he.

'She won't want to be managed. She'll be a great lady herself, I suppose. But, papa, where will the matron live ? She is not to live in the warden's house with you, is she ? '

' Well, I hope not, my dear.'

' Oh, papa, I tell you fairly, I won't have a matron for a new step-mother.'

' You shan't, my dear ; that is, if I can help it. But they are going to build another house for the matron and the women ; and I believe they haven't even fixed yet on the site of the building.'

' And have they appointed the matron ? ' said Eleanor.

' They haven't appointed the warden yet,' replied he.

' But there's no doubt about that, I suppose,' said his daughter.

Mr. Harding explained that he thought there was no doubt ; that the archdeacon had declared as much, saying that the bishop and his chaplain between them had not the power to appoint any one else, even if they had the will to do so, and sufficient impudence to carry out such a will. The archdeacon was of opinion, that though Mr. Harding had resigned his wardenship, and had done so unconditionally, he had done so under circumstances which left the bishop no choice as to his re-appointment, now that the affair of the hospital had been settled on a new basis by act of parliament. Such was the archdeacon's opinion, and his father-in-law received it without a shadow of doubt.

Dr. Grantly had always been strongly opposed to Mr. Harding's resignation of the place. He had done all in his power to dissuade him from it. He had considered that Mr. Harding was bound to withstand the popular clamour with which he was attacked for receiving so large an income as eight hundred a year from such a charity, and was not even yet satisfied that his father-in-law's conduct had not been pusillanimous and undignified. He looked also on this reduction of the warden's income as a shabby, paltry scheme on the part of government for escaping from a difficulty into which it had been brought by the public press. Dr. Grantly observed that the government had no more right to dispose of a sum of four hundred and fifty pounds a year out of the income of Hiram's legacy, than of nine hundred ; whereas, as he said, the bishop, dean, and chapter clearly had a right

to settle what sum should be paid. He also declared that
the government had no more right to saddle the charity
with twelve old women than with twelve hundred; and
he was, therefore, very indignant on the matter. He
probably forgot when so talking that government had
done nothing of the kind, and had never assumed any such
might or any such right. He made the common mistake
of attributing to the government, which in such matters
is powerless, the doings of parliament, which in such
matters is omnipotent.

But though he felt that the glory and honour of the
situation of warden of Barchester hospital were indeed
curtailed by the new arrangement; that the whole establishment had to a certain degree been made vile by the
touch of Whig commissioners; that the place with its
lessened income, its old women, and other innovations,
was very different from the hospital of former days;
still the archdeacon was too practical a man of the world
to wish that his father-in-law, who had at present little
more than 200l. per annum for all his wants, should refuse
the situation, defiled, undignified, and commission-ridden
as it was.

Mr. Harding had, accordingly, made up his mind that
he would return to his old home at the hospital, and to
tell the truth, had experienced almost a childish pleasure
in the idea of doing so. The diminished income was to
him not even the source of momentary regret. The matron
and the old women did rather go against the grain; but
he was able to console himself with the reflection, that,
after all, such an arrangement might be of real service
to the poor of the city. The thought that he must receive
his re-appointment as the gift of the new bishop, and
probably through the hands of Mr. Slope, annoyed him
a little; but his mind was set at rest by the assurance
of the archdeacon that there would be no favour in such
a presentation. The re-appointment of the old warden
would be regarded by all the world as a matter of course.
Mr. Harding, therefore, felt no hesitation in telling his
daughter that they might look upon his return to his old
quarters as a settled matter.

' And you won't have to ask for it, papa.'
' Certainly not, my dear. There is no ground on which

I could ask for any favour from the bishop, whom, indeed,
I hardly know. Nor would I ask a favour, the granting
of which might possibly be made a question to be settled
by Mr. Slope. No,' said he, moved for a moment by a spirit
very unlike his own, ' I certainly shall be very glad to go
back to the hospital; but I should never go there, if it
were necessary that my doing so should be the subject
of a request to Mr. Slope.'

This little outbreak of her father's anger jarred on the
present tone of Eleanor's mind. She had not learnt to
like Mr. Slope, but she had learnt to think that he had
much respect for her father; and she would, therefore,
willingly use her efforts to induce something like good
feeling between them.

' Papa,' said she, ' I think you somewhat mistake Mr.
Slope's character.'

' Do I ? ' said he, placidly.

' I think you do, papa. I think he intended no personal
disrespect to you when he preached the sermon which
made the archdeacon and the dean so angry ! '

' I never supposed he did, my dear. I hope I never
inquired within myself whether he did or no. Such a
matter would be unworthy of any inquiry, and very
unworthy of the consideration of the chapter. But I
fear he intended disrespect to the ministration of God's
services, as conducted in conformity with the rules of
the Church of England.'

' But might it not be that he thought it his duty to
express his dissent from that which you, and the dean,
and all of us here so much approve ? '

' It can hardly be the duty of a young man rudely to
assail the religious convictions of his elders in the church.
Courtesy should have kept him silent, even if neither
charity nor modesty could do so.'

' But Mr. Slope would say that on such a subject the
commands of his heavenly Master do not admit of his
being silent.'

' Nor of his being courteous, Eleanor ? '

' He did not say that, papa.'

' Believe me, my child, that Christian ministers are
never called on by God's word to insult the convictions,
or even the prejudices of their brethren ; and that religion

is at any rate not less susceptible of urbane and courteous conduct among men, than any other study which men may take up. I am sorry to say that I cannot defend Mr. Slope's sermon in the cathedral. But come, my dear, put on your bonnet, and let us walk round the dear old gardens at the hospital. I have never yet had the heart to go beyond the court-yard since we left the place. Now I think I can venture to enter.'

Eleanor rang the bell, and gave a variety of imperative charges as to the welfare of the precious baby, whom, all but unwillingly, she was about to leave for an hour or so, and then sauntered forth with her father to revisit the old hospital. It had been forbidden ground to her as well as to him since the day on which they had walked forth together from its walls.

CHAPTER IX

THE STANHOPE FAMILY

It is now three months since Dr. Proudie began his reign, and changes have already been effected in the diocese which show at least the energy of an active mind. Among other things absentee clergymen have been favoured with hints much too strong to be overlooked. Poor dear old Bishop Grantly had on this matter been too lenient, and the archdeacon had never been inclined to be severe with those who were absent on reputable pretences, and who provided for their duties in a liberal way.

Among the greatest of the diocesan sinners in this respect was Dr. Vesey Stanhope. Years had now passed since he had done a day's duty; and yet there was no reason against his doing duty except a want of inclination on his own part. He held a prebendal stall in the diocese; one of the best residences in the close; and the two large rectories of Crabtree Canonicorum, and Stogpingum. Indeed, he had the cure of three parishes, for that of Eiderdown was joined to Stogpingum. He had resided in Italy for twelve years. His first going there had been attributed to a sore throat; and that sore throat, though never repeated in any violent manner, had stood him in such stead, that it had enabled him to live in easy idleness ever since.

He had now been summoned home—not, indeed, with rough violence, or by any peremptory command, but by a mandate which he found himself unable to disregard. Mr. Slope had written to him by the bishop's desire. In the first place, the bishop much wanted the valuable co-operation of Dr. Vesey Stanhope in the diocese; in the next, the bishop thought it his imperative duty to become personally acquainted with the most conspicuous of his diocesan clergy; then the bishop thought it essentially necessary for Dr. Stanhope's own interests, that Dr. Stanhope should, at any rate for a time, return to Barchester; and lastly, it was said that so strong a feeling was at the present moment evinced by the hierarchs of the church with reference to the absence of its clerical members, that it behoved Dr. Vesey Stanhope not to allow his name to stand among those which would probably in a few months be submitted to the councils of the nation.

There was something so ambiguously frightful in this last threat that Dr. Stanhope determined to spend two or three summer months at his residence in Barchester. His rectories were inhabited by his curates, and he felt himself from disuse to be unfit for parochial duty; but his prebendal home was kept empty for him, and he thought it probable that he might be able now and again to preach a prebendal sermon. He arrived, therefore, with all his family at Barchester, and he and they must be introduced to my readers.

The great family characteristic of the Stanhopes might probably be said to be heartlessness; but this want of feeling was, in most of them, accompanied by so great an amount of good nature as to make itself but little noticeable to the world. They were so prone to oblige their neighbours that their neighbours failed to perceive how indifferent to them was the happiness and well-being of those around them. The Stanhopes would visit you in your sickness (provided it were not contagious), would bring you oranges, French novels, and the last new bit of scandal, and then hear of your death or your recovery

with an equally indifferent composure. Their conduct
to each other was the same as to the world; they bore
and forebore: and there was sometimes, as will be seen,
much necessity for forbearing: but their love among
themselves rarely reached above this. It is astonishing
how much each of the family was able to do, and how
much each did, to prevent the well-being of the other
four.

For there were five in all; the doctor, namely, and
Mrs. Stanhope, two daughters, and one son. The doctor,
perhaps, was the least singular and most estimable of
them all, and yet such good qualities as he possessed
were all negative. He was a good looking rather plethoric
gentleman of about sixty years of age. His hair was
snow white, very plentiful, and somewhat like wool of
the finest description. His whiskers were very large and
very white, and gave to his face the appearance of a
benevolent sleepy old lion. His dress was always unexceptionable. Although he had lived so many years in Italy
it was invariably of a decent clerical hue, but it never
was hyperclerical. He was a man not given to much
talking, but what little he did say was generally well
said. His reading seldom went beyond romances and
poetry of the lightest and not always most moral description. He was thoroughly a *bon vivant*; an accomplished
judge of wine, though he never drank to excess; and
a most inexorable critic in all affairs touching the kitchen.
He had had much to forgive in his own family, since a
family had grown up around him, and had forgiven
everything—except inattention to his dinner. His weakness in that respect was now fully understood, and his
temper but seldom tried. As Dr. Stanhope was a clergyman, it may be supposed that his religious convictions
made up a considerable part of his character; but this
was not so. That he had religious convictions must be
believed; but he rarely obtruded them, even on his
children. This abstinence on his part was not systematic,
but very characteristic of the man. It was not that he
had predetermined never to influence their thoughts;
but he was so habitually idle that his time for doing so
had never come till the opportunity for doing so was gone
for ever. Whatever conviction the father may have had,

the children were at any rate but indifferent members of the church from which he drew his income.

Such was Dr. Stanhope. The features of Mrs. Stanhope's character were even less plainly marked than those of her lord. The *far niente* of her Italian life had entered into her very soul, and brought her to regard a state of inactivity as the only earthly good. In manner and appearance she was exceedingly prepossessing. She had been a beauty, and even now, at fifty-five, she was a handsome woman. Her dress was always perfect: she never dressed but once in the day, and never appeared till between three and four; but when she did appear, she appeared at her best. Whether the toil rested partly with her, or wholly with her handmaid, it is not for such a one as the author even to imagine. The structure of her attire was always elaborate, and yet never over laboured. She was rich in apparel, but not bedizened with finery; her ornaments were costly, rare, and such as could not fail to attract notice, but they did not look as though worn with that purpose. She well knew the great architectural secret of decorating her constructions, and never descended to construct a decoration. But when we have said that Mrs. Stanhope knew how to dress, and used her knowledge daily, we have said all. Other purpose in life she had none. It was something, indeed, that she did not interfere with the purposes of others. In early life she had undergone great trials with reference to the doctor's dinners; but for the last ten or twelve years her eldest daughter Charlotte had taken that labour off her hands, and she had had little to trouble her;— little, that is, till the edict for this terrible English journey had gone forth: since, then, indeed, her life had been laborious enough. For such a one, the toil of being carried from the shores of Como to the city of Barchester is more than labour enough, let the care of the carriers be ever so vigilant. Mrs. Stanhope had been obliged to have every one of her dresses taken in from the effects of the journey.

Charlotte Stanhope was at this time about thirty-five years old; and, whatever may have been her faults, she had none of those which belong particularly to old young ladies. She neither dressed young, nor talked young, nor indeed looked young. She appeared to be perfectly content with her time of life, and in no way affected the graces of youth. She was a fine young woman; and had she been a man, would have been a very fine young man. All that was done in the house, and that was not done by servants, was done by her. She gave the orders, paid the bills, hired and dismissed the domestics, made the tea, carved the meat, and managed everything in the Stanhope household. She, and she alone, could ever induce her father to look into the state of his worldly concerns. She, and she alone, could in any degree control the absurdities of her sister. She, and she alone, prevented the whole family from falling into utter disrepute and beggary. It was by her advice that they now found themselves very unpleasantly situated in Barchester.

So far, the character of Charlotte Stanhope is not unprepossessing. But it remains to be said, that the influence which she had in her family, though it had been used to a certain extent for their worldly well-being, had not been used to their real benefit, as it might have been. She had aided her father in his indifference to his professional duties, counselling him that his livings were as much his individual property as the estates of his elder brother were the property of that worthy peer. She had for years past stifled every little rising wish for a return to England which the doctor had from time to time expressed. She had encouraged her mother in her idleness in order that she herself might be mistress and manager of the Stanhope household. She had encouraged and fostered the follies of her sister, though she was always willing, and often able, to protect her from their probable result. She had done her best, and had thoroughly succeeded in spoiling her brother, and turning him loose upon the world an idle man without a profession, and without a shilling that he could call his own.

Miss Stanhope was a clever woman, able to talk on most subjects, and quite indifferent as to what the subject was. She prided herself on her freedom from English prejudice, and she might have added, from feminine delicacy. On religion she was a pure freethinker, and with much want of true affection, delighted to throw out her own views before the troubled mind of her father.

To have shaken what remained of his Church of England faith would have gratified her much; but the idea of his abandoning his preferment in the church had never once presented itself to her mind. How could he indeed, when he had no income from any other source ?

But the two most prominent members of the family still remain to be described. The second child had been christened Madeline, and had been a great beauty. We need not say had been, for she was never more beautiful than at the time of which we write, though her person for many years had been disfigured by an accident. It is unnecessary that we should give in detail the early history of Madeline Stanhope. She had gone to Italy when about seventeen years of age, and had been allowed to make the most of her surpassing beauty in the saloons of Milan, and among the crowded villas along the shores of the Lake of Como. She had become famous for adventures in which her character was just not lost, and had destroyed the hearts of a dozen cavaliers without once being touched in her own. Blood had flowed in quarrels about her charms, and she heard of these encounters with pleasurable excitement. It had been told of her that on one occasion she had stood by in the disguise of a page, and had seen her lover fall.

As is so often the case, she had married the very worst of those who sought her hand. Why she had chosen Paulo Neroni, a man of no birth and no property, a mere captain in the pope's guard, one who had come up to Milan either simply as an adventurer or else as a spy, a man of harsh temper and oily manners, mean in figure, swarthy in face, and so false in words as to be hourly detected, need not now be told. When the moment for doing so came, she had probably no alternative, He, at any rate, had become her husband; and after a prolonged honeymoon among the lakes, they had gone together to Rome, the papal captain having vainly endeavoured to induce his wife to remain behind him.

Six months afterwards she arrived at her father's house a cripple, and a mother. She had arrived without even notice, with hardly clothes to cover her, and without one of those many ornaments which had graced her bridal *trousseau.* Her baby was in the arms of a poor girl from

Milan, whom she had taken in exchange for the Roman maid who had accompanied her thus far, and who had then, as her mistress said, become homesick and had returned. It was clear that the lady had determined that there should be no witness to tell stories of her life in Rome.

She had fallen, she said, in ascending a ruin, and had fatally injured the sinews of her knee; so fatally, that when she stood she lost eight inches of her accustomed height; so fatally, that when she essayed to move, she could only drag herself painfully along, with protruded hip and extended foot in a manner less graceful than that of a hunchback. She had consequently made up her mind, once and for ever, that she would never stand, and never attempt to move herself.

Stories were not slow to follow her, averring that she had been cruelly ill used by Neroni, and that to his violence had she owed her accident. Be that as it may, little had been said about her husband, but that little had made it clearly intelligible to the family that Signor Neroni was to be seen and heard of no more. There was no question as to re-admitting the poor ill used beauty to her old family rights, no question as to adopting her infant daughter beneath the Stanhope roof tree. Though heartless, the Stanhopes were not selfish. The two were taken in, petted, made' much of, for a time all but adored, and then felt by the two parents to be great nuisances in the house. But in the house the lady was, and there she remained, having her own way, though that way was not very conformable with the customary usages of an English clergyman.

Madame Neroni, though forced to give up all motion in the world, had no intention whatever of giving up the world itself. The beauty of her face was uninjured, and that beauty was of a peculiar kind. Her copious rich brown hair was worn in Grecian *bandeaux* round her head, displaying as much as possible of her forehead and cheeks. Her forehead, though rather low, was very beautiful from its perfect contour and pearly whiteness. Her eyes were long and large, and marvellously bright; might I venture to say, bright as Lucifer's, I should perhaps best express the depth of their brilliancy. They were dreadful eyes to look at, such as would absolutely deter any man of quiet mind and easy spirit from attempting a passage of arms with such foes. There was talent in them, and the fire of passion and the play of wit, but there was no love. Cruelty was there instead, and courage, a desire of masterhood, cunning, and a wish for mischief. And yet, as eyes, they were very beautiful. The eyelashes were long and perfect, and the long steady unabashed gaze, with which she would look into the face of her admirer, fascinated while it frightened him. She was a basilisk from whom an ardent lover of beauty could make no escape. Her nose and mouth and teeth and chin and neck and bust were perfect, much more so at twenty-eight than they had been at eighteen. What wonder that with such charms still glowing in her face, and with such deformity destroying her figure, she should resolve to be seen, but only to be seen reclining on a sofa.

Her resolve had not been carried out without difficulty. She had still frequented the opera at Milan; she had still been seen occasionally in the saloons of the *noblesse*; she had caused herself to be carried in and out from her carriage, and that in such a manner as in no wise to disturb her charms, disarrange her dress, or expose her deformities. Her sister always accompanied her and a maid, a man-servant also, and on state occasions, two. It was impossible that her purpose could have been achieved with less: and yet, poor as she was, she had achieved her purpose. And then again the more dissolute Italian youths of Milan frequented the Stanhope villa and surrounded her couch, not greatly to her father's satisfaction. Sometimes his spirit would rise, a dark spot would show itself on his cheek, and he would rebel; but Charlotte would assuage him with some peculiar triumph of her culinary art, and all again would be smooth for a while.

Madeline affected all manner of rich and quaint devices in the garniture of her room, her person, and her feminine belongings. In nothing was this more apparent than in the visiting card which she had prepared for her use. For such an article one would say that she, in her present state, could have but small need, seeing how improbable it was that she should make a morning call: but not such was her own opinion. Her card was surrounded by

a deep border of gilding; on this she had imprinted, in
three lines,—

> ' La Signora Madeline
>   ' Vesey Neroni.
> —Nata Stanhope.'

And over the name she had a bright gilt coronet, which
certainly looked very magnificent. How she had come
to concoct such a name for herself it would be difficult
to explain. Her father had been christened Vesey, as
another man is christened Thomas; and she had no more
right to assume it than would have the daughter of a
Mr. Josiah Jones to call herself Mrs. Josiah Smith, on
marrying a man of the latter name. The gold coronet
was equally out of place, and perhaps inserted with even
less excuse. Paulo Neroni had had not the faintest title
to call himself a scion of even Italian nobility. Had the
pair met in England Neroni would probably have been
a count; but they had met in Italy, and any such pretence
on his part would have been simply ridiculous. A coronet,
however, was a pretty ornament, and if it could solace
a poor cripple to have such on her card, who would
begrudge it to her?

Of her husband, or of his individual family, she never
spoke; but with her admirers she would often allude in
a mysterious way to her married life and isolated state,
and, pointing to her daughter, would call her the last of
the blood of the emperors, thus referring Neroni's extrac-
tion to the old Roman family from which the worst of
the Cæsars sprang.

The ' Signora ' was not without talent, and not without
a certain sort of industry; she was an indomitable letter
writer, and her letters were worth the postage: they
were full of wit, mischief, satire, love, latitudinarian
philosophy, free religion, and, sometimes, alas! loose
ribaldry. The subject, however, depended entirely on
the recipient, and she was prepared to correspond with
any one but moral young ladies or stiff old women. She
wrote also a kind of poetry, generally in Italian, and short
romances, generally in French. She read much of a
desultory sort of literature, and as a modern linguist had
really made great proficiency. Such was the lady who
had now come to wound the hearts of the men of Barchester.

Ethelbert Stanhope was in some respects like his younger sister, but he was less inestimable as a man than she as a woman. His great fault was an entire absence of that principle which should have induced him, as the son of a man without fortune, to earn his own bread. Many attempts had been made to get him to do so, but these had all been frustrated, not so much by idleness on his part, as by a disinclination to exert himself in any way not to his taste. He had been educated at Eton, and had been intended for the Church, but had left Cambridge in disgust after a single term, and notified to his father his intention to study for the bar. Preparatory to that, he thought it well that he should attend a German university, and consequently went to Leipsic. There he remained two years, and brought away a knowledge of German and a taste for the fine arts. He still, however, intended himself for the bar, took chambers, engaged himself to sit at the feet of a learned pundit, and spent a season in London. He there found that all his aptitudes inclined him to the life of an artist, and he determined to live by painting. With this object he returned to Milan, and had himself rigged out for Rome. As a painter he might have earned his bread, for he wanted only diligence to excel; but when at Rome his mind was carried away by other things: he soon wrote home for money, saying that he had been converted to the Mother Church, that he was already an acolyte of the Jesuits, and that he was about to start with others to Palestine on a mission for converting Jews. He did go to Judèa, but being unable to convert the Jews, was converted by them. He again wrote home, to say that Moses was the only giver of perfect laws to the world; that the coming of the true Messiah was at hand, that great things were doing in Palestine, and that he had met one of the family of Sidonia, a most remarkable man, who was now on his way to Western Europe, and whom he had induced to deviate from his route with the object of calling at the Stanhope villa. Ethelbert then expressed his hope that his mother and sisters would listen to this wonderful prophet. His father he knew could not do so from pecuniary considerations. This Sidonia, however, did not take so strong a fancy to him as another of that

family once did to a young English nobleman. At least
he provided him with no heaps of gold as large as lions;
so that the Judaised Ethelbert was again obliged to draw
on the revenues of the Christian Church.

It is needless to tell how the father swore that he would
send no more money and receive no Jew; nor how
Charlotte declared that Ethelbert could not be left penniless in Jerusalem, and how ' La Signora Neroni ' resolved
to have Sidonia at her feet. The money was sent, and
the Jew did come. The Jew did come, but he was not
at all to the taste of ' La Signora.' He was a dirty little
old man, and though he had provided no golden lions,
he had, it seems, relieved young Stanhope's necessities.
He positively refused to leave the villa till he had got
a bill from the doctor on his London bankers.

Ethelbert did not long remain a Jew. He soon reappeared at the villa without prejudices on the subject
of his religion, and with a firm resolve to achieve fame
and fortune as a sculptor. He brought with him some
models which he had originated at Rome, and which
really gave such fair promise that his father was induced
to go to further expense in furthering these views. Ethelbert opened an establishment, or rather took lodgings
and a workshop, at Carrara, and there spoilt much marble,
and made some few pretty images. Since that period,
now four years ago, he had alternated between Carrara
and the villa, but his sojourns at the workshop became
shorter and shorter, and those at the villa longer and
longer. 'Twas no wonder; for Carrara is not a spot in
which an Englishman would like to dwell.

When the family started for England he had resolved
not to be left behind, and with the assistance of his elder
sister had carried his point against his father's wishes.
It was necessary, he said, that he should come to England
for orders. How otherwise was he to bring his profession
to account ?

In personal appearance Ethelbert Stanhope was the
most singular of beings. He was certainly very handsome.
He · had his sister Madeline's eyes without their stare,
and without their hard cunning cruel firmness. They
were also very much lighter, and of so light and clear
a blue as to make his face remarkable, if nothing else did

so. On entering a room with him, Ethelbert's blue eyes
would be the first thing you would see, and on leaving
it almost the last you would forget. His light hair was
very long and silky, coming down over his coat. His
beard had been prepared in holy land, and was patriarchal.
He never shaved, and rarely trimmed it. It was glossy,
soft, clean, and altogether not unprepossessing. It was
such, that ladies might desire to reel it off and work it
into their patterns in lieu of floss silk. His complexion
was fair and almost pink, he was small in height, and
slender in limb, but well-made, and his voice was of
peculiar sweetness.

In manner and dress he was equally remarkable. He
had none of the *mauvaise honte* of an Englishman. He
required no introduction to make himself agreeable to
any person. He habitually addressed strangers, ladies
as well as men, without any such formality, and in doing
so never seemed to meet with rebuke. His costume
cannot be described, because it was so various ; but it
was always totally opposed in every principle of colour
and construction to the dress of those with whom he for
the time consorted.

He was habitually addicted to making love to ladies,
and did so without any scruple of conscience, or any idea
that such a practice was amiss. He had no heart to touch
himself, and was literally unaware that humanity was
subject to such an infliction. He had not thought much
about it ; but, had he been asked, would have said, that
ill-treating a lady's heart meant injuring her promotion
in the world. His principles therefore forbade him to
pay attention to a girl, if he thought any man was present
whom it might suit her to marry. In this manner, his
good nature frequently interfered with his amusement ;
but he had no other motive in abstaining from the fullest
declarations of love to every girl that pleased his eye.

Bertie Stanhope, as he was generally called, was,
however, popular with both sexes ; and with Italians
as well as English. His circle of acquaintance was very
large, and embraced people of all sorts. He had no
respect for rank, and no aversion to those below him.
He had lived on familiar terms with English peers, German
shopkeepers, and Roman priests. All people were nearly

alike to him. He was above, or rather below, all prejudices.
No virtue could charm him, no vice shock him. He had
about him a natural good manner, which seemed to
qualify him for the highest circles, and yet he was never
out of place in the lowest. He had no principle, no regard
for others, no self-respect, no desire to be other than a
drone in the hive, if only he could, as a drone, get what
honey was sufficient for him. Of honey, in his latter days,
it may probably be presaged, that he will have but short
allowance.

Such was the family of the Stanhopes, who, at this
period, suddenly joined themselves to the ecclesiastical
circle of Barchester close. Any stranger union, it would
be impossible perhaps to conceive. And it was not as
though they all fell down into the cathedral precincts
hitherto unknown and untalked of. In such case no
amalgamation would have been at all probable between
the new comers and either the Proudie set or the Grantly
set. But such was far from being the case. The Stanhopes
were all known by name in Barchester, and Barchester
was prepared to receive them with open arms. The
doctor was one of her prebendaries, one of her rectors,
one of her pillars of strength ; and was, moreover, counted
on, as a sure ally, both by Proudies and Grantlys.

He himself was the brother of one peer, and his wife
was the sister of another—and both these peers were
lords of whiggish tendency, with whom the new bishop
had some sort of alliance. This was sufficient to give to
Mr. Slope high hope that he might enlist Dr. Stanhope
on his side, before his enemies could out-manœuvre him.
On the other hand, the old dean had many many years
ago, in the days of the doctor's clerical energies, been
instrumental in assisting him in his views as to preferment ;
and many many years ago also, the two doctors, Stanhope
and Grantly, had, as young parsons, been joyous together
in the common rooms of Oxford. Dr. Grantly, consequently, did not doubt but that the new comer would
range himself under his banners.

Little did any of them dream of what ingredients the
Stanhope family was now composed.

CHAPTER X

MRS. PROUDIE'S RECEPTION—COMMENCED

THE bishop and his wife had only spent three or four days in Barchester on the occasion of their first visit. His lordship had, as we have seen, taken his seat on his throne; but his demeanour there, into which it had been his intention to infuse much hierarchal dignity, had been a good deal disarranged by the audacity of his chaplain's sermon. He had hardly dared to look his clergy in the face, and to declare by the severity of his countenance that in truth he meant all that his factotum was saying on his behalf; nor yet did he dare to throw Mr. Slope over, and show to those around him that he was no party to the sermon, and would resent it.

He had accordingly blessed his people in a shambling manner, not at all to his own satisfaction, and had walked back to his palace with his mind very doubtful as to what he would say to his chaplain on the subject. He did not remain long in doubt. He had hardly doffed his lawn when the partner of all his toils entered his study, and exclaimed even before she had seated herself—

'Bishop, did you ever hear a more sublime, more spirit-moving, more appropriate discourse than that?'

'Well, my love; ha—hum—he!' The bishop did not know what to say.

'I hope, my lord, you don't mean to say you disapprove?'

There was a look about the lady's eye which did not admit of my lord's disapproving at that moment. He felt that if he intended to disapprove, it must be now or never; but he also felt that it could not be now. It was not in him to say to the wife of his bosom that Mr. Slope's sermon was ill-timed, impertinent and vexatious.

'No, no,' replied the bishop. 'No, I can't say I disapprove—a very clever sermon and very well intended, and I dare say will do a great deal of good.' This last praise was added, seeing that what he had already said by no means satisfied Mrs. Proudie.

'I hope it will,' said she. 'I am sure it was well deserved.

Did you ever in your life, bishop, hear anything so like play-acting as the way in which Mr. Harding sings the litany ? I shall beg Mr. Slope to continue a course of sermons on the subject till all that is altered. We will have at any rate, in our cathedral, a decent, godly, modest morning service. There must be no more play-acting here now ; ' and so the lady rang for lunch.

The bishop knew more about cathedrals and deans, and precentors and church services than his wife did, and also more of a bishop's powers. But he thought it better at present to let the subject drop.

' My dear,' said he, ' I think we must go back to London on Tuesday. I find my staying here will be very inconvenient to the Government.'

The bishop knew that to this proposal his wife would not object ; and he also felt that by thus retreating from the ground of battle, the heat of the fight might be got over in his absence.

' Mr. Slope will remain here, of course ? ' said the lady.

' Oh, of course,' said the bishop.

Thus, after less than a week's sojourn in his palace, did the bishop fly from Barchester ; nor did he return to it for two months, the London season being then over. During that time Mr. Slope was not idle, but he did not again essay to preach in the cathedral. In answer to Mrs. Proudie's letters, advising a course of sermons, he had pleaded that he would at any rate wish to put off such an undertaking till she was there to hear them.

He had employed his time in consolidating a Proudie and Slope party—or rather a Slope and Proudie party, and he had not employed his time in vain. He did not meddle with the dean and chapter, except by giving them little teasing intimations of the bishop's wishes about this and the bishop's feelings about that, in a manner which was to them sufficiently annoying, but which they could not resent. He preached once or twice in a distant church in the suburbs of the city, but made no allusion to the cathedral service. He commenced the establishment of two ' Bishop's Barchester Sabbath-day Schools,' gave notice of a proposed ' Bishop's Barchester Young Men's Sabbath Evening Lecture Room,'—and wrote three or four letters to the manager of the Barchester branch railway, informing him how anxious the bishop was that the Sunday trains should be discontinued.

At the end of two months, however, the bishop and the lady reappeared; and as a happy harbinger of their return, heralded their advent by the promise of an evening party on the largest scale. The tickets of invitation were sent out from London—they were dated from Bruton Street, and were despatched by the odious Sabbath breaking railway, in a huge brown paper parcel to Mr. Slope. Everybody calling himself a gentleman, or herself a lady, within the city of Barchester, and a circle of two miles round it, was included. Tickets were sent to all the diocesan clergy, and also to many other persons of priestly note, of whose absence the bishop, or at least the bishop's wife, felt tolerably confident. It was intended, however, to be a thronged and noticeable affair, and preparations were made for receiving some hundreds.

And now there arose considerable agitation among the Grantlyites whether or no they would attend the episcopal bidding. The first feeling with them all was to send the briefest excuses both for themselves and their wives and daughters. But by degrees policy prevailed over passion. The archdeacon perceived that he would be making a false step if he allowed the cathedral clergy to give the bishop just ground of umbrage. They all met in conclave and agreed to go. They would show that they were willing to respect the office, much as they might dislike the man. They agreed to go. The old dean would crawl in, if it were but for half an hour. The chancellor, treasurer, archdeacon, prebendaries, and minor canons would all go, and would all take their wives. Mr. Harding was especially bidden to do so, resolving in his heart to keep himself far removed from Mrs. Proudie. And Mrs. Bold was determined to go, though assured by her father that there was no necessity for such a sacrifice on her part. When all Barchester was to be there, neither Eleanor nor Mary Bold understood why they should stay away. Had they not been invited separately? and had not a separate little note from the chaplain, couched in the most respectful language, been enclosed with the huge episcopal card?

And the Stanhopes would be there, one and all. Even

the lethargic mother would so far bestir herself on such an occasion. They had only just arrived. The card was at the residence waiting for them. No one in Barchester had seen them; and what better opportunity could they have of showing themselves to the Barchester world? Some few old friends, such as the archdeacon and his wife, had called, and had found the doctor and his eldest daughter; but the *élite* of the family were not yet known.

The doctor indeed wished in his heart to prevent the signora from accepting the bishop's invitation; but she herself had fully determined that she would accept it. If her father was ashamed of having his daughter carried into a bishop's palace, she had no such feeling.

' Indeed, I shall,' she had said to her sister who had gently endeavoured to dissuade her, by saying that the company would consist wholly of parsons and parsons' wives. ' Parsons, I suppose, are much the same as other men, if you strip them of their black coats; and as to their wives, I dare say they won't trouble me. You may tell papa I don't at all mean to be left at home.'

Papa was told, and felt that he could do nothing but yield. He also felt that it was useless for him now to be ashamed of his children. Such as they were, they had become such under his auspices; as he had made his bed, so he must lie upon it; as he had sown his seed, so must he reap his corn. He did not indeed utter such reflections in such language, but such was the gist of his thoughts. It was not because Madeline was a cripple that he shrank from seeing her make one of the bishop's guests; but because he knew that she would practise her accustomed lures, and behave herself in a way that could not fail of being distasteful to the propriety of Englishwomen. These things had annoyed but not shocked him in Italy. There they had shocked no one; but here in Barchester, here among his fellow parsons, he was ashamed that they should be seen. Such had been his feelings, but he repressed them. What if his brother clergymen were shocked! They could not take from him his preferment because the manners of his married daughter were too free.

La Signora Neroni had, at any rate, no fear that she would shock anybody. Her ambition was to create a sensation, to have parsons at her feet, seeing that the manhood of Barchester consisted mainly of parsons, and to send, if possible, every parson's wife home with a green fit of jealousy. None could be too old for her, and hardly any too young. None too sanctified, and none too worldly. She was quite prepared to entrap the bishop himself, and then to turn up her nose at the bishop's wife. She did not doubt of success, for she had always succeeded; but one thing was absolutely necessary, she must secure the entire use of a sofa.

The card sent to Dr. and Mrs. Stanhope and family, had been so sent in an envelope, having on the cover Mr. Slope's name. The signora soon learnt that Mrs. Proudie was not yet at the palace, and that the chaplain was managing everything. It was much more in her line to apply to him than to the lady, and she accordingly wrote him the prettiest little billet in the world. In five lines she explained everything, declared how impossible it was for her not to be desirous to make the acquaintance of such persons as the Bishop of Barchester and his wife, and she might add also of Mr. Slope, depicted her own grievous state, and concluded by being assured that Mrs. Proudie would forgive her extreme hardihood in petitioning to be allowed to be carried to a sofa. She then enclosed one of her beautiful cards. In return she received as polite an answer from Mr. Slope—a sofa should be kept in the large drawing-room, immediately at the top of the grand stairs, especially for her use.

And now the day of the party had arrived. The bishop and his wife came down from town, only on the morning of the eventful day, as behoved such great people to do; but Mr. Slope had toiled day and night to see that everything should be in right order. There had been much to do. No company had been seen in the palace since heaven knows when. New furniture had been required, new pots and pans, new cups and saucers, new dishes and plates. Mrs. Proudie had at first declared that she would condescend to nothing so vulgar as eating and drinking; but Mr. Slope had talked, or rather written her out of economy! Bishops should be given to hospitality, and hospitality meant eating and drinking. So the supper was conceded; the guests, however, were to stand as they consumed it.

There were four rooms opening into each other on the first floor of the house, which were denominated the drawing-rooms, the reception-room, and Mrs. Proudie's boudoir. In olden days one of these had been Bishop Grantly's bed-room, and another his common sitting-room and study. The present bishop, however, had been moved down into a back parlour, and had been given to understand, that he could very well receive his clergy in the dining-room, should they arrive in too large a flock to be admitted into his small sanctum. He had been un-willing to yield, but after a short debate had yielded.

Mrs. Proudie's heart beat high as she inspected her suite of rooms. They were really very magnificent, or at least would be so by candlelight; and they had never-theless been got up with commendable economy. Large rooms when full of people and full of light look well, because they are large, and are full, and are light. Small rooms are those which require costly fittings and rich furniture. Mrs. Proudie knew this, and made the most of it; she had therefore a huge gas lamp with a dozen burners hanging from each of the ceilings.

People were to arrive at ten, supper was to last from twelve till one, and at half-past one everybody was to be gone. Carriages were to come in at the gate in the town and depart at the gate outside. They were desired to take up at a quarter before one. It was managed excellently, and Mr. Slope was invaluable.

At half-past nine the bishop and his wife and their three daughters entered the great reception-room, and very grand and very solemn they were. Mr. Slope was down-stairs giving the last orders about the wine. He well understood that curates and country vicars with their belongings did not require so generous an article as the dignitaries of the close. There is a useful gradation in such things, and Marsala at 20s. a dozen did very well for the exterior supplementary tables in the corner.

' Bishop,' said the lady, as his lordship sat himself down, ' don't sit on that sofa, if you please; it is to be kept separate for a lady.'

The bishop jumped up and seated himself on a cane-bottomed chair. ' A lady?' he inquired meekly; ' do you mean one particular lady, my dear?'

' Yes, Bishop, one particular lady,' said his wife, disdaining to explain.

' She has got no legs, papa,' said the youngest daughter, tittering.

' No legs ! ' said the bishop, opening his eyes.

' Nonsense, Netta, what stuff you talk,' said Olivia. ' She has got legs, but she can't use them. She has always to be kept lying down, and three or four men carry her about everywhere.'

' Laws, how odd ! ' said Augusta. ' Always carried about by four men ! I'm sure I shouldn't like it. Am I right behind, mamma ? I feel as if I was open ; ' and she turned her back to her anxious parent.

' Open ! to be sure you are,' said she, ' and a yard of petticoat strings hanging out. I don't know why I pay such high wages to Mrs. Richards, if she can't take the trouble to see whether or no you are fit to be looked at,' and Mrs. Proudie poked the strings here, and twitched the dress there, and gave her daughter a shove and a shake, and then pronounced it all right.

' But,' rejoined the bishop, who was dying with curiosity about the mysterious lady and her legs, ' who is it that is to have the sofa ? What 's her name, Netta ? '

A thundering rap at the front door interrupted the conversation. Mrs. Proudie stood up and shook herself gently, and touched her cap on each side as she looked in the mirror. Each of the girls stood on tiptoe, and re-arranged the bows on their bosoms ; and Mr. Slope rushed up stairs three steps at a time.

' But who is it, Netta ? ' whispered the bishop to his youngest daughter.

' La Signora Madeline Vesey Neroni,' whispered back the daughter ; ' and mind you don't let any one sit upon the sofa.'

' La Signora Madeline Vicinironi ! ' muttered, to himself, the bewildered prelate. Had he been told that the Begum of Oude was to be there, or Queen Pomara of the Western Isles, he could not have been more astonished. La Signora Madeline Vicinironi, who, having no legs to stand on, had bespoken a sofa in his drawing-room !—who could she be ? He however could now make no further inquiry, as Dr. and Mrs. Stanhope were announced. They had been sent on out of the way a little before the time, in order that the signora might have plenty of time to get herself conveniently packed into the carriage.

The bishop was all smiles for the prebendary's wife, and the bishop's wife was all smiles for the prebendary. Mr. Slope was presented, and was delighted to make the acquaintance of one of whom he had heard so much. The doctor bowed very low, and then looked as though he could not return the compliment as regarded Mr. Slope, of whom, indeed, he had heard nothing. The doctor, in spite of his long absence, knew an English gentleman when he saw him.

And then the guests came in shoals: Mr. and Mrs. Quiverful and their three grown daughters. Mr. and Mrs. Chadwick and their three daughters. The burly chancellor and his wife and clerical son from Oxford. The meagre little doctor without incumbrance. Mr. Harding with Eleanor and Miss Bold. The dean leaning on a gaunt spinster, his only child now living with him, a lady very learned in stones, ferns, plants, and vermin, and who had written a book about petals. A wonderful woman in her way was Miss Trefoil. Mr. Finnie, the attorney, with his wife, was to be seen, much to the dismay of many who had never met him in a drawing-room before. The five Barchester doctors were all there, and old Scalpen, the retired apothecary and toothdrawer, who was first taught to consider himself as belonging to the higher orders by the receipt of the bishop's card. Then came the archdeacon and his wife, with their elder daughter Griselda, a slim pale retiring girl of seventeen, who kept close to her mother, and looked out on the world with quiet watchful eyes, one who gave promise of much beauty when time should have ripened it.

And so the rooms became full, and knots were formed, and every new comer paid his respects to my lord and passed on, not presuming to occupy too much of the great man's attention. The archdeacon shook hands very heartily with Doctor Stanhope, and Mrs. Grantly seated herself by the doctor's wife. And Mrs. Proudie moved about with well regulated grace, measuring out the quantity of her favours to the quality of her guests, just as Mr. Slope had been doing with the wine. But the sofa

was still empty, and five-and-twenty ladies and five
gentlemen had been courteously warned off it by the
mindful chaplain.

'Why doesn't she come?' said the bishop to himself.
His mind was so preoccupied with the signora, that he
hardly remembered how to behave himself *en bishop*.

At last a carriage dashed up to the hall steps with a
very different manner of approach from that of any other
vehicle that had been there that evening. A perfect
commotion took place. The doctor, who heard it as he
was standing in the drawing-room, knew that his daughter
was coming, and retired into the furthest corner, where
he might not see her entrance. Mrs. Proudie perked
herself up, feeling that some important piece of business
was in hand. The bishop was instinctively aware that
La Signora Vicinironi was come at last, and Mr. Slope
hurried into the hall to give his assistance.

He was, however, nearly knocked down and trampled
on by the cortège that he encountered on the hall steps.
He got himself picked up as well as he could, and followed
the cortège up stairs. The signora was carried head
foremost, her head being the care of her brother and an
Italian man-servant who was accustomed to the work;
her feet were in the care of the lady's maid and the lady's
Italian page; and Charlotte Stanhope followed to see
that all was done with due grace and decorum. In this
manner they climbed easily into the drawing-room, and
a broad way through the crowd having been opened, the
signora rested safely on her couch. She had sent a servant
beforehand to learn whether it was a right or a left hand
sofa, for it required that she should dress accordingly,
particularly as regarded her bracelets.

And very becoming her dress was. It was white velvet,
without any other garniture than rich white lace worked
with pearls across her bosom, and the same round the
armlets of her dress. Across her brow she wore a band
of red velvet, on the centre of which shone a magnificent
Cupid in mosaic, the tints of whose wings were of the most
lovely azure, and the colour of his chubby cheeks the
clearest pink. On the one arm which her position required
her to expose she wore three magnificent bracelets, each
of different stones. Beneath her on the sofa, and over the

cushion and head of it, was spread a crimson silk mantle or shawl, which went under her whole body and concealed her feet. Dressed as she was and looking as she did, so beautiful and yet so motionless, with the pure brilliancy of her white dress brought out and strengthened by the colour beneath it, with that lovely head, and those large bold bright staring eyes, it was impossible that either man or woman should do other than look at her.

Neither man nor woman for some minutes did do other.

Her bearers too were worthy of note. The three servants were Italian, and though perhaps not peculiar in their own country, were very much so in the palace at Barchester. The man especially attracted notice, and created a doubt in the mind of some whether he were a friend or a domestic. The same doubt was felt as to Ethelbert. The man was attired in a loose-fitting common black cloth morning coat. He had a jaunty fat well-pleased clean face, on which no atom of beard appeared, and he wore round his neck a loose black silk neckhandkerchief. The bishop essayed to make him a bow, but the man, who was well-trained, took no notice of him, and walked out of the room quite at his ease, followed by the woman and the boy.

Ethelbert Stanhope was dressed in light blue from head to foot. He had on the loosest possible blue coat, cut square like a shooting coat, and very short. It was lined with silk of azure blue. He had on a blue satin waistcoat, a blue neckhandkerchief which was fastened beneath his throat with a coral ring, and very loose blue trowsers which almost concealed his feet. His soft glossy beard was softer and more glossy than ever.

The bishop, who had made one mistake, thought that he also was a servant, and therefore tried to make way for him to pass. But Ethelbert soon corrected the error.

CHAPTER XI

MRS. PROUDIE'S RECEPTION—CONCLUDED

'BISHOP OF BARCHESTER, I presume?' said Bertie Stanhope, putting out his hand, frankly; 'I am delighted to make your acquaintance. We are in rather close quarters here, a'nt we?'

In truth they were. They had been crowded up behind the head of the sofa: the bishop in waiting to receive his guest, and the other in carrying her; and they now had hardly room to move themselves.

The bishop gave his hand quickly, and made his little studied bow, and was delighted to make——. He couldn't go on, for he did not know whether his friend was a signor, or a count, or a prince.

'My sister really puts you all to great trouble,' said Bertie.

'Not at all!' The bishop was delighted to have the opportunity of welcoming the Signora Vicinironi—so at least he said—and attempted to force his way round to the front of the sofa. He had, at any rate, learnt that his strange guests were brother and sister. The man, he presumed, must be Signor Vicinironi—or count, or prince, as it might be. It was wonderful what good English he spoke. There was just a twang of foreign accent, and no more.

'Do you like Barchester on the whole?' asked Bertie.

The bishop, looking dignified, said that he did like Barchester.

'You've not been here very long, I believe,' said Bertie.

'No—not long,' said the bishop, and tried again to make his way between the back of the sofa and a heavy rector, who was staring over it at the grimaces of the signora.

'You weren't a bishop before, were you?'

Dr. Proudie explained that this was the first diocese he had held.

'Ah—I thought so,' said Bertie; 'but you are changed about sometimes, a'nt you?'

'Translations are occasionally made,' said Dr. Proudie; 'but not so frequently as in former days.'

'They've cut them all down to pretty nearly the same figure, haven't they ? ' said Bertie.

To this the bishop could not bring himself to make any answer, but again attempted to move the rector.

'But the work, I suppose, is different ? ' continued Bertie. 'Is there much to do here, at Barchester ? ' This was said exactly in the tone that a young Admiralty clerk might use in asking the same question of a brother acolyte at the Treasury.

'The work of a bishop of the Church of England,' said Dr. Proudie, with considerable dignity, ' is not easy. The responsibility which he has to bear is very great indeed.'

'Is it ? ' said Bertie, opening wide his wonderful blue eyes. 'Well; I never was afraid of responsibility. I once had thoughts of being a bishop, myself.'

'Had thoughts of being a bishop ! ' said Dr. Proudie, much amazed.

'That is, a parson—a parson first, you know, and a bishop afterwards. If I had once begun, I'd have stuck to it. But, on the whole, I like the Church of Rome the best.'

The bishop could not discuss the point, so he remained silent.

'Now, there's my father,' continued Bertie; ' he hasn't stuck to it. I fancy he didn't like saying the same thing over so often. By the bye, Bishop, have you seen my father ? '

The bishop was more amazed than ever. Had he seen his father ? 'No,' he replied; ' he had not yet had the pleasure : he hoped he might; ' and, as he said so, he resolved to bear heavy on that fat, immovable rector, if ever he had the power of doing so.

'He's in the room somewhere,' said Bertie, ' and he'll turn up soon. By the bye, do you know much about the Jews ? '

At last the bishop saw a way out. ' I beg your pardon,' said he ; ' but I'm forced to go round the room.'

'Well—I believe I'll follow in your wake,' said Bertie. 'Terribly hot—isn't it ? ' This he addressed to the fat rector with whom he had brought himself into the closest contact. 'They've got this sofa into the worst possible part of the room; suppose we move it. Take care, Madeline.'

The sofa had certainly been so placed that those who were behind it found great difficulty in getting out ;— there was but a narrow gangway, which one person could stop. This was a bad arrangement, and one which Bertie thought it might be well to improve.

'Take care, Madeline,' said he ; and turning to the fat rector, added, ' Just help me with a slight push.'

The rector's weight was resting on the sofa, and unwittingly lent all its impetus to accelerate and increase the motion which Bertie intentionally originated. The sofa rushed from its moorings, and ran half-way into the middle of the room. Mrs. Proudie was standing with Mr. Slope in front of the signora, and had been trying to be condescending and sociable ; but she was not in the very best of tempers ; for she found that, whenever she spoke to the lady, the lady replied by speaking to Mr. Slope. Mr. Slope was a favourite, no doubt ; but Mrs. Proudie had no idea of being less thought of than the chaplain. She was beginning to be stately, stiff, and offended, when unfortunately the castor of the sofa caught itself in her lace train, and carried away there is no saying how much of her garniture. Gathers were heard to go, stitches to crack, plaits to fly open, flounces were seen to fall, and breadths to expose themselves ;— a long ruin of rent lace disfigured the carpet, and still clung to the vile wheel on which the sofa moved.

So, when a granite battery is raised, excellent to the eyes of warfaring men, is its strength and symmetry admired. It is the work of years. Its neat embrasures, its finished parapets, its casemated stories, show all the skill of modern science. But, anon, a small spark is applied to the treacherous fusee—a cloud of dust arises to the heavens—and then nothing is to be seen but dirt and dust and ugly fragments.

We know what was the wrath of Juno when her beauty was despised. We know too what storms of passion even celestial minds can yield. As Juno may have looked at Paris on Mount Ida, so did Mrs. Proudie look on Ethelbert Stanhope when he pushed the leg of the sofa into her lace train.

' Oh, you idiot, Bertie ! ' said the signora, seeing what
had been done, and what were to be the consequences.

' Idiot ! ' re-echoed Mrs. Proudie, as though the word
were not half strong enough to express the required
meaning ; ' I'll let him know——; ' and then looking
round to learn, at a glance, the worst, she saw that at
present it behoved her to collect the scattered *débris* of
her dress.

Bertie, when he saw what he had done, rushed over the
sofa, and threw himself on one knee before the offended
lady. His object, doubtless, was to liberate the torn
lace from the castor ; but he looked as though he were
imploring pardon from a goddess.

' Unhand it, sir ! ' said Mrs. Proudie. From what
scrap of dramatic poetry she had extracted the word
cannot be said ; but it must have rested on her memory,
and now seemed opportunely dignified for the occasion.

' I'll fly to the looms of the fairies to repair the damage,
if you'll only forgive me,' said Ethelbert, still on his
knees.

' Unhand it, sir ! ' said Mrs. Proudie, with redoubled
emphasis, and all but furious wrath. This allusion to
the fairies was a direct mockery, and intended to turn
her into ridicule. So at least it seemed to her. ' Unhand
it, sir ! ' she almost screamed.

' It 's not me ; it 's the cursed sofa,' said Bertie, looking
imploringly in her face, and holding up both his hands
to show that he was not touching her belongings, but
still remaining on his knees.

Hereupon the signora laughed ; not loud, indeed, but
yet audibly. And as the tigress bereft of her young will
turn with equal anger on any within reach, so did Mrs.
Proudie turn upon her female guest.

' Madam ! ' she said—and it is beyond the power of
prose to tell of the fire which flashed from her eyes.

The signora stared her full in the face for a moment,
and then turning to her brother said, playfully, ' Bertie,
you idiot, get up.'

By this time the bishop, and Mr. Slope, and her three
daughters were around her, and had collected together
the wide ruins of her magnificence. The girls fell into
circular rank behind their mother, and thus following

her and carrying out the fragments, they left the reception-rooms in a manner not altogether devoid of dignity. Mrs. Proudie had to retire and re-array herself.

As soon as the constellation had swept by, Ethelbert rose from his knees, and turning with mock anger to the fat rector, said: 'After all it was your doing, sir—not mine. But perhaps you are waiting for preferment, and so I bore it.'

Whereupon there was a laugh against the fat rector, in which both the bishop and the chaplain joined; and thus things got themselves again into order.

'Oh! my lord, I am so sorry for this accident,' said the signora, putting out her hand so as to force the bishop to take it. 'My brother is so thoughtless. Pray sit down, and let me have the pleasure of making your acquaintance. Though I am so poor a creature as to want a sofa, I am not so selfish as to require it all.' Madeline could always dispose herself so as to make room for a gentleman, though, as she declared, the crinoline of her lady friends was much too bulky to be so accommodated.

'It was solely for the pleasure of meeting you that I have had myself dragged here,' she continued. 'Of course, with your occupation, one cannot even hope that you should have time to come to us, that is, in the way of calling. And at your English dinner-parties all is so dull and so stately. Do you know, my lord, that in coming to England my only consolation has been the thought that I should know you;' and she looked at him with the look of a she-devil.

The bishop, however, thought that she looked very like an angel, and accepting the proffered seat, sat down beside her. He uttered some platitude as to his deep obligation for the trouble she had taken, and wondered more and more who she was.

'Of course you know my sad story?' she continued.

The bishop didn't know a word of it. He knew, however, or thought he knew, that she couldn't walk into a room like other people, and so made the most of that. He put on a look of ineffable distress, and said that he was aware how God had afflicted her.

The signora just touched the corner of her eyes with the most lovely of pocket-handkerchiefs. Yes, she said—

she had been sorely tried—tried, she thought, beyond
the common endurance of humanity; but while her child
was left to her, everything was left. 'Oh! my lord,'
she exclaimed, 'you must see that infant—the last bud
of a wondrous tree: you must let a mother hope that
you will lay your holy hands on her innocent head, and
consecrate her for female virtues. May I hope it?' said
she, looking into the bishop's eye, and touching the
bishop's arm with her hand.

The bishop was but a man, and said she might. After
all, what was it but a request that he would confirm her
daughter?—a request, indeed, very unnecessary to make,
as he should do so as a matter of course, if the young lady
came forward in the usual way.

'The blood of Tiberius,' said the signora, in all but
a whisper; 'the blood of Tiberius flows in her veins.
She is the last of the Neros!'

The bishop had heard of the last of the Visigoths, and
had floating in his brain some indistinct idea of the last
of the Mohicans, but to have the last of the Neros thus
brought before him for a blessing was very staggering.
Still he liked the lady: she had a proper way of thinking,
and talked with more propriety than her brother. But
who were they? It was now quite clear that that blue
madman with the silky beard was not a Prince Vicinironi.
The lady was married, and was of course one of the
Vicinironis by right of the husband. So the bishop went
on learning.

'When will you see her?' said the signora with a start.

'See whom?' said the bishop.

'My child,' said the mother.

'What is the young lady's age?' asked the bishop.

'She is just seven,' said the signora.

'Oh,' said the bishop, shaking his head; 'she is much
too young—very much too young.'

'But in sunny Italy you know, we do not count by
years,' and the signora gave the bishop one of her very
sweetest smiles.

'But indeed, she is a great deal too young,' persisted
the bishop; 'we never confirm before——'

'But you might speak to her; you might let her hear
from your consecrated lips, that she is not a castaway

because she is a Roman ; that she may be a Nero and
yet a Christian ; that she may owe her black locks and
dark cheeks to the blood of the pagan Cæsars, and yet
herself be a child of grace ; you will tell her this, won't
you, my friend ? '

The friend said he would, and asked if the child could
say her catechism.

' No,' said the signora, ' I would not allow her to learn
lessons such as those in a land ridden over by priests,
and polluted by the idolatry of Rome. It is here, here
in Barchester, that she must first be taught to lisp those
holy words. Oh, that you could be her instructor ! '

Now, Dr. Proudie certainly liked the lady, but, seeing
that he was a bishop, it was not probable that he was
going to instruct a little girl in the first rudiments of her
catechism ; so he said he'd send a teacher.

' But you'll see her, yourself, my lord ? '

The bishop said he would, but where should he call.

' At papa's house,' said the signora, with an air of some
little surprise at the question.

The bishop actually wanted the courage to ask her who
was her papa ; so he was forced at last to leave her without
fathoming the mystery. Mrs. Proudie, in her second
best, had now returned to the rooms, and her husband
thought it as well that he should not remain in too close
conversation with the lady whom his wife appeared to
hold in such slight esteem. Presently he came across.
his youngest daughter.

' Netta,' said he, ' do you know who is the father of
that Signora Vicinironi ? '

' It isn't Vicinironi, papa,' said Netta ; ' but Vesey
Neroni, and she's Doctor Stanhope's daughter. But
I must go and do the civil to Griselda Grantly ; I declare
nobody has spoken a word to the poor girl this evening.'

Dr. Stanhope ! Dr. Vesey Stanhope ! Dr. Vesey
Stanhope's daughter, of whose marriage with a dissolute
Italian scamp he now remembered to have heard something !
And that impertinent blue cub who had examined him
as to his episcopal bearings was old Stanhope's son, and
the lady who had entreated him to come and teach her
child the catechism was old Stanhope's daughter ! the
daughter of one of his own prebendaries ! As these things

flashed across his mind, he was nearly as angry as his wife had been. Nevertheless, he could not but own that the mother of the last of the Neros was an agreeable woman.

Dr. Proudie tripped out into the adjoining room, in which were congregated a crowd of Grantlyite clergymen, among whom the archdeacon was standing pre-eminent, while the old dean was sitting nearly buried in a huge arm-chair by the fire-place. The bishop was very anxious to be gracious, and, if possible, to diminish the bitterness which his chaplain had occasioned. Let Mr. Slope do the *fortiter in re*, he himself would pour in the *suaviter in modo*.

'Pray don't stir, Mr. Dean, pray don't stir,' he said, as the old man essayed to get up; 'I take it as a great kindness, your coming to such an *omnium gatherum* as this. But we have hardly got settled yet, and Mrs. Proudie has not been able to see her friends as she would wish to do. Well, Mr. Archdeacon, after all, we have not been so hard upon you at Oxford.'

'No,' said the archdeacon; 'you've only drawn our teeth and cut out our tongues; you've allowed us still to breathe and swallow.'

'Ha, ha, ha!' laughed the bishop; 'it's not quite so easy to cut out the tongue of an Oxford magnate,—and as for teeth,—ha, ha, ha! Why, in the way we've left the matter, it's very odd if the heads of colleges don't have their own way quite as fully as when the hebdomadal board was in all its glory; what do you say, Mr. Dean?'

'An old man, my lord, never likes changes,' said the dean.

'You must have been sad bunglers if it is so,' said the archdeacon; 'and indeed, to tell the truth, I think you have bungled it. At any rate, you must own this; you have not done the half what you boasted you would do.'

'Now, as regards your system of professors——' began the chancellor slowly. He was never destined to get beyond such beginning.

'Talking of professors,' said a soft clear voice, close behind the chancellor's elbow; 'how much you Englishmen might learn from Germany; only you are all too proud.'

The bishop looking round, perceived that that abominable young Stanhope had pursued him. The dean stared at him, as though he were some unearthly apparition; so also did two or three prebendaries and minor canons. The archdeacon laughed.

'The German professors are men of learning,' said Mr. Harding, 'but——'

'German professors!' groaned out the chancellor, as though his nervous system had received a shock which nothing but a week of Oxford air could cure.

'Yes,' continued Ethelbert; not at all understanding why a German professor should be contemptible in the eyes of an Oxford don. 'Not but what the name is best earned at Oxford. In Germany the professors do teach; at Oxford, I believe they only profess to do so, and sometimes not even that. You'll have those universities of yours about your ears soon, if you don't consent to take a lesson from Germany.'

There was no answering this. Dignified clergymen of sixty years of age could not condescend to discuss such a matter with a young man with such clothes and such a beard.

'Have you got good water out at Plumstead, Mr. Archdeacon?' said the bishop by way of changing the conversation.

'Pretty good,' said Dr. Grantly.

'But by no means so good as his wine, my lord,' said a witty minor canon.

'Nor so generally used,' said another; 'that is for inward application.'

'Ha, ha, ha!' laughed the bishop, 'a good cellar of wine is a very comfortable thing in a house.'

'Your German professors, sir, prefer beer, I believe,' said the sarcastic little meagre prebendary.

'They don't think much of either,' said Ethelbert; 'and that perhaps accounts for their superiority. Now the Jewish professor——'

The insult was becoming too deep for the spirit of Oxford to endure, so the archdeacon walked off one way and the chancellor another, followed by their disciples, and the bishop and the young reformer were left together on the hearth-rug.

'I was a Jew once myself,' began Bertie.

The bishop was determined not to stand another examination, or be led on any terms into Palestine; so he again remembered that he had to do something very particular, and left young Stanhope with the dean. The dean did not get the worst of it, for Ethelbert gave him a true account of his remarkable doings in the Holy Land.

'Oh, Mr. Harding,' said the bishop, overtaking the ci-devant warden; 'I wanted to say one word about the hospital. You know, of course, that it is to be filled up.'

Mr. Harding's heart beat a little, and he said that he had heard so.

'Of course,' continued the bishop; 'there can be only one man whom I could wish to see in that situation. I don't know what your own views may be, Mr. Harding—'

'They are very simply told, my lord,' said the other; 'to take the place if it be offered me, and to put up with the want of it should another man get it.'

The bishop professed himself delighted to hear it; Mr. Harding might be quite sure that no other man would get it. There were some few circumstances which would in a slight degree change the nature of the duties. Mr. Harding was probably aware of this, and would, perhaps, not object to discuss the matter with Mr. Slope. It was a subject to which Mr. Slope had given a good deal of attention.

Mr. Harding felt, he knew not why, oppressed and annoyed. What could Mr. Slope do to him? He knew that there were to be changes. The nature of them must be communicated to the warden through somebody, and through whom so naturally as the bishop's chaplain. 'Twas thus he tried to argue himself back to an easy mind, but in vain.

Mr. Slope in the mean time had taken the seat which the bishop had vacated on the signora's sofa, and remained with that lady till it was time to marshal the folk to supper. Not with contented eyes had Mrs. Proudie seen this. Had not this woman laughed at her distress, and had not Mr. Slope heard it? Was she not an intriguing Italian woman, half wife and half not, full of affectation, airs, and impudence? Was she not horribly bedizened with velvet and pearls, with velvet and pearls, too, which

had not been torn off her back ? Above all, did she not
pretend to be more beautiful than her neighbours ? To
say that Mrs. Proudie was jealous would give a wrong
idea of her feelings. She had not the slightest desire that
Mr. Slope should be in love with herself. But she desired
the incense of Mr. Slope's spiritual and temporal services,
and did not choose that they should be turned out of
their course to such an object as Signora Neroni. She
considered also that Mr. Slope ought in duty to hate the
signora ; and it appeared from his manner that he was
very far from hating her.

'Come, Mr. Slope,' she said, sweeping by, and looking
all that she felt ; ' can't you make yourself useful ? Do
pray take Mrs. Grantly down to supper.'

Mrs. Grantly heard and escaped. The words were
hardly out of Mrs. Proudie's mouth, before the intended
victim had stuck her hand through the arm of one of
her husband's curates, and saved herself. What would
the archdeacon have said had he seen her walking down
stairs with Mr. Slope ?

Mr. Slope heard also, but was by no means so obedient
as was expected. Indeed, the period of Mr. Slope's
obedience to Mrs. Proudie was drawing to a close. He
did not wish yet to break with her, nor to break with
her at all, if it could be avoided. But he intended to be
master in that palace, and as she had made the same
resolution it was not improbable that they might come
to blows.

Before leaving the signora he arranged a little table
before her, and begged to know what he should bring
her. She was quite indifferent, she said—nothing—
anything. It was now she felt the misery of her position,
now that she must be left alone. Well, a little chicken,
some ham, and a glass of champagne.

Mr. Slope had to explain, not without blushing for
his patron, that there was no champagne.

Sherry would do just as well. And then Mr. Slope
descended with the learned Miss Trefoil on his arm.
Could she tell him, he asked, whether the ferns of Barsetshire were equal to those of Cumberland ? His strongest
worldly passion was for ferns — and before she could
answer him he left her wedged between the door and the

sideboard. It was fifty minutes before she escaped, and even then unfed.

' You are not leaving us, Mr. Slope,' said the watchful lady of the house, seeing her slave escaping towards the door, with stores of provisions held high above the heads of the guests.

Mr. Slope explained that the Signora Neroni was in want of her supper.

' Pray, Mr. Slope, let her brother take it to her,' said Mrs. Proudie, quite out loud. ' It is out of the question that you should be so employed. Pray, Mr. Slope, oblige me ; I am sure Mr. Stanhope will wait upon his sister.'

Ethelbert was most agreeably occupied in the furthest corner of the room, making himself both useful and agreeable to Mrs. Proudie's youngest daughter.

' I couldn't get out, madam, if Madeline were starving for her supper,' said he ; ' I'm physically fixed, unless I could fly.'

The lady's anger was increased by seeing that her daughter also had gone over to the enemy ; and when she saw, that in spite of her remonstrances, in the teeth of her positive orders, Mr. Slope went off to the drawing-room, the cup of her indignation ran over, and she could not restrain herself. ' Such manners I never saw,' she said, muttering. ' I cannot, and will not permit it ; ' and then, after fussing and fuming for a few minutes, she pushed her way through the crowd, and followed Mr. Slope.

When she reached the room above, she found it absolutely deserted, except by the guilty pair. The signora was sitting very comfortably up to her supper, and Mr. Slope was leaning over her and administering to her wants. They had been discussing the merits of Sabbath-day schools, and the lady had suggested that as she could not possibly go to the children, she might be indulged in the wish of her heart by having the children brought to her.

' And when shall it be, Mr. Slope ? ' said she.

Mr. Slope was saved the necessity of committing himself to a promise by the entry of Mrs. Proudie. She swept close up to the sofa so as to confront the guilty pair, stared full at them for a moment, and then said as she passed on to the next room, 'Mr. Slope, his lordship is especially desirous of your attendance below; you will greatly oblige me if you will join him.' And so she stalked on.

Mr. Slope muttered something in reply, and prepared to go down stairs. As for the bishop's wanting him, he knew his lady patroness well enough to take that assertion at what it was worth; but he did not wish to make himself the hero of a scene, or to become conspicuous for more gallantry than the occasion required.

'Is she always like this?' said the signora.

'Yes—always—madam,' said Mrs. Proudie, returning; 'always the same—always equally adverse to impropriety of conduct of every description;' and she stalked back through the room again, following Mr. Slope out of the door.

The signora couldn't follow her, or she certainly would have done so. But she laughed loud, and sent the sound of it ringing through the lobby and down the stairs after Mrs. Proudie's feet. Had she been as active as Grimaldi, she could probably have taken no better revenge.

'Mr. Slope,' said Mrs. Proudie, catching the delinquent at the door, 'I am surprised that you should leave my company to attend on such a painted Jezebel as that.'

'But she's lame, Mrs. Proudie, and cannot move. Somebody must have waited upon her.'

'Lame,' said Mrs. Proudie; 'I'd lame her if she belonged to me. What business had she here at all?—such impertinence—such affectation.'

In the hall and adjacent rooms all manner of cloaking and shawling was going on, and the Barchester folk were getting themselves gone. Mrs. Proudie did her best to smirk at each and every one, as they made their adieux, but she was hardly successful. Her temper had been tried fearfully. By slow degrees, the guests went.

'Send back the carriage quick,' said Ethelbert, as Dr. and Mrs. Stanhope took their departure.

The younger Stanhopes were left to the very last, and an uncomfortable party they made with the bishop's family. They all went into the dining room, and then the bishop observing that 'the lady' was alone in the drawing-room, they followed him up. Mrs. Proudie kept Mr. Slope and her daughters in close conversation, resolving that he should not be indulged, nor they polluted. The bishop, in mortal dread of Bertie and the Jews, tried to converse with Charlotte Stanhope about the climate of Italy. Bertie and the signora had no resource but in each other.

' Did you get your supper, at last, Madeline ? ' said the impudent or else mischievous young man.

' Oh, yes,' said Madeline ; ' Mr. Slope was so very kind as to bring it me. I fear, however, he put himself to more inconvenience than I wished.'

Mrs. Proudie looked at her, but said nothing. The meaning of her look might have been thus translated : ' If ever you find yourself within these walls again, I'll give you leave to be as impudent and affected, and as mischievous as you please.'

At last the carriage returned with the three Italian servants, and La Signora Madeline Vesey Neroni was carried out, as she had been carried in.

The lady of the palace retired to her chamber by no means contented with the result of her first grand party at Barchester.

CHAPTER XII

SLOPE VERSUS HARDING

Two or three days after the party, Mr. Harding received a note, begging him to call on Mr. Slope, at the palace, at an early hour the following morning. There was nothing uncivil in the communication, and yet the tone of it was thoroughly displeasing. It was as follows :

' My dear Mr. Harding,—Will you favour me by calling on me at the palace to-morrow morning at 9.30 A.M. The bishop wishes me to speak to you touching the hospital. I hope you will excuse my naming so early an hour. I do so as my time is greatly occupied. If, however, it is positively inconvenient to you, I will change it to 10. You will, perhaps, be kind enough to let me have a note in reply.

' Believe me to be,
' My dear Mr. Harding,
' Your assured friend,
' OBH. SLOPE.

' The Palace, Monday morning,
' 20th August, 185—.'

Mr. Harding neither could nor would believe anything of the sort; and he thought, moreover, that Mr. Slope was rather impertinent to call himself by such a name. His assured friend, indeed! How many assured friends generally fall to the lot of a man in this world? And by what process are they made? and how much of such process had taken place as yet between Mr. Harding and Mr. Slope? Mr. Harding could not help asking himself these questions as he read and re-read the note before him. He answered it, however, as follows:

'Dear Sir,—I will call at the palace to-morrow at 9.30 A.M. as you desire.

'Truly yours,
'S. HARDING.

'High Street, Barchester, Monday.'

And on the following morning, punctually at half-past nine, he knocked at the palace door, and asked for Mr. Slope.

The bishop had one small room allotted to him on the ground-floor, and Mr. Slope had another. Into this latter Mr. Harding was shown, and asked to sit down. Mr. Slope was not yet there. The ex-warden stood up at the window looking into the garden, and could not help thinking how very short a time had passed since the whole of that house had been open to him, as though he had been a child of the family, born and bred in it. He remembered how the old servants used to smile as they opened the door to him; how the familiar butler would say, when he had been absent a few hours longer than usual, 'A sight of you, Mr. Harding, is good for sore eyes;' how the fussy housekeeper would swear that he couldn't have dined, or couldn't have breakfasted, or couldn't have lunched. And then, above all, he remembered the pleasant gleam of inward satisfaction which always spread itself over the old bishop's face, whenever his friend entered his room.

A tear came into each eye as he reflected that all this was gone. What use would the hospital be to him now? He was alone in the world, and getting old; he would soon, very soon have to go, and leave it all, as his dear old friend had gone;—go, and leave the hospital, and

his accustomed place in the cathedral, and his haunts
and pleasures, to younger and perhaps wiser men. That
chanting of his !—perhaps, in truth, the time for it had
gone by. He felt as though the world were sinking from
his feet ; as though this, this was the time for him to
turn with confidence to those hopes which he had preached
with confidence to others. ' What,' said he to himself,
' can a man's religion be worth, if it does not support him
against the natural melancholy of declining years ? '
And, as he looked out through his dimmed eyes into the
bright parterres of the bishop's garden, he felt that he
had the support which he wanted.

Nevertheless, he did not like to be thus kept waiting.
If Mr. Slope did not really wish to see him at half-past
nine o'clock, why force him to come away from his
lodgings with his breakfast in his throat ? To tell the
truth, it was policy on the part of Mr. Slope. Mr. Slope
had made up his mind that Mr. Harding should either
accept the hospital with abject submission, or else refuse
it altogether ; and had calculated that he would probably
be more quick to do the latter, if he could be got to enter
upon the subject in an ill-humour. Perhaps Mr. Slope
was not altogether wrong in his calculation.

It was nearly ten when Mr. Slope hurried into the room,
and, muttering something about the bishop and diocesan
duties, shook Mr. Harding's hand ruthlessly, and begged
him to be seated.

Now the air of superiority which this man assumed,
did go against the grain of Mr. Harding ; and yet he did
not know how to resent it. The whole tendency of his
mind and disposition was opposed to any contra-assump-
tion of grandeur on his own part, and he hadn't the worldly
spirit or quickness necessary to put down insolent pretensions by downright and open rebuke, as the archdeacon
would have done. There was nothing for Mr. Harding
but to submit, and he accordingly did so.

' About the hospital, Mr. Harding ? ' began Mr. Slope,
speaking of it as the head of a college at Cambridge might
speak of some sizarship which had to be disposed of.

Mr. Harding crossed one leg over another, and then
one hand over the other on the top of them, and looked
Mr. Slope in the face ; but he said nothing.

'It's to be filled up again,' said Mr. Slope. Mr. Harding said that he had understood so.

'Of course, you know, the income will be very much reduced,' continued Mr. Slope. 'The bishop wished to be liberal, and he therefore told the government that he thought it ought to be put at not less than £450. I think on the whole the bishop was right; for though the services required will not be of a very onerous nature, they will be more so than they were before. And it is, perhaps, well that the clergy immediately attached to the cathedral town should be made as comfortable as the extent of the ecclesiastical means at our disposal will allow. Those are the bishop's ideas, and I must say mine also.'

Mr. Harding sat rubbing one hand on the other, but said not a word.

'So much for the income, Mr. Harding. The house will, of course, remain to the warden, as before. It should, however, I think, be stipulated that he should paint inside every seven years, and outside every three years, and be subject to dilapidations, in the event of vacating, either by death or otherwise. But this is a matter on which the bishop must yet be consulted.'

Mr. Harding still rubbed his hands, and still sat silent, gazing up into Mr. Slope's unprepossessing face.

'Then, as to the duties,' continued he, 'I believe, if I am rightly informed, there can hardly be said to have been any duties hitherto,' and he gave a sort of half laugh, as though to pass off the accusation in the guise of a pleasantry.

Mr. Harding thought of the happy, easy years he had passed in his old home; of the worn-out, aged men whom he had succoured; of his good intentions; and of his work, which had certainly been of the lightest. He thought of these things, doubting for a moment whether he did or did not deserve the sarcasm. He gave his enemy the benefit of the doubt, and did not rebuke him. He merely observed, very tranquilly, and perhaps with too much humility, that the duties of the situation, such as they were, had, he believed, been done to the satisfaction of the late bishop.

Mr. Slope again smiled, and this time the smile was intended to operate against the memory of the late bishop, rather than against the energy of the ex-warden; and so it was understood by Mr. Harding. The colour rose to his cheeks, and he began to feel very angry.

' You must be aware, Mr. Harding, that things are a good deal changed in Barchester,' said Mr. Slope.

Mr. Harding said that he was aware of it. ' And not only in Barchester, Mr. Harding, but in the world at large. It is not only in Barchester that a new man is carrying out new measures and casting away the useless rubbish of past centuries. The same thing is going on throughout the country. Work is now required from every man who receives wages; and they who have to superintend the doing of work, and the paying of wages, are bound to see that this rule is carried out. New men, Mr. Harding, are now needed, and are now forthcoming in the church, as well as in other professions.'

All this was wormwood to our old friend. He had never rated very high his own abilities or activity; but all the feelings of his heart were with the old clergy, and any antipathies of which his heart was susceptible, were directed against those new, busy, uncharitable, self-lauding men, of whom Mr. Slope was so good an example.

' Perhaps,' said he, ' the bishop will prefer a new man at the hospital ? '

' By no means,' said Mr. Slope. ' The bishop is very anxious that you should accept the appointment; but he wishes you should understand beforehand what will be the required duties. In the first place, a Sabbath-day school will be attached to the hospital.'

' What ! for the old men ? ' asked Mr. Harding.

' No, Mr. Harding, not for the old men, but for the benefit of the children of such of the poor of Barchester as it may suit. The bishop will expect that you shall attend this school, and the teachers shall be under your inspection and care.'

Mr. Harding slipped his topmost hand off the other, and began to rub the calf of the leg which was supported.

' As to the old men,' continued Mr. Slope, ' and the old women who are to form a part of the hospital, the bishop is desirous that you shall have morning and evening service on the premises every Sabbath, and one week-day service ; that you shall preach to them once at least on

Sundays; and that the whole hospital be always collected for morning and evening prayer. The bishop thinks that this will render it unnecessary that any separate seats in the cathedral should be reserved for the hospital inmates.'

Mr. Slope paused, but Mr. Harding still said nothing.

'Indeed, it would be difficult to find seats for the women; and, on the whole, Mr. Harding, I may as well say at once, that for people of that class the cathedral service does not appear to me the most useful,—even if it be so for any class of people.'

'We will not discuss that, if you please,' said Mr. Harding.

'I am not desirous of doing so; at least, not at the present moment. I hope, however, you fully understand the bishop's wishes about the new establishment of the hospital; and if, as I do not doubt, I shall receive from you an assurance that you accord with his lordship's views, it will give me very great pleasure to be the bearer from his lordship to you of the presentation to the appointment.'

'But if I disagree with his lordship's views?' asked Mr. Harding.

'But I hope you do not,' said Mr. Slope.

'But if I do?' again asked the other.

'If such unfortunately should be the case, which I can hardly conceive, I presume your own feelings will dictate to you the propriety of declining the appointment.'

'But if I accept the appointment, and yet disagree with the bishop, what then?'

This question rather bothered Mr. Slope. It was true that he had talked the matter over with the bishop, and had received a sort of authority for suggesting to Mr. Harding the propriety of a Sunday school, and certain hospital services; but he had no authority for saying that these propositions were to be made peremptory conditions attached to the appointment. The bishop's idea had been that Mr. Harding would of course consent, and that the school would become, like the rest of those new establishments in the city, under the control of his wife and his chaplain. Mr. Slope's idea had been more correct. He intended that Mr. Harding should refuse the situation, and that an ally of his own should get it;

but he had not conceived the possibility of Mr. Harding openly accepting the appointment, and as openly rejecting the conditions.

' It is not, I presume, probable,' said he, ' that you will accept from the hands of the bishop a piece of preferment, with a fixed predetermination to disacknowledge the duties attached to it.'

' If I become warden,' said Mr. Harding, ' and neglect my duty, the bishop has means by which he can remedy the grievance.'

' I hardly expected such an argument from you, or I may say the suggestion of such a line of conduct,' said Mr. Slope, with a great look of injured virtue.

' Nor did I expect such a proposition.'

' I shall be glad at any rate to know what answer I am to make to his lordship,' said Mr. Slope.

' I will take an early opportunity of seeing his lordship myself,' said Mr. Harding.

' Such an arrangement,' said Mr. Slope, ' will hardly give his lordship satisfaction. Indeed, it is impossible that the bishop should himself see every clergyman in the diocese on every subject of patronage that may arise. The bishop, I believe, did see you on the matter, and I really cannot see why he should be troubled to do so again.'

' Do you know, Mr. Slope, how long I have been officiating as a clergyman in this city ? ' Mr. Slope's wish was now nearly fulfilled. Mr. Harding had become angry, and it was probable that he might commit himself.

' I really do not see what that has to do with the question. You cannot think the bishop would be justified in allowing you to regard as a sinecure a situation that requires an active man, merely because you have been employed for many years in the cathedral.'

' But it might induce the bishop to see me, if I asked him to do so. I shall consult my friends in this matter, Mr. Slope ; but I mean to be guilty of no subterfuge,—you may tell the bishop that as I altogether disagree·with his views about the hospital, I shall decline the situation if I find that any such conditions are attached to it as those you have suggested ; ' and so saying, Mr. Harding took his hat and went his way.

Mr. Slope was contented. He considered himself at liberty to accept Mr. Harding's last speech as an absolute refusal of the appointment. At least, he so represented it to the bishop and to Mrs. Proudie.

' That is very surprising,' said the bishop.

' Not at all,' said Mrs. Proudie ; ' you little know how determined the whole set of them are to withstand your authority.'

' But Mr. Harding was so anxious for it,' said the bishop.

' Yes,' said Mr. Slope, ' if he can hold it without the slightest acknowledgment of your lordship's jurisdiction.'

' That is out of the question,' said the bishop.

' I should imagine it to be quite so,' said the chaplain.

' Indeed, I should think so,' said the lady.

' I really am sorry for it,' said the bishop.

' I don't know that there is much cause for sorrow,' said the lady. ' Mr. Quiverful is a much more deserving man, more in need of it, and one who will make himself much more useful in the close neighbourhood of the palace.'

' I suppose I had better see Quiverful ? ' said the chaplain.

' I suppose you had,' said the bishop.

CHAPTER XIII

THE RUBBISH CART

MR. HARDING was not a happy man as he walked down the palace pathway, and stepped out into the close. His preferment and pleasant house were a second time gone from him ; but that he could endure. He had been schooled and insulted by a man young enough to be his son ; but that he could put up with. He could even draw from the very injuries, which had been inflicted on him, some of that consolation, which we may believe martyrs always receive from the injustice of their own sufferings, and which is generally proportioned in its strength to the extent of cruelty with which martyrs are treated. He had admitted to his daughter that he wanted the comfort of his old home, and yet he could have returned to his lodgings in the High Street, if not with exultation, at least with satisfaction, had that been all. But the venom of the chaplain's harangue had worked into his blood, and sapped the life of his sweet contentment.

'New men are carrying out new measures, and are carting away the useless rubbish of past centuries!' What cruel words these had been ; and how often are they now used with all the heartless cruelty of a Slope ! A man is sufficiently condemned if it can only be shown that either in politics or religion he does not belong to some new school established within the last score of years. He may then regard himself as rubbish and expect to be carted away. A man is nothing now unless he has within him a full appreciation of the new era ; an era in which it would seem that neither honesty nor truth is very desirable, but in which success is the only touchstone of merit. We must laugh at every thing that is established. Let the joke be ever so bad, ever so untrue to the real principles of joking ; nevertheless we must laugh—or else beware the cart. We must talk, think, and live up to the spirit of the times, and write up to it too, if that cacoethes be upon us, or else we are nought. New men and new measures, long credit and few scruples, great success or wonderful ruin, such are now the tastes of Englishmen who know how to live. Alas, alas ! under such circumstances Mr. Harding could not but feel that he was an Englishman who did not know how to live. This new doctrine of Mr. Slope and the rubbish cart, new at least at Barchester, sadly disturbed his equanimity.

'The same thing is going on throughout the whole country !' 'Work is now required from every man who receives wages !' And had he been living all his life receiving wages, and doing no work ? Had he in truth so lived as to be now in his old age justly reckoned as rubbish fit only to be hidden away in some huge dust hole ? The school of men to whom he professes to belong, the Grantlys, the Gwynnes, and the old high set of Oxford divines, are afflicted with no such self-accusations as these which troubled Mr. Harding. They, as a rule, are as satisfied with the wisdom and propriety of their own conduct as can be any Mr. Slope, or any Dr. Proudie, with his own. But unfortunately for himself Mr. Harding had little of this self-reliance. When he heard himself designated as rubbish by the Slopes of the world, he had no other resource than to make inquiry within his own bosom as to the truth of the designation. Alas, alas! the evidence seemed generally to go against him.

He had professed to himself in the bishop's parlour that in these coming sources of the sorrow of age, in these fits of sad regret from which the latter years of few reflecting men can be free, religion would suffice to comfort him. Yes, religion could console him for the loss of any worldly good; but was his religion of that active sort which would enable him so to repent of misspent years as to pass those that were left to him in a spirit of hope for the future? And such repentance itself, is it not a work of agony and of tears? It is very easy to talk of repentance; but a man has to walk over hot ploughshares before he can complete it; to be skinned alive as was St. Bartholomew; to be stuck full of arrows as was St. Sebastian; to lie broiling on a gridiron like St. Lorenzo! How if his past life required such repentance as this? had he the energy to go through with it?

Mr. Harding after leaving the palace, walked slowly for an hour or so beneath the shady elms of the close, and then betook himself to his daughter's house. He had at any rate made up his mind that he would go out to Plumstead to consult Dr. Grantly, and that he would in the first instance tell Eleanor what had occurred.

And now he was doomed to undergo another misery. Mr. Slope had forestalled him at the widow's house. He had called there on the preceding afternoon. He could not, he had said, deny himself the pleasure of telling Mrs. Bold that her father was about to return to the pretty house at Hiram's hospital. He had been instructed by the bishop to inform Mr. Harding that the appointment would now be made at once. The bishop was of course only too happy to be able to be the means of restoring to Mr. Harding the preferment which he had so long adorned. And then by degrees Mr. Slope had introduced the subject of the pretty school which he hoped before long to see attached to the hospital. He had quite fascinated Mrs. Bold by his description of this picturesque, useful, and charitable appendage, and she had gone so far as to say that she had no doubt her father would approve, and that she herself would gladly undertake a class.

Any one who had heard the entirely different tone, and seen the entirely different manner in which Mr. Slope had spoken of this projected institution to the daughter and to the father, could not have failed to own that Mr. Slope was a man of genius. He said nothing to Mrs. Bold about the hospital sermons and services, nothing about the exclusion of the old men from the cathedral, nothing about dilapidation and painting, nothing about carting away the rubbish. Eleanor had said to herself that certainly she did not like Mr. Slope personally, but that he was a very active, zealous clergyman, and would no doubt be useful in Barchester. All this paved the way for much additional misery to Mr. Harding.

Eleanor put on her happiest face as she heard her father on the stairs, for she thought she had only to congratulate him ; but directly she saw his face, she knew that there was but little matter for congratulation. She had seen him with the same weary look of sorrow on one or two occasions before, and remembered it well. She had seen him when he first read that attack upon himself in the Jupiter which had ultimately caused him to resign the hospital ; and she had seen him also when the archdeacon had persuaded him to remain there against his own sense of propriety and honour. She knew at a glance that his spirit was in deep trouble.

' Oh, papa, what is it ? ' said she, putting down her boy to crawl upon the floor.

' I came to tell you, my dear,' said he, ' that I am going out to Plumstead : you won't come with me, I suppose ? '

' To Plumstead, papa ? Shall you stay there ? '

' I suppose I shall, to night : I must consult the archdeacon about this weary hospital. Ah me ! I wish I had never thought of it again.'

' Why, papa, what is the matter ? '

' I've been with Mr. Slope, my dear, and he isn't the pleasantest companion in the world, at least not to me.' Eleanor gave a sort of half blush ; but she was wrong if she imagined that her father in any way alluded to her acquaintance with Mr. Slope.

' Well, papa.'

' He wants to turn the hospital into a Sunday school and a preaching house ; and I suppose he will have his way.

I do not feel myself adapted for such an establishment, and therefore, I suppose, I must refuse the appointment.'

' What would be the harm of the school, papa ? '

' The want of a proper schoolmaster, my dear.'

' But that would of course be supplied.'

' Mr. Slope wishes to supply it by making me his schoolmaster. But as I am hardly fit for such work, I intend to decline.'

' Oh, papa ! Mr. Slope doesn't intend that. He was here yesterday, and what he intends——'

' He was here yesterday, was he ? ' asked Mr. Harding.

' Yes, papa.'

' And talking about the hospital ? '

' He was saying how glad he would be, and the bishop too, to see you back there again. And then he spoke about the Sunday school ; and to tell the truth I agreed with him ; and I thought you would have done so too. Mr. Slope spoke of a school, not inside the hospital, but just connected with it, of which you would be the patron and visitor ; and I thought you would have liked such a school as that ; and I promised to look after it and to take a class —and it all seemed so very——. But, oh, papa ! I shall be so miserable if I find I have done wrong.'

' Nothing wrong at all, my dear,' said he, gently, very gently rejecting his daughter's caress. ' There can be nothing wrong in your wishing to make yourself useful ; indeed, you ought to do so by all means. Every one must now exert himself who would not choose to go to the wall.' Poor Mr. Harding thus attempted in his misery to preach the new doctrine to his child. ' Himself or herself, it 's all the same,' he continued ; ' you will be quite right, my dear, to do something of this sort ; but——'

' Well, papa.'

' I am not quite sure that if I were you I would select Mr. Slope for my guide.'

' But I never have done so, and never shall.'

' It would be very wicked of me to speak evil of him, for to tell the truth I know no evil of him ; but I am not quite sure that he is honest. That he is not gentleman-like in his manners, of that I am quite sure.'

' I never thought of taking him for my guide, papa.'

' As for myself, my dear,' continued he, ' we know the

old proverb—'It's bad teaching an old dog tricks.' I must decline the Sunday school, and shall therefore probably decline the hospital also. But I will first see your brother-in-law.' So he took up his hat, kissed the baby, and withdrew, leaving Eleanor in as low spirits as himself.

All this was a great aggravation to his misery. He had so few with whom to sympathise, that he could not afford to be cut off from the one whose sympathy was of the most value to him. And yet it seemed probable that this would be the case. He did not own to himself that he wished his daughter to hate Mr. Slope; yet had she expressed such a feeling there would have been very little bitterness in the rebuke he would have given her for so uncharitable a state of mind. The fact, however, was that she was on friendly terms with Mr. Slope, that she coincided with his views, adhered at once to his plans, and listened with delight to his teaching. Mr. Harding hardly wished his daughter to hate the man, but he would have preferred that to her loving him.

He walked away to the inn to order a fly, went home to put up his carpet bag, and then started for Plumstead. There was, at any rate, no danger that the archdeacon would fraternise with Mr. Slope; but then he would recommend internecine war, public appeals, loud reproaches, and all the paraphernalia of open battle. Now that alternative was hardly more to Mr. Harding's taste than the other.

When Mr. Harding reached the parsonage he found that the archdeacon was out, and would not be home till dinner-time, so he began his complaint to his elder daughter. Mrs. Grantly entertained quite as strong an antagonism to Mr. Slope as did her husband; she was also quite as alive to the necessity of combating the Proudie faction, of supporting the old church interest of the close, of keeping in her own set such of the loaves and fishes as duly belonged to it; and was quite as well prepared as her lord to carry on the battle without giving or taking quarter. Not that she was a woman prone to quarrelling, or ill inclined to live at peace with her clerical neighbours; but she felt, as did the archdeacon, that the presence of Mr. Slope in Barchester was an insult to every one connected with the late bishop, and that his assumed dominion in the diocese was a spiritual injury to her husband. Hitherto people had little guessed how bitter Mrs. Grantly could be. She lived on the best of terms with all the rectors' wives around her. She had been popular with all the ladies connected with the close. Though much the wealthiest of the ecclesiastical matrons of the county, she had so managed her affairs that her carriage and horses had given umbrage to none. She had never thrown herself among the county grandees so as to excite the envy of other clergymen's wives. She had never talked too loudly of earls and countesses, or boasted that she gave her governess sixty pounds a year, or her cook seventy. Mrs. Grantly had lived the life of a wise, discreet, peace-making woman ; and the people of Barchester were surprised at the amount of military vigour she displayed as general of the feminine Grantlyite forces.

Mrs. Grantly soon learnt that her sister Eleanor had promised to assist Mr. Slope in the affairs of the hospital ; and it was on this point that her attention soon fixed itself.

' How can Eleanor endure him ? ' said she.

' He is a very crafty man,' said her father, ' and his craft has been successful in making Eleanor think that he is a meek, charitable, good clergyman. God forgive me, if I wrong him, but such is not his true character in my opinion.'

' His true character, indeed ! ' said she, with something approaching to scorn for her father's moderation. ' I only hope he won't have craft enough to make Eleanor forget herself and her position.'

' Do you mean marry him ? ' said he, startled out of his usual demeanour by the abruptness and horror of so dreadful a proposition.

' What is there so improbable in it ? Of course that would be his own object if he thought he had any chance of success. Eleanor has a thousand a year entirely at her own disposal, and what better fortune could fall to Mr. Slope's lot than the transferring of the disposal of such a fortune to himself ? '

' But you can't think she likes him, Susan ? '

' Why not ? ' said Susan. ' Why shouldn't she like him ? He's just the sort of man to get on with a woman left as she is, with no one to look after her.'

' Look after her ! ' said the unhappy father ; ' don't we look after her ? '

'Ah, papa, how innocent you are! Of course it was to be expected that Eleanor should marry again. I should be the last to advise her against it, if she would only wait the proper time, and then marry at least a gentleman.'

'But you don't really mean to say that you suppose Eleanor has ever thought of marrying Mr. Slope? Why, Mr. Bold has only been dead a year.'

'Eighteen months,' said his daughter. 'But I don't suppose Eleanor has ever thought about it. It is very probable, though, that he has, and that he will try and make her do so; and that he will succeed too, if we don't take care what we are about.'

This was quite a new phase of the affair to poor Mr. Harding. To have thrust upon him as his son-in-law, as the husband of his favourite child, the only man in the world whom he really positively disliked, would be a misfortune which he felt he would not know how to endure patiently. But then, could there be any ground for so dreadful a surmise? In all worldly matters he was apt to look upon the opinion of his eldest daughter, as one generally sound and trustworthy. In her appreciation of character, of motives, and the probable conduct both of men and women, she was usually not far wrong. She had early foreseen the marriage of Eleanor and John Bold; she had at a glance deciphered the character of the new bishop and his chaplain; could it possibly be that her present surmise should ever come forth as true?

'But you don't think that she likes him?' said Mr. Harding again.

'Well, papa, I can't say that I think she dislikes him as she ought to do. Why is he visiting there as a confidential friend, when he never ought to have been admitted inside the house? Why is it that she speaks to him about your welfare and your position, as she clearly has done? At the bishop's party the other night, I saw her talking to him for half an hour at the stretch.'

'I thought Mr. Slope seemed to talk to nobody there but that daughter of Stanhope's,' said Mr. Harding, wishing to defend his child.

'Oh, Mr. Slope is a cleverer man than you think of, papa, and keeps more than one iron in the fire.'

To give Eleanor her due, any suspicion as to the slightest

inclination on her part towards Mr. Slope was a wrong to her. She had no more idea of marrying Mr. Slope than she had of marrying the bishop ; and the idea that Mr. Slope would present himself as a suitor had never occurred to her. Indeed, to give her her due again, she had never thought about suitors since her husband's death. But nevertheless it was true that she had overcome all that repugnance to the man which was so strongly felt for him by the rest of the Grantly faction. She had forgiven him his sermon. She had forgiven him his low church tendencies, his Sabbath schools, and puritanical observances. She had forgiven his pharisaical arrogance, and even his greasy face and oily vulgar manners. Having agreed to overlook such offences as these, why should she not in time be taught to regard Mr. Slope as a suitor ?

And as to him, it must also be affirmed that he was hitherto equally innocent of the crime imputed to him. How it had come to pass that a man whose eyes were generally so widely open to everything around him had not perceived that this young widow was rich as well as beautiful, cannot probably now be explained. But such was the fact. Mr. Slope had ingratiated himself with Mrs. Bold, merely as he had done with other ladies, in order to strengthen his party in the city. He subsequently amended his error ; but it was not till after the interview between him and Mr. Harding.

CHAPTER XIV

THE NEW CHAMPION

THE archdeacon did not return to the parsonage till close upon the hour of dinner, and there was therefore no time to discuss matters before that important ceremony. He seemed to be in an especial good humour, and welcomed his father-in-law with a sort of jovial earnestness that was usual with him when things on which he was intent were going on as he would have them.

' It 's all settled, my dear,' said he to his wife as he washed his hands in his dressing-room, while she, according to her wont, sat listening in the bedroom ; ' Arabin has agreed to accept the living. He'll be here next week.'

And the archdeacon scrubbed his hands and rubbed his face with a violent alacrity, which showed that Arabin's coming was a great point gained.

'Will he come here to Plumstead?' said the wife.

'He has promised to stay a month with us,' said the archdeacon, 'so that he may see what his parish is like. You'll like Arabin very much. He's a gentleman in every respect, and full of humour.'

'He's very queer, isn't he?' asked the lady.

'Well—he is a little odd in some of his fancies; but there's nothing about him you won't like. He is as staunch a churchman as there is at Oxford. I really don't know what we should do without Arabin. It's a great thing for me to have him so near me; and if anything can put Slope down, Arabin will do it.'

The Reverend Francis Arabin was a fellow of Lazarus, the favoured disciple of the great Dr. Gwynne, a high churchman at all points; so high, indeed, that at one period of his career he had all but toppled over into the cesspool of Rome; a poet and also a polemical writer, a great pet in the common rooms at Oxford, an eloquent clergyman, a droll, odd, humorous, energetic, conscientious man, and, as the archdeacon had boasted of him, a thorough gentleman. As he will hereafter be brought more closely to our notice, it is now only necessary to add, that he had just been presented to the vicarage of St. Ewold by Dr. Grantly, in whose gift as archdeacon the living lay. St. Ewold is a parish lying just without the city of Barchester. The suburbs of the new town, indeed, are partly within its precincts, and the pretty church and parsonage are not much above a mile distant from the city gate.

St. Ewold is not a rich piece of preferment—it is worth some three or four hundred a year at most, and has generally been held by a clergyman attached to the cathedral choir. The archdeacon, however, felt, when the living on this occasion became vacant, that it imperatively behoved him to aid the force of his party with some tower of strength, if any such tower could be got to occupy St. Ewold's. He had discussed the matter with his brethren in Barchester; not in any weak spirit as the holder of patronage to be used for his own or his family's benefit, but as one to whom was committed a trust, on the due ad-

ministration of which much of the church's welfare might
depend. He had submitted to them the name of Mr.
Arabin, as though the choice had rested with them all in
conclave, and they had unanimously admitted that, if
Mr. Arabin would accept St. Ewold's no better choice
could possibly be made.

If Mr. Arabin would accept St. Ewold's ! There lay the
difficulty. Mr. Arabin was a man standing somewhat
prominently before the world, that is, before the Church
of England world. He was not a rich man, it is true, for
he held no preferment but his fellowship ; but he was a
man not over anxious for riches, not married of course, and
one whose time was greatly taken up in discussing, both in
print and on platforms, the privileges and practices of the
church to which he belonged. As the archdeacon had done
battle for its temporalities, so did Mr. Arabin do battle for
its spiritualities ; and both had done so conscientiously ;
that is, not so much each for his own benefit as for that of
others.

Holding such a position as Mr. Arabin did, there was
much reason to doubt whether he would consent to become
the parson of St. Ewold's, and Dr. Grantly had taken the
trouble to go himself to Oxford on the matter. Dr. Gwynne
and Dr. Grantly together had succeeded in persuading this
eminent divine that duty required him to go to Barchester.
There were wheels within wheels in this affair. For some
time past Mr. Arabin had been engaged in a tremendous
controversy with no less a person than Mr. Slope, respecting the apostolic succession. These two gentlemen had
never seen each other, but they had been extremely bitter
in print. Mr. Slope had endeavoured to strengthen his
cause by calling Mr. Arabin an owl, and Mr. Arabin had
retaliated by hinting that Mr. Slope was an infidel. This
battle had been commenced in the columns of the daily
Jupiter, a powerful newspaper, the manager of which was
very friendly to Mr. Slope's view of the case. The matter,
however, had become too tedious for the readers of the
Jupiter, and a little note had therefore been appended to
one of Mr. Slope's most telling rejoinders, in which it had
been stated that no further letters from the reverend
gentleman could be inserted except as advertisements.

Other methods of publication were, however, found less

expensive than advertisements in the Jupiter; and the war went on merrily. Mr. Slope declared that the main part of the consecration of a clergyman was the self-devotion of the inner man to the duties of the ministry. Mr. Arabin contended that a man was not consecrated at all, had, indeed, no single attribute of a clergyman, unless he became so through the imposition of some bishop's hands, who had become a bishop through the imposition of other hands, and so on in a direct line to one of the apostles. Each had repeatedly hung the other on the horns of a dilemma; but neither seemed to be a whit the worse for the hanging; and so the war went on merrily.

Whether or no the near neighbourhood of the foe may have acted in any way as an inducement to Mr. Arabin to accept the living of St. Ewold, we will not pretend to say; but it had at any rate been settled in Dr. Gwynne's library, at Lazarus, that he would accept it, and that he would lend his assistance towards driving the enemy out of Barchester, or, at any rate, silencing him while he remained there. Mr. Arabin intended to keep his rooms at Oxford, and to have the assistance of a curate at St. Ewold; but he promised to give as much time as possible to the neighbourhood of Barchester, and from so great a man Dr. Grantly was quite satisfied with such a promise. It was no small part of the satisfaction derivable from such an arrangement that Bishop Proudie would be forced to institute into a living, immediately under his own nose, the enemy of his favourite chaplain.

All through dinner the archdeacon's good humour shone brightly in his face. He ate of the good things heartily, he drank wine with his wife and daughter, he talked pleasantly of his doings at Oxford, told his father-in-law that he ought to visit Dr. Gwynne at Lazarus, and launched out again in praise of Mr. Arabin.

'Is Mr. Arabin married, papa?' asked Griselda.

'No, my dear; the fellow of a college is never married.'

'Is he a young man, papa?'

'About forty, I believe,' said the archdeacon.

'Oh!' said Griselda. Had her father said eighty, Mr. Arabin would not have appeared to her to be very much older.

When the two gentlemen were left alone over their wine,

Mr. Harding told his tale of woe. But even this, sad as it was, did not much diminish the archdeacon's good humour, though it greatly added to his pugnacity.

'He can't do it,' said Dr. Grantly over and over again, as his father-in-law explained to him the terms on which the new warden of the hospital was to be appointed; 'he can't do it. What he says is not worth the trouble of listening to. He can't alter the duties of the place.'

'Who can't?' asked the ex-warden.

'Neither the bishop nor the chaplain, nor yet the bishop's wife, who, I take it, has really more to say to such matters than either of the other two. The whole body corporate of the palace together have no power to turn the warden of the hospital into a Sunday schoolmaster.'

'But the bishop has the power to appoint whom he pleases, and——'

'I don't know that; I rather think he'll find he has no such power. Let him try it, and see what the press will say. For once we shall have the popular cry on our side. But Proudie, ass as he is, knows the world too well to get such a hornet's nest about his ears.'

Mr. Harding winced at the idea of the press. He had had enough of that sort of publicity, and was unwilling to be shown up a second time either as a monster or as a martyr. He gently remarked that he hoped the newspapers would not get hold of his name again, and then suggested that perhaps it would be better that he should abandon his object. 'I am getting old,' said he; 'and after all I doubt whether I am fit to undertake new duties.'

'New duties!' said the archdeacon: 'don't I tell you there shall be no new duties?'

'Or, perhaps, old duties either,' said Mr. Harding; 'I think I will remain content as I am.' The picture of Mr. Slope carting away the rubbish was still present to his mind.

The archdeacon drank off his glass of claret, and prepared himself to be energetic. 'I do hope,' said he, 'that you are not going to be so weak as to allow such a man as Mr. Slope to deter you from doing what you know it is your duty to do. You know it is your duty to resume your place at the hospital now that parliament has so settled the stipend as to remove those difficulties which induced you to resign it. You cannot deny this; and should your timidity now prevent you from doing so, your conscience will hereafter never forgive you;' and as he finished this clause of his speech, he pushed over the bottle to his companion.

'Your conscience will never forgive you,' he continued. 'You resigned the place from conscientious scruples, scruples which I greatly respected, though I did not share them. All your friends respected them, and you left your old house as rich in reputation as you were ruined in fortune. It is now expected that you will return. Dr. Gwynne was saying only the other day——'

'Dr. Gwynne does not reflect how much older a man I am now than when he last saw me.'

'Old—nonsense!' said the archdeacon; 'you never thought yourself old till you listened to the impudent trash of that coxcomb at the palace.'

'I shall be sixty-five if I live till November,' said Mr. Harding.

'And seventy-five, if you live till November ten years,' said the archdeacon. 'And you bid fair to be as efficient then as you were ten years ago. But for heaven's sake let us have no pretence in this matter. Your plea of old age is only a pretence. But you're not drinking your wine. It is only a pretence. The fact is, you are half afraid of this Slope, and would rather subject yourself to comparative poverty and discomfort, than come to blows with a man who will trample on you, if you let him.'

'I certainly don't like coming to blows, if I can help it.'

'Nor I neither—but sometimes we can't help it. This man's object is to induce you to refuse the hospital, that he may put some creature of his own into it; that he may show his power, and insult us all by insulting you, whose cause and character are so intimately bound up with that of the chapter. You owe it to us all to resist him in this, even if you have no solicitude for yourself. But surely, for your own sake, you will not be so lily-livered as to fall into this trap which he has baited for you, and let him take the very bread out of your mouth without a struggle.'

Mr. Harding did not like being called lily-livered, and was rather inclined to resent it. 'I doubt there is any true courage,' said he, 'in squabbling for money.'

' If honest men did not squabble for money, in this
wicked world of ours, the dishonest men would get it all ;
and I do not see that the cause of virtue would be much
improved. No,—we must use the means which we have.
If we were to carry your argument home, we might give
away every shilling of revenue which the church has ; and
I presume you are not prepared to say that the church
would be strengthened by such a sacrifice.' The archdeacon filled his glass and then emptied it, drinking with
much reverence a silent toast to the well-being and
permanent security of those temporalities which were so
dear to his soul.

' I think all quarrels between a clergyman and his bishop
should be avoided,' said Mr. Harding.

' I think so too ; but it is quite as much the duty of the
bishop to look to that as of his inferior. I tell you what,
my friend ; I'll see the bishop in this matter, that is, if you
will allow me ; and you may be sure I will not compromise
you. My opinion is, that all this trash about the Sunday-
schools and the sermons has originated wholly with Slope
and Mrs. Proudie, and that the bishop knows nothing
about it. The bishop can't very well refuse to see me, and
I'll come upon him when he has neither his wife nor his
chaplain by him. I think you'll find that it will end in his
sending you the appointment without any condition whatever. And as to the seats in the cathedral, we may safely
leave that to Mr. Dean. I believe the fool positively thinks
that the bishop could walk away with the cathedral if he
pleased.'

And so the matter was arranged between them. Mr.
Harding had come expressly for advice, and therefore felt
himself bound to take the advice given him. He had
known, moreover, beforehand, that the archdeacon would
not hear of his giving the matter up, and accordingly
though he had in perfect good faith put forward his own
views, he was prepared to yield.

They therefore went into the drawing-room in good
humour with each other, and the evening passed pleasantly
in prophetic discussions on the future wars of Arabin and
Slope. The frogs and the mice would be nothing to them,
nor the angers of Agamemnon and Achilles. How the
archdeacon rubbed his hands, and plumed himself on the

success of his last move. He could not himself descend into the arena with Slope, but Arabin would have no such scruples. Arabin was exactly the man for such work, and the only man whom he knew that was fit for it.

The archdeacon's good humour and high buoyancy continued till, when reclining on his pillow, Mrs. Grantly commenced to give him her view of the state of affairs at Barchester. And then certainly he was startled. The last words he said that night were as follows :—

'If she does, by heaven I'll never speak to her again. She dragged me into the mire once, but I'll not pollute myself with such filth as that——' And the archdeacon gave a shudder which shook the whole room, so violently was he convulsed with the thought which then agitated his mind.

Now in this matter, the widow Bold was scandalously ill-treated by her relatives. She had spoken to the man three or four times, and had expressed her willingness to teach in a Sunday-school. Such was the full extent of her sins in the matter of Mr. Slope. Poor Eleanor ! But time will show.

The next morning Mr. Harding returned to Barchester, no further word having been spoken in his hearing respecting Mr. Slope's acquaintance with his younger daughter. But he observed that the archdeacon at breakfast was less cordial than he had been on the preceding evening.

CHAPTER XV

THE WIDOW'S SUITORS

MR. SLOPE lost no time in availing himself of the bishop's permission to see Mr. Quiverful, and it was in his interview with this worthy pastor that he first learned that Mrs. Bold was worth the wooing. He rode out to Puddingdale to communicate to the embryo warden the good will of the bishop in his favour, and during the discussion on the matter it was not unnatural that the pecuniary resources of Mr. Harding and his family should become the subject of remark.

Mr. Quiverful, with his fourteen children and his four hundred a year, was a very poor man, and the prospect of this new preferment, which was to be held together with his living, was very grateful to him. To what clergyman so circumstanced would not such a prospect be very grateful? But Mr. Quiverful had long been acquainted with Mr. Harding, and had received kindness at his hands, so that his heart misgave him as he thought of supplanting a friend at the hospital. Nevertheless, he was extremely civil, cringingly civil, to Mr. Slope; treated him quite as the great man; entreated this great man to do him the honour to drink a glass of sherry, at which, as it was very poor Marsala, the now pampered Slope turned up his nose; and ended by declaring his extreme obligation to the bishop and Mr. Slope, and his great desire to accept the hospital, if—if it were certainly the case that Mr. Harding had refused it.

What man, as needy as Mr. Quiverful, would have been more disinterested?

' Mr. Harding did positively refuse it,' said Mr. Slope, with a certain air of offended dignity, ' when he heard of the conditions to which the appointment is now subjected. Of course, you understand, Mr. Quiverful, that the same conditions will be imposed on yourself.'

Mr. Quiverful cared nothing for the conditions. He would have undertaken to preach any number of sermons Mr. Slope might have chosen to dictate, and to pass every remaining hour of his Sundays within the walls of a Sunday-school. What sacrifices, or, at any rate, what promises, would have been too much to make for such an addition to his income, and for such a house! But his mind still recurred to Mr. Harding.

' To be sure,' said he; ' Mr. Harding's daughter is very rich, and why should he trouble himself with the hospital?'

' You mean Mrs. Grantly,' said Slope.

' I meant his widowed daughter,' said the other. ' Mrs. Bold has twelve hundred a year of her own, and I suppose Mr. Harding means to live with her.'

' Twelve hundred a year of her own!' said Slope, and very shortly afterwards took his leave, avoiding, as far as it was possible for him to do, any further allusion to the hospital. Twelve hundred a year, said he to himself, as he rode slowly home. If it were the fact that Mrs. Bold had twelve hundred a year of her own, what a fool would he be

to oppose her father's return to his old place. The train of
Mr. Slope's ideas will probably be plain to all my readers.
Why should he not make the twelve hundred a year his
own ? and if he did so, would it not be well for him to have
a father-in-law comfortably provided with the good things
of this world ? would it not, moreover, be much more easy
for him to gain the daughter, if he did all in his power to
forward the father's views ?

These questions presented themselves to him in a very
forcible way, and yet there were many points of doubt.
If he resolved to restore to Mr. Harding his former place,
he must take the necessary steps for doing so at once; he
must immediately talk over the bishop, quarrel on the
matter with Mrs. Proudie whom he knew he could not talk
over, and let Mr. Quiverful know that he had been a little too
precipitate as to Mr. Harding's positive refusal. That he
could effect all this, he did not doubt; but he did not wish
to effect it for nothing. He did not wish to give way to
Mr. Harding, and then be rejected by the daughter. He
did not wish to lose one influential friend before he had
gained another.

And thus he rode home, meditating many things in his
mind. It occurred to him that Mrs. Bold was sister-in-law
to the archdeacon; and that not even for twelve hundred
a year would he submit to that imperious man. A rich
wife was a great desideratum to him, but success in his
profession was still greater; there were, moreover, other
rich women who might be willing to become wives; and
after all, this twelve hundred a year might, when inquired
into, melt away into some small sum utterly beneath his
notice. Then also he remembered that Mrs. Bold had
a son.

Another circumstance also much influenced him, though
it was one which may almost be said to have influenced
him against his will. The vision of the Signora Neroni was
perpetually before his eyes. It would be too much to say
that Mr. Slope was lost in love, but yet he thought, and
kept continually thinking, that he had never seen so
beautiful a woman. He was a man whose nature was open
to such impulses, and the wiles of the Italianised charmer
had been thoroughly successful in imposing upon his
thoughts. We will not talk about his heart: not that he

had no heart, but because his heart had little to do with
his present feelings. His taste had been pleased, his eyes
charmed, and his vanity gratified. He had been dazzled
by a sort of loveliness which he had never before seen, and
had been caught by an easy, free, voluptuous manner
which was perfectly new to him. He had never been so
tempted before, and the temptation was now irresistible.
He had not owned to himself that he cared for this woman
more than for others around him; but yet he thought
often of the time when he might see her next, and made,
almost unconsciously, little cunning plans for seeing her
frequently.

He had called at Dr. Stanhope's house the day after the
bishop's party, and then the warmth of his admiration had
been fed with fresh fuel. If the signora had been kind in
her manner and flattering in her speech when lying upon
the bishop's sofa, with the eyes of so many on her, she had
been much more so in her mother's drawing-room, with no
one present but her sister to repress either her nature or
her art. Mr. Slope had thus left her quite bewildered, and
could not willingly admit into his brain any scheme, a part
of which would be the necessity of his abandoning all
further special friendship with this lady.

And so he slowly rode along very meditative.

And here the author must beg it to be remembered that
Mr. Slope was not in all things a bad man. His motives,
like those of most men, were mixed; and though his
conduct was generally very different from that which we
would wish to praise, it was actuated perhaps as often as
that of the majority of the world by a desire to do his duty.
He believed in the religion which he taught, harsh, unpalatable, uncharitable as that religion was. He believed
those whom he wished to get under his hoof, the Grantlys
and Gwynnes of the church, to be the enemies of that
religion. He believed himself to be a pillar of strength,
destined to do great things; and with that subtle, selfish,
ambiguous sophistry to which the minds of all men are so
subject, he had taught himself to think that in doing much
for the promotion of his own interests he was doing much
also for the promotion of religion. But Mr. Slope had
never been an immoral man. Indeed, he had resisted
temptations to immorality with a strength of purpose that

was creditable to him. He had early in life devoted himself to works which were not compatible with the ordinary
pleasures of youth, and he had abandoned such pleasures
not without a struggle. It must therefore be conceived
that he did not admit to himself that he warmly admired
the beauty of a married woman without heartfelt stings of
conscience ; and to pacify that conscience, he had to teach
himself that the nature of his admiration was innocent.

And thus he rode along meditative and ill at ease. His
conscience had not a word to say against his choosing the
widow and her fortune. That he looked upon as a godly
work rather than otherwise ; as a deed which, if carried
through, would redound to his credit as a Christian. On
that side lay no future remorse, no conduct which he
might probably have to forget, no inward stings. If it
should turn out to be really the fact that Mrs. Bold had
twelve hundred a year at her own disposal, Mr. Slope
would rather look upon it as a duty which he owed his
religion to make himself the master of the wife and the
money ; as a duty too, in which some amount of self-
sacrifice would be necessary. He would have to give up
his friendship with the signora, his resistance to Mr.
Harding, his antipathy—no, he found on mature self-
examination, that he could not bring himself to give up his
antipathy to Dr. Grantly. He would marry the lady as the
enemy of her brother-in-law if such an arrangement suited
her ; if not, she must look elsewhere for a husband.

It was with such resolve as this that he reached Barchester. He would at once ascertain what the truth might
be as to the lady's wealth, and having done this, he would
be ruled by circumstances in his conduct respecting the
hospital. If he found that he could turn round and secure
the place for Mr. Harding without much self-sacrifice, he
would do so ; but if not, he would woo the daughter in
opposition to the father. But in no case would he succumb
to the archdeacon.

He saw his horse taken round to the stable, and immediately went forth to commence his inquiries. To give
Mr. Slope his due, he was not a man who ever let much
grass grow under his feet.

Poor Eleanor ! She was doomed to be the intended
victim of more schemes than one.

About the time that Mr. Slope was visiting the vicar of Puddingdale, a discussion took place respecting her charms and wealth at Dr. Stanhope's house in the close. There had been morning callers there, and people had told some truth and also some falsehood respecting the property which John Bold had left behind him. By degrees the visitors went, and as the doctor went with them, and as the doctor's wife had not made her appearance, Charlotte Stanhope and her brother were left together. He was sitting idly at the table, scrawling caricatures of Barchester notables, then yawning, then turning over a book or two, and evidently at a loss how to kill his time without much labour.

'You haven't done much, Bertie, about getting any orders,' said his sister.

'Orders!' said he; 'who on earth is there at Barchester to give one orders? Who among the people here could possibly think it worth his while to have his head done into marble?'

'Then you mean to give up your profession,' said she.

'No, I don't,' said he, going on with some absurd portrait of the bishop. 'Look at that, Lotte; isn't it the little man all over, apron and all? I'd go on with my profession at once, as you call it, if the governor would set me up with a studio in London; but as to sculpture at Barchester—I suppose half the people here don't know what a torso means.'

'The governor will not give you a shilling to start you in London,' said Lotte. 'Indeed, he can't give you what would be sufficient, for he has not got it. But you might start yourself very well, if you pleased.'

'How the deuce am I to do it?' said he.

'To tell you the truth, Bertie, you'll never make a penny by any profession.'

'That's what I often think myself,' said he, not in the least offended. 'Some men have a great gift of making money, but they can't spend it. Others can't put two shillings together, but they have a great talent for all sorts of outlay. I begin to think that my genius is wholly in the latter line.'

'How do you mean to live then?' asked the sister.

'I suppose I must regard myself as a young raven, and

look for heavenly manna; besides, we have all got something when the governor goes.'

'Yes—you'll have enough to supply yourself with gloves
and boots; that is, if the Jews have not got the possession
of it all. I believe they have the most of it already. I
wonder, Bertie, at your indifference; that you, with your
talents and personal advantages, should never try to settle
yourself in life. I look forward with dread to the time
when the governor must go. Mother, and Madeline, and
I,—we shall be poor enough, but you will have absolutely
nothing.'

'Sufficient for the day is the evil thereof,' said Bertie.

'Will you take my advice?' said his sister.

'*Cela dépend*,' said the brother.

'Will you marry a wife with money?'

'At any rate,' said he, 'I won't marry one without:
wives with money a'nt so easy to get now-a-days; the
parsons pick them all up.'

'And a parson will pick up the wife I mean for you, if
you do not look quickly about it; the wife I mean is
Mrs. Bold.'

'Whew-w-w-w!' whistled Bertie, 'a widow!'

'She is very beautiful,' said Charlotte.

'With a son and heir all ready to my hand,' said Bertie.

'A baby that will very likely die,' said Charlotte.

'I don't see that,' said Bertie. 'But however, he may
live for me—I don't wish to kill him; only, it must be
owned that a ready-made family is a drawback.'

'There is only one after all,' pleaded Charlotte.

'And that a very little one, as the maid-servant said,'
rejoined Bertie.

'Beggars mustn't be choosers, Bertie; you can't have
everything.'

'God knows I am not unreasonable,' said he, 'nor yet
opinionated; and if you'll arrange it all for me, Lotte, I'll
marry the lady. Only mark this; the money must be sure,
and the income at my own disposal, at any rate for the
lady's life.'

Charlotte was explaining to her brother that he must
make love for himself if he meant to carry on the matter,
and was encouraging him to do so, by warm eulogiums on
Eleanor's beauty, when the signora was brought into the

drawing-room. When at home, and subject to the gaze of none but her own family, she allowed herself to be dragged about by two persons, and her two bearers now deposited her on her sofa. She was not quite so grand in her apparel as she had been at the bishop's party, but yet she was dressed with much care, and though there was a look of care and pain about her eyes, she was, even by daylight, extremely beautiful.

' Well, Madeline ; so I'm going to be married,' Bertie began, as soon as the servants had withdrawn.

' There's no other foolish thing left, that you haven't done,' said Madeline, ' and therefore you are quite right to try that.'

' Oh, you think it 's a foolish thing, do you ? ' said he. ' There's Lotte advising me to marry by all means. But on such a subject your opinion ought to be the best ; you have experience to guide you.'

' Yes, I have,' said Madeline, with a sort of harsh sadness in her tone, which seemed to say—What is it to you if I am sad ? I have never asked your sympathy.

Bertie was sorry when he saw that she was hurt by what he said, and he came and squatted on the floor close before her face to make his peace with her.

' Come, Mad, I was only joking ; you know that. But in sober earnest, Lotte is advising me to marry. She wants me to marry this Mrs. Bold. She's a widow with lots of tin, a fine baby, a beautiful complexion, and the *George and Dragon* hotel up in the High Street. By Jove, Lotte, if I marry her, I'll keep the public house myself— it 's just the life to suit me.'

' What ? ' said Madeline, ' that vapid swarthy creature in the widow's cap, who looked as though her clothes had been stuck on her back with a pitchfork ! ' The signora never allowed any woman to be beautiful.

' Instead of being vapid,' said Lotte, ' I call her a very lovely woman. She was by far the loveliest woman in the rooms the other night ; that is, excepting you, Madeline.'

Even the compliment did not soften the asperity of the maimed beauty. ' Every woman is charming according to Lotte,' she said ; ' I never knew an eye with so little true appreciation. In the first place, what woman on earth could look well in such a thing as that she had on her head ? '

' Of course she wears a widow's cap ; but she'll put that off when Bertie marries her.'

' I don't see any of course in it,' said Madeline. ' The death of twenty husbands should not make me undergo such a penance. It is as much a relic of paganism as the sacrifice of a Hindoo woman at the burning of her husband's body. ·If not so bloody, it is quite as barbarous, and quite as useless.'

' But you don't blame her for that,' said Bertie. ' She does it because it 's the custom of the country. People would think ill of her if she didn't do it.'

' Exactly,' said Madeline. ' She is just one of those English nonentities who would tie her head up in a bag for three months every summer, if her mother and her grandmother had tied up their heads before her. It would never occur to her, to think whether there was any use in submitting to such a nuisance.'

' It 's very hard, in a country like England, for a young woman to set herself in opposition to prejudices of that sort,' said the prudent Charlotte.

' What you mean is, that it 's very hard for a fool not to be a fool,' said Madeline.

Bertie Stanhope had been so much knocked about the world from his earliest years, that he had not retained much respect for the gravity of English customs ; but even to his mind an idea presented itself, that, perhaps in a wife, true British prejudice would not in the long run be less agreeable than Anglo-Italian freedom from restraint. He did not exactly say so, but he expressed the idea in another way.

' I fancy,' said he, ' that if I were to die, and then walk, I should think that my widow looked better in one of those caps than any other kind of head-dress.'

' Yes—and you'd fancy also that she could do nothing better than shut herself up and cry for you, or else burn herself. But she would think differently. She'd probably wear one of those horrid she-helmets, because she'd want the courage not to do so ; but she'd wear it with a heart longing for the time when she might be allowed to throw it off. I hate such shallow false pretences. For my part, I would let the world say what it pleased, and show no grief if I felt none ;—and perhaps not, if I did.'

'But wearing a widow's cap won't lessen her fortune,' said Charlotte.

'Or increase it,' said Madeline. 'Then why on earth does she do it ? '

'But Lotte's object is to make her put it off,' said Bertie.

'If it be true that she has got twelve hundred a year quite at her own disposal, and she be not utterly vulgar in her manners, I would advise you to marry her. I dare say she is to be had for the asking : and as you are not going to marry her for love, it doesn't much matter whether she is good-looking or not. As to your really marrying a woman for love, I don't believe *you* are fool enough for that.'

'Oh, Madeline ! ' exclaimed her sister.

'And oh, Charlotte ! ' said the other.

'You don't mean to say that no man can love a woman unless he be a fool ? '

'I mean very much the same thing,—that any man who is willing to sacrifice his interest to get possession of a pretty face is a fool. Pretty faces are to be had cheaper than that. I hate your mawkish sentimentality, Lotte. You know as well as I do in what way husbands and wives generally live together ; you know how far the warmth of conjugal affection can withstand the trial of a bad dinner, of a rainy day, or of the least privation which poverty brings with it ; you know what freedom a man claims for himself, what slavery he would exact from his wife if he could ! And you know also how wives generally obey. Marriage means tyranny on one side and deceit on the other. I say that a man is a fool to sacrifice his interests for such a bargain. A woman, too generally, has no other way of living.'

'But Bertie has no other way of living,' said Charlotte.

'Then, in God's name, let him marry Mrs. Bold,' said Madeline. And so it was settled between them.

But let the gentle-hearted reader be under no apprehension whatsoever. It is not destined that Eleanor shall marry Mr. Slope or Bertie Stanhope. And here, perhaps, it may be allowed to the novelist to explain his views on a very important point in the art of telling tales. He

ventures to reprobate that system which goes so far to
violate all proper confidence between the author and his
readers, by maintaining nearly to the end of the third
volume a mystery as to the fate of their favourite personage. Nay, more, and worse than this, is too frequently
done. Have not often the profoundest efforts of genius
been used to baffle the aspirations of the reader, to raise
false hopes and false fears, and to give rise to expectations
which are never to be realised ? Are not promises all but
made of delightful horrors, in lieu of which the writer
produces nothing but most commonplace realities in his
final chapter ? And is there not a species of deceit in this
to which the honesty of the present age should lend no
countenance ?

And what can be the worth of that solicitude which a
peep into the third volume can utterly dissipate ? What
the value of those literary charms which are absolutely
destroyed by their enjoyment ? When we have once
learnt what was that picture before which was hung Mrs.
Radcliffe's solemn curtain, we feel no further interest about
either the frame or the veil. They are to us, merely a
receptacle for old bones, an inappropriate coffin, which we
would wish to have decently buried out of our sight.

And then, how grievous a thing it is to have the pleasure
of your novel destroyed by the ill-considered triumph of
a previous reader. ' Oh, you needn't be alarmed for
Augusta, of course she accepts Gustavus in the end.'
' How very ill-natured you are, Susan,' says Kitty, with
tears in her eyes ; ' I don't care a bit about it now.' Dear
Kitty, if you will read my book, you may defy the ill-
nature of your sister. There shall be no secret that she can
tell you. Nay, take the last chapter if you please—learn
from its pages all the results of our troubled story, and the
story shall have lost none of its interest, if indeed there be
any interest in it to lose.

Our doctrine is, that the author and the reader should
move along together in full confidence with each other.
Let the personages of the drama undergo ever so complete a
comedy of errors among themselves, but let the spectator
never mistake the Syracusan for the Ephesian ; otherwise
he is one of the dupes, and the part of a dupe is never
dignified.

I would not for the value of this chapter have it believed by a single reader that my Eleanor could bring herself to marry Mr. Slope, or that she should be sacrificed to a Bertie Stanhope. But among the good folk of Barchester many believed both the one and the other.

CHAPTER XVI

BABY WORSHIP

' DIDDLE, diddle, diddle, diddle, dum, dum, dum,' said or sung Eleanor Bold.

' Diddle, diddle, diddle, diddle, dum, dum, dum,' continued Mary Bold, taking up the second part in this concerted piece.

The only audience at the concert was the baby, who however gave such vociferous applause, that the performers presuming it to amount to an encore, commenced again.

' Diddle, diddle, diddle, diddle, dum, dum, dum : hasn't he got lovely legs ? ' said the rapturous mother.

' H'm 'm 'm 'm 'm,' simmered Mary, burying her lips in the little fellow's fat neck, by way of kissing him.

' H'm 'm 'm 'm 'm,' simmered the mamma, burying her lips also in his fat round short legs. ' He's a dawty little bold darling, so he is ; and he has the nicest little pink legs in all the world, so he has ; ' and the simmering and the kissing went on over again, and as though the ladies were very hungry, and determined to eat him.

' Well, then, he's his own mother's own darling : well, he shall—oh, oh—Mary, Mary—did you ever see ? What am I to do ? My naughty, naughty, naughty, naughty little Johnny.' All these energetic exclamations were elicited by the delight of the mother in finding that her son was strong enough, and mischievous enough, to pull all her hair out from under her cap. ' He's been and pulled down all mamma's hair, and he's the naughtiest, naughtiest, naughtiest little man that ever, ever, ever, ever, ever——'

A regular service of baby worship was going on. Mary Bold was sitting on a low easy chair, with the boy in her lap, and Eleanor was kneeling before the object of her idolatry. As she tried to cover up the little fellow's face

with her long, glossy, dark brown locks, and permitted him
to pull them hither and thither, as he would, she looked
very beautiful in spite of the widow's cap which she still
wore. There was a quiet, enduring, grateful sweetness
about her face, which grew so strongly upon those who
knew her, as to make the great praise of her beauty which
came from her old friends, appear marvellously exaggerated to those who were only slightly acquainted with
her. Her loveliness was like that of many landscapes,
which require to be often seen to be fully enjoyed. There
was a depth of dark clear brightness in her eyes which was
lost upon a quick observer, a character about her mouth
which only showed itself to those with whom she familiarly
conversed, a glorious form of head the perfect symmetry
of which required the eye of an artist for its appreciation.
She had none of that dazzling brilliancy, of that voluptuous
Rubens beauty, of that pearly whiteness, and those
vermilion tints, which immediately entranced with the
power of a basilisk men who came within reach of Madeline
Neroni. It was all but impossible to resist the signora, but
no one was called upon for any resistance towards Eleanor.
You might begin to talk to her as though she were your
sister, and it would not be till your head was on your pillow,
that the truth and intensity of her beauty would flash upon
you; that the sweetness of her voice would come upon
your ear. A sudden half-hour with the Neroni, was like
falling into a pit; an evening spent with Eleanor like an
unexpected ramble in some quiet fields of asphodel.

' We'll cover him up till there sha'n't be a morsel of his
little 'ittle 'ittle 'ittle nose to be seen,' said the mother,
stretching her streaming locks over the infant's face. The
child screamed with delight, and kicked till Mary Bold was
hardly able to hold him.

At this moment the door opened, and Mr. Slope was
announced. Up jumped Eleanor, and with a sudden quick
motion of her hands pushed back her hair over her shoulders. It would have been perhaps better for her that she
had not, for she thus showed more of her confusion than
she would have done had she remained as she was. Mr.
Slope, however, immediately recognised her loveliness, and
thought to himself, that irrespective of her fortune, she
would be an inmate that a man might well desire for his

house, a partner for his bosom's care very well qualified
to make care lie easy. Eleanor hurried out of the room to
re-adjust her cap, muttering some unnecessary apology
about her baby. And while she is gone, we will briefly go
back and state what had been hitherto the results of Mr.
Slope's meditations on his scheme of matrimony.

His inquiries as to the widow's income had at any rate
been so far successful as to induce him to determine to go
on with the speculation. As regarded Mr. Harding, he had
also resolved to do what he could without injury to himself.
To Mrs. Proudie he determined not to speak on the matter,
at least not at present. His object was to instigate a little
rebellion on the part of the bishop. He thought that such
a state of things would be advisable not only in respect to
Messrs. Harding and Quiverful, but also in the affairs of the
diocese generally. Mr. Slope was by no means of opinion
that Dr. Proudie was fit to rule, but he conscientiously
thought it wrong that his brother clergy should be subjected
to petticoat government. He therefore made up his mind
to infuse a little of his spirit into the bishop, sufficient to
induce him to oppose his wife, though not enough to make
him altogether insubordinate.

He had therefore taken an opportunity of again speaking
to his lordship about the hospital, and had endeavoured to
make it appear that after all it would be unwise to exclude
Mr. Harding from the appointment. Mr. Slope, however,
had a harder task than he had imagined. Mrs. Proudie,
anxious to assume to herself as much as possible of the
merit of patronage, had written to Mrs. Quiverful, request-
ing her to call at the palace; and had then explained to
that matron, with much mystery, condescension, and
dignity, the good that was in store for her and her progeny.
Indeed Mrs. Proudie had been so engaged at the very time
that Mr. Slope had been doing the same with the husband
at Puddingdale Vicarage, and had thus in a measure
committed herself. The thanks, the humility, the gratitude, the surprise of Mrs. Quiverful had been very overpowering; she had all but embraced the knees of her
patroness, and had promised that the prayers of fourteen
unprovided babes (so Mrs. Quiverful had described her
own family, the eldest of which was a stout young woman
of three-and-twenty) should be put up to heaven morning

and evening for the munificent friend whom God had sent
to them. Such incense as this was not unpleasing to Mrs.
Proudie, and she made the most of it. She offered her
general assistance to the fourteen unprovided babes, if,
as she had no doubt, she should find them worthy;
expressed a hope that the eldest of them would be fit to
undertake tuition in her Sabbath schools, and altogether
made herself a very great lady in the estimation of Mrs.
Quiverful.

Having done this, she thought it prudent to drop a few
words before the bishop, letting him know that she had
acquainted the Puddingdale family with their good
fortune; so that he might perceive that he stood committed to the appointment. The husband well understood
the *ruse* of his wife, but he did not resent it. He knew that
she was taking the patronage out of his hands; he was
resolved to put an end to her interference, and re-assume
his powers. But then he thought this was not the best
time to do it. He put off the evil hour, as many a man in
similar circumstances has done before him.

Such having been the case, Mr. Slope naturally encountered a difficulty in talking over the bishop, a difficulty
indeed which he found could not be overcome except at
the cost of a general outbreak at the palace. A general
outbreak at the present moment might be good policy, but
it also might not. It was at any rate not a step to be lightly
taken. He began by whispering to the bishop that he
feared that public opinion would be against him if Mr.
Harding did not reappear at the hospital. The bishop
answered with some warmth that Mr. Quiverful had been
promised the appointment on Mr. Slope's advice. 'Not
promised!' said Mr. Slope. 'Yes, promised,' replied the
bishop, 'and Mrs. Proudie has seen Mrs. Quiverful on the
subject.' This was quite unexpected on the part of Mr.
Slope, but his presence of mind did not fail him, and he
turned the statement to his own account.

'Ah, my lord,' said he, 'we shall all be in scrapes if the
ladies interfere.'

This was too much in unison with my lord's feelings
to be altogether unpalatable, and yet such an allusion to
interference demanded a rebuke. My lord was somewhat
astounded also, though not altogether made miserable, by

finding that there was a point of difference between his wife and his chaplain.

' I don't know what you mean by interference,' said the bishop mildly. ' When Mrs. Proudie heard that Mr. Quiverful was to be appointed, it was not unnatural that she should wish to see Mrs. Quiverful about the schools. I really cannot say that I see any interference.'

' I only speak, my lord, for your own comfort,' said Slope ; ' for your own comfort and dignity in the diocese. I can have no other motive. As far as personal feelings go, Mrs. Proudie is the best friend I have. I must always remember that. But still, in my present position, my first duty is to your lordship.'

' I'm sure of that, Mr. Slope, I am quite sure of that ; ' said the bishop mollified : ' and you really think that Mr. Harding should have the hospital ? '

' Upon my word, I'm inclined to think so. I am quite prepared to take upon myself the blame of first suggesting Mr. Quiverful's name. But since doing so, I have found that there is so strong a feeling in the diocese in favour of Mr. Harding, that I think your lordship should give way. I hear also that Mr. Harding has modified the objections he first felt to your lordship's propositions. And as to what has passed between Mrs. Proudie and Mrs. Quiverful, the circumstance may be a little inconvenient, but I really do not think that that should weigh in a matter of so much moment.'

And thus the poor bishop was left in a dreadfully un-decided state as to what he should do. His mind, however, slightly inclined itself to the appointment of Mr. Harding, seeing that by such a step, he should have the assistance of Mr. Slope in opposing Mrs. Proudie.

Such was the state of affairs at the palace, when Mr. Slope called at Mrs. Bold's house, and found her playing with her baby. When she ran out of the room, Mr. Slope began praising the weather to Mary Bold, then he praised the baby and kissed him, and then he praised the mother, and then he praised Miss Bold herself. Mrs. Bold, however, was not long before she came back.

' I have to apologise for calling at so very early an hour,' began Mr. Slope, ' but I was really so anxious to speak to you that I hope you and Miss Bold will excuse me.'

Eleanor muttered something in which the words
'certainly,' and 'of course,' and 'not early at all,' were
just audible, and then apologised for her own appearance,
declaring with a smile, that her baby was becoming such
a big boy that he was quite unmanageable.

'He's a great big naughty boy,' said she to the child;
'and we must send him away to a great big rough romping
school, where they have great big rods, and do terrible
things to naughty boys who don't do what their own
mammas tell them;' and she then commenced another
course of kissing, being actuated thereto by the terrible
idea of sending her child away which her own imagination
had depicted.

'And where the masters don't have such beautiful long
hair to be dishevelled,' said Mr. Slope, taking up the joke
and paying a compliment at the same time.

Eleanor thought he might as well have left the compliment alone; but she said nothing and looked nothing,
being occupied as she was with the baby.

'Let me take him,' said Mary. 'His clothes are nearly
off his back with his romping,' and so saying she left the
room with the child. Miss Bold had heard Mr. Slope say
he had something pressing to say to Eleanor, and thinking
that she might be de trop, took this opportunity of getting
herself out of the room.

'Don't be long, Mary,' said Eleanor, as Miss Bold shut
the door.

'I am glad, Mrs. Bold, to have the opportunity of having
ten minutes' conversation with you alone,' began Mr.
Slope. 'Will you let me openly ask you a plain question?'

'Certainly,' said she.

'And I am sure you will give me a plain and open
answer.'

'Either that or none at all,' said she, laughing.

'My question is this, Mrs. Bold; is your father really
anxious to go back to the hospital?'

'Why do you ask me?' said she. 'Why don't you ask
himself?'

'My dear Mrs. Bold, I'll tell you why. There are
wheels within wheels, all of which I would explain to you,
only I fear that there is not time. It is essentially necessary that I should have an answer to this question, other-

wise I cannot know how to advance your father's wishes;
and it is quite impossible that I should ask himself. No
one can esteem your father more than I do, but I doubt if
this feeling is reciprocal.' It certainly was not. 'I must
be candid with you as the only means of avoiding ultimate
consequences, which may be most injurious to Mr. Harding.
I fear there is a feeling, I will not even call it a prejudice,
with regard to myself in Barchester, which is not in my
favour. You remember that sermon——'

'Oh! Mr. Slope, we need not go back to that,' said
Eleanor.

'For one moment, Mrs. Bold. It is not that I may talk
of myself, but because it is so essential that you should
understand how matters stand. That sermon may have
been ill-judged,—it was certainly misunderstood; but
I will say nothing about that now; only this, that it did
give rise to a feeling against myself which your father
shares with others. It may be that he has proper cause,
but the result is that he is not inclined to meet me on
friendly terms. I put it to yourself whether you do not
know this to be the case.'

Eleanor made no answer, and Mr. Slope, in the eagerness
of his address, edged his chair a little nearer to the widow's
seat, unperceived by her.

'Such being so,' continued Mr. Slope, 'I cannot ask him
this question as I can ask it of you. In spite of my delin-
quencies since I came to Barchester you have allowed me
to regard you as a friend.' Eleanor made a little motion
with her head which was hardly confirmatory, but Mr.
Slope if he noticed it, did not appear to do so. 'To you
I can speak openly, and explain the feelings of my heart.
This your father would not allow. Unfortunately the
bishop has thought it right that this matter of the hospital
should pass through my hands. There have been some
details to get up with which he would not trouble himself,
and thus it has come to pass that I was forced to have an
interview with your father on the matter.'

'I am aware of that,' said Eleanor.

'Of course,' said he. 'In that interview Mr. Harding
left the impression on my mind that he did not wish to
return to the hospital.'

'How could that be?' said Eleanor, at last stirred up to

forget the cold propriety of demeanour which she had determined to maintain.

'My dear Mrs. Bold, I give you my word that such was the case,' said he, again getting a little nearer to her. 'And what is more than that, before my interview with Mr. Harding, certain persons at the palace, I do not mean the bishop, had told me that such was the fact. I own, I hardly believed it; I own, I thought that your father would wish on every account, for conscience' sake, for the sake of those old men, for old association, and the memory of dear days long gone by, on every account I thought that he would wish to resume his duties. But I was told that such was not his wish; and he certainly left me with the impression that I had been told the truth.'

'Well!' said Eleanor, now sufficiently roused on the matter.

'I hear Miss Bold's step,' said Mr. Slope; 'would it be asking too great a favour to beg you to——I know you can manage anything with Miss Bold.'

Eleanor did not like the word manage, but still she went out, and asked Mary to leave them alone for another quarter of an hour.

'Thank you, Mrs. Bold,—I am so very grateful for this confidence. Well, I left your father with this impression. Indeed, I may say that he made me understand that he declined the appointment.'

'Not the appointment,' said Eleanor. 'I am sure he did not decline the appointment. But he said that he would not agree,—that is, that he did not like the scheme about the schools and the services, and all that. I am quite sure he never said that he wished to refuse the place.'

'Oh, Mrs. Bold!' said Mr. Slope, in a manner almost impassioned. 'I would not, for the world, say to so good a daughter a word against so good a father. But you must, for his sake, let me show you exactly how the matter stands at present. Mr. Harding was a little flurried when I told him of the bishop's wishes about the school. I did so, perhaps, with the less caution because you yourself had so perfectly agreed with me on the same subject. He was a little put out and spoke warmly. 'Tell the bishop,' said he, ' that I quite disagree with him,—and shall not return to the hospital as such conditions are attached to it.' What he said was to that effect; indeed, his words were, if anything, stronger than those. I had no alternative but to repeat them to his lordship, who said that he could look on them in no other light than a refusal. He also had heard the report that your father did not wish for the appointment, and putting all these things together, he thought he had no choice but to look for some one else. He has consequently offered the place to Mr. Quiverful.'

' Offered the place to Mr. Quiverful ! ' repeated Eleanor, her eyes suffused with tears. ' Then, Mr. Slope, there is an end of it.'

' No, my friend—not so,' said he. ' It is to prevent such being the end of it that I am now here. I may at any rate presume that I have got an answer to my question, and that Mr. Harding is desirous of returning.'

' Desirous of returning—of course he is,' said Eleanor ; ' of course he wishes to have back his house and his income, and his place in the world ; to have back what he gave up with such self-denying honesty, if he can have them without restraints on his conduct to which at his age it would be impossible that he should submit. How can the bishop ask a man of his age to turn schoolmaster to a pack of children ? '

' Out of the question,' said Mr. Slope, laughing slightly ; ' of course no such demand shall be made on your father. I can at any rate promise you that I will not be the medium of any so absurd a requisition. We wished your father to preach in the hospital, as the inmates may naturally be too old to leave it ; but even that shall not be insisted on. We wished also to attach a Sabbath-day school to the hospital, thinking that such an establishment could not but be useful under the surveillance of so good a clergyman as Mr. Harding, and also under your own. But, dear Mrs. Bold ; we won't talk of these things now. One thing is clear ; we must do what we can to annul this rash offer the bishop has made to Mr. Quiverful. Your father wouldn't see Quiverful, would he ? Quiverful is an honourable man, and would not, for a moment, stand in your father's way.'

' What ? ' said Eleanor ; ' ask a man with fourteen children to give up his preferment ! I am quite sure he will do no such thing.'

' I suppose not,' said Slope ; and he again drew near to

Mrs. Bold, so that now they were very close to each other.
Eleanor did not think much about it, but instinctively
moved away a little. How greatly would she have increased the distance could she have guessed what had been
said about her at Plumstead! 'I suppose not. But it is
out of the question that Quiverful should supersede your
father,—quite out of the question. The bishop has been
too rash. An idea occurs to me, which may, perhaps.
with God's blessing, put us right. My dear Mrs. Bold,
would you object to seeing the bishop yourself?'

'Why should not my father see him?' said Eleanor.
She had once before in her life interfered in her father's
affairs, and then not to much advantage. She was older
now, and felt that she should take no step in a matter so
vital to him without his consent.

'Why, to tell the truth,' said Mr. Slope, with a look of
sorrow, as though he greatly bewailed the want of charity
in his patron, ' the bishop fancies that he has cause of
anger against your father. I fear an interview would lead
to further ill will.'

'Why,' said Eleanor, ' my father is the mildest, the
gentlest man living.'

'I only know,' said Slope, ' that he has the best of
daughters. So you would not see the bishop? As to
getting an interview, I could manage that for you without
the slightest annoyance to yourself.'

'I could do nothing, Mr. Slope, without consulting my
father.'

'Ah!' said he, ' that would be useless; you would then
only be your father's messenger. Does anything occur to
yourself? Something must be done. Your father shall
not be ruined by so ridiculous a misunderstanding.'

Eleanor said that nothing occurred to her, but that it
was very hard; and the tears came to her eyes and rolled
down her cheeks. Mr. Slope would have given much to
have had the privilege of drying them; but he had tact
enough to know that he had still a great deal to do before
he could even hope for any privilege with Mrs. Bold.

'It cuts me to the heart to see you so grieved,' said he.
' But pray let me assure you that your father's interests
shall not be sacrificed if it be possible for me to protect
them. I will tell the bishop openly what are the facts.

I will explain to him that he has hardly the right to appoint
any other than your father, and will show him that if he
does so he will be guilty of great injustice,—and you, Mrs.
Bold, you will have the charity at any rate to believe this
of me, that I am truly anxious for your father's welfare,—
for his and for your own.'

The widow hardly knew what answer to make. She
was quite aware that her father would not be at all thankful to Mr. Slope; she had a strong wish to share her
father's feelings; and yet she could not but acknowledge
that Mr. Slope was very kind. Her father, who was
generally so charitable to all men, who seldom spoke ill of
any one, had warned her against Mr. Slope, and yet she did
not know how to abstain from thanking him. What
interest could he have in the matter but that which he
professed? Nevertheless there was that in his manner
which even she distrusted. She felt, she did not know why,
that there was something about him which ought to put
her on her guard.

Mr. Slope read all this in her hesitating manner just as
plainly as though she had opened her heart to him. It was
the talent of the man that he could so read the inward
feelings of women with whom he conversed. He knew that
Eleanor was doubting him, and that if she thanked him
she would only do so because she could not help it; but
yet this did not make him angry or even annoy him.
Rome was not built in a day.

'I did not come for thanks,' continued he, seeing her
hesitation; 'and do not want them—at any rate before
they are merited. But this I do want, Mrs. Bold, that I
may make to myself friends in this fold to which it has
pleased God to call me as one of the humblest of his
shepherds. If I cannot do so, my task here must indeed be
a sad one. I will at any rate endeavour to deserve them.'

'I'm sure,' said she, 'you will soon make plenty of
friends.' She felt herself obliged to say something.

'That will be nothing unless they are such as will
sympathise with my feelings; unless they are such as I can
reverence and admire—and love. If the best and purest
turn away from me, I cannot bring myself to be satisfied
with the friendship of the less estimable. In such case
I must live alone.'

'Oh! I'm sure you will not do that, Mr. Slope.'
Eleanor meant nothing, but it suited him to appear to
think some special allusion had been intended.

'Indeed, Mrs. Bold, I shall live alone, quite alone as far
as the heart is concerned, if those with whom I yearn to
ally myself turn away from me. But enough of this; I
have called you my friend, and I hope you will not contradict me. I trust the time may come when I may also
call your father so. May God bless you, Mrs. Bold, you
and your darling boy. And tell your father from me that
what can be done for his interest shall be done.'

And so he took his leave, pressing the widow's hand
rather more closely than usual. Circumstances, however,
seemed just then to make this intelligible, and the lady did
not feel called on to resent it.

'I cannot understand him,' said Eleanor to Mary Bold,
a few minutes afterwards. 'I do not know whether he is
a good man or a bad man—whether he is true or false.'

'Then give him the benefit of the doubt,' said Mary,
'and believe the best.'

'On the whole, I think I do,' said Eleanor. 'I think I do
believe that he means well—and if so, it is a shame that we
should revile him, and make him miserable while he is
among us. But, oh, Mary, I fear papa will be disappointed
in the hospital.'

CHAPTER XVII

WHO SHALL BE COCK OF THE WALK?

ALL this time things were going on somewhat uneasily
at the palace. The hint or two which Mr. Slope had given
was by no means thrown away upon the bishop. He had
a feeling that if he ever meant to oppose the now almost
unendurable despotism of his wife, he must lose no further
time in doing so; that if he ever meant to be himself
master in his own diocese, let alone his own house, he
should begin at once. It would have been easier to have
done so from the day of his consecration than now, but
easier now than when Mrs. Proudie should have succeeded
in thoroughly mastering the diocesan details. Then the
proffered assistance of Mr. Slope was a great thing for him,

a most unexpected and invaluable aid. Hitherto he had looked on the two as allied forces; and had considered that as allies they were impregnable. He had begun to believe that his only chance of escape would be by the advancement of Mr. Slope to some distant and rich preferment. But now it seemed that one of his enemies, certainly the least potent of them, but nevertheless one very important, was willing to desert his own camp. Assisted by Mr. Slope what might he not do ? He walked up and down his little study, almost thinking that the time might come when he would be able to appropriate to his own use the big room up stairs, in which his predecessor had always sat.

As he revolved these things in his mind a note was brought to him from Archdeacon Grantly, in which that divine begged his lordship to do him the honour of seeing him on the morrow—would his lordship have the kindness to name an hour ? Dr. Grantly's proposed visit would have reference to the reappointment of Mr. Harding to the wardenship of Barchester hospital. The bishop having read his note was informed that the archdeacon's servant was waiting for an answer.

Here at once a great opportunity offered itself to the bishop of acting on his own responsibility. He bethought himself however of his new ally, and rang the bell for Mr. Slope. It turned out that Mr. Slope was not in the house ; and then, greatly daring, the bishop with his own unassisted spirit wrote a note to the archdeacon saying that he would see him, and naming an hour for doing so. Having watched from his study-window that the messenger got safely off from the premises with this despatch, he began to turn over in his mind what step he should next take.

To-morrow he would have to declare to the archdeacon either that Mr. Harding should have the appointment, or that he should not have it. The bishop felt that he could not honestly throw over the Quiverfuls without informing Mrs. Proudie, and he resolved at last to brave the lioness in her den and tell her that circumstances were such that it behoved him to reappoint Mr. Harding. He did not feel that he should at all derogate from his new courage by promising Mrs. Proudie that the very first piece of available preferment at his disposal should be given to Quiverful

to atone for the injury done to him. If he could mollify
the lioness with such a sop, how happy would he think his
first efforts to have been !

Not without many misgivings did he find himself in
Mrs. Proudie's boudoir. He had at first thought of sending
for her. But it was not at all impossible that she might
chose to take such a message amiss, and then also it might
be some protection to him to have his daughters present
at the interview. He found her sitting with her account
books before her nibbling the end of her pencil evidently
mersed in pecuniary difficulties, and harassed in mind by
the multiplicity of palatial expenses, and the heavy cost
of episcopal grandeur. Her daughters were around her.
Olivia was reading a novel, Augusta was crossing a note
to her bosom friend in Baker Street, and Netta was
working diminutive coach wheels for the bottom of a
petticoat. If the bishop could get the better of his wife in
her present mood, he would be a man indeed. He might
then consider the victory his own for ever. After all, in
such cases the matter between husband and wife stands
much the same as it does between two boys at the same
school, two cocks in the same yard, or two armies on the
same continent. The conqueror once is generally the
conqueror for ever after. The prestige of victory is every
thing.

' Ahem—my dear,' began the bishop, ' if you are dis-
engaged, I wished to speak to you.' Mrs. Proudie put her
pencil down carefully at the point to which she had dotted
her figures, marked down in her memory the sum she had
arrived at, and then looked up, sourly enough, into her
helpmate's face. ' If you are busy, another time will do
as well,' continued the bishop, whose courage like Bob
Acres' had oozed out, now that he found himself on the
ground of battle.

' What is it about, Bishop ? ' asked the lady.

' Well—it was about those Quiverfuls—but I see you
are engaged. Another time will do just as well for me.'

' What about the Quiverfuls ? It is quite understood
I believe, that they are to come to the hospital. There is
to be no doubt about that, is there ? ' and as she spoke she
kept her pencil sternly and vigorously fixed on the column
of figures before her.

' Why, my dear, there is a difficulty,' said the bishop.

' A difficulty ! ' said Mrs. Proudie, ' what difficulty ? The place has been promised to Mr. Quiverful, and of course he must have it. He has made all his arrangements. He has written for a curate for Puddingdale, he has spoken to the auctioneer about selling his farm, horses, and cows, and in all respects considers the place as his own. Of course he must have it.'

Now, bishop, look well to thyself, and call up all the manhood that is in thee. Think how much is at stake. If now thou art not true to thy guns, no Slope can hereafter aid thee. How can he who deserts his own colours at the first smell of gunpowder expect faith in any ally. Thou thyself hast sought the battle-field ; fight out the battle manfully now thou art there. Courage, bishop, courage ! Frowns cannot kill, nor can sharp words break any bones. After all the apron is thine own. She can appoint no wardens, give away no benefices, nominate no chaplains, an' thou art but true to thyself. Up, man, and at her with a constant heart.

Some little monitor within the bishop's breast so addressed him. But then there was another monitor there which advised him differently, and as follows. Remember, bishop, she is a woman, and such a woman too as thou well knowest : a battle of words with such a woman is the very mischief. Were it not better for thee to carry on this war, if it must be waged, from behind thine own table in thine own study ? Does not every cock fight best on his own dunghill ? Thy daughters also are here, the pledges of thy love, the fruits of thy loins ; is it well that they should see thee in the hour of thy victory over their mother ? nay, is it well that they should see thee in the possible hour of thy defeat ? Besides, hast thou not chosen thy opportunity with wonderful little skill, indeed with no touch of that sagacity for which thou art famous ? Will it not turn out that thou art wrong in this matter, and thine enemy right ; that thou hast actually pledged thy-self in this matter of the hospital, and that now thou wouldest turn upon thy wife because she requires from thee but the fulfilment of thy promise ? Art thou not a Christian bishop, and is not thy word to be held sacred whatever be the result ? Return, bishop, to thy sanctum

on the lower floor, and postpone thy combative propensities for some occasion in which at least thou mayest fight
the battle against odds less tremendously against thee.

All this passed within the bishop's bosom while Mrs.
Proudie still sat with her fixed pencil, and the figures
of her sum still enduring on the tablets of her memory.
' £4 17s. 7d.' she said to herself. ' Of course Mr. Quiverful
must have the hospital,' she said out loud to her lord.

' Well, my dear, I merely wanted to suggest to you that
Mr. Slope seems to think that if Mr. Harding be not
appointed, public feeling in the matter would be against
us, and that the press might perhaps take it up.'

' Mr. Slope seems to think ! ' said Mrs. Proudie, in a tone
of voice which plainly showed the bishop that he was right
in looking for a breach in that quarter. ' And what has
Mr. Slope to do with it ? I hope, my lord, you are not
going to allow yourself to be governed by a chaplain.' And
now in her eagerness the lady lost her place in her account.

' Certainly not, my dear. Nothing I can assure you is
less probable. But still Mr. Slope may be useful in finding
how the wind blows, and I really thought that if we could
give something else as good to the Quiverfuls——'

' Nonsense,' said Mrs. Proudie ; ' it would be years
before you could give them anything else that could suit
them half as well, and as for the press and the public, and
all that, remember there are two ways of telling a story.
If Mr. Harding is fool enough to tell his tale, we can also
tell ours. The place was offered to him, and he refused it.
It has now been given to some one else, and there's an end
of it. At least, I should think so.'

' Well, my dear, I rather believe you are right ; ' said the
bishop, and sneaking out of the room, he went down stairs,
troubled in his mind as to how he should receive the archdeacon on the morrow. He felt himself not very well just
at present ; and began to consider that he might, not
improbably, be detained in his room the next morning by
an attack of bile. He was, unfortunately, very subject to
bilious annoyances.

' Mr. Slope, indeed ! I'll Slope him,' said the indignant
matron to her listening progeny. ' I don't know what has
come to Mr. Slope. I believe he thinks he is to be Bishop
of Barchester himself, because I've taken him by the

hand, and got your father to make him his domestic chaplain.'

' He was always full of impudence,' said Olivia ; ' I told you so once before, mamma.' Olivia, however, had not thought him too impudent when once before he had proposed to make her Mrs. Slope.

' Well, Olivia, I always thought you liked him,' said Augusta, who at that moment had some grudge against her sister. ' I always disliked the man, because I think him thoroughly vulgar.'

' There you're wrong,' said Mrs. Proudie ; ' he's not vulgar at all ; and what is more, he is a soul-stirring, eloquent preacher ; but he must be taught to know his place if he is to remain in this house.'

' He has the horridest eyes I ever saw in a man's head,' said Netta ; ' and I tell you what, he's terribly greedy ; did you see all the currant pie he ate yesterday ? '

When Mr. Slope got home he soon learnt from the bishop, as much from his manner as his words, that Mrs. Proudie's behests in the matter of the hospital were to be obeyed. Dr. Proudie let fall something as to ' this occasion only,' and ' keeping all affairs about patronage exclusively in his own hands.' But he was quite decided about Mr. Harding ; and as Mr. Slope did not wish to have both the prelate and the prelatess against him, he did not at present see that he could do anything but yield.

He merely remarked that he would of course carry out the bishop's views, and that he was quite sure that if the bishop trusted to his own judgment things in the diocese would certainly be well ordered. Mr. Slope knew that if you hit a nail on the head often enough, it will penetrate at last.

He was sitting alone in his room on the same evening when a light knock was made on his door, and before he could answer it the door was opened, and his patroness appeared. He was all smiles in a moment, but so was not she also. She took, however, the chair that was offered to her, and thus began her expostulation :—

' Mr. Slope, I did not at all approve your conduct the other night with that Italian woman. Any one would have thought that you were her lover.'

' Good gracious, my dear madam,' said Mr. Slope, with a look of horror. ' Why, she is a married woman.'

'That's more than I know,' said Mrs. Proudie; 'however she chooses to pass for such. But married or not married, such attention as you paid to her was improper. I cannot believe that you would wish to give offence in my drawing-room, Mr. Slope; but I owe it to myself and my daughters to tell you that I disapprove your conduct.'

Mr. Slope opened wide his huge protruding eyes, and stared out of them with a look of well-feigned surprise. 'Why, Mrs. Proudie,' said he, 'I did but fetch her something to eat when she said she was hungry.'

'And you have called on her since,' continued she, looking at the culprit with the stern look of a detective policeman in the act of declaring himself.

Mr. Slope turned over in his mind whether it would be well for him to tell this termagant at once that he should call on whom he liked, and do what he liked; but he remembered that his footing in Barchester was not yet sufficiently firm, and that it would be better for him to pacify her.

'I certainly called since at Dr. Stanhope's house, and certainly saw Madame Neroni.'

'Yes, and you saw her alone,' said the episcopal Argus.

'Undoubtedly, I did,' said Mr. Slope, 'but that was because nobody else happened to be in the room. Surely it was no fault of mine if the rest of the family were out.'

'Perhaps not; but I assure you, Mr. Slope, you will fall greatly in my estimation if I find that you allow yourself to be caught by the lures of that woman. I know women better than you do, Mr. Slope, and you may believe me that that signora, as she calls herself, is not a fitting companion for a strict evangelical, unmarried young clergyman.'

How Mr. Slope would have liked to laugh at her, had he dared! But he did not dare. So he merely said, 'I can assure you, Mrs. Proudie, the lady in question is nothing to me.'

'Well, I hope not, Mr. Slope. But I have considered it my duty to give you this caution; and now there is another thing I feel myself called on to speak about; it is your conduct to the bishop, Mr. Slope.'

'My conduct to the bishop,' said he, now truly surprised and ignorant what the lady alluded to.

' Yes, Mr. Slope ; your conduct to the bishop. It is by no means what I would wish to see it.'

' Has the bishop said anything, Mrs. Proudie ? '

' No, the bishop has said nothing. He probably thinks that any remarks on the matter will come better from me, who first introduced you to his lordship's notice. The fact is, Mr. Slope, you are a little inclined to take too much upon yourself.'

An angry spot showed itself on Mr. Slope's cheeks, and it was with difficulty that he controlled himself. But he did do so, and sat quite silent while the lady went on.

' It is the fault of many young men in your position, and therefore the bishop is not inclined at present to resent it. You will, no doubt, soon learn what is required from you, and what is not. If you will take my advice, however, you will be careful not to obtrude advice upon the bishop in any matter touching patronage. If his lordship wants advice, he knows where to look for it.' And then having added to her counsel a string of platitudes as to what was desirable and what not desirable in the conduct of a strictly evangelical, unmarried young clergyman, Mrs. Proudie retreated, leaving the chaplain to his thoughts.

The upshot of his thoughts was this, that there certainly was not room in the diocese for the energies of both himself and Mrs. Proudie, and that it behoved him quickly to ascertain whether his energies or hers were to prevail.

CHAPTER XVIII

THE WIDOW'S PERSECUTION

EARLY on the following morning Mr. Slope was summoned to the bishop's dressing-room, and went there fully expecting that he should find his lordship very indignant, and spirited up by his wife to repeat the rebuke which she had administered on the previous day. Mr. Slope had resolved that at any rate from him he would not stand it, and entered the dressing-room in rather a combative disposition ; but he found the bishop in the most placid and gentlest of humours. His lordship complained of being rather unwell, had a slight headache, and was not quite the thing in his stomach ; but there was nothing the matter with his temper.

' Oh, Slope,' said he, taking the chaplain's proffered hand, ' Archdeacon Grantly is to call on me this morning, and I really am not fit to see him. I fear I must trouble you, to see him for me ; ' and then Dr. Proudie proceeded to explain what it was that must be said to Dr. Grantly. He was to be told in fact in the civilest words in which the tidings could be conveyed, that Mr. Harding having refused the wardenship, the appointment had been offered to Mr. Quiverful and accepted by him.

Mr. Slope again pointed out to his patron that he thought he was perhaps not quite wise in his decision, and this he did *sotto voce*. But even with this precaution it was not safe to say much, and during the little that he did say, the bishop made a very slight, but still a very ominous gesture with his thumb towards the door which opened from his dressing-room to some inner sanctuary. Mr. Slope at once took the hint, and said no more ; but he perceived that there was to be confidence between him and his patron, that the league desired by him was to be made, and that this appointment of Mr. Quiverful was to be the last sacrifice offered on the altar of conjugal obedience. All this Mr. Slope read in the slight motion of the bishop's thumb, and he read it correctly. There was no need of parchments and seals, of attestations, explanations, and professions. The bargain was understood between them, and Mr. Slope gave the bishop his hand upon it. The bishop understood the little extra squeeze, and an intelligible gleam of assent twinkled in his eye.

' Pray be civil to the archdeacon, Mr. Slope,' said he out loud ; ' but make him quite understand that in this matter Mr. Harding has put it out of my power to oblige him.'

It would be a calumny on Mrs. Proudie to suggest that she was sitting in her bed-room with her ear at the keyhole during this interview. She had within her a spirit of decorum which prevented her from descending to such baseness. To put her ear to a key-hole or to listen at a chink, was a trick for a housemaid.

Mrs. Proudie knew this, and therefore she did not do it ; but she stationed herself as near to the door as she well

could, that she might, if possible, get the advantage which
the housemaid would have had, without descending to the
housemaid's artifice.

It was little, however, that she heard, and that little was
only sufficient to deceive her. She saw nothing of that
friendly pressure, perceived nothing of that concluded
bargain ; she did not even dream of the treacherous
resolves which those two false men had made together to
upset her in the pride of her station, to dash the cup from
her lip before she had drank of it, to sweep away all her
power before she had tasted its sweets ! Traitors that they
were ; the husband of her bosom, and the outcast whom
she had fostered and brought to the warmth of the world's
brightest fireside ! But neither of them had the magnani-
mity of this woman. Though two men have thus leagued
themselves together against her, even yet the battle is not
lost.

Mr. Slope felt pretty sure that Dr. Grantly would
decline the honour of seeing him, and such turned out to be
the case. The archdeacon, when the palace door was
opened to him, was greeted by a note. Mr. Slope presented
his compliments, &c. &c. The bishop was ill in his room,
and very greatly regretted, &c. &c. Mr. Slope had been
charged with the bishop's views, and if agreeable to the
archdeacon, would do himself the honour, &c. &c. The
archdeacon, however, was not agreeable, and having read
his note in the hall, crumpled it up in his hand, and muttering something about sorrow for his lordship's illness, took
his leave, without sending as much as a verbal message in
answer to Mr. Slope's note.

' Ill ! ' said the archdeacon to himself as he flung himself
into his brougham. ' The man is absolutely a coward. He
is afraid to see me. Ill, indeed ! ' The archdeacon was
never ill himself, and did not therefore understand that any
one else could in truth be prevented by illness from keeping
an appointment. He regarded all such excuses as subter-
fuges, and in the present instance he was not far wrong.

Dr. Grantly desired to be driven to his father-in-law's
lodgings in the High Street, and hearing from the servant
that Mr. Harding was at his daughter's, followed him to
Mrs. Bold's house, and there found him. The archdeacon
was fuming with rage when he got into the drawing-room,

and had by this time nearly forgotten the pusillanimity of the bishop in the villany of the chaplain.

'Look at that,' said he, throwing Mr. Slope's crumpled note to Mr. Harding. 'I am to be told that if I choose I may have the honour of seeing Mr. Slope, and that too, after a positive engagement with the bishop.'

'But he says the bishop is ill,' said Mr. Harding.

'Pshaw! You don't mean to say that you are deceived by such an excuse as that. He was well enough yesterday. Now I tell you what, I will see the bishop; and I will tell him also very plainly what I think of his conduct. I will see him, or else Barchester will soon be too hot to hold him.'

Eleanor was sitting in the room, but Dr. Grantly had hardly noticed her in his anger. Eleanor now said to him, with the greatest innocence, 'I wish you had seen Mr. Slope, Dr. Grantly, because I think perhaps it might have done good.'

The archdeacon turned on her with almost brutal wrath. Had she at once owned that she had accepted Mr. Slope for her second husband, he could hardly have felt more convinced of her belonging body and soul to the Slope and Proudie party than he now did on hearing her express such a wish as this. Poor Eleanor!

'See him!' said the archdeacon glaring at her; 'and why am I to be called on to lower myself in the world's esteem and my own by coming in contact with such a man as that? I have hitherto lived among gentlemen, and do not mean to be dragged into other company by anybody.'

Poor Mr. Harding well knew what the archdeacon meant, but Eleanor was as innocent as her own baby. She could not understand how the archdeacon could consider himself to be dragged into bad company by condescending to speak to Mr. Slope for a few minutes when the interests of her father might be served by his doing so.

'I was talking for a full hour yesterday to Mr. Slope,' said she, with some little assumption of dignity, 'and I did not find myself lowered by it.'

'Perhaps not,' said he. 'But if you'll be good enough to allow me, I shall judge for myself in such matters. And I tell you what, Eleanor; it will be much better for you if you will allow yourself to be guided also by the advice of those who are your friends. If you do not you will be apt to find that you have no friends left who can advise you.'

Eleanor blushed up to the roots of her hair. But even now she had not the slightest idea of what was passing in the archdeacon's mind. No thought of love-making or love-receiving had yet found its way to her heart since the death of poor John Bold ; and if it were possible that such a thought should spring there, the man must be far different from Mr. Slope that could give it birth.

Nevertheless Eleanor blushed deeply, for she felt she was charged with improper conduct, and she did so with the more inward pain because her father did not instantly rally to her. side ; that father for whose sake and love she had submitted to be the receptacle of Mr. Slope's confidence. She had given a detailed account of all that had passed to her father ; and though he had not absolutely agreed with her about Mr. Slope's views touching the hospital, yet he had said nothing to make her think that she had been wrong in talking to him.

She was far too angry to humble herself before her brother-in-law. Indeed, she had never accustomed herself to be very abject before him, and they had never been confidential allies. ' I do not the least understand what you mean, Dr. Grantly,' said she. ' I do not know that I can accuse myself of doing anything that my friends should disapprove. Mr. Slope called here expressly to ask what papa's wishes were about the hospital ; and as I believe he called with friendly intentions I told him.'

' Friendly intentions ! ' sneered the archdeacon.

' I believe you greatly wrong Mr. Slope,' continued Eleanor ; ' but I have explained this to papa already ; and as you do not seem to approve of what I say, Dr. Grantly, I will with your permission leave you and papa together,' and so saying she walked slowly out of the room.

All this made Mr. Harding very unhappy. It was quite clear that the archdeacon and his wife had made up their minds that Eleanor was going to marry Mr. Slope. Mr. Harding could not really bring himself to think that she would do so, but yet he could not deny that circumstances made it appear that the man's company was not disagreeable to her. She was now constantly seeing him, and yet she received visits from no other unmarried gentleman.

She always took his part when his conduct was canvassed,
although she was aware how personally objectionable he
was to her friends. Then, again, Mr. Harding felt that if
she should choose to become Mrs. Slope, he had nothing
that he could justly urge against her doing so. She had
full right to please herself, and he, as a father, could not say
that she would disgrace herself by marrying a clergyman
who stood so well before the world as Mr. Slope did. As
for quarrelling with his daughter on account of such a
marriage, and separating himself from her as the archdeacon had threatened to do, that, with Mr. Harding,
would be out of the question. If she should determine to
marry this man, he must get over his aversion as best he
could. His Eleanor, his own old companion in their old
happy home, must still be the friend of his bosom, the child
of his heart. Let who would cast her off, he would not. If
it were fated that he should have to sit in his old age at the
same table with that man whom of all men he disliked the
most, he would meet his fate as best he might. Anything
to him would be preferable to the loss of his daughter.

Such being his feelings, he hardly knew how to take part
with Eleanor against the archdeacon, or with the archdeacon against Eleanor. It will be said that he should
never have suspected her.—Alas! he never should have
done so. But Mr. Harding was by no means a perfect
character. In his indecision, his weakness, his proneness
to be led by others, his want of self-confidence, he was very
far from being perfect. And then it must be remembered
that such a marriage as that which the archdeacon contemplated with disgust, which we who know Mr. Slope so
well would regard with equal disgust, did not appear so
monstrous to Mr. Harding, because in his charity he did
not hate the chaplain as the archdeacon did, and as we do.

He was, however, very unhappy when his daughter left
the room, and he had recourse to an old trick of his that
was customary to him in his times of sadness. He began
playing some slow tune upon an imaginary violoncello,
drawing one hand slowly backwards and forwards as
though he held a bow in it, and modulating the unreal
cords with the other.

'She'll marry that man as sure as two and two make
four,' said the practical archdeacon.

'I hope not, I hope not,' said the father. 'But if she does, what can I say to her ? I have no right to object to him.'

'No right !' exclaimed Dr. Grantly.

'No right as her father. He is in my own profession, and for aught we know a good man.'

To this the archdeacon would by no means assent. It was not well, however, to argue the case against Eleanor in her own drawing-room, and so they both walked forth and discussed the matter in all its bearings under the elm trees of the close. Mr. Harding also explained to his son-in-law what had been the purport, at any rate the alleged purport, of Mr. Slope's last visit to the widow. He, however, stated that he could not bring himself to believe that Mr. Slope had any real anxiety such as that he had pretended. 'I cannot forget his demeanour to myself,' said Mr. Harding, 'and it is not possible that his ideas should have changed so soon.'

'I see it all,' said the archdeacon. 'The sly *tartufe !* He thinks to buy the daughter by providing for the father. He means to show how powerful he is, how good he is, and how much he is willing to do for her *beaux yeux ;* yes, I see it all now. But we'll be too many for him yet, Mr. Harding ;' he said, turning to his companion with some gravity, and pressing his hand upon the other's arm. 'It would, perhaps, be better for you to lose the hospital than get it on such terms.'

'Lose it !' said Mr. Harding ; 'why I've lost it already. I don't want it. I've made up my mind to do without it. I'll withdraw altogether. I'll just go and write a line to the bishop and tell him that I withdraw my claim altogether.'

Nothing would have pleased him better than to be allowed to escape from the trouble and difficulty in such a manner. But he was now going too fast for the archdeacon.

'No—no—no ! we'll do no such thing,' said Dr. Grantly ; 'we'll still have the hospital. I hardly doubt but that we'll have it. But not by Mr. Slope's assistance. If that be necessary we'll lose it ; but we'll have it, spite of his teeth, if we can. Arabin will be at Plumstead to-morrow ; you must come over and talk to him.'

The two now turned into the cathedral library, which was used by the clergymen of the close as a sort of ecclesiastical club-room, for writing sermons and sometimes letters; also for reading theological works, and sometimes magazines and newspapers. The theological works were not disturbed, perhaps, quite as often as from the appearance of the building the outside public might have been led to expect. Here the two allies settled on their course of action. The archdeacon wrote a letter to the bishop, strongly worded, but still respectful, in which he put forward his father-in-law's claim to the appointment, and expressed his own regret that he had not been able to see his lordship when he called. Of Mr. Slope he made no mention whatsoever. It was then settled that Mr. Harding should go out to Plumstead on the following day; and after considerable discussion on the matter, the archdeacon proposed to ask Eleanor there also, so as to withdraw her, if possible, from Mr. Slope's attentions. 'A week or two,' said he, ' may teach her what he is, and while she is there she will be out of harm's way. Mr. Slope won't come there after her.'

Eleanor was not a little surprised when her brother-in-law came back and very civilly pressed her to go out to Plumstead with her father. She instantly perceived that her father had been fighting her battles for her behind her back. She felt thankful to him, and for his sake she would not show her resentment to the archdeacon by refusing his invitation. But she could not, she said, go on the morrow; she had an invitation to drink tea at the Stanhopes which she had promised to accept. She would, she added, go with her father on the next day, if he would wait; or she would follow him.

' The Stanhopes!' said Dr. Grantly; 'I did not know you were so intimate with them.'

' I did not know it myself,' said she, ' till Miss Stanhope called yesterday. However, I like her very much, and I have promised to go and play chess with some of them.'

' Have they a party there?' said the archdeacon, still fearful of Mr. Slope.

' Oh, no,' said Eleanor; ' Miss Stanhope said there was to be nobody at all. But she had heard that Mary had left me for a few weeks, and she had learnt from some one that

I play chess, and so she came over on purpose to ask me to go in.'

' Well, that's very friendly,' said the ex-warden. ' They certainly do look more like foreigners than English people, but I dare say they are none the worse for that.'

The archdeacon was inclined to look upon the Stanhopes with favourable eyes, and had nothing to object on the matter. It was therefore arranged that Mr. Harding should postpone his visit to Plumstead for one day, and then take with him Eleanor, the baby, and the nurse.

Mr. Slope is certainly becoming of some importance in Barchester.

CHAPTER XIX

BARCHESTER BY MOONLIGHT

THERE was much cause for grief and occasional perturbation of spirits in the Stanhope family, but yet they rarely seemed to be grieved or to be disturbed. It was the peculiar gift of each of them that each was able to bear his or her own burden without complaint, and perhaps without sympathy. They habitually looked on the sunny side of the wall, if there was a gleam on either side for them to look at ; and, if there was none, they endured the shade with an indifference which, if not stoical, answered the end at which the Stoics aimed. Old Stanhope could not but feel that he had ill-performed his duties as a father and a clergyman ; and could hardly look forward to his own death without grief at the position in which he would leave his family. His income for many years had been as high as 3000l. a year, and yet they had among them no other provision than their mother's fortune of 10,000l. He had not only spent his income, but was in debt. Yet with all this, he seldom showed much outward sign of trouble.

It was the same with the mother. If she added little to the pleasures of her children she detracted still less : she neither grumbled at her lot, nor spoke much of her past or future sufferings ; as long as she had a maid to adjust her dress, and had those dresses well made, nature with her was satisfied. It was the same with the children. Charlotte never rebuked her father with the prospect of their future poverty, nor did it seem to grieve her that she was becoming an old maid so quickly; her temper was rarely ruffled, and, if we might judge by her appearance, she was always happy. The signora was not so sweet-tempered, but she possessed much enduring courage; she seldom complained—never, indeed, to her family. Though she had a cause for affliction which would have utterly broken down the heart of most women as beautiful as she and as devoid of all religious support, yet, she bore her suffering in silence, or alluded to it only to elicit the sympathy and stimulate the admiration of the men with whom she flirted. As to Bertie, one would have imagined from the sound of his voice and the gleam of his eye that he had not a sorrow nor a care in the world. Nor had he. He was incapable of anticipating to-morrow's griefs. The prospect of future want no more disturbed his appetite than does that of the butcher's knife disturb the appetite of the sheep.

Such was the usual tenour of their way; but there were rare exceptions. Occasionally the father would allow an angry glance to fall from his eye, and the lion would send forth a low dangerous roar as though he meditated some deed of blood. Occasionally also Madame Neroni would become bitter against mankind, more than usually antagonistic to the world's decencies, and would seem as though she was about to break from her moorings and allow herself to be carried forth by the tide of her feelings to utter ruin and shipwreck. She, however, like the rest of them, had no real feelings, could feel no true passion. In that was her security. Before she resolved on any contemplated escapade she would make a small calculation, and generally summed up that the Stanhope villa or even Barchester close was better than the world at large.

They were most irregular in their hours. The father was generally the earliest in the breakfast-parlour, and Charlotte would soon follow and give him his coffee; but the others breakfasted anywhere, anyhow, and at any time. On the morning after the archdeacon's futile visit to the palace, Dr. Stanhope came down stairs with an ominously dark look about his eyebrows; his white locks were rougher than usual, and he breathed thickly and loudly as he took his seat in his arm-chair. He had open letters in his hand, and when Charlotte came into the room he was still reading them. She went up and kissed him as was her wont, but he hardly noticed her as she did so, and she knew at once that something was the matter.

' What's the meaning of that ? ' said he, throwing over the table a letter with a Milan post-mark. Charlotte was a little frightened as she took it up, but her mind was relieved when she saw that it was merely the bill of their Italian milliner. The sum total was certainly large, but not so large as to create an important row.

' It's for our clothes, papa, for six months before we came here. The three of us can't dress for nothing you know.'

' Nothing, indeed ! ' said he, looking at the figures, which in Milanese denominations were certainly monstrous.

' The man should have sent it to me,' said Charlotte.

' I wish he had with all my heart—if you would have paid it. I see enough in it, to know that three quarters of it are for Madeline.'

' She has little else to amuse her, sir,' said Charlotte with true good nature.

' And I suppose he has nothing else to amuse him,' said the doctor, throwing over another letter to his daughter. It was from some member of the family of Sidonia, and politely requested the father to pay a small trifle of 700*l.*, being the amount of a bill discounted in favour of Mr. Ethelbert Stanhope, and now overdue for a period of nine months.

Charlotte read the letter, slowly folded it up, and put it under the edge of the tea-tray.

' I suppose he has nothing to amuse him but discounting bills with Jews. Does he think I'll pay that ? '

' I am sure he thinks no such thing,' said she.

' And who does he think will pay it ? '

' As far as honesty goes I suppose it won't much matter if it is never paid,' said she. ' I dare say he got very little of it.'

' I suppose it won't much matter either,' said the father, ' if he goes to prison and rots there. It seems to me that that's the other alternative.'

Dr. Stanhope spoke of the custom of his youth. But his daughter, though she had lived so long abroad, was much more completely versed in the ways of the English world. 'If the man arrests him,' said she, 'he must go through the court.'

It is thus, thou great family of Sidonia—it is thus that we Gentiles treat thee, when, in our extremest need, thou and thine have aided us with mountains of gold as big as lions,—and occasionally with wine-warrants and orders for dozens of dressing-cases.

'What, and become an insolvent?' said the doctor.

'He's that already,' said Charlotte, wishing always to get over a difficulty.

'What a condition,' said the doctor, 'for the son of a clergyman of the Church of England.'

'I don't see why clergymen's sons should pay their debts more than other young men,' said Charlotte.

'He's had as much from me since he left school as is held sufficient for the eldest son of many a nobleman,' said the angry father.

'Well, sir,' said Charlotte, 'give him another chance.'

'What!' said the doctor, 'do you mean that I am to pay that Jew?'

'Oh no! I wouldn't pay him, he must take his chance; and if the worst comes to the worst, Bertie must go abroad. But I want you to be civil to Bertie, and let him remain here as long as we stop. He has a plan in his head, that may put him on his feet after all.'

'Has he any plan for following up his profession?'

'Oh, he'll do that too; but that must follow. He's thinking of getting married.'

Just at that moment the door opened, and Bertie came in whistling. The doctor immediately devoted himself to his egg, and allowed Bertie to whistle himself round to his sister's side without noticing him.

Charlotte gave a sign to him with her eye, first glancing at her father, and then at the letter, the corner of which peeped out from under the tea-tray. Bertie saw and understood, and with the quiet motion of a cat abstracted the letter, and made himself acquainted with its contents. The doctor, however, had seen him, deep as he appeared to be mersed in his egg-shell, and said in his harshest voice, 'Well, sir, do you know that gentleman?'

'Yes, sir.' said Bertie. 'I have a sort of acquaintance

with him, but none that can justify him in troubling you. If you will allow me, sir, I will answer this.'

'At any rate I sha'n't,' said the father, and then he added, after a pause, 'Is it true, sir, that you owe the man 700*l.* ?'

'Well,' said Bertie, 'I think I should be inclined to dispute the amount, if I were in a condition to pay him such of it as I really do owe him.'

'Has he your bill for 700*l.* ?' said the father, speaking very loudly and very angrily.

'Well, I believe he has,' said Bertie; 'but all the money I ever got from him was 150*l.*'

'And what became of the 550*l.* ?'

'Why, sir; the commission was 100*l.* or so, and I took the remainder in paving-stones and rocking-horses.'

'Paving-stones and rocking-horses!' said the doctor, 'where are they?'

'Oh, sir, I suppose they are in London somewhere—but I'll inquire if you wish for them.'

'He's an idiot,' said the doctor, 'and it's sheer folly to waste more money on him. Nothing can save him from ruin,' and so saying, the unhappy father walked out of the room.

'Would the governor like to have the paving-stones?' said Bertie to his sister.

'I'll tell you what,' said she. 'If you don't take care, you will find yourself loose upon the world without even a house over your head: you don't know him as well as I do. He's very angry.'

Bertie stroked his big beard, sipped his tea, chatted over his misfortunes in a half comic, half serious tone, and ended by promising his sister that he would do his very best to make himself agreeable to the widow Bold. Then Charlotte followed her father to his own room and softened down his wrath, and persuaded him to say nothing more about the Jew bill discounter, at any rate for a few weeks. He even went so far as to say he would pay the 700*l.*, or at any rate settle the bill, if he saw a certainty of his son's securing for himself anything like a decent provision in life. Nothing was said openly between them about poor Eleanor: but the father and the daughter understood each other.

They all met together in the drawing-room at nine
o'clock, in perfect good humour with each other; and
about that hour Mrs. Bold was announced. She had never
been in the house before, though she had of course called;
and now she felt it strange to find herself there in her usual
evening dress, entering the drawing-room of these strangers
in this friendly unceremonious way, as though she had
known them all her life. But in three minutes they made
her at home. Charlotte tripped down stairs and took her
bonnet from her, and Bertie came to relieve her from her
shawl, and the signora smiled on her as she could smile
when she chose to be gracious, and the old doctor shook
hands with her in a kind benedictory manner that went to
her heart at once, and made her feel that he must be a good
man.

She had not been seated for above five minutes when the
door again opened, and Mr. Slope was announced. She
felt rather surprised, because she was told that nobody was
to be there, and it was very evident from the manner of
some of them, that Mr. Slope was unexpected. But still
there was not much in it. In such invitations a bachelor
or two more or less are always spoken of as nobodies, and
there was no reason why Mr. Slope should not drink tea at
Dr. Stanhope's as well as Eleanor herself. He, however,
was very much surprised and not very much gratified at
finding that his own embryo spouse made one of the party.
He had come there to gratify himself by gazing on Madame
Neroni's beauty, and listening to and returning her flattery:
and though he had not owned as much to himself, he still
felt that if he spent the evening as he had intended to do,
he might probably not thereby advance his suit with
Mrs. Bold.

The signora, who had no idea of a rival, received Mr.
Slope with her usual marks of distinction. As he took her
hand, she made some confidential communication to him
in a low voice, declaring that she had a plan to communicate to him after tea, and was evidently prepared to go on
with her work of reducing the chaplain to a state of
captivity. Poor Mr. Slope was rather beside himself. He
thought that Eleanor could not but have learnt from his
demeanour that he was an admirer of her own, and he had
also flattered himself that the idea was not unacceptable

to her. What would she think of him if he now devoted himself to a married woman!

But Eleanor was not inclined to be severe in her criticisms on him in this respect, and felt no annoyance of any kind, when she found herself seated between Bertie and Charlotte Stanhope. She had no suspicion of Mr. Slope's intentions; she had no suspicion even of the suspicion of other people; but still she felt well pleased not to have Mr. Slope too near to her.

And she was not ill-pleased to have Bertie Stanhope near her. It was rarely indeed that he failed to make an agreeable impression on strangers. With a bishop indeed who thought much of his own dignity it was possible that he might fail, but hardly with a young and pretty woman· He possessed the tact of becoming instantly intimate with women without giving rise to any fear of impertinence. He had about him somewhat of the propensities of a tame cat. It seemed quite natural that he should be petted, caressed, and treated with familiar good nature, and that in return he should purr, and be sleek and graceful, and above all never show his claws. Like other tame cats, however, he had his claws, and sometimes made them dangerous.

When tea was over Charlotte went to the open window and declared loudly that the full harvest moon was much too beautiful to be disregarded, and called them all to look at it. To tell the truth, there was but one there who cared much about the moon's beauty, and that one was not Charlotte; but she knew how valuable an aid to her purpose the chaste goddess might become, and could easily create a little enthusiasm for the purpose of the moment. Eleanor and Bertie were soon with her. The doctor was now quiet in his arm-chair, and Mrs. Stanhope in hers, both prepared for slumber.

'Are you a Whewellite or a Brewsterite, or a t'othermanite, Mrs. Bold?' said Charlotte, who knew a little about everything, and had read about a third of each of the books to which she alluded.

'Oh!' said Eleanor; 'I have not read any of the books, but I feel sure that there is one man in the moon at least, if not more.'

'You don't believe in the pulpy gelatinous matter?' said Bertie.

'I heard about that,' said Eleanor; 'and I really think it's almost wicked to talk in such a manner. How can we argue about God's power in the other stars from the laws which he has given for our rule in this one?'

'How indeed!' said Bertie. 'Why shouldn't there be a race of salamanders in Venus? and even if there be nothing but fish in Jupiter, why shouldn't the fish there be as wide awake as the men and women here?'

'That would be saying very little for them,' said Charlotte. 'I am for Dr. Whewell myself; for I do not think that men and women are worth being repeated in such countless worlds. There may be souls in other stars, but I doubt their having any bodies attached to them. But come, Mrs. Bold, let us put our bonnets on and walk round the close. If we are to discuss sidereal questions, we shall do so much better under the towers of the cathedral, than stuck in this narrow window.'

Mrs. Bold made no objection, and a party was made to walk out. Charlotte Stanhope well knew the rule as to three being no company, and she had therefore to induce her sister to allow Mr. Slope to accompany them.

'Come, Mr. Slope,' she said; 'I'm sure you'll join us. We shall be in again in a quarter of an hour, Madeline.'

Madeline read in her eye all that she had to say, knew her object, and as she had to depend on her sister for so many of her amusements, she felt that she must yield. It was hard to be left alone while others of her own age walked out to feel the soft influence of the bright night, but it would be harder still to be without the sort of sanction which Charlotte gave to all her flirtations and intrigues. Charlotte's eye told her that she must give up just at present for the good of the family, and so Madeline obeyed.

But Charlotte's eyes said nothing of the sort to Mr. Slope. He had no objection at all to the *tête-à-tête* with the signora, which the departure of the other three would allow him, and gently whispered to her, 'I shall not leave you alone.'

'Oh, yes,' said she; 'go—pray go, pray go, for my sake. Do not think that I am so selfish. It is understood that nobody is kept within for me. You will understand this too when you know me better. Pray join them, Mr. Slope,

but when you come in speak to me for five minutes before
you leave us.'

Mr. Slope understood that he was to go, and he therefore
joined the party in the hall. He would have had no objection at all to this arrangement, if he could have secured
Mrs. Bold's arm; but this of course was out of the question.
Indeed, his fate was very soon settled, for no sooner had he
reached the hall-door than Miss Stanhope put her hand
within his arm, and Bertie walked off with Eleanor just
as naturally as though she were already his own property.

And so they sauntered forth: first they walked round
the close, according to their avowed intent; then they
went under the old arched gateway below St. Cuthbert's
little church, and then they turned behind the grounds of
the bishop's palace, and so on till they came to the bridge
just at the edge of the town, from which passers-by can
look down into the gardens of Hiram's Hospital; and here
Charlotte and Mr. Slope, who were in advance, stopped till
the other two came up to them. Mr. Slope knew that the
gable-ends and old brick chimneys which stood up so
prettily in the moonlight, were those of Mr. Harding's late
abode, and would not have stopped on such a spot, in such
company, if he could have avoided it; but Miss Stanhope
would not take the hint which he tried to give.

' This is a very pretty place, Mrs. Bold,' said Charlotte;
' by far the prettiest place near Barchester. I wonder your
father gave it up.'

It was a very pretty place, and now by the deceitful
light of the moon looked twice larger, twice prettier, twice
more antiquely picturesque than it would have done in
truth-telling daylight. Who does not know the air of
complex multiplicity and the mysterious interesting grace
which the moon always lends to old gabled buildings half
surrounded, as was the hospital, by fine trees! As seen
from the bridge on the night of which we are speaking,
Mr. Harding's late abode did look very lovely; and though
Eleanor did not grieve at her father's having left it, she felt
at the moment an intense wish that he might be allowed
to return.

' He is going to return to it almost immediately, is he
not?' asked Bertie.

Eleanor made no immediate reply. Many such a question

passes unanswered, without the notice of the questioner; but such was not now the case. They all remained silent as though expecting her to reply, and after a moment or two, Charlotte said, ' I believe it is settled that Mr. Harding returns to the hospital, is it not ? '

' I don't think anything about it is settled yet,' said Eleanor.

' But it must be a matter of course,' said Bertie ; ' that is, if your father wishes it ; who else on earth could hold it after what has occurred ? '

Eleanor quietly made her companion understand that the matter was one which she could not discuss in the present company ; and then they passed on ; Charlotte said she would go a short way up the hill out of the town so as to look back upon the towers of the cathedral, and as Eleanor leant upon Bertie's arm for assistance in the walk, she told him how the matter stood between her father and the bishop.

' And, he,' said Bertie, pointing on to Mr. Slope, ' what part does he take in it ? '

Eleanor explained how Mr. Slope had at first endeavoured to tyrannise over her father, but how he had latterly come round, and done all he could to talk the bishop over in Mr. Harding's favour. ' But my father,' said she, ' is hardly inclined to trust him ; they all say he is so arrogant to the old clergymen of the city.'

' Take my word for it,' said Bertie, ' your father is right. If I am not very much mistaken, that man is both arrogant and false.'

They strolled up to the top of the hill, and then returned through the fields by a footpath which leads by a small wooden bridge, or rather a plank with a rustic rail to it, over the river to the other side of the cathedral from that at which they had started. They had thus walked round the bishop's grounds, through which the river runs, and round the cathedral and adjacent fields, and it was past eleven before they reached the doctor's door.

' It is very late,' said Eleanor, ' it will be a shame to disturb your mother again at such an hour.'

' Oh,' said Charlotte, laughing, ' you won't disturb mamma ; I dare say she is in bed by this time, and Madeline would be furious if you did not come in and see her. Come, Bertie, take Mrs. Bold's bonnet from her.'

They went up stairs, and found the signora alone, reading. She looked somewhat sad and melancholy, but not more so perhaps than was sufficient to excite additional interest in the bosom of Mr. Slope ; and she was soon deep in whispered intercourse with that happy gentleman, who was allowed to find a resting-place on her sofa. The signora had a way of whispering that was peculiarly her own, and was exactly the reverse of that which prevails among great tragedians. The great tragedian hisses out a positive whisper, made with bated breath, and produced by inarticulated tongue-formed sounds, but yet he is audible through the whole house. The signora however used no hisses, and produced all her words in a clear silver tone, but they could only be heard by the ear into which they were poured.

Charlotte hurried and skurried about the room hither and thither, doing, or pretending to do many things ; and then saying something about seeing her mother, ran up stairs. Eleanor was thus left alone with Bertie, and she hardly felt an hour fly by her. To give Bertie his due credit, he could not have played his cards better. He did not make love to her, nor sigh, nor look languishing ; but he was amusing and familiar, yet respectful ; and when he left Eleanor at her own door at one o'clock, which he did by the bye with the assistance of the now jealous Slope, she thought that he was one of the most agreeable men, and the Stanhopes decidedly the most agreeable family, that she had ever met.

CHAPTER XX

MR. ARABIN

THE Rev. Francis Arabin, fellow of Lazarus, late professor of poetry at Oxford, and present vicar of St. Ewold, in the diocese of Barchester, must now be introduced personally to the reader. And as he will fill a conspicuous place in the volume, it is desirable that he should be made to stand before the reader's eye by the aid of such portraiture as the author is able to produce.

It is to be regretted that no mental method of daguerreotype or photography has yet been discovered, by which the characters of men can be reduced to writing and put into grammatical language with an unerring precision of truthful description. How often does the novelist feel, ay, and the historian also and the biographer, that he has conceived within his mind and accurately depicted on the tablet of his brain the full character and personage of a man, and that nevertheless, when he flies to pen and ink to perpetuate the portrait, his words forsake, elude, disappoint, and play the deuce with him, till at the end of a dozen pages the man described has no more resemblance to the man conceived than the sign board at the corner of the street has to the Duke of Cambridge ?

And yet such mechanical descriptive skill would hardly give more satisfaction to the reader than the skill of the photographer does to the anxious mother desirous to possess an absolute duplicate of her beloved child. The likeness is indeed true ; but it is a dull, dead, unfeeling, inauspicious likeness. The face is indeed there, and those looking at it will know at once whose image it is ; but the owner of the face will not be proud of the resemblance.

There is no royal road to learning ; no short cut to the acquirement of any valuable art. Let photographers and daguerreotypers do what they will, and improve as they may with further skill on that which skill has already done, they will never achieve a portrait of the human face divine. Let biographers, novelists, and the rest of us groan as we may under the burdens which we so often feel too heavy for our shoulders ; we must either bear them up like men, or own ourselves too weak for the work we have undertaken. There is no way of writing well and also of writing easily.

Labor omnia vincit improbus. Such should be the chosen motto of every labourer, and it may be that labour, if adequately enduring, may suffice at last to produce even some not untrue resemblance of the Rev. Francis Arabin.

Of his doings in the world, and of the sort of fame which he has achieved, enough has been already said. It has also been said that he is forty years of age, and still unmarried. He was the younger son of a country gentleman of small fortune in the north of England. At an early age he went to Winchester, and was intended by his father for New College ; but though studious as a boy, he was not studious within the prescribed limits ; and at the age of eighteen he left school with a character for talent, but without a scholarship. All that he had obtained, over and above the advantage of his character, was a gold medal for English verse, and hence was derived a strong presumption on the part of his friends that he was destined to add another name to the imperishable list of English poets.

From Winchester he went to Oxford, and was entered as a commoner at Balliol. Here his special career very soon commenced. He utterly eschewed the society of fast men, gave no wine parties, kept no horses, rowed no boats, joined no rows, and was the pride of his college tutor. Such at least was his career till he had taken his little go ; and then he commenced a course of action which, though not less creditable to himself as a man, was hardly so much to the taste of the tutor. He became a member of a vigorous debating society, and rendered himself remarkable there for humorous energy. Though always in earnest, yet his earnestness was always droll. To be true in his ideas, unanswerable in his syllogisms, and just in his aspirations was not enough for him. He had failed, failed in his own opinion as well as that of others when others came to know him, if he could not reduce the arguments of his opponents to an absurdity, and conquer both by wit and reason. To say that his object was ever to raise a laugh, would be most untrue. He hated such common and unnecessary evidence of satisfaction on the part of his hearers. A joke that required to be laughed at was, with him, not worth uttering. He could appreciate by a keener sense than that of his ears the success of his wit, and would see in the eyes of his auditory whether or no he was understood and appreciated.

He had been a religious lad before he left school. That is, he had addicted himself to a party in religion, and having done so had received that benefit which most men do who become partisans in such a cause. We are much too apt to look at schism in our church as an unmitigated

evil. Moderate schism, if there may be such a thing, at
any rate calls attention to the subject, draws in supporters
who would otherwise have been inattentive to the matter,
and teaches men to think upon religion. How great an
amount of good of this description has followed that
movement in the Church of England which commenced
with the publication of Froude's Remains !

As a boy young Arabin took up the cudgels on the side
of the Tractarians, and at Oxford he sat for a while at
the feet of the great Newman. To this cause he lent all
his faculties. For it he concocted verses, for it he made
speeches, for it he scintillated the brightest sparks of his
quiet wit. For it he ate and drank and dressed, and had
his being. In due process of time he took his degree, and
wrote himself B.A., but he did not do so with any remarkable amount of academical éclat. He had occupied
himself too much with high church matters, and the
polemics, politics, and outward demonstrations usually
concurrent with high churchmanship, to devote himself
with sufficient vigour to the acquisition of a double first.
He was not a double first, nor even a first class man ;
but he revenged himself on the university by putting
firsts and double firsts out of fashion for the year, and
laughing down a species of pedantry which at the age of
twenty-three leaves no room in a man's mind for graver
subjects than conic sections or Greek accents.

Greek accents, however, and conic sections were
esteemed necessaries at Balliol, and there was no admittance there for Mr. Arabin within the list of its fellows.
Lazarus, however, the richest and most comfortable
abode of Oxford dons, opened its bosom to the young
champion of a church militant. Mr. Arabin was ordained,
and became a fellow soon after taking his degree, and
shortly after that was chosen professor of poetry.

And now came the moment of his great danger. After
many mental struggles, and an agony of doubt which may
be well surmised, the great prophet of the Tractarians
confessed himself a Roman Catholic. Mr. Newman left
the Church of England, and with him carried many a
waverer. He did not carry off Mr. Arabin, but the escape
which that gentleman had was a very narrow one. He
left Oxford for a while that he might meditate in complete

peace on the step which appeared to him to be all but
unavoidable, and shut himself up in a little village on
the sea-shore of one of our remotest counties, that he
might learn by communing with his own soul whether
or no he could with a safe conscience remain within the
pale of his mother church.

Things would have gone badly with him there had he
been left entirely to himself. Every thing was against
him: all his worldly interests required him to remain
a Protestant; and he looked on his worldly interests as
a legion of foes, to get the better of whom was a point of
extremest honour. In his then state of ecstatic agony
such a conquest would have cost him little; he could
easily have thrown away all his livelihood; but it cost
him much to get over the idea that by choosing the Church
of England he should be open in his own mind to the
charge that he had been led to such a choice by unworthy
motives. Then his heart was against him: he loved
with a strong and eager love the man who had hitherto
been his guide, and yearned to follow his footsteps. His
tastes were against him: the ceremonies and pomps of
the Church of Rome, their august feasts and solemn fasts,
invited his imagination and pleased his eye. His flesh
was against him: how great an aid would it be to a poor,
weak, wavering man to be constrained to high moral
duties, self-denial, obedience, and chastity by laws which
were certain in their enactments, and not to be broken
without loud, palpable, unmistakable sin! Then his faith
was against him: he required to believe so much; panted
so eagerly to give signs of his belief; deemed it so insufficient to wash himself simply in the waters of Jordan;
that some great deed, such as that of forsaking everything
for a true church, had for him allurements almost past
withstanding.

Mr. Arabin was at this time a very young man, and
when he left Oxford for his far retreat was much too
confident in his powers of fence, and too apt to look down
on the ordinary sense of ordinary people, to expect aid
in the battle that he had to fight from any chance inhabitants of the spot which he had selected. But Providence
was good to him; and there, in that all but desolate place,
on the storm-beat shore of that distant sea, he met one

who gradually calmed his mind, quieted his imagination, and taught him something of a Christian's duty. When Mr. Arabin left Oxford, he was inclined to look upon the rural clergymen of most English parishes almost with contempt. It was his ambition, should he remain within the fold of their church, to do somewhat towards redeeming and rectifying their inferiority, and to assist in infusing energy and faith into the hearts of Christian ministers, who were, as he thought, too often satisfied to go through life without much show of either.

And yet it was from such a one that Mr. Arabin in his extremest need received that aid which he so much required. It was from the poor curate of a small Cornish parish that he first learnt to know that the highest laws for the governance of a Christian's duty must act from within and not from without; that no man can become a serviceable servant solely by obedience to written edicts; and that the safety which he was about to seek within the gates of Rome was no other than the selfish freedom from personal danger which the bad soldier attempts to gain who counterfeits illness on the eve of battle.

Mr. Arabin returned to Oxford a humbler but a better and a happier man; and from that time forth he put his shoulder to the wheel as a clergyman of the Church for which he had been educated. The intercourse of those among whom he familiarly lived kept him staunch to the principles of that system of the Church to which he had always belonged. Since his severance from Mr. Newman, no one had had so strong an influence over him as the head of his college. During the time of his expected apostacy, Dr. Gwynne had not felt much predisposition in favour of the young fellow. Though a High Churchman himself within moderate limits, Dr. Gwynne felt no sympathy with men who could not satisfy their faiths with the Thirty-nine Articles. He regarded the enthusiasm of such as Newman as a state of mind more nearly allied to madness than to religion; and when he saw it evinced by very young men, was inclined to attribute a good deal of it to vanity. Dr. Gwynne himself, though a religious man, was also a thoroughly practical man of the world, and he regarded with no favourable eye the tenets of any one who looked on the two things as incompatible. When he found that Mr. Arabin was a half Roman, he began to regret all he had done towards bestowing a fellowship on so unworthy a recipient; and when again he learnt that Mr. Arabin would probably complete his journey to Rome, he regarded with some satisfaction the fact that in such case the fellowship would be again vacant.

When, however, Mr. Arabin returned and professed himself a confirmed Protestant, the master of Lazarus again opened his arms to him, and gradually he became the pet of the college. For some little time he was saturnine, silent, and unwilling to take any prominent part in university broils; but gradually his mind recovered, or rather made its tone, and he became known as a man always ready at a moment's notice to take up the cudgels in opposition to anything that savoured of an evangelical bearing. He was great in sermons, great on platforms, great at after dinner conversations, and always pleasant as well as great. He took delight in elections, served on committees, opposed tooth and nail all projects of university reform, and talked jovially over his glass of port of the ruin to be anticipated by the Church, and of the sacrilege daily committed by the Whigs. The ordeal through which he had gone, in resisting the blandishments of the lady of Rome, had certainly done much towards the strengthening of his character. Although in small and outward matters he was self-confident enough, nevertheless in things affecting the inner man he aimed at a humility of spirit which would never have been attractive to him but for that visit to the coast of Cornwall. This visit he now repeated every year.

Such is an interior view of Mr. Arabin at the time when he accepted the living of St. Ewold. Exteriorly, he was not a remarkable person. He was above the middle height, well made, and very active. His hair which had been jet black, was now tinged with gray, but his face bore no sign of years. It would perhaps be wrong to say that he was handsome, but his face was, nevertheless, pleasant to look upon. The cheek bones were rather too high for beauty, and the formation of the forehead too massive and heavy: but the eyes, nose, and mouth were perfect. There was a continual play of lambent fire about

his eyes, which gave promise of either pathos or humour
whenever he essayed to speak, and that promise was
rarely broken. There was a gentle play about his mouth
which declared that his wit never descended to sarcasm,
and that there was no ill-nature in his repartee.

Mr. Arabin was a popular man among women, but more
so as a general than a special favourite. Living as a fellow
at Oxford, marriage with him had been out of the question,
and it may be doubted whether he had ever allowed his
heart to be touched. Though belonging to a Church in
which celibacy is not the required lot of its ministers, he
had come to regard himself as one of those clergymen to
whom to be a bachelor is almost a necessity. He had never
looked for parochial duty, and his career at Oxford was
utterly incompatible with such domestic joys as a wife
and nursery. He looked on women, therefore, in the same
light that one sees them regarded by many Romish
priests. He liked to have near him that which was pretty
and amusing, but women generally were little more to
him than children. He talked to them without putting
out all his powers, and listened to them without any idea
that what he should hear from them could either actuate
his conduct or influence his opinion.

Such was Mr. Arabin, the new vicar of St. Ewold, who
is going to stay with the Grantlys, at Plumstead Episcopi.

Mr. Arabin reached Plumstead the day before Mr.
Harding and Eleanor, and the Grantly family were thus
enabled to make his acquaintance and discuss his qualifications before the arrival of the other guests. Griselda
was surprised to find that he looked so young ; but she
told Florinda her younger sister, when they had retired
for the night, that he did not talk at all like a young man :
and she decided with the authority that seventeen has
over sixteen, that he was not at all nice, although his eyes
were lovely. As usual, sixteen implicitly acceded to the
dictum of seventeen in such a matter, and said that he
certainly was not nice. They then branched off on the
relative merits of other clerical bachelors in the vicinity,
and both determined without any feeling of jealousy
between them that a certain Rev. Augustus Green was
by many degrees the most estimable of the lot. The
gentleman in question had certainly much in his favour,

as, having a comfortable allowance from his father, he could devote the whole proceeds of his curacy to violet gloves and unexceptionable neck ties. Having thus fixedly resolved that the new comer had nothing about him to shake the pre-eminence of the exalted Green, the two girls went to sleep in each other's arms, contented with themselves and the world.

Mrs. Grantly at first sight came to much the same conclusion about her husband's favourite as her daughters had done, though, in seeking to measure his relative value, she did not compare him to Mr. Green; indeed, she made no comparison by name between him and any one else; but she remarked to her husband that one person's swans were very often another person's geese, thereby clearly showing that Mr. Arabin had not yet proved his qualifications in swanhood to her satisfaction.

'Well, Susan,' said he, rather offended at hearing his friend spoken of so disrespectfully, 'if you take Mr. Arabin for a goose, I cannot say that I think very highly of your discrimination.'

'A goose! No of course, he's not a goose. I've no doubt he's a very clever man. But you're so matter-of-fact, archdeacon, when it suits your purpose, that one can't trust oneself to any *façon de parler*. I've no doubt Mr. Arabin is a very valuable man—at Oxford, and that he'll be a good vicar at St. Ewold. All I mean is, that having passed one evening with him, I don't find him to be absolutely a paragon. In the first place, if I am not mistaken, he is a little inclined to be conceited.'

'Of all the men that I know intimately,' said the archdeacon, 'Arabin is, in my opinion, the most free from any taint of self-conceit. His fault is that he's too diffident.'

'Perhaps so,' said the lady; 'only I must own I did not find it out this evening.'

Nothing further was said about him. Dr. Grantly thought that his wife was abusing Mr. Arabin merely because he had praised him; and Mrs. Grantly knew that it was useless arguing for or against any person in favour of or in opposition to whom the archdeacon had already pronounced a strong opinion.

In truth they were both right. Mr. Arabin was a diffident man in social intercourse with those whom he did

not intimately know ; when placed in situations which
it was his business to fill, and discussing matters with
which it was his duty to be conversant, Mr. Arabin was
from habit brazen-faced enough. When standing on a
platform in Exeter Hall, no man would be less mazed
than he by the eyes of the crowd before him ; for such
was the work which his profession had called on him to
perform ; but he shrank from a strong expression of
opinion in general society, and his doing so not uncommonly made it appear that he considered the company
not worth the trouble of his energy. He was averse to
dictate when the place did not seem to him to justify
dictation ; and as those subjects on which people wished
to hear him speak were such as he was accustomed to
treat with decision, he generally shunned the traps there
were laid to allure him into discussion, and, by doing so,
not unfrequently subjected himself to such charges as
those brought against him by Mrs. Grantly.

Mr. Arabin, as he sat at his open window, enjoying the
delicious moonlight and gazing at the gray towers of the
church, which stood almost within the rectory grounds,
little dreamed that he was the subject of so many friendly
or unfriendly criticisms. Considering how much we are
all given to discuss the characters of others, and discuss
them often not in the strictest spirit of charity, it is singular
how little we are inclined to think that others can speak
ill-naturedly of us, and how angry and hurt we are when
proof reaches us that they have done so. It is hardly
too much to say, that we all of us occasionally speak of our
dearest friends in a manner in which those dearest friends
would very little like to hear themselves mentioned ;
and that we nevertheless expect that our dearest friends
shall invariably speak of us as though they were blind
to all our faults, but keenly alive to every shade of our
virtues.

It did not occur to Mr. Arabin that he was spoken of
at all. It seemed to him, when he compared himself with
his host, that he was a person of so little consequence
to any, that he was worth no one's words or thoughts.
He was utterly alone in the world as regarded domestic
ties and those inner familiar relations which are hardly
possible between others than husbands and wives, parents

and children, or brothers and sisters. He had often discussed with himself the necessity of such bonds for a
man's happiness in this world, and had generally satisfied
himself with the answer that happiness in this world is
not a necessity. Herein he deceived himself, or rather
tried to do so. He, like others, yearned for the enjoyment
of whatever he saw enjoyable ; and though he attempted,
with the modern stoicism of so many Christians, to make
himself believe that joy and sorrow were matters which here
should be held as perfectly indifferent, these things were not
indifferent to him. He was tired of his Oxford rooms and
his college life. He regarded the wife and children of
his friend with something like envy ; he all but coveted
the pleasant drawing-room, with its pretty windows
opening on to lawns and flower-beds, the apparel of the
comfortable house, and—above all—the air of home
which encompassed it all.

It will be said that no time can have been so fitted for
such desires on his part as this, when he had just possessed
himself of a country parish, of a living among fields and
gardens, of a house which a wife would grace. It is true
there was a difference between the opulence of Plumstead
and the modest economy of St. Ewold ; but surely Mr.
Arabin was not a man to sigh after wealth ! Of all men,
his friends would have unanimously declared he was the
last to do so. But how little our friends know us ! In
his period of stoical rejection of this world's happiness,
he had cast from him as utter dross all anxiety as to fortune.
He had, as it were, proclaimed himself to be indifferent
to promotion, and those who chiefly admired his talents,
and would mainly have exerted themselves to secure to
them their deserved reward, had taken him at his word.
And now, if the truth must out, he felt himself disappointed
—disappointed not by them but by himself. The day-
dream of his youth was over, and at the age of forty he
felt that he was not fit to work in the spirit of an apostle.
He had mistaken himself, and learned his mistake when
it was past remedy. He had professed himself indifferent
to mitres and diaconal residences, to rich livings and
pleasant glebes, and now he had to own to himself that
he was sighing for the good things of other men, on whom
in his pride he had ventured to look down.

Not for wealth, in its vulgar sense, had he ever sighed; not for the enjoyment of rich things had he ever longed; but for the allotted share of worldly bliss, which a wife, and children, and happy home could give him, for that usual amount of comfort which he had ventured to reject as unnecessary for him, he did now feel that he would have been wiser to have searched.

He knew that his talents, his position, and his friends would have won for him promotion, had he put himself in the way of winning it. Instead of doing so, he had allowed himself to be persuaded to accept a living which would give him an income of some 300*l*. a year, should he, by marrying, throw up his fellowship. Such, at the age of forty, was the worldly result of labour, which the world had chosen to regard as successful. The world also thought that Mr. Arabin was, in his own estimation, sufficiently paid. Alas! alas! the world was mistaken; and Mr. Arabin was beginning to ascertain that such was the case.

And here, may I beg the reader not to be hard in his judgment upon this man. Is not the state at which he has arrived, the natural result of efforts to reach that which is not the condition of humanity? Is not modern stoicism, built though it be on Christianity, as great an outrage on human nature as was the stoicism of the ancients? The philosophy of Zeno was built on true laws, but on true laws misunderstood, and therefore misapplied. It is the same with our Stoics here, who would teach us that wealth and worldly comfort and happiness on earth are not worth the search. Alas, for a doctrine which can find no believing pupils and no true teachers!

The case of Mr. Arabin was the more singular, as he belonged to a branch of the Church of England well inclined to regard its temporalities with avowed favour, and had habitually lived with men who were accustomed to much worldly comfort. But such was his idiosyncrasy, that these very facts had produced within him, in early life, a state of mind that was not natural to him. He was content to be a High Churchman, if he could be so on principles of his own, and could strike out a course showing a marked difference from those with whom he consorted. He was ready to be a partisan as long as he was allowed to have a course of action and of thought unlike that of his party. His party had indulged him, and he began to feel that his party was right and himself wrong, just when such a conviction was too late to be of service to him. He discovered, when such discovery was no longer serviceable, that it *would* have been worth his while to have worked for the usual pay assigned to work in this world, and have earned a wife and children, with a carriage for them to sit in ; to have earned a pleasant dining-room, in which his friends could drink his wine, and the power of walking up the high street of his country town, with the knowledge that all its tradesmen would have gladly welcomed him within their doors. Other men arrived at those convictions in their start in life, and so worked up to them. To him they had come when they were too late to be of use.

It has been said that Mr. Arabin was a man of pleasantry and it may be thought that such a state of mind as that described, would be antagonistic to humour. But surely such is not the case. Wit is the outward mental casing of the man, and has no more to do with the inner mind of thoughts and feelings than have the rich brocaded garments of the priest at the altar with the asceticism of the anchorite below them, whose skin is tormented with sackcloth, and whose body is half flayed with rods. Nay, will not such a one often rejoice more than any other in the rich show of his outer apparel ? Will it not be food for his pride to feel that he groans inwardly, while he shines outwardly ? So it is with the mental efforts which men make. Those which they show forth daily to the world are often the opposites of the inner workings of the spirit.

In the archdeacon's drawing-room, Mr. Arabin had sparkled with his usual unaffected brilliancy, but when he retired to his bed-room, he sat there sad, at his open window, repining within himself that he also had no wife, no bairns, no soft sward of lawn duly mown for him to lie on, no herd of attendant curates, no bowings from the banker's clerks, no rich rectory. That apostleship that he had thought of had evaded his grasp, and he was now only vicar of St. Ewold's, with a taste for a mitre. Truly he had fallen between two stools.

CHAPTER XXI

ST. EWOLD'S PARSONAGE

WHEN Mr. Harding and Mrs. Bold reached the rectory on the following morning, the archdeacon and his friend were at St. Ewold's. They had gone over that the new vicar might inspect his church, and be introduced to the squire, and were not expected back before dinner. Mr. Harding rambled out by himself, and strolled, as was his wont at Plumstead, about the lawn and round the church; and as he did so, the two sisters naturally fell into conversation about Barchester.

There was not much sisterly confidence between them. Mrs. Grantly was ten years older than Eleanor, and had been married while Eleanor was yet a child. They had never, therefore, poured into each other's ears their hopes and loves; and now that one was a wife and the other a widow, it was not probable that they would begin to do so. They lived too much asunder to be able to fall into that kind of intercourse which makes confidence between sisters almost a necessity; and, moreover, that which is so easy at eighteen is often very difficult at twenty-eight. Mrs. Grantly knew this, and did not, therefore, expect confidence from her sister; and yet she longed to ask her whether in real truth Mr. Slope was agreeable to her.

It was by no means difficult to turn the conversation to Mr. Slope. That gentleman had become so famous at Barchester, had so much to do with all clergymen connected with the city, and was so specially concerned in the affairs of Mr. Harding, that it would have been odd if Mr. Harding's daughters had not talked about him. Mrs. Grantly was soon abusing him, which she did with her whole heart; and Mrs. Bold was nearly as eager to defend him. She positively disliked the man, would have been delighted to learn that he had taken himself off so that she should never see him again, had indeed almost a fear of him, and yet she constantly found herself taking his part. The abuse of other people, and abuse of a nature that she felt to be unjust, imposed this necessity on her, and at last made Mr. Slope's defence an habitual course of argument with her.

From Mr. Slope the conversation turned to the Stanhopes, and Mrs. Grantly was listening with some interest to Eleanor's account of the family, when it dropped out that Mr. Slope made one of the party.

'What!' said the lady of the rectory, 'was Mr. Slope there too?'

Eleanor merely replied that such had been the case.

'Why, Eleanor, he must be very fond of you, I think; he seems to follow you everywhere.'

Even this did not open Eleanor's eyes. She merely laughed, and said that she imagined Mr. Slope found other attraction at Dr. Stanhope's. And so they parted. Mrs. Grantly felt quite convinced that the odious match would take place; and Mrs. Bold as convinced that that unfortunate chaplain, disagreeable as he must be allowed to be, was more sinned against than sinning.

The archdeacon of course heard before dinner that Eleanor had remained the day before in Barchester with the view of meeting Mr. Slope, and that she had so met him. He remembered how she had positively stated that there were to be no guests at the Stanhopes, and he did not hesitate to accuse her of deceit. Moreover, the fact, or rather presumed fact, of her being deceitful on such a matter, spoke but too plainly in evidence against her as to her imputed crime of receiving Mr. Slope as a lover.

'I am afraid that anything we can do will be too late,' said the archdeacon. 'I own I am fairly surprised. I never liked your sister's taste with regard to men; but still I did not give her credit for—ugh!'

'And so soon, too,' said Mrs. Grantly, who thought more, perhaps, of her sister's indecorum in having a lover before she had put off her weeds, than her bad taste in having such a lover as Mr. Slope.

'Well, my dear, I shall be sorry to be harsh, or to do anything that can hurt your father; but, positively, neither that man nor his wife shall come within my doors.'

Mrs. Grantly sighed, and then attempted to console herself and her lord by remarking that, after all, the thing was not accomplished yet. Now that Eleanor was at Plumstead, much might be done to wean her from her fatal passion. Poor Eleanor!

The evening passed off without anything to make it

remarkable. Mr. Arabin discussed the parish of St. Ewold
with the archdeacon, and Mrs. Grantly and Mr. Harding,
who knew the personages of the parish, joined in. Eleanor
also knew them, but she said little. Mr. Arabin did not
apparently take much notice of her, and she was not in
a humour to receive at that time with any special grace
any special favourite of her brother-in-law. Her first
idea on reaching her bed-room was that a much pleasanter
family party might be met at Dr. Stanhope's than at the
rectory. She began to think that she was getting tired
of clergymen and their respectable humdrum wearisome
mode of living, and that after all, people in the outer world,
who had lived in Italy, London, or elsewhere, need not
necessarily be regarded as atrocious and abominable.
The Stanhopes, she had thought, were a giddy, thoughtless,
extravagant set of people ; but she had seen nothing wrong
about them, and had, on the other hand, found that they
thoroughly knew how to make their house agreeable. It
was a thousand pities, she thought, that the archdeacon
should not have a little of the same *savoir vivre.* Mr.
Arabin, as we have said, did not apparently take much
notice of her ; but yet he did not go to bed without feeling
that he had been in company with a very pretty woman ;
and as is the case with most bachelors, and some married
men, regarded the prospect of his month's visit at Plumstead in a pleasanter light, when he learnt that a very
pretty woman was to share it with him.

Before they all retired it was settled that the whole
party should drive over on the following day to inspect
the parsonage at St. Ewold. The three clergymen were
to discuss dilapidations, and the two ladies were to lend
their assistance in suggesting such changes as might be
necessary for a bachelor's abode. Accordingly, soon after
breakfast, the carriage was at the door. There was only
room for four inside, and the archdeacon got upon the
box. Eleanor found herself opposite to Mr. Arabin, and
was, therefore, in a manner forced into conversation
with him. They were soon on comfortable terms together ;
and had she thought about it, she would have thought
that, in spite of his black cloth, Mr. Arabin would not
have been a bad addition to the Stanhope family party.

Now that the archdeacon was away, they could all

trifle. Mr. Harding began by telling them in the most innocent manner imaginable an old legend about Mr. Arabin's new parish. There was, he said, in days of yore, an illustrious priestess of St. Ewold, famed through the whole country for curing all manner of diseases. She had a well, as all priestesses have ever had, which well was extant to this day, and shared in the minds of many of the people the sanctity which belonged to the consecrated ground of the parish church. Mr. Arabin declared that he should look on such tenets on the part of his parishioners as anything but orthodox. And Mrs. Grantly replied that she so entirely disagreed with him as to think that no parish was in a proper state that had not its priestess as well as its priest. 'The duties are never well done,' said she, ' unless they are so divided.'

' I suppose, papa,' said Eleanor, ' that in the olden times the priestess bore all the sway herself. Mr. Arabin, perhaps, thinks that such might be too much the case now if a sacred lady were admitted within the parish.'

' I think, at any rate,' said he, ' that it is safer to run no such risk. No priestly pride has ever exceeded that of sacerdotal females. A very lowly curate I might, perhaps, essay to rule; but a curatess would be sure to get the better of me.'

' There are certainly examples of such accidents happening,' said Mrs. Grantly. 'They do say that there is a priestess at Barchester who is very imperious in all things touching the altar. Perhaps the fear of such a fate as that is before your eyes.

When they were joined by the archdeacon on the gravel before the vicarage, they descended again to grave dulness. Not that Archdeacon Grantly was a dull man; but his frolic humours were of a cumbrous kind; and his wit, when he was witty, did not generally extend itself to his auditory. On the present occasion he was soon making speeches about wounded roofs and walls, which he declared to be in want of some surgeon's art. There was not a partition that he did not tap, nor a block of chimneys that he did not narrowly examine; all water-pipes, flues, cisterns, and sewers underwent an investigation; and he even descended, in the care of his friend, so far as to bore sundry boards in the floors with a bradawl.

Mr. Arabin accompanied him through the rooms, trying
to look wise in such domestic matters, and the other
three also followed. Mrs. Grantly showed that she had
not herself been priestess of a parish twenty years for
nothing, and examined the bells and window panes in
a very knowing way.

'You will, at any rate, have a beautiful prospect out
of your own window, if this is to be your private sanctum,'
said Eleanor. She was standing at the lattice of a little
room up stairs, from which the view certainly was very
lovely. It was from the back of the vicarage, and there
was nothing to interrupt the eye between the house and
the glorious gray pile of the cathedral. The intermediate
ground, however, was beautifully studded with timber.
In the immediate foreground ran the little river which
afterwards skirted the city; and, just to the right of the
cathedral, the pointed gables and chimneys of Hiram's
Hospital peeped out of the elms which encompass it.

'Yes,' said he, joining her. 'I shall have a beautifully
complete view of my adversaries. I shall sit down before
the hostile town, and fire away at them at a very pleasant
distance. I shall just be able to lodge a shot in the hospital,
should the enemy ever get possession of it; and as for
the palace, I have it within full range.'

'I never saw anything like you clergymen,' said Eleanor;
'you are always thinking of fighting each other.'

'Either that,' said he, 'or else supporting each other.
The pity is that we cannot do the one without the other.
But are we not here to fight? Is not ours a church militant? What is all our work but fighting, and hard
fighting, if it be well done?'

'But not with each other.'

'That's as it may be. The same complaint which you
make of me for battling with another clergyman of our
own church, the Mohammedan would make against me
for battling with the error of a priest of Rome. Yet,
surely, you would not be inclined to say that I should
be wrong to do battle with such as him. A pagan, too,
with his multiplicity of gods, would think it equally odd
that the Christian and the Mohammedan should disagree.'

'Ah! but you wage your wars about trifles so bitterly.'

'Wars about trifles,' said he, 'are always bitter,

especially among neighbours. When the differences are
great, and the parties comparative strangers, men quarrel
with courtesy. What combatants are ever so eager as
two brothers ? '

' But do not such contentions bring scandal on the
church ? '

' More scandal would fall on the church if there were
no such contentions. We have but one way to avoid
them—that of acknowledging a common head of our
church, whose word on all points of doctrine shall be
authoritative. Such a termination of our difficulties
is alluring enough. It has charms which are irresistible
to many, and all but irresistible, I own, to me.'

' You speak now of the Church of Rome ? ' said Eleanor.

' No,' said he, ' not necessarily of the Church of Rome ;
but of a church with a head. Had it pleased God to
vouchsafe to us such a church our path would have been
easy. But easy paths have not been thought good for
us.' He paused and stood silent for a while, thinking of
the time when he had so nearly sacrificed all he had, his
powers of mind, his free agency, the fresh running waters
of his mind's fountain, his very inner self, for an easy
path in which no fighting would be needed ; and then
he continued :—' What you say is partly true ; our contentions do bring on us some scandal. The outer world,
though it constantly reviles us for our human infirmities,
and throws in our teeth the fact that being clergymen we
are still no more than men, demands of us that we should
do our work with godlike perfection. There is nothing
godlike about us : we differ from each other with the
acerbity common to man—we triumph over each other
with human frailty—we allow differences on subjects
of divine origin to produce among us antipathies and
enmities which are anything but divine. This is all true.
But what would you have in place of it ? There is no
infallible head for a church on earth. This dream of
believing man has been tried, and we see in Italy and in
Spain what has come of it. Grant that there are and have
been no bickerings within the pale of the Pope's Church.
Such an assumption would be utterly untrue ; but let
us grant it, and then let us say which church has incurred
the heavier scandals.'

There was a quiet earnestness about Mr. Arabin, as he half acknowledged and half defended himself from the charge brought against him, which surprised Eleanor. She had been used all her life to listen to clerical discussion ; but the points at issue between the disputants had so seldom been of more than temporal significance as to have left on her mind no feeling of reverence for such subjects. There had always been a hard worldly leaven of the love either of income or of power in the strains she had heard ; there had been no panting for the truth ; no aspirations after religious purity. It had always been taken for granted by those around her that they were indubitably right, that there was no ground for doubt, that the hard uphill work of ascertaining what the duty of a clergyman should be had been already accomplished in full ; and that what remained for an active militant parson to do, was to hold his own against all comers. Her father, it is true, was an exception to this ; but then he was so essentially anti-militant in all things, that she classed him in her own mind apart from all others. She had never argued the matter within herself, or considered whether this common tone was or was not faulty ; but she was sick of it without knowing that she was so. And now she found to her surprise and not without a certain pleasurable excitement, that this new comer among them spoke in a manner very different from that to which she was accustomed.

'It is so easy to condemn,' said he, continuing the thread of his thoughts. 'I know no life that must be so delicious as that of a writer for newspapers, or a leading member of the opposition—to thunder forth accusations against men in power ; show up the worst side of everything that is produced ; to pick holes in every coat ; to be indignant, sarcastic, jocose, moral, or supercilious ; to damn with faint praise, or crush with open calumny ! What can be so easy as this when the critic has to be responsible for nothing ? You condemn what I do ; but put yourself in my position and do the reverse, and then see if I cannot condemn you.'

'Oh ! Mr. Arabin, I do not condemn you.'

'Pardon me, you do, Mrs. Bold—you as one of the world ; you are now the opposition member ; you are now composing your leading article, and well and bitterly

you do it. "Let dogs delight to bark and bite;" you
fitly begin with an elegant quotation; "but if we are
to have a church at all, in heaven's name let the pastors
who preside over it keep their hands from each other's
throats. Lawyers can live without befouling each other's
names; doctors do not fight duels. Why is it that clergymen alone should indulge themselves in such unrestrained
liberty of abuse against each other?" and so you go on
reviling us for our ungodly quarrels, our sectarian propensities, and scandalous differences. It will, however,
give you no trouble to write another article next week
in which we, or some of us, shall be twitted with an unseemly apathy in matters of our vocation. It will not
fall on you to reconcile the discrepancy; your readers
will never ask you how the poor parson is to be urgent
in season and out of season, and yet never come in contact
with men who think widely differently from him. You,
when you condemn this foreign treaty, or that official
arrangement, will have to incur no blame for the graver
faults of any different measure. It is so easy to condemn;
and so pleasant too; for eulogy charms no listeners as
detraction does.'

Eleanor only half followed him in his raillery, but she
caught his meaning. 'I know I ought to apologise for
presuming to criticise you,' she said; 'but I was thinking
with sorrow of the ill-will that has lately come among us
at Barchester, and I spoke more freely than I should have
done.'

'Peace on earth and good-will among men, are, like
heaven, promises for the future;' said he, following
rather his own thoughts than hers. 'When that prophecy
is accomplished, there will no longer be any need for
clergymen.'

Here they were interrupted by the archdeacon, whose
voice was heard from the cellar shouting to the vicar.

'Arabin, Arabin,'—and then turning to his wife, who
was apparently at his elbow—'where has he gone to?
This cellar is perfectly abominable. It would be murder
to put a bottle of wine into it till it has been roofed, walled,
and floored. How on earth old Goodenough ever got on
with it, I cannot guess. But then Goodenough never
had a glass of wine that any man could drink.'

'What is it, archdeacon?' said the vicar, running down stairs, and leaving Eleanor above to her meditations.

'This cellar must be roofed, walled, and floored,' repeated the archdeacon. 'Now mind what I say, and don't let the architect persuade you that it will do; half of these fellows know nothing about wine. This place as it is now would be damp and cold in winter, and hot and muggy in summer. I wouldn't give a straw for the best wine that ever was vinted, after it had lain here a couple of years.'

Mr. Arabin assented, and promised that the cellar should be reconstructed according to the archdeacon's receipt.

'And, Arabin, look here; was such an attempt at a kitchen grate ever seen?'

'The grate is really very bad,' said Mrs. Grantly; 'I am sure the priestess won't approve of it, when she is brought home to the scene of her future duties. Really, Mr. Arabin, no priestess accustomed to such an excellent well as that above could put up with such a grate as this.'

'If there must be a priestess at St. Ewold's at all, Mrs. Grantly, I think we will leave her to her well, and not call down her divine wrath on any of the imperfections rising from our human poverty. However, I own I am amenable to the attractions of a well-cooked dinner, and the grate shall certainly be changed.'

By this time the archdeacon had again ascended, and was now in the dining-room. 'Arabin,' said he, speaking in his usual loud clear voice, and with that tone of dictation which was so common to him; 'you must positively alter this dining-room, that is, remodel it altogether; look here, it is just sixteen feet by fifteen; did anybody ever hear of a dining-room of such proportions!' and the archdeacon stepped the room long-ways and cross-ways with ponderous steps, as though a certain amount of ecclesiastical dignity could be imparted even to such an occupation as that by the manner of doing it. 'Barely sixteen; you may call it a square.'

'It would do very well for a round table,' suggested the ex-warden.

Now there was something peculiarly unorthodox in the archdeacon's estimation in the idea of a round table.

He had always been accustomed to a goodly board of
decent length, comfortably elongating itself according
to the number of the guests, nearly black with perpetual
rubbing, and as bright as a mirror. Now round dinner
tables are generally of oak, or else of such new construction as not to have acquired the peculiar hue which was
so pleasing to him. He connected them with what he
called the nasty new fangled method of leaving a cloth
on the table, as though to warn people that they were
not to sit long. In his eyes there was something democratic
and parvenue in a round table. He imagined that dissenters and calico-printers chiefly used them, and perhaps
a few literary lions more conspicuous for their wit than
their gentility. He was a little flurried at the idea of
such an article being introduced into the diocese by a
protégé of his own, and at the instigation of his father-
in-law.

'A round dinner-table,' said he, with some heat, 'is
the most abominable article of furniture that ever was
invented. I hope that Arabin has more taste than to
allow such a thing in his house.'

Poor Mr. Harding felt himself completely snubbed, and
of course said nothing further; but Mr. Arabin, who had
yielded submissively in the small matters of the cellar
and kitchen grate, found himself obliged to oppose reforms
which might be of a nature too expensive for his pocket.

'But it seems to me, archdeacon, that I can't very well
lengthen the room without pulling down the wall, and
if I pull down the wall, I must build it up again; then
if I throw out a bow on this side, I must do the same on
the other, then if I do it for the ground floor, I must
carry it up to the floor above. That will be putting a new
front to the house, and will cost, I suppose, a couple of
hundred pounds. The ecclesiastical commissioners will
hardly assist me when they hear that my grievance consists
in having a dining-room only sixteen feet long.'

The archdeacon proceeded to explain that nothing
would be easier than adding six feet to the front of the
dining-room, without touching any other in the house.
Such irregularities of construction in small country houses
were, he said, rather graceful than otherwise, and he
offered to pay for the whole thing out of his own pocket.

if it cost more than forty pounds. Mr. Arabin, however,
was firm, and, although the archdeacon fussed and fumed
about it, would not give way.

Forty pounds, he said, was a matter of serious moment
to him, and his friends, if under such circumstances they
would be good-natured enough to come to him at all, must
put up with the misery of a square room. He was willing
to compromise matters by disclaiming any intention
of having a round table.

' But,' said Mrs. Grantly, ' what if the priestess insists
on having both the rooms enlarged ? '

' The priestess in that case must do it for herself, Mrs.
Grantly.'

' I have no doubt she will be well able to do so,' replied
the lady ; ' to do that and many more wonderful things.
I am quite sure that the priestess of St. Ewold, when she
does come, won't come empty-handed.'

Mr. Arabin, however, did not appear well inclined to
enter into speculative expenses on such a chance as this,
and therefore, any material alterations in the house, the
cost of which could not fairly be made to lie at the door
either of the ecclesiastical commissioners or of the estate
of the late incumbent, were tabooed. With this essential
exception, the archdeacon ordered, suggested, and carried
all points before him in a manner very much to his own
satisfaction. A close observer, had there been one there,
might have seen that his wife had been quite as useful
in the matter as himself. No one knew better than Mrs.
Grantly the appurtenances necessary to a comfortable
house. She did not, however, think it necessary to lay
claim to any of the glory which her lord and master was
so ready to appropriate as his own.

Having gone through their work effectually and
systematically, the party returned to Plumstead well
satisfied with their expedition.

CHAPTER XXII

THE THORNES OF ULLATHORNE

ON the following Sunday Mr. Arabin was to read himself in at his new church. It was agreed at the rectory that the archdeacon should go over with him and assist at the reading-desk, and that Mr. Harding should take the archdeacon's duty at Plumstead Church. Mrs. Grantly had her school and her buns to attend to, and professed that she could not be spared; but Mrs. Bold was to accompany them. It was further agreed also, that they would lunch at the squire's house, and return home after the afternoon service.

Wilfred Thorne, Esq., of Ullathorne, was the squire of St. Ewold's; or rather the squire of Ullathorne; for the domain of the modern landlord was of wider notoriety than the fame of the ancient saint. He was a fair specimen of what that race has come to in our days, which a century ago was, as we are told, fairly represented by Squire Western. If that representation be a true one, few classes of men can have made faster strides in improvement. Mr. Thorne, however, was a man possessed of quite a sufficient number of foibles to lay him open to much ridicule. He was still a bachelor, being about fifty, and was not a little proud of his person. When living at home at Ullathorne there was not much room for such pride, and there therefore he always looked like a gentleman, and like that which he certainly was, the first man in his parish. But during the month or six weeks which he annually spent in London, he tried so hard to look like a great man there also, which he certainly was not, that he was put down as a fool by many at his club. He was a man of considerable literary attainment in a certain way and on certain subjects. His favourite authors were Montaigne and Burton, and he knew more perhaps than any other man in his own county, and the next to it, of the English essayists of the two last centuries. He possessed complete sets of the 'Idler,' the 'Spectator,' the 'Tatler,' the 'Guardian,' and the 'Rambler;' and would discourse by hours together on the superiority of such publications to anything which has since been

produced in our Edinburghs and Quarterlies. He was a
great proficient in all questions of genealogy, and knew
enough of almost every gentleman's family in England
to say of what blood and lineage were descended all those
who had any claim to be considered as possessors of any
such luxuries. For blood and lineage he himself had a
most profound respect. He counted back his own ancestors
to some period long antecedent to the Conquest; and
could tell you, if you would listen to him, how it had come
to pass that they, like Cedric the Saxon, had been permitted to hold their own among the Norman barons.
It was not, according to his showing, on account of any
weak complaisance on the part of his family towards their
Norman neighbours. Some Ealfried of Ullathorne once
fortified his own castle, and held out, not only that, but
the then existing cathedral of Barchester also, against
one Geoffrey De Burgh, in the time of King John; and
Mr. Thorne possessed the whole history of the siege
written on vellum, and illuminated in a most costly
manner. It little signified that no one could read the
writing, as, had that been possible, no one could have
understood the language. Mr. Thorne could, however,
give you all the particulars in good English, and had no
objection to do so.

It would be unjust to say that he looked down on men
whose families were of recent date. He did not do so.
He frequently consorted with such, and had chosen many
of his friends from among them. But he looked on them
as great millionaires are apt to look on those who have
small incomes; as men who have Sophocles at their
fingers' ends regard those who know nothing of Greek.
They might doubtless be good sort of people, entitled to
much praise for virtue, very admirable for talent, highly
respectable in every way; but they were without the one
great good gift. Such was Mr. Thorne's way of thinking
on this matter; nothing could atone for the loss of good
blood; nothing could neutralise its good effects. Few
indeed were now possessed of it, but the possession was
on that account the more precious. It was very pleasant
to hear Mr. Thorne descant on this matter. Were you
in your ignorance to surmise that such a one was of a
good family because the head of his family was a baronet

of an old date, he would open his eyes with a delightful
look of affected surprise, and modestly remind you that
baronetcies only dated from James I. He would gently
sigh if you spoke of the blood of the Fitzgeralds and De
Burghs ; would hardly allow the claims of the Howards
and Lowthers ; and has before now alluded to the Talbots
as a family who had hardly yet achieved the full honours
of a pedigree.

In speaking once of a wide spread race whose name
had received the honours of three coronets, scions from
which sat for various constituencies, some one of whose
members had been in almost every cabinet formed during
the present century, a brilliant race such as there are
few in England, Mr. Thorne had called them all ' dirt.' He
had not intended any disrespect to these men. He admired
them in many senses, and allowed them their privileges
without envy. He had merely meant to express his feeling
that the streams which ran through their veins were not
yet purified by time to that perfection, had not become
so genuine an ichor, as to be worthy of being called blood
in the genealogical sense.

When Mr. Arabin was first introduced to him, Mr.
Thorne had immediately suggested that he was one of the
Arabins of Uphill Stanton. Mr. Arabin replied that he
was a very distant relative of the family alluded to. To
this Mr. Thorne surmised that the relationship could not
be very distant. Mr. Arabin assured him that it was so
distant that the families knew nothing of each other.
Mr. Thorne laughed his gentle laugh at this, and told
Mr. Arabin that there was now existing no branch of his
family separated from the parent stock at an earlier date
than the reign of Elizabeth ; and that therefore Mr.
Arabin could not call himself distant. Mr. Arabin himself
was quite clearly an Arabin of Uphill Stanton.

' But,' said the vicar, ' Uphill Stanton has been sold
to the De Greys, and has been in their hands for the last
fifty years.'

' And when it has been there one hundred and firty,
if it unluckily remain there so long,' said Mr. Thorne,
' your descendants will not be a whit the less entitled
to describe themselves as being of the family of Uphill Stanton. Thank God, no De Grey can buy that

—and, thank God—no Arabin, and no Thorne, can
sell it.'

In politics, Mr. Thorne was an unflinching conservative.
He looked on those fifty-three Trojans, who, as Mr. Dod
tells us, censured free trade in November, 1852, as the
only patriots left among the public men of England.
When that terrible crisis of free trade had arrived, when
the repeal of the corn laws was carried by those very men
whom Mr. Thorne had hitherto regarded as the only
possible saviours of his country, he was for a time paralysed.
His country was lost ; but that was comparatively a small
thing.   Other countries had flourished and fallen, and
the human race still went on improving under God's
providence.   But now all trust in human faith must for
ever be at an end.   Not only must ruin come, but it must
come through the apostasy of those who had been regarded as the truest of true believers.   Politics in England,
as a pursuit for gentlemen, must be at an end.   Had Mr.
Thorne been trodden under foot by a Whig, he could
have borne it as a Tory and a martyr ; but to be so utterly
thrown over and deceived by those he had so earnestly
supported, so thoroughly trusted, was more than he could
endure and live.   He therefore ceased to live as a politician,
and refused to hold any converse with the world at large
on the state of the country.

Such were Mr. Thorne's impressions for the first two
or three years after Sir Robert Peel's apostasy ; but by
degrees his temper, as did that of others, cooled down.
He began once more to move about, to frequent the bench
and the market, and to be seen at dinners, shoulder to
shoulder with some of those who had so cruelly betrayed
him.   It was a necessity for him to live, and that plan of
his for avoiding the world did not answer.   He, however,
and others around him who still maintained the same
staunch principles of protection—men like himself, who
were too true to flinch at the cry of a mob—had their
own way of consoling themselves.   They were, and felt
themselves to be, the only true depositaries left of certain
Eleusinian mysteries, of certain deep and wondrous
services of worship by which alone the gods could be
rightly approached.   To them and them only was it now
given to know these things, and to perpetuate them, if

that might still be done, by the careful and secret education
of their children.

We have read how private and peculiar forms of worship
have been carried on from age to age in families, which
to the outer world have apparently adhered to the services
of some ordinary church. And so by degrees it was with
Mr. Thorne. He learnt at length to listen calmly while
protection was talked of as a thing dead, although he
knew within himself that it was still quick with a mystic
life. Nor was he without a certain pleasure that such
knowledge though given to him should be debarred from
the multitude. He became accustomed to hear, even
among country gentlemen, that free trade was after all
not so bad, and to hear this without dispute, although
conscious within himself that everything good in England
had gone with his old palladium. He had within him
something of the feeling of Cato, who gloried that he
could kill himself because Romans were no longer worthy
of their name. Mr. Thorne had no thought of killing
himself, being a Christian, and still possessing his 4000*l.*
a year; but the feeling was not on that account the less
comfortable.

Mr. Thorne was a sportsman, and had been active
though not outrageous in his sports. Previous to the
great downfall of politics in his country, he had supported
the hunt by every means in his power. He had preserved
game till no goose or turkey could show a tail in the parish
of St. Ewold's. He had planted gorse covers with more
care than oaks and larches. He had been more anxious
for the comfort of his foxes than of his ewes and lambs.
No meet had been more popular than Ullathorne; no
man's stables had been more liberally open to the horses
of distant men than Mr. Thorne's; no man had said
more, written more, or done more to keep the club up.
The theory of protection could expand itself so thoroughly
in the practices of a country hunt! But when the great
ruin came; when the noble master of the Barsetshire
hounds supported the recreant minister in the House of
Lords, and basely surrendered his truth, his manhood,
his friends, and his honour for the hope of a garter, then
Mr. Thorne gave up the hunt. He did not cut his covers,
for that would not have been the act of a gentleman. He

did not kill his foxes, for that according to his light would
have been murder. He did not say that his covers should
not be drawn, or his earths stopped, for that would have
been illegal according to the by-laws prevailing among
country gentlemen. But he absented himself from home
on the occasion of every meet at Ullathorne, left the covers
to their fate, and could not be persuaded to take his pink
coat out of the press, or his hunters out of his stable.
This lasted for two years, and then by degrees he came
round. He first appeared at a neighbouring meet on a
pony, dressed in his shooting coat, as though he had
trotted in by accident; then he walked up one morning
on foot to see his favourite gorse drawn, and when his
groom brought his mare out by chance, he did not refuse
to mount her. He was next persuaded, by one of the
immortal fifty-three, to bring his hunting materials over
to the other side of the county, and take a fortnight with
the hounds there; and so gradually he returned to his
old life. But in hunting as in other things he was only
supported by an inward feeling of mystic superiority to
those with whom he shared the common breath of outer
life.

Mr. Thorne did not live in solitude at Ullathorne. He
had a sister, who was ten years older than himself, and
who participated in his prejudices and feelings so strongly,
that she was a living caricature of all his foibles. She
would not open a modern quarterly, did not choose to
see a magazine in her drawing-room, and would not have
polluted her fingers with a shred of the 'Times' for any
consideration. She spoke of Addison, Swift, and Steele,
as though they were still living, regarded De Foe as the
best known novelist of his country, and thought of
Fielding as a young but meritorious novice in the fields
of romance. In poetry, she was familiar with names as
late as Dryden, and had once been seduced into reading
the 'Rape of the Lock;' but she regarded Spenser as
the purest type of her country's literature in this line.
Genealogy was her favourite insanity. Those things
which are the pride of most genealogists were to her contemptible. Arms and mottoes set her beside herself.
Ealfried of Ullathorne had wanted no motto to assist him
in cleaving to the brisket Geoffrey De Burgh; and

Ealfried's great grandfather, the gigantic Ullafrid, had required no other arms than those which nature gave him to hurl from the top of his own castle a cousin of the base invading Norman. To her all modern English names were equally insignificant: Hengist, Horsa, and such like, had for her ears the only true savour of nobility. She was not contented unless she could go beyond the Saxons; and would certainly have christened her children, had she had children, by the names of the ancient Britons. In some respects she was not unlike Scott's Ulrica, and had she been given to cursing, she would certainly have done so in the names of Mista, Skogula, and Zernebock. Not having submitted to the embraces of any polluting Norman, as poor Ulrica had done, and having assisted no parricide, the milk of human kindness was not curdled in her bosom. She never cursed, therefore, but blessed rather. This, however, she did in a strange uncouth Saxon manner that would have been unintelligible to any peasants but her own.

As a politician, Miss Thorne had been so thoroughly disgusted with public life by base deeds long antecedent to the Corn Law question, that that had but little moved her. In her estimation her brother had been a fast young man, hurried away by a too ardent temperament into democratic tendencies. Now happily he was brought to sounder views by seeing the iniquity of the world. She had not yet reconciled herself to the Reform Bill, and still groaned in spirit over the defalcations of the Duke as touching the Catholic Emancipation. If asked whom she thought the Queen should take as her counsellor, she would probably have named Lord Eldon; and when reminded that that venerable man was no longer present in the flesh to assist us, she would probably have answered with a sigh that none now could help us but the dead.

In religion, Miss Thorne was a pure Druidess. We would not have it understood by that, that she did actually in these latter days assist at any human sacrifices, or that she was in fact hostile to the Church of Christ. She had adopted the Christian religion as a milder form of the worship of her ancestors, and always appealed to her doing so as evidence that she had no prejudices against reform, when it could be shown that reform was salutary.

This reform was the most modern of any to which she had
as yet acceded, it being presumed that British ladies
had given up their paint and taken to some sort of petticoats before the days of St. Augustine. That further
feminine step in advance which combines paint and
petticoats together, had not found a votary in Miss Thorne.

But she was a Druidess in this, that she regretted she
knew not what in the usages and practices of her Church.
She sometimes talked and constantly thought of good
things gone by, though she had but the faintest idea of
what those good things had been. She imagined that
a purity had existed which was now gone ; that a piety
had adorned our pastors and a simple docility our people,
for which it may be feared history gave her but little true
warrant. She was accustomed to speak of Cranmer as
though he had been the firmest and most simple-minded
of martyrs, and of Elizabeth as though the pure Protestant
faith of her people had been the one anxiety of her life.
It would have been cruel to undeceive her, had it been
possible ; but it would have been impossible to make her
believe that the one was a time-serving priest, willing
to go any length to keep his place, and that the other was
in heart a papist, with this sole proviso, that she should
be her own pope.

And so Miss Thorne went on sighing and regretting,
looking back to the divine right of kings as the ruling
axiom of a golden age, and cherishing, low down in the
bottom of her heart of hearts, a dear unmentioned wish
for the restoration of some exiled Stuart. Who would
deny her the luxury of her sighs, or the sweetness of her
soft regrets !

In her person and her dress she was perfect, and well
she knew her own perfection. She was a small elegantly
made old woman, with a face from which the glow of her
youth had not departed without leaving some streaks of
a roseate hue. She was proud of her colour, proud of her
grey hair which she wore in short crisp curls peering out
all around her face from the dainty white lace cap. To
think of all the money that she spent in lace used to break
the heart of poor Mrs. Quiverful with her seven daughters.
She was proud of her teeth, which were still white and
numerous, proud of her bright cheery eye, proud of her

short jaunty step, and very proud of the neat, precise, small feet with which those steps were taken. She was proud also, ay, very proud, of the rich brocaded silk in which it was her custom to ruffle through her drawing-room.

We know what was the custom of the lady of Brank-some—

> Nine-and-twenty knights of fame
> Hung their shields in Branksome Hall.

The lady of Ullathorne was not so martial in her habits, but hardly less costly. She might have boasted that nine-and-twenty silken skirts might have been produced in her chamber, each fit to stand alone. The nine-and-twenty shields of the Scottish heroes were less independent, and hardly more potent to withstand any attack that might be made on them. Miss Thorne when fully dressed might be said to have been armed cap-a-pie, and she was always fully dressed, as far as was ever known to mortal man.

For all this rich attire Miss Thorne was not indebted to the generosity of her brother. She had a very comfortable independence of her own, which she divided among juvenile relatives, the milliners, and the poor, giving much the largest share to the latter. It may be imagined, therefore, that with all her little follies she was not unpopular. All her follies have, we believe, been told. Her virtues were too numerous to describe, and not sufficiently interesting to deserve description.

While we are on the subject of the Thornes, one word must be said of the house they lived in. It was not a large house, nor a fine house, nor perhaps to modern ideas a very commodious house; but by those who love the peculiar colour and peculiar ornaments of genuine Tudor architecture it was considered a perfect gem. We beg to own ourselves among the number, and therefore take this opportunity to express our surprise that so little is known by English men and women of the beauties of English architecture. The ruins of the Colosseum, the Campanile at Florence, St. Mark's, Cologne, the Bourse and Notre Dame, are with our tourists as familiar as household words; but they know nothing of the glories of Wiltshire, Dorsetshire, and Somersetshire. Nay, we much question whether many noted travellers, men who have pitched their tents perhaps under Mount Sinai, are not still ignorant that there are glories in Wiltshire, Dorsetshire, and Somersetshire. We beg that they will go and see.

Mr. Thorne's house was called Ullathorne Court, and was properly so called; for the house itself formed two sides of a quadrangle, which was completed on the other two sides by a wall about twenty feet high. This wall was built of cut stone, rudely cut indeed, and now much worn, but of a beautiful rich tawny yellow colour, the effect of that stonecrop of minute growth, which it had taken three centuries to produce. The top of this wall was ornamented by huge round stone balls of the same colour as the wall itself. Entrance into the court was had through a pair of iron gates, so massive that no one could comfortably open or close them, consequently they were rarely disturbed. From the gateway two paths led obliquely across the court; that to the left reaching the hall-door, which was in the corner made by the angle of the house, and that to the right leading to the back entrance, which was at the further end of the longer portion of the building.

With those who are now adepts in contriving house accommodation, it will militate much against Ullathorne Court, that no carriage could be brought to the hall-door. If you enter Ullathorne at all, you must do so, fair reader, on foot, or at least in a bath-chair. No vehicle drawn by horses ever comes within that iron gate. But this is nothing to the next horror that will encounter you. On entering the front door, which you do by no very grand portal, you find yourself immediately in the dining-room. What,—no hall? exclaims my luxurious friend, accustomed to all the comfortable appurtenances of modern life. Yes, kind sir; a noble hall, if you will but observe it; a true old English hall of excellent dimensions for a country gentleman's family; but, if you please, no dining-parlour.

Both Mr. and Miss Thorne were proud of this peculiarity of their dwelling, though the brother was once all but tempted by his friends to alter it. They delighted in the knowledge that they, like Cedric, positively dined in their true hall, even though they so dined tête-à-tête. But though they had never owned, they had felt and endeavoured to remedy the discomfort of such an arrangement. A huge screen partitioned off the front door and a portion of the hall, and from the angle so screened off a second door led into a passage, which ran along the larger side of the house next to the courtyard. Either my reader or I must be a bad hand at topography, if it be not clear that the great hall forms the ground-floor of the smaller portion of the mansion, that which was to your left as you entered the iron gate, and that it occupies the whole of this wing of the building. It must be equally clear that it looks out on a trim mown lawn, through three quadrangular windows with stone mullions, each window divided into a larger portion at the bottom, and a smaller portion at the top, and each portion again divided into five by perpendicular stone supporters. There may be windows which give a better light than such as these, and it may be, as my utilitarian friend observes, that the giving of light is the desired object of a window. I will not argue the point with him. Indeed I cannot. But I shall not the less die in the assured conviction that no sort of description of window is capable of imparting half so much happiness to mankind as that which had been adopted at Ullathorne Court. What—not an oriel? says Miss Diana de Midellage. No, Miss Diana; not even an oriel, beautiful as is an oriel window. It has not about it so perfect a feeling of quiet English homely comfort. Let oriel windows grace a college, or the half public mansion of a potent peer; but for the sitting room of quiet country ladies, of ordinary homely folk, nothing can equal the square mullioned windows of the Tudor architects.

The hall was hung round with family female insipidities by Lely, and unprepossessing male Thornes in red coats by Kneller; each Thorne having been let into a panel in the wainscoting, in the proper manner. At the further end of the room was a huge fire-place, which afforded much ground of difference between the brother and sister. An antiquated grate that would hold about a hundred weight of coal, had been stuck on to the hearth, by Mr.

Thorne's father. This hearth had of course been intended for the consumption of wood fagots, and the iron dogs for the purpose were still standing, though half buried in the masonry of the grate. Miss Thorne was very anxious to revert to the dogs. The dear good old creature was always glad to revert to anything, and had she been systematically indulged, would doubtless in time have reflected that fingers were made before forks, and have reverted accordingly. But in the affairs of the fire-place, Mr. Thorne would not revert. Country gentlemen around him, all had comfortable grates in their dining-rooms. He was not exactly the man to have suggested a modern usage; but he was not so far prejudiced as to banish those which his father had prepared for his use. Mr. Thorne had, indeed, once suggested that with very little contrivance the front door might have been so altered, as to open at least into the passage; but on hearing this, his sister Monica, such was Miss Thorne's name, had been taken ill, and had remained so for a week. Before she came down stairs she received a pledge from her brother that the entrance should never be changed in her lifetime.

At the end of the hall opposite to the fire-place a door led into the drawing-room, which was of equal size, and lighted with precisely similar windows. But yet the aspect of the room was very different. It was papered, and the ceiling, which in the hall showed the old rafters, was whitened and finished with a modern cornice. Miss Thorne's drawing-room, or, as she always called it, with-drawing-room, was a beautiful apartment. The windows opened on to the full extent of the lovely trim garden; immediately before the windows were plots of flowers in stiff, stately, stubborn little beds, each bed surrounded by a stone coping of its own; beyond, there was a low parapet wall, on which stood urns and images, fawns, nymphs, satyrs, and a whole tribe of Pan's followers; and then again, beyond that, a beautiful lawn sloped away to a sunk fence which divided the garden from the park. Mr. Thorne's study was at the end of the drawing room, and beyond that were the kitchen and the offices. Doors opened into both Miss Thorne's withdrawing-room and Mr. Thorne's sanctum from the passage above alluded to; which, as it came to the latter room, widened itself so as to make space for the huge black oak stairs, which led to the upper regions.

Such was the interior of Ullathorne Court. But having thus described it, perhaps somewhat too tediously, we beg to say that it is not the interior to which we wish to call the English tourist's attention, though we advise him to lose no legitimate opportunity of becoming acquainted with it in a friendly manner. It is the outside of Ullathorne that is so lovely. Let the tourist get admission at least into the garden, and fling himself on that soft sward just opposite to the exterior angle of the house. He will there get the double frontage, and enjoy that which is so lovely—the expanse of architectural beauty without the formal dulness of one long line.

It is the colour of Ullathorne that is so remarkable. It is all of that delicious tawny hue which no stone can give, unless it has on it the vegetable richness of centuries. Strike the wall with your hand, and you will think that the stone has on it no covering, but rub it carefully, and you will find that the colour comes off upon your finger. No colourist that ever yet worked from a palette has been able to come up to this rich colouring of years crowding themselves on years.

Ullathorne is a high building for a country house, for it possesses three stories ; and in each story, the windows are of the same sort as that described, though varying in size, and varying also in their lines athwart the house. Those of the ground floor are all uniform in size and position. But those above are irregular both in size and place, and this irregularity gives a bizarre and not unpicturesque appearance to the building. Along the top, on every side, runs a low parapet, which nearly hides the roof, and at the corners are more figures of fawns and satyrs.

Such is Ullathorne House. But we must say one word of the approach to it, which shall include all the description which we mean to give of the church also. The picturesque old church of St. Ewold's stands immediately opposite to the iron gates which open into the court, and is all but surrounded by the branches of the lime trees, which form the avenue leading up to the house from both sides. This avenue is magnificent, but it would lose much of its value in the eyes of many proprietors, by the fact that the road through it is not private property. It is a public lane between hedge rows, with a broad grass margin on each side of the road, from which the lime trees spring. Ulla-thorne Court, therefore, does not stand absolutely sur-rounded by its own grounds, though Mr. Thorne is owner of all the adjacent land. This, however, is the source of very little annoyance to him. Men, when they are acquiring property, think much of such things, but they who live where their ancestors have lived for years, do not feel the misfortune. It never occurred either to Mr. or Miss Thorne that they were not sufficiently private, because the world at large might, if it so wished, walk or drive by their iron gates. That part of the world which availed itself of the privilege was however very small.

Such a year or two since were the Thornes of Ullathorne. Such, we believe, are the inhabitants of many an English country home. May it be long before their number diminishes.

CHAPTER XXIII

MR. ARABIN READS HIMSELF IN AT ST. EWOLD'S

ON the Sunday morning the archdeacon with his sister-in-law and Mr. Arabin drove over to Ullathorne, as had been arranged. On their way thither the new vicar declared himself to be considerably disturbed in his mind at the idea of thus facing his parishioners for the first time. He had, he said, been always subject to *mauvaise honte* and an annoying degree of bashfulness, which often unfitted him for any work of a novel description ; and now he felt this so strongly that he feared he should acquit himself badly in St. Ewold's reading-desk. He knew, he said, that those sharp little eyes of Miss Thorne would be on him, and that they would not approve. All this the archdeacon greatly ridiculed. He himself knew not, and had never known, what it was to be shy. He could not conceive that Miss Thorne, surrounded as she would be by the peasants of Ullathorne, and a few of the poorer inhabitants of the suburbs of Barchester, could in any way affect the com-posure of a man well accustomed to address the learned congregation of St. Mary's at Oxford, and he laughed accordingly at the idea of Mr. Arabin's modesty.

Thereupon Mr. Arabin commenced to subtilise. The change, he said, from St. Mary's to St. Ewold's was quite as powerful on the spirits as would be that from St. Ewold's to St. Mary's.. Would not a peer who, by chance of fortune, might suddenly be driven to herd among navvies be as afraid of the jeers of his companions, as would any navvy suddenly exalted to a seat among the peers ? Whereupon the archdeacon declared with a loud laugh that he would tell Miss Thorne that her new minister had likened her to a navvy. Eleanor, however, pronounced such a conclusion to be unfair ; a comparison might be very just in its proportions which did not at all assimilate the things compared. But Mr. Arabin went on subtilising, regarding neither the archdeacon's raillery nor Eleanor's defence. A young lady, he said, would execute with most perfect self-possession a difficult piece of music in a room crowded with strangers, who would not be able to express herself in intelligible language, even on any ordinary subject and among her most intimate friends, if she were required to do so standing on a box somewhat elevated among them. It was all an affair of education, and he at forty found it difficult to educate himself anew.

Eleanor dissented on the matter of the box ; and averred she could speak very well about dresses, or babies, or legs of mutton from any box, provided it were big enough for her to stand upon without fear, even though all her friends were listening to her. The archdeacon was sure she would not be able to say a word ; but this proved nothing in favour of Mr. Arabin. Mr. Arabin said that he would try the question out with Mrs. Bold, and get her on a box some day when the rectory might be full of visitors. To this Eleanor assented, making condition that the visitors should be of their own set, and the archdeacon cogitated in his mind, whether by such a condition it was intended that Mr. Slope should be included, resolving also that, if so, the trial would certainly never take place in the rectory drawing-room at Plumstead.

And so arguing, they drove up to the iron gates of Ullathorne Court.

Mr. and Miss Thorne were standing ready dressed for

church in the hall, and greeted their clerical visitors with
cordiality. The archdeacon was an old favourite. He was
a clergyman of the old school, and this recommended him
to the lady. He had always been an opponent of free trade
as long as free trade was an open question ; and now that
it was no longer so, he, being a clergyman, had not been
obliged, like most of his lay Tory companions, to read his
recantation. He could therefore be regarded as a supporter
of the immaculate fifty-three, and was on this account a
favourite with Mr. Thorne. The little bell was tinkling,
and the rural population of the parish were standing about
the lane, leaning on the church stile, and against the walls
of the old court, anxious to get a look at their new minister
as he passed from the house to the rectory. The archdeacon's servant had already preceded them thither with
the vestments.

They all went forth together ; and when the ladies
passed into the church the three gentlemen tarried a
moment in the lane, that Mr. Thorne might name to the
vicar with some kind of one-sided introduction, the most
leading among his parishioners.

' Here are our churchwardens, Mr. Arabin ; Farmer
Greenacre and Mr. Stiles. Mr. Stiles has the mill as you go
into Barchester ; and very good churchwardens they are.'

' Not very severe, I hope,' said Mr. Arabin : the two
ecclesiastical officers touched their hats, and each made a leg
in the approved rural fashion, assuring the vicar that they
were very glad to have the honour of seeing him, and
adding that the weather was very good for the harvest.
Mr. Stiles being a man somewhat versed in town life, had an
impression of his own dignity, and did not quite like leaving
his pastor under the erroneous idea that he being a church-
warden kept the children in order during church time.
'Twas thus he understood Mr. Arabin's allusion to his
severity, and hastened to put matters right by observing
that ' Sexton Clodheve looked to the younguns, and
perhaps sometimes there may be a thought too much stick
going on during sermon.' Mr. Arabin's bright eye twinkled
as he caught that of the archdeacon ; and he smiled to
himself as he observed how ignorant his officers were of the
nature of their authority, and of the surveillance which it
was their duty to keep even over himself.

Mr. Arabin read the lessons and preached. It was enough to put a man a little out, let him have been ever so used to pulpit reading, to see the knowing way in which the farmers cocked their ears, and set about a mental criticism as to whether their new minister did or did not fall short of the excellence of him who had lately departed from them. A mental and silent criticism it was for the existing moment, but soon to be made public among the elders of St. Ewold's over the green graves of their children and forefathers. The excellence, however, of poor old Mr. Goodenough had not been wonderful, and there were few there who did not deem that Mr. Arabin did his work sufficiently well, in spite of the slightly nervous affection which at first impeded him, and which nearly drove the archdeacon beside himself.

But the sermon was the thing to try the man. It often surprises us that very young men can muster courage to preach for the first time to a strange congregation. Men who are as yet but little more than boys, who have but just left, what indeed we may not call a school, but a seminary intended for their tuition as scholars, whose thoughts have been mostly of boating, cricketing, and wine parties, ascend a rostrum high above the heads of the submissive crowd, not that they may read God's word to those below, but that they may preach their own word for the edification of their hearers. It seems strange to us that they are not stricken dumb by the new and awful solemnity of their position. How am I, just turned twenty-three, who have never yet passed ten thoughtful days since the power of thought first came to me, how am I to instruct these greybeards, who with the weary thinking of so many years have approached so near the grave ? Can I teach them their duty ? Can I explain to them that which I so imperfectly understand, that which years of study may have made so plain to them ? Has my newly acquired privilege, as one of God's ministers, imparted to me as yet any fitness for the wonderful work of a preacher ?

It must be supposed that such ideas do occur to young clergymen, and yet they overcome, apparently with ease, this difficulty which to us appears to be all but insurmountable. We have never been subjected in the way of ordination to the power of a bishop's hands. It may be that there is in them something that sustains the spirit and banishes the natural modesty of youth. But for ourselves we must own that the deep affection which Dominie Sampson felt for his young pupils has not more endeared him to us than the bashful spirit which sent him mute and inglorious from the pulpit when he rose there with the futile attempt to preach God's gospel.

There is a rule in our church which forbids the younger order of our clergymen to perform a certain portion of the service. The absolution must be read by a minister in priest's orders. If there be no such minister present, the congregation can have the benefit of no absolution but that which each may succeed in administering to himself. The rule may be a good one, though the necessity for it hardly comes home to the general understanding. But this forbearance on the part of youth would be much more appreciated if it were extended likewise to sermons. The only danger would be that congregations would be too anxious to prevent their young clergymen from advancing themselves in the ranks of the ministry. Clergymen who could not preach would be such blessings that they would be bribed to adhere to their incompetence.

Mr. Arabin, however, had not the modesty of youth to impede him, and he succeeded with his sermon even better than with the lessons. He took for his text two verses out of the second epistle of St. John, ' Whosoever transgresseth, and abideth not in the doctrine of Christ, hath not God. He that abideth in the doctrine of Christ he hath both the Father and Son. If there come any unto you and bring not this doctrine, receive him not into your house, neither bid him God speed.' He told them that the house of theirs to which he alluded was this their church in which he now addressed them for the first time ; that their most welcome and proper manner of bidding him God speed would be their patient obedience to his teaching of the gospel ; but that he could put forward no claim to such conduct on their part unless he taught them the great Christian doctrine of works and faith combined. On this he enlarged, but not very amply, and after twenty minutes succeeded in sending his new friends home to their baked mutton and pudding well pleased with their new minister.

Then came the lunch at Ullathorne. As soon as they

were in the hall Miss Thorne took Mr. Arabin's hand, and
assured him that she received him into her house, into
the temple, she said, in which she worshipped, and bade
him God speed with all her heart. Mr. Arabin was touched,
and squeezed the spinster's hand without uttering a
word in reply. Then Mr. Thorne expressed a hope
that Mr. Arabin found the church easy to fill, and
Mr. Arabin having replied that he had no doubt he
should do so as soon as he had learnt to pitch his voice
to the building, they all sat down to the good things before
them.

Miss Thorne took special care of Mrs. Bold. Eleanor
still wore her widow's weeds, and therefore had about
her that air of grave and sad maternity which is the lot
of recent widows. This opened the soft heart of Miss
Thorne, and made her look on her young guest as though
too much could not be done for her. She heaped chicken
and ham upon her plate, and poured out for her a full
bumper of port wine. When Eleanor, who was not sorry
to get it, had drunk a little of it, Miss Thorne at once
essayed to fill it again. To this Eleanor objected, but in
vain. Miss Thorne winked and nodded and whispered,
saying that it was the proper thing and must be done,
and that she knew all about it; and so she desired Mrs.
Bold to drink it up, and not mind any body.

' It is your duty, you know, to support yourself,' she
said into the ear of the young mother; ' there's more
than yourself depending on it; ' and thus she coshered
up Eleanor with cold fowl and port wine. How it is that
poor men's wives, who have no cold fowl and port wine
on which to be coshered up, nurse their children without
difficulty, whereas the wives of rich men, who eat and
drink everything that is good, cannot do so, we will for
the present leave to the doctors and the mothers to settle
between them.

And then Miss Thorne was great about teeth. Little
Johnny Bold had been troubled for the last few days with
his first incipient masticator, and with that freemasonry
which exists among ladies, Miss Thorne became aware
of the fact before Eleanor had half finished her wing.
The old lady prescribed at once a receipt which had been
much in vogue in the young days of her grandmother,

and warned Eleanor with solemn voice against the fallacies
of modern medicine.

' Take his coral, my dear,' said she, ' and rub it well with
carrot-juice ; rub it till the juice dries on it, and then
give it him to play with——'

' But he hasn't got a coral,' said Eleanor.

' Not got a coral ! ' said Miss Thorne, with almost angry
vehemence. ' Not got a coral—how can you expect that
he should cut his teeth ? Have you got Daffy's Elixir ? '

Eleanor explained that she had not. It had not been
ordered by Mr. Rerechild, the Barchester doctor whom
she employed ; and then the young mother mentioned
some shockingly modern succedaneum, which Mr. Rerechild's new lights had taught him to recommend.

Miss Thorne looked awfully severe. ' Take care, my
dear,' said she, ' that the man knows what he's about ;
take care he doesn't destroy your little boy. But '—and
she softened into sorrow as she said it, and spoke more in
pity than in anger—' but I don't know who there is in
Barchester now that you can trust. Poor dear old Doctor
Bumpwell, indeed——'

' Why, Miss Thorne, he died when I was a little
girl.'

' Yes, my dear, he did, and an unfortunate day it was
for Barchester. As to those young men that have come
up since ' (Mr. Rerechild, by the bye, was quite as old as
Miss Thorne herself), ' one doesn't know where they came
from or who they are, or whether they know anything
about their business or not.'

' I think there are very clever men in Barchester,'
said Eleanor.

' Perhaps there may be ; only I don't know them ; and
it's admitted on all sides that medical men arn't now
what they used to be. They used to be talented, observing,
educated men. But now any whipper-snapper out of an
apothecary's shop can call himself a doctor. I believe
no kind of education is now thought necessary.'

Eleanor was herself the widow of a medical man, and
felt a little inclined to resent all these hard sayings. But
Miss Thorne was so essentially good-natured that it was
impossible to resent anything she said. She therefore
sipped her wine and finished her chicken.

' At any rate, my dear, don't forget the carrot-juice,
and by all means get him a coral at once. My grandmother Thorne had the best teeth in the county, and
carried them to the grave with her at eighty. I have
heard her say it was all the carrot-juice. She couldn't
bear the Barchester doctors. Even poor old Dr. Bumpwell
didn't please her.' It clearly never occurred to Miss Thorne
that some fifty years ago Dr. Bumpwell was only a rising
man, and therefore as much in need of character in the
eyes of the then ladies of Ullathorne, as the present doctors
were in her own.

The archdeacon made a very good lunch, and talked
to his host about turnip-drillers and new machines for
reaping ; while the host, thinking it only polite to attend
to a stranger, and fearing that perhaps he might not care
about turnip crops on a Sunday, mooted all manner of
ecclesiastical subjects.

' I never saw a heavier lot of wheat, Thorne, than
you've got there in that field beyond the copse. I suppose
that's guano,' said the archdeacon.

' Yes, guano. I get it from Bristol myself. You'll find
you often have a tolerable congregation of Barchester
people out here, Mr. Arabin. They are very fond of St.
Ewold's, particularly of an afternoon, when the weather
is not too hot for the walk.'

' I am under an obligation to them for staying away
to-day, at any rate,' said the vicar. ' The congregation
can never be too small for a maiden sermon.'

' I got a ton and a half at Bradley's in High Street,'
said the archdeacon, ' and it was a complete take in.
I don't believe there was five hundred-weight of guano
in it.'

' That Bradley never has anything good,' said Miss
Thorne, who had just caught the name during her whisper-
ings with Eleanor. ' And such a nice shop as there used
to be in that very house before he came. Wilfred, don't
you remember what good things old Ambleoff used to
have ? '

' There have been three men since Ambleoff's time,'
said the archdeacon, ' and each as bad as the other. But
who gets it for you at Bristol, Thorne ? '

' I ran up myself this year and bought it out of the

ship. I am afraid as the evenings get shorter, Mr. Arabin,
you'll find the reading desk too dark. I must send a
fellow with an axe and make him lop off some of those
branches.'

Mr. Arabin declared that the morning light at any rate
was perfect, and deprecated any interference with the
lime trees. And then they took a stroll out among the
trim parterres, and Mr. Arabin explained to Mrs. Bold
the difference between a naiad and a dryad, and dilated
on vases and the shapes of urns. Miss Thorne busied
herself among her pansies ; and her brother, finding it
quite impracticable to give anything of a peculiarly
Sunday tone to the conversation, abandoned the attempt,
and had it out with the archdeacon about the Bristol
guano.

At three o'clock they again went into church ; and now
Mr. Arabin read the service and the archdeacon preached.
Nearly the same congregation was present, with some
adventurous pedestrians from the city, who had not
thought the heat of the mid-day August sun too great to
deter them. The archdeacon took his text from the
Epistle of Philemon. ' I beseech thee for my son Onesimus,
whom I have begotten in my bonds.' From such a text
it may be imagined the kind of sermon which Dr. Grantly
preached, and on the whole it was neither dull, nor bad,
nor out of place.

He told them that it had become his duty to look about
for a pastor for them, to supply the place of one who had
been long among them ; and that in this manner he
regarded as a son him whom he had selected, as St. Paul
had regarded the young disciple whom he sent forth. Then
he took a little merit to himself for having studiously
provided the best man he could without reference to
patronage or favour ; but he did not say that the best
man according to his views was he who was best able to
subdue Mr. Slope, and make that gentleman's situation
in Barchester too hot to be comfortable. As to the bonds,
they had consisted in the exceeding struggle which he had
made to get a good clergyman for them. He deprecated
any comparison between himself and St. Paul, but said
that he was entitled to beseech them for their good will
towards Mr. Arabin, in the same manner that the apostle

had besought Philemon and his household with regard
to Onesimus.

The archdeacon's sermon, text, blessing and all, was
concluded within the half hour. Then they shook hands
with their Ullathorne friends, and returned to Plumstead.
'Twas thus that Mr. Arabin read himself in at St. Ewold's.

CHAPTER XXIV

MR. SLOPE MANAGES MATTERS VERY CLEVERLY AT
PUDDINGDALE

THE next two weeks passed pleasantly enough at
Plumstead. The whole party there assembled seemed
to get on well together. Eleanor made the house agreeable,
and the archdeacon and Mrs. Grantly seemed to have
forgotten her iniquity as regarded Mr. Slope. Mr. Harding
had his violoncello, and played to them while his daughters
accompanied him. Johnny Bold, by the help either of
Mr. Rerechild or else by that of his coral and carrot-juice,
got through his teething troubles. There had been
gaieties too of all sorts. They had dined at Ullathorne,
and the Thornes had dined at the Rectory. Eleanor had
been duly put to stand on her box, and in that position
had found herself quite unable to express her opinion on
the merits of flounces, such having been the subject given
to try her elocution. Mr. Arabin had of course been much
in his own parish, looking to the doings at his vicarage,
calling on his parishioners, and taking· on himself the
duties of his new calling. But still he had been every
evening at Plumstead, and Mrs. Grantly was partly willing
to agree with her husband that he was a pleasant inmate
in a house.

They had also been at a dinner party at Dr. Stanhope's,
of which Mr. Arabin had made one. He also, moth-like,
burnt his wings in the flames of the signora's candle. Mrs.
Bold, too, had been there, and had felt somewhat displeased with the taste, want of taste she called it, shown
by Mr. Arabin in paying so much attention to Madame
Neroni. It was as infallible that Madeline should displease
and irritate the women, as that she should charm and

captivate the men. The one result followed naturally
on the other. It was quite true that Mr. Arabin had been
charmed. He thought her a very clever and a very
handsome woman; he thought also that her peculiar
affliction entitled her to the sympathy of all. He had
never, he said, met so much suffering joined to such
perfect beauty and so clear a mind. 'Twas thus he spoke
of the signora coming home in the archdeacon's carriage;
and Eleanor by no means liked to hear the praise. It was,
however, exceedingly unjust of her to be angry with
Mr. Arabin, as she had herself spent a very pleasant
evening with Bertie Stanhope, who had taken her down
to dinner, and had not left her side for one moment after
the gentlemen came out of the dining-room. It was unfair
that she should amuse herself with Bertie and yet begrudge
her new friend his license of amusing himself with Bertie's
sister. And yet she did so. She was half angry with him
in the carriage, and said something about meretricious
manners. Mr. Arabin did not understand the ways of
women very well, or else he might have flattered himself
that Eleanor was in love with him.

But Eleanor was not in love with him. How many
shades there are between love and indifference, and how
little the graduated scale is understood! She had now
been nearly three weeks in the same house with Mr. Arabin,
and had received much of his attention, and listened daily
to his conversation. He had usually devoted at least
some portion of his evening to her exclusively. At Dr.
Stanhope's he had devoted himself exclusively to another.
It does not require that a woman should be in love to be
irritated at this; it does not require that she should even
acknowledge to herself that it is unpleasant to her.
Eleanor had no such self-knowledge. She thought in her
own heart that it was only on Mr. Arabin's account that
she regretted that he could condescend to be amused by
the signora. 'I thought he had more mind,' she said to
herself, as she sat watching her baby's cradle on her return
from the party. 'After all, I believe Mr. Stanhope is the
pleasanter man of the two.' Alas for the memory of poor
John Bold! Eleanor was not in love with Bertie Stanhope,
nor was she in love with Mr. Arabin. But her devotion
to her late husband was fast fading, when she could revolve

in her mind, over the cradle of his infant, the faults and
failings of other aspirants to her favour.

Will any one blame my heroine for this ? Let him or
her rather thank God for all His goodness,—for His mercy
endureth for ever.

Eleanor, in truth, was not in love ; neither was Mr.
Arabin. Neither indeed was Bertie Stanhope, though he
had already found occasion to say nearly as much as that
he was. The widow's cap had prevented him from making
a positive declaration, when otherwise he would have
considered himself entitled to do so on a third or fourth
interview. It was, after all, but a small cap now, and had
but little of the weeping-willow left in its construction.
It is singular how these emblems of grief fade away by
unseen gradations. Each pretends to be the counterpart
of the forerunner, and yet the last little bit of crimped
white crape that sits so jauntily on the back of the head,
is as dissimilar to the first huge mountain of woe which
disfigured the face of the weeper, as the state of the
Hindoo is to the jointure of the English dowager.

But let it be clearly understood that Eleanor was in
love with no one, and that no one was in love with Eleanor.
Under these circumstances her anger against Mr. Arabin
did not last long, and before two days were over they were
both as good friends as ever. She could not but like him,
for every hour spent in his company was spent pleasantly.
And yet she could not quite like him, for there was always
apparent in his conversation a certain feeling on his part
that he hardly thought it worth his while to be in earnest.
It was almost as though he were playing with a child.
She knew well enough that he was in truth a sober thoughtful man, who in some matters and on some occasions could
endure an agony of earnestness. And yet to her he was
always gently playful. Could she have seen his brow once
clouded she might have learnt to love him.

So things went on at Plumstead, and on the whole
not unpleasantly, till a huge storm darkened the horizon,
and came down upon the inhabitants of the rectory with
all the fury of a water-spout. It was astonishing how in
a few minutes the whole face of the heavens was changed.
The party broke up from breakfast in perfect harmony ;
but fierce passions had arisen before the evening, which

did not admit of their sitting at the same board for
dinner. To explain this, it will be necessary to go back
a little.

It will be remembered that the bishop expressed to
Mr. Slope in his dressing-room, his determination that
Mr. Quiverful should be confirmed in his appointment to
the hospital, and that his lordship requested Mr. Slope
to communicate this decision to the archdeacon. It will
also be remembered that the archdeacon had indignantly
declined seeing Mr. Slope, and had, instead, written a
strong letter to the bishop, in which he all but demanded
the situation of warden for Mr. Harding. To this letter
the archdeacon received an immediate formal reply from
Mr. Slope, in which it was stated, that the bishop had
received and would give his best consideration to the
archdeacon's letter.

The archdeacon felt himself somewhat checkmated
by this reply. What could he do with a man who would
neither see him, nor argue with him by letter, and who
had undoubtedly the power of appointing any clergyman
he pleased ? He had consulted with Mr. Arabin, who had
suggested the propriety of calling in the aid of the master
of Lazarus. ' If,' said he, ' you and Dr. Gwynne formally
declare your intention of waiting upon the bishop, the
bishop will not dare to refuse to see you ; and if two such
men as you are see him together, you will probably not
leave him without carrying your point.'

The archdeacon did not quite like admitting the
necessity of his being backed by the master of Lazarus
before he could obtain admission into the episcopal palace
of Barchester ; but still he felt that the advice was good,
and he resolved to take it. He wrote again to the bishop,
expressing a hope that nothing further would be done in
the matter of the hospital, till the consideration promised
by his lordship had been given, and then sent off a warm
appeal to his friend the master, imploring him to come
to Plumstead and assist in driving the bishop into compliance. The master had rejoined, raising some difficulty,
but not declining ; and the archdeacon had again pressed
his point, insisting on the necessity for immediate action.
Dr. Gwynne unfortunately had the gout, and could therefore name no immediate day, but still agreed to come,

if it should be finally found necessary. So the matter stood, as regarded the party at Plumstead.

But Mr. Harding had another friend fighting his battle for him, quite as powerful as the master of Lazarus, and this was Mr. Slope. Though the bishop had so pertinaciously insisted on giving way to his wife in the matter of the hospital, Mr. Slope did not think it necessary to abandon his object. He had, he thought, daily more and more reason to imagine that the widow would receive his overtures favourably, and he could not but feel that Mr. Harding at the hospital, and placed there by his means, would be more likely to receive him as a son-in-law, than Mr. Harding growling in opposition and disappointment under the archdeacon's wing at Plumstead. Moreover, to give Mr. Slope due credit, he was actuated by greater motives even than these. He wanted a wife, and he wanted money, but he wanted power more than either. He had fully realised the fact that he must come to blows with Mrs. Proudie. He had no desire to remain in Barchester as her chaplain. Sooner than do so, he would risk the loss of his whole connection with the diocese. What! was he to feel within him the possession of no ordinary talents; was he to know himself to be courageous, firm, and, in matters where his conscience did not interfere, unscrupulous; and yet be contented to be the working factotum of a woman-prelate ? Mr. Slope had higher ideas of his own destiny. Either he or Mrs. Proudie must go to the wall; and now had come the time when he would try which it should be.

The bishop had declared that Mr. Quiverful should be the new warden. As Mr. Slope went down stairs prepared to see the archdeacon if necessary, but fully satisfied that no such necessity would arise, he declared to himself that Mr. Harding should be warden. With the object of carrying this point, he rode over to Puddingdale, and had a further interview with the worthy expectant of clerical good things. Mr. Quiverful was on the whole a worthy man. The impossible task of bringing up as ladies and gentlemen fourteen children on an income which was insufficient to give them with decency the common necessaries of life, had had an effect upon him not beneficial either to his spirit, or his keen sense of

honour. Who can boast that he would have supported
such a burden with a different result ? Mr. Quiverful
was an honest, pains-taking, drudging man ; anxious,
indeed, for bread and meat, anxious for means to quiet
his butcher and cover with returning smiles the now sour
countenance of the baker's wife, but anxious also to be
right with his own conscience. He was not careful, as
another might be who sat on an easier worldly seat, to
stand well with those around him, to shun a breath which
might sully his name, or a rumour which might affect
his honour. He could not afford such niceties of conduct,
such moral luxuries. It must suffice for him to be
ordinarily honest according to the ordinary honesty of
the world's ways, and to let men's tongues wag as they
would.

He had felt that his brother clergymen, men whom
he had known for the last twenty years, looked coldly
on him from the first moment that he had shown himself
willing to sit at the feet of Mr. Slope ; he had seen that
their looks grew colder still, when it became bruited
about that he was to be the bishop's new warden at
Hiram's hospital. This was painful enough ; but it was
the cross which he was doomed to bear. He thought of his
wife, whose last new silk dress was six years in wear.
He thought of all his young flock, whom he could hardly
take to church with him on Sundays, for there were not
decent shoes and stockings for them all to wear. He
thought of the well-worn sleeves of his own black coat,
and of the stern face of the draper from whom he would
fain ask for cloth to make another, did he not know that
the credit would be refused him. Then he thought of
the comfortable house in Barchester, of the comfortable
income, of his boys sent to school, of his girls with books
in their hands instead of darning needles, of his wife's
face again covered with smiles, and of his daily board
again covered with plenty. He thought of these things ;
and do thou also, reader, think of them, and then wonder,
if thou canst, that Mr. Slope had appeared to him to
possess all those good gifts which could grace a bishop's
chaplain. ' How beautiful upon the mountains are the
feet of him that bringeth good tidings.'

Why, moreover, should the Barchester clergy have

looked coldly on Mr. Quiverful ? Had they not all shown
that they regarded with complacency the loaves and
fishes of their mother church ? Had they not all, by some
hook or crook, done better for themselves than he had
done ? They were not burdened as he was burdened.
Dr. Grantly had five children, and nearly as many thousands a year on which to feed them. It was very well for
him to turn up his nose at a new bishop who could do
nothing for him, and a chaplain who was beneath his
notice ; but it was cruel in a man so circumstanced to
set the world against the father of fourteen children
because he was anxious to obtain for them an honourable
support ! He, Mr. Quiverful, had not asked for the
wardenship ; he had not even accepted it till he had
been assured that Mr. Harding had refused it. How hard
then that he should be blamed for doing that which not to
have done would have argued a most insane imprudence ?

Thus in this matter of the hospital poor Mr. Quiverful
had his trials ; and he had also his consolations. On the
whole the consolations were the more vivid of the two.
The stern draper heard of the coming promotion, and
the wealth of his warehouse was at Mr. Quiverful's disposal.
Coming events cast their shadows before, and the coming
event of Mr. Quiverful's transference to Barchester produced a delicious shadow in the shape of a new outfit for
Mrs. Quiverful and her three elder daughters. Such consolations come home to the heart of a man, and quite
home to the heart of a woman. Whatever the husband
might feel, the wife cared nothing for frowns of dean,
archdeacon, or prebendary. To her the outsides and
insides of her husband and fourteen children were everything. In her bosom every other ambition had been
swallowed up in that maternal ambition of seeing them
and him and herself duly clad and properly fed. It had
come to that with her that life had now no other purpose.
She recked nothing of the imaginary rights of others.
She had no patience with her husband when he declared
to her that he could not accept the hospital unless he
knew that Mr. Harding had refused it. Her husband had
no right to be Quixotic at the expense of fourteen children.
The narrow escape of throwing away his good fortune
which her lord had had, almost paralysed her. Now,

indeed, they had received the full promise not only from
Mr. Slope, but also from Mrs. Proudie. Now, indeed,
they might reckon with safety on their good fortune.
But what if all had been lost? What if her fourteen
bairns had been resteeped to the hips in poverty by the
morbid sentimentality of their father? Mrs. Quiverful
was just at present a happy woman, but yet it nearly
took her breath away when she thought of the risk they
had run.

' I don't know what your father means when he talks
so much of what is due to Mr. Harding,' she said to her
eldest daughter. ' Does he think that Mr. Harding would
give him 450*l.* a year out of fine feeling? And what
signifies it whom he offends, as long as he gets the place?
He does not expect anything better. It passes me to
think how your father can be so soft, while everybody
around him is so griping.'

Thus, while the outer world was accusing Mr. Quiverful
of rapacity for promotion and of disregard to his honour,
the inner world of his own household was falling foul of
him, with equal vehemence, for his willingness to sacrifice
their interest to a false feeling of sentimental pride. It
is astonishing how much difference the point of view
makes in the aspect of all that we look at!

Such were the feelings of the different members of the
family at Puddingdale on the occasion of Mr. Slope's
second visit. Mrs. Quiverful, as soon as she saw his horse
coming up the avenue from the vicarage gate, hastily
packed up her huge basket of needlework, and hurried
herself and her daughter out of the room in which she
was sitting with her husband. ' It's Mr. Slope,' she said.
' He's come to settle with you about the hospital. I do
hope we shall now be able to move at once.' And she
hastened to bid the maid of all work go to the door, so
that the welcome great man might not be kept waiting.

Mr. Slope thus found Mr. Quiverful alone. Mrs. Quiverful went off to her kitchen and back settlements with
anxious beating heart, almost dreading that there might
be some slip between the cup of her happiness and the
lip of her fruition, but yet comforting herself with the
reflection that after what had taken place, any such slip
could hardly be possible.

Mr. Slope was all smiles as he shook his brother clergyman's hand, and said that he had ridden over because he
thought it right at once to put Mr. Quiverful in possession
of the facts of the matter regarding the wardenship of the
hospital. As he spoke, the poor expectant husband and
father saw at a glance that his brilliant hopes were to
be dashed to the ground, and that his visitor was now
there for the purpose of unsaying what on his former visit
he had said. There was something in the tone of the
voice, something in the glance of the eye, which told the
tale. Mr. Quiverful knew it all at once. He maintained
his self-possession, however, smiled with a slight unmeaning smile, and merely said that he was obliged to Mr. Slope
for the trouble he was taking.

'It has been a troublesome matter from first to last,'
said Mr. Slope ; ' and the bishop has hardly known how
to act. Between ourselves—but mind this of course must
go no further, Mr. Quiverful.'

Mr. Quiverful said that of course it should not. ' The
truth is, that poor Mr. Harding has hardly known his
own mind. You remember our last conversation, no
doubt.'

Mr. Quiverful assured him that he remembered it very
well indeed.

' You will remember that I told you that Mr. Harding
had refused to return to the hospital.'

Mr. Quiverful declared that nothing could be more
distinct on his memory.

' And acting on this refusal, I suggested that you should
take the hospital,' continued Mr. Slope.

' I understood you to say that the bishop had authorised
you to offer it to me.'

' Did I ? did I go so far as that ? Well, perhaps it may
be, that in my anxiety in your behalf I did commit myself
further than I should have done. So far as my own
memory serves me, I don't think I did go quite so far as
that. But I own I was very anxious that you should get
it ; and I may have said more than was quite prudent.'

' But,' said Mr. Quiverful, in his deep anxiety to prove
his case, ' my wife received as distinct a promise from
Mrs. Proudie as one human being could give to another.'

Mr. Slope smiled, and gently shook his head. He meant

that smile for a pleasant smile, but it was diabolical in the eyes of the man he was speaking to. 'Mrs. Proudie!' he said. 'If we are to go to what passes between the ladies in these matters, we shall really be in a nest of troubles from which we shall never extricate ourselves. Mrs. Proudie is a most excellent lady, kind-hearted, charitable, pious, and in every way estimable. But, my dear Mr. Quiverful, the patronage of the diocese is not in her hands.'

Mr. Quiverful for a moment sat panic-stricken and silent. 'Am I to understand, then, that I have received no promise?' he said, as soon as he had sufficiently collected his thoughts.

'If you will allow me, I will tell you exactly how the matter rests. You certainly did receive a promise conditional on Mr. Harding's refusal. I am sure you will do me the justice to remember that you yourself declared that you could accept the appointment on no other condition than the knowledge that Mr. Harding had declined it.'

'Yes,' said Mr. Quiverful; 'I did say that, certainly.'

'Well; it now appears that he did not refuse it.'

'But surely you told me, and repeated it more than once, that he had done so in your own hearing.'

'So I understood him. But it seems I was in error. But don't for a moment, Mr. Quiverful, suppose that I mean to throw you over. No. Having held out my hand to a man in your position, with your large family and pressing claims, I am not now going to draw it back again. I only want you to act with me fairly and honestly.'

'Whatever I do, I shall endeavour at any rate to act fairly,' said the poor man, feeling that he had to fall back for support on the spirit of martyrdom within him.

'I am sure you will,' said the other. 'I am sure you have no wish to obtain possession of an income which belongs by all right to another. No man knows better than you do Mr. Harding's history, or can better appreciate his character. Mr. Harding is very desirous of returning to his old position, and the bishop feels that he is at the present moment somewhat hampered, though of course he is not bound, by the conversation which took place on the matter between you and me.'

' Well,' said Mr. Quiverful, dreadfully doubtful as to
what his conduct under such circumstances should be,
and fruitlessly striving to harden his nerves with some
of that instinct of self-preservation which made his wife
so bold.

' The wardenship of this little hospital is not the only
thing in the bishop's gift, Mr. Quiverful, nor is it by many
degrees the best. And his lordship is not the man to forget any one whom he has once marked with approval.
If you would allow me to advise you as a friend——'

' Indeed I shall be most grateful to you,' said the poor
vicar of Puddingdale——

' I should advise you to withdraw from any opposition
to Mr. Harding's claims. If you persist in your demand,
I do not think you will ultimately succeed. Mr. Harding
has all but a positive right to the place. But if you will
allow me to inform the bishop that you decline to stand
in Mr. Harding's way, I think I may promise you—though,
by the bye, it must not be taken as a formal promise—
that the bishop will not allow you to be a poorer man
than you would have been had you become warden.'

Mr. Quiverful sat in his arm chair silent, gazing at
vacancy. What was he to say ? All this that came from
Mr. Slope was so true. Mr. Harding had a right to the
hospital. The bishop had a great many good things to
give away. Both the bishop and Mr. Slope would be
excellent friends and terrible enemies to a man in his
position. And then he had no proof of any promise ; he
could not force the bishop to appoint him.

' Well, Mr. Quiverful, what do you say about it ? '

' Oh, of course, whatever you think fit, Mr. Slope. It's
a great disappointment, a very great disappointment.
I won't deny that I am a very poor man, Mr. Slope.'

' In the end, Mr. Quiverful, you will find that it will
have been better for you.'

The interview ended in Mr. Slope receiving a full
renunciation from Mr. Quiverful of any claim he might
have to the appointment in question. It was only given
verbally and without witnesses ; but then the original
promise was made in the same way.

Mr. Slope again assured him that he should not be
forgotten, and then rode back to Barchester, satisfied that
he would now be able to mould the bishop to his wishes.

CHAPTER XXV

FOURTEEN ARGUMENTS IN FAVOUR OF MR. QUIVERFUL'S CLAIMS

WE have most of us heard of the terrible anger of a lioness when, surrounded by her cubs, she guards her prey. Few of us wish to disturb the mother of a litter of puppies when mouthing a bone in the midst of her young family. Medea and her children are familiar to us, and so is the grief of Constance. Mrs. Quiverful, when she first heard from her husband the news which he had to impart, felt within her bosom all the rage of a lioness, the rapacity of the hound, the fury of the tragic queen, and the deep despair of the bereaved mother.

Doubting, but yet hardly fearing, what might·have been the tenor of Mr. Slope's discourse, she rushed back to her husband as soon as the front door was closed behind the visitor. It was well for Mr. Slope that he so escaped,— the anger of such a woman, at such a moment, would have cowed even him. As a general rule, it is highly desirable that ladies should keep their temper; a woman when she storms always makes herself ugly, and usually ridiculous also. There is nothing so odious to man as a virago. Though Theseus loved an Amazon, he showed his love but roughly; and from the time of Theseus downward, no man ever wished to have his wife remarkable rather for forward prowess than retiring gentleness. A low voice ' is an excellent thing in woman.'

Such may be laid down as a very general rule; and few women should allow themselves to deviate from it, and then only on rare occasions. But if there be a time when a woman may let her hair to the winds, when she may loose her arms, and scream out trumpet-tongued to the ears of men, it is when nature calls out within her not for her own wants, but for the wants of those whom her womb has borne, whom her breasts have suckled, for those who look to her for their daily bread as naturally as man looks to his Creator.

There was nothing poetic in the nature of Mrs. Quiverful. She was neither a Medea nor a Constance. When angry, she spoke out her anger in plain words, and in a tone which might have been modulated with advantage; but she did so, at any rate, without affectation. Now, without knowing it, she rose to a tragic vein.

' Well, my dear; we are not to have it.' Such were the words with which her ears were greeted when she entered the parlour, still hot from the kitchen fire. And the face of her husband spoke even more plainly than his words :—

> E'en such a man, so faint, so spiritless,
> So dull, so dead in look, so woe-begone,
> Drew Priam's curtain in the dead of night.

' What ! ' said she,—and Mrs. Siddons could not have put more passion into a single syllable,—' What ! not have it ? who says so ? ' And she sat opposite to her husband, with her elbows on the table, her hands clasped together, and her coarse, solid, but once handsome face stretched over it towards him.

She sat as silent as death while he told his story, and very dreadful to him her silence was. He told it very lamely and badly, but still in such a manner that she soon understood the whole of it.

' And so you have resigned it ? ' said she.

' I have had no opportunity of accepting it,' he replied. ' I had no witnesses to Mr. Slope's offer, even if that offer would bind the bishop. It was better for me, on the whole, to keep on good terms with such men than to fight for what I should never get ! '

' Witnesses ! ' she screamed, rising quickly to her feet, and walking up and down the room. ' Do clergymen require witnesses to their words ? He made the promise in the bishop's name, and if it is to be broken I'll know the reason why. Did he not positively say that the bishop had sent him to offer you the place ? '

' He did, my dear. But that is now nothing to the purpose.'

' It is everything to the purpose, Mr. Quiverful. Witnesses indeed ! and then to talk of *your* honour being questioned, because you wish to provide for fourteen children. It is everything to the purpose; and so they shall know, if I scream it into their ears from the town cross of Barchester.'

' You rorget, Letitia, that the bishop has so many things in his gift. We must wait a little longer. That is all.'

' Wait! Shall we feed the children by waiting? Will waiting put George, and Tom, and Sam, out into the world? Will it enable my poor girls to give up some of their drudgery? Will waiting make Bessy and Jane fit even to be governesses? Will waiting pay for the things we got in Barchester last week?'

' It is all we can do, my dear. The disappointment is as much to me as to you; and yet, God knows, I feel it more for your sake than my own.'

Mrs. Quiverful was looking full into her husband's face, and saw a small hot tear appear on each of those furrowed cheeks. This was too much for her woman's heart. He also had risen, and was standing with his back to the empty grate. She rushed towards him, and, seizing him in her arms, sobbed aloud upon his bosom.

' You are too good, too soft, too yielding,' she said at last. ' These men, when they want you, they use you like a cat's-paw; and when they want you no longer, they throw you aside like an old shoe. This is twice they have treated you so.'

' In one way this will be all for the better,' argued he. ' It will make the bishop feel that he is bound to do something for me.'

' At any rate, he shall hear of it,' said the lady, again reverting to her more angry mood. ' At any rate he shall hear of it, and that loudly; and so shall she. She little knows Letitia Quiverful, if she thinks I will sit down quietly with the loss after all that passed between us at the palace. If there's any feeling within her, I'll make her ashamed of herself,'—and she paced the room again, stamping the floor as she went with her fat heavy foot. ' Good heavens! what a heart she must have within her to treat in such a way as this the father of fourteen unprovided children!'

Mr. Quiverful proceeded to explain that he didn't think that Mrs. Proudie had had anything to do with it.

' Don't tell me,' said Mrs. Quiverful; ' I know more about it than that. Doesn't all the world know that Mrs. Proudie is bishop of Barchester, and that Mr. Slope is merely her creature? Wasn't it she that made me the promise, just as though the thing was in her own particular gift? I tell you, it was that woman who sent him over here to-day, because, for some reason of her own, she wants to go back from her word.'

' My dear, you're wrong—'

' Now, Q., don't be so soft,' she continued. ' Take my word for it, the bishop knows no more about it than Jemima does.' Jemima was the two-year-old. ' And if you'll take my advice, you'll lose no time in going over and seeing him yourself.'

Soft, however, as Mr. Quiverful might be, he would not allow himself to be talked out of his opinion on this occasion; and proceeded with much minuteness to explain to his wife the tone in which Mr. Slope had spoken of Mrs. Proudie's interference in diocesan matters. As he did so, a new idea gradually instilled itself into the matron's head, and a new course of conduct presented itself to her judgment. What if, after all, Mrs. Proudie knew nothing of this visit of Mr. Slope's? In that case, might it not be possible that that lady would still be staunch to her in this matter, still stand her friend, and, perhaps, possibly carry her through in opposition to Mr. Slope? Mrs. Quiverful said nothing as this vague hope occurred to her, but listened with more than ordinary patience to what her husband had to say. While he was still explaining that in all probability the world was wrong in its estimation of Mrs. Proudie's power and authority, she had fully made up her mind as to her course of action. She did not, however, proclaim her intention. She shook her head ominously as he continued his narration; and when he had completed she rose to go, merely observing that it was cruel, cruel treatment. She then asked him if he would mind. waiting for a late dinner instead of dining at their usual hour of three, and, having received from him a concession on this point, she proceeded to carry her purpose into execution.

She determined that she would at once go to the palace; that she would do so, if possible, before Mrs. Proudie could have had an interview with Mr. Slope; and that she would be either submissive piteous and pathetic, or else indignant violent and exacting, according to the manner in which she was received.

She was quite confident in her own power. Strengthened
as she was by the pressing wants of fourteen children,
she felt that she could make her way through legions of
episcopal servants, and force herself, if need be, into the
presence of the lady who had so wronged her. She had
no shame about it, no *mauvaise honte*, no dread of archdeacons. She would, as she declared to her husband,
make her wail heard in the market-place if she did not
get redress and justice. It might be very well for an
unmarried young curate to be shamefaced in such matters ;
it might be all right that a snug rector, really in want of
nothing, but still looking for better preferment, should
carry on his affairs decently under the rose. But Mrs.
Quiverful, with fourteen children, had given over being
shamefaced, and, in some things, had given over being
decent. If it were intended that she should be ill used in
the manner proposed by Mr. Slope, it should not be done
under the rose. All the world should know of it.

In her present mood, Mrs. Quiverful was not over
careful about her attire. She tied her bonnet under her
chin, threw her shawl over her shoulders, armed herself
with the old family cotton umbrella, and started for
Barchester. A journey to the palace was not quite so
easy a thing for Mrs. Quiverful as for our friend at Plumstead. Plumstead is nine miles from Barchester, and
Puddingdale is but four. But the archdeacon could
order round his brougham, and his high-trotting fast bay
gelding would take him into the city within the hour.
There was no brougham in the coach-house of Puddingdale
Vicarage, no bay horse in the stables. There was no
method of locomotion for its inhabitants but that which
nature has assigned to man.

Mrs. Quiverful was a broad heavy woman, not young,
nor given to walking. In her kitchen, and in the family
dormitories, she was active enough ; but her pace and
gait were not adapted for the road. A walk into Barchester
and back in the middle of an August day would be to
her a terrible task, if not altogether impracticable. There
was living in the parish, about half a mile from the
vicarage on the road to the city, a decent, kindly farmer,
well to do as regards this world, and so far mindful of the
next that he attended his parish church with decent

regularity. To him Mrs. Quiverful had before now appealed in some of her more pressing family troubles, and had not appealed in vain. At his door she now presented herself, and, having explained to his wife that most urgent business required her to go at once to Barchester, begged that Farmer Subsoil would take her thither in his tax-cart. The farmer did not reject her plan ; and, as soon as Prince could be got into his collar, they started on their journey.

Mrs. Quiverful did not mention the purpose of her business, nor did the farmer alloy his kindness by any unseemly questions. She merely begged to be put down at the bridge going into the city, and to be taken up again at the same place in the course of two hours. The farmer promised to be punctual to his appointment, and the lady, supported by her umbrella, took the short cut to the close, and in a few minutes was at the bishop's door.

Hitherto she had felt no dread with regard to the coming interview. She had felt nothing but an indignant longing to pour forth her claims, and declare her wrongs, if those claims were not fully admitted. But now the difficulty of her situation touched her a little. She had been at the palace once before, but then she went to give grateful thanks. Those who have thanks to return for favours received find easy admittance to the halls of the great. Such is not always the case with men, or even with women, who have favours to beg. Still less easy is access for those who demand the fulfilment of promises already made.

Mrs. Quiverful had not been slow to learn the ways of the world. She knew all this, and she knew also that her cotton umbrella and all but ragged shawl would not command respect in the eyes of the palatial servants. If she were too humble, she knew well that she would never succeed. To overcome by imperious overbearing with such a shawl as hers upon her shoulders, and such a bonnet on her head, would have required a personal bearing very superior to that with which nature had endowed her. Of this also Mrs. Quiverful was aware. She must make it known that she was the wife of a gentleman and a clergyman, and must yet condescend to conciliate.

The poor lady knew but one way to overcome these difficulties at the very threshold of her enterprise, and to

this she resorted. Low as were the domestic funds at
Puddingdale, she still retained possession of half-a-crown,
and this she sacrificed to the avarice of Mrs. Proudie's
metropolitan sesquipedalian serving-man. She was, she
said, Mrs. Quiverful of Puddingdale, the wife of the Rev.
Mr. Quiverful. She wished to see Mrs. Proudie. It was
indeed quite indispensable that she should see Mrs.
Proudie. James Fitzplush looked worse than dubious,
did not know whether his lady were out, or engaged, or in
her bed-room ; thought it most probable she was subject
to one of these or to some other cause that would make
her invisible ; but Mrs. Quiverful could sit down in the
waiting-room while inquiry was being made of Mrs.
Proudie's maid.

' Look here, my man,' said Mrs. Quiverful ; ' I must
see her ; ' and she put her card and half-a-crown—think
of it, my reader, think of it ; her last half-crown—into
the man's hand, and sat herself down on a chair in the
waiting-room.

Whether the bribe carried the day, or whether the
bishop's wife really chose to see the vicar's wife, it boots
not now to inquire. The man returned, and begging
Mrs. Quiverful to follow him, ushered her into the presence
of the mistress of the diocese.

Mrs. Quiverful at once saw that her patroness was in
a smiling humour. Triumph sat throned upon her brow,
and all the joys of dominion hovered about her curls.
Her lord had that morning contested with her a great
point. He had received an invitation to spend a couple
of days with the archbishop. His soul longed for the
gratification. Not a word, however, in his grace's note
alluded to the fact of his being a married man ; and, if
he went at all, he must go alone. This necessity would
have presented no insurmountable bar to the visit, or
have militated much against the pleasure, had he been
able to go without any reference to Mrs. Proudie. But
this he could not do. He could not order his portmanteau
to be packed, and start with his own man, merely telling
the lady of his heart that he would probably be back on
Saturday. There are men—may we not rather say
monsters ?—who do such things ; and there are wives—
may we not rather say slaves ?—who put up with such

usage. But Doctor and Mrs. Proudie were not among the number.

The bishop, with some beating about the bush, made the lady understand that he very much wished to go. The lady, without any beating about the bush, made the bishop understand that she wouldn't hear of it. It would be useless here to repeat the arguments that were used on each side, and needless to record the result. Those who are married will understand very well how the battle was lost and won; and those who are single will never understand it till they learn the lesson which experience alone can give. When Mrs. Quiverful was shown into Mrs. Proudie's room, that lady had only returned a few minutes from her lord. But before she left him she had seen the answer to the archbishop's note written and sealed. No wonder that her face was wreathed with smiles as she received Mrs. Quiverful.

She instantly spoke of the subject which was so near the heart of her visitor. ' Well, Mrs. Quiverful,' said she, ' is it decided yet when you are to move into Barchester ? '

' That woman,' as she had an hour or two since been called, became instantly re-endowed with all the graces that can adorn a bishop's wife. Mrs. Quiverful immediately saw that her business was to be piteous, and that nothing was to be gained by indignation; nothing, indeed, unless she could be indignant in company with her patroness.

' Oh, Mrs. Proudie,' she began, ' I fear we are not to move to Barchester at all.'

' Why not ? ' said that lady sharply, dropping at a moment's notice her smiles and condescension, and turning with her sharp quick way to business which she saw at a glance was important.

And then Mrs. Quiverful told her tale. As she progressed in the history of her wrongs she perceived that the heavier she leant upon Mr. Slope the blacker became Mrs. Proudie's brow, but that such blackness was not injurious to her own cause. When Mr. Slope was at Puddingdale vicarage that morning she had regarded him as the creature of the lady-bishop; now she perceived that they were enemies. She admitted her mistake to herself without any pain or humiliation. She had but one feeling, and that was

confined to her family. She cared little how she twisted
and turned among these new comers at the bishop's
palace so long as she could twist her husband into the
warden's house. She cared not which was her friend or
which was her enemy, if only she could get this preferment
which she so sorely wanted.

She told her tale, and Mrs. Proudie listened to it almost
in silence. She told how Mr. Slope had cozened her
husband into resigning his claim, and had declared that
it was the bishop's will that none but Mr. Harding should
be warden. Mrs. Proudie's brow became blacker and
blacker. At last she started from her chair, and begging
Mrs. Quiverful to sit and wait for her return, marched out
of the room.

'Oh, Mrs. Proudie, it's for fourteen children—for
fourteen children.' Such was the burden that fell on her
ear as she closed the door behind her.

CHAPTER XXVI

MRS. PROUDIE WRESTLES AND GETS A FALL

IT was hardly an hour since Mrs. Proudie had left her
husband's apartment victorious, and yet so indomitable
was her courage that she now returned thither panting
for another combat. She was greatly angry with what
she thought was his duplicity. He had so clearly given
her a promise on this matter of the hospital. He had been
already so absolutely vanquished on that point. Mrs.
Proudie began to feel that if every affair was to be thus
discussed and battled about twice and even thrice, the
work of the diocese would be too much even for her.

Without knocking at the door she walked quickly into
her husband's room, and found him seated at his office
table, with Mr. Slope opposite to him. Between his
fingers was the very note which he had written to the
archbishop in her presence——and it was open! Yes,
he had absolutely violated the seal which had been made
sacred by her approval. They were sitting in deep conclave, and it was too clear that the purport of the archbishop's invitation had been absolutely canvassed again,

after it had been already debated and decided on in obedience to her behests ! Mr. Slope rose from his chair, and bowed slightly. The two opposing spirits looked each other fully in the face, and they knew that they were looking each at an enemy.

'What is this, bishop, about Mr. Quiverful ? ' said she, coming to the end of the table and standing there.

Mr. Slope did not allow the bishop to answer, but replied himself. ' I have been out to Puddingdale this morning, ma'am, and have seen Mr. Quiverful. Mr. Quiverful has abandoned his claim to the hospital, because he is now aware that Mr. Harding is desirous to fill his old place. Under these circumstances I have strongly advised his lordship to nominate Mr. Harding.'

' Mr. Quiverful has not abandoned anything,' said the lady, with a very imperious voice. ' His lordship's word has been pledged to him, and it must be respected.'.

The bishop still remained silent. He was anxiously desirous of making his old enemy bite the dust beneath his feet. His new ally had told him that nothing was more easy for him than to do so. The ally was there now at his elbow to help him, and yet his courage failed him. It is so hard to conquer when the prestige of former victories is all against one. It is so hard for the cock who has once been beaten out of his yard to resume his courage and again take a proud place upon a dunghill.

' Perhaps I ought not to interfere,' said Mr. Slope, ' but yet——— '

' Certainly you ought not,' said the infuriated dame.

' But yet,' continued Mr. Slope, not regarding the interruption, ' I have thought it my imperative duty to recommend the bishop not to slight Mr. Harding's claims.'

' Mr. Harding should have known his own mind,' said the lady.

' If Mr. Harding be not replaced at the hospital, his lordship will have to encounter much ill will, not only in the diocese, but in the world at large. Besides, taking a higher ground, his lordship, as I understood, feels it to be his duty to gratify, in this matter, so very worthy a man and so good a clergyman as Mr. Harding.'

' And what is to become of the Sabbath-day school, and of the Sunday services in the hospital ? ' said Mrs. Proudie,

with something very nearly approaching to a sneer on
her face.

'I understand that Mr. Harding makes no objection
to the Sabbath-day school,' said Mr. Slope. 'And as to
the hospital services, that matter will be best discussed
after his appointment. If he has any permanent objection,
then, I fear, the matter must rest.'

'You have a very easy conscience in such matters,
Mr. Slope,' said she.

'I should not have an easy conscience,' he rejoined,
' but a conscience very far from being easy, if anything
said or done by me should lead the bishop to act un-
advisedly in this matter. It is clear that in the interview
I had with Mr. Harding, I misunderstood him——'

'And it is equally clear that you have misunderstood
Mr. Quiverful,' said she, now at the top of her wrath.
'What business have you at all with these interviews?
Who desired you to go to Mr. Quiverful this morning?
Who commissioned you to manage this affair? Will you
answer me, sir?—who sent you to Mr. Quiverful this
morning?'

There was a dead pause in the room. Mr. Slope had
risen from his chair, and was standing with his hand on
the back of it, looking at first very solemn and now very
black. Mrs. Proudie was standing as she had at first
placed herself, at the end of the table, and as she interrogated her foe she struck her hand upon it with almost
more than feminine vigour. The bishop was sitting in
his easy chair twiddling his thumbs, turning his eyes now
to his wife, and now to his chaplain, as each took up the
cudgels. How comfortable it would be if they could
fight it out between them without the necessity of any
interference on his part; fight it out so that one should
kill the other utterly, as far as diocesan life was concerned,
so that he, the bishop, might know clearly by whom it
behoved him to be led. There would be the comfort of
quiet in either case; but if the bishop had a wish as to
which might prove the victor, that wish was certainly
not antagonistic to Mr. Slope.

'Better the d—— you know than the d—— you don't
know,' is an old saying, and perhaps a true one; but the
bishop had not yet realised the truth of it.

' Will you answer me, sir ? ' she repeated. ' Who instructed you to call on Mr. Quiverful this morning ? ' There was another pause. ' Do you intend to answer me, sir ? '

' I think, Mrs. Proudie, that under all the circumstances it will be better for me not to answer such a question,' said Mr. Slope. Mr. Slope had many tones in his voice, all duly under his command ; among them was a sanctified low tone, and a sanctified loud tone ; and he now used the former.

' Did any one send you, sir ? '

' Mrs. Proudie,' said Mr. Slope, ' I am quite aware how much I owe to your kindness. I am aware also what is due by courtesy from a gentleman to a lady. But there are higher considerations than either of those, and I hope I shall be forgiven if I now allow myself to be actuated solely by them. My duty in this matter is to his lordship, and I can admit of no questioning but from him. He has approved of what I have done, and you must excuse me if I say, that having that approval and my own, I want none other.'

What horrid words were these which greeted the ear of Mrs. Proudie ? The matter was indeed too clear. There was premeditated mutiny in the camp. Not only had ill-conditioned minds become insubordinate by the fruition of a little power, but sedition had been overtly taught and preached. The bishop had not yet been twelve months in his chair, and rebellion had already reared her hideous head within the palace. Anarchy and misrule would quickly follow, unless she took immediate and strong measures to put down the conspiracy which she had detected.

' Mr. Slope,' she said, with slow and dignified voice, differing much from that which she had hitherto used, ' Mr. Slope, I will trouble you, if you please, to leave the apartment. I wish to speak to my lord alone.'

Mr. Slope also felt that everything depended on the present interview. Should the bishop now be repetticoated, his thraldom would be complete and for ever. The present moment was peculiarly propitious for rebellion. The bishop had clearly committed himself by breaking the seal of the answer to the archbishop ; he had therefore

fear to influence him. Mr. Slope had told him that no
consideration ought to induce him to refuse the archbishop's invitation ; he had therefore hope to influence
him. He had accepted Mr. Quiverful's resignation, and
therefore dreaded having to renew that matter with his
wife. He had been screwed up to the pitch of asserting
a will of his own, and might possibly be carried on till
by an absolute success he should have been taught how
possible it was to succeed. Now was the moment for
victory or rout. It was now that Mr. Slope must make
himself master of the diocese, or else resign his place and
begin his search for fortune again. He saw all this plainly.
After what had taken place any compromise between
him and the lady was impossible. Let him once leave the
room at her bidding, and leave the bishop in her hands, and
he might at once pack up his portmanteau and bid adieu
to episcopal honours, Mrs. Bold, and the Signora Neroni.

And yet it was not so easy to keep his ground when he
was bidden by a lady to go ; or to continue to make a
third in a party between a husband and wife when the
wife expressed a wish for a *tête-à-tête* with her husband.

' Mr. Slope,' she repeated, ' I wish to be alone with
my lord.'

' His lordship has summoned me on most important
diocesan business,' said Mr. Slope, glancing with uneasy
eye at Dr. Proudie. He felt that he must trust something
to the bishop, and yet that trust was so woefully ill-placed.
' My leaving him at the present moment is, I fear, impossible.'

' Do you bandy words with me, you ungrateful man ? '
said she. ' My lord, will you do me the favour to beg
Mr. Slope to leave the room ? '

My lord scratched his head, but for the moment said
nothing. This was as much as Mr. Slope expected from
him, and was on the whole, for him, an active exercise
of marital rights.

' My lord,' said the lady, ' is Mr. Slope to leave this
room, or am I ? '

Here Mrs. Proudie made a false step. She should not
have alluded to the possibility of retreat on her part.
She should not have expressed the idea that her order
for Mr. Slope's expulsion could be treated otherwise than

by immediate obedience. In answer to such a question
the bishop naturally said in his own mind, that as it was
necessary that one should leave the room, perhaps it
might be as well that Mrs. Proudie did so. He did say so
in his own mind, but externally he again scratched his
head and again twiddled his thumbs.

Mrs. Proudie was boiling over with wrath. Alas, alas!
could she but have kept her temper as her enemy did,
she would have conquered as she had ever conquered.
But divine anger got the better of her, as it has done of
other heroines, and she fell.

'My lord,' said she, ' am I to be vouchsafed an answer
or am I not ? '

At last he broke his deep silence and proclaimed himself
a Slopeite. ' Why, my dear,' said he, ' Mr. Slope and
I are very busy.'

That was all. There was nothing more necessary. He
had gone to the battle-field, stood the dust and heat of
the day, encountered the fury of the foe, and won the
victory. How easy is success to those who will only be
true to themselves !

Mr. Slope saw at once the full amount of his gain, and
turned on the vanquished lady a look of triumph which
she never forgot and never forgave. Here he was wrong.
He should have looked humbly at her, and with meek
entreating eye have deprecated her anger. He should
have said by his glance that he asked pardon for his
success, and that he hoped forgiveness for the stand which
he had been forced to make in the cause of duty. So
might he perchance have somewhat mollified that imperious bosom, and prepared the way for future terms.
But Mr. Slope meant to rule without terms. Ah, forgetful,
inexperienced man ! Can you cause that little trembling
victim to be divorced from the woman that possesses
him ? Can you provide that they shall be separated at
bed and board ? Is he not flesh of her flesh and bone of
her bone, and must he not so continue ? It is very well
now for you to stand your ground, and triumph as she is
driven ignominiously from the room ; but can you be
present when those curtains are drawn, when that awful
helmet of proof has been tied beneath the chin, when the
small remnants of the bishop's prowess shall be cowed

by the tassel above his head ? Can you then intrude
yourself when the wife wishes ' to speak to my lord alone ' ?

But for the moment Mr. Slope's triumph was complete ;
for Mrs. Proudie without further parley left the room,
and did not forget to shut the door after her. Then
followed a close conference between the new allies, in
which was said much which it astonished Mr. Slope to
say and the bishop to hear. And yet the one said it and
the other heard it without ill will. There was no mincing
of matters now. The chaplain plainly told the bishop
that the world gave him credit for being under the governance of his wife ; that his credit and character in the
diocese were suffering ; that he would surely get himself
into hot water if he allowed Mrs. Proudie to interfere in
matters which were not suitable for a woman's powers ;
and in fact that he would become contemptible if he did
not throw off the yoke under which he groaned. The
bishop at first hummed and hawed, and affected to deny
the truth of what was said. But his denial was not stout
and quickly broke down. He soon admitted by silence
his state of vassalage, and pledged himself, with Mr. Slope's
assistance, to change his courses. Mr. Slope also did not
make out a bad case for himself. He explained how it
grieved him to run counter to a lady who had always been
his patroness, who had befriended him in so many ways,
who had, in fact, recommended him to the bishop's
notice ; but, as he stated, his duty was now imperative ;
he held a situation of peculiar confidence, and was immediately and especially attached to the bishop's person.
In such a situation his conscience required that he should
regard solely the bishop's interests, and therefore he had
ventured to speak out.

The bishop took this for what it was worth, and Mr.
Slope only intended that he should do so. It gilded the
pill which Mr. Slope had to administer, and which the
bishop thought would be less bitter than that other pill
which he had so long been taking.

' My lord,' had his immediate reward, like a good child.
He was instructed to write and at once did write another
note to the archbishop accepting his grace's invitation.
This note Mr. Slope, more prudent than the lady, himself
took away and posted with his own hands. Thus he made

sure that this act of self-jurisdiction should be as nearly
as possible a *fait accompli*. He begged, and coaxed, and
threatened the bishop with a view of making him also
write at once to Mr. Harding; but the bishop, though
temporarily emancipated from his wife, was not yet
enthralled to Mr. Slope. He said, and probably said truly,
that such an offer must be made in some official form;
that he was not yet prepared to sign the form; and that
he should prefer seeing Mr. Harding before he did so.
Mr. Slope might, however, beg Mr. Harding to call upon
him. Not disappointed with his achievement Mr. Slope
went his way. He first posted the precious note which
he had in his pocket, and then pursued other enterprises
in which we must follow him in other chapters.

Mrs. Proudie, having received such satisfaction as was
to be derived from slamming her husband's door, did not
at once betake herself to Mrs. Quiverful. Indeed for the
first few moments after her repulse she felt that she could
not again see that lady. She would have to own that she
had been beaten, to confess that the diadem had passed
from her brow, and the sceptre from her hand! No, she
would send a message to her with the promise of a letter
on the next day or the day after. Thus resolving, she
betook herself to her bed-room; but here she again
changed her mind. The air of that sacred enclosure
somewhat restored her courage, and gave her more heart.
As Achilles warmed at the sight of his armour, as Don
Quixote's heart grew strong when he grasped his lance,
so did Mrs. Proudie look forward to fresh laurels, as her
eye fell on her husband's pillow. She would not despair.
Having so resolved, she descended with dignified mien
and refreshed countenance to Mrs. Quiverful.

This scene in the bishop's study took longer m the
acting than in the telling. We have not, perhaps, had the
whole of the conversation. At any rate Mrs. Quiverful
was beginning to be very impatient, and was thinking
that farmer Subsoil would be tired of waiting for her,
when Mrs. Proudie returned. Oh! who can tell the
palpitations of that maternal heart, as the suppliant
looked into the face of the great lady to see written there
either a promise of house, income, comfort and future
competence, or else the doom of continued and ever

increasing poverty. Poor mother ! poor wife ! there was
little there to comfort you !

'Mrs. Quiverful,' thus spoke the lady with considerable
austerity, and without sitting down herself, 'I find that
your husband has behaved in this matter in a very weak
and foolish manner.'

Mrs. Quiverful immediately rose upon her feet, thinking
it disrespectful to remain sitting while the wife of the
bishop stood. But she was desired to sit down again,
and made to do so, so that Mrs. Proudie might stand
and preach over her. It is generally considered an offensive
thing for a gentleman to keep his seat while another is
kept standing before him, and we presume the same law
holds with regard to ladies. It often is so felt ; but we
are inclined to say that it never produces half the discomfort or half the feeling of implied inferiority that is
shown by a great man who desires his visitor to be seated
while he himself speaks from his legs. Such a solecism
in good breeding, when construed into English, means
this : ' The accepted rules of courtesy in the world require
that I should offer you a seat ; if I did not do so, you
would bring a charge against me in the world of being
arrogant and ill-mannered ; I will obey the world ; but,
nevertheless, I will not put myself on an equality with
you. You may sit down, but I won't sit with you. Sit,
therefore, at my bidding, and I'll stand and talk at you ! '

This was just what Mrs. Proudie meant to say ; and
Mrs. Quiverful, though she was too anxious and too
flurried thus to translate the full meaning of the manœuvre,
did not fail to feel its effect. She was cowed and uncomfortable, and a second time essayed to rise from her chair.

'Pray be seated, Mrs. Quiverful, pray keep your seat.
Your husband, I say, has been most weak and most
foolish. It is impossible, Mrs. Quiverful, to help people
who will not help themselves. I much fear that I can
now do nothing for you in this matter.'

'Oh ! Mrs. Proudie—don't say so,' said the poor woman
again jumping up.

'*Pray* be seated Mrs. Quiverful. I much fear that I
can do nothing further for you in this matter. Your
husband has, in a most unaccountable manner, taken upon
himself to resign that which I was empowered to offer

him. As a matter of course, the bishop expects that his clergy shall know their own minds. What he may ulti-mately do—what we may finally decide on doing—I cannot now say. Knowing the extent of your family—'

' Fourteen children, Mrs. Proudie, fourteen of them ! and barely bread,—barely, bread ! It's hard for the children of a clergyman, it's hard for one who has always done his duty respectably ! ' Not a word fell from her about herself ; but the tears came streaming down her big coarse cheeks, on which the dust of the August road had left its traces.

Mrs. Proudie has not been portrayed in these pages as an agreeable or an amiable lady. There has been no intention to impress the reader much in her favour. It is ordained that all novels should have a male and a female angel, and a male and a female devil. If it be considered that this rule is obeyed in these pages, the latter character must be supposed to have fallen to the lot of Mrs. Proudie. But she was not all devil. There was a heart inside that stiff-ribbed bodice, though not, perhaps, of large dimen-sions, and certainly not easily accessible. Mrs. Quiverful, however, did gain access, and Mrs. Proudie proved herself a woman. Whether it was the fourteen children with their probable bare bread and their possible bare backs, or the respectability of the father's work, or the mingled dust and tears on the mother's face, we will not pretend to say. But Mrs. Proudie was touched.

She did not show it as other women might have done. She did not give Mrs. Quiverful eau-de-Cologne, or order her a glass of wine. She did not take her to her toilet table, and offer her the use of brushes and combs, towels and water. She did not say soft little speeches and coax her kindly back to equanimity. Mrs. Quiverful, despite her rough appearance, would have been as amenable to such little tender cares as any lady in the land. But none such were forthcoming. Instead of this, Mrs. Proudie slapped one hand upon the other, and declared—not with an oath ; for as a lady and a Sabbatarian and a she-bishop, she could not swear,—but with an adjuration, that ' she wouldn't have it done.'

The meaning of this was that she wouldn't have Mr. Quiverful's promised appointment cozened away by the

treachery of Mr. Slope and the weakness of her husband.
This meaning she very soon explained to Mrs. Quiverful.

' Why was your husband such a fool,' said she, now
dismounted from her high horse and sitting confidentially
down close to her visitor, ' as to take the bait which that
man threw to him ? If he had not been so utterly foolish,
nothing could have prevented your going to the hospital.'

Poor Mrs. Quiverful was ready enough with her own
tongue in accusing her husband to his face of being soft,
and perhaps did not always speak of him to her children
quite so respectfully as she might have done. But she
did not at all like to hear him abused by others, and began
to vindicate him, and to explain that of course he had
taken Mr. Slope to be an emissary from Mrs. Proudie
herself ; that Mr. Slope was thought to be peculiarly her
friend ; and that, therefore, Mr. Quiverful would have
been failing in respect to her had he assumed to doubt
what Mr. Slope had said.

Thus mollified Mrs. Proudie again declared that ' she
would not have it done,' and at last sent Mrs. Quiverful
home with an assurance that, to the furthest stretch of
her power and influence in the palace, the appointment
of Mr. Quiverful should be insisted on. As she repeated
the word ' insisted,' she thought of the bishop in his
night-cap, and with compressed lips slightly shook her
head. Oh ! my aspiring pastors, divines to whose ears
nolo episcopari are the sweetest of words, which of you
would be a bishop on such terms as these ?

Mrs. Quiverful got home in the farmer's cart, not indeed
with a light heart, but satisfied that she had done right
in making her visit.

CHAPTER XXVII

A LOVE SCENE

Mr. Slope, as we have said, left the palace with a
feeling of considerable triumph. Not that he thought that
his difficulties were all over ; he did not so deceive himself ;
but he felt that he had played his first move well, as well
as the pieces on the board would allow ; and that he had
nothing with which to reproach himself. He first of all

posted the letter to the archbishop, and having made that
sure he proceeded to push the advantage which he had
gained. Had Mrs. Bold been at home, he would have
called on her; but he knew that she was at Plumstead,
so he wrote the following note. It was the beginning of
what, he trusted, might be a long and tender series of
epistles.

'My dear Mrs. Bold,—You will understand perfectly
that I cannot at present correspond with your father.
I heartily wish that I could, and hope the day may be
not long distant when mists shall have cleared away, and
we may know each other. But I cannot preclude myself
from the pleasure of sending you these few lines to say
that Mr. Q. has to-day, in my presence, resigned any
title that he ever had to the wardenship of the hospital,
and that the bishop has assured me that it is his intention
to offer it to your esteemed father.

'Will you, with my respectful compliments, ask him,
who I believe is now a fellow-visitor with you, to call on
the bishop either on Wednesday or Thursday, between
ten and one. *This is by the bishop's desire.* If you will
so far oblige me as to let me have a line naming either
day, and the hour which will suit Mr. Harding, I will
take care that the servants shall have orders to show him
in without delay. Perhaps I should say no more,—but
still I wish you could make your father understand that
no subject will be mooted between his lordship and him,
which will refer at all to the method in which he may
choose to perform his duty. I for one, am persuaded that
no clergyman could perform it more satisfactorily than he
did, or than he will do again.

'On a former occasion I was indiscreet and much too
impatient, considering your father's age and my own.
I hope he will not now refuse my apology. I still hope
also that with your aid and sweet pious labours, we may
live to attach such a Sabbath school to the old endowment,
as may, by God's grace and furtherance, be a blessing to
the poor of this city.

'You will see at once that this letter is confidential.
The subject, of course, makes it so. But, equally of
course, it is for your parent's eye as well as for your own,
should you think proper to show it to him.

'I hope my darling little friend Johnny is as strong as
ever,—dear little fellow. Does he still continue his rude
assaults on those beautiful long silken tresses ?

'I can assure you your friends miss you from Barchester
sorely; but it would be cruel to begrudge you your
sojourn among flowers and fields during this truly sultry
weather.

'Pray believe me, my dear Mrs. Bold,

'Yours most sincerely,

'OBADIAH SLOPE.

'Barchester, Friday.'

Now this letter, taken as a whole, and with the consideration that Mr. Slope wished to assume a great degree
of intimacy with Eleanor, would not have been bad, but
for the allusion to the tresses. Gentlemen do not write to
ladies about their tresses, unless they are on very intimate
terms indeed. But Mr. Slope could not be expected to be
aware of this. He longed to put a little affection into his
epistle, and yet he thought it injudicious, as the letter
would, he knew, be shown to Mr. Harding. He would have
insisted that the letter should be strictly private and
seen by no eyes but Eleanor's own, had he not felt that
such an injunction would have been disobeyed. He
therefore restrained his passion, did not sign himself
'yours affectionately,' and contented himself instead
with the compliment to the tresses.

Having finished his letter, he took it to Mrs. Bold's
house, and learning there, from the servant, that things
were to be sent out to Plumstead that afternoon, left it,
with many injunctions, in her hands.

We will now follow Mr. Slope so as to complete the day
with him, and then return to his letter and its momentous
fate in the next chapter.

There is an old song which gives us some very good
advice about courting :—

It's gude to be off with the auld luve
Before ye be on wi' the new.

Of the wisdom of this maxim Mr. Slope was ignorant,
and accordingly, having written his letter to Mrs. Bold,
he proceeded to call upon the Signora Neroni. Indeed it

was hard to say which was the old love and which the new,
Mr. Slope having been smitten with both so nearly at the
same time. Perhaps he thought it not amiss to have two
strings to his bow. But two strings to Cupid's bow are
always dangerous to him on whose behalf they are to be
used. A man should remember that between two stools
he may fall to the ground.

But in sooth Mr. Slope was pursuing Mrs. Bold in
obedience to his better instincts, and the signora in
obedience to his worser. Had he won the widow and worn
her, no one could have blamed him. You, O reader, and
I, and Eleanor's other friends would have received the
story of such a winning with much disgust and disappointment; but we should have been angry with Eleanor,
not with Mr. Slope. Bishop, male and female, dean and
chapter and diocesan clergy in full congress, could have
found nothing to disapprove of in such an alliance. Convocation itself, that mysterious and mighty synod, could
in no wise have fallen foul of it. The possession of 1000*l.*
a year and a beautiful wife would not at all have hurt
the voice of the pulpit charmer, or lessened the grace and
piety of the exemplary clergyman.

But not of such a nature were likely to be his dealings
with the Signora Neroni. In the first place he knew that
her husband was living, and therefore he could not woo
her honestly. Then again she had nothing to recommend
her to his honest wooing had such been possible. She was
not only portionless, but also from misfortune unfitted to be
chosen as the wife of any man who wanted a useful mate.
Mr. Slope was aware that she was a helpless hopeless
cripple.

But Mr. Slope could not help himself. He knew that
he was wrong in devoting his time to the back drawing-
room in Dr. Stanhope's house. He knew that what took
place there would if divulged utterly ruin him with Mrs.
Bold. He knew that scandal would soon come upon his
heels and spread abroad among the black coats of Barchester some tidings, exaggerated tidings, of the sighs
which he poured into the lady's ears. He knew that he
was acting against the recognised principles of his life,
against those laws of conduct by which he hoped to achieve
much higher success. But as we have said, he could not

help himself. Passion, for the first time in his life, passion was too strong for him.

As for the signora, no such plea can be put forward for her, for in truth she cared no more for Mr. Slope than she did for twenty others who had been at her feet before him. She willingly, nay greedily, accepted his homage. He was the finest fly that Barchester had hitherto afforded to her web; and the signora was a powerful spider that made wondrous webs, and could in no way live without catching flies. Her taste in this respect was abominable, for she had no use for the victims when caught. She could not eat them matrimonially, as young lady-flies do whose webs are most frequently of their mothers' weaving. Nor could she devour them by any escapade of a less legitimate description. Her unfortunate affliction precluded her from all hope of levanting with a lover. It would be impossible to run away with a lady who required three servants to move her from a sofa.

The signora was subdued by no passion. Her time for love was gone. She had lived out her heart, such heart as she had ever had, in her early years, at an age when Mr. Slope was thinking of the second book of Euclid and his unpaid bill at the buttery hatch. In age the lady was younger than the gentleman; but in feelings, in knowledge of the affairs of love, in intrigue, he was immeasurably her junior. It was necessary to her to have some man at her feet. It was the one customary excitement of her life. She delighted in the exercise of power which this gave her; it was now nearly the only food for her ambition; she would boast to her sister that she could make a fool of any man, and the sister, as little imbued with feminine delicacy as herself, good naturedly thought it but fair that such amusement should be afforded to a poor invalid who was debarred from the ordinary pleasures of life.

Mr. Slope was madly in love, but hardly knew it. The signora spitted him, as a boy does a cockchafer on a cork, that she might enjoy the energetic agony of his gyrations. And she knew very well what she was doing.

Mr. Slope having added to his person all such adornments as are possible to a clergyman making a morning visit, such as a clean neck tie, clean handkerchief, new gloves, and a *soupçon* of not unnecessary scent called about three o'clock at the doctor's door. At about this hour the signora was almost always alone in the back drawing-room. The mother had not come down. The doctor was out or in his own room. Bertie was out, and Charlotte at any rate left the room if any one called whose object was specially with her sister. Such was her idea of being charitable and sisterly.

Mr. Slope, as was his custom, asked for Mr. Stanhope, and was told, as was the servant's custom, that the signora was in the drawing-room. Upstairs he accordingly went. He found her, as he always did, lying on her sofa with a French volume before her, and a beautiful little inlaid writing case open on her table. At the moment of his entrance she was in the act of writing.

' Ah my friend,' said she, putting out her left hand to him across her desk, ' I did not expect you to-day and was this very instant writing to you——'

Mr. Slope, taking the soft fair delicate hand in his, and very soft and fair and delicate it was, bowed over it his huge red head and kissed it. It was a sight to see, a deed to record if the author could fitly do it, a picture to put on canvass. Mr. Slope was big, awkward, cumbrous, and having his heart in his pursuit was ill at ease. The lady was fair, as we have said, and delicate ; every thing about her was fine and refined ; her hand in his looked like a rose lying among carrots, and when he kissed it he looked as a cow might do on finding such a flower among her food. She was graceful as a couchant goddess, and, moreover, as self-possessed as Venus must have been when courting Adonis.

Oh, that such grace and such beauty should have condescended to waste itself on such a pursuit !

' I was in the act of writing to you,' said she, ' but now my scrawl may go into the basket ; ' and she raised the sheet of gilded note paper from off her desk as though to tear it.

' Indeed it shall not,' said he, laying the embargo of half a stone weight of human flesh and blood upon the devoted paper. ' Nothing that you write for my eyes, signora, shall be so desecrated,' and he took up the letter, put that also among the carrots and fed on it, and then proceeded to read it.

' Gracious me ! Mr. Slope,' said she, ' I hope you don't mean to say that you keep all the trash I write to you. Half my time I don't know what I write, and when I do, I know it is only fit for the back of the fire. I hope you have not that ugly trick of keeping letters.'

' At any rate, I don't throw them into a waste-paper basket. If destruction is their doomed lot, they perish worthily, and are burnt on a pyre, as Dido was of old.'

' With a steel pen stuck through them, of course,' said she, ' to make the simile more complete. Of all the ladies of my acquaintance I think Lady Dido was the most absurd. Why did she not do as Cleopatra did ? Why did she not take out her ships and insist on going with him ? She could not bear to lose the land she had got by a swindle ; and then she could not bear the loss of her lover. So she fell between two stools. Mr. Slope, whatever you do, never mingle love and business.'

Mr. Slope blushed up to his eyes, and over his mottled forehead to the very roots of his hair. He felt sure that the signora knew all about his intentions with reference to Mrs. Bold. His conscience told him that he was detected. His doom was to be spoken ; he was to be punished for his duplicity, and rejected by the beautiful creature before him. Poor man. He little dreamt that had all his intentions with reference to Mrs. Bold been known to the signora, it would only have added zest to that lady's amusement. It was all very well to have Mr. Slope at her feet, to show her power by making an utter fool of a clergyman, to gratify her own infidelity by thus proving the little strength which religion had in controlling the passions even of a religious man ; but it would be an increased gratification if she could be made to understand that she was at the same time alluring her victim away from another, whose love if secured would be in every way beneficent and salutary.

The signora had indeed discovered with the keen instinct of such a woman, that Mr. Slope was bent on matrimony with Mrs. Bold, but in alluding to Dido she had not thought of it. She instantly perceived, however, from her lover's blushes, what was on his mind, and was not slow in taking advantage of it.

She looked him full in the face, not angrily, nor yet

in the face, Mr. Slope. Am I to understand that you say you love me ? '

Mr. Slope never had said so. If he had come there with any formed plan at all, his intention was to make love to the lady without uttering any such declaration. It was, however, quite impossible that he should now deny his love. He had, therefore, nothing for it, but to go down on his knees distractedly against the sofa, and swear that he did love her with a love passing the love of man.

The signora received the assurance with very little palpitation or appearance of surprise. 'And now answer me another question,' said she; 'when are you to be married to my dear friend Eleanor Bold ? '

Poor Mr. Slope went round and round in mortal agony. In such a condition as his it was really very hard for him to know what answer to give. And yet no answer would be his surest condemnation. He might as well at once plead guilty to the charge brought against him.

'And why do you accuse me of such dissimulation ? ' said he.

'Dissimulation! I said nothing of dissimulation. I made no charge against you, and make none. Pray don't defend yourself to me. You swear that you are devoted to my beauty, and yet you are on the eve of matrimony with another. I feel this to be rather a compliment. It is to Mrs. Bold that you must defend yourself. That you may find difficult; unless, indeed, you can keep her in the dark. You clergymen are cleverer than other men.'

'Signora, I have told you that I loved you, and now you rail at me ? '

'Rail at you. God bless the man; what would he have ? Come, answer me this at your leisure,—not without thinking now, but leisurely and with consideration,— Are you not going to be married to Mrs. Bold ? '

'I am not,' said he. And as he said it, he almost hated, with an exquisite hatred, the woman whom he could not help loving with an exquisite love.

'But surely you are a worshipper of hers ? '

'I am not,' said Mr. Slope, to whom the word worshipper was peculiarly distasteful. The signora had conceived that it would be so.

'I wonder at that,' said she. 'Do you not admire her

with a smile, but with an intense and overpowering gaze; and then holding up her forefinger, and slightly shaking her head she said :—

'Whatever you do, my friend, do not mingle love and business. Either stick to your treasure and your city of wealth, or else follow your love like a true man. But never attempt both. If you do, you'll have to die with a broken heart as did poor Dido. Which is it to be with you, Mr. Slope, love or money ? '

Mr. Slope was not so ready with a pathetic answer as he usually was with touching episodes in his extempore sermons. He felt that he ought to say something pretty, something also that should remove the impression on the mind of his lady love. But he was rather put about how to do it.

'Love,' said he, 'true overpowering love, must be the strongest passion a man can feel; it must control every other wish, and put aside every other pursuit. But with me love will never act in that way unless it be returned; ' and he threw upon the signora a look of tenderness which was intended to make up for all the deficiencies of his speech.

'Take my advice,' said she. 'Never mind love. After all, what is it ? The dream of a few weeks. That is all its joy. The disappointment of a life is its Nemesis. Who was ever successful in true love ? Success in love argues that the love is false. True love is always despondent or tragical. Juliet loved, Haidee loved, Dido loved, and what came of it ? Troilus loved and ceased to be a man.'

'Troilus loved and was fooled,' said the more manly chaplain. 'A man may love and yet not be a Troilus. All women are not Cressids.'

'No; all women are not Cressids. The falsehood is not always on the woman's side. Imogen was true, but how was she rewarded ? Her lord believed her to be the paramour of the first he who came near her in his absence. Desdemona was true and was smothered. Ophelia was true and went mad. There is no happiness in love, except at the end of an English novel. But in wealth, money, houses, lands, goods and chattels, in the good things of this world, yes, in them there is something tangible, something that can be retained and enjoyed.'

'Oh, no,' said Mr. Slope, feeling himself bound to enter some protest against so very unorthodox a doctrine, 'this world's wealth will make no one happy.'

'And what will make you happy—you—you?' said she, raising herself up, and speaking to him with energy across the table. 'From what source do you look for happiness? Do not say that you look for none? I shall not believe you. It is a search in which every human being spends an existence.'

'And the search is always in vain,' said Mr. Slope. 'We look for happiness on earth, while we ought to be content to hope for it in heaven.'

'Pshaw! you preach a doctrine which you know you don't believe. It is the way with you all. If you know that there is no earthly happiness, why do you long to be a bishop or a dean? Why do you want lands and income?'

'I have the natural ambition of a man,' said he.

'Of course you have, and the natural passions; and therefore I say that you don't believe the doctrine you preach. St. Paul was an enthusiast. He believed so that his ambition and passions did not war against his creed. So does the Eastern fanatic who passes half his life erect upon a pillar. As for me, I will believe in no belief that does not make itself manifest by outward signs. I will think no preaching sincere that is not recommended by the practice of the preacher.'

Mr. Slope was startled and horrified, but he felt that he could not answer. How could he stand up and preach the lessons of his Master, being there as he was, on the devil's business? He was a true believer, otherwise this would have been nothing to him. He had audacity for most things, but he had not audacity to make a plaything of the Lord's word. All this the signora understood, and felt much interest as she saw her cockchafer whirl round upon her pin.

'Your wit delights in such arguments,' said he, 'but your heart and your reason do not go along with them.'

'My heart!' said she; 'you quite mistake the principles of my composition if you imagine that there is such a thing about me.' After all, there was very little that was false in anything that the signora said. If Mr. Slope allowed himself to be deceived it was his own fault.

Nothing could have been more open than her declarati about herself.

The little writing table with her desk was still standi before her, a barrier, as it were, against the enemy. S was sitting as nearly upright as she ever did, and he ha brought a chair close to the sofa, so that there was onl the corner of the table between him and her. It s happened that as she spoke her hand lay upon the table and as Mr. Slope answered her he put his hand upon hers.

'No heart!' said he. 'That is a heavy charge which you bring against yourself, and one of which I cannot find you guilty——'

She withdrew her hand, not quickly and angrily, as though insulted by his touch, but gently and slowly.

'You are in no condition to give a verdict on the matter,' said she, 'as you have not tried me. No; don't say that you intend doing so, for you know you have no intention of the kind; nor indeed have I either. As for you, you will take your vows where they will result in something more substantial than the pursuit of such a ghostlike, ghastly love as mine——'

'Your love should be sufficient to satisfy the dream of a monarch,' said Mr. Slope, not quite clear as to the meaning of his words.

'Say an archbishop, Mr. Slope,' said she. Poor fellow! she was very cruel to him. He went round again upon his cork on this allusion to his profession. He tried, however, to smile, and gently accused her of joking on a matter, which was, he said, to him of such vital moment.

'Why—what gulls do you men make of us,' she replied. 'How you fool us to the top of our bent; and of all men you clergymen are the most fluent of your honeyed caressing words. Now look me in the face, Mr. Slope, boldly and openly.'

Mr. Slope did look at her with a languishing loving eye, and as he did so, he again put forth his hand to get hold of hers.

'I told you to look at me boldly, Mr. Slope; but confine your boldness to your eyes.'

'Oh, Madeline!' he sighed.

'Well, my name is Madeline,' said she; 'but none except my own family usually call me so. Now look me

To my eye she is the perfection of English beauty. And then she is rich too. I should have thought she was just the person to attract you. Come, Mr. Slope, let me give you advice on this matter. Marry the charming widow! she will be a good mother to your children, and an excellent mistress of a clergyman's household.'

' Oh, signora, how can you be so cruel ? '

' Cruel,' said she, changing the voice of banter which she had been using for one which was expressively earnest in its tone ; ' is that cruelty ? '

' How can I love another, while my heart is entirely your own ? '

' If that were cruelty, Mr. Slope, what might you say of me if I were to declare that I returned your passion ? What would you think if I bound you even by a lover's oath to do daily penance at this couch of mine ? What can I give in return for a man's love ? Ah, dear friend, you have not realised the conditions of my fate.'

Mr. Slope was not on his knees all this time. After his declaration of love he had risen from them as quickly as he thought consistent with the new position which he now filled, and as he stood was leaning on the back of his chair. This outburst of tenderness on the Signora's part quite overcame him, and made him feel for the moment that he could sacrifice everything to be assured of the love of the beautiful creature before him, maimed, lame, and already married as she was,

' And can I not sympathise with your lot ? ' said he, now seating himself on her sofa, and pushing away the table with his foot.

' Sympathy is so near to pity ! ' said she. ' If you pity me, cripple as I am, I shall spurn you from me.'

' Oh, Madeline, I will only love you,' and again he caught her hand and devoured it with kisses. Now she did not draw it from him, but sat there as he kissed it, looking at him with her great eyes, just as a great spider would look at a great fly that was quite securely caught.

' Suppose Signor Neroni were to come to Barchester,' said she, ' would you make his acquaintance ? '

' Signor Neroni ! ' said he.

' Would you introduce him to the bishop, and Mrs. Proudie, and the young ladies ? ' said she, again having

recourse to that horrid quizzing voice which Mr. Slope
so particularly hated.

'Why do you ask such a question ? ' said he.

'Because it is necessary that you should know that
there is a Signor Neroni. I think you had forgotten it.'

'If I thought that you retained for that wretch one
particle of the love of which he was never worthy, I would
die before I would distract you by telling you what I feel.
No ! were your husband the master of your heart, I might
perhaps love you ; but you should never know it.'

'My heart again ! how you talk. And you consider
then, that if a husband be not master of his wife's heart,
he has no right to her fealty ; if a wife ceases to love,
she may cease to be true. Is that your doctrine on this
matter, as a minister of the Church of England ? '

Mr. Slope tried hard within himself to cast off the
pollution with which he felt that he was defiling his soul.
He strove to tear himself away from the noxious siren
that had bewitched him. But he could not do it. He
could not be again heart free. He had looked for rapturous
joy in loving this lovely creature, and he already found
that he met with little but disappointment and self-rebuke.
He had come across the fruit of the Dead Sea, so sweet
and delicious to the eye, so bitter and nauseous to the
taste. He had put the apple to his mouth, and it had
turned to ashes between his teeth. Yet he could not tear
himself away. He knew, he could not but know, that
she jeered at him, ridiculed his love, and insulted the
weakness of his religion. But she half permitted his
adoration, and that half permission added such fuel to
his fire that all the fountain of his piety could not quench
it. He began to feel savage, irritated, and revengeful.
He meditated some severity of speech, some taunt that
should cut her, as her taunts cut him. He reflected as
he stood there for a moment, silent before her, that if he
desired to quell her proud spirit, he should do so by being
prouder even than herself ; that if he wished to have her
at his feet suppliant for his love it behoved him to conquer
her by indifference. All this passed through his mind.
As far as dead knowledge went, he knew, or thought he
knew, how a woman should be tamed. But when he
essayed to bring his tactics to bear, he failed like a child.

What chance has dead knowledge with experience in any of the transactions between man and man? What possible chance between man and woman? Mr. Slope loved furiously, insanely, and truly; but he had never played the game of love. The signora did not love at all, but she was up to every move of the board. It was Philidor pitted against a school-boy.

And so she continued to insult him, and he continued to bear it.

' Sacrifice the world for love!' said she, in answer to some renewed vapid declaration of his passion, ' how often has the same thing been said, and how invariably with the same falsehood!'

' Falsehood,' said he. ' Do you say that I am false to you? do you say that my love is not real?'

' False? of course it is false, false as the father of false-hood—if indeed falsehoods need a sire and are not self-begotten since the world began. You are ready to sacrifice the world for love? Come let us see what you will sacrifice. I care nothing for nuptial vows. The wretch, I think you were kind enough to call him so, whom I swore to love and obey, is so base that he can only be thought of with repulsive disgust. In the council chamber of my heart I have divorced him. To me that is as good as though aged lords had gloated for months over the details of his licentious life. I care nothing for what the world can say. Will you be as frank? Will you take me to your home as your wife? Will you call me Mrs. Slope before bishop, dean, and prebendaries?' The poor tortured wretch stood silent, not knowing what to say. ' What! you won't do that. Tell me, then, what part of the world is it that you will sacrifice for my charms?'

' Were you free to marry, I would take you to my house to-morrow and wish no higher privilege.'

' I am free;' said she, almost starting up in her energy. For though there was no truth in her pretended regard for her clerical admirer, there was a mixture of real feeling in the scorn and satire with which she spoke of love and marriage generally. ' I am free; free as the winds. Come; will you take me as I am? Have your wish sacrifice the world, and prove yourself a true man.'

Mr. Slope should have taken her at her word. She

would have drawn back, and he would have had the full advantage of the offer. But he did not. Instead of doing so, he stood wrapt in astonishment, passing his fingers through his lank red hair, and thinking as he stared upon her animated countenance that her wondrous beauty grew more and more wonderful as he gazed on it. 'Ha! ha! ha!' she laughed out loud. 'Come Mr. Slope; don't talk of sacrificing the world again. People beyond one-and-twenty should never dream of such a thing. You and I, if we have the dregs of any love left in us, if we have the remnants of a passion remaining in our hearts, should husband our resources better. We are not in our *première jeunesse*. The world is a very nice place. Your world, at any rate, is so. You have all manner of fat rectories to get, and possible bishoprics to enjoy. Come, confess; on second thoughts you would not sacrifice such things for the smiles of a lame lady?'

It was impossible for him to answer this. In order to be in any way dignified, he felt that he must be silent.

'Come,' said she—'don't boody with me: don't be angry because I speak out some home truths. Alas, the world, as I have found it, has taught me bitter truths. Come, tell me that I am forgiven. Are we not to be friends?' and she again put out her hand to him.

He sat himself down in the chair beside her, and took her proffered hand and leant over her.

'There,' said she, with her sweetest softest smile—a smile to withstand which a man should be cased in triple steel, 'there; seal your forgiveness on it,' and she raised it towards his face. He kissed it again and again, and stretched over her as though desirous of extending the charity of his pardon beyond the hand that was offered to him. She managed, however, to check his ardour. For one so easily allured as this poor chaplain, her hand was surely enough.

'Oh, Madeline!' said he, 'tell me that you love me—do you—do you love me?'

'Hush,' said she. 'There is my mother's step. Our *tête-à-tête* has been of monstrous length. Now you had better go. But we shall see you soon again, shall we not?'

Mr. Slope promised that he would call again on the following day.

' And, Mr. Slope,' she continued, ' pray answer my note. You have it in your hand, though I declare during these two hours you have not been gracious enough to read it. It is about the Sabbath school and the children. You know how anxious I am to have them here. I have been learning the catechism myself, on purpose. You must manage it for me next week. I will teach them, at any rate, to submit themselves to their spiritual pastors and masters.'

Mr. Slope said but little on the subject of Sabbath schools, but he made his adieu, and betook himself home with a sad heart, troubled mind, and uneasy conscience.

CHAPTER XXVIII

MRS. BOLD IS ENTERTAINED BY DR. AND MRS. GRANTLY AT PLUMSTEAD

IT will be remembered that Mr. Slope, when leaving his *billet doux* at the house of Mrs. Bold, had been informed that it would be sent out to her at Plumstead that afternoon. The archdeacon and Mr. Harding had in fact come into town together in the brougham, and it had been arranged that they should call for Eleanor's parcels as they left on their way home. Accordingly they did so call, and the maid, as she handed to the coachman a small basket and large bundle carefully and neatly packed, gave in at the carriage window Mr. Slope's epistle. The archdeacon, who was sitting next to the window, took it, and immediately recognised the hand-writing of his enemy.

' Who left this ? ' said he.

' Mr. Slope called with it himself, your reverence,' said the girl ; ' and was very anxious that missus should have it to-day.'

So the brougham drove off, and the letter was left in the archdeacon's hand. He looked at it as though he held a basket of adders. He could not have thought worse of the document had he read it and discovered it to be licentious and atheistical. He did, moreover, what so many wise people are accustomed to do in similar circumstances ; he immediately condemned the person to whom the letter was written, as though she were necessarily a *particeps criminis*.

Poor Mr. Harding, though by no means inclined to forward Mr. Slope's intimacy with his daughter, would have given anything to have kept the letter from his son-in-law. But that was now impossible. There it was in his hand; and he looked as thoroughly disgusted as though he were quite sure that it contained all the rhapsodies of a favoured lover.

' It's very hard on me,' said he, after awhile, ' that this should go on under my roof.'

Now here the archdeacon was certainly most unreasonable. Having invited his sister-in-law to his house, it was a natural consequence that she should receive her letters there. And if Mr. Slope chose to write to her, his letter would, as a matter of course, be sent after her. Moreover, the very fact of an invitation to one's house implies confidence on the part of the inviter. He had shown that he thought Mrs. Bold to be a fit person to stay with him by his asking her to do so, and it was most cruel to her that he should complain of her violating the sanctity of his roof-tree, when the laches committed were none of her committing.

Mr. Harding felt this; and felt also that when the archdeacon talked thus about his roof, what he said was most offensive to himself as Eleanor's father. If Eleanor did receive a letter from Mr. Slope, what was there in that to pollute the purity of Dr. Grantly's household? He was indignant that his daughter should be so judged and so spoken of; and he made up his mind that even as Mrs. Slope she must be dearer to him than any other creature on God's earth. He almost broke out, and said as much; but for the moment he restrained himself.

' Here,' said the archdeacon, handing the offensive missile to his father-in-law; ' I am not going to be the bearer of his love letters. You are her father, and may do as you think fit with it.'

By doing as he thought fit with it, the archdeacon certainly meant that Mr. Harding would be justified in opening and reading the letter, and taking any steps which might in consequence be necessary. To tell the truth, Dr. Grantly did feel rather a stronger curiosity than was justified by his outraged virtue, to see the contents of the letter. Of course he could not open it himself, but he

wished to make Mr. Harding understand that he, as
Eleanor's father, would be fully justified in doing so. The
idea of such a proceeding never occurred to Mr. Harding.
His authority over Eleanor ceased when she became the
wife of John Bold. He had not the slightest wish to pry
into her correspondence. He consequently put the letter
into his pocket, and only wished that he had been able to
do so without the archdeacon's knowledge. They both sat
silent during half the journey home, and then Dr. Grantly
said, ' Perhaps Susan had better give it to her. She can
explain to her sister, better than either you or I can do,
how deep is the disgrace of such an acquaintance.'

' I think you are very hard upon Eleanor,' replied Mr.
Harding. ' I will not allow that she has disgraced herself,
nor do I think it likely that she will do so. She has a right
to correspond with whom she pleases, and I shall not take
upon myself to blame her because she gets a letter from
Slope.'

' I suppose,' said Dr. Grantly, ' you don't wish her to
marry the man. I suppose you'll admit that she would
disgrace herself if she did do so.'

' I do not wish her to marry him,' said the perplexed
father ; ' I do not like him, and do not think he would
make a good husband. But if Eleanor chooses to do so, I
shall certainly not think that she disgraces herself.'

' Good heavens ! ' exclaimed Dr. Grantly, and threw
himself back into the corner of his brougham. Mr. Harding
said nothing more, but commenced playing a dirge, with
an imaginary fiddle bow upon an imaginary violoncello,
for which there did not appear to be quite room enough in
the carriage ; and he continued the tune, with sundry
variations, till he arrived at the rectory door.

The archdeacon had been meditating sad things in his
mind. Hitherto he had always looked on his father-in-law
as a true partisan, though he knew him to be a man devoid
of all the combative qualifications for that character. He
had felt no fear that Mr. Harding would go over to the
enemy, though he had never counted much on the ex-
warden's prowess in breaking the hostile ranks. Now,
however, it seemed that Eleanor, with her wiles, had
completely trepanned and bewildered her father, cheated
him out of his judgment, robbed him of the predilections

and tastes of his life, and caused him to be tolerant of a man whose arrogance and vulgarity would, a few years since, have been unendurable to him. That the whole thing was as good as arranged between Eleanor and Mr. Slope there was no longer any room to doubt. That Mr. Harding knew that such was the case, even this could hardly be doubted. It was too manifest that he at any rate suspected it, and was prepared to sanction it.

And to tell the truth, such was the case. Mr. Harding disliked Mr. Slope as much as it was in his nature to dislike any man. Had his daughter wished to do her worst to displease him by a second marriage, she could hardly have succeeded better than by marrying Mr. Slope. But, as he said to himself now very often, what right had he to condemn her if she did nothing that was really wrong ? If she liked Mr. Slope it was her affair. It was indeed miraculous to him that a woman with such a mind, so educated, so refined, so nice in her tastes, should like such a man. Then he asked himself whether it was possible that she did so ?

Ah, thou weak man ; most charitable, most Christian, but weakest of men ! Why couldst thou not have asked herself ? Was she not the daughter of thy loins, the child of thy heart, the best beloved to thee of all humanity ? Had she not proved to thee, by years of closest affection, her truth and goodness and filial obedience ? And yet, knowing and feeling all this, thou couldst endure to go groping in darkness, hearing her named in strains which wounded thy loving heart, and being unable to defend her as thou shouldst have done !

Mr. Harding had not believed, did not believe, that his daughter meant to marry this man ; but he feared to commit himself to such an opinion. If she did do it there would be then no means of retreat. The wishes of his heart were—First, that there should be no truth in the arch- deacon's surmises ; and in this wish he would have fain trusted entirely, had he dared so to do ; Secondly, that the match might be prevented, if unfortunately, it had been contemplated by Eleanor ; Thirdly, that should she be so infatuated as to marry this man, he might justify his con- duct, and declare that no cause existed for his separating himself from her.

He wanted to believe her incapable of such a marriage; he wanted to show that he so believed of her; but he wanted also to be able to say hereafter, that she had done nothing amiss, if she should unfortunately prove herself to be different from what he thought her to be.

Nothing but affection could justify such fickleness; but affection did justify it. There was but little of the Roman about Mr. Harding. He could not sacrifice his Lucretia even though she should be polluted by the accepted addresses of the clerical Tarquin at the palace. If Tarquin could be prevented, well and good; but if not, the father would still open his heart to his daughter, and accept her as she presented herself, Tarquin and all.

Dr. Grantly's mind was of a stronger calibre, and he was by no means deficient in heart. He loved with an honest genuine love his wife and children and friends. He loved his father-in-law; and was quite prepared to love Eleanor too, if she would be one of his party, if she would be on his side, if she would regard the Slopes and the Proudies as the enemies of mankind, and acknowledge and feel the comfortable merits of the Gwynnes and Arabins. He wished to be what he called ' safe ' with all those whom he had admitted to the penetralia of his house and heart. He could luxuriate in no society that was deficient in a certain feeling of faithful staunch high-churchism, which to him was tantamount to freemasonry. He was not strict in his lines of definition. He endured without impatience many different shades of Anglo-church conservatism; but with the Slopes and Proudies he could not go on all fours.

He was wanting in, moreover, or perhaps it would be more correct to say, he was not troubled by that womanly tenderness which was so peculiar to Mr. Harding. His feelings towards his friends were, that while they stuck to him he would stick to them; that he would work with them shoulder and shoulder; that he would be faithful to the faithful. He knew nothing of that beautiful love which can be true to a false friend.

And thus these two men, each miserable enough in his own way, returned to Plumstead.

It was getting late when they arrived there, and the ladies had already gone up to dress. Nothing more was said as the two parted in the hall. As Mr. Harding passed to his own room he knocked at Eleanor's door and handed in the letter. The archdeacon hurried to his own territory, there to unburden his heart to his faithful partner.

What colloquy took place between the marital chamber and the adjoining dressing-room shall not be detailed. The reader, now intimate with the persons concerned, can well imagine it. The whole tenor of it also might be read in Mrs. Grantly's brow as she came down to dinner.

Eleanor, when she received the letter from her father's hand, had no idea from whom it came. She had never seen Mr. Slope's hand-writing, or if so had forgotten it; and did not think of him as she twisted the letter as people do twist letters when they do not immediately recognise their correspondents either by the writing or the seal. She was sitting at her glass brushing her hair, and rising every other minute to play with her boy who was sprawling on the bed, and who engaged pretty nearly the whole attention of the maid as well as of his mother.

At last, sitting before her toilet table, she broke the seal, and turning over the leaf saw Mr. Slope's name. She first felt surprised, and then annoyed, and then anxious. As she read it she became interested. She was so delighted to find that all obstacles to her father's return to the hospital were apparently removed that she did not observe the fulsome language in which the tidings were conveyed. She merely perceived that she was commissioned to tell her father that such was the case, and she did not realise the fact that such a communication should not have been made, in the first instance, to her by an unmarried young clergyman. She felt, on the whole, grateful to Mr. Slope, and anxious to get on her dress that she might run with the news to her father. Then she came to the allusion to her own pious labours, and she said in her heart that Mr. Slope was an affected ass. Then she went on again and was offended by her boy being called Mr. Slope's darling—he was nobody's darling but her own; or at any rate not the darling of a disagreeable stranger like Mr. Slope. Lastly she arrived at the tresses and felt a qualm of disgust. She looked up in the glass, and there they were before her, long and silken, certainly, and very beautiful. I will not say but that she knew them to be so, but she felt angry with them and brushed them roughly and carelessly. She crumpled the letter up with angry violence, and resolved, almost without thinking of it, that she would not show it to her father. She would merely tell him the contents of it. She then comforted herself again with her boy, had her dress fastened, and went down to dinner.

As she tripped down the stairs she began to ascertain that there was some difficulty in her situation. She could not keep from her father the news about the hospital, nor could she comfortably confess the letter from Mr. Slope before the Grantlys. Her father had already gone down. She had heard his step upon the lobby. She resolved therefore to take him aside, and tell him her little bit of news. Poor girl! she had no idea how severely the unfortunate letter had already been discussed.

When she entered the drawing-room the whole party were there, including Mr. Arabin, and the whole party looked glum and sour. The two girls sat silent and apart as though they were aware that something was wrong. Even Mr. Arabin was solemn and silent. Eleanor had not seen him since breakfast. He had been the whole day at St. Ewold's, and such having been the case it was natural that he should tell how matters were going on there. He did nothing of the kind, however, but remained solemn and silent. They were all solemn and silent. Eleanor knew in her heart that they had been talking about her, and her heart misgave her as she thought of Mr. Slope and his letter. At any rate she felt it to be quite impossible to speak to her father alone while matters were in this state.

Dinner was soon announced, and Dr. Grantly, as was his wont, gave Eleanor his arm. But he did so as though the doing it were an outrage on his feelings rendered necessary by sternest necessity. With quick sympathy Eleanor felt this, and hardly put her fingers on his coat sleeve. It may be guessed in what way the dinner-hour was passed. Dr. Grantly said a few words to Mr. Arabin, Mr. Arabin said a few words to Mrs. Grantly, she said a few words to her father, and he tried to say a few words to Eleanor. She felt that she had been tried and found guilty of something, though she knew not what. She longed to say out to them all, ' Well, what is it that I have done; out with it, and let me know my crime; for heaven's sake let me hear the worst of it; ' but she could not. She could say nothing, but sat there silent, half feeling that she was guilty, and trying in vain to pretend even to eat her dinner.

At last the cloth was drawn, and the ladies were not long following it. When they were gone the gentlemen were somewhat more sociable but not much so. They could not of course talk over Eleanor's sins. The archdeacon had indeed so far betrayed his sister-in-law as to whisper into Mr. Arabin's ear in the study, as they met there before dinner, a hint of what he feared. He did so with the gravest and saddest of fears, and Mr. Arabin became grave and apparently sad enough as he heard it. He opened his eyes and his mouth and said in a sort of whisper ' Mr. Slope ! ' in the same way as he might have said ' The Cholera ! ' had his friend told him that that horrid disease was in his nursery. ' I fear so, I fear so,' said the archdeacon, and then together they left the room.

We will not accurately analyse Mr. Arabin's feelings on receipt of such astounding tidings. It will suffice to say that he was surprised, vexed, sorrowful, and ill at ease. He had not perhaps thought very much about Eleanor, but he had appreciated her influence, and had felt that close intimacy with her in a country house was pleasant to him, and also beneficial. He had spoken highly of her intelligence to the archdeacon, and had walked about the shrubberies with her, carrying her boy on his back. When Mr. Arabin had called Johnny his darling, Eleanor was not angry.

Thus the three men sat over their wine, all thinking of the same subject, but unable to speak of it to each other. So we will leave them, and follow the ladies into the drawing-room.

Mrs. Grantly had received a commission from her husband, and had undertaken it with some unwillingness. He had desired her to speak gravely to Eleanor, and to tell her that, if she persisted in her adherence to Mr. Slope, she could no longer look-for the countenance of her present friends. Mrs. Grantly probably knew her sister better than the doctor did, and assured him that it would be in vain to talk to her. The only course likely to be of any service in her opinion was to keep Eleanor away from Barchester. Perhaps she might have added, for she had a very keen eye in such things, that there might also be ground for hope in keeping Eleanor near Mr. Arabin. Of this, however, she said nothing. But the archdeacon would not be talked over ; he spoke much of his conscience, and declared that if Mrs. Grantly would not do it he would. So instigated, the lady undertook the task, stating, however, her full conviction that her interference would be worse than useless. And so it proved.

As soon as they were in the drawing-room Mrs. Grantly found some excuse for sending her girls away, and then began her task. She knew well that she could exercise but very slight authority over her sister. Their various modes of life, and the distance between their residences, had prevented any very close confidence. They had hardly lived together since Eleanor was a child. Eleanor had moreover, especially in latter years, resented in a quiet sort of way the dictatorial authority which the archdeacon seemed to exercise over her father, and on this account had been unwilling to allow the archdeacon's wife to exercise authority over herself.

' You got a note just before dinner, I believe,' began the eldest sister.

Eleanor acknowledged that she had done so, and felt that she turned red as she acknowledged it. She would have given anything to have kept her colour, but the more she tried to do so the more signally she failed.

' Was it not from Mr. Slope ? '

Eleanor said that the letter was from Mr. Slope.

' Is he a regular correspondent of yours, Eleanor ? '

' Not exactly,' said she, already beginning to feel angry at the cross-examination. She determined, and why it would be difficult to say, that nothing should induce her to tell her sister Susan what was the subject of the letter. Mrs. Grantly, she knew, was instigated by the archdeacon, and she would not plead to any arraignment made against her by him.

' But, Eleanor dear, why do you get letters from Mr. Slope at all, knowing, as you do, he is a person so distasteful to papa, and to the archdeacon, and indeed to all your friends ? '

' In the first place, Susan, I don't get letters from him ; and in the next place, as Mr. Slope wrote the one letter which I have got, and as I only received it, which I could not very well help doing, as papa handed it to me, I think you had better ask Mr. Slope instead of me.'

' What was his letter about, Eleanor ? '

' I cannot tell you,' said she, ' because it was confidential. It was on business respecting a third person.'

' It was in no way personal to yourself, then ? '

' I won't exactly say that, Susan,' said she, getting more and more angry at her sister's questions.

' Well, I must say it's rather singular,' said Mrs. Grantly, affecting to laugh, ' that a young lady in your position should receive a letter from an unmarried gentleman of which she will not tell the contents, and which she is ashamed to show to her sister.'

' I am not ashamed,' said Eleanor blazing up ; ' I am not ashamed of anything in the matter ; only I do not choose to be cross-examined as to my letters by any one.'

' Well, dear,' said the other, ' I cannot but tell you that I do not think Mr. Slope a proper correspondent for you.'

' If he be ever so improper, how can I help his having written to me ? But you are all prejudiced against him to such an extent, that that which would be kind and generous in another man is odious and impudent in him. I hate a religion that teaches one to be so onesided in one's charity.'

' I am sorry, Eleanor, that you hate the religion you find here ; but surely you should remember that in such matters the archdeacon must know more of the world than you do. I don't ask you to respect or comply with me, although I am, unfortunately, so many years your senior ; but surely, in such a matter as this, you might consent to be guided by the archdeacon. He is most anxious to be your friend if you will let him.'

' In such a matter as what ? ' said Eleanor very testily. ' Upon my word I don't know what this is all about.'

' We all want you to drop Mr. Slope.'

' You all want me to be as illiberal as yourselves. That I shall never be. I see no harm in Mr. Slope's acquaintance, and I shall not insult the man by telling him that I do. He has thought it necessary to write to me, and I do not want the archdeacon's advice about the letter. If I did I would ask it.'

' Then, Eleanor, it is my duty to tell you,' and now she
spoke with a tremendous gravity, ' that the archdeacon
thinks that such a correspondence is disgraceful, and that
he cannot allow it to go on in his house.'

Eleanor's eyes flashed fire as she answered her sister,
jumping up from her seat as she did so. ' You may tell the
archdeacon that wherever I am I shall receive what letters
I please and from whom I please. And as for the word
disgraceful, if Dr. Grantly has used it of me he has been
unmanly and inhospitable,' and she walked off to the door.
' When papa comes from the dining-room I will thank you
to ask him to step up to my bed-room. I will show him
Mr. Slope's letter, but I will show it to no one else.' And
so saying she retreated to her baby.

She had no conception of the crime with which she was
charged. The idea that she could be thought by her
friends to regard Mr. Slope as a lover, had never flashed
upon her. She conceived that they were all prejudiced
and illiberal in their persecution of him, and therefore she
would not join in the persecution, even though she greatly
disliked the man.

Eleanor was very angry as she seated herself in a low
chair by her open window at the foot of her child's bed.
' To dare to say I have disgraced myself,' she repeated to
herself more than once. ' How papa can put up with that
man's arrogance ! I will certainly not sit down to dinner
in his house again unless he begs my pardon for that word.'
And then a thought struck her that Mr. Arabin might
perchance hear of her ' disgraceful ' correspondence with
Mr. Slope, and she turned crimson with pure vexation.
Oh, if she had known the truth ? If she could have
conceived that Mr. Arabin had been informed as a fact that
she was going to marry Mr. Slope !

She had not been long in her room before her father
joined her. As he left the drawing-room Mrs. Grantly took
her husband into the recess of the window, and told him
how signally she had failed.

' I will speak to her myself before I go to bed,' said the
archdeacon.

' Pray do no such thing,' said she ; ' you can do no good
and will only make an unseemly quarrel in the house. You
have no idea how headstrong she can be.'

The archdeacon declared that as to that he was quite indifferent. He knew his duty and would do it. Mr. Harding was weak in the extreme in such matters. He would not have it hereafter on his conscience that he had not done all that in him lay to prevent so disgraceful an alliance. It was in vain that Mrs. Grantly assured him that speaking to Eleanor angrily would only hasten such a crisis, and render it certain if at present there were any doubt. He was angry, self-willed, and sore. The fact that a lady of his household had received a letter from Mr. Slope had wounded his pride in the sorest place, and nothing could control him.

Mr. Harding looked worn and woebegone as he entered his daughter's room. These sorrows worried him sadly. He felt that if they were continued he must go to the wall in the manner so kindly prophesied to him by the chaplain. He knocked gently at his daughter's door, waited till he was distinctly bade to enter, and then appeared as though he and not she were the suspected criminal.

Eleanor's arm was soon within his, and she had soon kissed his forehead and caressed him, not with joyous but with eager love. ' Oh, papa,' she said, ' I do so want to speak to you. They have been talking about me down stairs to-night; don't you know they have, papa ? '

Mr. Harding confessed with a sort of murmur that the archdeacon had been speaking of her.

' I shall hate Dr. Grantly soon—'

' Oh my dear ! '

' Well ; I shall. I cannot help it. He is so uncharitable, so unkind, so suspicious of every one that does not worship himself : and then he is so monstrously arrogant to other people who have a right to their opinions as well as he has to his own.'

' He is an earnest eager man, my dear : but he never means to be unkind.'

' He is unkind, papa, most unkind. There, I got that letter from Mr. Slope before dinner. It was you yourself who gave it to me. There ; pray read it. It is all for you. It should have been addressed to you. You know how they have been talking about it down stairs. You know how they behaved to me at dinner. And since dinner Susan has been preaching to me, till I could not remain

in the room with her. Read it, papa; and then say
whether that is a letter that need make Dr. Grantly so
outrageous.'

Mr. Harding took his arm from his daughter's waist, and
slowly read the letter. She expected to see his countenance
lit with joy as he learnt that his path back to the hospital
was made so smooth; but she was doomed to disappointment, as had once been the case before on a somewhat
similar occasion. His first feeling was one of unmitigated
disgust that Mr. Slope should have chosen to interfere in
his behalf. He had been anxious to get back to the
hospital, but he would have infinitely sooner resigned all
pretensions to the place, than have owed it in any manner
to Mr. Slope's influence in his favour. Then he thoroughly
disliked the tone of Mr. Slope's letter; it was unctuous,
false, and unwholesome, like the man. He saw, which
Eleanor had failed to see, that much more had been
intended than was expressed. The appeal to Eleanor's
pious labours as separate from his own grated sadly against
his feelings as a father. And then when he came to the
' darling boy ' and the ' silken tresses,' he slowly closed
and folded the letter in despair. It was impossible that
Mr. Slope should so write unless he had been encouraged.
It was impossible Eleanor should have received such a
letter, and have received it without annoyance, unless she
were willing to encourage him. So at least Mr. Harding
argued to himself.

How hard it is to judge accurately of the feelings of
others. Mr. Harding, as he came to the close of the letter,
in his heart condemned his daughter for indelicacy, and
it made him miserable to do so. She was not responsible
for what Mr. Slope might write. True. But then she
expressed no disgust at it. She had rather expressed
approval of the letter as a whole. She had given it to him
to read, as a vindication for herself and also for him. The
father's spirits sank within him as he felt that he could not
acquit her.

And yet it was the true feminine delicacy of Eleanor's
mind which brought her on this condemnation. Listen
to me, ladies, and I beseech *you* to acquit her. She thought
of this man, this lover of whom she was so unconscious,
exactly as her father did, exactly as the Grantlys did.

At least she esteemed him personally as they did. But she believed him to be in the main an honest man, and one truly inclined to assist her father. She felt herself bound, after what had passed, to show this letter to Mr. Harding. She thought it necessary that he should know what Mr. Slope had to say. But she did not think it necessary to apologise for, or condemn, or even allude to the vulgarity of the man's tone, which arose, as does all vulgarity, from ignorance. It was nauseous to her to have a man like Mr. Slope commenting on her personal attractions; and she did not think it necessary to dilate with her father upon what was nauseous. She never supposed they could disagree on such a subject. It would have been painful for her to point it out, painful for her to speak strongly against a man of whom, on the whole, she was anxious to think and speak well. In encountering such a man she had encountered what was disagreeable, as she might do in walking the streets. But in such encounters she never thought it necessary to dwell on what disgusted her.

And he, foolish weak loving man, would not say one word, though one word would have cleared up everything. There would have been a deluge of tears, and in ten minutes every one in the house would have understood how matters really were. The father would have been delighted. The sister would have kissed her sister and begged a thousand pardons. The archdeacon would have apologised and wondered, and raised his eyebrows, and gone to bed a happy man. And Mr. Arabin—Mr. Arabin would have dreamt of Eleanor, have awoke in the morning with ideas of love, and retired to rest the next evening with schemes of marriage. But, alas! all this was not to be.

Mr. Harding slowly folded the letter, handed it back to her, kissed her forehead and bade God bless her. He then crept slowly away to his own room.

As soon as he had left the passage another knock was given at Eleanor's door, and Mrs. Grantly's very demure own maid, entering on tiptoe, wanted to know would Mrs. Bold be so kind as to speak to the archdeacon for two minutes, in the archdeacon's study, if not disagreeable. The archdeacon's compliments, and he wouldn't detain her two minutes.

Eleanor thought it was very disagreeable; she was

tired and fagged and sick at heart; her present feelings towards Dr. Grantly were anything but those of affection. She was, however, no coward, and therefore promised to be in the study in five minutes. So she arranged her hair, tied on her cap, and went down with a palpitating heart.

CHAPTER XXIX

A SERIOUS INTERVIEW

THERE are people who delight in serious interviews, especially when to them appertains the part of offering advice or administering rebuke, and perhaps the archdeacon was one of these. Yet on this occasion he did not prepare himself for the coming conversation with much anticipation of pleasure. Whatever might be his faults he was not an inhospitable man, and he almost felt that he was sinning against hospitality in upbraiding Eleanor in his own house. Then, also he was not quite sure that he would get the best of it. His wife had told him that he decidedly would not, and he usually gave credit to what his wife said. He was, however, so convinced of what he considered to be the impropriety of Eleanor's conduct, and so assured also of his own duty in trying to check it, that his conscience would not allow him to take his wife's advice and go to bed quietly.

Eleanor's face as she entered the room was not such as to reassure him. As a rule she was always mild in manner and gentle in conduct; but there was that in her eye which made it not an easy task to scold her. In truth she had been little used to scolding. No one since her childhood had tried it but the archdeacon, and he had generally failed when he did try it. He had never done so since her marriage; and now, when he saw her quiet easy step, as she entered his room, he almost wished that he had taken his wife's advice.

He began by apologising for the trouble he was giving her. She begged him not to mention it, assured him that walking down stairs was no trouble to her at all, and then took a seat and waited patiently for him to begin his attack.

' My dear Eleanor,' he said, ' I hope you believe me when I assure you that you have no sincerer friend than

I am.' To this Eleanor answered nothing, and therefore
he proceeded. ' If you had a brother of your own I should
not probably trouble you with what I am going to say.
But as it is I cannot but think that it must be a comfort
to you to know that you have near you one who is as
anxious for your welfare as any brother of your own
could be.'

' I never had a brother,' said she.

' I know you never had, and it is therefore that I speak
to you.'

' I never had a brother,' she repeated ; ' but I have
hardly felt the want. Papa has been to me both father
and brother.'

' Your father is the fondest and most affectionate of
men. But—'

' He is—the fondest and most affectionate of men, and
the best of counsellors. While he lives I can never want
advice.'

This rather put the archdeacon out. He could not
exactly contradict what his sister-in-law said about her
father ; and yet he did not at all agree with her. He
wanted her to understand that he tendered his assistance
because her father was a soft good-natured gentleman, not
sufficiently knowing in the ways of the world ; but he
could not say this to her. So he had to rush into the
subject-matter of his proffered counsel without any
acknowledgment on her part that she could need it, or
would be grateful for it.

' Susan tells me that you received a letter this evening
from Mr. Slope.'

' Yes ; papa brought it in the brougham. Did he not
tell you ? '

' And Susan says that you objected to let her know what
it was about.'

' I don't think she asked me. But had she done so I
should not have told her. I don't think it nice to be asked
about one's letters. If one wishes to show them one does
so without being asked.'

' True. Quite so. What you say is quite true. But is
not the fact of your receiving letters from Mr. Slope, which
you do not wish to show to your friends, a circumstance
which must excite some—some surprise—some suspicion—'

' Suspicion ! ' said she, not speaking above her usual voice, speaking still in a soft womanly tone, but yet with indignation ; ' suspicion ! and who suspects me, and of what ? ' And then there was a pause, for the arch-deacon was not quite ready to explain the ground of his suspicion. ' No, Dr. Grantly, I did not choose to show Mr. Slope's letter to Susan. I could not show it to any one till papa had seen it. If you have any wish to read it now, you can do so,' and she handed the letter to him over the table.

This was an amount of compliance which he had not at all expected, and which rather upset him in his tactics. However, he took the letter, perused it carefully, and then refolding it, kept it on the table under his hand. To him it appeared to be in almost every respect the letter of a declared lover; it seemed to corroborate his worst suspicions ; and the fact of Eleanor's showing it to him was all but tantamount to a declaration on her part, that it was her pleasure to receive love-letters from Mr. Slope. He almost entirely overlooked the real subject-matter of the epistle ; so intent was he on the forthcoming courtship and marriage.

' I'll thank you to give it me back, if you please, Dr. Grantly.'

He took it in his hand and held it up, but made no immediate overture to return it. ' And Mr. Harding has seen this ? ' said he.

' Of course he has,' said she ; ' it was written that he might see it. It refers solely to his business—of course I showed it to him.'

' And, Eleanor, do you think that that is a proper letter for you—for a person in your condition—to receive from Mr. Slope ? '

' Quite a proper letter,' said she, speaking, perhaps, a little out of obstinacy ; probably forgetting at the moment the objectionable mention of her silken curls.

' Then, Eleanor, it is my duty to tell you that I wholly differ from you.'

' So I suppose,' said she, instigated now by sheer opposition and determination not to succumb. ' You think Mr. Slope is a messenger direct from Satan. I think he is an industrious, well meaning clergyman It's a pity that

we differ as we do. But, as we do differ, we had probably
better not talk about it.'

Here Eleanor undoubtedly put herself in the wrong.
She might probably have refused to talk to Dr. Grantly
on the matter in dispute without any impropriety; but
having consented to listen to him, she had no business to
tell him that he regarded Mr. Slope as an emissary from the
evil one; nor was she justified in praising Mr. Slope, seeing
that in her heart of hearts she did not think well of him.
She was, however, wounded in spirit, and angry and bitter.
She had been subjected to contumely and cross-questioning
and ill-usage through the whole evening. No one, not even
Mr. Arabin, not even her father, had been kind to her.
All this she attributed to the prejudice and conceit of the
archdeacon, and therefore she resolved to set no bounds
to her antagonism to him. She would neither give nor
take quarter. He had greatly presumed in daring to
question her about her correspondence, and she was
determined to show that she thought so.

'Eleanor, you are forgetting yourself,' said he, looking
very sternly at her. 'Otherwise you would never tell me
that I conceive any man to be a messenger from Satan.'

'But you do,' said she. 'Nothing is too bad for him.
Give me that letter, if you please;' and she stretched out
her hand and took it from him. 'He has been doing his
best to serve papa, doing more than any of papa's friends
could do; and yet, because he is the chaplain of a bishop
whom you don't like, you speak of him as though he had
no right to the usage of a gentleman.'

'He has done nothing for your father.'

'I believe that he has done a great deal; and, as far as
I am concerned, I am grateful to him. Nothing that you
can say can prevent my being so. I judge people by their
acts, and his, as far as I can see them, are good.' She then
paused for a moment. 'If you have nothing further to
say, I shall be obliged by being permitted to say good
night—I am very tired.'

Dr. Grantly had, as he thought, done his best to be
gracious to his sister-in-law. He had endeavoured not to
be harsh to her, and had striven to pluck the sting from his
rebuke. But he did not intend that she should leave him
without hearing him.

'I have something to say, Eleanor; and I fear I must trouble you to hear it. You profess that it is quite proper that you should receive from Mr. Slope such letters as that you have in your hand. Susan and I think very differently. You are, of course, your own mistress, and much as we both must grieve should anything separate you from us, we have no power to prevent you from taking steps which may lead to such a separation. If you are so wilful as to reject the counsel of your friends, you must be allowed to cater for yourself. But Eleanor, I may at any rate ask you this. Is it worth your while to break away from all those you have loved—from all who love you—for the sake of Mr. Slope?'

'I don't know what you mean, Dr. Grantly; I don't know what you're talking about. I don't want to break away from anybody.'

'But you will do so if you connect yourself with Mr. Slope. Eleanor, I must speak out to you. You must choose between your sister and myself and our friends, and Mr. Slope and his friends. I say nothing of your father, as you may probably understand his feelings better than I do.'

'What do you mean, Dr. Grantly? What am I to understand? I never heard such wicked prejudice in my life.'

'It is no prejudice, Eleanor. I have known the world longer than you have done. Mr. Slope is altogether beneath you. You ought to know and feel that he is so. Pray—pray think of this before it is too late.'

'Too late!'

'Or if you will not believe me, ask Susan; you cannot think she is prejudiced against you. Or even consult your father, he is not prejudiced against you. Ask Mr. Arabin——,'

'You haven't spoken to Mr. Arabin about this!' said she, jumping up and standing before him.

'Eleanor, all the world in and about Barchester will be speaking of it soon.'

'But have you spoken to Mr. Arabin about me and Mr. Slope?'

'Certainly I have, and he quite agrees with me.'

'Agrees with what?' said she. 'I think you are trying to drive me mad.'

' He agrees with me and Susan that it is quite impossible you should be received at Plumstead as Mrs. Slope.'

Not being favourites with the tragic muse we do not dare to attempt any description of Eleanor's face when she first heard the name of Mrs. Slope pronounced as that which would or should or might at some time appertain to herself. The look, such as it was, Dr. Grantly did not soon forget. For a moment or two she could find no words to express her deep anger and deep disgust ; and, indeed, at this conjuncture, words did not come to her very freely.

' How dare you be so impertinent ? ' at last she said ; and then hurried out of the room, without giving the archdeacon the opportunity of uttering another word. It was with difficulty she contained herself till she reached her own room ; and then locking the door, she threw herself on her bed and sobbed as though her heart would break.

But even yet she had no conception of the truth. She had no idea that her father and her sister had for days past conceived in sober earnest the idea that she was going to marry this man. She did not even then believe that the archdeacon thought that she would do so. By some manœuvre of her brain, she attributed the origin of the accusation to Mr. Arabin, and as she did so her anger against him was excessive, and the vexation of her spirit almost unendurable. She could not bring herself to think that the charge was made seriously. It appeared to her most probable that the archdeacon and Mr. Arabin had talked over her objectionable acquaintance with Mr. Slope ; that Mr. Arabin, in his jeering, sarcastic way, had suggested the odious match as being the severest way of treating with contumely her acquaintance with his enemy ; and that the archdeacon, taking the idea from him, thought proper to punish her by the allusion. The whole night she lay awake thinking of what had been said, and this appeared to be the most probable solution.

But the reflection that Mr. Arabin should have in any way mentioned her name in connection with that of Mr. Slope was overpowering ; and the spiteful ill-nature of the archdeacon, in repeating the charge to her, made her wish to leave his house almost before the day had broken. One thing was certain : nothing should make her stay there beyond the following morning, and nothing should make

her sit down to breakfast in company with Dr. Grantly.
When she thought of the man whose name had been linked
with her own, she cried from sheer disgust. It was only
because she would be thus disgusted, thus pained and
shocked and cut to the quick, that the archdeacon had
spoken the horrid word. He wanted to make her quarrel
with Mr. Slope, and therefore he had outraged her by his
abominable vulgarity. She determined that at any rate
he should know that she appreciated it.

Nor was the archdeacon a bit better satisfied with the
result of his serious interview than was Eleanor. He
gathered from it, as indeed he could hardly fail to do, that
she was very angry with him ; but he thought that she
was thus angry, not because she was suspected of an
intention to marry Mr. Slope, but because such an intention
was imputed to her as a crime. Dr. Grantly regarded this
supposed union with disgust ; but it never occurred to
him that Eleanor was outraged, because she looked at it
exactly in the same light.

He returned to his wife vexed and somewhat discon-
solate, but, nevertheless, confirmed in his wrath against
his sister-in-law. ' Her whole behaviour,' said he, ' has
been most objectionable. She handed me his love letter
to read as though she were proud of it. And she is proud
of it. She is proud of having this slavering, greedy man
at her feet. She will throw herself and John Bold's money
into his lap ; she will ruin her boy, disgrace her father and
you, and be a wretched miserable woman.'

His spouse who was sitting at her toilet table, continued
her avocations, making no answer to all this. She had
known that the archdeacon would gain nothing by interfering ; but she was too charitable to provoke him by
saying so while he was in such deep sorrow.

' This comes of a man making such a will as that of
Bold's,' he continued. ' Eleanor is no more fitted to be
trusted with such an amount of money in her own hands
than is a charity-school girl.' Still Mrs. Grantly made no
reply. ' But I have done my duty ; I can do nothing
further. I have told her plainly that she cannot be allowed
to form a link of connection between me and that man.
From henceforward it will not be in my power to make her
welcome at Plumstead. I cannot have Mr. Slope's love

letters coming here. Susan, I think you had better let her understand that as her mind on this subject seems to be irrevocably fixed, it will be better for all parties that she should return to Barchester.'

Now Mrs. Grantly was angry with Eleanor, nearly as angry as her husband ; but she had no idea of turning her sister out of the house. She, therefore, at length spoke out, and explained to the archdeacon in her own mild seducing way, that he was fuming and fussing and fretting himself very unnecessarily. She declared that things, if left alone, would arrange themselves much better than he could arrange them ; and at last succeeded in inducing him to go to bed in a somewhat less inhospitable state of mind.

On the following morning Eleanor's maid was commissioned to send word into the dining-room that her mistress was not well enough to attend prayers, and that she would breakfast in her own room. Here she was visited by her father and declared to him her intention of returning immediately to Barchester. He was hardly surprised by the announcement. All the household seemed to be aware that something had gone wrong. Every one walked about with subdued feet, and people's shoes seemed to creak more than usual. There was a look of conscious intelligence on the faces of the women : and the men attempted, but in vain, to converse as though nothing were the matter. All this had weighed heavily on the heart of Mr. Harding ; and when Eleanor told him that her immediate return to Barchester was a necessity, he merely sighed piteously, and said that he would be ready to accompany her.

But here she objected strenuously. She had a great wish, she said, to go alone ; a great desire that it might be seen that her father was not implicated in her quarrel with Dr. Grantly. To this at last he gave way ; but not a word passed between them about Mr. Slope—not a word was said, not a question asked as to the serious interview on the preceding evening. There was, indeed, very little confidence between them, though neither of them knew why it should be so. Eleanor once asked him whether he would not call upon the bishop ; but he answered rather tartly that he did not know—he did not think he should, but he could not say just at present. And so they parted.

Each was miserably anxious for some show of affection, for some return of confidence, for some sign of the feeling that usually bound them together. But none was given. The father could not bring himself to question his daughter about her supposed lover ; and the daughter would not sully her mouth by repeating the odious word with which Dr. Grantly had roused her wrath. And so they parted.

There was some trouble in arranging the method of Eleanor's return. She begged her father to send for a postchaise ; but when Mrs. Grantly heard of this, she objected strongly. If Eleanor would go away in dudgeon with the archdeacon, why should she let all the servants and all the neighbourhood know that she had done so ? So at last Eleanor consented to make use of the Plumstead carriage ; and as the archdeacon had gone out immediately after breakfast and was not to return till dinnertime, she also consented to postpone her journey till after lunch, and to join the family at that time. As to the subject of the quarrel not a word was said by any one. The affair of the carriage was arranged by Mr. Harding, who acted as Mercury between the two ladies ; they, when they met, kissed each other very lovingly, and then sat down each to her crochet work as though nothing was amiss in all the world.

CHAPTER XXX

ANOTHER LOVE SCENE

But there was another visitor at the rectory whose feelings in this unfortunate matter must be somewhat strictly analysed. Mr. Arabin had heard from his friend of the probability of Eleanor's marriage with Mr. Slope with amazement, but not with incredulity. It has been said that he was not in love with Eleanor, and up to this period this certainly had been true. But as soon as he heard that she loved some one else, he began to be very fond of her himself. He did not make up his mind that he wished to have her for his wife ; he had never thought of her, and did not now think of her, in connection with himself ; but he experienced an inward indefinable feeling of deep regret, a gnawing sorrow, an unconquerable

depression of spirits, and also a species of self-abasement
that he—he Mr. Arabin—had not done something to
prevent that other he, that vile he, whom he so thoroughly
despised, from carrying off this sweet prize.

Whatever man may have reached the age of forty
unmarried without knowing something of such feelings
must have been very successful or else very cold hearted.

Mr. Arabin had never thought of trimming the sails of
his bark so that he might sail as convoy to this rich argosy.
He had seen that Mrs. Bold was beautiful, but he had not
dreamt of making her beauty his own. He knew that
Mrs. Bold was rich, but he had had no more idea of
appropriating her wealth than that of Dr. Grantly. He
had discovered that Mrs. Bold was intelligent, warm-
hearted, agreeable, sensible, all, in fact, that a man could
wish his wife to be ; but the higher were her attractions,
the greater her claims to consideration, the less had he
imagined that he might possibly become the possessor of
them. Such had been his instinct rather than his thoughts,
so humble and so diffident. Now his diffidence was to be
rewarded by his seeing this woman, whose beauty was to
his eyes perfect, whose wealth was such as to have deterred
him from thinking of her, whose widowhood would have
silenced him had he not been so deterred, by his seeing her
become the prey of——Obadiah Slope !

On the morning of Mrs. Bold's departure he got on his
horse to ride over to St. Ewold's. As he rode he kept
muttering to himself a line from Van Artevelde,

> How little flattering is woman's love.

And then he strove to recall his mind and to think of other
affairs, his parish, his college, his creed—but his thoughts
would revert to Mr. Slope and the Flemish chieftain.—

> When we think upon it,
> How little flattering is woman's love,
> Given commonly to whosoe'er is nearest
> And propped with most advantage.

It was not that Mrs. Bold should marry any one but him ;
he had not put himself forward as a suitor ; but that she
should marry Mr. Slope—and so he repeated over again—

> Outward grace
> Nor inward light is needful—day by day

Men wanting both are mated with the best
And loftiest of God's feminine creation,
Whose love takes no distinction but of gender,
And ridicules the very name of choice.

And so he went on, troubled much in his mind.

He had but an uneasy ride of it that morning, and little good did he do at St. Ewold's.

The necessary alterations in his house were being fast completed, and he walked through the rooms, and went up and down the stairs and rambled through the garden; but he could not wake himself to much interest about them. He stood still at every window to look out and think upon Mr. Slope. At almost every window he had before stood and chatted with Eleanor. She and Mrs. Grantly had been there continually, and while Mrs. Grantly had been giving orders, and seeing that orders had been complied with, he and Eleanor had conversed on all things appertaining to a clergyman's profession. He thought how often he had laid down the law to her, and how sweetly she had borne with his somewhat dictatorial decrees. He remembered her listening intelligence, her gentle but quick replies, her interest in all that concerned the church, in all that concerned him; and then he struck his riding whip against the window sill, and declared to himself that it was impossible that Eleanor Bold should marry Mr. Slope.

And yet he did not really believe, as he should have done, that it was impossible. He should have known her well enough to feel that it was truly impossible. He should have been aware that Eleanor had that within her which would surely protect her from such degradation. But he, like so many others, was deficient in confidence in woman. He said to himself over and over again that it was impossible that Eleanor Bold should become Mrs. Slope, and yet he believed that she would do so. And so he rambled about, and could do and think of nothing. He was thoroughly uncomfortable, thoroughly ill at ease, cross with himself and every body else, and feeding in his heart on animosity towards Mr. Slope. This was not as it should be, as he knew and felt; but he could not help himself. In truth Mr. Arabin was now in love with Mrs. Bold, though ignorant of the fact himself. He was in love, and, though forty years old, was in love without being aware of it. He

fumed and fretted, and did not know what was the matter,
as a youth might do at one-and-twenty. And so having
done no good at St. Ewold's, he rode back much earlier
than was usual with him, instigated by some inward
unacknowledged hope that he might see Mrs. Bold before
she left.

Eleanor had not passed a pleasant morning. She was
irritated with every one, and not least with herself. She
felt that she had been hardly used, but she felt also that
she had not played her own cards well. She should have
held herself so far above suspicion as to have received her
sister's innuendoes and the archdeacon's lecture with
indifference. She had not done this, but had shown herself
angry and sore, and was now ashamed of her own petu-
lance, and yet unable to discontinue it.

The greater part of the morning she had spent alone ;
but after a while her father joined her. He had fully made
up his mind that, come what come might, nothing should
separate him from his younger daughter. It was a hard
task for him to reconcile himself to the idea of seeing her
at the head of Mr. Slope's table ; but he got through it.
Mr. Slope, as he argued to himself, was a respectable man
and a clergyman ; and he, as Eleanor's father, had no
right even to endeavour to prevent her from marrying
such a one. He longed to tell her how he had determined
to prefer her to all the world, how he was prepared to
admit that she was not wrong, how thoroughly he differed
from Dr. Grantly ; but he could not bring himself to
mention Mr. Slope's name. There was yet a chance that
they were all wrong in their surmise ! and, being thus in
doubt, he could not bring himself to speak openly to her
on the subject.

He was sitting with her in the drawing-room, with his
arm round her waist, saying every now and then some
little soft words of affection, and working hard with his
imaginary fiddle-bow, when Mr. Arabin entered the room.
He immediately got up, and the two made some trite
remarks to each other, neither thinking of what he was
saying, while Eleanor kept her seat on the sofa mute and
moody. Mr. Arabin was included in the list of those
against whom her anger was excited. He, too, had dared
to talk about her acquaintance with Mr. Slope ; he, too,

had dared to blame her for not making an enemy of his enemy. She had not intended to see him before her departure, and was now but little inclined to be gracious.

There was a feeling through the whole house that something was wrong. Mr. Arabin, when he saw Eleanor, could not succeed in looking or in speaking as though he knew nothing of all this. He could not be cheerful and positive and contradictory with her, as was his wont. He had not been two minutes in the room before he felt that he had done wrong to return; and the moment he heard her voice, he thoroughly wished himself back at St. Ewold's. Why, indeed, should he have wished to have aught further to say to the future wife of Mr. Slope ?

' I am sorry to hear that you are to leave us so soon,' said he, striving in vain to use his ordinary voice. In answer to this she muttered something about the necessity of her being in Barchester, and betook herself most industriously to her crochet work.

Then there was a little more trite conversation between Mr. Arabin and Mr. Harding ; trite, and hard, and vapid, and senseless. Neither of them had anything to say to the other, and yet neither at such a moment liked to remain silent. At last Mr. Harding, taking advantage of a pause, escaped out of the room, and Eleanor and Mr. Arabin were left together.

' Your going will be a great break-up to our party,' said he.

She again muttered something which was all but inaudible ; but kept her eyes fixed upon her work.

' We have had a very pleasant month here,' said he ; ' at least I have ; and I am sorry it should be so soon over.'

' I have already been from home longer than I intended,' said she ; ' and it is time that I should return.'

' Well, pleasant hours and pleasant days must come to an end. It is a pity that so few of them are pleasant ; or perhaps, rather '——

' It is a pity, certainly, that men and women do so much to destroy the pleasantness of their days,' said she, interrupting him. ' It is a pity that there should be so little charity abroad.'

' Charity should begin at home,' said he ; and he was proceeding to explain that he as a clergyman could not be what she would call charitable at the expense of those principles which he considered it his duty to teach, when he remembered that it would be worse than vain to argue on such a matter with the future wife of Mr. Slope. ' But you are just leaving us,' he continued, ' and I will not weary your last hour with another lecture. As it is, I fear I have given you too many.'

' You should practise as well as preach, Mr. Arabin ? '

' Undoubtedly I should. So should we all. All of us who presume to teach are bound to do our utmost towards fulfilling our own lessons. I thoroughly allow my deficiency in doing so : but I do not quite know now to what you allude. Have you any special reason for telling me now that I should practise as well as preach ? '

Eleanor made no answer. She longed to let him know the cause of her anger, to upbraid him for speaking of her disrespectfully, and then at last to forgive him, and so part friends. She felt that she would be unhappy to leave him in her present frame of mind ; but yet she could hardly bring herself to speak to him of Mr. Slope. And how could she allude to the innuendo thrown out by the archdeacon, and thrown out, as she believed, at the instigation of Mr. Arabin ? She wanted to make him know that he was wrong, to make him aware that he had ill-treated her, in order that the sweetness of her forgiveness might be enhanced. She felt that she liked him too well to be contented to part with him in displeasure ; and yet she could not get over her deep displeasure without some explanation, some acknowledgment on his part, some assurance that he would never again so sin against her.

' Why do you tell me that I should practise what I preach ? ' continued he.

' All men should do so.'

' Certainly. That is as it were understood and acknowledged. But you do not say so to all men, or to all clergymen. The advice, good as it is, is not given except in allusion to some special deficiency. If you will tell me my special deficiency, I will endeavour to profit by the advice.'

She paused for a while, and then looking full in his face, she said, ' You are not bold enough, Mr. Arabin, to speak out to me openly and plainly, and yet you expect me, a woman, to speak openly to you. Why did you speak calumny of me to Dr. Grantly behind my back ? '

' Calumny ! ' said he, and his whole face became suffused with blood ; ' what calumny ? If I have spoken calumny of you, I will beg your pardon, and his to whom I spoke it, and God's pardon also. But what calumny have I spoken of you to Dr. Grantly ? '

She also blushed deeply. She could not bring herself to ask him whether he had not spoken of her as another man's wife. ' You know that best yourself,' said she ; ' but I ask you as a man of honour, if you have not spoken of me as you would not have spoken of your own sister ; or rather I will not ask you,' she continued, finding that he did not immediately answer her. ' I will not put you to the necessity of answering such a question. Dr. Grantly has told me what you said.'

' Dr. Grantly certainly asked me for my advice, and I gave it. He asked me '——

' I know he did, Mr. Arabin. He asked you whether he would be doing right to receive me at Plumstead, if I continued my acquaintance with a gentleman who happens to be personally disagreeable to yourself and to him ? '

' You are mistaken, Mrs. Bold. I have no personal knowledge of Mr. Slope ; I never met him in my life.'

' You are not the less individually hostile to him. It is not for me to question the propriety of your enmity ; but I had a right to expect that my name should not have been mixed up in your hostilities. This has been done, and been done by you in a manner the most injurious and the most distressing to me as a woman. I must confess, Mr. Arabin, that from you I expected a different sort of usage.'

As she spoke she with difficulty restrained her tears ; but she did restrain them. Had she given way and sobbed aloud, as in such cases a woman should do, he would have melted at once, implored her pardon, perhaps knelt at her feet and declared his love. Everything would have been explained, and Eleanor would have gone back to Barchester with a contented mind. How easily would she have forgiven and forgotten the archdeacon's suspicions had she but heard the whole truth from Mr. Arabin. But then where would have been my novel ? She did not cry, and Mr. Arabin did not melt.

'You do me an injustice,' said he. 'My advice was asked by Dr. Grantly, and I was obliged to give it.'

'Dr. Grantly has been most officious, most impertinent. I have as complete a right to form my acquaintance as he has to form his. What would you have said, had I consulted you as to the propriety of my banishing Dr. Grantly from my house because he knows Lord Tattenham Corner? I am sure Lord Tattenham is quite as objectionable an acquaintance for a clergyman as Mr. Slope is for a clergyman's daughter.'

'I do not know Lord Tattenham Corner.'

'No; but Dr. Grantly does. It is nothing to me if he knows all the young lords on every racecourse in England. I shall not interfere with him; nor shall he with me.'

'I am sorry to differ with you, Mrs. Bold; but as you have spoken to me on this matter, and especially as you blame me for what little I said on the subject, I must tell you that I do differ from you. Dr. Grantly's position as a man in the world gives him a right to choose his own acquaintances, subject to certain influences. If he chooses them badly, those influences will be used. If he consorts with persons unsuitable to him, his bishop will interfere. What the bishop is to Dr. Grantly, Dr. Grantly is to you.'

'I deny it. I utterly deny it,' said Eleanor, jumping from her seat, and literally flashing before Mr. Arabin, as she stood on the drawing-room floor. He had never seen her so excited, he had never seen her look half so beautiful.

'I utterly deny it,' said she. 'Dr. Grantly has no sort of jurisdiction over me whatsoever. Do you and he forget that I am not altogether alone in the world? Do you forget that I have a father? Dr. Grantly, I believe, always has forgotten it.'

'From you, Mr. Arabin,' she continued, 'I would have listened to advice because I should have expected it to have been given as one friend may advise another; not as a schoolmaster gives an order to a pupil. I might have differed from you; on this matter I should have done so; but had you spoken to me in your usual manner and with your usual freedom I should not have been angry. But now——was it manly of you, Mr. Arabin, to speak of me in this way——, so disrespectful—so—— ? I cannot bring myself to repeat what you said. You must understand what I feel. Was it just of you to speak of me in such a way, and to advise my sister's husband to turn me out of my sister's house, because I chose to know a man of whose doctrine you disapprove ? '

' I have no alternative left to me, Mrs. Bold,' said he, standing with his back to the fire-place, looking down intently at the carpet pattern, and speaking with a slow measured voice, ' but to tell you plainly what did take place between me and Dr. Grantly.'

' Well,' said she, finding that he paused for a moment.

' I am afraid that what I may say may pain you.'

' It cannot well do so more than what you have already done,' said she.

' Dr. Grantly asked me whether I thought it would be prudent for him to receive you in his house as the wife of Mr. Slope, and I told him that I thought it would be imprudent. Believing it to be utterly impossible that Mr. Slope and —— '

' Thank you, Mr. Arabin, that is sufficient. I do not want to know your reasons,' said she, speaking with a terribly calm voice. ' I have shown to this gentleman the common-place civility of a neighbour ; and because I have done so, because I have not indulged against him in all the rancour and hatred which you and Dr. Grantly consider due to all clergymen who do not agree with yourselves, you conclude that I am to marry him ;—or rather you do not conclude so—no rational man could really come to such an outrageous conclusion without better ground ; —you have not thought so—but, as I am in a position in which such an accusation must be peculiarly painful, it is made in order that I may be terrified into hostility against this enemy of yours.'

As she finished speaking, she walked to the drawing-room window and stepped out into the garden. Mr. Arabin was left in the room, still occupied in counting the pattern on the carpet. He had, however, distinctly heard and accurately marked every word that she had spoken. Was it not clear from what she had said, that the archdeacon had been wrong in imputing to her any attachment to Mr. Slope ? Was it not clear that Eleanor was still free to make another choice ? It may seem strange that he should for a moment have had a doubt ; and yet he did doubt. She had not absolutely denied the charge ; she had not expressly said that it was untrue. Mr. Arabin understood little of the nature of a woman's feelings, or he would have known how improbable it was that she should make any clearer declaration than she had done. Few men do understand the nature of a woman's heart, till years have robbed such understanding of its value. And it is well that it should be so, or men would triumph too easily.

Mr. Arabin stood counting the carpet, unhappy, wretchedly unhappy, at the hard words that had been spoken to him ; and yet happy, exquisitely happy, as he thought that after all the woman whom he so regarded was not to become the wife of the man whom he so much disliked. As he stood there he began to be aware that he was himself in love. Forty years had passed over his head, and as yet woman's beauty had never given him an uneasy hour. His present hour was very uneasy.

Not that he remained there for half or a quarter of that time. In spite of what Eleanor had said, Mr. Arabin was, in truth, a manly man. Having ascertained that he loved this woman, and having now reason to believe that she was free to receive his love, at least if she pleased to do so, he followed her into the garden to make such wooing as he could.

He was not long in finding her. She was walking to and fro beneath the avenue of elms that stood in the archdeacon's grounds, skirting the churchyard. What had passed between her and Mr. Arabin, had not, alas, tended to lessen the acerbity of her spirit. She was very angry ; more angry with him than with any one. How could he have so misunderstood her ? She had been so intimate with him, had allowed him such latitude in what he had chosen to say to her, had complied with his ideas, cherished his views, fostered his precepts, cared for his comforts, made much of him in every way in which a pretty woman can make much of an unmarried man without committing herself or her feelings ! She had been doing this, and while she had been doing it he had regarded her as the affianced wife of another man.

As she passed along the avenue, every now and then an unbidden tear would force itself on her cheek, and as she raised her hand to brush it away she stamped with her little foot upon the sward with very spite to think that she had been so treated.

Mr. Arabin was very near to her when she first saw him, and she turned short round and retraced her steps down the avenue, trying to rid her cheeks of all trace of the tell-tale tears. It was a needless endeavour, for Mr. Arabin was in a state of mind that hardly allowed him to observe such trifles. He followed her down the walk, and overtook her just as she reached the end of it.

He had not considered how he would address her; he had not thought what he would say. He had only felt that it was wretchedness to him to quarrel with her, and that it would be happiness to be allowed to love her. And yet he could not lower himself by asking her pardon. He had done her no wrong. He had not calumniated her, not injured her, as she had accused him of doing. He could not confess sins of which he had not been guilty. He could only let the past be past, and ask her as to her and his hopes for the future.

'I hope we are not to part as enemies?' said he.

'There shall be no enmity on my part,' said Eleanor; 'I endeavour to avoid all enmities. It would be a hollow pretence were I to say that there can be true friendship between us after what has just passed. People cannot make their friends of those whom they despise.'

'And am I despised?'

'*I* must have been so before you could have spoken of me as you did. And I was deceived, cruelly deceived. I believed that you thought well of me; I believed that you esteemed me.'

'Thought well of you and esteemed you!' said he. 'In justifying myself before you, I must use stronger words than those.' He paused for a moment, and Eleanor's heart beat with painful violence within her bosom as she waited for him to go on. 'I have esteemed, do esteem you, as I never yet esteemed any woman. Think well of you! I never thought to think so well, so much of any human creature. Speak calumny of you! Insult you! Wilfully injure you! I wish it were my privilege to shield you from calumny, insult, and injury. Calumny! ah, me. 'Twere almost better that it were so. Better than to worship with a sinful worship; sinful and vain also.' And then he walked along beside her, with his hands clasped behind his back, looking down on the grass beneath his feet, and utterly at a loss how to express his meaning. And Eleanor walked beside him determined at least to give him no assistance.

' Ah me ! ' he uttered at last, speaking rather to himself than to her. ' Ah me ! these Plumstead walks were pleasant enough, if one could have but heart's ease ; but without that the dull dead stones of Oxford were far preferable ; and St. Ewold's too ; Mrs. Bold, I am beginning to think that I mistook myself when I came hither. A Romish priest now would have escaped all this. Oh, Father of heaven ! how good for us would it be, if thou couldest vouchsafe to us a certain rule.'

' And have we not a certain rule, Mr. Arabin ? '

' Yes—yes, surely ; ' Lead us not into temptation but deliver us from evil.' But what is temptation ? what is evil ? Is this evil,—is this temptation ? '

Poor Mr. Arabin ! It would not come out of him, that deep true love of his. He could not bring himself to utter it in plain language that would require and demand an answer. He knew not how to say to the woman by his side, ' Since the fact is that you do not love that other man, that you are not to be his wife, can you love me, will you be my wife ? ' These were the words which were in his heart, but with all his sighs he could not draw them to his lips. He would have given anything, everything for power to ask this simple question ; but glib as was his tongue in pulpits and on platforms, now he could not find a word wherewith to express the plain wish of his heart.

And yet Eleanor understood him as thoroughly as though he had declared his passion with all the elegant fluency of a practised Lothario. With a woman's instinct she followed every bend of his mind, as he spoke of the pleasantness of Plumstead and the stones of Oxford, as he alluded to the safety of the Romish priest and the hidden perils of temptation. She knew that it all meant love. She knew that this man at her side, this accomplished scholar, this practised orator, this great polemical combatant, was striving and striving in vain to tell her that his heart was no longer his own.

She knew this, and felt a sort of joy in knowing it ; and

yet she would not come to his aid. He had offended her
deeply, had treated her unworthily, the more unworthily
seeing that he had learnt to love her, and Eleanor could
not bring herself to abandon her revenge. She did not ask
herself whether or no she would ultimately accept his love.
She did not even acknowledge to herself that she now
perceived it with pleasure. At the present moment it did
not touch her heart ; it merely appeased her pride and
flattered her vanity. Mr. Arabin had dared to associate
her name with that of Mr. Slope, and now her spirit was
soothed by finding that he would fain associate it with his
own. And so she walked on beside him inhaling incense,
but giving out no sweetness in return.

' Answer me this,' said Mr. Arabin, stopping suddenly
in his walk, and stepping forward so that he faced his
companion. ' Answer me this one question. You do not
love Mr. Slope ? you do not intend to be his wife ? '

Mr. Arabin certainly did not go the right way to win
such a woman as Eleanor Bold. Just as her wrath was
evaporating, as it was disappearing before the true
warmth of his untold love, he re-kindled it by a most useless repetition of his original sin. Had he known what he
was about he should never have mentioned Mr. Slope's
name before Eleanor Bold, till he had made her all his own.
Then, and not till then, he might have talked of Mr. Slope
with as much triumph as he chose.

' I shall answer no such question,' said she ; ' and what
is more, I must tell you that nothing can justify your
asking it. Good morning ! '

And so saying she stepped proudly across the lawn, and
passing through the drawing-room window joined her
father and sister at lunch in the dining-room. Half an
hour afterwards she was in the carriage, and so she left
Plumstead without again seeing Mr. Arabin.

His walk was long and sad among the sombre trees that
overshadowed the churchyard. He left the archdeacon's
grounds that he might escape attention, and sauntered
among the green hillocks under which lay at rest so many
of the once loving swains and forgotten beauties of
Plumstead. To his ears Eleanor's last words sounded like
a knell never to be reversed. He could not comprehend
that she might be angry with him, indignant with him,

remorseless with him, and yet love him. He could not
make up his mind whether or no Mr. Slope was in truth a
favoured rival. If not, why should she not have answered
his question ?

Poor Mr. Arabin—untaught, illiterate, boorish, ignorant
man ! That at forty years of age you should know so little
of the workings of a woman's heart !

CHAPTER XXXI

THE BISHOP'S LIBRARY

AND thus the pleasant party at Plumstead was broken
up. It had been a very pleasant party as long as they had
all remained in good humour with one another. Mrs.
Grantly had felt her house to be gayer and brighter than
it had been for many a long day, and the archdeacon had
been aware that the month had passed pleasantly without
attributing the pleasure to any other special merits than
those of his own hospitality. Within three or four days
of Eleanor's departure Mr. Harding had also returned,
and Mr. Arabin had gone to Oxford to spend one week
there previous to his settling at the vicarage of St. Ewold's.
He had gone laden with many messages to Dr. Gwynne
touching the iniquity of the doings in Barchester palace,
and the peril in which it was believed the hospital still
stood in spite of the assurances contained in Mr. Slope's
inauspicious letter.

During Eleanor's drive into Barchester she had not
much opportunity of reflecting on Mr. Arabin. She had
been constrained to divert her mind both from his sins
and his love by the necessity of conversing with her sister,
and maintaining the appearance of parting with her on
good terms. When the carriage reached her own door,
and while she was in the act of giving her last kiss to
her sister and nieces, Mary Bold ran out and exclaimed,

'Oh ! Eleanor,—have you heard ?—oh ! Mrs. Grantly,
have you heard what has happened ? The poor dean !'

'Good heavens !' said Mrs. Grantly ; 'what—what has
happened ?'

'This morning at nine he had a fit of apoplexy, and he

has not spoken since. I very much fear that by this time he is no more.'

Mrs. Grantly had been very intimate with the dean, and was therefore much shocked. Eleanor had not known him so well; nevertheless she was sufficiently acquainted with his person and manners to feel startled and grieved also at the tidings she now received. 'I will go at once to the deanery,' said Mrs. Grantly; 'the archdeacon, I am sure, will be there. If there is any news to send you I will let Thomas call before he leaves town.' And so the carriage drove off, leaving Eleanor and her baby with Mary Bold.

Mrs. Grantly had been quite right. The archdeacon was at the deanery. He had come into Barchester that morning by himself, not caring to intrude himself upon Eleanor, and he also immediately on his arrival had heard of the dean's fit. There was, as we have before said, a library or reading room connecting the cathedral with the dean's house. This was generally called the bishop's library, because a certain bishop of Barchester was supposed to have added it to the cathedral. It was built immediately over a portion of the cloisters, and a flight of stairs descended from it into the room in which the cathedral clergymen put their surplices on and off. As it also opened directly into the dean's house, it was the passage through which that dignitary usually went to his public devotions. Who had or had not the right of entry into it, it might be difficult to say; but the people of Barchester believed that it belonged to the dean, and the clergymen of Barchester believed that it belonged to the chapter.

On the morning in question most of the resident clergymen who constituted the chapter, and some few others, were here assembled, and among them as usual the archdeacon towered with high authority. He had heard of the dean's fit before he was over the bridge which led into the town, and had at once come to the well known clerical trysting place. He had been there by eleven o'clock, and had remained ever since. From time to time the medical men who had been called in came through from the deanery into the library, uttered little bulletins, and then returned. There was it appears very little hope of the old man's rallying, indeed no hope of any thing like a final recovery. The only question was whether he must die at once speechless, unconscious, stricken to death by his first heavy fit; or whether by due aid of medical skill he might not be so far brought back to this world as to become conscious of his state, and enabled to address one prayer to his Maker before he was called to meet Him face to face at the judgment seat.

Sir Omicron Pie had been sent for from London. That great man had shown himself a wonderful adept at keeping life still moving within an old man's heart in the case of good old Bishop Grantly, and it might be reasonably expected that he would be equally successful with a dean. In the mean time Dr. Fillgrave and Mr. Rerechild were doing their best; and poor Miss Trefoil sat at the head of her father's bed, longing, as in such cases daughters do long, to be allowed to do something to show her love; if it were only to chafe his feet with her hands, or wait in menial offices on those autocratic doctors; anything so that now in the time of need she might be of use.

The archdeacon alone of the attendant clergy had been admitted for a moment into the sick man's chamber. He had crept in with creaking shoes, had said with smothered voice a word of consolation to the sorrowing daughter, had looked on the distorted face of his old friend with solemn but yet eager scrutinising eye, as though he said in his heart ' and so some day it will probably be with me;' and then having whispered an unmeaning word or two to the doctors, had creaked his way back again into the library.

' He'll never speak again, I fear,' said the archdeacon as he noiselessly closed the door, as though the unconscious dying man, from whom all sense had fled, would have heard in his distant chamber the spring of the lock which was now so carefully handled.

' Indeed! indeed! is he so bad?' said the meagre little prebendary, turning over in his own mind all the probable candidates for the deanery, and wondering whether the archdeacon would think it worth his while to accept it. ' The fit must have been very violent.'

' When a man over seventy has a stroke of apoplexy, it seldom comes very lightly,' said the burly chancellor.

' He was an excellent, sweet-tempered man,' said one of the vicars choral. ' Heaven knows how we shall repair his loss.'

' He was indeed,' said a minor canon ; ' and a great blessing to all those privileged to take a share of the services of our cathedral. I suppose the government will appoint, Mr. Archdeacon. I trust we may have no stranger.'

' We will not talk about his successor,' said the archdeacon, ' while there is yet hope.'

' Oh no, of course not,' said the minor canon. ' It would be exceedingly indecorous ? but——'

' I know of no man,' said the meagre little prebendary, ' who has better interest with the present government than Mr. Slope.'

' Mr. Slope,' said two or three at once almost sotto voce. ' Mr. Slope dean of Barchester ! '

' Pooh ! ' exclaimed the burly chancellor.

' The bishop would do anything for him,' said the little prebendary.

' And so would Mrs. Proudie,' said the vicar choral.

' Pooh ! ' said the chancellor.

The archdeacon had almost turned pale at the idea. What if Mr. Slope should become dean of Barchester ? To be sure there was no adequate ground, indeed no ground at all, for presuming that such a desecration could even be contemplated. But nevertheless it was on the cards. Dr. Proudie had interest with the government, and the man carried as it were Dr. Proudie in his pocket. How should they all conduct themselves if Mr. Slope were to become dean of Barchester ? The bare idea for a moment struck even Dr. Grantly dumb.

' It would certainly not be very pleasant for us to have Mr. Slope at the deanery,' said the little prebendary, chuckling inwardly at the evident consternation which his surmise had created.

' About as pleasant and as probable as having you in the palace,' said the chancellor.

' I should think such an appointment highly improbable,' said the minor canon, ' and, moreover, extremely injudicious. Should not you, Mr. Archdeacon ? '

' I should presume such a thing to be quite out of the question,' said the archdeacon ; ' but at the present moment I am thinking rather of our poor friend who is lying so near us than of Mr. Slope.'

'Of course, of course,' said the vicar choral with a very solemn air ; ' of course you are. So are we all. Poor Dr. Trefoil ; the best of men, but——'

' It's the most comfortable dean's residence in England,' said a second prebendary. ' Fifteen acres in the grounds. It is better than many of the bishops' palaces.'

' And full two thousand a year,' said the meagre doctor.

' It is cut down to 1200*l.*' said the chancellor.

' No,' said the second prebendary. ' It is to be fifteen. A special case was made.'

' No such thing,' said the chancellor.

' You'll find I'm right,' said the prebendary.

' I'm sure I read it in the report,' said the minor canon.

' Nonsense,' said the chancellor. ' They couldn't do it. There were to be no exceptions but London and Durham.'

' And Canterbury and York,' said the vicar choral, modestly.

' What do you say, Grantly ? ' said the meagre little doctor.

' Say about what ? ' said the archdeacon, who had been looking as though he were thinking about his friend the dean, but who had in reality been thinking about Mr. Slope.

' What is the next dean to have, twelve or fifteen ? '

' Twelve,' said the archdeacon authoritatively, thereby putting an end at once to all doubt and dispute among his subordinates as far as that subject was concerned.

' Well, I certainly thought it was fifteen,' said the minor canon.

' Pooh ! ' said the burly chancellor. At this moment the door opened, and in came Dr. Fillgrave.

' How is he ? ' ' Is he conscious ? ' ' Can he speak ? ' ' I hope not dead ? ' ' No worse news, doctor, I trust ? ' ' I hope, I trust, something better, doctor ? ' said half a dozen voices all at once, each in a tone of extremest anxiety. It was pleasant to see how popular the good old dean was among his clergy.

' No change, gentlemen ; not the slightest change—but a telegraphic message has arrived—Sir Omicron Pie will be here by the 9.15 P.M. train. If any man can do any-

thing Sir Omicron Pie will do it. But all that skill can do
has been done.'

'We are sure of that Dr. Fillgrave,' said the archdeacon;
'we are quite sure of that. But yet you know——'

'Oh! quite right,' said the doctor, 'quite right—I
should have done just the same—I advised it at once.
I said to Rerechild at once that with such a life and such
a man, Sir Omicron should be summoned—of course I
knew the expense was nothing—so distinguished, you
know, and so popular. Nevertheless, all that human skill
can do has been done.'

Just at this period Mrs. Grantly's carriage drove into the
close, and the archdeacon went down to confirm the news
which she had heard before.

By the 9.15 P.M. train Sir Omicron Pie did arrive. And
in the course of the night a sort of consciousness returned
to the poor old dean. Whether this was due to Sir Omicron
Pie is a question on which it may be well not to offer an
opinion. Dr. Fillgrave was very clear in his own mind, but
Sir Omicron himself is thought to have differed from that
learned doctor. At any rate Sir Omicron expressed an
opinion that the dean had yet some days to live.

For the eight or ten next days, accordingly, the poor
dean remained in the same state, half conscious and half
comatose, and the attendant clergy began to think that
no new appointment would be necessary for some few
months to come.

CHAPTER XXXII

A NEW CANDIDATE FOR ECCLESIASTICAL HONOURS

THE dean's illness occasioned much mental turmoil in
other places besides the deanery and adjoining library;
and the idea which occurred to the meagre little prebendary
about Mr. Slope did not occur to him alone.

The bishop was sitting listlessly in his study when the
news reached him of the dean's illness. It was brought to
him by Mr. Slope, who of course was not the last person
in Barchester to hear it. It was also not slow in finding
its way to Mrs. Proudie's ears. It may be presumed that
there was not just then much friendly intercourse between

these two rival claimants for his lordship's obedience. Indeed, though living in the same house, they had not met since the stormy interview between them in the bishop's study on the preceding day.

On that occasion Mrs. Proudie had been defeated. That the prestige of continual victory should have been torn from her standards was a subject of great sorrow to that militant lady ; but though defeated, she was not overcome. She felt that she might yet recover her lost ground, that she might yet hurl Mr. Slope down to the dust from which she had picked him, and force her sinning lord to sue for pardon in sackcloth and ashes.

On that memorable day, memorable for his mutiny and rebellion against her high behests, he had carried his way with a high hand, and had really begun to think it possible that the days of his slavery were counted. He had begun to hope that he was now about to enter into a free land, a land delicious with milk which he himself might quaff, and honey which would not tantalise him by being only honey to the eye. When Mrs. Proudie banged the door, as she left his room, he felt himself every inch a bishop. To be sure his spirit had been a little cowed by his chaplain's subsequent lecture ; but on the whole he was highly pleased with himself, and flattered himself that the worst was over. ' Ce n'est que le premier pas qui coûte,' he reflected ; and now that the first step had been so magnanimously taken, all the rest would follow easily.

He met his wife as a matter of course at dinner, where little or nothing was said that could ruffle the bishop's happiness. His daughters and the servants were present and protected him.

He made one or two trifling remarks on the subject of his projected visit to the archbishop, in order to show to all concerned that he intended to have his own way ; and the very servants perceiving the change transferred a little of their reverence from their mistress to their master. All which the master perceived ; and so also did the mistress. But Mrs. Proudie bided her time.

After dinner he returned to his study where Mr. Slope soon found him, and there they had tea together and planned many things. For some few minutes the bishop was really happy ; but as the clock on the chimney piece warned him that the stilly hours of night were drawing on, as he looked at his chamber candlestick and knew that he must use it, his heart sank within him again. He was as a ghost, all whose power of wandering free through these upper regions ceases at cock-crow; or rather he was the opposite of the ghost, for till cock-crow he must again be a serf. And would that be all? Could he trust himself to come down to breakfast a free man in the morning.

He was nearly an hour later than usual, when he betook himself to his rest. Rest! what rest? However, he took a couple of glasses of sherry, and mounted the stairs. Far be it from us to follow him thither. There are some things which no novelist, no historian, should attempt; some few scenes in life's drama which even no poet should dare to paint. Let that which passed between Dr. Proudie and his wife on this night be understood to be among them.

He came down the following morning a sad and thoughtful man. He was attenuated in appearance; one might almost say emaciated. I doubt whether his now grizzled locks had not palpably become more grey than on the preceding evening. At any rate he had aged materially. Years do not make a man old gradually and at an even pace. Look through the world and see if this is not so always, except in those rare cases in which the human being lives and dies without joys and without sorrows, like a vegetable. A man shall be possessed of florid youthful blooming health till, it matters not what age. Thirty— forty—fifty, then comes some nipping frost, some period of agony, that robs the fibres of the body of their succulence, and the hale and hearty man is counted among the old.

He came down and breakfasted alone; Mrs. Proudie being indisposed took her coffee in her bed-room, and her daughters waited upon her there. He ate his breakfast alone, and then, hardly knowing what he did, he betook himself to his usual seat in his study. He tried to solace himself with his coming visit to the archbishop. That effort of his own free will at any rate remained to him as an enduring triumph. But somehow, now that he had achieved it, he did not seem to care so much about it. It was his ambition that had prompted him to take his place

at the archi-episcopal table, and his ambition was now
quite dead within him.

He was thus seated when Mr. Slope made his appearance,
with breathless impatience.

' My lord, the dean is dead.'

' Good heavens ! ' exclaimed the bishop, startled out of
his apathy by an announcement so sad and so sudden.

' He is either dead or now dying. He has had an
apoplectic fit, and I am told that there is not the slightest
hope ; indeed, I do not doubt that by this time he is no
more.'

Bells were rung, and servants were immediately sent to
inquire. In the course of the morning, the bishop, leaning
on his chaplain's arm, himself called at the deanery door.
Mrs. Proudie sent to Miss Trefoil all manner of offers of
assistance. The Miss Proudies sent also, and there was
immense sympathy between the palace and the deanery.
The answer to all inquiries was unvaried. The dean was
just the same ; and Sir Omicron Pie was expected down
by the 9.15 P.M. train.

And then Mr. Slope began to meditate, as others also
had done, as to who might possibly be the new dean ; and
it occurred to him, as it had also occurred to others, that
it might be possible that he should be the new dean himself. And then the question as to the twelve hundred, or
fifteen hundred, or two thousand, ran in his mind, as it
had run through those of the other clergymen in the
cathedral library.

Whether it might be two thousand, or fifteen or twelve
hundred, it would in any case undoubtedly be a great
thing for him, if he could get it. The gratification to his
ambition would be greater even than that of his covetous-
ness. How glorious to out-top the archdeacon in his own
cathedral city ; to sit above prebendaries and canons,
and have the cathedral pulpit and all the cathedral services altogether at his own disposal !

But it might be easier to wish for this than to obtain
it. Mr. Slope, however, was not without some means of
forwarding his views, and he at any rate did not let the
grass grow under his feet. In the first place he thought—
and not vainly—that he could count upon what assistance
the bishop could give him. He immediately changed his

views with regard to his patron; he made up his mind
that if he became dean, he would hand his lordship back
again to his wife's vassalage; and he thought it possible
that his lordship might not be sorry to rid himself of one
of his mentors. Mr. Slope had also taken some steps
towards making his name known to other men in power.
There was a certain chief-commissioner of national schools
who at the present moment was presumed to stand
especially high in the good graces of the government big
wigs, and with him Mr. Slope had contrived to establish
a sort of epistolary intimacy. He thought that he might
safely apply to Sir Nicholas Fitzwhiggin; and he felt
sure that if Sir Nicholas chose to exert himself, the promise of such a piece of preferment would be had for the
asking for.

Then he also had the press at his bidding, or flattered
himself that he had so. The daily Jupiter had taken his
part in a very thorough manner in those polemical contests
of his with Mr. Arabin; he had on more than one occasion
absolutely had an interview with a gentleman on the
staff of that paper, who, if not the editor, was as good as
the editor; and had long been in the habit of writing
telling letters on all manner of ecclesiastical abuses, which
he signed with his initials, and sent to his editorial friend
with private notes signed in his own name. Indeed, he
and Mr. Towers—such was the name of the powerful
gentleman of the press with whom he was connected—
were generally very amiable with each other. Mr. Slope's
little productions were always printed and occasionally
commented upon; and thus, in a small sort of way, he
had become a literary celebrity. This public life had
great charms for him, though it certainly also had its
drawbacks. On one occasion, when speaking in the
presence of reporters, he had failed to uphold and praise
and swear by that special line of conduct which had been
upheld and praised and sworn by in the Jupiter, and then
he had been much surprised and at the moment not a
little irritated to find himself lacerated most unmercifully
by his old ally. He was quizzed and bespattered and
made a fool of, just as though, or rather worse than if, he
had been a constant enemy instead of a constant friend.
He had hitherto not learnt that a man who aspires to be

on the staff of the Jupiter must surrender all individuality.
But ultimately this little castigation had broken no bones
between him and his friend Mr. Towers. Mr. Slope was
one of those who understood the world too well to show
himself angry with such a potentate as the Jupiter. He
had kissed the rod that scourged him, and now thought
that he might fairly look for his reward. He determined
that he would at once let Mr. Towers know that he was
a candidate for the place which was about to become
vacant. More than one piece of preferment had lately
been given away much in accordance with advice tendered
to the government in the columns of the Jupiter.

But it was incumbent on Mr. Slope first to secure the
bishop. He specially felt that it behoved him to do this
before the visit to the archbishop was made. It was really
quite providential that the dean should have fallen ill
just at the very nick of time. If Dr. Proudie could be
instigated to take the matter up warmly, he might manage
a good deal while staying at the archbishop's palace.
Feeling this very strongly Mr. Slope determined to sound
the bishop that very afternoon. He was to start on the
following morning to London, and therefore not a moment
could be lost with safety.

He went into the bishop's study about five o'clock, and
found him still sitting alone. It might have been supposed
that he had hardly moved since the little excitement
occasioned by his walk to the dean's door. He still wore
on his face that dull dead look of half unconscious suffering.
He was doing nothing, reading nothing, thinking of
nothing, but simply gazing on vacancy when Mr. Slope
for the second time that day entered his room.

' Well, Slope,' said he, somewhat impatiently ; for, to
tell the truth, he was not anxious just at present to have
much conversation with Mr. Slope.

' Your lordship will be sorry to hear that as yet the poor
dean has shown no sign of amendment.'

' Oh—ah—hasn't he ? Poor man ! I'm sure I'm very
sorry. I suppose Sir Omicron has not arrived yet ? '

' No ; not till the 9.15 P.M. train.'

' I wonder they didn't have a special. They say Dr.
Trefoil is very rich.'

' Very rich, I believe,' said Mr. Slope. ' But the truth

is, all the doctors in London can do no good; no other
good than to show that every possible care has been
taken. Poor Dr. Trefoil is not long for this world, my lord.'

' I suppose not—I suppose not.'

' Oh no; indeed, his best friends could not wish that
he should outlive such a shock, for his intellects cannot
possibly survive it.'

' Poor man! poor man!' said the bishop.

' It will naturally be a matter of much moment to your
lordship who is to succeed him,' said Mr. Slope. ' It would
be a great thing if you could secure the appointment for
some person of your own way of thinking on important
points. The party hostile to us are very strong here in
Barchester—much too strong.'

' Yes, yes. If poor Dr. Trefoil is to go, it will be a great
thing to get a good man in his place.'

' It will be everything to your lordship to get a man on
whose co-operation you can reckon. Only think what
trouble we might have if Dr. Grantly, or Dr. Hyandry, or
any of that way of thinking, were to get it.'

' It is not very probable that Lord —— will give it to
any of that school; why should he?'

' No. Not probable; certainly not; but it's possible.
Great interest will probably be made. If I might venture
to advise your lordship, I would suggest that you should
discuss the matter with his grace next week. I have no
doubt that your wishes, if made known and backed by
his grace, would be paramount with Lord ——.'

' Well, I don't know that; Lord —— has always been
very kind to me, very kind. But I am unwilling to interfere in such matters unless asked. And indeed if asked,
I don't know whom, at this moment, I should recommend.'

Mr. Slope, even Mr. Slope, felt at the present rather
abashed. He hardly knew how to frame his little request
in language sufficiently modest. He had recognised and
acknowledged to himself the necessity of shocking the
bishop in the first instance by the temerity of his application, and his difficulty was how best to remedy that by
his adroitness and eloquence. ' I doubted myself,' said
he, ' whether your lordship would have any one immediately in your eye, and it is on this account that I venture
to submit to you an idea that I have been turning over

in my own mind. If poor Dr. Trefoil must go, I really
do not see why, with your lordship's assistance, I should
not hold the preferment myself.'

'You!' exclaimed the bishop, in a manner that Mr.
Slope could hardly have considered complimentary.

The ice was now broken, and Mr. Slope became fluent
enough. 'I have been thinking of looking for it. If your
lordship will press the matter on the archbishop, I do not
doubt but I shall succeed. You see I shall be the first to
move, which is a great matter. Then I can count upon
assistance from the public press: my name is known,
I may say, somewhat favourably known to that portion
of the press which is now most influential with the government, and I have friends also in the government. But,
nevertheless, it is to you, my lord, that I look for assistance.
It is from your hands that I would most willingly receive
the benefit. And, which should ever be the chief consideration in such matters, you must know better than any other
person whatsoever what qualifications I possess.'

The bishop sat for a while dumbfounded. Mr. Slope
dean of Barchester! The idea of such a transformation
of character would never have occurred to his own unaided
intellect. At first he went on thinking why, for what
reasons, on what account, Mr. Slope should be dean of
Barchester. But by degrees the direction of his thoughts
changed, and he began to think why, for what reasons,
on what account, Mr. Slope should not be dean of Barchester. As far as he himself, the bishop, was concerned,
he could well spare the services of his chaplain. That
little idea of using Mr. Slope as a counterpoise to his wife
had well nigh evaporated. He had all but acknowledged
the futility of the scheme. If indeed he could have slept
in his chaplain's bed-room instead of his wife's there
might have been something in it. But ————. And
thus as Mr. Slope was speaking, the bishop began to
recognise the idea that that gentleman might become
dean of Barchester without impropriety; not moved,
indeed, by Mr. Slope's eloquence, for he did not follow
the tenor of his speech; but led thereto by his own
cogitations.

'I need not say,' continued Mr. Slope, 'that it would
be my chief desire to act in all matters connected with the

cathedral as far as possible in accordance with your views. I know your lordship so well (and I hope you know me well enough to have the same feelings), that I am satisfied that my being in that position would add materially to your own comfort, and enable you to extend the sphere of your useful influence. As I said before, it is most desirable that there should be but one opinion among the dignitaries of the same diocese. I doubt much whether I would accept such an appointment in any diocese in which I should be constrained to differ much from the bishop. In this case there would be a delightful uniformity of opinion.'

Mr. Slope perfectly well perceived that the bishop did not follow a word that he said, but nevertheless he went on talking. He knew it was necessary that Dr. Proudie should recover from his surprise, and he knew also that he must give him the opportunity of appearing to have been persuaded by argument. So he went on, and produced a multitude of fitting reasons all tending to show that no one on earth could make so good a dean of Barchester as himself, that the government and the public would assuredly coincide in desiring that he, Mr. Slope, should be dean of Barchester; but that for high considerations of ecclesiastical polity it would be especially desirable that this piece of preferment should be so bestowed through the instrumentality of the bishop of the diocese.

' But I really don't know what I could do in the matter,' said the bishop.

' If you would mention it to the archbishop; if you could tell his grace that you consider such an appointment very desirable, that you have it much at heart with a view to putting an end to schism in the diocese; if you did this with your usual energy, you would probably find no difficulty in inducing his grace to promise that he would mention it to Lord ——. Of course you would let the archbishop know that I am not looking for the preferment solely through his intervention; that you do not exactly require him to ask it as a favour; that you expect that I shall get it through other sources, as is indeed the case; but that you are very anxious that his grace should express his approval of such an arrangement to Lord ——'

It ended in the bishop promising to do as he was bid.
Not that he so promised without a stipulation. ' About
that hospital,' he said, in the middle of the conference.
' I was never so troubled in my life ; ' which was about
the truth. ' You haven't spoken to Mr. Harding since
I saw you ? '

Mr. Slope assured his patron that he had not.

' Ah well, then—I think upon the whole it will be
better to let Quiverful have it. It has been half promised
to him, and he has a large family and is very poor. I think
on the whole it will be better to make out the nomination
for Mr. Quiverful.'

' But, my lord,' said Mr. Slope, still thinking that he
was bound to make a fight for his own view on this matter,
and remembering that it still behoved him to maintain
his lately acquired supremacy over Mrs. Proudie, lest he
should fail in his views regarding the deanery,—' but my
lord, I am really much afraid——'

' Remember, Mr. Slope,' said the bishop, ' I can hold
out no sort of hope to you in this matter of succeeding
poor Dr. Trefoil. I will certainly speak to the archbishop,
as you wish it, but I cannot think——'

' Well, my lord,' said Mr. Slope, fully understanding
the bishop, and in his turn interrupting him, ' perhaps
your lordship is right about Mr. Quiverful. I have no
doubt I can easily arrange matters with Mr. Harding, and
I will make out the nomination for your signature as-you
direct.'

' Yes, Slope, I think that will be best ; and you may
be sure that any little that I can do to forward your views
shall be done.'

And so they parted.

Mr. Slope had now much business on his hands. He
had to make his daily visit to the signora. This common
prudence should have now induced him to omit, but he
was infatuated ; and could not bring himself to be commonly prudent. He determined therefore that he would
drink tea at the Stanhopes' ; and he determined also,
or thought that he determined, that having done so he
would go thither no more. He had also to arrange his
matters with Mrs. Bold. He was of opinion that Eleanor
would grace the deanery as perfectly as she would the

chaplain's cottage; and he thought, moreover, that Eleanor's fortune would excellently repair any dilapidations and curtailments in the dean's stipend which might have been made by that ruthless ecclesiastical commission.

Touching Mrs. Bold his hopes now soared high. Mr. Slope was one of that numerous multitude of swains who think that all is fair in love, and he had accordingly not refrained from using the services of Mrs. Bold's own maid. From her he had learnt much of what had taken place at Plumstead; not exactly with truth, for ' the own maid' had not been able to divine the exact truth, but with some sort of similitude to it. He had been told that the archdeacon and Mrs. Grantly and Mr. Harding and Mr. Arabin had all quarrelled with ' missus' for having received a letter from Mr. Slope; that ' missus' had positively refused to give the letter up; that she had received from the archdeacon the option of giving up either Mr. Slope and his letter, or else the society of Plumstead rectory; and that ' missus' had declared with much indignation, that ' she didn't care a straw for the society of Plumstead rectory,' and that she wouldn't give up Mr. Slope for any of them.

Considering the source from whence this came, it was not quite so untrue as might have been expected. It showed pretty plainly what had been the nature of the conversation in the servants' hall; and coupled as it was with the certainty of Eleanor's sudden return, it appeared to Mr. Slope to be so far worthy of credit as to justify him in thinking that the fair widow would in all human probability accept his offer.

All this work was therefore to be done. It was desirable he thought that he should make his offer before it was known that Mr. Quiverful was finally appointed to the hospital. In his letter to Eleanor he had plainly declared that Mr. Harding was to have the appointment. It would be very difficult to explain this away; and were he to write another letter to Eleanor, telling the truth and throwing the blame on the bishop, it would naturally injure him in her estimation. He determined therefore to let that matter disclose itself as it would, and to lose no time in throwing himself at her feet.

Then he had to solicit the assistance of Sir Nicholas

Fitzwhiggin and Mr. Towers, and he went directly from
the bishop's presence to compose his letters to those
gentlemen. As Mr. Slope was esteemed an adept at letter
writing, they shall be given in full.

' (Private.)   ' Palace, Barchester, Sept. 185—.

' My dear Sir Nicholas,—I hope that the intercourse
which has been between us will preclude you from regarding my present application as an intrusion. You cannot
I imagine have yet heard that poor dear old Dr. Trefoil
has been seized with apoplexy. It is a subject of profound
grief to every one in Barchester, for he has always been
an excellent man—excellent as a man and as a clergyman.
He is, however, full of years, and his life could not under
any circumstances have been much longer spared. You
may probably have known him.

' There is, it appears, no probable chance of his recovery.
Sir Omicron Pie is, I believe, at present with him. At
any rate the medical men here have declared that one
or two days more must limit the tether of his mortal
coil. I sincerely trust that his soul may wing its flight
to that haven where it may for ever be at rest and
for ever be happy.

' The bishop has been speaking to me about the preferment, and he is anxious that it should be conferred on
me. I confess that I can hardly venture, at my age, to
look for such advancement; but I am so far encouraged
by his lordship, that I believe I shall be induced to do so.
His lordship goes to —— to-morrow, and is intent on
mentioning the subject to the archbishop.

' I know well how deservedly great is your weight with
the present government. In any matter touching church
preferment you would of course be listened to. Now that
the matter has been put into my head, I am of course
anxious to be successful. If you can assist me by your
good word, you will confer on me one additional favour.

' I had better add, that Lord —— cannot as yet know of
this piece of preferment having fallen in, or rather of its
certainty of falling (for poor dear Dr. Trefoil is past hope).
Should Lord —— first hear it from you, that might probably
be thought to give you a fair claim to express your opinion.

' Of course our grand object is, that we should all be

of one opinion in church matters. This is most desirable
at Barchester ; it is this that makes our good bishop so
anxious about it. You may probably think it expedient
to point this out to Lord —— if it shall be in your power
to oblige me by mentioning the subject to his lordship.

> 'Believe me, my dear Sir Nicholas,
> 'Your most faithful servant,
> 'OBADIAH SLOPE.'

His letter to Mr. Towers was written in quite a different
strain. Mr. Slope conceived that he completely understood
the difference in character and position of the two men
whom he addressed. He knew that for such a man as
Sir Nicholas Fitzwhiggin a little flummery was necessary,
and that it might be of the easy everyday description.
Accordingly his letter to Sir Nicholas was written *currente
calamo*, with very little trouble. But to such a man as
Mr. Towers it was not so easy to write a letter that should
be effective and yet not offensive, that should carry its
point without undue interference. It was not difficult
to flatter Dr. Proudie or Sir Nicholas Fitzwhiggin, but
very difficult to flatter Mr. Towers without letting the
flattery declare itself. This, however, had to be done.
Moreover, this letter must, in appearance at least, be
written without effort, and be fluent, unconstrained, and
demonstrative of no doubt or fear on the part of the
writer. Therefore the epistle to Mr. Towers was studied,
and recopied, and elaborated at the cost of so many
minutes, that Mr. Slope had hardly time to dress himself
and reach Dr. Stanhope's that evening.

When despatched it ran as follows :—

'(Private.)   'Barchester. Sept. 185—.'

(He purposely omitted any allusion to the 'palace,'
thinking that Mr. Towers might not like it. A great man,
he remembered, had been once much condemned for
dating a letter from Windsor Castle.)

'My dear Sir,—We were all a good deal shocked here
this morning by hearing that poor old Dean Trefoil had
been stricken with apoplexy. The fit took him about
9 A.M. I am writing now to save the post, and he is still
alive, but past all hope, or possibility I believe, of living.

Sir Omicron Pie is here, or will be very shortly; but all
that even Sir Omicron can do, is to ratify the sentence of
his less distinguished brethren that nothing can be done.
Poor Dr. Trefoil's race on this side the grave is run. I do
not know whether you knew him. He was a good, quiet,
charitable man, of the old school of course, as any clergyman over seventy years of age must necessarily be.

' But I do not write merely with the object of sending
you such news as this: doubtless some one of your
Mercuries will have seen and heard and reported so much;
I write, as you usually do yourself, rather with a view to
the future than to the past.

' Rumour is already rife here as to Dr. Trefoil's successor,
and among those named as possible future deans your
humble servant is, I believe, not the least frequently
spoken of; in short I am looking for the preferment.
You may probably know that since Bishop Proudie came
to this diocese I have exerted myself here a good deal;
and I may certainly say not without some success. He
and I are nearly always of the same opinion on points of
doctrine as well as church discipline, and therefore I have
had, as his confidential chaplain, very much in my own
hands; but I confess to you that I have a higher ambition
than to remain the chaplain of any bishop.

' There are no positions in which more energy is now
needed than those of our deans. The whole of our enormous cathedral establishments have been allowed to go
to sleep,—nay, they are all but dead and ready for the
sepulchre! And yet of what prodigious moment they
might be made, if, as was intended, they were so managed
as to lead the way and show an example for all our
parochial clergy!

' The bishop here is most anxious for my success;
indeed, he goes to-morrow to press the matter on the
archbishop. I believe also I may count on the support
of at least one most effective member of the government.
But I confess that the support of the Jupiter, if I be
thought worthy of it, would be more gratifying to me
than any other; more gratifying if by it I should be
successful; and more gratifying also, if, although so
supported, I should be unsuccessful.

' The time has, in fact, come in which no government

can venture to fill up the high places of the Church in defiance of the public press. The age of honourable bishops and noble deans has gone by ; and any clergyman however humbly born can now hope for success, if his industry, talent, and character be sufficient to call forth the manifest opinion of the public in his favour.

' At the present moment we all feel that any counsel given in such matters by the Jupiter has the greatest weight—is, indeed, generally followed ; and we feel also—I am speaking of clergymen of my own age and standing—that it should be so. There can be no patron less interested than the Jupiter, and none that more thoroughly understands the wants of the people.

' I am sure you will not suspect me of asking from you any support which the paper with which you are connected cannot conscientiously give me. My object in writing is to let you know that I am a candidate for the appointment. It is for you to judge whether or no you can assist my views. I should not, of course, have written to you on such a matter had I not believed (and I have had good reason so to believe) that the Jupiter approves of my views on ecclesiastical polity.

' The bishop expresses a fear that I may be considered too young for such a station, my age being thirty-six. I cannot think that at the present day any hesitation need be felt on such a point. The public has lost its love for antiquated servants. If a man will ever be fit to do good work he will be fit at thirty-six years of age.

'Believe me very faithfully yours,
'OBADIAH SLOPE.

'T. TOWERS, ESQ
'———Court,
'Middle Temple.'

Having thus exerted himself, Mr. Slope posted his letters, and passed the remainder of the evening at the feet of his mistress.

Mr. Slope will be accused of deceit in his mode of canvassing. It will be said that he lied in the application he made to each of his three patrons. I believe it must be owned that he did so. He could not hesitate on account of his youth, and yet be quite assured that he

was not too young. He could not count chiefly on the
bishop's support, and chiefly also on that of the newspaper.
He did not think that the bishop was going to —— to press
the matter on the archbishop. It must be owned that in
his canvassing Mr. Slope was as false as he well could be.

Let it, however, be asked of those who are conversant
with such matters, whether he was more false than men
usually are on such occasions. We English gentlemen
hate the name of a lie; but how often do we find public
men who believe each other's words ?

CHAPTER XXXIII

MRS. PROUDIE VICTRIX

THE next week passed over at Barchester with much
apparent tranquillity. The hearts, however, of some of
the inhabitants were not so tranquil as the streets of the
city. The poor old dean still continued to live, just as
Sir Omicron Pie had prophesied that he would do, much
to the amazement, and some thought disgust, of Dr.
Fillgrave. The bishop still remained away. He had
stayed a day or two in town, and had also remained
longer at the archbishop's than he had intended. Mr.
Slope had as yet received no line in answer to either of
his letters; but he had learnt the cause of this. Sir
Nicholas was stalking a deer, or attending the Queen, in
the Highlands; and even the indefatigable Mr. Towers
had stolen an autumn holiday, and had made one of the
yearly tribe who now ascend Mont Blanc. Mr. Slope
learnt that he was not expected back till the last day of
September.

Mrs. Bold was thrown much with the Stanhopes, of
whom she became fonder and fonder. If asked, she would
have said that Charlotte Stanhope was her especial friend,
and so she would have thought. But, to tell the truth,
she liked Bertie nearly as well; she had no more idea of
regarding him as a lover than she would have had of
looking at a big tame dog in such a light. Bertie had
become very intimate with her, and made little speeches
to her, and said little things of a sort very different from

the speeches and sayings of other men. But then this was almost always done before his sisters; and he, with his long silken beard, his light blue eyes and strange dress, was so unlike other men. She admitted him to a kind of familiarity which she had never known with any one else, and of which she by no means understood the danger. She blushed once at finding that she had called him Bertie, and on the same day only barely remembered her position in time to check herself from playing upon him some personal practical joke to which she was instigated by Charlotte.

In all this Eleanor was perfectly innocent, and Bertie Stanhope could hardly be called guilty. But every familiarity into which Eleanor was entrapped was deliberately planned by his sister. She knew well how to play her game, and played it without mercy; she knew, none so well, what was her brother's character, and she would have handed over to him the young widow, and the young widow's money, and the money of the widow's child, without remorse. With her pretended friendship and warm cordiality, she strove to connect Eleanor so closely with her brother as to make it impossible that she should go back even if she wished it. But Charlotte Stanhope knew really nothing of Eleanor's character; did not even understand that there were such characters. She did not comprehend that a young and pretty woman could be playful and familiar with a man such as Bertie Stanhope, and yet have no idea in her head, no feeling in her heart that she would have been ashamed to own to all the world. Charlotte Stanhope did not in the least conceive that her new friend was a woman whom nothing could entrap into an inconsiderate marriage, whose mind would have revolted from the slightest impropriety had she been aware that any impropriety existed.

Miss Stanhope, however, had tact enough to make herself and her father's house very agreeable to Mrs. Bold. There was with them all an absence of stiffness and formality which was peculiarly agreeable to Eleanor after the great dose of clerical arrogance which she had lately been constrained to take. She played chess with them, walked with them, and drank tea with them; studied or pretended to study astronomy; assisted them in writing stories in rhyme, in turning prose tragedy into comic verse, or comic stories into would-be tragic poetry. She had no idea before that she had any such talents. She had not conceived the possibility of her doing such things as she now did. She found with the Stanhopes new amusements and employments, new pursuits, which in themselves could not be wrong, and which were exceedingly alluring.

Is it not a pity that people who are bright and clever should so often be exceedingly improper ? and that those who are never improper should so often be dull and heavy ? Now Charlotte Stanhope was always bright, and never heavy : but her propriety was doubtful.

But during all this time Eleanor by no means forgot Mr. Arabin, nor did she forget Mr. Slope. She had parted from Mr. Arabin in her anger. She was still angry at what she regarded as his impertinent interference ; but nevertheless she looked forward to meeting him again, and also looked forward to forgiving him. The words that Mr. Arabin had uttered still sounded in her ears. She knew that if not intended for a declaration of love, they did signify that he loved her ; and she felt also that if he ever did make such a declaration, it might be that she should not receive it unkindly. She was still angry with him, very angry with him ; so angry that she would bite her lip and stamp her foot as she thought of what he had said and done. But nevertheless she yearned to let him know that he was forgiven ; all that she required was that he should own that he had sinned.

She was to meet him at Ullathorne on the last day of the present month. Miss Thorne had invited all the country round to a breakfast on the lawn. There were to be tents, and archery, and dancing for the ladies on the lawn, and for the swains and girls in the paddock. There were to be fiddlers and fifers, races for the boys, poles to be climbed, ditches full of water to be jumped over, horse-collars to be grinned through (this latter amusement was an addition of the stewards, and not arranged by Miss Thorne in the original programme), and every game to be played which, in a long course of reading, Miss Thorne could ascertain to have been played in the good days of Queen Elizabeth. Everything of more

modern growth was to be tabooed, if possible. On one
subject Miss Thorne was very unhappy. She had been
turning in her mind the matter of a bull-ring, but could
not succeed in making anything of it. She would not for
the world have done, or allowed to be done, anything that
was cruel; as to the promoting the torture of a bull for
the amusement of her young neighbours, it need hardly
be said that Miss Thorne would be the last to think of it.
And yet there was something so charming in the name.
A bull-ring, however, without a bull would only be a
memento of the decadence of the times, and she felt herself
constrained to abandon the idea. Quintains, however,
she was determined to have, and had poles and swivels
and bags of flour prepared accordingly. She would no
doubt have been anxious for something small in the way
of a tournament; but, as she said to her brother, that had
been tried, and the age had proved itself too decidedly
inferior to its fore-runners to admit of such a pastime.
Mr. Thorne did not seem to participate much in her regret,
feeling perhaps that a full suit of chain-armour would
have added but little to his own personal comfort.

This party at Ullathorne had been planned in the first
place as a sort of welcoming to Mr. Arabin on his entrance
into St. Ewold's parsonage; an intended harvest-home
gala for the labourers and their wives and children had
subsequently been amalgamated with it, and thus it had
grown to its present dimensions. All the Plumstead
party had of course been asked, and at the time of the
invitation Eleanor had intended to have gone with her
sister. Now her plans were altered, and she was going
with the Stanhopes. The Proudies were also to be there;
and as Mr. Slope had not been included in the invitation to the palace, the signora, whose impudence never
deserted her, asked permission of Miss Thorne to bring
him.

This permission Miss Thorne gave, having no other
alternative; but she did so with a trembling heart, fearing
Mr. Arabin would be offended. Immediately on his
return she apologised, almost with tears, so dire an enmity
was presumed to rage between the two gentlemen. But
Mr. Arabin comforted her by an assurance that he should
meet Mr. Slope with the greatest pleasure imaginable

and made her promise that she would introduce them to each other.

But this triumph of Mr. Slope's was not so agreeable to Eleanor, who since her return to Barchester had done her best to avoid him. She would not give way to the Plumstead folk when they so ungenerously accused her of being in love with this odious man; but, nevertheless, knowing that she was so accused, she was fully alive to the expediency of keeping out of his way and dropping him by degrees. She had seen very little of him since her return. Her servant had been instructed to say to all visitors that she was out. She could not bring herself to specify Mr. Slope particularly, and in order to avoid him she had thus debarred herself from all her friends. She had excepted Charlotte Stanhope, and by degrees a few others also. Once she had met him at the Stanhopes'; but, as a rule, Mr. Slope's visits there were made in the morning, and hers in the evening. On that one occasion Charlotte had managed to preserve her from any annoyance. This was very good-natured on the part of Charlotte, as Eleanor thought, and also very sharp-witted, as Eleanor had told her friend nothing of her reasons for wishing to avoid that gentleman. The fact, however, was, that Charlotte had learnt from her sister that Mr. Slope would probably put himself forward as a suitor for the widow's hand, and she was consequently sufficiently alive to the expediency of guarding Bertie's future wife from any danger in that quarter.

Nevertheless the Stanhopes were pledged to take Mr. Slope with them to Ullathorne. An arrangement was therefore necessarily made, which was very disagreeable to Eleanor. Dr. Stanhope, with herself, Charlotte, and Mr. Slope, were to go together, and Bertie was to follow with his sister Madeline. It was clearly visible by Eleanor's face that this assortment was very disagreeable to her; and Charlotte, who was much encouraged thereby in her own little plan, made a thousand apologies.

'I see you don't like it, my dear,' said she, 'but we could not manage otherwise. Bertie would give his eyes to go with you, but Madeline cannot possibly go without him. Nor could we possibly put Mr. Slope and Madeline in the same carriage without any one else. They'd both

be ruined for ever, you know, and not admitted inside
Ullathorne gates, I should imagine, after such an impropriety.'

' Of course that wouldn't do,' said Eleanor ; ' but
couldn't I go in the carriage with the signora and your
brother ? '

' Impossible ! ' said Charlotte. ' When she is there,
there is only room for two.' The signora, in truth, did
not care to do her travelling in the presence of strangers.

' Well, then,' said Eleanor, ' you are all so kind, Charlotte,
and so good to me, that I am sure you won't be offended ;
but I think I'll not go at all.'

' Not go at all !—what nonsense !—indeed you shall.'
It had been absolutely determined in family council that
Bertie should propose on that very occasion.

' Or I can take a fly,' said Eleanor. ' You know I am
not embarrassed by so many difficulties as you young
ladies ; I can go alone.'

' Nonsense ! my dear.   Don't think of such a thing ;
after all it is only for an hour or so ; and, to tell the truth,
I don't know what it is you dislike so. I thought you and
Mr. Slope were great friends. What is it you dislike ? '

' Oh ! nothing particular,' said Eleanor ; ' only I thought
it would be a family party.'

' Of course it would be much nicer, much more snug,
if Bertie could go with us.   It is he that is badly treated.
I can assure you he is much more afraid of Mr. Slope than
you are.   But you see Madeline cannot go out without
him,—and she, poor creature, goes out so seldom ! I am
sure you don't begrudge her this, though her vagary does
knock about our own party a little.'

Of course Eleanor made a thousand protestations, and
uttered a thousand hopes that Madeline would enjoy
herself. And of course she had to give way, and undertake
to go in the carriage with Mr. Slope. In fact, she was
driven either to do this, or to explain why she would not
do so. Now she could not bring herself to explain to
Charlotte Stanhope all that had passed at Plumstead.

But it was to her a sore necessity. She thought of a
thousand little schemes for avoiding it ; she would plead
illness, and not go at all ; she would persuade Mary Bold
to go although not asked, and then make a necessity of

having a carriage of her own to take her sister-in-law; anything, in fact, she could do rather than be seen by Mr. Arabin getting out of the same carriage with Mr. Slope. However, when the momentous morning came she had no scheme matured, and then Mr. Slope handed her into Dr. Stanhope's carriage, and following her steps, sat opposite to her.

The bishop returned on the eve of the Ullathorne party, and was received at home with radiant smiles by the partner of all his cares. On his arrival he crept up to his dressing-room with somewhat of a palpitating heart; he had overstayed his allotted time by three days, and was not without much fear of penalties. Nothing, however, could be more affectionately cordial than the greeting he received : the girls came out and kissed him in a manner that was quite soothing to his spirit; and Mrs. Proudie, 'albeit, unused to the melting mood,' squeezed him in her arms, and almost in words called him her dear, darling, good, pet, little bishop. All this was a very pleasant surprise.

Mrs. Proudie had somewhat changed her tactics; not that she had seen any cause to disapprove of her former line of conduct, but she had now brought matters to such a point that she calculated that she might safely do so. She had got the better of Mr. Slope, and she now thought well to show her husband that when allowed to get the better of everybody, when obeyed by him and permitted to rule over others, she would take care that he should have his reward. Mr. Slope had not a chance against her; not only could she stun the poor bishop by her midnight anger, but she could assuage and soothe him, if she so willed, by daily indulgences. She could furnish his room for him, turn him out as smart a bishop as any on the bench, give him good dinners, warm fires, and an easy life; all this she would do if he would but be quietly obedient. But if not —— ! To speak sooth, however, his sufferings on that dreadful night had been so poignant, as to leave him little spirit for further rebellion.

As soon as he had dressed himself she returned to his room. ' I hope you enjoyed yourself at ——' said she, seating herself on one side of the fire while he remained in his arm-chair on the other, stroking the calves of his

legs. It was the first time he had had a fire in his room
since the summer, and it pleased him; for the good
bishop loved to be warm and cozy. Yes, he said, he had
enjoyed himself very much. Nothing could be more
polite than the archbishop; and Mrs. Archbishop had
been equally charming.

Mrs. Proudie was delighted to hear it; nothing, she
declared, pleased her so much as to think

> Her bairn respectit like the lave.

She did not put it precisely in these words, but what she
said came to the same thing; and then, having petted
and fondled her little man sufficiently, she proceeded
to business.

'The poor dean is still alive,' said she.

'So I hear, so I hear,' said the bishop. 'I'll go to the
deanery directly after breakfast to-morrow.'

'We are going to this party at Ullathorne to-morrow
morning, my dear; we must be there early, you know,—
by twelve o'clock I suppose.'

'Oh,—ah!' said the bishop; 'then I'll certainly call
the next day.'

'Was much said about it at,——?' asked Mrs. Proudie.

'About what?' said the bishop.

'Filling up the dean's place,' said Mrs. Proudie. As
she spoke a spark of the wonted fire returned to her eye,
and the bishop felt himself to be a little less comfortable
than before.

'Filling up the dean's place; that is, if the dean
dies?—very little, my dear. It was mentioned, just
mentioned.'

'And what did you say about it, bishop?'

'Why, I said that I thought that if, that is, should—
should the dean die, that is, I said I thought——' As he
went on stammering and floundering, he saw that his
wife's eye was fixed sternly on him. Why should he
encounter such evil for a man whom he loved so slightly
as Mr. Slope? Why should he give up his enjoyments
and his ease, and such dignity as might be allowed to
him, to fight a losing battle for a chaplain? The chaplain
after all, if successful, would be as great a tyrant as his
wife. Why fight at all? why contend? why be uneasy?

From that moment he determined to fling Mr. Slope to
the winds, and take the goods the gods provided.

' I am told,' said Mrs. Proudie, speaking very slowly,
' that Mr. Slope is looking to be the new dean.'

' Yes,—certainly, I believe he is,' said the bishop.

' And what does the archbishop say about that ? '
asked Mrs. Proudie.

' Well, my dear, to tell the truth, I promised Mr. Slope
to speak to the archbishop. Mr. Slope spoke to me about
it. It is very arrogant of him, I must say,—but that is
nothing to me.'

' Arrogant ! ' said Mrs. Proudie ; ' it is the most impudent piece of pretension I ever heard of in my life. Mr.
Slope dean of Barchester, indeed ! And what did you do
in the matter, bishop ? '

' Why, my dear, I did speak to the archbishop.'

' You don't mean to tell me,' said Mrs. Proudie, ' that
you are going to make yourself ridiculous by lending
your name to such a preposterous attempt as this ? Mr.
Slope dean of Barchester, indeed ! ' And she tossed her
head, and put her arms a-kimbo, with an air of confident
defiance that made her husband quite sure that Mr. Slope
never would be Dean of Barchester. In truth, Mrs.
Proudie was all but invincible ; had she married Petruchio,
it may be doubted whether that arch wife-tamer would
have been able to keep her legs out of those garments
which are presumed by men to be peculiarly unfitted for
feminine use.

' It is preposterous, my dear.'

' Then why have you endeavoured to assist him ? '

' Why,—my dear, I haven't assisted him—much.'

' But why have you done it at all ? why have you mixed
your name up in any thing so ridiculous ? What was it
you did say to the archbishop ? '

' Why, I just did mention it ; I just did say that—that
in the event of the poor dean's death, Mr. Slope would—
would——'

' Would what ? '

' I forget how I put it,—would take it if he could get it ;
something of that sort. I didn't say much more than that.'

' You shouldn't have said anything at all. And what
did the archbishop say ? '

' He didn't say anything; he just bowed and rubbed his hands. Somebody else came up at the moment, and as we were discussing the new parochial universal school committee, the matter of the new dean dropped; after that I didn't think it wise to renew it.'

' Renew it! I am very sorry you ever mentioned it. What will the archbishop think of you ? '

' You may be sure, my dear, the archbishop thought very little about it.'

' But why did you think about it, bishop ? how could you think of making such a creature as that Dean of Barchester ?—Dean of Barchester ! I suppose he'll be looking for a bishopric some of these days—a man that hardly knows who his own father was; a man that I found without bread to his mouth, or a coat to his back. Dean of Barchester, indeed ! I'll dean him.'

Mrs. Proudie considered herself to be in politics a pure Whig; all her family belonged to the Whig party. Now among all ranks of Englishmen and Englishwomen (Mrs. Proudie should, I think, be ranked among the former, on the score of her great strength of mind), no one is so hostile to lowly born pretenders to high station as the pure Whig.

The bishop thought it necessary to exculpate himself. ' Why, my dear,' said he, ' it appeared to me that you and Mr. Slope did not get on quite so well as you used to do.'

' Get on ! ' said Mrs. Proudie, moving her foot uneasily on the hearth-rug, and compressing her lips in a manner that betokened much danger to the subject of their discourse.

' I began to find that he was objectionable to you,'— Mrs. Proudie's foot worked on the hearth-rug with great rapidity,—' and that you would be more comfortable if he was out of the palace,'—Mrs. Proudie smiled, as a hyena may probably smile before he begins his laugh,— ' and therefore I thought that if he got this place, and so ceased to be my chaplain, you might be pleased at such an arrangement.'

And then the hyena laughed out. Pleased at such an arrangement ! pleased at having her enemy converted into a dean with twelve hundred a year ! Medea, when she describes the customs of her native country (I am quoting from Robson's edition), assures her astonished auditor that in her land captives, when taken, are eaten.

'You pardon them?' says Medea. 'We do indeed,' says the mild Grecian. 'We eat them!' says she of Colchis, with terrific energy. Mrs. Proudie was the Medea of Barchester; she had no idea of not eating Mr. Slope. Pardon him! merely get rid of him! make a dean of him! It was not so they did with their captives in her country, among people of her sort! Mr. Slope had no such mercy to expect; she would pick him to the very last bone.

'Oh, yes, my dear, of course he'll cease to be your chaplain,' said she. 'After what has passed, that must be a matter of course. I couldn't for a moment think of living in the same house with such a man. Besides, he has shown himself quite unfit for such a situation; making broils and quarrels among the clergy, getting you, my dear, into scrapes, and taking upon himself as though he were as good as bishop himself. Of course he'll go. But because he leaves the palace, that is no reason why he should get into the deanery.'

'Oh, of course not!' said the bishop; 'but to save appearances you know, my dear——'

'I don't want to save appearances; I want Mr. Slope to appear just what he is—a false, designing, mean, intriguing man. I have my eye on him; he little knows what I see. He is misconducting himself in the most disgraceful way with that lame Italian woman. That family is a disgrace to Barchester, and Mr. Slope is a disgrace to Barchester! If he doesn't look well to it, he'll have his gown stripped off his back instead of having a dean's hat on his head. Dean, indeed! The man has gone mad with arrogance.'

The bishop said nothing further to excuse either himself or his chaplain, and having shown himself passive and docile was again taken into favour. They soon went to dinner, and he spent the pleasantest evening he had had in his own house for a long time. His daughter played and sang to him as he sipped his coffee and read his newspaper, and Mrs. Proudie asked good-natured little questions about the archbishop; and then he went happily to bed, and slept as quietly as though Mrs. Proudie had been Griselda herself. While shaving himself in the morning and preparing for the festivities of Ullathorne, he fully resolved to run no more tilts against a warrior so fully armed at all points as was Mrs. Proudie.

CHAPTER XXXIV

OXFORD—THE MASTER AND TUTOR OF LAZARUS

MR. ARABIN, as we have said, had but a sad walk of it under the trees of Plumstead churchyard. He did not appear to any of the family till dinner time, and then he seemed, as far as their judgment went, to be quite himself. He had, as was his wont, asked himself a great many questions, and given himself a great many answers; and the upshot of this was that he had set himself down for an ass. He had determined that he was much too old and much too rusty to commence the manœuvres of love-making; that he had let the time slip through his hands which should have been used for such purposes; and that now he must lie on his bed as he had made it. Then he asked himself whether in truth he did love this woman; and he answered himself, not without a long struggle, but at last honestly, that he certainly did love her. He then asked himself whether he did not also love her money; and he again answered himself that he did so. But here he did not answer honestly. It was and ever had been his weakness to look for impure motives for his own con- duct. No doubt, circumstanced as he was, with a small living and a fellowship, accustomed as he had been to collegiate luxuries and expensive comforts, he might have hesitated to marry a penniless woman had he felt ever so strong a predilection for the woman herself; no doubt Eleanor's fortune put all such difficulties out of the question; but it was equally without doubt that his love for her had crept upon him without the slightest idea on his part that he could ever benefit his own con- dition by sharing her wealth.

When he had stood on the hearth-rug, counting the pattern, and counting also the future chances of his own life, the remembrances of Mrs. Bold's comfortable income had not certainly damped his first assured feeling of love for her. And why should it have done so? Need it have done so with the purest of men? Be that as it may, Mr. Arabin decided against himself; he decided that it had done so in his case, and that he was not the purest of men.

He also decided, which was more to his purpose, that Eleanor did not care a straw for him, and that very probably she did care a straw for his rival. Then he made up his mind not to think of her any more, and went on thinking of her till he was almost in a state to drown himself in the little brook which ran at the bottom of the archdeacon's grounds.

And ever and again his mind would revert to the Signora Neroni, and he would make comparisons between her and Eleanor Bold, not always in favour of the latter. The signora had listened to him, and flattered him, and believed in him ; at least she had told him so. Mrs. Bold had also listened to him, but had never flattered him ; had not always believed in him : and now had broken from him in violent rage. The signora, too, was the more lovely woman of the two, and had also the additional attraction of her affliction ; for to him it was an attraction.

But he never could have loved the Signora Neroni as he felt that he now loved Eleanor ! and so he flung stones into the brook, instead of flinging in himself, and sat down on its margin as sad a gentleman as you shall meet in a summer's day.

He heard the dinner-bell ring from the churchyard, and he knew that it was time to recover his self-possession. He felt that he was disgracing himself in his own eyes, that he had been idling his time and neglecting the high duties which he had taken upon himself to perform. He should have spent this afternoon among the poor at St. Ewold's, instead of wandering about at Plumstead, an ancient love-lorn swain, dejected and sighing, full of imaginary sorrows and Wertherian grief. He was thoroughly ashamed of himself, and determined to lose no time in retrieving his character, so damaged in his own eyes. Thus when he appeared at dinner he was as animated as ever, and was the author of most of the conversation which graced the archdeacon's board on that evening. Mr. Harding was ill at ease and sick at heart, and did not care to appear more comfortable than he really was ; what little he did say was said to his daughter. He thought that the archdeacon and Mr. Arabin had leagued together against Eleanor's comfort ; and his wish now was to break away from the pair, and undergo in his Barchester lodgings whatever Fate had in store for him. He hated the name of the hospital; his attempt to regain his lost inheritance there had brought upon him so much suffering. As far as he was concerned, Mr. Quiverful was now welcome to the place.

And the archdeacon was not very lively. The poor dean's illness was of course discussed in the first place. Dr. Grantly did not mention Mr. Slope's name in connexion with the expected event of Dr. Trefoil's death; he did not wish to say anything about Mr. Slope just at present, nor did he wish to make known his sad surmises; but the idea that his enemy might possibly become Dean of Barchester made him very gloomy. Should such an event take place, such a dire catastrophe come about, there would be an end to his life as far as his life was connected with the city of Barchester. He must give up all his old haunts, all his old habits, and live quietly as a retired rector at Plumstead. It had been a severe trial for him to have Dr. Proudie in the palace; but with Mr. Slope also in the deanery, he felt that he should be unable to draw his breath in Barchester close.

Thus it came to pass that in spite of the sorrow at his heart, Mr. Arabin was apparently the gayest of the party. Both Mr. Harding and Mrs. Grantly were in a slight degree angry with him on account of his want of gloom. To the one it appeared as though he were triumphing at Eleanor's banishment, and to the other that he was not affected as he should have been by all the sad circumstances of the day, Eleanor's obstinacy, Mr. Slope's success, and the poor dean's apoplexy. And so they were all at cross purposes.

Mr. Harding left the room almost together with the ladies, and then the archdeacon opened his heart to Mr. Arabin. He still harped upon the hospital. 'What did that fellow mean,' said he, 'by saying in his letter to Mrs. Bold, that if Mr. Harding would call on the bishop it would be all right? Of course I would not be guided by anything he might say; but still it may be well that Mr. Harding should see the bishop. It would be foolish to let the thing slip through our fingers because Mrs. Bold is determined to make a fool of herself.'

Mr. Arabin hinted that he was not quite so sure that

Mrs. Bold would make a fool of herself. He said that he
was not convinced that she did regard Mr. Slope so warmly
as she was supposed to do. The archdeacon questioned
and cross-questioned him about this, but elicited nothing;
and at last remained firm in his own conviction that he
was destined, *malgré lui*, to be the brother-in-law of Mr.
Slope. Mr. Arabin strongly advised that Mr. Harding
should take no step regarding the hospital in connexion
with, or in consequence of, Mr. Slope's letter. ' If the
bishop really means to confer the appointment on Mr.
Harding,' argued Mr. Arabin, ' he will take care to let
him have some other intimation than a message conveyed
through a letter to a lady. Were Mr. Harding to present
himself at the palace he might merely be playing Mr.
Slope's game;' and thus it was settled that nothing
should be done till the great Dr. Gwynne's arrival, or at
any rate without that potentate's sanction.

It was droll to observe how these men talked of Mr.
Harding as though he were a puppet, and planned their
intrigues and small ecclesiastical manœuvres in reference
to Mr. Harding's future position, without dreaming of
taking him into their confidence. There was a comfortable
house and income in question, and it was very desirable,
and certainly very just, that Mr. Harding should have
them; but that, at present, was not the main point;
it was expedient to beat the bishop, and if possible to
smash Mr. Slope. Mr. Slope had set up, or was supposed
to have set up, a rival candidate. Of all things the most
desirable would have been to have had Mr. Quiverful's
appointment published to the public, and then annulled
by the clamour of an indignant world, loud in the defence
of Mr. Harding's rights. But of such an event the chance
was small; a slight fraction only of the world would be
indignant, and that fraction would be one not accustomed
to loud speaking. And then the preferment had in a sort
of way been offered to Mr. Harding, and had in a sort of
way been refused by him.

Mr. Slope's wicked, cunning hand had been peculiarly
conspicuous in the way in which this had been brought
to pass, and it was the success of Mr. Slope's cunning which
was so painfully grating to the feelings of the archdeacon.
That which of all things he most dreaded was that he

should be out-generalled by Mr. Slope : and just at present
it appeared probable that Mr. Slope would turn his flank,
steal a march on him, cut off his provisions, carry his strong
town by a *coup de main*, and at last beat him thoroughly
in a regular pitched battle. The archdeacon felt that
his flank had been turned when desired to wait on Mr. Slope
instead of the bishop, that a march had been stolen when
Mr. Harding was induced to refuse the bishop's offer, that
his provisions would be cut off when Mr. Quiverful got
the hospital, that Eleanor was the strong town doomed
to be taken, and that Mr. Slope, as Dean of Barchester,
would be regarded by all the world as the conqueror in
the final conflict.

Dr. Gwynne was the *Deus ex machinâ* who was to come
down upon the Barchester stage, and bring about deliver-
ance from these terrible evils. But how can melodramatic
dénouements be properly brought about, how can vice and
Mr. Slope be punished, and virtue and the archdeacon be
rewarded, while the avenging god is laid up with the
gout ? In the mean time evil may be triumphant, and
poor innocence, transfixed to the earth by an arrow from
Dr. Proudie's quiver, may lie dead upon the ground, not
to be resuscitated even by Dr. Gwynne.

Two or three days after Eleanor's departure, Mr. Arabin
went to Oxford, and soon found himself closeted with
the august head of his college. It was quite clear that
Dr. Gwynne was not very sanguine as to the effects of
his journey to Barchester, and not over anxious to interfere
with the bishop. He had had the gout but was very
nearly convalescent, and Mr. Arabin at once saw that had
the mission been one of which the master thoroughly
approved, he would before this have been at Plumstead.

As it was, Dr. Gwynne was resolved on visiting his
friend, and willingly promised to return to Barchester
with Mr. Arabin. He could not bring himself to believe
that there was any probability that Mr. Slope would be
made Dean of Barchester. Rumour, he said, had reached
even his ears, not at all favourable to that gentleman's
character, and he expressed himself strongly of opinion
that any such appointment was quite out of the question.
At this stage of the proceedings, the master's right-hand
man, Tom Staple, was called in to assist at the conference.

Tom Staple was the Tutor of Lazarus, and moreover a
great man at Oxford. Though universally known by a
species of nomenclature so very undignified, Tom Staple
was one who maintained a high dignity in the University.
He was, as it were, the leader of the Oxford tutors, a body
of men who consider themselves collectively as being by
very little, if at all, second in importance to the heads
themselves. It is not always the case that the master,
or warden, or provost, or principal can hit it off exactly
with his tutor. A tutor is by no means indisposed to have
a will of his own. But at Lazarus they were great friends
and firm allies at the time of which we are writing.

Tom Staple was a hale strong man of about forty-five;
short in stature, swarthy in face, with strong sturdy black
hair, and crisp black beard, of which very little was allowed
to show itself in shape of whiskers. He always wore a
white neckcloth, clean indeed, but not tied with that
scrupulous care which now distinguishes some of our
younger clergy. He was, of course, always clothed in
a seemly suit of solemn black. Mr. Staple was a decent
cleanly liver, not over addicted to any sensuality; but
nevertheless a somewhat warmish hue was beginning to
adorn his nose, the peculiar effect, as his friends averred,
of a certain pipe of port introduced into the cellars of
Lazarus the very same year in which the tutor entered
it as a freshman. There was also, perhaps, a little redolence
of port wine, as it were the slightest possible twang, in
Mr. Staple's voice.

In these latter days Tom Staple was not a happy man;
University reform had long been his bugbear, and now
was his bane. It was not with him as with most others,
an affair of politics, respecting which, when the need
existed, he could, for parties' sake or on behalf of principle,
maintain a certain amount of necessary zeal; it was not
with him a subject for dilettante warfare, and courteous
common-place opposition. To him it was life and death.
The *statu quo* of the University was his only idea of life,
and any reformation was as bad to him as death. He
would willingly have been a martyr in the cause, had the
cause admitted of martyrdom.

At the present day, unfortunately, public affairs will
allow of no martyrs, and therefore it is that there is such

a deficiency of zeal. Could gentlemen of 10,000*l.* a year have died on their own door-steps in defence of protection, no doubt some half-dozen glorious old baronets would have so fallen, and the school of protection would at this day have been crowded with scholars. Who can fight strenuously in any combat in which there is no danger ? Tom Staple would have willingly been impaled before a Committee of the House, could he by such self-sacrifice have infused his own spirit into the component members of the hebdomadal board.

Tom Staple was one of those who in his heart approved of the credit system which had of old been in vogue between the students and tradesmen of the University. He knew and acknowledged to himself that it was useless in these degenerate days publicly to contend with the Jupiter on such a subject. The Jupiter had undertaken to rule the University, and Tom Staple was well aware that the Jupiter was too powerful for him. But in secret, and among his safe companions, he would argue that the system of credit was an ordeal good for young men to undergo.

The bad men, said he, the weak and worthless, blunder into danger and burn their feet ; but the good men, they who have any character, they who have that within them which can reflect credit on their Alma Mater, they come through scatheless. What merit will there be to a young man to get through safely, if he be guarded and protected and restrained like a school-boy ? By so doing, the period of the ordeal is only postponed, and the manhood of the man will be deferred from the age of twenty to that of twenty-four. If you bind him with leading-strings at college, he will break loose while eating for the bar in London ; bind him there, and he will break loose after- wards, when he is a married man. The wild oats must be sown somewhere. 'Twas thus that Tom Staple would argue of young men ; not, indeed, with much consistency, but still with some practical knowledge of the subject gathered from long experience.

And now Tom Staple proffered such wisdom as he had for the assistance of Dr. Gwynne and Mr. Arabin.

' Quite out of the question,' said he, arguing that Mr. Slope could not possibly be made the new Dean of Barchester.

'So I think,' said the master. 'He has no standing, and, if all I hear be true, very little character.'

'As to character,' said Tom Staple, 'I don't think much of that. They rather like loose parsons for deans; a little fast living, or a dash of infidelity, is no bad recommendation to a cathedral close. But they couldn't make Mr. Slope; the last two deans have been Cambridge men; you'll not show me an instance of their making three men running from the same University. We don't get our share, and never shall, I suppose; but we must at least have one out of three.'

'Those sort of rules are all gone by now,' said Mr. Arabin.

'Everything has gone by, I believe,' said Tom Staple. 'The cigar has been smoked out, and we are the ashes.'

'Speak for yourself, Staple,' said the master.

'I speak for all,' said the tutor, stoutly. 'It is coming to that, that there will be no life left anywhere in the country. No one is any longer fit to rule himself, or those belonging to him. The Government is to find us all in everything, and the press is to find the Government. Nevertheless, Mr. Slope won't be Dean of Barchester.'

'And who will be warden of the hospital?' said Mr. Arabin.

'I hear that Mr. Quiverful is already appointed,' said Tom Staple.

'I think not,' said the master. 'And I think, moreover, that Dr. Proudie will not be so short-sighted as to run against such a rock: Mr. Slope should himself have sense enough to prevent it.'

'But perhaps Mr. Slope may have no objection to see his patron on a rock,' said the suspicious tutor.

'What could he get by that?' asked Mr. Arabin.

'It is impossible to see the doubles of such a man,' said Mr. Staple. 'It seems quite clear that Bishop Proudie is altogether in his hands, and it is equally clear that he has been moving heaven and earth to get this Mr. Quiverful into the hospital, although he must know that such an appointment would be most damaging to the bishop. It is impossible to understand such a man, and dreadful to think,' added Tom Staple, sighing deeply, 'that the welfare and fortunes of good men may depend on his intrigues.'

Dr. Gwynne or Mr. Staple were not in the least aware, nor even was Mr. Arabin, that this Mr. Slope, of whom they were talking, had been using his utmost efforts to put their own candidate into the hospital ; and that in lieu of being permanent in the palace, his own expulsion therefrom had been already decided on by the high powers of the diocese.

' I'll tell you what,' said the tutor, ' if this Quiverful is thrust into the hospital and Dr. Trefoil does die, I should not wonder if the Government were to make Mr. Harding Dean of Barchester. They would feel bound to do something for him after all that was said when he resigned.'

Dr. Gwynne at the moment made no reply to this suggestion ; but it did not the less impress itself on his mind. If Mr. Harding could not be warden of the hospital, why should he not be Dean of Barchester ?

And so the conference ended without any very fixed resolution, and Dr. Gwynne and Mr. Arabin prepared for their journey to Plumstead on the morrow.

CHAPTER XXXV

MISS THORNE'S FÊTE CHAMPÊTRE

THE day of the Ullathorne party arrived, and all the world were there ; or at least so much of the world as had been included in Miss Thorne's invitation. As we have said, the bishop returned home on the previous evening, and on the same evening, and by the same train, came Dr. Gwynne and Mr. Arabin from Oxford. The archdeacon with his brougham was in waiting for the Master of Lazarus, so that there was a goodly show of church dignitaries on the platform of the railway.

The Stanhope party was finally arranged in the odious manner already described, and Eleanor got into the doctor's carriage full of apprehension and presentiment of further misfortune, whereas Mr. Slope entered the vehicle elate with triumph.

He had received that morning a very civil note from Sir Nicholas Fitzwhiggin ; not promising much indeed ; but then Mr. Slope knew, or fancied that he knew, that it was

not etiquette for government officers to make promises.
Though Sir Nicholas promised nothing he implied a good
deal; declared his conviction that Mr. Slope would make
an excellent dean, and wished him every kind of success.
To be sure he added that, not being in the cabinet, he was
never consulted on such matters, and that even if he spoke
on the subject his voice would go for nothing. But all this
Mr. Slope took for the prudent reserve of official life. To
complete his anticipated triumphs, another letter was
brought to him just as he was about to start to Ullathorne.

Mr. Slope also enjoyed the idea of handing Mrs. Bold
out of Dr. Stanhope's carriage before the multitude at
Ullathorne gate, as much as Eleanor dreaded the same
ceremony. He had fully made up his mind to throw himself and his fortune at the widow's feet, and had almost
determined to select the present propitious morning for
doing so. The signora had of late been less than civil to
him. She had indeed admitted his visits, and listened, at
any rate without anger, to his love; but she had tortured
him and reviled him, jeered at him and ridiculed him,
while she allowed him to call her the most beautiful of
living women, to kiss her hand, and to proclaim himself
with reiterated oaths her adorer, her slave, and worshipper.

Miss Thorne was in great perturbation, yet in great
glory, on the morning of the gala day. Mr. Thorne also,
though the party was none of his giving, had much heavy
work on his hands. But perhaps the most overtasked, the
most anxious, and the most effective of all the Ullathorne
household was Mr. Plomacy, the steward. This last
personage had, in the time of Mr. Thorne's father, when
the Directory held dominion in France, gone over to Paris
with letters in his boot heel for some of the royal party;
and such had been his good luck that he had returned safe.
He had then been very young and was now very old, but
the exploit gave him a character for political enterprise
and secret discretion which still availed him as thoroughly
as it had done in its freshest gloss. Mr. Plomacy had been
steward of Ullathorne for more than fifty years, and a very
easy life he had had of it. Who could require much
absolute work from a man who had carried safely at his
heel that which if discovered would have cost him his
head? Consequently Mr. Plomacy had never worked

hard, and of latter years had never worked at all. He had a taste for timber, and therefore he marked the trees that were to be cut down; he had a taste for gardening, and would therefore allow no shrub to be planted or bed to be made without his express sanction. In these matters he was sometimes driven to run counter to his mistress, but he rarely allowed his mistress to carry the point against him.

But on occasions such as the present Mr. Plomacy came out strong. He had the honour of the family at heart; he thoroughly appreciated the duties of hospitality; and therefore, when gala doings were going on, always took the management into his own hands and reigned supreme over master and mistress.

To give Mr. Plomacy his due, old as he was, he thoroughly understood such work as he had in hand, and did it well.

The order of the day was to be as follows. The quality, as the upper classes in rural districts are designated by the lower with so much true discrimination, were to eat a breakfast, and the non-quality were to eat a dinner. Two marquees had been erected for these two banquets, that for the quality on the esoteric or garden side of a certain deep ha-ha; and that for the non-quality on the exoteric or paddock side of the same. Both were of huge dimensions; that on the outer side was, one may say, on an egregious scale; but Mr. Plomacy declared that neither would be sufficient. To remedy this, an auxiliary banquet was prepared in the dining-room, and a subsidiary board was to be spread *sub dio* for the accommodation of the lower class of yokels on the Ullathorne property.

No one who has not had a hand in the preparation of such an affair can understand the manifold difficulties which Miss Thorne encountered in her project. Had she not been made throughout of the very finest whalebone, riveted with the best Yorkshire steel, she must have sunk under them. Had not Mr. Plomacy felt how much was justly expected from a man who at one time carried the destinies of Europe in his boot, he would have given way; and his mistress, so deserted, must have perished among her poles and canvass.

In the first place there was a dreadful line to be drawn.

Who were to dispose themselves within the ha-ha, and who without ? To this the unthinking will give an off-hand answer, as they will to every ponderous question. Oh, the bishop and such like within the ha-ha ; and Farmer Greenacre and such like without. True, my unthinking friend ; but who shall define these such-likes ? It is in such definitions that the whole difficulty of society consists. To seat the bishop on an arm chair on the lawn and place Farmer Greenacre at the end of a long table in the paddock is easy enough ; but where will you put Mrs. Lookaloft, whose husband, though a tenant on the estate, hunts in a red coat, whose daughters go to a fashionable seminary in Barchester, who calls her farm house Rosebank, and who has a pianoforte in her drawing-room ? The Misses Lookaloft, as they call themselves, won't sit contented among the bumpkins. Mrs. Lookaloft won't squeeze her fine clothes on a bench and talk familiarly about cream and ducklings to good Mrs. Greenacre. And yet Mrs. Lookaloft is no fit companion and never has been the associate of the Thornes and the Grantlys. And if Mrs. Lookaloft be admitted within the sanctum of fashionable life, if she be allowed with her three daughters to leap the ha-ha, why not the wives and daughters of other families also ? Mrs. Greenacre is at present well contented with the paddock, but she might cease to be so if she saw Mrs. Lookaloft on the lawn. And thus poor Miss Thorne had a hard time of it.

And how was she to divide her guests between the marquee and the parlour ? She had a countess coming, an Honourable John and an Honourable George, and a whole bevy of Ladies Amelia, Rosina, Margaretta, &c. ; she had a leash of baronets with their baronnettes ; and, as we all know, she had a bishop. If she put them on the lawn, no one would go into the parlour ; if she put them into the parlour, no one would go into the tent. She thought of keeping the old people in the house, and leaving the lawn to the lovers. She might as well have seated herself at once in a hornet's nest. Mr. Plomacy knew better than this. ' Bless your soul, Ma'am,' said he, ' there won't be no old ladies ; not one, barring yourself and old Mrs. Clantantram.'

Personally Miss Thorne accepted this distinction in her

favour as a compliment to her good sense; but nevertheless she had no desire to be closeted on the coming occasion with Mrs. Clantantram. She gave up all idea of any arbitrary division of her guests, and determined if possible to put the bishop on the lawn and the countess in the house, to sprinkle the baronets, and thus divide the attractions. What to do with the Lookalofts even Mr. Plomacy could not decide. They must take their chance. They had been specially told in the invitation that all the tenants had been invited; and they might probably have the good sense to stay away if they objected to mix with the rest of the tenantry.

Then Mr. Plomacy declared his apprehension that the Honourable Johns and Honourable Georges would come in a sort of amphibious costume, half morning half evening, satin neckhandkerchiefs, frock coats, primrose gloves, and polished boots; and that, being so dressed, they would decline riding at the quintain, or taking part in any of the athletic games which Miss Thorne had prepared with so much fond care. If the Lord Johns and Lord Georges didn't ride at the quintain, Miss Thorne might be sure that nobody else would.

' But,' said she in dolorous voice, all but overcome by her cares; ' it was specially signified that there were to be sports.'

' And so there will be, of course,' said Mr. Plomacy. ' They'll all be sporting with the young ladies in the laurel walks. Them's the sports they care most about now-a-days. If you gets the young men at the quintain, you'll have all the young women in the pouts.'

' Can't they look on, as their great grandmothers did before them ? ' said Miss Thorne.

' It seems to me that the ladies ain't contented with looking now-a-days. Whatever the men do they'll do. If you'll have side saddles on the nags, and let them go at the quintain too, it'll answer capital, no doubt.'

Miss Thorne made no reply. She felt that she had no good ground on which to defend her sex of the present generation from the sarcasm of Mr. Plomacy. She had once declared, in one of her warmer moments, ' that now-a-days the gentlemen were all women, and the ladies all men.' She could not alter the debased character of the age. But, such being the case, why should she take on herself to cater for the amusement of people of such degraded tastes ? This question she asked herself more than once, and she could only answer herself with a sigh. There was her own brother Wilfred, on whose shoulders rested all the ancient honours of Ullathorne house ; it was very doubtful whether even he would consent to ' go at the quintain,' as Mr. Plomacy not injudiciously expressed it.

And now the morning arrived. The Ullathorne household was early on the move. Cooks were cooking in the kitchen long before daylight, and men were dragging out tables and hammering red baize on to benches at the earliest dawn. With what dread eagerness did Miss Thorne look out at the weather as soon as the parting veil of night permitted her to look at all ! In this respect at any rate there was nothing to grieve her. The glass had been rising for the last three days, and the morning broke with that dull chill steady grey haze which in autumn generally presages a clear and dry day. By seven she was dressed and down. Miss Thorne knew nothing of the modern luxury of *déshabilles*. She would as soon have thought of appearing before her brother without her stockings as without her stays ; and Miss Thorne's stays were no trifle.

And yet there was nothing for her to do when down. She fidgeted out to the lawn, and then back into the kitchen. She put on her high-heeled clogs, and fidgeted out into the paddock. Then she went into the small home park where the quintain was erected. The pole and cross bar and the swivel, and the target and the bag of flour were all complete. She got up on a carpenter's bench and touched the target with her hand ; it went round with beautiful ease ; the swivel had been oiled to perfection. She almost wished to take old Plomacy at his word, to get on a side saddle and have a tilt at it herself. What must a young man be, thought she, who could prefer maundering among laurel trees with a wishy-washy school girl to such fun as this ? ' Well,' said she aloud to herself, ' one man can take a horse to water, but a thousand can't make him drink. There it is. If they haven't the spirit to enjoy it, the fault shan't be mine ; ' and so she returned to the house.

At a little after eight her brother came down, and they had a sort of scrap breakfast in his study. The tea, was made without the customary urn, and they dispensed with the usual rolls and toast. Eggs also were missing, for every egg in the parish had been whipped into custards, baked into pies, or boiled into lobster salad. The allowance of fresh butter was short, and Mr. Thorne was obliged to eat the leg of a fowl without having it devilled in the manner he loved.

' I have been looking at the quintain, Wilfred,' said she, ' and it appears to be quite right.'

' Oh,—ah ; yes ; ' said he. ' It seemed to be so yesterday when I saw it.' Mr. Thorne was beginning to be rather bored by his sister's love of sports, and had especially no affection for this quintain post.

' I wish you'd just try it after breakfast,' said she. ' You could have the saddle put on Mark Antony, and the pole is there all handy. You can take the flour bag off, you know, if you think Mark Antony won't be quick enough,' added Miss Thorne, seeing that her brother's countenance was not indicative of complete accordance with her little proposition.

Now Mark Antony was a valuable old hunter, excellently suited to Mr. Thorne's usual requirements, steady indeed at his fences, but extremely sure, very good in deep ground, and safe on the roads. But he had never yet been ridden at a quintain, and Mr. Thorne was not inclined to put him to the trial, either with or without the bag of flour. He hummed and hawed, and finally declared that he was afraid Mark Antony would shy.

' Then try the cob,' said the indefatigable Miss Thorne.

' He's in physic,' said Wilfred.

' There's the Beelzebub colt,' said his sister ; ' I know he's in the stable, because I saw Peter exercising him just now.'

' My dear Monica, he's so wild, that it's as much as I can do to manage him at all. He'd destroy himself and me too, if I attempted to ride him at such a rattletrap as that.'

A rattletrap ! The quintain that she had put up with so much anxious care ; the game that she had prepared for the amusement of the stalwart yeomen of the country ; the sport that had been honoured by the affection of so many of their ancestors ! It cut her to the heart to hear it so denominated by her own brother. There were but the two of them left together in the world ; and it had ever been one of the rules by which Miss Thorne had regulated her conduct through life, to say nothing that could provoke her brother. She had often had to suffer from his indifference to time-honoured British customs ; but she had always suffered in silence. It was part of her creed that the head of the family should never be upbraided in his own house ; and Miss Thorne had lived up to her creed. Now, however, she was greatly tried. The colour mounted to her ancient cheek, and the fire blazed in her still bright eye ; but yet she said nothing. She resolved that at any rate, to him nothing more should be said about the quintain that day.

She sipped her tea in silent sorrow, and thought with painful regret of the glorious days when her great ancestor Ealfried had successfully held Ullathorne against a Norman invader. There was no such spirit now left in her family except that small useless spark which burnt in her own bosom. And she herself, was not she at this moment intent on entertaining a descendant of those very Normans, a vain proud countess with a frenchified name, who would only think that she graced Ullathorne too highly by entering its portals ? Was it likely that an honourable John, the son of an Earl De Courcy, should ride at a quintain in company with Saxon yeomen ? And why should she expect her brother to do that which her brother's guests would decline to do ?

Some dim faint idea of the impracticability of her own views flitted across her brain. Perhaps it was necessary that races doomed to live on the same soil should give way to each other, and adopt each other's pursuits. Perhaps it was impossible that after more than five centuries of close intercourse, Normans should remain Normans, and Saxons, Saxons. Perhaps after all her neighbours were wiser than herself. Such ideas did occasionally present themselves to Miss Thorne's mind, and make her sad enough. But it never occurred to her that her favourite quintain was but a modern copy of a Norman knight's amusement, an adaptation of the noble tourney to the tastes and habits of the Saxon yeomen. Of this she was entertain! Who shall have sufficient self-assurance, who shall feel sufficient confidence in his own powers to dare to boast that he can entertain his company? A clown can sometimes do so, and sometimes a dancer in short petticoats and stuffed pink legs; occasionally, perhaps, a singer. But beyond these, success in this art of entertaining is not often achieved. Young men and women linking themselves kind with kind, pairing like birds in spring because nature wills it, they, after a simple fashion, do entertain each other. Few others even try. Ladies, when they open their houses, modestly confessing, it may be presumed, their own incapacity, mainly trust to wax candles and upholstery. Gentlemen seem to rely on their white waistcoats. To these are added, for the delight of the more sensual, champagne and such good things of the table as fashion allows to be still considered as comestible. Even in this respect the world is deteriorating. All the good soups are now tabooed; and in the houses of one's accustomed friends, small barristers, doctors, government clerks, and such like, (for we cannot all of us always live as grandees, surrounded by an elysium of livery servants), one gets a cold potato handed to one as a sort of finale to one's slice of mutton. Alas! for those happy days when one could say to one's neighbour-maid, 'Jones, shall I give you some mashed turnip?—may I trouble you for a little cabbage?' And then the pleasure of drinking wine with Mrs. Jones and Miss Smith; with all the Joneses and all the Smiths! These latter-day habits are certainly more economical.

Miss Thorne, however, boldly attempted to leave the modern beaten track, and made a positive effort to entertain her guests. Alas! she did so with but moderate success. They had all their own way of going, and would go her way. She piped to them, but they would not dance. She offered to them good honest household cake, made of currants and flour and eggs and sweetmeat; but they would feed themselves on trashy wafers from the shop of the Barchester pastry-cook, on chalk and gum and adulterated sugar. Poor Miss Thorne! yours is not the first honest soul that has vainly striven to recall the glories of happy days gone by! If fashion suggests to a Lady De Courcy that when invited to a *déjeûner* at

ignorant, and it would have been cruelty to instruct her.

When Mr. Thorne saw the tear in her eye, he repented himself of his contemptuous expression. By him also it was recognised as a binding law that every whim of his sister was to be respected. He was not perhaps so firm in his observances to her, as she was in hers to him. But his intentions were equally good, and whenever he found that he had forgotten them it was matter of grief to him.

'My dear Monica,' said he, 'I beg your pardon; I don't in the least mean to speak ill of the game. When I called it a rattletrap, I merely meant that it was so for a man of my age. You know you always forget that I an't a young man.'

'I am quite sure you are not an old man, Wilfred,' said she, accepting the apology in her heart, and smiling at him with the tear still on her cheek.

'If I was five-and-twenty, or thirty,' continued he, 'I should like nothing better than riding at the quintain all day.'

'But you are not too old to hunt or to shoot,' said she. 'If you can jump over a ditch and hedge I am sure you could turn the quintain round.'

'But when I ride over the hedges, my dear—and it isn't very often I do that—but when I do ride over the hedges there isn't any bag of flour coming after me. Think how I'd look taking the countess out to breakfast with the back of my head all covered with meal.'

Miss Thorne said nothing further. She didn't like the allusion to the countess. She couldn't be satisfied with the reflection that the sports of Ullathorne should be interfered with by the personal attentions necessary for a Lady De Courcy. But she saw that it was useless for her to push the matter further. It was conceded that Mr. Thorne was to be spared the quintain; and Miss Thorne determined to trust wholly to a youthful knight of hers, an immense favourite, who, as she often declared, was a pattern to the young men of the age, and an excellent sample of an English yeoman.

This was Farmer Greenacre's eldest son; who, to tell the truth, had from his earliest years taken the exact measure of Miss Thorne's foot. In his boyhood he had never failed to obtain from her, apples, pocket money, and forgiveness for his numerous trespasses ; and now in his early manhood he got privileges and immunities which were equally valuable. He was allowed a day or two's shooting in September ; he schooled the squire's horses ; got slips of trees out of the orchard, and roots of flowers out of the garden ; and had the fishing of the little river altogether in his own hands. He had undertaken to come mounted on a nag of his father's, and show the way at the quintain post. Whatever young Greenacre did the others would do after him. The juvenile Lookalofts might stand aloof, but the rest of the youth of Ullathorne would be sure to venture if Harry Greenacre showed the way. And so Miss Thorne made up her mind to dispense with the noble Johns and Georges, and trust, as her ancestors had done before her, to the thews and sinews of native Ullathorne growth.

At about nine the lower orders began to congregate in the paddock and park, under the surveillance of Mr. Plomacy and the head gardener and head groom, who were sworn in as his deputies, and were to assist him in keeping the peace and promoting the sports. Many of the younger inhabitants of the neighbourhood, thinking that they could not have too much of a good thing, had come at a very early hour, and the road between the house and the church had been thronged for some time before the gates were thrown open.

And then another difficulty of huge dimensions arose, a difficulty which Mr. Plomacy had indeed foreseen and for which he was in some sort provided. Some of those who wished to share Miss Thorne's hospitality were not so particular as they should have been as to the preliminary ceremony of an invitation. They doubtless conceived that they had been overlooked by accident ; and instead of taking this in dudgeon, as their betters would have done, they good-naturedly put up with the slight, and showed that they did so by presenting themselves at the gate in their Sunday best.

Mr. Plomacy, however, well knew who were welcome and who were not. To some, even though uninvited, he allowed ingress. ' Don't be too particular, Plomacy,' his

mistress had said ; ' especially with the childre live anywhere near, let them in.'

Acting on this hint, Mr. Plomacy did let in eager urchin, and a few tidily dressed girls swains, who in no way belonged to the propert the denizens of the city he was inexorable. Ma chester apprentice made his appearance there and urged with piteous supplication that he working all the week in making saddles and boo use of Ullathorne, in compounding doses for th or cutting up carcases for the kitchen. No such allowed. Mr. Plomacy knew nothing about apprentices ; he was to admit the tenants and on the estate ; Miss Thorne wasn't going to tal whole city of Barchester ; and so on.

Nevertheless, before the day was half over, all found to be useless. Almost anybody who chose made his way into the park, and the care of the g was transferred to the tables on which the banq spread. Even here there was many an unaut claimant for a place, of whom it was impossible to without more commotion than the place and foo worth.

CHAPTER XXXVI

ULLATHORNE SPORTS—ACT I

THE trouble in civilised life of entertaining com as it is called too generally without much regard to veracity, is so great that it cannot but be matter of w that people are so fond of attempting it. It is difficu ascertain what is the *quid pro quo.* If they who give laborious parties, and who endure such toil and tur in the vain hope of giving them successfully, really enj the parties given by others, the matter could be un stood. A sense of justice would induce men and wo to undergo, in behalf of others, those miseries which otl had undergone in their behalf. But they all profess t going out is as great a bore as receiving ; and to look them when they are out, one cannot but believe them.

twelve she ought to come at three, no eloquence of thine will teach her the advantage of a nearer approach to punctuality.

She had fondly thought that when she called on her friends to come at twelve, and specially begged them to believe that she meant it, she would be able to see them comfortably seated in their tents at two. Vain woman—or rather ignorant woman—ignorant of the advances of that civilisation which the world had witnessed while she was growing old. At twelve she found herself alone, dressed in all the glory of the newest of her many suits of raiment; with strong shoes however, and a serviceable bonnet on her head, and a warm rich shawl on her shoulders. Thus clad she peered out into the tent, went to the ha-ha, and satisfied herself that at any rate the youngsters were amusing themselves, spoke a word to Mrs. Greenacre over the ditch, and took one look at the quintain. Three or four young farmers were turning the machine round and round, and poking at the bag of flour in a manner not at all intended by the inventor of the game; but no mounted sportsmen were there. Miss Thorne looked at her watch. It was only fifteen minutes past twelve, and it was understood that Harry Greenacre was not to begin till the half hour.

Miss Thorne returned to her drawing-room rather quicker than was her wont, fearing that the countess might come and find none to welcome her. She need not have hurried, for no one was there. At half-past twelve she peeped into the kitchen; at a quarter to one she was joined by her brother; and just then the first fashionable arrival took place. Mrs. Clantantram was announced.

No announcement was necessary, indeed; for the good lady's voice was heard as she walked across the court-yard to the house scolding the unfortunate postilion who had driven her from Barchester. At the moment, Miss Thorne could not but be thankful that the other guests were more fashionable, and were thus spared the fury of Mrs. Clantantram's indignation.

' Oh Miss Thorne, look here ! ' said she, as soon as she found herself in the drawing-room ; ' do look at my roquelaure ! It's clean spoilt, and for ever. I wouldn't but wear it because I knew you wished us all to be grand to-day; and yet I had my misgivings. Oh dear, oh dear! It was five-and-twenty shillings a yard.'

The Barchester post horses had misbehaved in some unfortunate manner just as Mrs. Clantantram was getting out of the chaise and had nearly thrown her under the wheel.

Mrs. Clantantram belonged to other days, and therefore, though she had but little else to recommend her, Miss Thorne was to a certain extent fond of her. She sent the roquelaure away to be cleaned, and lent her one of her best shawls out of her own wardrobe.

The next comer was Mr. Arabin, who was immediately informed of Mrs. Clantantram's misfortune, and of her determination to pay neither master nor post-boy; although, as she remarked, she intended to get her lift home before she made known her mind upon that matter. Then a good deal of rustling was heard in the sort of lobby that was used for the ladies' outside cloaks; and the door having been thrown wide open, the servant announced, not in the most confident of voices, Mrs. Lookaloft, and the Miss Lookalofts, and Mr. Augustus Lookaloft.

Poor man!—we mean the footman. He knew, none better, that Mrs. Lookaloft had no business there, that she was not wanted there, and would not be welcome. But he had not the courage to tell a stout lady with a low dress, short sleeves, and satin at eight shillings a yard, that she had come to the wrong tent; he had not dared to hint to young ladies with white dancing shoes and long gloves, that there was a place ready for them in the paddock. And thus Mrs. Lookaloft carried her point, broke through the guards, and made her way into the citadel. That she would have to pass an uncomfortable time there, she had surmised before. But nothing now could rob her of the power of boasting that she had consorted on the lawn with the squire and Miss Thorne, with a countess, a bishop, and the country grandees, while Mrs. Greenacre and such like were walking about with the ploughboys in the park. It was a great point gained by Mrs. Lookaloft, and it might be fairly expected that from this time forward the tradesmen of Barchester would, with undoubting pens, address her husband as T. Lookaloft, Esquire.

Mrs. Lookaloft's pluck carried her through everything, and she walked triumphant into the Ullathorne drawing-room ; but her children did feel a little abashed at the sort of reception they met with. It was not in Miss Thorne's heart to insult her own guests ; but neither was it in her disposition to overlook such effrontery.

' Oh, Mrs. Lookaloft, is this you,' said she ; ' and your daughters and son ? Well, we're very glad to see you ; but I'm sorry you've come in such low dresses, as we are all going out of doors. Could we lend you anything ? '

' Oh dear no ! thank ye, Miss Thorne,' said the mother ; ' the girls and myself are quite used to low dresses, when we're out.'

' Are you, indeed ? ' said Miss Thorne shuddering ; but the shudder was lost on Mrs. Lookaloft.

' And where's Lookaloft ? ' said the master of the house, coming up to welcome his tenant's wife. Let the faults of the family be what they would, he could not but remember that their rent was well paid ; he was therefore not willing to give them a cold shoulder.

' Such a headache, Mr. Thorne ! ' said Mrs. Lookaloft. ' In fact he couldn't stir, or you may be certain on such a day he would not have absented hisself.'

' Dear me,' said Miss Thorne. ' If he is so ill, I'm sure you'd wish to be with him.'

' Not at all ! ' said Mrs. Lookaloft. ' Not at all, Miss Thorne. It is only bilious you know, and when he's that way he can bear nobody nigh him.'

The fact however was that Mr. Lookaloft, having either more sense or less courage than his wife, had not chosen to intrude on Miss Thorne's drawing-room ; and as he could not very well have gone among the plebeians while his wife was with the patricians, he thought it most expedient to remain at Rosebank.

Mrs. Lookaloft soon found herself on a sofa, and the Miss Lookalofts on two chairs, while Mr. Augustus stood near the door ; and here they remained till in due time they were seated all four together at the bottom of the dining-room table.

Then the Grantlys came ; the archdeacon and Mrs. Grantly and the two girls, and Dr. Gwynne and Mr. Harding ; and as ill luck would have it, they were closely

followed by Dr. Stanhope's carriage. As Eleanor looked
out of the carriage window, she saw her brother-in-law
helping the ladies out, and threw herself back into her
seat, dreading to be discovered. She had had an odious
journey. Mr. Slope's civility had been more than ordinarily
greasy ; and now, though he had not in fact said anything
which she could notice, she had for the first time entertained a suspicion that he was intending to make love
to her. Was it after all true that she had been conducting
herself in a way that justified the world in thinking that
she liked the man ? After all, could it be possible that
the archdeacon and Mr. Arabin were right, and that she
was wrong ? Charlotte Stanhope had also been watching
Mr. Slope, and had come to the conclusion that it behoved
her brother to lose no further time, if he meant to gain
the widow. She almost regretted that it had not been
contrived that Bertie should be at Ullathorne before them.

Dr. Grantly did not see his sister-in-law in company
with Mr. Slope, but Mr. Arabin did. Mr. Arabin came
out with Mr. Thorne to the front door to welcome Mrs.
Grantly, and he remained in the courtyard till all their
party had passed on. Eleanor hung back in the carriage
as long as she well could, but she was nearest to the door,
and when Mr. Slope, having alighted, offered her his
hand, she had no alternative but to take it. Mr. Arabin
standing at the open door, while Mrs. Grantly was shaking
hands with some one·within, saw a clergyman alight
from the carriage whom he at once knew to be Mr. Slope,
and then he saw this clergyman hand out Mrs. Bold.
Having seen so much, Mr. Arabin, rather sick at heart,
followed Mrs. Grantly into the house.

Eleanor was, however, spared any further immediate
degradation, for Dr. Stanhope gave her his arm across
the courtyard, and Mr. Slope was fain to throw away his
attention upon Charlotte.

They had hardly passed into the house, and from the
house to the lawn, when, with a loud rattle and such noise
as great men and great women are entitled to make in
their passage through the world, the Proudies drove up.
It was soon apparent that no every day comer was at the
door. One servant whispered to another that it was the
bishop, and the word soon ran through all the hangers-on

and strange grooms and coachmen about the place. There was quite a little cortége to see the bishop and his ' lady ' walk across the courtyard, and the good man was pleased to see that the church was held in such respect in the parish of St. Ewold's.

And now the guests came fast and thick, and the lawn began to be crowded, and the room to be full. Voices buzzed, silk rustled against silk, and muslin crumpled against muslin. Miss Thorne became more happy than she had been, and again bethought her of her sports. There were targets and bows and arrows prepared at the further end of the lawn. Here the gardens of the place encroached with a somewhat wide sweep upon the paddock, and gave ample room for the doings of the toxophilites. Miss Thorne got together such daughters of Diana as could bend a bow, and marshalled them to the targets. There were the Grantly girls and the Proudie girls and the Chadwick girls, and the two daughters of the burly chancellor, and Miss Knowle; and with them went Frederick and Augustus Chadwick, and young Knowle of Knowle park, and Frank Foster of the Elms, and Mr. Vellem Deeds the dashing attorney of the High Street, and the Rev. Mr. Green, and the Rev. Mr. Brown, and the Rev. Mr. White, all of whom, as in duty bound, attended the steps of the three Miss Proudies.

' Did you ever ride at the quintain, Mr. Foster ? ' said Miss Thorne, as she walked with her party, across the lawn.

' The quintain ? ' said young Foster, who considered himself a dab at horsemanship. ' Is it a sort of gate, Miss Thorne ? '

Miss Thorne had to explain the noble game she spoke of, and Frank Foster had to own that he never had ridden at the quintain.

' Would you like to come and see ? ' said Miss Thorne. ' There'll be plenty here without you, if you like it.'

' Well, I don't mind,' said Frank ; ' I suppose the ladies can come too.'

' Oh yes,' said Miss Thorne ; ' those who like it ; I have no doubt they'll go to see your prowess, if you'll ride, Mr. Foster.'

Mr. Foster looked down at a most unexceptionable

pair of pantaloons, which had arrived from London only
the day before. They were the very things, at least he
thought so, for a picnic or fête champêtre; but he was
not prepared to ride in them. Nor was he more encouraged
than had been Mr. Thorne, by the idea of being attacked
from behind by the bag of flour which Miss Thorne had
graphically described to him.

'Well, I don't know about riding, Miss Thorne,' said
he; 'I fear I'm not quite prepared.'

Miss Thorne sighed, but said nothing further. She
left the toxophilites to their bows and arrows, and returned
towards the house. But as she passed by the entrance to
the small park, she thought that she might at any rate
encourage the yeomen by her presence, as she could not
induce her more fashionable guests to mix with them in
their manly amusements. Accordingly she once more
betook herself to the quintain post.

Here to her great delight she found Harry Greenacre
ready mounted, with his pole in his hand, and a lot of
comrades standing round him, encouraging him to the
assault. She stood at a little distance and nodded to him
in token of her good pleasure.

'Shall I begin, ma'am?' said Harry fingering his long
staff in a rather awkward way, while his horse moved
uneasily beneath him, not accustomed to a rider armed
with such a weapon.

'Yes, yes,' said Miss Thorne, standing triumphant as
the queen of beauty, on an inverted tub which some chance
had brought thither from the farm-yard.

'Here goes then,' said Harry as he wheeled his horse
round to get the necessary momentum of a sharp gallop.
The quintain post stood right before him, and the square
board at which he was to tilt was fairly in his way. If he
hit that duly in the middle, and maintained his pace as
he did so, it was calculated that he would be carried out
of reach of the flour bag, which, suspended at the other
end of the cross-bar on the post, would swing round when
the board was struck. It was also calculated that if the
rider did not maintain his pace, he would get a blow from
the flour bag just at the back of his head, and bear about
him the signs of his awkwardness to the great amusement
of the lookers-on.

Harry Greenacre did not object to being powdered with flour in the service of his mistress, and therefore gallantly touched his steed with his spur, having laid his lance in rest to the best of his ability. But his ability in this respect was not great, and his appurtenances probably not very good; consequently, he struck his horse with his pole unintentionally on the side of the head as he started. The animal swerved and shied, and galloped off wide of the quintain. Harry well accustomed to manage a horse, but not to do so with a twelve-foot rod on his arm, lowered his right hand to the bridle and thus the end of the lance came to the ground, and got between the legs of the steed. Down came rider and steed and staff. Young Greenacre was thrown some six feet over the horse's head, and poor Miss Thorne almost fell off her tub in a swoon.

' Oh gracious, he's killed,' shrieked a woman who was near him when he fell.

' The Lord be good to him! his poor mother, his poor mother!' said another.

' Well, drat them dangerous plays all the world over,' said an old crone.

' He has broke his neck sure enough, if ever man did,' said a fourth.

Poor Miss Thorne. She heard all this and yet did not quite swoon. She made her way through the crowd as best she could, sick herself almost to death. Oh, his mother—his poor mother! how could she ever forgive herself. The agony of that moment was terrific. She could hardly get to the place where the poor lad was lying, as three or four men in front were about the horse which had risen with some difficulty; but at last she found herself close to the young farmer.

' Has he marked himself? for heaven's sake tell me that; has he marked his knees?' said Harry, slowly rising and rubbing his left shoulder with his right hand, and thinking only of his horse's legs. Miss Thorne soon found that he had not broken his neck, nor any of his bones, nor been injured in any essential way. But from that time forth she never instigated any one to ride at a quintain.

Eleanor left Dr. Stanhope as soon as she could do so civilly, and went in quest of her father whom she found on the lawn in company with Mr. Arabin. She was not sorry

to find them together. She was anxious to disabuse at
any rate her father's mind as to this report which had got
abroad respecting her, and would have been well pleased
to have been able to do the same with regard to Mr.
Arabin. She put her own through her father's arm,
coming up behind his back, and then tendered her hand
also to the vicar of St. Ewold's.

'And how did you come ? ' said Mr. Harding, when the
first greeting was over.

' The Stanhopes brought me,' said she ; ' their carriage
was obliged to come twice, and has now gone back for
the signora.' As she spoke she caught Mr. Arabin's eye,
and saw that he was looking pointedly at her with a
severe expression. She understood at once the accusation
contained in his glance. It said as plainly as an eye could
speak, ' Yes, you came with the Stanhopes, but you did
so in order that you might be in company with Mr. Slope.'

' Our party,' said she, still addressing her father ' consisted of the doctor and Charlotte Stanhope, myself, and
Mr. Slope.' As she mentioned the last name she felt her
father's arm quiver slightly beneath her touch. At the
same moment Mr. Arabin turned away from them, and
joining his hands behind his back strolled slowly away by
one of the paths.

' Papa,' said she, ' it was impossible to help coming in
the same carriage with Mr. Slope ; it was quite impossible.
I had promised to come with them before I dreamt of his
coming, and afterwards I could not get out of it without
explaining and giving rise to talk. You weren't at home,
you know, I couldn't possibly help it.' She said all this
so quickly that by the time her apology was spoken she
was quite out of breath.

' I don't know why you should have wished to help it,
my dear,' said her father.

' Yes, papa, you do ; you must know, you do know all
the things they said at Plumstead. I am sure you do.
You know all the archdeacon said. How unjust he was ;
and Mr. Arabin too. He's a horrid man, a horrid odious
man, but——'

' Who is an odious man, my dear ? Mr. Arabin ? '

' No ; but Mr. Slope. You know I mean Mr. Slope.
He's the most odious man I ever met in my life, and it

was most unfortunate my having to come here in the same carriage with him. But how could I help it ? '

A great weight began to move itself off Mr. Harding's mind. So, after all, the archdeacon with all his wisdom, and Mrs. Grantly with all her tact, and Mr. Arabin with all his talent, were in the wrong. His own child, his Eleanor, the daughter of whom he was so proud was not to become the wife of a Mr. Slope. He had been about to give his sanction to the marriage, so certified had he been of the fact; and now he learnt that this imputed lover of Eleanor's was at any rate as much disliked by her as by any one of the family. Mr. Harding, however, was by no means sufficiently a man of the world to conceal the blunder he had made. He could not pretend that he had entertained no suspicion ; he could not make believe that he had never joined the archdeacon in his surmises. He was greatly surprised, and gratified beyond measure, and he could not help showing that such was the case.

' My darling girl,' said he, ' I am so delighted, so overjoyed. My own child ; you have taken such a weight off my mind.'

' But surely, papa, *you* didn't think——'

' I didn't know what to think, my dear. The archdeacon told me that——'

' The archdeacon ! ' said Eleanor, her face lighting up with passion. ' A man like the archdeacon might, one would think, be better employed than in traducing his sister-in-law, and creating bitterness between a father and his daughter ! '

' He didn't mean to do that, Eleanor.'

' What did he mean then ? Why did he interfere with me, and fill your mind with such falsehood ? '

' Never mind it now, my child; never mind it now. We shall all know you better now.'

' Oh, papa, that you should have thought it ! that you should have suspected me ! '

' I don't know what you mean by suspicion, Eleanor. There would be nothing disgraceful, you know ; nothing wrong in such a marriage. Nothing that could have justified my interfering as your father.' And Mr. Harding would have proceeded in his own defence to make out that Mr. Slope after all was a very good sort of man, and a very

fitting second husband for a young widow, had he not been
interrupted by Eleanor's greater energy.

'It would be disgraceful,' said she; 'it would be wrong;
it would be abominable. Could I do such a horrid thing,
I should expect no one to speak to me. Ugh——' and
she shuddered as she thought of the matrimonial torch
which her friends had been so ready to light on her behalf.
'I don't wonder at Dr. Grantly; I don't wonder at Susan;
but, oh, papa, I do wonder at you. How could you, how
could you believe it?' Poor Eleanor, as she thought of
her father's defalcation, could resist her tears no longer,
and was forced to cover her face with her handkerchief.

The place was not very opportune for her grief. They
were walking through the shrubberies, and there were
many people near them. Poor Mr. Harding stammered
out his excuse as best he could, and Eleanor with an effort
controlled her tears, and returned her handkerchief to
her pocket. She did not find it difficult to forgive her
father, nor could she altogether refuse to join him in the
returning gaiety of spirit to which her present avowal
gave rise. It was such a load off his heart to think that
he should not be called on to welcome Mr. Slope as his
son-in-law. It was such a relief to him to find that his
daughter's feelings and his own were now, as they ever
had been, in unison. He had been so unhappy for the
last six weeks about this wretched Mr. Slope! He was
so indifferent as to the loss of the hospital, so thankful
for the recovery of his daughter, that, strong as was the
ground for Eleanor's anger, she could not find it in her
heart to be long angry with him.

'Dear papa,' she said, hanging closely to his arm,
'never suspect me again: promise me that you never will.
Whatever I do, you may be sure I shall tell you first;
you may be sure I shall consult you.'

And Mr. Harding did promise, and owned his sin, and
promised again. And so, while he promised amendment
and she uttered forgiveness, they returned together to
the drawing-room windows.

And what had Eleanor meant when she declared that
whatever she did, she would tell her father first? What
was she thinking of doing?

So ended the first act of the melodrama which Eleanor
was called on to perform this day at Ullathorne.

CHAPTER XXXVII

THE SIGNORA NERONI, THE COUNTESS DE COURCY, AND MRS. PROUDIE MEET EACH OTHER AT ULLATHORNE

AND now there were new arrivals. Just as Eleanor reached the drawing-room the signora was being wheeled into it. She had been brought out of the carriage into the dining-room and there placed on a sofa, and was now in the act of entering the other room, by the joint aid of her brother and sister, Mr. Arabin, and two servants in livery. She was all in her glory, and looked so pathetically happy, so full of affliction and grace, was so beautiful, so pitiable, and so charming, that it was almost impossible not to be glad she was there.

Miss Thorne was unaffectedly glad to welcome her. In fact, the signora was a sort of lion; and though there was no drop of the Leohunter blood in Miss Thorne's veins, she nevertheless did like to see attractive people at her house. The signora was attractive, and on her first settlement in the dining-room she had whispered two or three soft feminine words into Miss Thorne's ear, which, at the moment, had quite touched that lady's heart.

'Oh, Miss Thorne; where is Miss Thorne?' she said, as soon as her attendants had placed her in her position just before one of the windows, from whence she could see all that was going on upon the lawn; 'How am I to thank you for permitting a creature like me to be here? But if you knew the pleasure you give me, I am sure you would excuse the trouble I bring with me.' And as she spoke she squeezed the spinster's little hand between her own.

'We are delighted to see you here,' said Miss Thorne; 'you give us no trouble at all, and we think it a great favour conferred by you to come and see us; don't we, Wilfred?'

'A very great favour indeed,' said Mr. Thorne, with a gallant bow, but of a somewhat less cordial welcome than that conceded by his sister. Mr. Thorne had heard perhaps more of the antecedents of his guest than his

sister had done, and had not as yet undergone the power
of the signora's charms.

But while the mother of the last of the Neros was thus
in her full splendour, with crowds of people gazing at her
and the *élite* of the company standing round her couch,
her glory was paled by the arrival of the Countess De
Courcy. Miss Thorne had now been waiting three hours
for the countess, and could not therefore but show very
evident gratification when the arrival at last took place.
She and her brother of course went off to welcome the
titled grandees, and with them, alas, went many of the
signora's admirers.

'Oh, Mr. Thorne,' said the countess, while in the act
of being disrobed of her fur cloaks, and re-robed in her
gauze shawls, 'what dreadful roads you have; perfectly
frightful.'

It happened that Mr. Thorne was way-warden for the
district, and not liking the attack, began to excuse his
roads.

'Oh yes, indeed they are,' said the countess, not minding
him in the least, 'perfectly dreadful; are they not,
Margaretta? Why, my dear Miss Thorne, we left Courcy
Castle just at eleven; it was only just past eleven, was
it not, John? and——'

'Just past one, I think you mean,' said the Honourable
John, turning from the group and eyeing the signora
through his glass. The signora gave him back his own,
as the saying is, and more with it; so that the young
nobleman was forced to avert his glance, and drop his glass.

'I say, Thorne,' whispered he, 'who the deuce is that
on the sofa?'

'Dr. Stanhope's daughter,' whispered back Mr. Thorne.
'Signora Neroni, she calls herself.'

'Whew-ew-ew!' whistled the Honourable John. 'The
devil she is! I have heard no end of stories about that
filly. You must positively introduce me, Thorne; you
positively must.'

Mr. Thorne, who was respectability itself, did not
quite like having a guest about whom the Honourable
John De Courcy had heard no end of stories; but he
couldn't help himself. He merely resolved that before
he went to bed he would let his sister know somewhat

of the history of the lady she was so willing to welcome. The innocence of Miss Thorne, at her time of life was perfectly charming ; but even innocence may be dangerous.

'John may say what he likes,' continued the countess, urging her excuses to Miss Thorne ; 'I am sure we were past the castle gate before twelve, weren't we, Margaretta?'

'Upon my word I don't know,' said the Lady Margaretta, 'for I was half asleep. But I do know that I was called sometime in the middle of the night, and was dressing myself before daylight.'

Wise people, when they are in the wrong, always put themselves right by finding fault with the people against whom they have sinned. Lady De Courcy was a wise woman ; and therefore, having treated Miss Thorne very badly by staying away till three o'clock, she assumed the offensive and attacked Mr. Thorne's roads. Her daughter, not less wise, attacked Miss Thorne's early hours. The art of doing this is among the most precious of those usually cultivated by persons who know how to live. There is no withstanding it. Who can go systematically to work, and having done battle with the primary accusation and settled that, then bring forward a counter-charge and support that also ? Life is not long enough for such labours. A man in the right relies easily on his rectitude, and therefore goes about unarmed. His very strength is his weakness. A man in the wrong knows that he must look to his weapons ; his very weakness is his strength. The one is never prepared for combat, the other is always ready. Therefore it is that in this world the man that is in the wrong almost invariably conquers the man that is in the right, and invariably despises him.

A man must be an idiot or else an angel, who after the age of forty shall attempt to be just to his neighbours. Many like the Lady Margaretta have learnt their lesson at a much earlier age. But this of course depends on the school in which they have been taught.

Poor Miss Thorne was altogether overcome. She knew very well that she had been ill treated, and yet she found herself making apologies to Lady De Courcy. To do her ladyship justice, she received them very graciously, and allowed herself with her train of daughters to be led towards the lawn.

There were two windows in the drawing-room wide open for the countess to pass through; but she saw that there was a woman on a sofa, at the third window, and that that woman had, as it were, a following attached to her. Her ladyship therefore determined to investigate the woman. The De Courcys were hereditarily short sighted, and had been so for thirty centuries at least. So Lady De Courcy, who when she entered the family had adopted the family habits, did as her son had done before her, and taking her glass to investigate the Signora Neroni, pressed in among the gentlemen who surrounded the couch, and bowed slightly to those whom she chose to honour by her acquaintance.

In order to get to the window she had to pass close to the front of the couch, and as she did so she stared hard at the occupant. The occupant in return stared hard at the countess. The countess who since her countess-ship commenced had been accustomed to see all eyes, not royal, ducal or marquesal, fall before her own, paused as she went on, raised her eyebrows, and stared even harder than before. But she had now to do with one who cared little for countesses. It was, one may say, impossible for mortal man or woman to abash Madeline Neroni. She opened her large bright lustrous eyes wider and wider, till she seemed to be all eyes. She gazed up into the lady's face, not as though she did it with an effort, but as if she delighted in doing it. She used no glass to assist her effrontery, and needed none. The faintest possible smile of derision played round her mouth, and her nostrils were slightly dilated, as if in sure anticipation of her triumph. And it was sure. The Countess De Courcy, in spite of her thirty centuries and De Courcy castle, and the fact that Lord De Courcy was grand master of the ponies to the Prince of Wales, had not a chance with her. At first the little circlet of gold wavered in the countess's hand, then the hand shook, then the circlet fell, the countess's head tossed itself into the air, and the countess's feet shambled out to the lawn. She did not however go so fast but what she heard the signora's voice, asking—

'Who on earth is that woman, Mr. Slope?'

'That is Lady De Courcy.'

'Oh, ah. I might have supposed so. Ha, ha, ha. Well, that's as good as a play.'

It was as good as a play to any there who had eyes to observe it, and wit to comment on what they observed.

But the Lady De Courcy soon found a congenial spirit on the lawn. There she encountered Mrs. Proudie, and as Mrs. Proudie was not only the wife of a bishop, but was also the cousin of an earl, Lady De Courcy considered her to be the fittest companion she was likely to meet in that assemblage. They were accordingly delighted to see each other. Mrs. Proudie by no means despised a countess, and as this countess lived in the county and within a sort of extensive visiting distance of Barchester, she was glad to have this opportunity of ingratiating herself.

'My dear Lady De Courcy, I am so delighted,' said she, looking as little grim as it was in her nature to do. 'I hardly expected to see you here. It is such a distance, and then you know, such a crowd.'

'And such roads, Mrs. Proudie! I really wonder how the people ever get about. But I don't suppose they ever do.'

'Well, I really don't know; but I suppose not. The Thornes don't, I know,' said Mrs. Proudie. 'Very nice person, Miss Thorne, isn't she?'

'Oh, delightful, and so queer; I've known her these twenty years. A great pet of mine is dear Miss Thorne. She is so very strange, you know. She always makes me think of the Esquimaux and the Indians. Isn't her dress quite delightful?'

'Delightful,' said Mrs. Proudie; 'I wonder now whether she paints. Did you ever see such colour?'

'Oh, of course,' said Lady De Courcy; 'that is, I have no doubt she does. But, Mrs. Proudie, who is that woman on the sofa by the window? just step this way and you'll see her, there——' and the countess led her to a spot where she could plainly see the signora's well-remembered face and figure.

She did not however do so without being equally well seen by the signora. 'Look, look,' said that lady to Mr. Slope, who was still standing near to her; 'see the high spiritualities and temporalities of the land in league together, and all against poor me. I'll wager my bracelet,

Mr. Slope, against your next sermon, that they've taken up their position there on purpose to pull me to pieces. Well, I can't rush to the combat, but I know how to protect myself if the enemy come near me.'

But the enemy knew better. They could gain nothing by contact with the Signora Neroni, and they could abuse her as they pleased at a distance from her on the lawn.

'She's that horrid Italian woman, Lady De Courcy; you must have heard of her.'

'What Italian woman?' said her ladyship, quite alive to the coming story; 'I don't think I've heard of any Italian woman coming into the country. She doesn't look Italian either.'

'Oh, you must have heard of her,' said Mrs. Proudie. 'No, she's not absolutely Italian. She is Dr. Stanhope's daughter—Dr. Stanhope the prebendary; and she calls herself the Signora Neroni.'

'Oh-h-h-h!' exclaimed the countess.

'I was sure you had heard of her,' continued Mrs. Proudie. 'I don't know anything about her husband. They do say that some man named Neroni is still alive. I believe she did marry such a man abroad, but I do not at all know who or what he was.'

'Ah-h-h-h!' said the countess, shaking her head with much intelligence, as every additional 'h' fell from her lips. 'I know all about it now. I have heard George mention her. George knows all about her. George heard about her in Rome.'

'She's an abominable woman, at any rate,' said Mrs. Proudie.

'Insufferable,' said the countess.

'She made her way into the palace once, before I knew anything about her; and I cannot tell you how dreadfully indecent her conduct was.'

'Was it?' said the delighted countess.

'Insufferable,' said the prelatess.

'But why does she lie on a sofa?' asked Lady De Courcy.

'She has only one leg,' replied Mrs. Proudie.

'Only one leg!' said Lady De Courcy, who felt to a certain degree dissatisfied that the signora was thus incapacitated. 'Was she born so?'

'Oh, no,' said Mrs. Proudie,—and her ladyship felt somewhat recomforted by the assurance,—'she had two. But that Signor Neroni beat her, I believe, till she was obliged to have one amputated. At any rate, she entirely lost the use of it.'

'Unfortunate creature!' said the countess, who herself knew something of matrimonial trials.

'Yes,' said Mrs. Proudie; 'one would pity her, in spite of her past bad conduct, if she now knew how to behave herself. But she does not. She is the most insolent creature I ever put my eyes on.'

'Indeed she is,' said Lady De Courcy.

'And her conduct with men is so abominable, that she is not fit to be admitted into any lady's drawing-room.'

'Dear me!' said the countess, becoming again excited, happy, and merciless.

'You saw that man standing near her,—the clergyman with the red hair?'

'Yes, yes.'

'She has absolutely ruined that man. The bishop, or I should rather take the blame on myself, for it was I,—I brought him down from London to Barchester. He is a tolerable preacher, an active young man, and I therefore introduced him to the bishop. That woman, Lady De Courcy, has got hold of him, and has so disgraced him, that I am forced to require that he shall leave the palace; and I doubt very much whether he won't lose his gown!'

'Why what an idiot the man must be!' said the countess.

'You don't know the intriguing villainy of that woman,' said Mrs. Proudie, remembering her torn flounces.

'But you say she has only got one leg!'

'She is as full of mischief as tho' she had ten. Look at her eyes, Lady De Courcy. Did you ever see such eyes in a decent woman's head?'

'Indeed I never did, Mrs. Proudie.'

'And her effrontery, and her voice; I quite pity her poor father, who is really a good sort of man.'

'Dr. Stanhope, isn't he?'

'Yes, Dr. Stanhope. He is one of our prebendaries,— a good quiet sort of man himself. But I am surprised that he should let his daughter conduct herself as she does.'

'I suppose he can't help it,' said the countess.

'But a clergyman, you know, Lady De Courcy! He should at any rate prevent her from exhibiting in public, if he cannot induce her to behave at home. But he is to be pitied. I believe he has a desperate life of it with the lot of them. That apish-looking man there, with the long beard and the loose trousers,—he is the woman's brother. He is nearly as bad as she is. They are both of them infidels.'

'Infidels!' said Lady De Courcy, 'and their father a prebendary!'

'Yes, and likely to be the new dean too,' said Mrs. Proudie.

'Oh, yes, poor dear Dr. Trefoil!' said the countess, who had once in her life spoken to that gentleman; 'I was so distressed to hear it, Mrs. Proudie. And so Dr. Stanhope is to be the new dean! He comes of an excellent family, and I wish him success in spite of his daughter. Perhaps, Mrs. Proudie, when he is dean they'll be better able to see the error of their ways.'

To this Mrs. Proudie said nothing. Her dislike of the Signora Neroni was too deep to admit of her even hoping that that lady should see the error of her ways. Mrs. Proudie looked on the signora as one of the lost,—one of those beyond the reach of Christian charity, and was therefore able to enjoy the luxury of hating her, without the drawback of wishing her eventually well out of her sins.

Any further conversation between these congenial souls was prevented by the advent of Mr. Thorne, who came to lead the countess to the tent. Indeed, he had been desired to do so some ten minutes since; but he had been delayed in the drawing-room by the signora. She had contrived to detain him, to get him near to her sofa, and at last to make him seat himself on a chair close to her beautiful arm. The fish took the bait, was hooked, and caught, and landed. Within that ten minutes he had heard the whole of the signora's history in such strains as she chose to use in telling it. He learnt from the lady's own lips the whole of that mysterious tale to which the Honourable George had merely alluded. He discovered that the beautiful creature lying before him had been more sinned against than sinning. She had owned to

him that she had been weak, confiding and indifferent
to the world's opinion, and that she had therefore been
ill-used, deceived and evil spoken of. She had spoken to
him of her mutilated limb, her youth destroyed in its
fullest bloom, her beauty robbed of its every charm, her
life blighted, her hopes withered ; and as she did so, a
tear dropped from her eye to her cheek. She had told
him of these things, and asked for his sympathy.

What could a good-natured genial Anglo-Saxon Squire
Thorne do but promise to sympathise with her ? Mr.
Thorne did promise to sympathise ; promised also to come
and see the last of the Neros, to hear more of those fearful
Roman days, of those light and innocent but dangerous
hours which flitted by so fast on the shores of Como, and
to make himself the confidant of the signora's sorrows.

We need hardly say that he dropped all idea of warning
his sister against the dangerous lady. He had been
mistaken ; never so much mistaken in his life. He had
always regarded that Honourable George as a coarse
brutal-minded young man ; now he was more convinced
than ever that he was so. It was by such men as the
Honourable George that the reputations of such women
as Madeline Neroni were imperilled and damaged. He
would go and see the lady in her own house ; he was fully
sure in his own mind of the soundness of his own judgment ;
if he found her, as he believed he should do, an injured
well-disposed warm-hearted woman, he would get his
sister Monica to invite her out to Ullathorne.

' No,' said she, as at her instance he got up to leave her,
and declared that he himself would attend upon her wants ;
' no, no, my friend ; I positively put a veto upon your
doing so. What, in your own house, with an assemblage
round you such as there is here ! Do you wish to make
every woman hate me and every man stare at me ? I lay
a positive order on you not to come near me again to-day.
Come and see me at home. It is only at home that I can
talk ; it is only at home that I really can live and enjoy
myself. My days of going out, days such as these, are
rare indeed. Come and see me at home, Mr. Thorne, and
then I will not bid you to leave me.'

It is, we believe, common with young men of five and
twenty to look on their seniors—on men of, say, double

their own age—as so many stocks and stones,—stocks
and stones, that is, in regard to feminine beauty. There
never was a greater mistake. Women, indeed, generally
know better; but on this subject men of one age are
thoroughly ignorant of what is the very nature of mankind
of other ages. No experience of what goes on in the world,
no reading of history, no observation of life, has any effect
in teaching the truth. Men of fifty don't dance mazurkas,
being generally too fat and wheezy; nor do they sit for
the hour together on river banks at their mistresses' feet,
being somewhat afraid of rheumatism. But for real true
love, love at first sight, love to devotion, love that robs
a man of his sleep, love that ' will gaze an eagle blind,'
love that ' will hear the lowest sound when the suspicious
tread of theft is stopped,' love that is ' like a Hercules,
still climbing trees in the Hesperides,'—we believe the
best age is from forty-five to seventy; up to that, men
are generally given to mere flirting.

At the present moment Mr. Thorne, *ætat.* fifty, was
over head and ears in love at first sight with the Signora
Madeline Vesey Neroni, *nata* Stanhope.

Nevertheless he was sufficiently master of himself to
offer his arm with all propriety to Lady De Courcy, and
the countess graciously permitted herself to be led to
the tent. Such had been Miss Thorne's orders, as she had
succeeded in inducing the bishop to lead old Lady Knowle
to the top of the dining-room. One of the baronets was
sent off in quest of Mrs. Proudie, and found that lady on
the lawn not in the best of humours. Mr. Thorne and
the countess had left her too abruptly; she had in vain
looked about for an attendant chaplain, or even a stray
curate; they were all drawing long bows with the young
ladies at the bottom of the lawn, or finding places for
their graceful co-toxophilites in some snug corner of the
tent. In such position Mrs. Proudie had been wont in
earlier days to fall back upon Mr. Slope; but now she
could never fall back upon him again. She gave her head
one shake as she thought of her lone position, and that
shake was as good as a week deducted from Mr. Slope's
longer sojourn in Barchester. Sir Harkaway Gorse,
however, relieved her present misery, though his doing so
by no means mitigated the sinning chaplain's doom.

And now the eating and drinking began in earnest.
Dr. Grantly, to his great horror, found himself leagued
to Mrs. Clantantram. Mrs. Clantantram had a great
regard ·for the archdeacon, which was not cordially
returned ; and when she, coming up to him, whispered
in his ear, ' Come, archdeacon, I'm sure you won't begrudge
an old friend the favour of your arm,' and then proceeded
to tell him the whole history of her roquelaure, he resolved
that he would shake her off before he was fifteen minutes
older. But latterly the archdeacon had not been successful
in his resolutions ; and on the present occasion Mrs.
Clantantram stuck to him till the banquet was over.

Dr. Gwynne got a baronet's wife, and Mrs. Grantly
fell to the lot of a baronet. Charlotte Stanhope attached
herself to Mr. Harding in order to make room for Bertie,
who succeeded in sitting down in the dining-room next
to Mrs. Bold. To speak sooth, now that he had love in
earnest to make, his heart almost failed him.

Eleanor had been right glad to avail herself of his arm,
seeing that Mr. Slope was hovering nigh her. In striving
to avoid that terrible Charybdis of a Slope she was in
great danger of falling into an unseen Scylla on the other
hand, that Scylla being Bertie Stanhope. Nothing could
be more gracious than she was to Bertie. She almost
jumped at his proffered arm. Charlotte perceived this
from a distance, and triumphed in her heart ; Bertie
felt it, and was encouraged ; Mr. Slope saw it, and glowered
with jealousy. Eleanor and Bertie sat down to table in
the dining-room ; and as she took her seat at his right
hand, she found that Mr. Slope was already in possession
of the chair at her own.

As these things were going on in the dining-room, Mr.
Arabin was hanging enraptured and alone over the
signora's sofa ; and Eleanor from her seat could look
through the open door and see that he was doing so.

CHAPTER XXXVIII

THE BISHOP SITS DOWN TO BREAKFAST, AND THE DEAN DIES

THE bishop of Barchester said grace over the well-spread board in the Ullathorne dining-room; and while he did so the last breath was flying from the dean of Barchester as he lay in his sick room in the deanery. When the bishop of Barchester raised his first glass of champagne to his lips, the deanship of Barchester was a good thing in the gift of the prime minister. Before the bishop of Barchester had left the table, the minister of the day was made aware of the fact at his country seat in Hampshire, and had already turned over in his mind the names of five very respectable aspirants for the preferment. It is at present only necessary to say that Mr. Slope's name was not among the five.

' 'Twas merry in the hall when the beards wagged all; ' and the clerical beards wagged merrily in the hall of Ullathorne that day. It was not till after the last cork had been drawn, the last speech made, the last nut cracked, that tidings reached and were whispered about that the poor dean was no more. It was well for the happiness of the clerical beards that this little delay took place, as otherwise decency would have forbidden them to wag at all.

But there was one sad man among them that day. Mr. Arabin's beard did not wag as it should have done. He had come there hoping the best, striving to think the best, about Eleanor; turning over in his mind all the words he remembered to have fallen from her about Mr. Slope, and trying to gather from them a conviction unfavourable to his rival. He had not exactly resolved to come that day to some decisive proof as to the widow's intention; but he had meant, if possible, to re-cultivate his friendship with Eleanor; and in his present frame of mind any such re-cultivation must have ended in a declaration of love.

He had passed the previous night alone at his new parsonage, and it was the first night that he had so passed. It had been dull and sombre enough. Mrs. Grantly had been right in saying that a priestess would be wanting at St. Ewold's. He had sat there alone with his glass before him, and then with his teapot, thinking about Eleanor Bold. As is usual in such meditations, he did little but blame her; blame her for liking Mr. Slope, and blame her for not liking him; blame her for her cordiality to himself, and blame her for her want of cordiality; blame her for being stubborn, headstrong, and passionate; and yet the more he thought of her the higher she rose in his affection. If only it should turn out, if only it could be made to turn out, that she had defended Mr. Slope, not from love, but on principle, all would be right. Such principle in itself would be admirable, loveable, womanly; he felt that he could be pleased to allow Mr. Slope just so much favour as that. But if—— And then Mr. Arabin poked his fire most unnecessarily, spoke crossly to his new parlour-maid who came in for the tea-things, and threw himself back in his chair determined to go to sleep. Why had she been so stiffnecked when asked a plain question? She could not but have known in what light he regarded her. Why had she not answered a plain question, and so put an end to his misery? Then, instead of going to sleep in his arm-chair, Mr. Arabin walked about the room as though he had been possessed.

On the following morning, when he attended Miss Thorne's behests, he was still in a somewhat confused state. His first duty had been to converse with Mrs. Clantantram, and that lady had found it impossible to elicit the slightest sympathy from him on the subject of her roquelaure. Miss Thorne had asked him whether Mrs. Bold was coming with the Grantlys; and the two names of Bold and Grantly together had nearly made him jump from his seat.

He was in this state of confused uncertainty, hope, and doubt, when he saw Mr. Slope, with his most polished smile, handing Eleanor out of her carriage. He thought of nothing more. He never considered whether the carriage belonged to her or to Mr. Slope, or to any one else to whom they might both be mutually obliged without any concert between themselves. This sight in his present state of mind was quite enough to upset him and his resolves. It was clear as noonday. Had he seen her handed into

a carriage by Mr. Slope at a church door with a white
veil over her head, the truth could not be more manifest.
He went into the house, and, as we have seen, soon found
himself walking with Mr. Harding. Shortly afterwards
Eleanor came up; and then he had to leave his companion, and either go about alone or find another. While
in this state he was encountered by the archdeacon.

'I wonder,' said Dr. Grantly, 'if it be true that Mr.
Slope and Mrs. Bold came here together. Susan says she
is almost sure she saw their faces in the same carriage
as she got out of her own.'

Mr. Arabin had nothing for it but to bear his testimony
to the correctness of Mrs. Grantly's eyesight.

'It is perfectly shameful,' said the archdeacon; 'or
I should rather say, shameless. She was asked here as
my guest; and if she be determined to disgrace herself,
she should have feeling enough not to do so before my
immediate friends. I wonder how that man got himself
invited. I wonder whether she had the face to bring him.'

To this Mr. Arabin could answer nothing, nor did he
wish to answer anything. Though he abused Eleanor
to himself, he did not choose to abuse her to any one else,
nor was he well pleased to hear any one else speak ill of
her. Dr. Grantly, however, was very angry, and did not
spare his sister-in-law. Mr. Arabin therefore left him as
soon as he could, and wandered back into the house.

He had not been there long, when the signora was
brought in. For some time he kept himself out of temptation, and merely hovered round her at a distance; but
as soon as Mr. Thorne had left her, he yielded himself
up to the basilisk, and allowed himself to be made prey of.

It is impossible to say how the knowledge had been
acquired, but the signora had a sort of instinctive knowledge that Mr. Arabin was an admirer of Mrs. Bold. Men
hunt foxes by the aid of dogs, and are aware that they
do so by the strong organ of smell with which the dog is
endowed. They do not, however, in the least comprehend
how such a sense can work with such acuteness. The
organ by which women instinctively, as it were, know
and feel how other women are regarded by men, and how
also men are regarded by other women, is equally strong,
and equally incomprehensible. A glance, a word, a

motion, suffices: by some such acute exercise of her
feminine senses the signora was aware that Mr. Arabin
loved Eleanor Bold; and therefore, by a further exercise
of her peculiar feminine propensities, it was quite natural
for her to entrap Mr. Arabin into her net.

The work was half done before she came to Ullathorne,
and when could she have a better opportunity of completing it? She had had almost enough of Mr. Slope,
though she could not quite resist the fun of driving a very
sanctimonious clergyman to madness by a desperate and
ruinous passion. Mr. Thorne had fallen too easily to give
much pleasure in the chase. His position as a man of
wealth might make his alliance of value, but as a lover he
was very second-rate. We may say that she regarded
him somewhat as a sportsman does a pheasant. The
bird is so easily shot, that he would not be worth the
shooting were it not for the very respectable appearance
that he makes in a larder. The signora would not waste
much time in shooting Mr. Thorne, but still he was worth
bagging for family uses.

But Mr. Arabin was game of another sort. The signora
was herself possessed of quite sufficient intelligence to
know that Mr. Arabin was a man more than usually
intellectual. She knew also, that as a clergyman he was
of a much higher stamp than Mr. Slope, and that as a
gentleman he was better educated than Mr. Thorne. She
would never have attempted to drive Mr. Arabin into
ridiculous misery as she did Mr. Slope, nor would she
think it possible to dispose of him in ten minutes as she
had done with Mr. Thorne.

Such were her reflections about Mr. Arabin. As to
Mr. Arabin, it cannot be said that he reflected at all about
the signora. He knew that she was beautiful, and he felt
that she was able to charm him. He required charming
in his present misery, and therefore he went and stood
at the head of her couch. She knew all about it. Such
were her peculiar gifts. It was her nature to see that
he required charming, and it was her province to charm
him. As the Eastern idler swallows his dose of opium, as
the London reprobate swallows his dose of gin, so with
similar desires and for similar reasons did Mr. Arabin
prepare to swallow the charms of the Signora Neroni.

'Why an't you shooting with bows and arrows, Mr. Arabin?' said she, when they were nearly alone together in the drawing-room; 'or talking with young ladies in shady bowers, or turning your talents to account in some way? What was a bachelor like you asked here for? Don't you mean to earn your cold chicken and champagne? Were I you, I should be ashamed to be so idle.'

Mr. Arabin murmured some sort of answer. Though he wished to be charmed, he was hardly yet in a mood to be playful in return.

'Why, what ails you, Mr. Arabin?' said she, 'here you are in your own parish; Miss Thorne tells me that her party is given expressly in your honour; and yet you are the only dull man at it. Your friend Mr. Slope was with me a few minutes since, full of life and spirits; why don't you rival him?'

It was not difficult for so acute an observer as Madeline Neroni to see that she had hit the nail on the head and driven the bolt home. Mr. Arabin winced visibly before her attack, and she knew at once that he was jealous of Mr. Slope.

'But I look on you and Mr. Slope as the very antipodes of men,' said she. 'There is nothing in which you are not each the reverse of the other, except in belonging to the same profession; and even in that you are so unlike as perfectly to maintain the rule. He is gregarious, you are given to solitude. He is active, you are passive. He works, you think. He likes women, you despise them. He is fond of position and power, and so are you, but for directly different reasons. He loves to be praised, you very foolishly abhor it. He will gain his rewards, which will be an insipid useful wife, a comfortable income, and a reputation for sanctimony. You will also gain yours.'

'Well, and what will they be?' said Mr. Arabin, who knew that he was being flattered, and yet suffered himself to put up with it. 'What will be my rewards?'

'The heart of some woman whom you will be too austere to own that you love, and the respect of some few friends which you will be too proud to own that you value.'

'Rich rewards,' said he; 'but of little worth if they are to be so treated.'

' Oh, you are not to look for such success as awaits Mr. Slope. He is born to be a successful man. He suggests to himself an object, and then starts for it with eager intention. Nothing will deter him from his pursuit. He will have no scruples, no fears, no hesitation. His desire is to be a bishop with a rising family, the wife will come first, and in due time the apron. You will see all this, and then——'

' Well, and what then ? '

' Then you will begin to wish that you had done the same.'

Mr. Arabin looked placidly out at the lawn, and resting his shoulder on the head of the sofa, rubbed his chin with his hand. It was a trick he had when he was thinking deeply; and what the signora said made him think. Was it not all true ? Would he not hereafter look back, if not at Mr. Slope, at some others, perhaps not equally gifted with himself, who had risen in the world while he had lagged behind, and then wish that he had done the same ?

' Is not such the doom of all speculative men of talent ? ' said she. ' Do they not all sit rapt as you now are, cutting imaginary silken cords with their fine edges, while those not so highly tempered sever the every-day Gordian knots of the world's struggle, and win wealth and renown ? Steel too highly polished, edges too sharp, do not do for this world's work, Mr. Arabin.'

Who was this woman that thus read the secrets of his heart, and re-uttered to him the unwelcome bodings of his own soul ? He looked full into her face when she had done speaking, and said, ' Am I one of those foolish blades, too sharp and too fine to do a useful day's work ? '

' Why do you let the Slopes of the world out-distance you ? ' said she. ' Is not the blood in your veins as warm as his ? does not your pulse beat as fast ? Has not God made you a man, and intended you to do a man's work here, ay, and to take a man's wages also ? '

Mr. Arabin sat ruminating and rubbing his face, and wondering why these things were said to him; but he replied nothing. The signora went on—

' The greatest mistake any man ever made is to suppose that the good things of the world are not worth the winning. And it is a mistake so opposed to the religion which you preach! Why does God permit his bishops one after another to have their five thousands and ten thousands a year if such wealth be bad and not worth having? Why are beautiful things given to us, and luxuries and pleasant enjoyments, if they be not intended to be used? They must be meant for some one, and what is good for a layman cannot surely be bad for a clerk. You try to despise these good things, but you only try; you don't succeed.'

'Don't I?' said Mr. Arabin, still musing, and not knowing what he said.

'I ask you the question; do you succeed?'

Mr. Arabin looked at her piteously. It seemed to him as though he were being interrogated by some inner spirit of his own, to whom he could not refuse an answer, and to whom he did not dare to give a false reply.

'Come, Mr. Arabin, confess; do you succeed? Is money so contemptible? Is worldly power so worthless? Is feminine beauty a trifle to be so slightly regarded by a wise man?'

'Feminine beauty!' said he, gazing into her face, as though all the feminine beauty in the world were concentrated there. 'Why do you say I do not regard it?'

'If you look at me like that, Mr. Arabin, I shall alter my opinion—or should do so, were I not of course aware that I have no beauty of my own worth regarding.'

The gentleman blushed crimson, but the lady did not blush at all. A slightly increased colour animated her face, just so much so as to give her an air of special interest. She expected a compliment from her admirer, but she was rather grateful than otherwise by finding that he did not pay it to her. Messrs. Slope and Thorne, Messrs. Brown, Jones and Robinson, they all paid her compliments. She was rather in hopes that she would ultimately succeed in inducing Mr. Arabin to abuse her.

'But your gaze,' said she, 'is one of wonder, and not of admiration. You wonder at my audacity in asking you such questions about yourself.'

'Well, I do rather,' said he.

'Nevertheless I expect an answer, Mr. Arabin. Why

were women made beautiful if men are not to regard them ? '

' But men do regard them,' he replied.

' And why not you ? '

' You are begging the question, Madame Neroni.'

' I am sure I shall beg nothing, Mr. Arabin, which you will not grant, and I do beg for an answer. Do you not as a rule think women below your notice as companions ? Let us see. There is the widow Bold looking round at you from her chair this minute. What would you say to her as a companion for life ? '

Mr. Arabin, rising from his position, leaned over the sofa and looked through the drawing-room door to the place where Eleanor was seated between Bertie Stanhope and Mr. Slope. She at once caught his glance, and averted her own. She was not pleasantly placed in her present position. Mr. Slope was doing his best to attract her attention ; and she was striving to prevent his doing so by talking to Mr. Stanhope, while her mind was intently fixed on Mr. Arabin and Madame Neroni. Bertie Stanhope endeavoured to take advantage of her favours, but he was thinking more of the manner in which he would by-and-by throw himself at her feet, than of amusing her at the present moment.

' There,' said the signora. ' She was stretching her beautiful neck to look at you, and now you have disturbed her. Well I declare, I believe I am wrong about you ; I believe that you do think Mrs. Bold a charming woman. Your looks seem to say so ; and by her looks I should say that she is jealous of me. Come, Mr. Arabin, confide in me, and if it is so, I'll do all in my power to make up the match.'

It is needless to say that the signora was not very sincere in her offer. She was never sincere on such subjects. She never expected others to be so, nor did she expect others to think her so. Such matters were her playthings, her billiard table, her hounds and hunters, her waltzes and polkas, her picnics and summer-day excursions. She had little else to amuse her, and therefore played at love-making in all its forms. She was now playing at it with Mr. Arabin, and did not at all expect the earnestness and truth of his answer.

'All in your power would be nothing,' said he; 'for Mrs. Bold is, I imagine, already engaged to another.'

'Then you own the impeachment yourself.'

'You cross-question me rather unfairly,' he replied, 'and I do not know why I answer you at all. Mrs. Bold is a very beautiful woman, and as intelligent as beautiful. It is impossible to know her without admiring her.'

'So you think the widow a very beautiful woman?'

'Indeed I do.'

'And one that would grace the parsonage of St. Ewold's.'

'One that would well grace any man's house.'

'And you really have the effrontery to tell me this,' said she; 'to tell me, who, as you very well know, set up to be a beauty myself, and who am at this very moment taking such an interest in your affairs, you really have the effrontery to tell me that Mrs. Bold is the most beautiful woman you know.'

'I did not say so,' said Mr. Arabin; 'you are more beautiful——'

'Ah, come now, that is something like. I thought you could not be so unfeeling.'

'You are more beautiful, perhaps more clever.'

'Thank you, thank you, Mr. Arabin. I knew that you and I should be friends.'

'But——'

'Not a word further. I will not hear a word further. If you talk till midnight, you cannot improve what you have said.'

'But Madame Neroni, Mrs. Bold——'

'I will not hear a word about Mrs. Bold. Dread thoughts of strychnine did pass across my brain, but she is welcome to the second place.'

'Her place——'

'I won't hear anything about her or her place. I am satisfied, and that is enough. But, Mr. Arabin, I am dying with hunger; beautiful and clever as I am, you know I cannot go to my food, and yet you do not bring it to me.'

This at any rate was so true as to make it necessary that Mr. Arabin should act upon it, and he accordingly went into the dining-room and supplied the signora's wants.

'And yourself?' said she.

'Oh,' said he, 'I am not hungry; I never eat at this hour.'

'Come, come, Mr. Arabin, don't let love interfere with your appetite. It never does with mine. Give me half a glass more champagne, and then go to the table. Mrs. Bold will do me an injury if you stay talking to me any longer.'

Mr. Arabin did as he was bid. He took her plate and glass from her, and going into the dining-room, helped himself to a sandwich from the crowded table and began munching it in a corner.

As he was doing so, Miss Thorne, who had hardly sat down for a moment, came into the room, and seeing him standing, was greatly distressed.

'Oh, my dear Mr. Arabin,' said she, 'have you never sat down yet? I am so distressed. You of all men too.'

Mr. Arabin assured her that he had only just come into the room.

'That is the very reason why you should lose no more time. Come, I'll make room for you. Thank'ee, my dear,' she said, seeing that Mrs. Bold was making an attempt to move from her chair, 'but I would not for worlds see you stir, for all the ladies would think it necessary to follow. But, perhaps, if Mr. Stanhope has done—just for a minute, Mr. Stanhope—till I can get another chair.'

And so Bertie had to rise to make way for his rival. This he did, as he did everything, with an air of good-humoured pleasantry which made it impossible for Mr. Arabin to refuse the proffered seat.

'His bishopric let another take,' said Bertie; the quotation being certainly not very appropriate, either for the occasion or the person spoken to. 'I have eaten and am satisfied; Mr. Arabin, pray take my chair. I wish for your sake that it really was a bishop's seat.'

Mr. Arabin did sit down, and as he did so, Mrs. Bold got up as though to follow her neighbour.

'Pray, pray don't move,' said Miss Thorne, almost forcing Eleanor back into her chair. 'Mr. Stanhope is not going to leave us. He will stand behind you like a true knight as he is. And now I think of it, Mr. Arabin, let me introduce you to Mr. Slope. Mr. Slope, Mr. Arabin.' And the two gentlemen bowed stiffly to each other across the lady whom they both intended to marry, while the other gentleman who also intended to marry her stood behind, watching them.

The two had never met each other before, and the present was certainly not a good opportunity for much cordial conversation, even if cordial conversation between them had been possible. As it was, the whole four who formed the party seemed as though their tongues were tied. Mr. Slope, who was wide awake to what he hoped was his coming opportunity, was not much concerned in the interest of the moment. His wish was to see Eleanor move, that he might pursue her. Bertie was not exactly in the same frame of mind; the evil day was near enough; there was no reason why he should precipitate it. He had made up his mind to marry Eleanor Bold if he could, and was resolved to-day to take the first preliminary step towards doing so. But there was time enough before him. He was not going to make an offer of marriage over the table-cloth. Having thus good-naturedly made way for Mr. Arabin, he was willing also to let him talk to the future Mrs. Stanhope as long as they remained in their present position.

Mr. Arabin having bowed to Mr. Slope, began eating his food without saying a word further. He was full of thought, and though he ate he did so unconsciously.

But poor Eleanor was the most to be pitied. The only friend on whom she thought she could rely, was Bertie Stanhope, and he, it seemed, was determined to desert her. Mr. Arabin did not attempt to address her. She said a few words in reply to some remarks from Mr. Slope, and then feeling the situation too much for her, started from her chair in spite of Miss Thorne, and hurried from the room. Mr. Slope followed her, and young Stanhope lost the occasion.

Madeline Neroni, when she was left alone, could not help pondering much on the singular interview she had had with this singular man. Not a word that she had spoken to him had been intended by her to be received as true, and yet he had answered her in the very spirit of truth. He had done so, and she had been aware that he had so done. She had wormed from him his secret; and he, debarred as it would seem from man's usual privilege of lying, had innocently laid bare his whole soul to her. He loved Eleanor Bold, but Eleanor was not in his eye so beautiful as herself. He would fain have Eleanor for his wife, but yet he had acknowledged that she was the less gifted of the two. The man had literally been unable to falsify his thoughts when questioned, and had been compelled to be true *malgrè lui*, even when truth must have been so disagreeable to him.

This teacher of men, this Oxford pundit, this double-distilled quintessence of university perfection, this writer of religious treatises, this speaker of ecclesiastical speeches, had been like a little child in her hands ; she had turned him inside out, and read his very heart as she might have done that of a young girl. She could not but despise him for his facile openness, and yet she liked him for it too. It was a novelty to her, a new trait in a man's character. She felt also that she could never so completely make a fool of him as she did of the Slopes and Thornes. She felt that she never could induce Mr. Arabin to make protestations to her that were not true, or to listen to nonsense that was mere nonsense.

It was quite clear that Mr. Arabin was heartily in love with Mrs. Bold, and the signora, with very unwonted good nature, began to turn it over in her mind whether she could not do him a good turn. Of course Bertie was to have the first chance. It was an understood family arrangement that her brother was, if possible, to marry the widow Bold. Madeline knew too well his necessities and what was due to her sister to interfere with so excellent a plan, as long as it might be feasible. But she had strong suspicion that it was not feasible. She did not think it likely that Mrs. Bold would accept a man in her brother's position, and she had frequently said so to Charlotte. She was inclined to believe that Mr. Slope had more chance of success ; and with her it would be a labour of love to rob Mr. Slope of his wife.

And so the signora resolved, should Bertie fail, to do a good-natured act for once in her life, and give up Mr. Arabin to the woman whom he loved.

CHAPTER XXXIX

THE LOOKALOFTS AND THE GREENACRES

On the whole, Miss Thorne's provision for the amusement and feeding of the outer classes in the exoteric paddock was not unsuccessful.

Two little drawbacks to the general happiness did take place, but they were of a temporary nature, and apparent rather than real. The first was the downfall of young Harry Greenacre, and the other the uprise of Mrs. Lookaloft and her family.

As to the quintain, it became more popular among the boys on foot, than it would ever have been among the men on horseback, even had young Greenacre been more successful. It was twirled round and round till it was nearly twirled out of the ground; and the bag of flour was used with great gusto in powdering the backs and heads of all who could be coaxed within its vicinity.

Of course it was reported all through the assemblage that Harry was dead, and there was a pathetic scene between him and his mother when it was found that he had escaped scatheless from the fall. A good deal of beer was drunk on the occasion, and the quintain was 'dratted' and 'bothered,' and very generally anathematised by all the mothers who had young sons likely to be placed in similar jeopardy. But the affair of Mrs. Lookaloft was of a more serious nature.

'I do tell 'ee plainly,—face to face,—she be there in madam's drawing-room; herself and Gussy, and them two walloping gals, dressed up to their very eyeses.' This was said by a very positive, very indignant, and very fat farmer's wife, who was sitting on the end of a bench leaning on the handle of a huge cotton umbrella.

'But you didn't zee her, Dame Guffern?' said Mrs. Greenacre, whom this information, joined to the recent peril undergone by her son, almost overpowered. Mr. Greenacre held just as much land as Mr. Lookaloft, paid his rent quite as punctually, and his opinion in the vestry-room was reckoned to be every whit as good. Mrs. Lookaloft's rise in the world had been wormwood to Mrs.

Greenacre. She had no taste herself for the sort of finery which had converted Barleystubb farm into Rosebank, and which had occasionally graced Mr. Lookaloft's letters with the dignity of esquirehood. She had no wish to convert her own homestead into Violet Villa, or to see her goodman go about with a new-fangled handle to his name. But it was a mortal injury to her that Mrs. Lookaloft should be successful in her hunt after such honours. She had abused and ridiculed Mrs. Lookaloft to the extent of her little power. She had pushed against her going out of church, and had excused herself with all the easiness of equality. 'Ah, dame, I axes pardon ; but you be grown so mortal stout these times.' She had inquired with apparent cordiality of Mr. Lookaloft, after 'the woman that owned him,' and had, as she thought, been on the whole able to hold her own pretty well against her aspiring neighbour. Now, however, she found herself distinctly put into a separate and inferior class. Mrs. Lookaloft was asked into the Ullathorne drawing-room merely because she called her house Rosebank, and had talked over her husband into buying pianos and silk dresses instead of putting his money by to stock farms for his sons.

Mrs. Greenacre, much as she reverenced Miss Thorne, and highly as she respected her husband's landlord, could not but look on this as an act of injustice done to her and hers. Hitherto the Lookalofts had never been recognised as being of a different class from the Greenacres. Their pretensions were all self-pretensions, their finery was all paid for by themselves and not granted to them by others. The local sovereigns of the vicinity, the district fountains of honour, had hitherto conferred on them the stamp of no rank. Hitherto their crinoline petticoats, late hours, and mincing gait had been a fair subject of Mrs. Green-acre's raillery, and this raillery had been a safety valve for her envy. Now, however, and from henceforward, the case would be very different. Now the Lookalofts would boast that their aspirations had been sanctioned by the gentry of the country ; now they would declare with some show of truth that their claims to peculiar consideration had been recognised. They had sat as equal guests in the presence of bishops and baronets ; they had been curtseyed to by Miss Thorne on her own drawing-room carpet; they were about to sit down to table in company with a live countess! Bab Lookaloft, as she had always been called by the young Greenacres in the days of their juvenile equality, might possibly sit next to the Honourable George, and that wretched Gussy might be permitted to hand a custard to the Lady Margaretta De Courcy.

The fruition of those honours, or such of them as fell to the lot of the envied family, was not such as should have caused much envy. The attention paid to the Lookalofts by the De Courcys was very limited, and the amount of entertainment which they received from the bishop's society was hardly in itself a recompense for the dull monotony of their day. But of what they endured Mrs. Greenacre took no account; she thought only of what she considered they must enjoy, and of the dreadfully exalted tone of living which would be manifested by the Rosebank family, as the consequence of their present distinction.

'But did 'ee zee 'em there, dame, did 'ee zee 'em there with your own eyes?' asked poor Mrs. Greenacre; still hoping that there might be some ground for doubt.

'And how could I do that, unless so be I was there myself?' asked Mrs. Guffern. 'I didn't zet eyes on none of them this blessed morning, but I zee'd them as did. You know our John; well, he will be for keeping company with Betsey Rusk, madam's own maid, you know. And Betsey isn't none of your common kitchen wenches. So Betsey, she came out to our John, you know, and she's always vastly polite to me, is Betsey Rusk, I must say. So before she took so much as one turn with John, she told me every ha'porth that was going on up in the house.'

'Did she now?' said Mrs. Greenacre.

'Indeed she did,' said Mrs. Guffern.

'And she told you them people was up there in the drawing-room?'

'She told me she zee'd them come in,—that they was dressed finer by half nor any of the family, with all their neckses and buzoms stark naked as a born babby.'

'The minxes!' exclaimed Mrs. Greenacre, who felt herself more put about by this than any other mark of aristocratic distinction which her enemies had assumed.

'Yes, indeed,' continued Mrs. Guffern, 'as naked as

you please, while all the quality was dressed just as you
and I be, Mrs. Greenacre.'

'Drat their impudence,' said Mrs. Greenacre, from
whose well-covered bosom all milk of human kindness
was receding, as far as the family of the Lookalofts were
concerned.

'So says I,' said Mrs. Guffern; 'and so says my goodman, Thomas Guffern, when he hear'd it. "Molly," says
he to me, "if ever you takes to going about o' mornings
with yourself all naked in them ways, I begs you won't
come back no more to the old house." So says I, "Thomas,
no more I wull." "But," says he, "drat it, how the deuce
does she manage with her rheumatiz, and she not a rag
on her:"' and Mrs. Guffern laughed loudly as she thought
of Mrs. Lookaloft's probable sufferings from rheumatic
attacks.

'But to liken herself that way to folk that ha' blood
in their veins,' said Mrs. Greenacre.

'Well, but that warn't all neither that Betsey told.
There they all swelled into madam's drawing-room, like
so many turkey cocks, as much as to say, "and who dare
say no to us?" and Gregory was thinking of telling of
'em to come down here, only his heart failed him 'cause
of the grand way they was dressed. So in they went;
but madam looked at them as glum as death.'

'Well now,' said Mrs. Greenacre, greatly relieved, 'so
they wasn't axed different from us at all then?'

'Betsey says that Gregory says that madam wasn't
a bit too well pleased to see them where they was, and
that, to his believing, they was expected to come here
just like the rest of us.'

There was great consolation in this. Not that Mrs.
Greenacre was altogether satisfied. She felt that justice
to herself demanded that Mrs. Lookaloft should not only
not be encouraged, but that she should also be absolutely
punished. What had been done at that scriptural banquet,
of which Mrs. Greenacre so often read the account to her
family? Why had not Miss Thorne boldly gone to the
intruder and said, 'Friend, thou hast come up hither to
high places not fitted to thee. Go down lower, and thou
wilt find thy mates.' Let the Lookalofts be treated at the
present moment with ever so cold a shoulder, they would

still be enabled to boast hereafter of their position, their aspirations, and their honour.

'Well, with all her grandeur, I do wonder that she be so mean,' continued Mrs. Greenacre, unable to dismiss the subject. 'Did you hear, goodman?' she went on, about to repeat the whole story to her husband who then came up. 'There's dame Lookaloft and Bab and Gussy and the lot of 'em all sitting as grand as fivepence in madam's drawing-room, and they not axed no more nor you nor me. Did you ever hear tell the like o' that?'

'Well, and what for shouldn't they?' said Farmer Greenacre.

'Likening theyselves to the quality, as though they was estated folk, or the like o' that!' said Mrs. Guffern.

'Well, if they likes it and madam likes it, they's welcome for me,' said the farmer. 'Now I likes this place better, cause I be more at home like, and don't have to pay for them fine clothes for the missus. Every one to his taste, Mrs. Guffern, and if neighbour Lookaloft thinks that he has the best of it, he's welcome.'

Mrs. Greenacre sat down by her husband's side to begin the heavy work of the banquet, and she did so in some measure with restored tranquillity, but nevertheless she shook her head at her gossip to show that in this instance she did not quite approve of her husband's doctrine.

'And I'll tell 'ee what, dames,' continued he; 'if so be that we cannot enjoy the dinner that madam gives us because Mother Lookaloft is sitting up there on a grand sofa, I think we ought all to go home. If we greet at that, what'll we do when true sorrow comes across us? How would you be now, dame, if the boy there had broke his neck when he got the tumble?'

Mrs. Greenacre was humbled and said nothing further on the matter. But let prudent men, such as Mr. Green-acre, preach as they will, the family of the Lookalofts certainly does occasion a good deal of heart-burning in the world at large.

It was pleasant to see Mr. Plomacy, as leaning on his stout stick he went about among the rural guests, acting as a sort of head constable as well as master of the revels. 'Now, young 'un, if you can't manage to get along without that screeching, you'd better go to the other side of the twelve-acre field, and take your dinner with you. Come, girls, what do you stand there for, twirling of your thumbs? come out, and let the lads see you ; you've no need to be so ashamed of your faces. Hollo ! there, who are you ? how did you make your way in here ? '

This last disagreeable question was put to a young man of about twenty-four, who did not, in Mr. Plomacy's eye, bear sufficient vestiges of a rural education and residence.

' If you please, your worship, Master Barrell the coach-man let me in at the church wicket, 'cause I do be working mostly al'ays for the family.'

' Then Master Barrell the coachman may let you out again,' said Mr. Plomacy, not even conciliated by the magisterial dignity which had been conceded to him. ' What 's your name ? and what trade are you, and who do you work for ? '

' I'm Stubbs, your worship, Bob Stubbs ; and—and—and——'

' And what's your trade, Stubbs ? '

' Plaisterer, please your worship.'

' I'll plaister you, and Barrell too ; you'll just walk out of this 'ere field as quick as you walked in. We don't want no plaisterers ; when we do, we'll send for 'em. Come, my buck, walk.'

Stubbs the plasterer was much downcast at this dread-ful edict. He was a sprightly fellow, and had contrived since his egress into the Ullathorne elysium to attract to himself a forest nymph, to whom he was whispering a plasterer's usual soft nothings, when he was encountered by the great Mr. Plomacy. It was dreadful to be thus dissevered from his dryad, and sent howling back to a Barchester pandemonium just as the nectar and ambrosia were about to descend on the fields of asphodel. He began to try what prayers would do, but city prayers were vain against the great rural potentate. Not only did Mr. Plomacy order his exit, but raising his stick to show the way which led to the gate that had been left in the custody of that false Cerberus Barrell, proceeded himself to see the edict of banishment carried out.

The goddess Mercy, however, the sweetest goddess that ever sat upon a cloud, and the dearest to poor frail erring man, appeared on the field in the person of Mr. Greenacre. Never was interceding goddess more welcome.

'Come, man,' said Mr. Greenacre, 'never stick at trifles such a day as this. I know the lad well. Let him bide at my axing. Madam won't miss what he can eat and drink, I know.'

Now Mr. Plomacy and Mr. Greenacre were sworn friends. Mr. Plomacy had at his own disposal as comfortable a room as there was in Ullathorne House; but he was a bachelor, and alone there; and, moreover, smoking in the house was not allowed even to Mr. Plomacy. His moments of truest happiness were spent in a huge arm-chair in the warmest corner of Mrs. Greenacre's beautifully clean front kitchen. 'Twas there that the inner man dissolved itself, and poured itself out in streams of pleasant chat; 'twas there that he was respected and yet at his ease; 'twas there, and perhaps there only, that he could unburden himself from the ceremonies of life without offending the dignity of those above him, or incurring the familiarity of those below. 'Twas there that his long pipe was always to be found on the accustomed chimney board, not only permitted but encouraged.

Such being the state of the case, it was not to be supposed that Mr. Plomacy could refuse such a favour to Mr. Greenacre; but nevertheless he did not grant it without some further show of austere authority.

'Eat and drink, Mr. Greenacre! No. It's not what he eats and drinks; but the example such a chap shows, coming in where he's not invited—a chap of his age too. He too that never did a day's work about Ullathorne since he was born. Plaisterer! I'll plaister him!'

'He worked long enough for me, then, Mr. Plomacy. And a good hand he is at setting tiles as any in Barchester,' said the other, not sticking quite to veracity, as indeed mercy never should. 'Come, come, let him alone to-day, and quarrel with him to-morrow. You wouldn't shame him before his lass there?'

'It goes against the grain with me, then,' said Mr. Plomacy 'And take care, you Stubbs, and behave yourself. If I hear a row I shall know where it comes from. I'm up to you Barchester journeymen; I know what stuff you're made of.'

And so Stubbs went off happy, pulling at the forelock of his shock head of hair in honour of the steward's clemency, and giving another double pull at it in honour of the farmer's kindness. And as he went he swore within his grateful heart, that if ever Farmer Greenacre wanted a day's work done for nothing, he was the lad to do it for him. Which promise it was not probable that he would ever be called on to perform.

But Mr. Plomacy was not quite happy in his mind, for he thought of the unjust steward, and began to reflect whether he had not made for himself friends of the mammon of unrighteousness. This, however, did not interfere with the manner in which he performed his duties at the bottom of the long board; nor did Mr. Greenacre perform his the worse at the top on account of the good wishes of Stubbs the plasterer. Moreover, the guests did not think it anything amiss when Mr. Plomacy, rising to say grace, prayed that God would make them all truly thankful for the good things which Madam Thorne in her great liberality had set before them!

All this time the quality in the tent on the lawn were getting on swimmingly; that is, if champagne without restriction can enable quality folk to swim. Sir Harkaway Gorse proposed the health of Miss Thorne, and likened her to a blood race-horse, always in condition, and not to be tired down by any amount of work. Mr. Thorne returned thanks, saying he hoped his sister would always be found able to run when called upon, and then gave the health and prosperity of the De Courcy family. His sister was very much honoured by seeing so many of them at her poor board. They were all aware that important avocations made the absence of the earl necessary. As his duty to his prince had called him from his family hearth, he, Mr. Thorne, could not venture to regret that he did not see him at Ullathorne; but nevertheless he would venture to say—that was to express a wish—an opinion he meant to say—— And so Mr. Thorne became somewhat gravelled, as country gentlemen in similar circumstances usually do; but he ultimately sat down, declaring that he had much satisfaction in drinking the noble earl's health, together with that of the countess, and all the family of De Courcy castle.

And then the Honourable George returned thanks. We will not follow him through the different periods of his somewhat irregular eloquence. Those immediately in his neighbourhood found it at first rather difficult to get him on his legs, but much greater difficulty was soon experienced in inducing him to resume his seat. One of two arrangements should certainly be made in these days : either let all speech-making on festive occasions be utterly tabooed and made as it were impossible ; or else let those who are to exercise the privilege be first subjected to a competing examination before the civil service examining commissioners. As it is now, the Honourable Georges do but little honour to our exertions in favour of British education.

In the dining-room the bishop went through the honours of the day with much more neatness and propriety. He also drank Miss Thorne's health, and did it in a manner becoming the bench which he adorned. The party there, was perhaps a little more dull, a shade less lively than that in the tent. But what was lost in mirth, was fully made up in decorum.

And so the banquets passed off at the various tables with great eclat and universal delight.

CHAPTER XL

ULLATHORNE SPORTS—ACT II

' THAT which has made them drunk, has made me bold.' 'Twas thus that Mr. Slope encouraged himself, as he left the dining-room in pursuit of Eleanor. He had not indeed seen in that room any person really intoxicated; but there had been a good deal of wine drunk, and Mr. Slope had not hesitated to take his share, in order to screw himself up to the undertaking which he had in hand. He is not the first man who has thought it expedient to call in the assistance of Bacchus on such an occasion.

Eleanor was out through the window, and on the grass before she perceived that she was followed. Just at that moment the guests were nearly all occupied at the tables. Here and there were to be seen a constant couple or two, who preferred their own sweet discourse to the jingle of glasses, or the charms of rhetoric which fell from the mouths of the Honourable George and the bishop of Barchester; but the grounds were as nearly vacant as Mr. Slope could wish them to be.

Eleanor saw that she was pursued, and as a deer, when escape is no longer possible, will turn to bay and attack the hounds, so did she turn upon Mr. Slope.

' Pray don't let me take you from the room,' said she, speaking with all the stiffness which she knew how to use. ' I have come out to look for a friend. I must beg of you, Mr. Slope, to go back.'

But Mr. Slope would not be thus entreated. He had observed all day that Mrs. Bold was not cordial to him, and this had to a certain extent oppressed him. But he did not deduce from this any assurance that his aspirations were in vain. He saw that she was angry with him. Might she not be so because he had so long tampered with her feelings,—might it not arise from his having, as he knew was the case, caused her name to be bruited about in conjunction with his own, without having given her the opportunity of confessing to the world that henceforth their names were to be one and the same? Poor lady! He had within him a certain Christian conscience-stricken feeling of remorse on this head. It might be that he had wronged her by his tardiness. He had, however, at the present moment imbibed too much of Mr. Thorne's champagne to have any inward misgivings. He was right in repeating the boast of Lady Macbeth: he was not drunk; but he was bold enough for anything. It was a pity that in such a state he could not have encountered Mrs. Proudie.

' You must permit me to attend you,' said he; ' I could not think of allowing you to go alone.'

' Indeed you must, Mr. Slope,' said Eleanor still very stiffly; ' for it is my special wish to be alone.'

The time for letting the great secret escape him had already come. Mr. Slope saw that it must be now or never, and he was determined that it should be now. This was not his first attempt at winning a fair lady. He had been on his knees, looked unutterable things with his eyes, and whispered honeyed words before this. Indeed he was somewhat an adept at these things, and had only to adapt

to the perhaps different taste of Mrs. Bold the well-
remembered rhapsodies which had once so much gratified
Olivia Proudie.

' Do not ask me to leave you, Mrs. Bold,' said he with
an impassioned look, impassioned and sanctified as well,
with that sort of look which is not uncommon with gentlemen of Mr. Slope's school, and which may perhaps be called
the tender-pious. ' Do not ask me to leave you, till I have
spoken a few words with which my heart is full ; which
I have come hither purposely to say.'

Eleanor saw how it was now. She knew directly what
it was she was about to go through, and very miserable the
knowledge made her. Of course she could refuse Mr. Slope,
and there would be an end of that, one might say. But
there would not be an end of it as far as Eleanor was
concerned. The very fact of Mr. Slope's making an offer
to her would be a triumph to the archdeacon, and in a
great measure a vindication of Mr. Arabin's conduct. The
widow could not bring herself to endure with patience the
idea that she had been in the wrong. She had defended Mr.
Slope, she had declared herself quite justified in admitting
him among her acquaintance, had ridiculed the idea of his
considering himself as more than an acquaintance, and had
resented the archdeacon's caution in her behalf : now it
was about to be proved to her in a manner sufficiently
disagreeable that the archdeacon had been right, and she
herself had been entirely wrong.

' I don't know what you can have to say to me, Mr.
Slope, that you could not have said when we were sitting
at table just now ; ' and she closed her lips, and steadied
her eyeballs, and looked at him in a manner that ought to
have frozen him.

But gentlemen are not easily frozen when they are full
of champagne, and it would not at any time have been
easy to freeze Mr. Slope.

' There are things, Mrs. Bold, which a man cannot well
say before a crowd ; which perhaps he cannot well say at
any time ; which indeed he may most fervently desire to
get spoken, and which he may yet find it almost impossible
to utter. It is such things as these, that I now wish to say
to you ; ' and then the tender-pious look was repeated,
with a little more emphasis even than before.

Eleanor had not found it practicable to stand stock still before the dining-room window, and there receive his offer in full view of Miss Thorne's guests. She had therefore in self-defence walked on, and thus Mr. Slope had gained his object of walking with her. He now offered her his arm.

' Thank you, Mr. Slope, I am much obliged to you ; but for the very short time that I shall remain with you I shall prefer walking alone.'

' And must it be so short ? ' said he ; ' must it be—'

' Yes,' said Eleanor, interrupting him ; ' as short as possible, if you please, sir.'

' I had hoped, Mrs. Bold—I had hoped—'

' Pray hope nothing, Mr. Slope, as far as I am concerned ; pray do not ; I do not know, and need not know what hope you mean. Our acquaintance is very slight, and will probably remain so. Pray, pray let that be enough ; there is at any rate no necessity for us to quarrel.'

Mrs. Bold was certainly treating Mr. Slope rather cavalierly, and he felt it so. She was rejecting him before he had offered himself, and informed him at the same time that he was taking a great deal too much on himself to be so familiar. She did not even make an attempt

> From such a sharp and waspish word as ' no '
> To pluck the sting.

He was still determined to be very tender and very pious, seeing that in spite of all Mrs. Bold had said to him, he not yet abandoned hope ; but he was inclined also to be somewhat angry. The widow was bearing herself, as he thought, with too high a hand, was speaking of herself in much too imperious a tone. She had clearly no idea that an honour was being conferred on her. Mr. Slope would be tender as long as he could, but he began to think, if that failed, it would not be amiss if he also mounted himself for a while on his high horse. Mr. Slope could undoubtedly be very tender, but he could be very savage also, and he knew his own abilities.

' That is cruel,' said he, ' and unchristian too. The worst of us are all still bidden to hope. What have I done that you should pass on me so severe a sentence ? ' and then he paused a moment, during which the widow walked steadily on with measured step, saying nothing further.

'Beautiful woman,' at last he burst forth; 'beautiful woman, you cannot pretend to be ignorant that I adore you. Yes, Eleanor, yes, I love you. I love you with the truest affection which man can bear to woman. Next to my hopes of heaven are my hopes of possessing you.' (Mr. Slope's memory here played him false, or he would not have omitted the deanery.) 'How sweet to walk to heaven with you by my side, with you for my guide, mutual guides. Say, Eleanor, dearest Eleanor, shall we walk that sweet path together?'

Eleanor had no intention of ever walking together with Mr. Slope on any other path than that special one of Miss Thorne's which they now occupied; but as she had been unable to prevent the expression of Mr. Slope's wishes and aspirations, she resolved to hear him out to the end, before she answered him.

'Ah! Eleanor,' he continued, and it seemed to be his idea that as he had once found courage to pronounce her Christian name, he could not utter it often enough. 'Ah! Eleanor, will it not be sweet, with the Lord's assistance, to travel hand in hand through this mortal valley which his mercies will make pleasant to us, till hereafter we shall dwell together at the foot of his throne?' And then a more tenderly pious glance than ever beamed from the lover's eyes. 'Ah! Eleanor—'

'My name, Mr. Slope, is Mrs. Bold,' said Eleanor, who, though determined to hear out the tale of his love, was too much disgusted by his blasphemy to be able to bear much more of it.

'Sweetest angel, be not so cold,' said he, and as he said it the champagne broke forth, and he contrived to pass his arm round her waist. He did this with considerable cleverness, for up to this point Eleanor had contrived with tolerable success to keep her distance from him. They had got into a walk nearly enveloped by shrubs, and Mr. Slope therefore no doubt considered that as they were now alone it was fitting that he should give her some outward demonstration of that affection of which he talked so much. It may perhaps be presumed that the same stamp of measures had been found to succeed with Olivia Proudie. Be this as it may, it was not successful with Eleanor Bold.

She sprang from him as she would have jumped from an adder, but she did not spring far ; not, indeed, beyond arm's length ; and then, quick as thought, she raised her little hand and dealt him a box on the ear with such right good will, that it sounded among the trees like a miniature thunder-clap.

And now it is to be feared that every well-bred reader of these pages will lay down the book with disgust, feeling that, after all, the heroine is unworthy of sympathy. She is a hoyden, one will say. At any rate she is not a lady, another will exclaim. I have suspected her all through, a third will declare ; she has no idea of the dignity of a matron ; or of the peculiar propriety which her position demands. At one moment she is romping with young Stanhope ; then she is making eyes at Mr. Arabin ; anon she comes to fisty-cuffs with a third lover ; and all before she is yet a widow of two years' standing.

She cannot altogether be defended ; and yet it may be averred that she is not a hoyden, not given to romping, nor prone to boxing. It were to be wished devoutly that she had not struck Mr. Slope in the face. In doing so she derogated from her dignity and committed herself. Had she been educated in Belgravia, had she been brought up by any sterner mentor than that fond father, had she lived longer under the rule of a husband, she might, perhaps, have saved herself from this great fault. As it was, the provocation was too much for her, the temptation to instant resentment of the insult too strong. She was too keen in the feeling of independence, a feeling dangerous for a young woman, but one in which her position pecu-liarly tempted her to indulge. And then Mr. Slope's face, tinted with a deeper dye than usual by the wine he had drunk, simpering and puckering itself with pseudo piety and tender grimaces, seemed specially to call for such punishment. She had, too, a true instinct as to the man ; he was capable of rebuke in this way and in no other. To him the blow from her little hand was as much an insult as a blow from a man would have been to another. It went direct to his pride. He conceived himself lowered in his dignity, and personally outraged. He could almost have struck at her again in his rage. Even the pain was a great annoyance to him, and the feeling that his clerical character had been wholly disregarded, sorely vexed him.

There are such men; men who can endure no taint on their personal self-respect, even from a woman;—men whose bodies are to themselves such sacred temples, that a joke against them is desecration, and a rough touch downright sacrilege. Mr. Slope was such a man; and, therefore, the slap on the face that he got from Eleanor was, as far as he was concerned, the fittest rebuke which could have been administered to him.

But, nevertheless, she should not have raised her hand against the man. Ladies' hands, so soft, so sweet, so delicious to the touch, so grateful to the eye, so gracious in their gentle doings, were not made to belabour men's faces. The moment the deed was done Eleanor felt that she had sinned against all propriety, and would have given little worlds to recall the blow. In her first agony of sorrow she all but begged the man's pardon. Her next impulse, however, and the one which she obeyed, was to run away.

'I never, never will speak another word to you,' she said, gasping with emotion and the loss of breath which her exertion and violent feelings occasioned her, and so saying she put foot to the ground and ran quickly back along the path to the house.

But how shall I sing the divine wrath of Mr. Slope, or how invoke the tragic muse to describe the rage which swelled the celestial bosom of the bishop's chaplain? Such an undertaking by no means befits the low-heeled buskin of modern fiction. The painter put a veil over Agamemnon's face when called on to depict the father's grief at the early doom of his devoted daughter. The god, when he resolved to punish the rebellious winds, abstained from mouthing empty threats. We will not attempt to tell with what mighty surgings of the inner heart Mr. Slope swore to revenge himself on the woman who had disgraced him, nor will we vainly strive to depict his deep agony of soul.

There he is, however, alone in the garden walk, and we must contrive to bring him out of it. He was not willing to come forth quite at once. His cheek was stinging with the weight of Eleanor's fingers, and he fancied that every one who looked at him would be able to see on his face the traces of what he had endured. He stood awhile, becoming redder and redder with rage. He stood motionless, undecided, glaring with his eyes, thinking of the pains and penalties of Hades, and meditating how he might best devote his enemy to the infernal gods with all the passion of his accustomed eloquence. He longed in his heart to be preaching at her. 'Twas thus that he was ordinarily avenged of sinning mortal men and women. Could he at once have ascended his Sunday rostrum and fulminated at her such denunciations as his spirit delighted in, his bosom would have been greatly eased.

But how preach to Mr. Thorne's laurels, or how preach indeed at all in such a vanity fair as this now going on at Ullathorne ? And then he began to feel a righteous disgust at the wickedness of the doings around him. He had been justly chastised for lending, by his presence, a sanction to such worldly lures. The gaiety of society, the mirth of banquets, the laughter of the young, and the eating and drinking of the elders were, for awhile, without excuse in his sight. What had he now brought down upon himself by sojourning thus in the tents of the heathen ? He had consorted with idolaters round the altars of Baal ; and therefore a sore punishment had come upon him. He then thought of the Signora Neroni, and his soul within him was full of sorrow. He had an inkling—a true inkling— that he was a wicked, sinful man ; but it led him in no right direction ; he could admit no charity in his heart. He felt debasement coming on him, and he longed to shake it off, to rise up in his stirrup, to mount to high places and great power, that he might get up into a mighty pulpit and preach to the world a loud sermon against Mrs. Bold.

There he stood fixed to the gravel for about ten minutes. Fortune favoured him so far that no prying eyes came to look upon him in his misery. Then a shudder passed over his whole frame ; he collected himself, and slowly wound his way round to the lawn, advancing along the path and not returning in the direction which Eleanor had taken. When he reached the tent he found the bishop standing there in conversation with the master of Lazarus. His lordship had come out to air himself after the exertion of his speech.

' This is very pleasant—very pleasant, my lord, is it

not ? ' said Mr. Slope with his most gracious smile, and pointing to the tent; ' very pleasant. It is delightful to see so many persons enjoying themselves so thoroughly.'

Mr. Slope thought he might force the bishop to introduce him to Dr. Gwynne. A very great example had declared and practised the wisdom of being everything to everybody, and Mr. Slope was desirous of following it. His maxim was never to lose a chance. The bishop, however, at the present moment was not very anxious to increase Mr. Slope's circle of acquaintance among his clerical brethren. He had his own reasons for dropping any marked allusion to his domestic chaplain, and he therefore made his shoulder rather cold for the occasion.

' Very, very,' said he without turning round, or even deigning to look at Mr. Slope. ' And therefore, Dr. Gwynne, I really think that you will find that the hebdomadal board will exercise as wide and as general an authority as at the present moment. I, for one, Dr. Gwynne——'

' Dr. Gwynne,' said Mr. Slope, raising his hat, and resolving not to be outwitted by such an insignificant little goose as the bishop of Barchester.

The master of Lazarus also raised his hat and bowed very politely to Mr. Slope. There is not a more courteous gentleman in the queen's dominions than the master of Lazarus.

' My lord,' said Mr. Slope ; ' pray do me the honour of introducing me to Dr. Gwynne. The opportunity is too much in my favour to be lost.'

The bishop had no help for it. ' My chaplain, Dr. Gwynne,' said he ; ' my present chaplain, Mr. Slope.' He certainly made the introduction as unsatisfactory to the chaplain as possible, and by the use of the word present, seemed to indicate that Mr. Slope might probably not long enjoy the honour which he now held. But Mr. Slope cared nothing for this. He understood the innuendo, and disregarded it. It might probably come to pass that he would be in a situation to resign his chaplaincy before the bishop was in a situation to dismiss him from it. What need the future dean of Barchester care for the bishop, or for the bishop's wife ? Had not Mr. Slope, just as he was entering Dr. Stanhope's carriage, received an all important note from Tom Towers of the Jupiter ? had he not that note this moment in his pocket ?

So disregarding the bishop, he began to open out a conversation with the master of Lazarus.

But suddenly an interruption came, not altogether unwelcome to Mr. Slope. One of the bishop's servants came up to his master's shoulder with a long, grave face, and whispered into the bishop's ear.

' What is it, John ? ' said the bishop.

' The dean, my lord ; he is dead.'

Mr. Slope had no further desire to converse with the master of Lazarus, and was very soon on his road back to Barchester.

Eleanor, as we have said, having declared her intention of never holding further communication with Mr. Slope, ran hurriedly back towards the house. The thought, however, of what she had done grieved her greatly, and she could not abstain from bursting into tears. 'Twas thus she played the second act in that day's melodrame.

CHAPTER XLI

MRS. BOLD CONFIDES HER SORROW TO HER FRIEND MISS STANHOPE

WHEN Mrs. Bold came to the end of the walk and faced the lawn, she began to bethink herself what she should do. Was she to wait there till Mr. Slope caught her, or was she to go in among the crowd with tears in her eyes and passion in her face ? She might in truth have stood there long enough without any reasonable fear of further immediate persecution from Mr. Slope ; but we are all inclined to magnify the bugbears which frighten us. In her present state of dread she did not know of what atrocity he might venture to be guilty. Had any one told her a week ago that he would have put his arm round her waist at this party of Miss Thorne's, she would have been utterly incredulous. Had she been informed that he would be seen on the following Sunday walking down the High-street in a scarlet coat and top-boots, she would not have thought such a phenomenon more improbable.

But this improbable iniquity he had committed; and now there was nothing she could not believe of him. In the first place it was quite manifest that he was tipsy; in the next place, it was to be taken as proved that all his religion was sheer hypocrisy; and finally the man was utterly shameless. She therefore stood watching for the sound of his footfall, not without some fear that he might creep out at her suddenly from among the bushes.

As she thus stood, she saw Charlotte Stanhope at a little distance from her walking quickly across the grass. Eleanor's handkerchief was in her hand, and putting it to her face so as to conceal her tears, she ran across the lawn and joined her friend.

' Oh, Charlotte,' she said, almost too much out of breath to speak very plainly; ' I am so glad I have found you.'

' Glad you have found me! ' said Charlotte, laughing: ' that's a good joke. Why Bertie and I have been looking for you everywhere. He swears that you have gone off with Mr. Slope, and is now on the point of hanging himself.'

' Oh, Charlotte, don't,' said Mrs. Bold.

' Why, my child, what on earth is the matter with you! ' said Miss Stanhope, perceiving that Eleanor's hand trembled on her own arm, and finding also that her companion was still half choked by tears. ' Goodness heaven! something has distressed you. What is it? What can I do for you? '

Eleanor answered her only by a sort of spasmodic gurgle in her throat. She was a good deal upset, as people say, and could not at the moment collect herself.

' Come here, this way, Mrs. Bold; come this way, and we shall not be seen. What has happened to vex you so? What can I do for you? Can Bertie do anything? '

' Oh, no, no, no, no,' said Eleanor. ' There is nothing to be done. Only that horrid man——'

' What horrid man? ' asked Charlotte.

There are some moments in life in which both men and women feel themselves imperatively called on to make a confidence; in which not to do so requires a disagreeable resolution and also a disagreeable suspicion. There are people of both sexes who never make confidences; who are never tempted by momentary circumstances to disclose their secrets; but such are generally dull, close, unimpassioned spirits, ' gloomy gnomes, who live in cold dark mines.' There was nothing of the gnome about Eleanor; and she therefore resolved to tell Charlotte Stanhope the whole story about Mr. Slope.

' That horrid man ; that Mr. Slope,' said she : ' did you not see that he followed me out of the dining-room ? '

' Of course I did, and was sorry enough ; but I could not help it. I knew you would be annoyed. But you and Bertie managed it badly between you.'

' It was not his fault nor mine either. You know how I disliked the idea of coming in the carriage with that man.'

' I am sure I am very sorry if that has led to it.'

' I don't know what has led to it,' said Eleanor, almost crying again. ' But it has not been my fault.'

' But what has he done, my dear ? '

' He's an abominable, horrid, hypocritical man, and it would serve him right to tell the bishop all about it.'

' Believe me, if you want to do him an injury, you had far better tell Mrs. Proudie. But what did he do, Mrs. Bold ? '

' Ugh ! ' exclaimed Eleanor.

' Well, I must confess he's not very nice,' said Charlotte Stanhope.

' Nice ! ' said Eleanor. ' He is the most fulsome, fawning, abominable man I ever saw. What business had he to come to me ?—I that never gave him the slightest tittle of encouragement—I that always hated him, though I did take his part when others ran him down.'

' That's just where it is, my dear. He has heard that, and therefore fancied that of course you were in love with him.'

This was wormwood to Eleanor. It was in fact the very thing which all her friends had been saying for the last month past ; and which experience now proved to be true. Eleanor resolved within herself that she would never again take any man's part. The world with all its villainy, and all its ill-nature, might wag as it liked ; she would not again attempt to set crooked things straight.

' But what did he do, my dear ? ' said Charlotte, who was really rather interested in the subject.

' He—he—he—'

'Well—come, it can't have been anything so very horrid, for the man was not tipsy.'

'Oh, I am sure he was,' said Eleanor. 'I am sure he must have been tipsy.'

'Well, I declare I didn't observe it. But what was it, my love?'

'Why, I believe I can hardly tell you. He talked such horrid stuff that you never heard the like; about religion, and heaven, and love.—Oh, dear,—he is such a nasty man.'

'I can easily imagine the sort of stuff he would talk. Well,—and then—?'

'And then—he took hold of me.'

'Took hold of you?'

'Yes,—he somehow got close to me, and took hold of me—'

'By the waist?'

'Yes,' said Eleanor shuddering.

'And then—'

'Then I jumped away from him, and gave him a slap on the face; and ran away along the path, till I saw you.'

'Ha, ha, ha!' Charlotte Stanhope laughed heartily at the finale to the tragedy. It was delightful to her to think that Mr. Slope had had his ears boxed. She did not quite appreciate the feeling which made her friend so unhappy at the result of the interview. To her thinking, the matter had ended happily enough as regarded the widow, who indeed was entitled to some sort of triumph among her friends. Whereas to Mr. Slope would be due all those jibes and jeers which would naturally follow such an affair. His friends would ask him whether his ears tingled whenever he saw a widow; and he would be cautioned that beautiful things were made to be looked at, and not to be touched.

Such were Charlotte Stanhope's views on such matters; but she did not at the present moment clearly explain them to Mrs. Bold. Her object was to endear herself to her friend; and therefore, having had her laugh, she was ready enough to offer sympathy. Could Bertie do anything? Should Bertie speak to the man, and warn him that in future he must behave with more decorum? Bertie, indeed, she declared, would be more angry than any one else when he heard to what insult Mrs. Bold had been subjected.

'But you won't tell him?' said Mrs. Bold with a look of horror.

'Not if you don't like it,' said Charlotte; 'but considering everything, I would strongly advise it. If you had a brother, you know, it would be unnecessary. But it is very right that Mr. Slope should know that you have somebody by you that will, and can protect you.'

'But my father is here.'

'Yes, but it is so disagreeable for clergymen to have to quarrel with each other; and circumstanced as your father is just at this moment, it would be very inexpedient that there should be anything unpleasant between him and Mr. Slope. Surely you and Bertie are intimate enough for you to permit him to take your part.'

Charlotte Stanhope was very anxious that her brother should at once on that very day settle matters with his future wife. Things had now come to that point between him and his father, and between him and his creditors, that he must either do so, or leave Barchester; either do that, or go back to his unwashed associates, dirty lodgings, and poor living at Carrara. Unless he could provide himself with an income, he must go to Carrara, or to ——. His father the prebendary had not said this in so many words, but had he done so, he could not have signified it more plainly.

Such being the state of the case, it was very necessary that no more time should be lost. Charlotte had seen her brother's apathy, when he neglected to follow Mrs. Bold out of the room, with anger which she could hardly suppress. It was grievous to think that Mr. Slope should have so distanced him. Charlotte felt that she had played her part with sufficient skill. She had brought them together and induced such a degree of intimacy, that her brother was really relieved from all trouble and labour in the matter. And moreover, it was quite plain that Mrs. Bold was very fond of Bertie. And now it was plain enough also that he had nothing to fear from his rival Mr. Slope.

There was certainly an awkwardness in subjecting Mrs. Bold to a second offer on the same day. It would have

been well perhaps to have put the matter off for a week,
could a week have been spared. But circumstances are
frequently too peremptory to be arranged as we would
wish to arrange them ; and such was the case now. This
being so, could not this affair of Mr. Slope's be turned to
advantage ? Could it not be made the excuse for bringing
Bertie and Mrs. Bold into still closer connection ; into such
close connection that they could not fail to throw themselves into each other's arms ? Such was the game which
Miss Stanhope now at a moment's notice resolved to play.

And very well she played it. In the first place, it was
arranged that Mr. Slope should not return in the Stanhopes' carriage to Barchester. It so happened that Mr.
Slope was already gone, but of that of course they knew
nothing. The signora should be induced to go first, with
only the servants and her sister, and Bertie should take
Mr. Slope's place in the second journey. Bertie was to be
told in confidence of the whole affair, and when the carriage
was gone off with its first load, Eleanor was to be left under
Bertie's special protection, so as to insure her from any
further aggression from Mr. Slope. While the carriage
was getting ready, Bertie was to seek out that gentleman
and make him understand that he must provide himself
with another conveyance back to Barchester. Their
immediate object should be to walk about together in
search of Bertie. Bertie, in short, was to be the Pegasus
on whose wings they were to ride out of their present
dilemma.

There was a warmth of friendship and cordial kindliness
in all this, that was very soothing to the widow ; but yet,
though she gave way to it, she was hardly reconciled to
doing so. It never occurred to her, that now that she had
killed one dragon, another was about to spring up in her
path ; she had no remote idea that she would have to
encounter another suitor in her proposed protector, but
she hardly liked the thought of putting herself so much
into the hands of young Stanhope. She felt that if she
wanted protection, she should go to her father. She felt
that she should ask him to provide a carriage for her back
to Barchester. Mrs. Clantantram she knew would give her
a seat. She knew that she should not throw herself
entirely upon friends whose friendship dated as it were but

from yesterday. But yet she could not say 'no,' to one who was so sisterly in her kindness, so eager in her good nature, so comfortably sympathetic as Charlotte Stanhope. And thus she gave way to all the propositions made to her.

They first went into the dining-room, looking for their champion, and from thence to the drawing-room. Here they found Mr. Arabin, still hanging over the signora's sofa ; or, rather, they found him sitting near her head, as a physician might have sat, had the lady been his patient. There was no other person in the room. The guests were some in the tent, some few still in the dining-room, some at the bows and arrows, but most of them walking with Miss Thorne through the park, and looking at the games that were going on.

All that had passed, and was passing between Mr. Arabin and the lady, it is unnecessary to give in detail. She was doing with him as she did with all others. It was her mission to make fools of men, and she was pursuing her mission with Mr. Arabin. She had almost got him to own his love for Mrs. Bold, and had subsequently almost induced him to acknowledge a passion for herself. He, poor man, was hardly aware what he was doing or saying, hardly conscious whether he was in heaven or hell. So little had he known of female attractions of that peculiar class which the signora owned, that he became affected with a kind of temporary delirium, when first subjected to its power. He lost his head rather than his heart, and toppled about mentally, reeling in his ideas as a drunken man does on his legs. She had whispered to him words that really meant nothing, but which coming from such beautiful lips, and accompanied by such lustrous glances, seemed to have a mysterious significance, which he felt though he could not understand.

In being thus be-sirened, Mr. Arabin behaved himself very differently from Mr. Slope. The signora had said truly, that the two men were the contrasts of each other ; that the one was all for action, the other all for thought. Mr. Slope, when this lady laid upon his senses the over-powering breath of her charms, immediately attempted to obtain some fruition, to achieve some mighty triumph. He began by catching at her hand, and progressed by kissing it. He made vows of love, and asked for vows in

return. He promised everlasting devotion, knelt before
her, and swore that had she been on Mount Ida, Juno
would have had no cause to hate the offspring of Venus.
But Mr. Arabin uttered no oaths, kept his hand mostly in
his trowsers pocket, and had no more thought of kissing
Madam Neroni, than of kissing the Countess De Courcy.

As soon as Mr. Arabin saw Mrs. Bold enter the room, he
blushed and rose from his chair; then he sat down again,
and then again got up. The signora saw the blush at once,
and smiled at the poor victim, but Eleanor was too much
confused to see anything.

'Oh, Madeline,' said Charlotte, 'I want to speak to you
particularly; we must arrange about the carriage, you
know,' and she stooped down to whisper to her sister.
Mr. Arabin immediately withdrew to a little distance, and
as Charlotte had in fact much to explain before she could
make the new carriage arrangement intelligible, he had
nothing to do but to talk to Mrs. Bold.

'We have had a very pleasant party,' said he, using the
tone he would have used had he declared that the sun was
shining very brightly, or the rain falling very fast.

'Very,' said Eleanor, who never in her life had passed
a more unpleasant day.

'I hope Mr. Harding has enjoyed himself.'

'Oh, yes, very much,' said Eleanor, who had not seen
her father since she parted from him soon after her arrival.

'He returns to Barchester to-night, I suppose.'

'Yes, I believe so; that is, I think he is staying at
Plumstead.'

'Oh, staying at Plumstead,' said Mr. Arabin.

'He came from there this morning. I believe he is going
back; he didn't exactly say, however.'

'I hope Mrs. Grantly is quite well.'

'She seemed to be quite well. She is here; that is,
unless she has gone away.'

'Oh, yes, to be sure. I was talking to her. Looking
very well indeed.' Then there was a considerable pause;
for Charlotte could not at once make Madeline understand
why she was to be sent home in a hurry without her
brother.

'Are you returning to Plumstead, Mrs. Bold?' Mr.
Arabin merely asked this by way of making conversation,

but he immediately perceived that he was approaching dangerous ground.

'No,' said Mrs. Bold, very quietly; 'I am going home to Barchester.'

'Oh, ah, yes. I had forgotten that you had returned.' And then Mr. Arabin, finding it impossible to say anything further, stood silent till Charlotte had completed her plans, and Mrs. Bold stood equally silent, intently occupied as it appeared in the arrangement of her rings.

And yet these two people were thoroughly in love with each other; and though one was a middle-aged clergyman, and the other a lady at any rate past the wishy-washy bread-and-butter period of life, they were as unable to tell their own minds to each other as any Damon and Phillis, whose united ages would not make up that to which Mr. Arabin had already attained.

Madeline Neroni consented to her sister's proposal, and then the two ladies again went off in quest of Bertie Stanhope.

CHAPTER XLII

ULLATHORNE SPORTS—ACT III

AND now Miss Thorne's guests were beginning to take their departure, and the amusement of those who remained was becoming slack. It was getting dark, and ladies in morning costumes were thinking that if they were to appear by candle-light they ought to readjust themselves. Some young gentlemen had been heard to talk so loud that prudent mammas determined to retire judiciously, and the more discreet of the male sex, whose libations had been moderate, felt that there was not much more left for them to do.

Morning parties, as a rule, are failures. People never know how to get away from them gracefully. A picnic on an island or a mountain or in a wood may perhaps be permitted. There is no master of the mountain bound by courtesy to bid you stay while in his heart he is longing for your departure. But in a private house or in private grounds a morning party is a bore. One is called on to eat and drink at unnatural hours. One is obliged to give up the day which is useful, and is then left without resource for the evening which is useless. One gets home fagged and *désœuvré*, and yet at an hour too early for bed. There is no comfortable resource left. Cards in these genteel days are among the things tabooed, and a rubber of whist is impracticable.

All this began now to be felt. Some young people had come with some amount of hope that they might get up a dance in the evening, and were unwilling to leave till all such hope was at an end. Others, fearful of staying longer than was expected, had ordered their carriages early, and were doing their best to go, solicitous for their servants and horses. The countess and her noble brood were among the first to leave, and as regarded the Hon. George, it was certainly time that he did so. Her ladyship was in a great fret and fume. Those horrid roads would, she was sure, be the death of her if unhappily she were caught in them by the dark night. The lamps she was assured were good, but no lamp could withstand the jolting of the roads of East Barsetshire. The De Courcy property lay in the western division of the county.

Mrs. Proudie could not stay when the countess was gone. So the bishop was searched for by the Revs. Messrs. Grey and Green, and found in one corner of the tent enjoying himself thoroughly in a disquisition on the hebdomadal board. He obeyed, however, the behests of his lady without finishing the sentence in which he was promising to Dr. Gwynne that his authority at Oxford should remain unimpaired; and the episcopal horses turned their noses towards the palatial stables. Then the Grantlys went. Before they did so, Mr. Harding managed to whisper a word into his daughter's ear. Of course, he said he would undeceive the Grantlys as to that foolish rumour about Mr. Slope.

'No, no, no,' said Eleanor; 'pray do not—pray wait till I see you. You will be home in a day or two, and then I will explain to you everything.'

'I shall be home to-morrow,' said he.

'I am so glad,' said Eleanor. 'You will come and dine with me, and then we shall be so comfortable.'

Mr. Harding promised. He did not exactly know what there was to be explained, or why Dr. Grantly's mind

should not be disabused of the mistake into which he had
fallen ; but nevertheless he promised. He owed some
reparation to his daughter, and he thought that he might
best make it by obedience.

And thus the people were thinning off by degrees, as
Charlotte and Eleanor walked about in quest of Bertie.
Their search might have been long, had they not happened
to hear his voice. He was comfortably ensconced in the
ha-ha, with his back to the sloping side, smoking a cigar,
and eagerly engaged in conversation with some youngster
from the further side of the county, whom he had never
met before, who was also smoking under Bertie's pupilage,
and listening with open ears to an account given by his
companion of some of the pastimes of Eastern clime.

' Bertie, I am seeking you everywhere,' said Charlotte.
' Come up here at once.'

Bertie looked up out of the ha-ha, and saw the two ladies
before him. As there was nothing for him but to obey, he
got up and threw away his cigar. From the first moment
of his acquaintance with her he had liked Eleanor Bold.
Had he been left to his own devices, had she been penniless,
and had it then been quite out of the question that he
should marry her, he would most probably have fallen
violently in love with her. But now he could not help
regarding her somewhat as he did the marble workshops
at Carrara, as he had done his easel and palette, as he had
done the lawyer's chambers in London ; in fact, as he had
invariably regarded everything by which it had been
proposed to him to obtain the means of living. Eleanor
Bold appeared before him, no longer as a beautiful woman,
but as a new profession called matrimony. It was a
profession indeed requiring but little labour, and one in
which an income was insured to him. But nevertheless he
had been as it were goaded on to it ; his sister had talked
to him of Eleanor, just as she had talked of busts and
portraits. Bertie did not dislike money, but he hated the
very thought of earning it. He was now called away from
his pleasant cigar to earn it, by offering himself as a
husband to Mrs. Bold. The work indeed was made easy
enough ; for in lieu of his having to seek the widow, the
widow had apparently come to seek him.

He made some sudden absurd excuse to his auditor, and

then throwing away his cigar, climbed up the wall of the ha-ha and joined the ladies on the lawn.

'Come and give Mrs. Bold an arm,' said Charlotte, 'while I set you on a piece of duty which, as a preux chevalier, you must immediately perform. Your personal danger will, I fear, be insignificant, as your antagonist is a clergyman.'

Bertie immediately gave his arm to Eleanor, walking between her and his sister. He had lived too long abroad to fall into the Englishman's habit of offering each an arm to two ladies at the same time ; a habit, by the bye, which foreigners regard as an approach to bigamy, or a sort of incipient Mormonism.

The little history of Mr. Slope's misconduct was then told to Bertie by his sister, Eleanor's ears tingling the while. And well they might tingle. If it were necessary to speak of the outrage at all, why should it be spoken of to such a person as Mr. Stanhope, and why in her own hearing ? She knew she was wrong, and was unhappy and dispirited, and yet she could think of no way to extricate herself, no way to set herself right. Charlotte spared her as much as she possibly could, spoke of the whole thing as though Mr. Slope had taken a glass of wine too much, said that of course there would be nothing more about it, but that steps must be taken to exclude Mr. Slope from the carriage.

'Mrs. Bold need be under no alarm about that,' said Bertie, 'for Mr. Slope has gone this hour past. He told me that business made it necessary that he should start at once for Barchester.'

'He is not so tipsy, at any rate, but what he knows his fault,' said Charlotte. 'Well, my dear, that is one difficulty over. Now I'll leave you with your true knight, and get Madeline off as quickly as I can. The carriage is here, I suppose, Bertie ?'

'It has been here for the last hour.'

'That's well. Good bye, my dear. Of course you'll come in to tea. I shall trust to you to bring her, Bertie ; even by force if necessary.' And so saying, Charlotte ran off across the lawn, leaving her brother alone with the widow.

As Miss Stanhope went off, Eleanor bethought herself

that, as Mr. Slope had taken his departure, there no longer existed any necessity for separating Mr. Stanhope from his sister Madeline, who so much needed his aid. It had been arranged that he should remain so as to preoccupy Mr. Slope's place in the carriage, and act as a social policeman to effect the exclusion of that disagreeable gentleman. But Mr. Slope had effected his own exclusion, and there was no possible reason now why Bertie should not go with his sister. At least Eleanor saw none, and she said as much.

'Oh, let Charlotte have her own way,' said he. 'She has arranged it, and there will be no end of confusion, if we make another change. Charlotte always arranges everything in our house; and rules us like a despot.'

'But the signora?' said Eleanor.

'Oh, the signora can do very well without me. Indeed, she will have to do without me,' he added, thinking rather of his studies in Carrara, than of his Barchester hymeneals.

'Why, you are not going to leave us?' asked Eleanor.

It has been said that Bertie Stanhope was a man without principle. He certainly was so. He had no power of using active mental exertion to keep himself from doing evil. Evil had no ugliness in his eyes; virtue no beauty. He was void of any of those feelings which actuate men to do good. But he was perhaps equally void of those which actuate men to do evil. He got into debt with utter recklessness, thinking nothing as to whether the tradesmen would ever be paid or not. But he did not invent active schemes of deceit for the sake of extracting the goods of others. If a man gave him credit, that was the man's look-out; Bertie Stanhope troubled himself nothing further. In borrowing money he did the same; he gave people references to 'his governor;' told them that the 'old chap' had a good income; and agreed to pay sixty per cent. for the accommodation. All this he did without a scruple of conscience; but then he never contrived active villainy.

In this affair of his marriage, it had been represented to him as a matter of duty that he ought to put himself in possession of Mrs. Bold's hand and fortune; and at first he had so regarded it. About her he had thought but little. It was the customary thing for men situated as he was to marry for money, and there was no reason why he should not do what others around him did. And so he consented. But now he began to see the matter in another light. He was setting himself down to catch this woman, as a cat sits to catch a mouse. He was to catch her, and swallow her up, her and her child, and her houses and land, in order that he might live on her instead of on his father. There was a cold, calculating, cautious cunning about this quite at variance with Bertie's character. The prudence of the measure was quite as antagonistic to his feelings as the iniquity.

And then, should he be successful, what would be the reward ? Having satisfied his creditors with half of the widow's fortune, he would be allowed to sit down quietly at Barchester, keeping economical house with the remainder. His duty would be to rock the cradle of the late Mr. Bold's child, and his highest excitement a demure party at Plumstead rectory, should it ultimately turn out that the archdeacon would be sufficiently reconciled to receive him.

There was very little in the programme to allure such a man as Bertie Stanhope. Would not the Carrara workshop, or whatever worldly career fortune might have in store for him, would not almost anything be better than this ? The lady herself was undoubtedly all that was desirable ; but the most desirable lady becomes nauseous when she has to be taken as a pill. He was pledged to his sister, however, and let him quarrel with whom he would, it behoved him not to quarrel with her. If she were lost to him all would be lost that he could ever hope to derive henceforward from the paternal roof-tree. His mother was apparently indifferent to his weal or woe, to his wants or his warfare. His father's brow got blacker and blacker from day to day, as the old man looked at his hopeless son. And as for Madeline—poor Madeline, whom of all of them he liked the best,—she had enough to do to shift for herself. No ; come what might, he must cling to his sister and obey her behests, let them be ever so stern ; or at the very least seem to obey them. Could not some happy deceit bring him through in this matter, so that he might save appearances with his sister, and yet not betray the widow to her ruin ? What if he made a confederate of

Eleanor ? 'Twas in this spirit that Bertie Stanhope set about his wooing.

'But you are not going to leave Barchester ? ' asked Eleanor.

'I do not know,' he replied ; ' I hardly know yet what I am going to do. But it is at any rate certain that I must do something.'

'You mean about your profession ? ' said she.

'Yes, about my profession, if you can call it one.'

'And is it not one ? ' said Eleanor. ' Were I a man, I know none I should prefer to it, except painting. And I believe the one is as much in your power as the other.'

'Yes, just about equally so,' said Bertie, with a little touch of inward satire directed at himself. He knew in his heart that he would never make a penny by either.

'I have often wondered, Mr. Stanhope, why you do not exert yourself more,' said Eleanor, who felt a friendly fondness for the man with whom she was walking. ' But I know it is very impertinent in me to say so.'

'Impertinent !' said he. ' Not so, but much too kind. It is much too kind in you to take any interest in so idle a scamp.'

'But you are not a scamp, though you are perhaps idle ; and I do take an interest in you ; a very great interest,' she added, in a voice which almost made him resolve to change his mind. ' And when I call you idle, I know you are only so for the present moment. Why can't you settle steadily to work here in Barchester ? '

'And make busts of the bishop, dean and chapter ? or perhaps, if I achieve a great success, obtain a commission to put up an elaborate tombstone over a prebendary's widow, a dead lady with a Grecian nose, a bandeau, and an intricate lace veil ; lying of course on a marble sofa, from among the legs of which Death will be creeping out and poking at his victim with a small toasting-fork.'

Eleanor laughed ; but yet she thought that if the surviving prebendary paid the bill, the object of the artist as a professional man would, in a great measure. be obtained.

'I don't know about the dean and chapter and the prebendary's widow,' said Eleanor. ' Of course you must take them as they come. But the fact of your having a great cathedral in which such ornaments are required, could not but be in your favour.'

' No real artist could descend to the ornamentation of a cathedral,' said Bertie, who had his ideas of the high ecstatic ambition of art, as indeed all artists have, who are not in receipt of a good income. ' Buildings should be fitted to grace the sculpture, not the sculpture to grace the building.'

' Yes, when the work of art is good enough to merit it. Do you, Mr. Stanhope, do something sufficiently excellent, and we ladies of Barchester will erect for it a fitting receptacle. Come, what shall the subject be ? '

' I'll put you in your pony chair, Mrs. Bold, as Dannecker put Ariadne on her lion. Only you must promise to sit for me.'

' My ponies are too tame, I fear, and my broad-rimmed straw hat will not look so well in marble as the lace veil of the prebendary's wife.'

' If you will not consent to that, Mrs. Bold, I will consent to try no other subject in Barchester.'

' You are determined, then, to push your fortune in other lands ? '

' I am determined,' said Bertie, slowly and significantly, as he tried to bring up his mind to a great resolve ; ' I am determined in this matter to be guided wholly by you.'

' Wholly by me ! ' said Eleanor, astonished at, and not quite liking, his altered manner.

' Wholly by you,' said Bertie, dropping his companion's arm, and standing before her on the path. In their walk they had come exactly to the spot in which Eleanor had been provoked into slapping Mr. Slope's face. Could it be possible that this place was peculiarly unpropitious to her comfort ? could it be possible that she should here have to encounter yet another amorous swain ?

' If you will be guided by me, Mr. Stanhope, you will set yourself down to steady and persevering work, and you will be ruled by your father as to the place in which it will be most advisable for you to do so.'

' Nothing could be more prudent, if only it were practicable. But now, if you will let me, I will tell you how it is that I will be guided by you, and why. Will you let me tell you ? '

' I really do not know what you can have to tell.'

' No,—you cannot know. It is impossible that you should. But we have been very good friends, Mrs. Bold, have we not ? '

' Yes, I think we have,' said she, observing in his demeanour an earnestness very unusual with him.

' You were kind enough to say just now that you took an interest in me, and I was perhaps vain enough to believe you.'

' There is no vanity in that ; I do so as your sister's brother,—and as my own friend also.'

' Well, I don't deserve that you should feel so kindly towards me,' said Bertie ; ' but upon my word I am very grateful for it,' and he paused awhile, hardly knowing how to introduce the subject that he had in hand.

And it was no wonder that he found it difficult. He had to make known to his companion the scheme that had been prepared to rob her of her wealth ; he had to tell her that he intended to marry her without loving her, or else that he loved her without intending to marry her ; and he had also to bespeak from her not only his own pardon, but also that of his sister, and induce Mrs. Bold to protest in her future communion with Charlotte that an offer had been duly made to her and duly rejected.

Bertie Stanhope was not prone to be very diffident of his own conversational powers, but it did seem to him that he was about to tax them almost too far. He hardly knew where to begin, and he hardly knew where he should end.

By this time Eleanor was again walking on slowly by his side, not taking his arm as she had heretofore done, but listening very intently for whatever Bertie might have to say to her.

' I wish to be guided by you,' said he ; ' and, indeed, in this matter, there is no one else who can set me right.'

' Oh, that must be nonsense,' said she.

' Well, listen to me now, Mrs. Bold ; and if you can help it, pray don't be angry with me.'

' Angry ! ' said she.

' Oh, indeed you will have cause to be so. You know how very much attached to you my sister Charlotte is.'

Eleanor acknowledged that she did.

' Indeed she is ; I never knew her to love any one so

warmly on so short an acquaintance. You know also how well she loves me ? '

Eleanor now made no answer, but she felt the blood tingle in her cheek as she gathered from what he said the probable result of this double-barrelled love on the part of Miss Stanhope.

' I am her only brother, Mrs. Bold, and it is not to be wondered at that she should love me. But you do not yet know Charlotte,—you do not know how entirely the well-being of our family hangs on her. Without her to manage for us, I do not know how we should get on from day to day. You cannot yet have observed all this.'

Eleanor had indeed observed a good deal of this ; she did not however now say so, but allowed him to proceed with his story.

' You cannot therefore be surprised that Charlotte should be most anxious to do the best for us all.'

Eleanor said that she was not at all surprised.

' And she has had a very difficult game to play, Mrs. Bold—a very difficult game. Poor Madeline's unfortunate marriage and terrible accident, my mother's ill health, my father's absence from England, and last, and worst perhaps, my own roving, idle spirit have almost been too much for her. You cannot wonder if among all her cares one of the foremost is to see me settled in the world.'

Eleanor on this occasion expressed no acquiescence. She certainly supposed that a formal offer was to be made, and could not but think that so singular an exordium was never before made by a gentleman in a similar position. Mr. Slope had annoyed her by the excess of his ardour. It was quite clear that no such danger was to be feared from Mr. Stanhope. Prudential motives alone actuated him. Not only was he about to make love because his sister told him, but he also took the precaution of explaining all this before he began. 'Twas thus, we may presume, that the matter presented itself to Mrs. Bold.

When he had got so far, Bertie began poking the gravel with a little cane which he carried. He still kept moving on, but very slowly, and his companion moved slowly by his side, not inclined to assist him in the task the performance of which appeared to be difficult to him.

' Knowing how fond she is of yourself, Mrs. Bold, cannot

you imagine what scheme should have occurred to her ? '

' I can imagine no better scheme, Mr. Stanhope, than the one I proposed to you just now.'

' No,' said he, somewhat lack-a-daisically ; ' I suppose that would be the best ; but Charlotte thinks another plan might be joined with it.—She wants me to marry you.'

A thousand remembrances flashed across Eleanor's mind all in a moment,—how Charlotte had talked about and praised her brother, how she had continually contrived to throw the two of them together, how she had encouraged all manner of little intimacies, how she had with singular cordiality persisted in treating Eleanor as one of the family. All this had been done to secure her comfortable income for the benefit of one of the family !

Such a feeling as this is very bitter when it first impresses itself on a young mind. To the old such plots and plans, such matured schemes for obtaining the goods of this world without the trouble of earning them, such long-headed attempts to convert ' tuum ' into ' meum,' are the ways of life to which they are accustomed. 'Tis thus that many live, and it therefore behoves all those who are well to do in the world to be on their guard against those who are not. With them it is the success that disgusts, not the attempt. But Eleanor had not yet learnt to look on her money as a source of danger ; she had not begun to regard herself as fair game to be hunted down by hungry gentlemen. She had enjoyed the society of the Stanhopes, she had greatly liked the cordiality of Charlotte, and had been happy in her new friends. Now she saw the cause of all this kindness, and her mind was opened to a new phase of human life.

' Miss Stanhope,' said she, haughtily, ' has been contriving for me a great deal of honour, but she might have saved herself the trouble. I am not sufficiently ambitious.'

' Pray don't be angry with her, Mrs. Bold,' said he, ' or with me either.'

' Certainly not with you, Mr. Stanhope,' said she, with considerable sarcasm in her tone. ' Certainly not with you.'

' No,—nor with her,' said he, imploringly.

' And why, may I ask you, Mr. Stanhope, have you told me this singular story ? For I may presume I may judge by your manner of telling it, that—that—that you and your sister are not exactly of one mind on the subject.'

' No, we are not.'

' And if so,' said Mrs. Bold, who was now really angry with the unnecessary insult which she thought had been offered to her, ' and if so, why has it been worth your while to tell me all this ? '

' I did once think, Mrs. Bold,—that you—that you——'

The widow now again became entirely impassive, and would not lend the slightest assistance to her companion.

' I did once think that you perhaps might,—might have been taught to regard me as more than a friend.'

' Never ! ' said Mrs. Bold, ' never. If I have ever allowed myself to do anything to encourage such an idea, I have been very much to blame,—very much to blame indeed.'

' You never have,' said Bertie, who really had a good-natured anxiety to make what he said as little unpleasant as possible. ' You never have, and I have seen for some time that I had no chance ; but my sister's hopes ran higher. I have not mistaken you, Mrs. Bold, though perhaps she has.'

' Then why have you said all this to me ? '

' Because I must not anger her.'

' And will not this anger her ? Upon my word, Mr. Stanhope, I do not understand the policy of your family. Oh, how I wish I was at home ! ' And as she expressed the wish, she could restrain herself no longer, but burst out into a flood of tears.

Poor Bertie was greatly moved. ' You shall have the carriage to yourself going home,' said he ; ' at least you and my father. As for me I can walk, or for the matter of that it does not much signify what I do.' He perfectly understood that part of Eleanor's grief arose from the apparent necessity of going back to Barchester in the carriage with her second suitor.

This somewhat mollified her. ' Oh, Mr. Stanhope,' said she, ' why should you have made me so miserable ? What will you have gained by telling me all this ? '

He had not even yet explained to her the most difficult part of his proposition ; he had not told her that she was to be a party to the little deception which he intended to play off upon his sister. This suggestion had still to be

made, and as it was absolutely necessary, he proceeded to
make it.

We need not follow him through the whole of his statement. At last, and not without considerable difficulty, he
made Eleanor understand why he had let her into his
confidence, seeing that he no longer intended her the
honour of a formal offer. At last he made her comprehend
the part which she was destined to play in this little family
comedy.

But when she did understand it, she was only more
angry with him than ever : more angry, not only with him,
but with Charlotte also. Her fair name was to be bandied
about between them in different senses, and each sense
false. She was to be played off by the sister against the
father ; and then by the brother against the sister. Her
dear friend Charlotte, with all her agreeable sympathy and
affection, was striving to sacrifice her for the Stanhope
family welfare ; and Bertie, who, as he now proclaimed
himself, was over head and ears in debt, completed the
compliment of owning that he did not care to have his
debts paid at so great a sacrifice of himself. Then she
was asked to conspire together with this unwilling suitor,
for the sake of making the family believe that he had in
obedience to their commands done his best to throw himself thus away !

She lifted up her face when he had finished, and looking
at him with much dignity, even through her tears, she
said—

' I regret to say it, Mr. Stanhope ; but after what has
passed, I believe that all intercourse between your family
and myself had better cease.'

' Well, perhaps it had,' said Bertie naïvely ; ' perhaps
that will be better, at any rate for a time ; and then
Charlotte will think you are offended at what I have done.'

' And now I will go back to the house, if you please,' said
Eleanor. ' I can find my way by myself, Mr. Stanhope :
after what has passed,' she added, ' I would rather go
alone.'

' But I must find the carriage for you, Mrs. Bold, and
I must tell my father that you will return with him alone,
and I must make some excuse to him for not going with
you ; and I must bid the servant put you down at your

own house, for I suppose you will not now choose to see
them again in the close.'

There was a truth about this, and a perspicuity in
making arrangements for lessening her immediate embarrassment, which had some effect in softening Eleanor's
anger. So she suffered herself to walk by his side over the
now deserted lawn, till they came to the drawing-room
window. There was something about Bertie Stanhope
which gave him, in the estimation of every one, a different
standing from that which any other man would occupy
under similar circumstances. Angry as Eleanor was, and
great as was her cause for anger, she was not half as angry
with him as she would have been with any one else. He
was apparently so simple, so good-natured, so unaffected
and easy to talk to, that she had already half-forgiven him
before he was at the drawing-room window. When they
arrived there, Dr. Stanhope was sitting nearly alone with
Mr. and Miss Thorne ; one or two other unfortunates were
there, who from one cause or another were still delayed in
getting away ; but they were every moment getting fewer
in number.

As soon as he had handed Eleanor over to his father,
Bertie started off to the front gate, in search of the carriage,
and there waited leaning patiently against the front wall,
and comfortably smoking a cigar, till it came up. When
he returned to the room Dr. Stanhope and Eleanor were
alone with their hosts.

' At last, Miss Thorne,' said he cheerily, ' I have come to
relieve you. Mrs. Bold and my father are the last roses
of the very delightful summer you have given us, and
desirable as Mrs. Bold's society always is, now at least you
must be glad to see the last flowers plucked from the tree.'

Miss Thorne declared that she was delighted to have
Mrs. Bold and Dr. Stanhope still with her ; and Mr.
Thorne would have said the same, had he not been checked
by a yawn, which he could not suppress.

' Father, will you give your arm to Mrs. Bold ? ' said
Bertie : and so the last adieux were made, and the
prebendary led out Mrs. Bold, followed by his son.

' I shall be home soon after you,' said he, as the two
got into the carriage.

' Are you not coming in the carriage ? ' said the father,

'No, no; I have some one to see on the road, and shall walk. John, mind you drive to Mrs. Bold's house first.'

Eleanor looking out of the window, saw him with his hat in his hand, bowing to her with his usual gay smile, as though nothing had happened to mar the tranquillity of the day. It was many a long year before she saw him again. Dr. Stanhope hardly spoke to her on her way home; and she was safely deposited by John at her own hall-door, before the carriage drove into the close.

And thus our heroine played the last act of that day's melodrame.

CHAPTER XLIII

MR. AND MRS. QUIVERFUL ARE MADE HAPPY. MR. SLOPE IS ENCOURAGED BY THE PRESS

BEFORE she started for Ullathorne, Mrs. Proudie, careful soul, caused two letters to be written, one by herself and one by her lord, to the inhabitants of Puddingdale vicarage, which made happy the hearth of those within it.

As soon as the departure of the horses left the bishop's stable-groom free for other services, that humble denizen of the diocese started on the bishop's own pony with the two despatches. We have had so many letters lately that we will spare ourselves these. That from the bishop was simply a request that Mr. Quiverful would wait upon his lordship the next morning at 11 A.M.; and that from the lady was as simply a request that Mrs. Quiverful would do the same by her, though it was couched in somewhat longer and more grandiloquent phraseology.

It had become a point of conscience with Mrs. Proudie to urge the settlement of this great hospital question. She was resolved that Mr. Quiverful should have it. She was resolved that there should be no more doubt or delay, no more refusals and resignations, no more secret negotiations carried on by Mr. Slope on his own account in opposition to her behests.

'Bishop,' she said, immediately after breakfast, on the morning of that eventful day, 'have you signed the appointment yet?'

'No, my dear, not yet; it is not exactly signed as yet.'
'Then do it,' said the lady.

The bishop did it; and a very pleasant day indeed he
spent at Ullathorne. And when he got home he had a
glass of hot negus in his wife's sitting-room, and read the
last number of the 'Little Dorrit' of the day with great
inward satisfaction. Oh, husbands, oh, my marital
friends, what great comfort is there to be derived from
a wife well obeyed!

Much perturbation and flutter, high expectation and
renewed hopes, were occasioned at Puddingdale, by the
receipt of these episcopal despatches. Mrs. Quiverful,
whose careful ear caught the sound of the pony's feet as he
trotted up to the vicarage kitchen door, brought them in
hurriedly to her husband. She was at the moment
concocting the Irish stew destined to satisfy the noonday
wants of fourteen young birds, let alone the parent couple.
She had taken the letters from the man's hands between
the folds of her capacious apron, so as to save them from
the contamination of the stew, and in this guise she
brought them to her husband's desk.

They at once divided the spoil, each taking that
addressed to the other. 'Quiverful,' said she with impressive voice, 'you are to be at the palace at eleven to-
morrow.'

'And so are you, my dear,' said he, almost gasping with
the importance of the tidings: and then they exchanged
letters.

'She'd never have sent for me again,' said the lady, 'if
it wasn't all right.'

'Oh! my dear, don't be too certain,' said the gentleman. 'Only think if it should be wrong.'

'She'd never have sent for me, Q., if it wasn't all right,'
again argued the lady. 'She's stiff and hard and proud
as pie-crust, but I think she's right at bottom.' Such was
Mrs. Quiverful's verdict about Mrs. Proudie, to which in
after times she always adhered. People when they get
their income doubled usually think that those through
whose instrumentality this little ceremony is performed
are right at bottom.

'Oh Letty!' said Mr. Quiverful, rising from his well-
worn seat.

'Oh Q.!' said Mrs. Quiverful: and then the two, unmindful of the kitchen apron, the greasy fingers, and the adherent Irish stew, threw themselves warmly into each other's arms.

'For heaven's sake don't let any one cajole you out of it again,' said the wife.

'Let me alone for that,' said the husband, with a look of almost fierce determination, pressing his fist as he spoke rigidly on his desk, as though he had Mr. Slope's head below his knuckles, and meant to keep it there.

'I wonder how soon it will be,' said she.

'I wonder whether it will be at all,' said he, still doubtful.

'Well, I won't say too much,' said the lady. 'The cup has slipped twice before, and it may fall altogether this time; but I'll not believe it. He'll give you the appointment to-morrow. You'll find he will.'

'Heaven send he may,' said Mr. Quiverful, solemnly. And who that considers the weight of the burden on this man's back, will say that the prayer was an improper one? There were fourteen of them—fourteen of them living—as Mrs. Quiverful had so powerfully urged in the presence of the bishop's wife. As long as promotion cometh from any human source, whether north or south, east or west, will not such a claim as this hold good, in spite of all our examination tests, *detur digniori's* and optimist tendencies? It is fervently to be hoped that it may. Till we can become divine we must be content to be human, lest in our hurry for a change we sink to something lower.

And then the pair sitting down lovingly together, talked over all their difficulties, as they so often did, and all their hopes, as they so seldom were enabled to do.

'You had better call on that man, Q., as you come away from the palace,' said Mrs. Quiverful, pointing to an angry call for money from the Barchester draper, which the postman had left at the vicarage that morning. Cormorant that he was, unjust, hungry cormorant! When rumour first got abroad that the Quiverfuls were to go to the hospital. this fellow with fawning eagerness had pressed his goods upon the wants of the poor clergyman. He had done so, feeling that he should be paid from the hospital funds, and flattering himself that a man with fourteen children, and money wherewithal to clothe them, could not but be an excellent customer. As soon as the second rumour reached him, he applied for his money angrily.

And 'the fourteen'—or such of them as were old enough to hope and discuss their hopes, talked over their golden future. The tall-grown girls whispered to each other of possible Barchester parties, of possible allowances for dress, of a possible piano—the one they had in the vicarage was so weather-beaten with the storms of years and children as to be no longer worthy of the name—of the pretty garden, and the pretty house. 'Twas of such things it most behoved them to whisper.

And the younger fry, they did not content themselves with whispers, but shouted to each other of their new play-ground beneath our dear ex-warden's well-loved elms, of their future own gardens, of marbles to be procured in the wished-for city, and of the rumour which had reached them of a Barchester school.

'Twas in vain that their cautious mother tried to instil into their breasts the very feeling she had striven to banish from that of their father; 'twas in vain that she repeated to the girls that ' there's many a slip 'twixt the cup and the lip; ' 'twas in vain she attempted to make the children believe that they were to live at Puddingdale all their lives. Hopes mounted high and would not have themselves quelled. The neighbouring farmers heard the news, and came in to congratulate them. 'Twas Mrs. Quiverful herself who had kindled the fire, and in the first outbreak of her renewed expectations she did it so thoroughly, that it was quite past her power to put it out again.

Poor matron! good honest matron! doing thy duty in the state to which thou hast been called, heartily if not contentedly; let the fire burn on;—on this occasion the flames will not scorch; they shall warm thee and thine. 'Tis ordained that that husband of thine, that Q. of thy bosom, shall reign supreme for years to come over the bedesmen of Hiram's hospital.

And the last in all Barchester to mar their hopes, had he heard and seen all that passed at Puddingdale that day, would have been Mr. Harding. What wants had he to set in opposition to those of such a regiment of young ravens ? There are fourteen of them living ! with him at any rate, let us say, that that argument would have been sufficient for the appointment of Mr. Quiverful.

In the morning, Q. and his wife kept their appointments with that punctuality which bespeaks an expectant mind. The friendly farmer's gig was borrowed, and in that they went, discussing many things by the way. They had instructed the household to expect them back by one, and injunctions were given to the eldest pledge to have ready by that accustomed hour the remainder of the huge stew which the provident mother had prepared on the previous day. The hands of the kitchen clock came round to two, three, four, before the farmer's gig-wheels were again heard at the vicarage gate. With what palpitating hearts were the returning wanderers greeted !

'I suppose, children, you all thought we were never coming back any more ?' said the mother, as she slowly let down her solid foot till it rested on the step of the gig. 'Well, such a day as we've had !' and then leaning heavily on a big boy's shoulder, she stepped once more on terra firma.

There was no need for more than the tone of her voice to tell them that all was right. The Irish stew might burn itself to cinders now.

Then there was such kissing and hugging, such crying and laughing. Mr. Quiverful could not sit still at all, but kept walking from room to room, then out into the garden, then down the avenue into the road, and then back again to his wife. She, however, lost no time so idly.

'We must go to work at once, girls ; and that in earnest. Mrs. Proudie expects us to be in the hospital house on the 15th of October.'

Had Mrs. Proudie expressed a wish that they should all be there on the next morning, the girls would have had nothing so say against it.

'And when will the pay begin ?' asked the eldest boy.

'To-day, my dear,' said the gratified mother.

'Oh,—that is jolly,' said the boy.

'Mrs. Proudie insisted on our going down to the house,' continued the mother ; ' and when there I thought I might save a journey by measuring some of the rooms and windows; so I got a knot of tape from Bobbins. Bobbins is as civil as you please, now.'

'I wouldn't thank him,' said Letty the younger.

'Oh, it's the way of the world, my dear. They all do just the same. You might just as well be angry with the turkey cock for gobbling at you. It's the bird's nature.' And as she enunciated to her bairns the upshot of her practical experience, she pulled from her pocket the portions of tape which showed the length and breadth of the various rooms at the hospital house.

And so we will leave her happy in her toils.

The Quiverfuls had hardly left the palace, and Mrs. Proudie was still holding forth on the matter to her husband, when another visitor was announced in the person of Dr. Gwynne. The master of Lazarus had asked for the bishop, and not for Mrs. Proudie, and therefore, when he was shown into the study, he was surprised rather than rejoiced to find the lady there.

But we must go back a little, and it shall be but a little, for a difficulty begins to make itself manifest in the necessity of disposing of all our friends in the small remainder of this one volume. Oh, that Mr. Longman would allow me a fourth! It should transcend the other three as the seventh heaven transcends all the lower stages of celestial bliss.

Going home in the carriage that evening from Ulla-thorne, Dr. Gwynne had not without difficulty brought round his friend the archdeacon to a line of tactics much less bellicose than that which his own taste would have preferred. 'It will be unseemly in us to show ourselves in a bad humour: and moreover we have no power in this matter, and it will therefore be bad policy to act as though we had.' 'Twas thus the master of Lazarus argued. 'If,' he continued, 'the bishop be determined to appoint another to the hospital, threats will not prevent him, and threats should not be lightly used by an archdeacon to his bishop. If he will place a stranger in the hospital, we can only leave him to the indignation of others. It is probable that such a step may not eventually injure your father-in-law. I will see the bishop, if you will allow me,—alone.' At this the archdeacon winced visibly; 'yes, alone; for so I shall be calmer: and then I shall at any rate learn what he does mean to do in the matter.'

The archdeacon puffed and blew, put up the carriage window and then put it down again, argued the matter up to his own gate, and at last gave way. Everybody was against him, his own wife, Mr. Harding, and Dr. Gwynne. . 'Pray keep him out of hot water, Dr. Gwynne,' Mrs. Grantly had said to her guest. 'My dearest madam, I'll do my best,' the courteous master had replied. 'Twas thus he did it; and earned for himself the gratitude of Mrs. Grantly.

And now we may return to the bishop's study.

Dr. Gwynne had certainly not foreseen the difficulty which here presented itself. He,—together with all the clerical world of England,—had heard it rumoured about that Mrs. Proudie did not confine herself to her wardrobes, still-rooms, and laundries; but yet it had never occurred to him that if he called on a bishop at one o'clock in the day, he could by any possibility find him closeted with his wife; or that if he did so, the wife would remain longer than necessary to make her curtsey. It appeared, however, as though in the present case Mrs. Proudie had no idea of retreating.

The bishop had been very much pleased with Dr. Gwynne on the preceding day, and of course thought that Dr. Gwynne had been as much pleased with him. He attributed the visit solely to compliment, and thought it an extremely gracious and proper thing for the master of Lazarus to drive over from Plumstead specially to call at the palace so soon after his arrival in the country. The fact that they were not on the same side either in politics or doctrines made the compliment the greater. The bishop, therefore, was all smiles. And Mrs. Proudie, who liked people with good handles to their names, was also very well disposed to welcome the master of Lazarus.

'We had a charming party at Ullathorne, Master, had we not?' said she. 'I hope Mrs. Grantly got home without fatigue.'

Dr. Gwynne said that they had all been a little tired, but were none the worse this morning.

'An excellent person, Miss Thorne,' suggested the bishop.

'And an exemplary Christian, I am told,' said Mrs. Proudie.

Dr. Gwynne declared that he was very glad to hear it.

'I have not seen her Sabbath-day schools yet,' continued the lady, 'but I shall make a point of doing so before long.'

Dr. Gwynne merely bowed at this intimation. He had heard something of Mrs. Proudie and her Sunday schools, both from Dr. Grantly and Mr. Harding.

'By the bye, Master,' continued the lady, 'I wonder whether Mrs. Grantly would like me to drive over and inspect her Sabbath-day school. I hear that it is most excellently kept.'

Dr. Gwynne really could not say. He had no doubt Mrs. Grantly would be most happy to see Mrs. Proudie any day Mrs. Proudie would do her the honour of calling : that was, of course, if Mrs. Grantly should happen to be at home.

A slight cloud darkened the lady's brow. She saw that her offer was not taken in good part. This generation of unregenerated vipers was still perverse, stiffnecked, and hardened in their iniquity. 'The archdeacon, I know,' said she, ' sets his face against these institutions.'

At this Dr. Gwynne laughed slightly. It was but a smile. Had he given his cap for it he could not have helped it.

Mrs. Proudie frowned again. ' "Suffer little children, and forbid them not," ' said she. ' Are we not to remember that, Dr. Gwynne ? "Take heed that ye despise not one of these little ones." Are we not to remember that, Dr. Gwynne ?' And at each of these questions she raised at him her menacing forefinger.

'Certainly, madam, certainly,' said the master, ' and so does the archdeacon, I am sure, on week days as well as on Sundays.'

'On week days you can't take heed not to despise them,' said Mrs. Proudie, ' because then they are out in the fields. On week days they belong to their parents, but on Sundays they ought to belong to the clergyman.' And the finger was again raised.

The master began to understand and to share the intense disgust which the archdeacon always expressed when Mrs. Proudie's name was mentioned. What was he to do with such a woman as this ? To take his hat and go would have been his natural resource; but then he did not wish to be foiled in his object.

'My lord,' said he, 'I wanted to ask you a question on business, if you could spare me one moment's leisure. I know I must apologise for so disturbing you; but in truth I will not detain you five minutes.'

'Certainly, Master, certainly,' said the bishop; 'my time is quite yours,—pray make no apology, pray make no apology.'

'You have a great deal to do just at the present moment, bishop. Do not forget how extremely busy you are at present,' said Mrs. Proudie, whose spirit was now up; for she was angry with her visitor.

'I will not delay his lordship much above a minute,' said the master of Lazarus, rising from his chair, and expecting that Mrs. Proudie would now go, or else that the bishop would lead the way into another room.

But neither event seemed likely to occur, and Dr. Gwynne stood for a moment silent in the middle of the room.

'Perhaps it's about Hiram's hospital?' suggested Mrs. Proudie.

Dr. Gwynne, lost in astonishment, and not knowing what else on earth to do, confessed that his business with the bishop was connected with Hiram's hospital.

'His lordship has finally conferred the appointment on Mr. Quiverful this morning,' said the lady

Dr. Gwynne made a simple reference to the bishop, and finding that the lady's statement was formally confirmed, he took his leave. 'That comes of the reform bill,' he said to himself as he walked down the bishop's avenue. 'Well, at any rate the Greek play bishops were not so bad as that.'

It has been said that Mr. Slope, as he started for Ullathorne, received a despatch from his friend, Mr. Towers, which had the effect of putting him in that high good-humour which subsequent events somewhat untowardly damped. It ran as follows. Its shortness will be its sufficient apology.

'My dear Sir,—I wish you every success. I don't know that I can help you, but if I can, I will.

'Yours ever,
'T. T.
'30/9/185—'

There was more in this than in all Sir Nicholas Fitzwhiggin's flummery; more than in all the bishop's
promises, even had they been ever so sincere; more than
in any archbishop's good word, even had it been possible
to obtain it. Tom Towers would do for him what he could.

Mr. Slope had from his youth upwards been a firm
believer in the public press. He had dabbled in it himself
ever since he had taken his degree, and regarded it as the
great arranger and distributor of all future British terres-
trial affairs whatever. He had not yet arrived at the age,
an age which sooner or later comes to most of us, which
dissipates the golden dreams of youth. He delighted in
the idea of wresting power from the hands of his country's
magnates, and placing it in a custody which was at any
rate nearer to his own reach. Sixty thousand broad sheets
dispersing themselves daily among his reading fellow-
citizens, formed in his eyes a better depôt for supremacy
than a throne at Windsor, a cabinet in Downing Street,
or even an assembly at Westminster. And on this subject
we must not quarrel with Mr. Slope, for the feeling is too
general to be met with disrespect.

Tom Towers was as good, if not better than his promise.
On the following morning the Jupiter, spouting forth
public opinion with sixty thousand loud clarions, did
proclaim to the world that Mr. Slope was the fitting man
for the vacant post. It was pleasant for Mr. Slope to read
the following lines in the Barchester news-room, which
he did within thirty minutes after the morning train from
London had reached the city.

' It is just now five years since we called the attention
of our readers to the quiet city of Barchester. From that
day to this, we have in no way meddled with the affairs of
that happy ecclesiastical community. Since then, an old
bishop has died there, and a young bishop has been
installed; but we believe we did not do more than give
some customary record of the interesting event. Nor are
we now about to meddle very deeply in the affairs of the
diocese. If any of the chapter feel a qualm of conscience
on reading thus far, let it be quieted. Above all, let the
mind of the new bishop be at rest. We are now not armed
for war, but approach the reverend towers of the old
cathedral with an olive-branch in our hands.

' It will be remembered that at the time alluded to, now five years past, we had occasion to remark on the state of a charity in Barchester called Hiram's Hospital. We thought that it was maladministered, and that the very estimable and reverend gentleman who held the office of warden was somewhat too highly paid for duties which were somewhat too easily performed. This gentleman—and we say it in all sincerity and with no touch of sarcasm —had never looked on the matter in this light before. We do not wish to take praise to ourselves whether praise be due to us or not. But the consequence of our remark was, that the warden did look into the matter, and finding on so doing that he himself could come to no other opinion than that expressed by us, he very creditably threw up the appointment. The then bishop as creditably declined to fill the vacancy till the affair was put on a better footing. Parliament then took it up ; and we have now the satisfaction of informing our readers that Hiram's hospital will be immediately re-opened under new auspices. Heretofore, provision was made for the maintenance of twelve old men. This will now be extended to the fair sex, and twelve elderly women, if any such can be found in Barchester, will be added to the establishment. There will be a matron ; there will, it is hoped, be schools attached for the poorest of the children of the poor, and there will be a steward. The warden, for there will still be a warden, will receive an income more in keeping with the extent of the charity than that heretofore paid. The stipend we believe will be 450*l.* We may add that the excellent house which the former warden inhabited will still be attached to the situation.

' Barchester hospital cannot perhaps boast a world-wide reputation ; but as we adverted to its state of decadence, we think it right also to advert to its renaissance. May it go on and prosper. Whether the salutary reform which has been introduced within its walls has been carried as far as could have been desired, may be doubtful. The important question of the school appears to be somewhat left to the discretion of the new warden. This might have been made the most important part of the establishment, and the new warden, whom we trust we shall not offend by the freedom of our remarks, might have been selected with some view to his fitness as schoolmaster. But we will not now look a gift horse in the mouth. May the hospital go on and prosper! The situation of warden has of course been offered to the gentleman who so honourably vacated it five years since; but we are given to understand that he has declined it. Whether the ladies who have been introduced, be in his estimation too much for his powers of control, whether it be that the diminished income does not offer to him sufficient temptation to resume his old place, or that he has in the meantime assumed other clerical duties, we do not know. We are, however, informed that he has refused the offer, and that the situation has been accepted by Mr. Quiverful, the vicar of Puddingdale.

'So much we think is due to Hiram redivivus. But while we are on the subject of Barchester, we will venture with all respectful humility to express our opinion on another matter, connected with the ecclesiastical polity of that ancient city. Dr. Trefoil, the dean, died yesterday. A short record of his death, giving his age, and the various pieces of preferment which he has at different times held, will be found in another column of this paper. The only fault we knew in him was his age, and as that is a crime of which we all hope to be guilty, we will not bear heavily on it. May he rest in peace! But though the great age of an expiring dean cannot be made matter of reproach, we are not inclined to look on such a fault as at all pardonable in a dean just brought to the birth. We do hope that the days of sexagenarian appointments are past. If we want deans, we must want them for some purpose. That purpose will necessarily be better fulfilled by a man of forty than by a man of sixty. If we are to pay deans at all, we are to pay them for some sort of work. That work, be it what it may, will be best performed by a workman in the prime of life. Dr. Trefoil, we see, was eighty when he died. As we have as yet completed no plan for pensioning superannuated clergymen, we do not wish to get rid of any existing deans of that age. But we prefer having as few such as possible. If a man of seventy be now appointed, we beg to point out to Lord —— that he will be past all use in a year or two, if indeed he be not so at the present moment. His lordship will allow us to remind him that all men are not evergreens like himself.

'We hear that Mr. Slope's name has been mentioned for this preferment. Mr. Slope is at present chaplain to the bishop. A better man could hardly be selected. He is a man of talent, young, active, and conversant with the affairs of the cathedral ; he is moreover, we conscientiously believe, a truly pious clergyman. We know that his services in the city of Barchester have been highly appreciated. He is an eloquent preacher and a ripe scholar. Such a selection as this would go far to raise the confidence of the public in the present administration of church patronage, and would teach men to believe that from henceforth the establishment of our church will not afford easy couches to worn-out clerical voluptuaries.'

Standing at a reading-desk in the Barchester newsroom, Mr. Slope digested this article with considerable satisfaction. What was therein said as to the hospital was now comparatively matter of indifference to him. He was certainly glad that he had not succeeded in restoring to the place the father of that virago who had so audaciously outraged all decency in his person ; and was so far satisfied. But Mrs. Proudie's nominee was appointed, and he was so far dissatisfied. His mind, however, was now soaring above Mrs. Bold or Mrs. Proudie. He was sufficiently conversant with the tactics of the Jupiter to know that the pith of the article would lie in the last paragraph. The place of honour was given to him, and it was indeed as honourable as even he could have wished. He was very grateful to his friend Mr. Towers, and with full heart looked forward to the day when he might entertain him in princely style at his own full-spread board in the deanery dining-room.

It had been well for Mr. Slope that Dr. Trefoil had died in the autumn. Those caterers for our morning repast, the staff of the Jupiter, had been sorely put to it for the last month to find a sufficiency of proper pabulum. Just then there was no talk of a new American president. No wonderful tragedies had occurred on railway trains in Georgia, or elsewhere. There was a dearth of broken banks, and a dead dean with the necessity for a live one was a godsend. Had Dr. Trefoil died in June, Mr. Towers would probably not have known so much about the piety of Mr. Slope.

And here we will leave Mr. Slope for a while in his triumph; explaining, however, that his feelings were not altogether of a triumphant nature. His rejection by the widow, or rather the method of his rejection, galled him terribly. For days to come he positively felt the sting upon his cheek, whenever he thought of what had been done to him. He could not refrain from calling her by harsh names, speaking to himself as he walked through the streets of Barchester. When he said his prayers, he could not bring himself to forgive her. When he strove to do so, his mind recoiled from the attempt, and in lieu of forgiving ran off in a double spirit of vindictiveness, dwelling on the extent of the injury he had received. And so his prayers dropped senseless from his lips.

And then the signora; what would he not have given to be able to hate her also ? As it was, he worshipped the very sofa on which she was ever lying. And thus it was not all rose colour with Mr. Slope, although his hopes ran high.

CHAPTER XLIV

MRS. BOLD AT HOME

Poor Mrs. Bold, when she got home from Ullathorne on the evening of Miss Thorne's party, was very unhappy, and moreover, very tired. Nothing fatigues the body so much as weariness of spirit, and Eleanor's spirit was indeed weary.

Dr. Stanhope had civilly but not very cordially asked her in to tea, and her manner of refusal convinced the worthy doctor that he need not repeat the invitation. He had not exactly made himself a party to the intrigue which was to convert the late Mr. Bold's patrimony into an income for his hopeful son, but he had been well aware what was going on. And he was well aware also, when he perceived that Bertie declined accompanying them home in the carriage, that the affair had gone off.

Eleanor was very much afraid that Charlotte would have darted out upon her, as the prebendary got out at his own door, but Bertie had thoughtfully saved her from this, by causing the carriage to go round by her own house. This also Dr. Stanhope understood, and allowed to pass by without remark.

When she got home, she found Mary Bold in the drawing-room with the child in her lap. She rushed forward, and, throwing herself on her knees, kissed the little fellow till she almost frightened him.

'Oh, Mary, I am so glad you did not go. It was an odious party.'

Now the question of Mary's going had been one greatly mooted between them. Mrs. Bold, when invited, had been the guest of the Grantlys, and Miss Thorne, who had chiefly known Eleanor at the hospital or at Plumstead rectory, had forgotten all about Mary Bold. Her sister-in-law had implored her to go under her wing, and had offered to write to Miss Thorne, or to call on her. But Miss Bold had declined. In fact, Mr. Bold had not been very popular with such people as the Thornes, and his sister would not go among them unless she were specially asked to do so.

'Well then,' said Mary, cheerfully, 'I have the less to regret.'

'You have nothing to regret; but oh! Mary, I have—so much—so much;'—and then she began kissing her boy, whom her caresses had aroused from his slumbers. When she raised her head, Mary saw that the tears were running down her cheeks.

'Good heavens, Eleanor, what is the matter? what has happened to you?—Eleanor—dearest Eleanor—what is the matter?' and Mary got up with the boy still in her arms.

'Give him to me—give him to me,' said the young mother. 'Give him to me, Mary,' and she almost tore the child out of her sister's arms. The poor little fellow murmured somewhat at the disturbance, but nevertheless nestled himself close into his mother's bosom.

'Here, Mary, take the cloak from me. My own, own darling, darling, darling jewel. You are not false to me. Everybody else is false; everybody else is cruel. Mamma will care for nobody, nobody, nobody, but her own, own, own little man;' and she again kissed and pressed the

baby, and cried till the tears ran down over the child's
face.

'Who has been cruel to you, Eleanor?' said Mary.
'I hope I have not.'

Now, in this matter, Eleanor had great cause for mental
uneasiness. She could not certainly accuse her loving
sister-in-law of cruelty; but she had to do that which was
more galling; she had to accuse herself of imprudence
against which her sister-in-law had warned her. Miss
Bold had never encouraged Eleanor's acquaintance with
Mr. Slope, and she had positively discouraged the friendship of the Stanhopes as far as her usual gentle mode of
speaking had permitted. Eleanor had only laughed at her,
however, when she said that she disapproved of married
women who lived apart from their husbands, and suggested
that Charlotte Stanhope never went to church. Now,
however, Eleanor must either hold her tongue, which was
quite impossible, or confess herself to have been utterly
wrong, which was nearly equally so. So she staved off the
evil day by more tears, and consoled herself by inducing
little Johnny to rouse himself sufficiently to return her
caresses.

'He is a darling—as true as gold. What would mamma
do without him? Mamma would lie down and die if she
had not her own Johnny Bold to give her comfort.' This
and much more she said of the same kind, and for a time
made no other answer to Mary's inquiries.

This kind of consolation from the world's deceit is very
common.

Mothers obtain it from their children, and men from
their dogs. Some men even do so from their walking-
sticks, which is just as rational. How is it that we can take
joy to ourselves in that we are not deceived by those who
have not attained the art to deceive us? In a true man,
if such can be found, or a true woman, much consolation
may indeed be taken.

In the caresses of her child, however, Eleanor did receive
consolation; and may ill befall the man who would
begrudge it to her. The evil day, however, was only
postponed. She had to tell her disagreeable tale to Mary,
and she had also to tell it to her father. Must it not,
indeed, be told to the whole circle of her acquaintance

before she could be made to stand all right with them ?
At the present moment there was no one to whom she
could turn for comfort. She hated Mr. Slope ; that was
a matter of course, in that feeling she revelled. She hated
and despised the Stanhopes ; but that feeling distressed
her greatly. She had, as it were, separated herself from her
old friends to throw herself into the arms of this family ;
and then how had they intended to use her ? She could
hardly reconcile herself to her own father, who had
believed ill of her. Mary Bold had turned Mentor. That
she could have forgiven had the Mentor turned out to be
in the wrong ; but Mentors in the right are not to be
pardoned. She could not but hate the archdeacon ; and
now she hated him worse than ever, for she must in some
sort humble herself before him. She hated her sister, for
she was part and parcel of the archdeacon. And she would
have hated Mr. Arabin if she could. He had pretended to
regard her, and yet before her face he had hung over that
Italian woman as though there had been no beauty in the
world but hers—no other woman worth a moment's
attention. And Mr. Arabin would have to learn all this
about Mr. Slope ! She told herself that she hated him,
and she knew that she was lying to herself as she did so.
She had no consolation but her baby, and of that she made
the most. Mary, though she could not surmise what it
was that had so violently affected her sister-in-law, saw
at once that her grief was too great to be kept under
control, and waited patiently till the child should be in
his cradle.

' You'll have some tea, Eleanor,' she said.

' Oh, I don't care,' said she ; though in fact she must
have been very hungry, for she had eaten nothing at
Ullathorne.

Mary quietly made the tea, and buttered the bread, laid
aside the cloak, and made things look comfortable.

' He's fast asleep,' said she, ' you're very tired ; let me
take him up to bed.'

But Eleanor would not let her sister touch him. She
looked wistfully at her baby's eyes, saw that they were
lost in the deepest slumber, and then made a sort of couch
for him on the sofa. She was determined that nothing
should prevail upon her to let him out of her sight that night.

'Come, Nelly,' said Mary, 'don't be cross with me.
I at least have done nothing to offend you.'

'I an't cross,' said Eleanor.

'Are you angry then ? Surely you can't be angry with
me.'

'No, I an't angry ; at least not with you.'

'If you are not, drink the tea I have made for you.
I am sure you must want it.'

Eleanor did drink it, and allowed herself to be persuaded.
She ate and drank, and as the inner woman was recruited
she felt a little more charitable towards the world at large.
At last she found words to begin her story, and before she
went to bed, she had made a clean breast of it and told
everything—everything, that is, as to the lovers she had
rejected : of Mr. Arabin she said not a word.

'I know I was wrong,' said she, speaking of the blow
she had given to Mr. Slope ; 'but I didn't know what he
might do, and I had to protect myself.'

'He richly deserved it,' said Mary.

'Deserved it !' said Eleanor, whose mind as regarded
Mr. Slope was almost bloodthirsty. 'Had I stabbed him
with a dagger, he would have deserved it. But what will
they say about it at Plumstead ?'

'I don't think I should tell them,' said Mary. Eleanor
began to think that she would not.

There could have been no kinder comforter than Mary
Bold. There was not the slightest dash of triumph about
her when she heard of the Stanhope scheme, nor did she
allude to her former opinion when Eleanor called her late
friend Charlotte a base, designing woman. She re-echoed
all the abuse that was heaped on Mr. Slope's head, and
never hinted that she had said as much before. 'I told
you so, I told you so !' is the croak of a true Job's comforter. But Mary, when she found her friend lying in her
sorrow and scraping herself with potsherds, forbore to
argue and to exult. Eleanor acknowledged the merit of
the forbearance, and at length allowed herself to be
tranquilised.

On the next day she did not go out of the house.
Barchester she thought would be crowded with Stanhopes
and Slopes ; perhaps also with Arabins and Grantlys.
Indeed there was hardly any one among her friends

whom she could have met, without some cause of uneasiness.

In the course of the afternoon she heard that the dean
was dead; and she also heard that Mr. Quiverful had been
finally appointed to the hospital.

In the evening her father came to her, and then the
story, or as much of it as she could bring herself to tell him,
had to be repeated. He was not in truth much surprised
at Mr. Slope's effrontery; but he was obliged to act as
though he had been, to save his daughter's feelings. He
was, however, anything but skilful in his deceit, and she
saw through it.

'I see,' said she, ' that you think it only in the common
course of things that Mr. Slope should have treated me in
this way.' She had said nothing to him about the embrace,
nor yet of the way in which it had been met.

'I do not think it at all strange,' said he, ' that any one
should admire my Eleanor.'

'It is strange to me,' said she, ' that any man should
have so much audacity, without ever having received the
slightest encouragement.'

To this Mr. Harding answered nothing. With the
archdeacon it would have been the text for a rejoinder,
which would not have disgraced Bildad the Shuhite.

'But you'll tell the archdeacon?' asked Mr. Harding.

'Tell him what?' said she sharply.

'Or Susan?' continued Mr. Harding. ' You'll tell
Susan; you'll let them know that they wronged you in
supposing that this man's addresses would be agreeable
to you.'

'They may find that out their own way,' said she;
'I shall not ever willingly mention Mr. Slope's name to
either of them.'

'But I may.'

'I have no right to hinder you from doing anything that
may be necessary to your own comfort, but pray do not do
it for my sake. Dr. Grantly never thought well of me,
and never will. I don't know now that I am even anxious
that he should do so.'

And then they went to the affair of the hospital. ' But
is it true, papa?'

'What, my dear?' said he. ' About the dean? Yes,

I fear quite true. Indeed I know there is no doubt about it.'

'Poor Miss Trefoil. I am so sorry for her. But I did not mean that,' said Eleanor. 'But about the hospital, papa ? '

'Yes, my dear. I believe it is true that Mr. Quiverful is to have it.'

'Oh, what a shame ! '

'No, my dear, not at all, not at all a shame : I am sure I hope it will suit him.'

'But, papa, you know it is a shame. After all your hopes, all your expectations to get back to your old house, to see it given away in this way to a perfect stranger ! '

'My dear, the bishop had a right to give it to whom he pleased.'

'I deny that, papa. He had no such right. It is not as though you were a candidate for a new piece of preferment. If the bishop has a grain of justice—'

'The bishop offered it to me on his terms, and as I did not like the terms, I refused it. After that, I cannot complain.'

'Terms ! he had no right to make terms.'

'I don't know about that ; but it seems he had the power. But to tell you the truth, Nelly, I am as well satisfied as it is. When the affair became the subject of angry discussion, I thoroughly wished to be rid of it altogether.'

'But you did want to go back to the old house, papa. You told me so yourself.'

'Yes, my dear, I did. For a short time I did wish it. And I was foolish in doing so. I am getting old now ; and my chief worldly wish is for peace and rest. Had I gone back to the hospital, I should have had endless contentions with the bishop, contentions with his chaplain, and con-tentions with the archdeacon. I am not up to this now, I am not able to meet such troubles ; and therefore I am not ill-pleased to find myself left to the little church of St. Cuthbert's. I shall never starve,' added he, laughing, ' as long as you are here.'

'But will you come and live with me, papa ? ' she said earnestly, taking him by both his hands. ' If you will do that, if you will promise that, I will own that you are right.'

' I will dine with you to-day at any rate.'

' No, but live here altogether. Give up that close, odious little room in High Street.'

' My dear, it's a very nice little room ; and you are really quite uncivil.'

' Oh, papa, don't joke. It's not a nice place for you. You say you are growing old, though I am sure you are not.'

' Am not I, my dear ? '

' No, papa, not old—not to say old. But you are quite old enough to feel the want of a decent room to sit in. You know how lonely Mary and I are here. You know nobody ever sleeps in the big front bed-room. It is really unkind of you to remain up there alone, when you are so much wanted here.'

' Thank you, Nelly—thank you. But, my dear—'

' If you had been living here, papa, with us, as I really think you ought to have done, considering how lonely we are, there would have been none of all this dreadful affair about Mr. Slope.'

Mr. Harding, however, did not allow himself to be talked over into giving up his own and only little *pied à terre* in the High Street. He promised to come and dine with his daughter, and stay with her, and visit her, and do every-thing but absolutely live with her. It did not suit the peculiar feelings of the man to tell his daughter that though she had rejected Mr. Slope, and been ready to reject Mr. Stanhope, some other more favoured suitor would probably soon appear ; and that on the appearance of such a suitor the big front bed-room might perhaps be more frequently in requisition than at present. But doubtless such an idea crossed his mind, and added its weight to the other reasons which made him decide on still keeping the close, odious little room in High Street.

The evening passed over quietly and in comfort. Eleanor was always happier with her father than with any one else. He had not, perhaps, any natural taste for baby-worship, but he was always ready to sacrifice himself, and therefore made an excellent third in a trio with his daughter and Mary Bold in singing the praises of the wonderful child.

They were standing together over their music in the evening, the baby having again been put to bed upon the sofa, when the servant brought in a very small note in a beautiful pink envelope. It quite filled the room with perfume as it lay upon the small salver. Mary Bold and Mrs. Bold were both at the piano, and Mr. Harding was sitting close to them, with the violoncello between his legs; so that the elegancy of the epistle was visible to them all.

'Please, ma'am, Dr. Stanhope's coachman says he is to wait for an answer,' said the servant.

Eleanor got very red in the face as she took the note in her hand. She had never seen the writing before. Charlotte's epistles, to which she was well accustomed, were of a very different style and kind. She generally wrote on large note-paper; she twisted up her letters into the shape and sometimes into the size of cocked hats; she addressed them in a sprawling manly hand, and not unusually added a blot or a smudge, as though such were her own peculiar sign-manual. The address of this note was written in a beautiful female hand, and the gummed wafer bore on it an impress of a gilt coronet. Though Eleanor had never seen such a one before, she guessed that it came from the signora. Such epistles were very numerously sent out from any house in which the signora might happen to be dwelling, but they were rarely addressed to ladies. When the coachman was told by the lady's maid to take the letter to Mrs. Bold, he openly expressed his opinion that there was some mistake about it. Whereupon the lady's maid boxed the coachman's ears. Had Mr. Slope seen in how meek a spirit the coachman took the rebuke, he might have learnt a useful lesson, both in philosophy and religion.

The note was as follows. It may be taken as a faithful promise that no further letter whatever shall be transcribed at length in these pages.

'My dear Mrs. Bold,—May I ask you, as a great favour, to call on me to-morrow? You can say what hour will best suit you; but quite early, if you can. I need hardly say that if I could call upon you I should not take this liberty with you.

'I partly know what occurred the other day, and I promise you that you shall meet with no annoyance if you will come to me. My brother leaves us for London to-day; from thence he goes to Italy.

'It will probably occur to you that I should not thus intrude on you, unless I had that to say to you which may be of considerable moment. Pray therefore excuse me, even if you do not grant my request, and believe me,

'Very sincerely yours,
'M. VESEY NERONI.

'Thursday Evening.'

The three of them sat in consultation on this epistle for some ten or fifteen minutes, and then decided that Eleanor should write a line saying that she would see the signora the next morning, at twelve o'clock.

CHAPTER XLV

THE STANHOPES AT HOME

WE must now return to the Stanhopes, and see how they behaved themselves on their return from Ullathorne. Charlotte, who came back in the first homeward journey with her sister, waited in palpitating expectation till the carriage drove up to the door a second time. She did not run down or stand at the window, or show in any outward manner that she looked for anything wonderful to occur; but, when she heard the carriage-wheels, she stood up with erect ears, listening for Eleanor's footfall on the pavement or the cheery sound of Bertie's voice welcoming her in. Had she heard either, she would have felt that all was right; but neither sound was there for her to hear. She heard only her father's slow step, as he ponderously let himself down from the carriage, and slowly walked along the hall, till he got into his own private room on the ground floor. 'Send Miss Stanhope to me,' he said to the servant.

'There's something wrong now,' said Madeline, who was lying on her sofa in the back drawing-room.

'It's all up with Bertie,' replied Charlotte. 'I know, I know,' she said to the servant, as he brought up the message. 'Tell my father I will be with him immediately.'

'Bertie's wooing has gone astray,' said Madeline; 'I knew it would.'

'It has been his own fault then. She was ready enough, I am quite sure,' said Charlotte, with that sort of ill-nature which is not uncommon when one woman speaks of another.

'What will you say to him now?' By 'him,' the signora meant their father.

'That will be as I find him. He was ready to pay two hundred pounds for Bertie, to stave off the worst of his creditors, if this marriage had gone on. Bertie must now have the money instead, and go and take his chance.'

'Where is he now?'

'Heaven knows! smoking in the bottom of Mr. Thorne's ha-ha, or philandering with some of those Miss Chadwicks. Nothing will ever make an impression on him. But he'll be furious if I don't go down.'

'No; nothing ever will. But don't be long, Charlotte, for I want my tea.'

And so Charlotte went down to her father. There was a very black cloud on the old man's brow; blacker than his daughter could ever yet remember to have seen there. He was sitting in his own arm-chair, not comfortably over the fire, but in the middle of the room, waiting till she should come and listen to him.

'What has become of your brother?' he said, as soon as the door was shut.

'I should rather ask you,' said Charlotte. 'I left you both at Ullathorne, when I came away. What have you done with Mrs. Bold?'

'Mrs. Bold! nonsense. The woman has gone home as she ought to do. And heartily glad I am that she should not be sacrificed to so heartless a reprobate.'

'Oh, papa!'

'A heartless reprobate! Tell me now where he is, and what he is going to do. I have allowed myself to be fooled between you. Marriage, indeed! Who on earth that has money, or credit, or respect in the world to lose, would marry him?'

'It is no use your scolding me, papa. I have done the best I could for him and you.'

'And Madeline is nearly as bad,' said the prebendary, who was in truth very, very angry.

'Oh, I suppose we are all bad,' replied Charlotte.

The old man emitted a huge leonine sigh. If they were all bad, who had made them so? If they were unprincipled, selfish, and disreputable, who was to be blamed for the education which had had so injurious an effect?

'I know you'll ruin me among you,' said he.

'Why, papa, what nonsense that is. You are living within your income this minute, and if there are any new debts, I don't know of them. I am sure there ought to be none, for we are dull enough here.'

'Are those bills of Madeline's paid?'

'No, they are not. Who was to pay them?'

'Her husband may pay them.'

'Her husband! would you wish me to tell her you say so? Do you wish to turn her out of your house?'

'I wish she would know how to behave herself.'

'Why, what on earth has she done now? Poor Madeline! To-day is only the second time she has gone out since we came to this vile town.'

He then sat silent for a time, thinking in what shape he would declare his resolve. 'Well, papa,' said Charlotte, 'shall I stay here, or may I go up-stairs and give mamma her tea?'

'You are in your brother's confidence. Tell me what he is going to do?'

'Nothing, that I am aware of.'

'Nothing—nothing! nothing but eat and drink, and spend every shilling of my money he can lay his hands upon. I have made up my mind, Charlotte. He shall eat and drink no more in this house.'

'Very well. Then I suppose he must go back to Italy.'

'He may go where he pleases.'

'That's easily said, papa; but what does it mean? You can't let him——'

'It means this,' said the doctor, speaking more loudly than was his wont, and with wrath flashing from his eyes; 'that as sure as God rules in heaven, I will not maintain him any longer in idleness.'

'Oh, ruling in heaven!' said Charlotte. 'It is no use talking about that. You must rule him here on earth; and the question is, how you can do it. You can't turn him out of the house penniless, to beg about the street.'

'He may beg where he likes.'

'He must go back to Carrara. That is the cheapest place he can live at, and nobody there will give him credit for above two or three hundred pauls. But you must let him have the means of going.'

'As sure as——'

'Oh, papa, don't swear. You know you must do it. You were ready to pay two hundred pounds for him if this marriage came off. Half that will start him to Carrara.'

'What? give him a hundred pounds!'

'You know we are all in the dark, papa,' said she, thinking it expedient to change the conversation. 'For anything we know, he may be at this moment engaged to Mrs. Bold.'

'Fiddlestick,' said the father, who had seen the way in which Mrs. Bold had got into the carriage, while his son stood apart without even offering her his hand.

'Well, then, he must go to Carrara,' said Charlotte.

Just at this moment the lock of the front door was heard, and Charlotte's quick ears detected her brother's cat-like step in the hall. She said nothing, feeling that for the present Bertie had better keep out of her father's way. But Dr. Stanhope also heard the sound of the lock.

'Who's that?' he demanded. Charlotte made no reply, and he asked again, 'Who is that that has just come in? Open the door. Who is it?'

'I suppose it is Bertie.'

'Bid him come here,' said the father. But Bertie, who was close to the door and heard the call, required no further bidding, but walked in with a perfectly unconcerned and cheerful air. It was this peculiar *insouciance* which angered Dr. Stanhope, even more than his son's extravagance.

'Well, sir?' said the doctor.

'And how did you get home, sir, with your fair companion?' said Bertie. 'I suppose she is not up-stairs, Charlotte?'

'Bertie,' said Charlotte, 'papa is in no humour for joking. He is very angry with you.'

'Angry!' said Bertie, raising his eyebrows, as though he had never yet given his parent cause for a single moment's uneasiness.

'Sit down, if you please, sir,' said Dr. Stanhope very sternly, but not now very loudly. 'And I'll trouble you to sit down too, Charlotte. Your mother can wait for her tea a few minutes.'

Charlotte sat down on the chair nearest to the door, in somewhat of a perverse sort of manner; as much as though she would say—Well, here I am; you shan't say I don't do what I am bid; but I'll be whipped if I give way to you. And she was determined not to give way. She too was angry with Bertie; but she was not the less ready on that account to defend him from his father. Bertie also sat down. He drew his chair close to the library-table, upon which he put his elbow, and then resting his face comfortably on one hand, he began drawing little pictures on a sheet of paper with the other. Before the scene was over he had completed admirable figures of Miss Thorne, Mrs. Proudie, and Lady De Courcy, and begun a family piece to comprise the whole set of the Lookalofts.

'Would it suit you, sir,' said the father, 'to give me some idea as to what your present intentions are?—what way of living you propose to yourself?'

'I'll do anything you can suggest, sir,' replied Bertie.

'No, I shall suggest nothing further. My time for suggesting has gone by. I have only one order to give, and that is, that you leave my house.'

'To-night?' said Bertie; and the simple tone of the question left the doctor without any adequately dignified method of reply.

'Papa does not quite mean to-night,' said Charlotte, 'at least I suppose not.'

'To-morrow, perhaps,' suggested Bertie.

'Yes, sir, to-morrow,' said the doctor. 'You shall leave this to-morrow.'

'Very well, sir. Will the 4.30 P.M. train be soon enough?' and Bertie, as he asked, put the finishing touch to Miss Thorne's high-heeled boots.

'You may go how and when and where you please, so

that you leave my house to-morrow. You have disgraced me, sir; you have disgraced yourself, and me, and your sisters.'

'I am glad at least, sir, that I have not disgraced my mother,' said Bertie.

Charlotte could hardly keep her countenance; but the doctor's brow grew still blacker than ever. Bertie was executing his *chef d'œuvre* in the delineation of Mrs. Proudie's nose and mouth.

'You are a heartless reprobate, sir; a heartless, thankless, good-for-nothing reprobate. I have done with you. You are my son—that I cannot help; but you shall have no more part or parcel in me as my child, nor I in you as your father.'

'Oh, papa, papa! you must not, shall not say so,' said Charlotte.

'I will say so, and do say so,' said the father, rising from his chair. 'And now leave the room, sir.'

'Stop, stop,' said Charlotte; 'why don't you speak, Bertie? why don't you look up and speak? It is your manner that makes papa so angry.'

'He is perfectly indifferent to all decency, to all propriety,' said the doctor; and then he shouted out, 'Leave the room, sir! Do you hear what I say?'

'Papa, papa, I will not let you part so. I know you will be sorry for it.' And then she added, getting up and whispering into his ear, 'Is he only to blame? Think of that. We have made our own bed, and, such as it is, we must lie on it. It is no use for us to quarrel among ourselves,' and as she finished her whisper Bertie finished off the countess's bustle, which was so well done that it absolutely seemed to be swaying to and fro on the paper with its usual lateral motion.

'My father is angry at the present time,' said Bertie, looking up for a moment from his sketches, 'because I am not going to marry Mrs. Bold. What can I say on the matter? It is true that I am not going to marry her. In the first place——'

'That is not true, sir,' said Dr. Stanhope; 'but I will not argue with you.'

'You were angry just this moment because I would not speak,' said Bertie, going on with a young Lookaloft.

'Give over drawing,' said Charlotte, going up to him and taking the paper from under his hand. The caricatures, however, she preserved, and showed them afterwards to the friends of the Thornes, the Proudies, and De Courcys. Bertie, deprived of his occupation, threw himself back in his chair and waited further orders.

'I think it will certainly be for the best that Bertie should leave this at once, perhaps to-morrow,' said Charlotte; 'but pray, papa, let us arrange some scheme together.'

'If he will leave this to-morrow, I will give him 10*l*., and he shall be paid 5*l*. a month by the banker at Carrara as long as he stays permanently in that place.'

'Well, sir! it won't be long,' said Bertie; 'for I shall be starved to death in about three months.'

'He must have marble to work with,' said Charlotte.

'I have plenty there in the studio to last me three months,' said Bertie. 'It will be no use attempting anything large in so limited a time; unless I do my own tombstone.'

Terms, however, were ultimately come to, somewhat more liberal than those proposed, and the doctor was induced to shake hands with his son, and bid him good night. Dr. Stanhope would not go up to tea, but had it brought to him in his study by his daughter.

But Bertie went up-stairs and spent a pleasant evening. He finished the Lookalofts, greatly to the delight of his sisters, though the manner of portraying their *décolleté* dresses was not the most refined. Finding how matters were going, he by degrees allowed it to escape from him that he had not pressed his suit upon the widow in a very urgent way.

'I suppose, in point of fact, you never proposed at all?' said Charlotte.

'Oh, she understood that she might have me if she wished,' said he.

'And she didn't wish,' said the signora.

'You have thrown me over in the most shameful manner,' said Charlotte. 'I suppose you told her all about my little plan?'

'Well, it came out somehow; at least the most of it.'

'There's an end of that alliance,' said Charlotte; 'but

it doesn't matter much. I suppose we shall all be back at Como soon.'

'I am sure I hope so,' said the signora; 'I'm sick of the sight of black coats. If that Mr. Slope comes here any more, he'll be the death of me.'

'You've been the ruin of him, I think,' said Charlotte.

'And as for a second black-coated lover of mine, I am going to make a present of him to another lady with most singular disinterestedness.'

The next day, true to his promise, Bertie packed up and went off by the 4.30 P.M. train, with 20*l.* in his pocket, bound for the marble quarries of Carrara. And so he disappears from our scene.

At twelve o'clock on the day following that on which Bertie went, Mrs. Bold, true also to her word, knocked at Dr. Stanhope's door with a timid hand and palpitating heart. She was at once shown up to the back drawing-room, the folding doors of which were closed, so that in visiting the signora Eleanor was not necessarily thrown into any communion with those in the front room. As she went up the stairs, she saw none of the family, and was so far saved much of the annoyance which she had dreaded.

'This is very kind of you, Mrs. Bold; very kind, after what has happened,' said the lady on the sofa with her sweetest smile.

'You wrote in such a strain that I could not but come to you.'

'I did, I did; I wanted to force you to see me.'

'Well, signora; I am here.'

'How cold you are to me. But I suppose I must put up with that. I know you think you have reason to be displeased with us all. Poor Bertie! if you knew all, you would not be angry with him.'

'I am not angry with your brother—not in the least. But I hope you did not send for me here to talk about him.'

'If you are angry with Charlotte, that is worse; for you have no warmer friend in all Barchester. But I did *not* send for you to talk about this,—pray bring your chair nearer, Mrs. Bold, so that I may look at you. It is so unnatural to see you keeping so far off from me.'

Eleanor did as she was bid, and brought her chair close to the sofa.

'And now, Mrs. Bold, I am going to tell you something which you may perhaps think indelicate ; but yet I know that I am right in doing so.'

Hereupon Mrs. Bold said nothing, but felt inclined to shake in her chair. The signora, she knew, was not very particular, and that which to her appeared to be indelicate might to Mrs. Bold appear to be extremely indecent.

'I believe you know Mr. Arabin ? '

Mrs. Bold would have given the world not to blush, but her blood was not at her own command. She did blush up to her forehead, and the signora, who had made her sit in a special light in order that she might watch her, saw that she did so.

'Yes,—I am acquainted with him. That is, slightly. He is an intimate friend of Dr. Grantly, and Dr. Grantly is my brother-in-law.'

'Well; if you know Mr. Arabin, I am sure you must like him. I know and like him much. Everybody that knows him must like him.'

Mrs. Bold felt it quite impossible to say anything in reply to this. Her blood was rushing about her body she knew not how or why. She felt as though she were swinging in her chair ; and she knew that she was not only red in the face, but also almost suffocated with heat. However, she sat still and said nothing.

'How stiff you are with me, Mrs. Bold,' said the signora ; ' and I the while am doing for you all that one woman can do to serve another.'

A kind of thought came over the widow's mind that perhaps the signora's friendship was real, and that at any rate it could not hurt her ; and another kind of thought, a glimmering of a thought, came to her also,—that Mr. Arabin was too precious to be lost. She despised the signora ; but might she not stoop to conquer ? It should be but the smallest fraction of a stoop !

'I don't want to be stiff,' she said, ' but your questions are so very singular.'

'Well, then, I will ask you one more singular still,' said Madeline Neroni, raising herself on her elbow and turning her own face full upon her companion's. 'Do you love him, love him with all your heart and soul, with all the love your bosom can feel ? For I can tell you that he loves

you, adores you, worships you, thinks of you and nothing
else, is now thinking of you as he attempts to write his
sermon for next Sunday's preaching. What would I not
give to be loved in such a way by such a man, that is, if
I were an object fit for any man to love!'

Mrs. Bold got up from her seat and stood speechless
before the woman who was now addressing her in this
impassioned way. When the signora thus alluded to
herself, the widow's heart was softened, and she put her
own hand, as though caressingly, on that of her companion
which was resting on the table. The signora grasped it
and went on speaking.

'What I tell you is God's own truth; and it is for you
to use it as may be best for your own happiness. But you
must not betray me. He knows nothing of this. He
knows nothing of my knowing his inmost heart. He is
simple as a child in these matters. He told me his secret
in a thousand ways because he could not dissemble; but
he does not dream that he has told it. You know it now,
and I advise you to use it.'

Eleanor returned the pressure of the other's hand with
an infinitesimal *soupçon* of a squeeze.

'And remember,' continued the signora, 'he is not like
other men. You must not expect him to come to you with
vows and oaths and pretty presents, to kneel at your feet,
and kiss your shoe-strings. If you want that, there are
plenty to do it; but he won't be one of them.' Eleanor's
bosom nearly burst with a sigh; but Madeline, not heeding
her, went on. 'With him, yea will stand for yea, and nay
for nay. Though his heart should break for it, the woman
who shall reject him once, will have rejected him once and
for all. Remember that. And now, Mrs. Bold, I will not
keep you, for you are fluttered. I partly guess what use
you will make of what I have said to you. If ever you are
a happy wife in that man's house, we shall be far away;
but I shall expect you to write me one line to say that you
have forgiven the sins of the family.'

Eleanor half whispered that she would, and then,
without uttering another word, crept out of the room, and
down the stairs, opened the front door for herself without
hearing or seeing any one, and found herself in the close.
It would be difficult to analyse Eleanor's feelings as she

walked home. She was nearly stupefied by the things
that had been said to her. She felt sore that her heart
should have been so searched and riddled by a comparative
stranger, by a woman whom she had never liked and never
could like. She was mortified that the man whom she
owned to herself that she loved should have concealed his
love from her and shown it to another. There was much
to vex her proud spirit. But there was, nevertheless, an
under-stratum of joy in all this which buoyed her up
wondrously. She tried if she could disbelieve what
Madame Neroni had said to her; but she found that she
could not. It was true; it must be true. She could not,
would not, did not doubt it.

On one point she fully resolved to follow the advice
given her. If it should ever please Mr. Arabin to put such
a question to her as that suggested, her ' yea ' should be
' yea '. Would not all her miseries be at an end, if she
could talk of them to him openly, with her head resting on
his shoulder ?

CHAPTER XLVI

MR. SLOPE'S PARTING INTERVIEW WITH THE SIGNORA

ON the following day the signora was in her pride.
She was dressed in her brightest of morning dresses, and
had quite a *levée* round her couch. It was a beautifully
bright October afternoon ; all the gentlemen of the neighbourhood were in Barchester, and those who had the entry
of Dr. Stanhope's house were in the signora's back drawing-
room. Charlotte and Mrs. Stanhope were in the front
room, and such of the lady's squires as could not for the
moment get near the centre of attraction had to waste
their fragrance on the mother and sister.

The first who came and the last to leave was Mr. Arabin.
This was the second visit he had paid to Madame Neroni
since he had met her at Ullathorne. He came he knew
not why, to talk about he knew not what. But, in truth,
the feelings which now troubled him were new to him,
and he could not analyse them. It may seem strange that
he should thus come dangling about Madame Neroni
because he was in love with Mrs. Bold ; but it was never-

theless the fact; and though he could not understand why he did so, Madame Neroni understood it well enough. She had been gentle and kind to him, and had encouraged his staying. Therefore he stayed on. She pressed his hand when he first greeted her; she made him remain near her; and whispered to him little nothings. And then her eye, brilliant and bright, now mirthful, now melancholy, and invincible in either way! What man with warm feelings, blood unchilled, and a heart not guarded by a triple steel of experience could have withstood those eyes! The lady, it is true, intended to do him no mortal injury; she merely chose to inhale a slight breath of incense before she handed the casket over to another. Whether Mrs. Bold would willingly have spared even so much is another question.

And then came Mr. Slope. All the world now knew that Mr. Slope was a candidate for the deanery, and that he was generally considered to be the favourite. Mr. Slope, therefore, walked rather largely upon the earth. He gave to himself a portly air, such as might become a dean, spoke but little to other clergymen, and shunned the bishop as much as possible. How the meagre little prebendary, and the burly chancellor, and all the minor canons and vicars choral, ay, and all the choristers too, cowered and shook and walked about with long faces when they read or heard of that article in the Jupiter. Now were coming the days when nothing would avail to keep the impure spirit from the cathedral pulpit. That pulpit would indeed be his own. Precentors, vicars, and choristers might hang up their harps on the willows. Ichabod! Ichabod! the glory of their house was departing from them.

Mr. Slope, great as he was with embryo grandeur, still came to see the signora. Indeed, he could not keep himself away. He dreamed of that soft hand which he had kissed so often, and of that imperial brow which his lips had once pressed, and he then dreamed also of further favours.

And Mr. Thorne was there also. It was the first visit he had ever paid to the signora, and he made it not without due preparation. Mr. Thorne was a gentleman usually precise in his dress, and prone to make the most of himself in an unpretending way. The grey hairs in his whiskers were eliminated perhaps once a month; those on his head were softened by a mixture which we will not call a dye; it was only a wash. His tailor lived in St. James's Street, and his bootmaker at the corner of that street and Piccadilly. He was particular in the article of gloves, and the getting up of his shirts was a matter not lightly thought of in the Ullathorne laundry. On the occasion of the present visit he had rather overdone his usual efforts, and caused some little uneasiness to his sister, who had not hitherto received very cordially the proposition for a lengthened visit from the signora at Ullathorne.

There were others also there—young men about the city who had not much to do, and who were induced by the lady's charms to neglect that little; but all gave way to Mr. Thorne, who was somewhat of a grand signior, as a country gentleman always is in a provincial city.

'Oh, Mr. Thorne, this is so kind of you!' said the signora. 'You promised to come; but I really did not expect it. I thought you country gentlemen never kept your pledges.'

'Oh, yes, sometimes,' said Mr. Thorne, looking rather sheepish, and making his salutations a little too much in the style of the last century.

'You deceive none but your consti—stit—stit; what do you call the people that carry you about in chairs and pelt you with eggs and apples when they make you a member of Parliament?'

'One another also, sometimes, signora,' said Mr. Slope, with a deanish sort of smirk on his face. 'Country gentlemen do deceive one another sometimes, don't they, Mr. Thorne?'

Mr. Thorne gave him a look which undeaned him completely for the moment; but he soon remembered his high hopes, and recovering himself quickly, sustained his probable coming dignity by a laugh at Mr. Thorne's expense.

'I never deceive a lady, at any rate,' said Mr. Thorne; 'especially when the gratification of my own wishes is so strong an inducement to keep me true, as it now is.'

Mr. Thorne went on thus awhile with antediluvian grimaces and compliments which he had picked up from

Sir Charles Grandison, and the signora at every grimace and at every bow smiled a little smile and bowed a little bow. Mr. Thorne, however, was kept standing at the foot of the couch, for the new dean sat in the seat of honour near the table. Mr. Arabin the while was standing with his back to the fire, his coat tails under his arms, gazing at her with all his eyes—not quite in vain, for every now and again a glance came up at him, bright as a meteor out of heaven.

' Oh, Mr. Thorne, you promised to let me introduce my little girl to you. Can you spare a moment ?—will you see her now ? '

Mr. Thorne assured her that he could, and would see the young lady with the greatest pleasure in life. ' Mr. Slope, might I trouble you to ring the bell ? ' said she ; and when Mr. Slope got up she looked at Mr. Thorne and pointed to the chair. Mr. Thorne, however, was much too slow to understand her, and Mr. Slope would have recovered his seat had not the signora, who never chose to be unsuccessful, somewhat summarily ordered him out of it.

' Oh, Mr. Slope, I must ask you to let Mr. Thorne sit here just for a moment or two. I am sure you will pardon me. We can take a liberty with you this week. Next week, you know, when you move into the dean's house, we shall all be afraid of you.'

Mr. Slope, with an air of much indifference, rose from his seat, and, walking into the next room, became greatly interested in Mrs. Stanhope's worsted work.

And then the child was brought in. She was a little girl, about eight years of age, like her mother, only that her enormous eyes were black, and her hair quite jet. Her complexion, too, was very dark, and bespoke her foreign blood. She was dressed in the most outlandish and extravagant way in which clothes could be put on a child's back. She had great bracelets on her naked little arms, a crimson fillet braided with gold round her head, and scarlet shoes with high heels. Her dress was all flounces, and stuck out from her as though the object were to make it lie off horizontally from her little hips. It did not nearly cover her knees ; but this was atoned for by a loose pair of drawers, which seemed made through-

out of lace; then she had on pink silk stockings. It was
thus that the last of the Neros was habitually dressed
at the hour when visitors were wont to call.

'Julia, my love,' said the mother,—Julia was ever a
favourite name with the ladies of that family. 'Julia,
my love, come here. I was telling you about the beautiful
party poor mamma went to. This is Mr. Thorne; will
you give him a kiss, dearest?'

Julia put up her face to be kissed, as she did to all her
mother's visitors; and then Mr. Thorne found that he
had got her, and, which was much more terrific to him,
all her finery, into his arms. The lace and starch crumpled
against his waistcoat and trowsers, the greasy black curls
hung upon his cheek, and one of the bracelet clasps
scratched his ear. He did not at all know how to hold
so magnificent a lady, nor holding her what to do with
her. However, he had on other occasions been compelled
to fondle little nieces and nephews, and now set about the
task in the mode he always had used.

'Diddle, diddle, diddle, diddle,' said he, putting the
child on one knee, and working away with it as though
he were turning a knife-grinder's wheel with his foot.

'Mamma, mamma,' said Julia, crossly, 'I don't want
to be diddle diddled. Let me go, you naughty old man,
you.'

Poor Mr. Thorne put the child down quietly on the
ground, and drew back his chair; Mr. Slope, who had
returned to the pole star that attracted him, laughed
aloud; Mr. Arabin winced and shut his eyes; and the
signora pretended not to hear her daughter.

'Go to Aunt Charlotte, lovey,' said the mamma, 'and
ask her if it is not time for you to go out.'

But little Miss Julia, though she had not exactly liked
the nature of Mr. Thorne's attention, was accustomed to
be played with by gentlemen, and did not relish the idea
of being sent so soon to her aunt.

'Julia, go when I tell you, my dear.' But Julia still
went pouting about the room. 'Charlotte, do come and
take her,' said the signora. 'She must go out; and the
days get so short now.' And thus ended the much-talked
of interview between Mr. Thorne and the last of the Neros.

Mr. Thorne recovered from the child's crossness sooner

than from Mr. Slope's laughter. He could put up with being called an old man by an infant, but he did not like to be laughed at by the bishop's chaplain, even though that chaplain was about to become a dean. He said nothing, but he showed plainly enough that he was angry.

The signora was ready enough to avenge him. 'Mr. Slope,' said she, 'I hear that you are triumphing on all sides.'

'How so?' said he, smiling. He did not dislike being talked to about the deanery, though, of course, he strongly denied the imputation.

'You carry the day both in love and war.' Mr. Slope hereupon did not look quite so satisfied as he had done.

'Mr. Arabin,' continued the signora, 'don't you think Mr. Slope is a very lucky man?'

'Not more so than he deserves, I am sure,' said Mr. Arabin.

'Only think, Mr. Thorne, he is to be our new dean; of course we all know that.'

'Indeed, signora,' said Mr. Slope, 'we all know nothing about it. I can assure you I myself——'

'He *is* to be the new dean—there is no manner of doubt of it, Mr. Thorne.'

'Hum!' said Mr. Thorne.

'Passing over the heads of old men like my father and Archdeacon Grantly——'

'Oh—oh!' said Mr. Slope.

'The archdeacon would not accept it,' said Mr. Arabin; whereupon Mr. Slope smiled abominably, and said, as plainly as a look could speak, that the grapes were sour.

'Going over all our heads,' continued the signora; 'for, of course, I consider myself one of the chapter.'

'If I am ever dean,' said Mr. Slope—'that is, were I ever to become so, I should glory in such a canoness.'

'Oh, Mr. Slope, stop; I haven't half done. There is another canoness for you to glory in. Mr. Slope is not only to have the deanery, but a wife to put in it.'

Mr. Slope again looked disconcerted.

'A wife with a large fortune too. It never rains but it pours, does it, Mr. Thorne?'

'No, never,' said Mr. Thorne, who did not quite relish talking about Mr. Slope and his affairs.

' When will it be, Mr. Slope ? '

' When will what be ? ' said he.

' Oh ! we know when the affair of the dean will be : a week will settle that. The new hat, I have no doubt, has been already ordered. But when will the marriage come off ? '

' Do you mean mine or Mr. Arabin's ? ' said he, striving to be facetious.

' Well, just then I meant yours, though, perhaps, after all, Mr. Arabin's may be first. But we know nothing of him. He is too close for any of us. Now all is open and above board with you ; which, by the bye, Mr. Arabin, I beg to tell you I like much the best. He who runs can read that Mr. Slope is a favoured lover. Come, Mr. Slope, when is the widow to be made Mrs. Dean ? '

To Mr. Arabin this badinage was peculiarly painful ; and yet he could not tear himself away and leave it. He believed, still believed with that sort of belief which the fear of a thing engenders, that Mrs. Bold would probably become the wife of Mr. Slope. Of Mr. Slope's little adventure in the garden he knew nothing. For aught he knew, Mr. Slope might have had an adventure of quite a different character. He might have thrown himself at the widow's feet, been accepted, and then returned to town a jolly, thriving wooer. The signora's jokes were bitter enough to Mr. Slope, but they were quite as bitter to Mr. Arabin. He still stood leaning against the fire-place, fumbling with his hands in his trowsers pockets.

' Come, come, Mr. Slope, don't be so bashful,' continued the signora. ' We all know that you proposed to the lady the other day at Ullathorne. Tell us with what words she accepted you. Was it with a simple " yes," or with two " no no's," which make an affirmative ? or did silence give consent ? or did she speak out with that spirit which so well becomes a widow, and say openly, " By my troth, sir, you shall make me Mrs. Slope as soon as it is your pleasure to do so ? " '

Mr. Slope had seldom in his life felt himself less at his ease. There sat Mr. Thorne, laughing silently. There stood his old antagonist, Mr. Arabin, gazing at him with all his eyes. There round the door between the two rooms were clustered a little group of people, including Miss

Stanhope and the Rev. Messrs. Gray and Green, all listening to his discomfiture. He knew that it depended solely on his own wit whether or no he could throw the joke back upon the lady. He knew that it stood him to do so if he possibly could; but he had not a word. ' 'Tis conscience that makes cowards of us all.' He felt on his cheek the sharp points of Eleanor's fingers, and did not know who might have seen the blow, who might have told the tale to this pestilent woman who took such delight in jeering him. He stood there, therefore, red as a carbuncle and mute as a fish; grinning just sufficiently to show his teeth; an object of pity.

But the signora had no pity; she knew nothing of mercy. Her present object was to put Mr. Slope down, and she was determined to do it thoroughly, now that she had him in her power.

' What, Mr. Slope, no answer? Why it can't possibly be that the woman has been fool enough to refuse you? She can't surely be looking out after a bishop. But I see how it is, Mr. Slope. Widows are proverbially cautious. You should have let her alone till the new hat was on your head; till you could show her the key of the deanery.'

' Signora,' said he at last, trying to speak in a tone of dignified reproach, ' you really permit yourself to talk on solemn subjects in a very improper way.'

' Solemn subjects—what solemn subject? Surely a dean's hat is not such a solemn subject.'

' I have no aspirations such as those you impute to me. Perhaps you will drop the subject.'

' Oh certainly, Mr. Slope; but one word first. Go to her again with the prime minister's letter in your pocket. I'll wager my shawl to your shovel she does not refuse you then.'

' I must say, signora, that I think you are speaking of the lady in a very unjustifiable manner.'

' And one other piece of advice, Mr. Slope; I'll only offer you one other; ' and then she commenced singing—

' It's gude to be merry and wise, Mr. Slope;
    It's gude to be honest and true;
  It's gude to be off with the old love—Mr. Slope,
    Before you are on with the new.—

' Ha, ha, ha!'

And the signora, throwing herself back on her sofa, laughed merrily. She little recked how those who heard her would, in their own imaginations, fill up the little history of Mr. Slope's first love. She little cared that some among them might attribute to her the honour of his earlier admiration. She was tired of Mr. Slope and wanted to get rid of him; she had ground for anger with him, and she chose to be revenged.

How Mr. Slope got out of that room he never himself knew.. He did succeed ultimately, and probably with some assistance, in getting his hat and escaping into the air. At last his love for the signora was cured. Whenever he again thought of her in his dreams, it was not as of an angel with azure wings. He connected her rather with fire and brimstone, and though he could still believe her to be a spirit, he banished her entirely out of heaven, and found a place for her among the infernal gods. When he weighed in the balance, as he not seldom did, the two women to whom he had attached himself in Barchester, the pre-eminent place in his soul's hatred was usually allotted to the signora.

CHAPTER XLVII

THE DEAN ELECT

DURING the entire next week Barchester was ignorant who was to be its new dean on Sunday morning. Mr. Slope was decidedly the favourite; but he did not show himself in the cathedral, and then he sank a point or two in the betting. On Monday, he got a scolding from the bishop in the hearing of the servants, and down he went till nobody would have him at any price; but on Tuesday he received a letter, in an official cover, marked private, by which he fully recovered his place in the public favour. On Wednesday, he was said to be ill, and that did not look well; but on Thursday morning he went down to the railway station, with a very jaunty air; and when it was ascertained that he had taken a first-class ticket for London, there was no longer any room for doubt on the matter.

While matters were in this state of ferment at Barchester, there was not much mental comfort at Plumstead. Our friend the archdeacon had many grounds for inward grief. He was much displeased at the result of Dr. Gwynne's diplomatic mission to the palace, and did not even scruple to say to his wife that had he gone himself, he would have managed the affair much better. His wife did not agree with him, but that did not mend the matter.

Mr. Quiverful's appointment to the hospital was, however, a *fait accompli*, and Mr. Harding's acquiescence in that appointment was not less so. Nothing would induce Mr. Harding to make a public appeal against the bishop; and the Master of Lazarus quite approved of his not doing so.

' I don't know what has come to the Master,' said the archdeacon over and over again. ' He used to be ready enough to stand up for his order.'

' My dear archdeacon,' Mrs. Grantly would say in reply, ' what is the use of always fighting ? I really think the Master is right.' The Master, however, had taken steps of his own, of which neither the archdeacon nor his wife knew anything.

Then Mr. Slope's successes were henbane to Dr. Grantly; and Mrs. Bold's improprieties were as bad. What would be all the world to Archdeacon Grantly if Mr. Slope should become Dean of Barchester and marry his wife's sister ! He talked of it, and talked of it till he was nearly ill. Mrs. Grantly almost wished that the marriage were done and over, so that she might hear no more about it.

And there was yet another ground of misery which cut him to the quick, nearly as closely as either of the others. That paragon of a clergyman, whom he had bestowed upon St. Ewold's, that college friend of whom he had boasted so loudly, that ecclesiastical knight before whose lance Mr. Slope was to fall and bite the dust, that worthy bulwark of the church as it should be, that honoured representative of Oxford's best spirit, was—so at least his wife had told him half a dozen times—misconducting himself !

Nothing had been seen of Mr. Arabin at Plumstead for the last week, but a good deal had, unfortunately, been heard of him. As soon as Mrs. Grantly had found herself

alone with the archdeacon, on the evening of the Ullathorne
party, she had expressed herself very forcibly as to Mr.
Arabin's conduct on that occasion. He had, she declared,
looked and acted and talked very unlike a decent parish
clergyman. At first the archdeacon had laughed at this,
and assured her that she need not trouble herself; that
Mr. Arabin would be found to be quite safe. But by
degrees he began to find that his wife's eyes had been
sharper than his own. Other people coupled the signora's
name with that of Mr. Arabin. The meagre little prebendary who lived in the close, told him to a nicety how
often Mr. Arabin had visited at Dr. Stanhope's, and how
long he had remained on the occasion of each visit. He
had asked after Mr. Arabin at the cathedral library, and
an officious little vicar choral had offered to go and see
whether he could be found at Dr. Stanhope's. Rumour,
when she has contrived to sound the first note on her
trumpet, soon makes a loud peal audible enough. It was
too clear that Mr. Arabin had succumbed to the Italian
woman, and that the archdeacon's credit would suffer
fearfully if something were not done to rescue the brand
from the burning. Besides, to give the archdeacon his
due, he was really attached to Mr. Arabin, and grieved
greatly at his backsliding.

They were sitting, talking over their sorrows, in the
drawing-room before dinner on the day after Mr. Slope's
departure for London; and on this occasion Mrs. Grantly
spoke out her mind freely. She had opinions of her own
about parish clergymen, and now thought it right to give
vent to them.

'If you would have been led by me, archdeacon, you
would never have put a bachelor into St. Ewold's.'

'But, my dear, you don't mean to say that all bachelor
clergymen misbehave themselves.'

'I don't know that clergymen are so much better than
other men,' said Mrs. Grantly. 'It's all very well with
a curate whom you have under your own eye, and whom
you can get rid of if he persists in improprieties.'

'But Mr. Arabin was a fellow, and couldn't have had
a wife.'

'Then I would have found some one who could.'

'But, my dear, are fellows never to get livings?'

'Yes, to be sure they are, when they get engaged. I never would put a young man into a living unless he were married, or engaged to be married. Now here is Mr. Arabin. The whole responsibility lies upon you.'

'There is not at this moment a clergyman in all Oxford more respected for morals and conduct than Arabin.'

'Oh, Oxford!' said the lady, with a sneer. 'What men choose to do at Oxford, nobody ever hears of. A man may do very well at Oxford who would bring disgrace on a parish; and, to tell you the truth, it seems to me that Mr. Arabin is just such a man.'

The archdeacon groaned deeply, but he had no further answer to make.

'You really must speak to him, archdeacon. Only think what the Thornes will say if they hear that their parish clergyman spends his whole time philandering with this woman.'

The archdeacon groaned again. He was a courageous man, and knew well enough how to rebuke the younger clergymen of the diocese, when necessary. But there was that about Mr. Arabin which made the doctor feel that it would be very difficult to rebuke him with good effect.

'You can advise him to find a wife for himself, and he will understand well enough what that means,' said Mrs. Grantly.

The archdeacon had nothing for it but groaning. There was Mr. Slope; he was going to be made dean; he was going to take a wife; he was about to achieve respectability and wealth; an excellent family mansion, and a family carriage; he would soon be among the comfortable *élite* of the ecclesiastical world of Barchester; whereas his own *protégé*, the true scion of the true church, by whom he had sworn, would be still but a poor vicar, and that with a very indifferent character for moral conduct! It might be all very well recommending Mr. Arabin to marry, but how would Mr. Arabin when married support a wife!

Things were ordering themselves thus in Plumstead drawing-room when Dr. and Mrs. Grantly were disturbed in their sweet discourse by the quick rattle of a carriage and pair of horses on the gravel sweep. The sound was not that of visitors, whose private carriages are generally brought up to country-house doors with demure propriety, but betokened rather the advent of some person or persons who were in a hurry to reach the house, and had no intention of immediately leaving it. Guests invited to stay a week, and who were conscious of arriving after the first dinner bell, would probably approach in such a manner. So might arrive an attorney with the news of a granduncle's death, or a son from college with all the fresh honours of a double first. No one would have had himself driven up to the door of a country house in such a manner who had the slightest doubt of his own right to force an entry.

'Who is it ?' said Mrs. Grantly, looking at her husband.

'Who on earth can it be ?' said the archdeacon to his wife. He then quietly got up and stood with the drawing-room door open in his hand. 'Why, it's your father !'

It was indeed Mr. Harding, and Mr. Harding alone. He had come by himself in a post-chaise with a couple of horses from Barchester, arriving almost after dark, and evidently full of news. His visits had usually been made in the quietest manner ; he had rarely presumed to come without notice, and had always been driven up in a modest old green fly, with one horse, that hardly made itself heard as it crawled up to the hall door.

'Good gracious, Warden, is it you ?' said the arch-deacon, forgetting in his surprise the events of the last few years. 'But come in ; nothing the matter, I hope.'

'We are very glad you are come, papa,' said his daughter. 'I'll go and get your room ready at once.'

'I an't warden, archdeacon,' said Mr. Harding. 'Mr. Quiverful is warden.'

'Oh, I know, I know,' said the archdeacon, petulantly. 'I forgot all about it at the moment. Is anything the matter ?'

'Don't go this moment, Susan,' said Mr. Harding ; 'I have something to tell you.'

'The dinner bell will ring in five minutes,' said she.

'Will it ?' said Mr. Harding. 'Then, perhaps, I had better wait.' He was big with news which he had come to tell, but which he knew could not be told without much discussion. He had hurried away to Plumstead as fast as two horses could bring him ; and now, finding himself there, he was willing to accept the reprieve which dinner would give him.

'If you have anything of moment to tell us,' said the archdeacon, 'pray let us hear it at once. Has Eleanor gone off?'

'No, she has not,' said Mr. Harding, with a look of great displeasure.

'Has Slope been made dean?'

'No, he has not; but—'

'But what?' said the archdeacon, who was becoming very impatient.

'They have—'

'They have what?' said the archdeacon.

'They have offered it to me,' said Mr. Harding, with a modesty which almost prevented his speaking.

'Good heavens!' said the archdeacon, and sank back exhausted in an easy-chair.

'My dear, dear father,' said Mrs. Grantly, and threw her arms round her father's neck.

'So I thought I had better come out and consult with you at once,' said Mr. Harding.

'Consult!' shouted the archdeacon. 'But, my dear Harding, I congratulate you with my whole heart—with my whole heart; I do indeed. I never heard anything in my life that gave me so much pleasure;' and he got hold of both his father-in-law's hands, and shook them as though he were going to shake them off, and walked round and round the room, twirling a copy of the Jupiter over his head, to show his extreme exultation.

'But—' began Mr. Harding.

'But me no buts,' said the archdeacon. 'I never was so happy in my life. It was just the proper thing to do. Upon my honour, I'll never say another word against Lord —— the longest day I have to live.'

'That's Dr. Gwynne's doing, you may be sure,' said Mrs. Grantly, who greatly liked the Master of Lazarus, he being an orderly married man with a large family.

'I suppose it is,' said the archdeacon.

'Oh, papa, I am so truly delighted!' said Mrs. Grantly, getting up and kissing her father.

'But, my dear,' said Mr. Harding.—It was all in vain that he strove to speak; nobody would listen to him.

'Well, Mr. Dean,' said the archdeacon, triumphing; 'the deanery gardens will be some consolation for the hospital elms. Well, poor Quiverful! I won't begrudge him his good fortune any longer.'

'No, indeed,' said Mrs. Grantly. 'Poor woman, she has fourteen children. I am sure I am very glad they have got it.'

'So am I,' said Mr. Harding.

'I would give twenty pounds,' said the archdeacon, 'to see how Mr. Slope will look when he hears it.' The idea of Mr. Slope's discomfiture formed no small part of the archdeacon's pleasure.

At last Mr. Harding was allowed to go up-stairs and wash his hands, having, in fact, said very little of all that he had come out to Plumstead on purpose to say. Nor could anything more be said till the servants were gone after dinner. The joy of Dr. Grantly was so uncontrollable that he could not refrain from calling his father-in-law Mr. Dean before the men; and therefore it was soon matter of discussion in the lower regions how Mr. Harding, instead of his daughter's future husband, was to be the new dean, and various were the opinions on the matter. The cook and butler, who were advanced in years, thought that it was just as it should be; but the footman and lady's maid, who were younger, thought it was a great shame that Mr. Slope should lose his chance.

'He's a mean chap all the same,' said the footman; 'and it an't along of him that I says so. But I always did admire the missus's sister; and she'd well become the situation.'

While these were the ideas down-stairs, a very great difference of opinion existed above. As soon as the cloth was drawn and the wine on the table, Mr. Harding made for himself an opportunity of speaking. It was, however, with much inward troubling that he said :—

'It's very kind of Lord —— very kind, and I feel it deeply, most deeply. I am, I must confess, gratified by the offer—'

'I should think so,' said the archdeacon.

'But, all the same, I am afraid that I can't accept it.'

The decanter almost fell from the archdeacon's hand upon the table; and the start he made was so great as to make his wife jump up from her chair. Not accept the deanship! If it really ended in this, there would be no longer any doubt that his father-in-law was demented. The question now was whether a clergyman with low rank, and preferment amounting to less than 200*l.* a year, should accept high rank, 1200*l.* a year, and one of the most desirable positions which his profession had to afford!

'What!' said the archdeacon, gasping for breath, and staring at his guest as though the violence of his emotion had almost thrown him into a fit.

'What!'

'I do not find myself fit for new duties,' urged Mr. Harding.

'New duties! what duties?' said the archdeacon, with unintended sarcasm.

'Oh, papa,' said Mrs. Grantly, 'nothing can be easier than what a dean has to do. Surely you are more active than Dr. Trefoil.'

'He won't have half as much to do as he has at present,' said Dr. Grantly.

'Did you see what the Jupiter said the other day about young men?'

'Yes; and I saw that the Jupiter said all that it could to induce the appointment of Mr. Slope. Perhaps you would wish to see Mr. Slope made dean.'

Mr. Harding made no reply to this rebuke, though he felt it strongly. He had not come over to Plumstead to have further contention with his son-in-law about Mr. Slope, so he allowed it to pass by.

'I know I cannot make you understand my feeling,' he said, 'for we have been cast in different moulds. I may wish that I had your spirit and energy and power of combating; but I have not. Every day that is added to my life increases my wish for peace and rest.'

'And where on earth can a man have peace and rest if not in a deanery?' said the archdeacon.

'People will say that I am too old for it.'

'Good heavens! people! what people? What need you care for any people?'

'But I think myself I am too old for any new place.'

'Dear papa,' said Mrs. Grantly, 'men ten years older

than you are appointed to new situations day after day.'

' My dear,' said he, ' it is impossible that I should make you understand my feelings, nor do I pretend to any great virtue in the matter. The truth is, I want the force of character which might enable me to stand against the spirit of the times. The call on all sides now is for young men, and I have not the nerve to put myself in opposition to the demand. Were the Jupiter, when it hears of my appointment, to write article after article, setting forth my incompetency, I am sure it would cost me my reason. I ought to be able to bear with such things, you will say. Well, my dear, I own that I ought. But I feel my weakness, and I know that I can't. And, to tell you the truth, I know no more than a child what the dean has to do.'

' Pshaw ! ' exclaimed the archdeacon.

' Don't be angry with me, archdeacon: don't let us quarrel about it, Susan. If you knew how keenly I feel the necessity of having to disoblige you in this matter, you would not be angry with me.'

This was a dreadful blow to Dr. Grantly. Nothing could possibly have suited him better than having Mr. Harding in the deanery. Though he had never looked down on Mr. Harding on account of his recent poverty, he did fully recognise the satisfaction of having those belonging to him in comfortable positions. It would be much more suitable that Mr. Harding should be dean of Barchester than vicar of St. Cuthbert's and precentor to boot. And then the great discomfiture of that arch enemy of all that was respectable in Barchester, of that new low-church clerical *parvenu* that had fallen amongst them, that alone would be worth more, almost, than the situation itself. It was frightful to think that such un-hoped-for good fortune should be marred by the absurd crotchets and unwholesome hallucinations by which Mr. Harding allowed himself to be led astray. To have the cup so near his lips and then to lose the drinking of it, was more than Dr. Grantly could endure.

And yet it appeared as though he would have to endure it. In vain he threatened and in vain he coaxed. Mr. Harding did not indeed speak with perfect decision of refusing the proffered glory, but he would not speak with

anything like decision of accepting it. When pressed
again and again, he would again and again allege that he
was wholly unfitted to new duties. It was in vain that
the archdeacon tried to insinuate, though he could not
plainly declare, that there were no new duties to perform.
It was in vain he hinted that in all cases of difficulty he,
the archdeacon, was willing and able to guide a weak-
minded dean. Mr. Harding seemed to have a foolish
idea, not only that there were new duties to do, but that
no one should accept the place who was not himself
prepared to do them.

The conference ended in an understanding that Mr.
Harding should at once acknowledge the letter he had
received from the minister's private secretary, and should
beg that he might be allowed two days to make up his
mind ; and that during those two days the matter should
be considered.

On the following morning the archdeacon was to drive
Mr. Harding back to Barchester.

CHAPTER XLVIII

MISS THORNE SHOWS HER TALENT AT MATCH-MAKING

ON Mr. Harding's return to Barchester from Plumstead,
which was effected by him in due course in company with
the archdeacon, more tidings of a surprising nature met
him. He was, during the journey, subjected to such a
weight of unanswerable argument, all of which went to
prove that it was his bounden duty not to interfere with
the paternal government that was so anxious to make
him a dean, that when he arrived at the chemist's door
in High Street, he hardly knew which way to turn himself
in the matter. But, perplexed as he was, he was doomed
to further perplexity. He found a note there from his
daughter begging him most urgently to come to her immediately. But we must again go back a little in our story.

Miss Thorne had not been slow to hear the rumours
respecting Mr. Arabin, which had so much disturbed the
happiness of Mrs. Grantly. And she, also, was unhappy
to think that her parish clergyman should be accused of

worshipping a strange goddess. She, also, was of opinion, that rectors and vicars should all be married, and with that good-natured energy which was characteristic of her, she put her wits to work to find a fitting match for Mr. Arabin. Mrs. Grantly, in this difficulty, could think of no better remedy than a lecture from the archdeacon. Miss Thorne thought that a young lady, marriageable, and with a dowry, might be of more efficacy. In looking through the catalogue of her unmarried friends, who might possibly be in want of a husband, and might also be fit for such promotion as a country parsonage affords, she could think of no one more eligible than Mrs. Bold; and, consequently, losing no time, she went into Barchester on the day of Mr. Slope's discomfiture, the same day that her brother had had his interesting interview with the last of the Neros, and invited Mrs. Bold to bring her nurse and baby to Ullathorne and make them a protracted visit.

Miss Thorne suggested a month or two, intending to use her influence afterwards in prolonging it so as to last out the winter, in order that Mr. Arabin might have an opportunity of becoming fairly intimate with his intended bride. 'We'll have Mr. Arabin too,' said Miss Thorne to herself; 'and before the spring they'll know each other; and in twelve or eighteen months' time, if all goes well, Mrs. Bold will be domiciled at St. Ewold's;' and then the kind-hearted lady gave herself some not undeserved praise for her match-making genius.

Eleanor was taken a little by surprise, but the matter ended in her promising to go to Ullathorne for at any rate a week or two; and on the day previous to that on which her father drove out to Plumstead, she had had herself driven out to Ullathorne.

Miss Thorne would not perplex her with her embryo lord on that same evening, thinking that she would allow her a few hours to make herself at home; but on the following morning Mr. Arabin arrived. 'And now,' said Miss Thorne to herself, 'I must contrive to throw them in each other's way.' That same day, after dinner, Eleanor, with an assumed air of dignity which she could not maintain, with tears that she could not suppress, with a flutter which she could not conquer, and a joy which she could not hide, told Miss Thorne that she was engaged to marry Mr. Arabin, and that it behoved her to get back home to Barchester as quick as she could.

To say simply that Miss Thorne was rejoiced at the success of the scheme, would give a very faint idea of her feelings on the occasion. My readers may probably have dreamt before now that they have had before them some terribly long walk to accomplish, some journey of twenty or thirty miles, an amount of labour frightful to anticipate, and that immediately on starting they have ingeniously found some accommodating short cut which has brought them without fatigue to their work's end in five minutes. Miss Thorne's waking feelings were somewhat of the same nature. My readers may perhaps have had to do with children, and may on some occasion have promised to their young charges some great gratification intended to come off, perhaps at the end of the winter, or at the beginning of summer. The impatient juveniles, however, will not wait, and clamorously demand their treat before they go to bed. Miss Thorne had a sort of feeling that her children were equally unreasonable. She was like an inexperienced gunner, who has ill calculated the length of the train that he has laid. The gunpowder exploded much too soon, and poor Miss Thorne felt that she was blown up by the strength of her own petard.

Miss Thorne had had lovers of her own, but they had been gentlemen of old-fashioned and deliberate habits. Miss Thorne's heart also had not always been hard, though she was still a virgin spinster; but it had never yielded in this way at the first assault. She had intended to bring together a middle-aged studious clergyman, and a discreet matron who might possibly be induced to marry again; and in doing so she had thrown fire among tinder. Well, it was all as it should be, but she did feel perhaps a little put out by the precipitancy of her own success; and perhaps a little vexed at the readiness of Mrs. Bold to be wooed.

She said, however, nothing about it to any one, and ascribed it all to the altered manners of the new age. Their mothers and grandmothers were perhaps a little more deliberate; but it was admitted on all sides that things were conducted very differently now than in former times. For aught Miss Thorne knew of the matter, a couple of hours might be quite sufficient under the new régime to complete that for which she in her ignorance had allotted twelve months.

But we must not pass over the wooing so cavalierly. It has been told, with perhaps tedious accuracy, how Eleanor disposed of two of her lovers at Ullathorne; and it must also be told with equal accuracy, and if possible with less tedium, how she encountered Mr. Arabin.

It cannot be denied that when Eleanor accepted Miss Thorne's invitation, she remembered that Ullathorne was in the parish of St. Ewold's. Since her interview with the signora she had done little else than think about Mr. Arabin, and the appeal that had been made to her. She could not bring herself to believe or try to bring herself to believe, that what she had been told was untrue. Think of it how she would, she could not but accept it as a fact that Mr. Arabin was fond of her; and then when she went further, and asked herself the question, she could not but accept it as a fact also that she was fond of him. If it were destined for her to be the partner of his hopes and sorrows, to whom could she look for friendship so properly as to Miss Thorne ? This invitation was like an ordained step towards the fulfilment of her destiny, and when she also heard that Mr. Arabin was expected to be at Ullathorne on the following day, it seemed as though all the world were conspiring in her favour. Well, did she not deserve it ? In that affair of Mr. Slope, had not all the world conspired against her ?

She could not, however, make herself easy and at home. When in the evening after dinner Miss Thorne expatiated on the excellence of Mr. Arabin's qualities, and hinted that any little rumour which might be ill-naturedly spread abroad concerning him really meant nothing, Mrs. Bold found herself unable to answer. When Miss Thorne went a little further and declared that she did not know a prettier vicarage-house in the county than St. Ewold's, Mrs. Bold remembering the projected bow-window and the projected priestess still held her tongue; though her ears tingled with the conviction that all the world knew that she was in love with Mr Arabin.

Well; what would that matter if they could only meet and tell each other what each now longed to tell?

And they did meet. Mr. Arabin came early in the day, and found the two ladies together at work in the drawing-room. Miss Thorne, who had she known all the truth would have vanished into air at once, had no conception that her immediate absence would be a blessing, and remained chatting with them till luncheon-time. Mr. Arabin could talk about nothing but the Signora Neroni's beauty, would discuss no people but the Stanhopes. This was very distressing to Eleanor, and not very satisfactory to Miss Thorne. But yet there was evidence of innocence in his open avowal of admiration.

And then they had lunch, and then Mr. Arabin went out on parish duty, and Eleanor and Miss Thorne were left to take a walk together.

'Do you think the Signora Neroni is so lovely as people say?' Eleanor asked as they were coming home.

'She is very beautiful certainly, very beautiful,' Miss Thorne answered; 'but I do not know that any one considers her lovely. She is a woman all men would like to look at; but few I imagine would be glad to take her to their hearths, even were she unmarried and not afflicted as she is.'

There was some little comfort in this. Eleanor made the most of it till she got back to the house. She was then left alone in the drawing-room, and just as it was getting dark Mr. Arabin came in.

It was a beautiful afternoon in the beginning of October, and Eleanor was sitting in the window to get the advantage of the last daylight for her novel. There was a fire in the comfortable room, but the weather was not cold enough to make it attractive; and as she could see the sun set from where she sat, she was not very attentive to her book.

Mr. Arabin when he entered stood awhile with his back to the fire in his usual way, merely uttering a few common-place remarks about the beauty of the weather, while he plucked up courage for more interesting converse. It cannot probably be said that he had resolved then and there to make an offer to Eleanor. Men we believe seldom make such resolves. Mr. Slope and Mr. Stanhope had done so, it is true; but gentlemen generally propose without any absolutely defined determination as to their doing so. Such was now the case with Mr. Arabin.

'It is a lovely sunset,' said Eleanor, answering him on the dreadfully trite subject which he had chosen.

Mr. Arabin could not see the sunset from the hearth-rug, so he had to go close to her.

'Very lovely,' said he, standing modestly so far away from her as to avoid touching the flounces of her dress. Then it appeared that he had nothing further to say; so after gazing for a moment in silence at the brightness of the setting sun, he returned to the fire.

Eleanor found that it was quite impossible for herself to commence a conversation. In the first place she could find nothing to say; words, which were generally plenty enough with her, would not come to her relief. And, moreover, do what she would, she could hardly prevent herself from crying.

'Do you like Ullathorne?' said Mr. Arabin, speaking from the safely distant position which he had assumed on the hearth-rug.

'Yes, indeed, very much!'

'I don't mean Mr. and Miss Thorne. I know you like them; but the style of the house. There is something about old-fashioned mansions, built as this is, and old-fashioned gardens, that to me is especially delightful.'

'I like everything old-fashioned,' said Eleanor; 'old-fashioned things are so much the honestest.'

'I don't know about that,' said Mr. Arabin, gently laughing. 'That is an opinion on which very much may be said on either side. It is strange how widely the world is divided on a subject which so nearly concerns us all, and which is so close beneath our eyes. Some think that we are quickly progressing towards perfection, while others imagine that virtue is disappearing from the earth.'

'And you, Mr. Arabin, what do you think?' said Eleanor. She felt somewhat surprised at the tone which his conversation was taking, and yet she was relieved at his saying something which enabled herself to speak without showing her own emotion.

'What do I think, Mrs. Bold?' and then he rumbled his money with his hands in his trowsers pockets, and looked and spoke very little like a thriving lover. 'It is the bane of my life that on important subjects I acquire no fixed opinion. I think, and think, and go on thinking; and yet my thoughts are running ever in different directions. I hardly know whether or no we do lean more confidently than our fathers did on those high hopes to which we profess to aspire.'

'I think the world grows more worldly every day,' said Eleanor.

'That is because you see more of it than when you were younger. But we should hardly judge by what we see,—we see so very very little.' There was then a pause for a while, during which Mr. Arabin continued to turn over his shillings and half-crowns. 'If we believe in Scripture, we can hardly think that mankind in general will now be allowed to retrograde.'

Eleanor, whose mind was certainly engaged otherwise than on the general state of mankind, made no answer to this. She felt thoroughly dissatisfied with herself. She could not force her thoughts away from the topic on which the signora had spoken to her in so strange a way, and yet she knew that she could not converse with Mr. Arabin in an unrestrained natural tone till she did so. She was most anxious not to show to him any special emotion, and yet she felt that if he looked at her he would at once see that she was not at ease.

But he did not look at her. Instead of doing so, he left the fire-place and began walking up and down the room. Eleanor took up her book resolutely; but she could not read, for there was a tear in her eye, and do what she would it fell on her cheek. When Mr. Arabin's back was turned to her she wiped it away; but another was soon coursing down her face in its place. They would come; not a deluge of tears that would have betrayed her at once, but one by one, single monitors. Mr. Arabin did not observe her closely, and they passed unseen.

Mr. Arabin, thus pacing up and down the room, took four or five turns before he spoke another word, and Eleanor sat equally silent with her face bent over her book. She was afraid that her tears would get the better of her, and was preparing for an escape from the room, when Mr Arabin in his walk stood opposite to her. He

did not come close up, but stood exactly on the spot to
which his course brought him, and then, with his hands
under his coat tails, thus made his confession.

'Mrs. Bold,' said he, 'I owe you retribution for a great
offence of which I have been guilty towards you.' Eleanor's
heart beat so that she could not trust herself to say that
he had never been guilty of any offence. So Mr. Arabin
thus went on.

'I have thought much of it since, and I am now aware
that I was wholly unwarranted in putting to you a question
which I once asked you. It was indelicate on my part,
and perhaps unmanly. No intimacy which may exist
between myself and your connection, Dr. Grantly, could
justify it. Nor could the acquaintance which existed
between ourselves.' This word acquaintance struck cold
on Eleanor's heart. Was this to be her doom after all?
'I therefore think it right to beg your pardon in a humble
spirit, and I now do so.'

What was Eleanor to say to him? She could not say
much, because she was crying, and yet she must say
something. She was most anxious to say that something
graciously, kindly, and yet not in such a manner as to
betray herself. She had never felt herself so much at
a loss for words.

'Indeed I took no offence, Mr. Arabin.'

'Oh, but you did! And had you not done so, you
would not have been yourself. You were as right to be
offended, as I was wrong so to offend you. I have not
forgiven myself, but I hope to hear that you forgive me.'

She was now past speaking calmly, though she still continued to hide her tears, and Mr. Arabin, after pausing a
moment in vain for her reply, was walking off towards the
door. She felt that she could not allow him to go unanswered without grievously sinning against all charity;
so, rising from her seat, she gently touched his arm and
said: 'Oh, Mr. Arabin, do not go till I speak to you!
I do forgive you. You know that I forgive you.'

He took the hand that had so gently touched his arm,
and then gazed into her face as if he would peruse there,
as though written in a book, the whole future destiny
of his life; and as he did so, there was a sober sad seriousness in his own countenance, which Eleanor found herself

unable to sustain. She could only look down upon the carpet, let her tears trickle as they would, and leave her hand within his.

It was but for a minute that they stood so, but the duration of that minute was sufficient to make it ever memorable to them both. Eleanor was sure now that she was loved. No words, be their eloquence what it might, could be more impressive than that eager, melancholy gaze.

Why did he look so into her eyes? Why did he not speak to her? Could it be that he looked for her to make the first sign?

And he, though he knew but little of women, even he knew that he was loved. He had only to ask and it would be all his own, that inexpressible loveliness, those ever speaking but yet now mute eyes, that feminine brightness and eager loving spirit which had so attracted him since first he had encountered it at St. Ewold's. It might, must all be his own now. On no other supposition was it possible that she should allow her hand to remain thus clasped within his own. He had only to ask. Ah! but that was the difficulty. Did a minute suffice for all this? Nay, perhaps it might be more than a minute.

'Mrs. Bold—' at last he said, and then stopped himself.

If he could not speak, how was she to do so? He had called her by her name, the same name that any merest stranger would have used! She withdrew her hand from his, and moved as though to return to her seat. 'Eleanor!' he then said, in his softest tone, as though the courage of a lover were as yet but half assumed, as though he were still afraid of giving offence by the freedom which he took. She looked slowly, gently, almost piteously up into his face. There was at any rate no anger there to deter him.

'Eleanor!' he again exclaimed; and in a moment he had her clasped to his bosom. How this was done, whether the doing was with him or her, whether she had flown thither conquered by the tenderness of his voice, or he with a violence not likely to give offence had drawn her to his breast, neither of them knew; nor can I declare. There was now that sympathy between them which

hardly admitted of individual motion. They were one
and the same,—one flesh,—one spirit,—one life.

'Eleanor, my own Eleanor, my own, my wife!' She
ventured to look up at him through her tears, and he,
bowing his face down over hers, pressed his lips upon her
brow; his virgin lips, which since a beard first grew upon
his chin, had never yet tasted the luxury of a woman's
cheek.

She had been told that her yea must be yea, or her
nay, nay; but she was called on for neither the one nor
the other. She told Miss Thorne that she was engaged
to Mr. Arabin, but no such words had passed between
them, no promises had been asked or given.

'Oh, let me go,' said she; 'let me go now. I am too
happy to remain,—let me go, that I may be alone.' He
did not try to hinder her; he did not repeat the kiss;
he did not press another on her lips. He might have done
so had he been so minded. She was now all his own. He
took his arm from round her waist, his arm that was
trembling with a new delight, and let her go. She fled
like a roe to her own chamber, and then, having turned
the bolt, she enjoyed the full luxury of her love. She
idolised, almost worshipped this man who had so meekly
begged her pardon. And he was now her own. Oh, how
she wept and cried and laughed, as the hopes and fears
and miseries of the last few weeks passed in remembrance
through her mind.

Mr. Slope! That any one should have dared to think
that she who had been chosen by him could possibly
have mated herself with Mr. Slope! That they should
have dared to tell him, also, and subject her bright happiness to such needless risk! And then she smiled with joy
as she thought of all the comforts that she could give
him; not that he cared for comforts, but that it would
be so delicious for her to give.

She got up and rang for her maid that she might tell
her little boy of his new father; and in her own way she
did tell him. She desired her maid to leave her, in order
that she might be alone with her child; and then, while
he lay sprawling on the bed, she poured forth the praises,
all unmeaning to him, of the man she had selected to
guard his infancy.

She could not be happy, however, till she had made Mr. Arabin take the child to himself, and thus, as it were, adopt him as his own. The moment the idea struck her she took the baby up in her arms, and, opening her door, ran quickly down to the drawing-room. She at once found, by his step still pacing on the floor, that he was there; and a glance within the room told her that he was alone. She hesitated a moment, and then hurried in with her precious charge.

Mr. Arabin met her in the middle of the room. 'There,' said she, breathless with her haste; 'there, take him—take him and love him.'

Mr. Arabin took the little fellow from her, and kissing him again and again, prayed God to bless him. 'He shall be all as my own—all as my own,' said he. Eleanor, as she stooped to take back her child, kissed the hand that held him, and then rushed back with her treasure to her chamber.

It was thus that Mr. Harding's younger daughter was won for the second time. At dinner neither she nor Mr. Arabin were very bright, but their silence occasioned no remark. In the drawing-room, as we have before said, she told Miss Thorne what had occurred. The next morning she returned to Barchester, and Mr. Arabin went over with his budget of news to the archdeacon. As Doctor Grantly was not there, he could only satisfy himself by telling Mrs. Grantly how that he intended himself the honour of becoming her brother-in-law. In the ecstasy of her joy at hearing such tidings, Mrs. Grantly vouchsafed him a warmer welcome than any he had yet received from Eleanor.

'Good heavens!' she exclaimed—it was the general exclamation of the rectory. 'Poor Eleanor! Dear Eleanor! What a monstrous injustice has been done her! —Well, it shall all be made up now.' And then she thought of the signora. 'What lies people tell,' she said to herself. But people in this matter had told no lies at all.

CHAPTER XLIX

THE BELZEBUB COLT

WHEN Miss Thorne left the dining-room, Eleanor had formed no intention of revealing to her what had occurred ; but when she was seated beside her hostess on the sofa the secret dropped from her almost unawares. Eleanor was but a bad hypocrite, and she found herself quite unable to continue talking about Mr. Arabin as though he were a stranger, while her heart was full of him. When Miss Thorne, pursuing her own scheme with discreet zeal, asked the young widow whether, in her opinion, it would not be a good thing for Mr. Arabin to get married, she had nothing for it but to confess the truth. ' I suppose it would,' said Eleanor, rather sheepishly. Whereupon Miss Thorne amplified on the idea. ' Oh, Miss Thorne,' said Eleanor, ' he is going to be married : I am engaged to him.'

Now Miss Thorne knew very well that there had been no such engagement when she had been walking with Mrs. Bold in the morning. She had also heard enough to be tolerably sure that there had been no preliminaries to such an engagement. She was, therefore, as we have before described, taken a little by surprise. But, nevertheless, she embraced her guest, and cordially congratulated her.

Eleanor had no opportunity of speaking another word to Mr. Arabin that evening, except such words as all the world might hear ; and these, as may be supposed, were few enough. Miss Thorne did her best to leave them in privacy ; but Mr. Thorne, who knew nothing of what had occurred, and another guest, a friend of his, entirely interfered with her good intentions. So poor Eleanor had to go to bed without one sign of affection. Her state, nevertheless, was not to be pitied.

The next morning she was up early. It was probable, she thought, that by going down a little before the usual hour of breakfast, she might find Mr. Arabin alone in the dining-room. Might it not be that he also would calculate that an interview would thus be possible ? Thus thinking, Eleanor was dressed a full hour before

the time fixed in the Ullathorne household for morning
prayers. She did not at once go down. She was afraid
to seem to be too anxious to meet her lover; though,
heaven knows, her anxiety was intense enough. She
therefore sat herself down at her window, and repeatedly
looking at her watch, nursed her child till she thought
she might venture forth.

When she found herself at the dining-room door, she
stood a moment, hesitating to turn the handle; but
when she heard Mr. Thorne's voice inside she hesitated
no longer. Her object was defeated, and she might now
go in as soon as she liked without the slightest imputation
on her delicacy. Mr. Thorne and Mr. Arabin were standing
on the hearth-rug, discussing the merits of the Belzebub
colt; or rather, Mr. Thorne was discussing, and Mr. Arabin
was listening. That interesting animal had rubbed the
stump of his tail against the wall of his stable, and occasioned much uneasiness to the Ullathorne master of
the horse. Had Eleanor but waited another minute,
Mr. Thorne would have been in the stables.

Mr. Thorne, when he saw his lady guest, repressed his
anxiety. The Belzebub colt must do without him. And
so the three stood, saying little or nothing to each other,
till at last the master of the house, finding that he could
no longer bear his present state of suspense respecting
his favourite young steed, made an elaborate apology
to Mrs. Bold, and escaped. As he shut the door behind
him, Eleanor almost wished that he had remained. It
was not that she was afraid of Mr. Arabin, but she hardly
yet knew how to address him.

He, however, soon relieved her from her embarrassment.
He came up to her, and taking both her hands in his, he
said: 'So, Eleanor, you and I are to be man and wife.
Is it so?'

She looked up into his face, and her lips formed themselves into a single syllable. She uttered no sound, but
he could read the affirmative plainly in her face.

'It is a great trust,' said he; 'a very great trust.'

'It is—it is,' said Eleanor, not exactly taking what he
had said in the sense that he had meant. 'It is a very,
very great trust, and I will do my utmost to deserve it.'

'And I also will do my utmost to deserve it,' said Mr.

Arabin, very solemnly. And then, winding his arm round her waist, he stood there gazing at the fire, and she with her head leaning on his shoulder, stood by him, well satisfied with her position. They neither of them spoke, or found any want of speaking. All that was needful for them to say had been said. The yea, yea, had been spoken by Eleanor in her own way—and that way had been perfectly satisfactory to Mr. Arabin.

And now it remained to them each to enjoy the assurance of the other's love. And how great that luxury is! How far it surpasses any other pleasure which God has allowed to his creatures! And to a woman's heart how doubly delightful!

When the ivy has found its tower, when the delicate creeper has found its strong wall, we know how the parasite plants grow and prosper. They were not created to stretch forth their branches alone, and endure without protection the summer's sun and the winter's storm. Alone they but spread themselves on the ground, and cower unseen in the dingy shade. But when they have found their firm supporters, how wonderful is their beauty; how all pervading and victorious! What is the turret without its ivy, or the high garden-wall without the jasmine which gives it its beauty and fragrance? The hedge without the honeysuckle is but a hedge.

There is a feeling still half existing, but now half conquered by the force of human nature, that a woman should be ashamed of her love till the husband's right to her compels her to acknowledge it. We would fain preach a different doctrine. A woman should glory in her love; but on that account let her take the more care that it be such as to justify her glory.

Eleanor did glory in hers, and she felt, and had cause to feel, that it deserved to be held as glorious. She could have stood there for hours with his arm round her, had fate and Mr. Thorne permitted it. Each moment she crept nearer to his bosom, and felt more and more certain that there was her home. What now to her was the archdeacon's arrogance, her sister's coldness, or her dear father's weakness? What need she care for the duplicity of such friends as Charlotte Stanhope? She had found the strong shield that should guard her from all wrongs, the trusty pilot that should henceforward guide her through the shoals and rocks. She would give up the heavy burden of her independence, and once more assume the position of a woman, and the duties of a trusting and loving wife.

And he, too, stood there fully satisfied with his place. They were both looking intently on the fire, as though they could read there their future fate, till at last Eleanor turned her face towards his. 'Hów sad you are,' she said, smiling; and indeed his face was, if not sad, at least serious. 'How sad you are, love!'

'Sad,' said he, looking down at her; 'no, certainly not sad.' Her sweet loving eyes were turned towards him, and she smiled softly as he answered her. The temptation was too strong even for the demure propriety of Mr. Arabin, and, bending over her, he pressed his lips to hers.

Immediately after this, Mr. Thorne appeared, and they were both delighted to hear that the tail of the Belzebub colt was not materially injured.

It had been Mr. Harding's intention to hurry over to Ullathorne as soon as possible after his return to Barchester, in order to secure the support of his daughter in his meditated revolt against the archdeacon as touching the deanery; but he was spared the additional journey by hearing that Mrs. Bold had returned unexpectedly home. As soon as he had read her note he started off, and found her waiting for him in her own house.

How much each of them had to tell the other, and how certain each was that the story which he or she had to tell would astonish the other!

'My dear, I am so anxious to see you,' said Mr. Harding, kissing his daughter.

'Oh, papa, I have so much to tell you!' said the daughter, returning the embrace.

'My dear, they have offered me the deanery!' said Mr. Harding, anticipating by the suddenness of the revelation the tidings which Eleanor had to give him.

'Oh, papa,' said she, forgetting her own love and happiness in her joy at the surprising news; 'oh, papa, can it be possible? Dear papa, how thoroughly, thoroughly happy that makes me!'

'But, my dear, I think it best to refuse it.'

'Oh, papa!'

'I am sure you will agree with me, Eleanor, when I explain it to you. You know, my dear, how old I am. If I live, I——'

'But, papa, I must tell you about myself.'

'Well, my dear.'

'I do so wonder how you'll take it.'

'Take what?'

'If you don't rejoice at it, if it doesn't make you happy, if you don't encourage me, I shall break my heart.'

'If that be the case, Nelly, I certainly will encourage you.'

'But I fear you won't. I do so fear you won't. And yet you can't but think I am the most fortunate woman living on God's earth.'

'Are you, dearest? Then I certainly will rejoice with you. Come, Nelly, come to me, and tell me what it is.'

'I am going——'

He led her to the sofa, and seating himself beside her, took both her hands in his. 'You are going to be married, Nelly. Is not that it?'

'Yes,' she said, faintly. 'That is if you will approve;' and then she blushed as she remembered the promise which she had so lately volunteered to him, and which she had so utterly forgotten in making her engagement with Mr. Arabin.

Mr. Harding thought for a moment who the man could be whom he was to be called upon to welcome as his son-in-law. A week since he would have had no doubt whom to name. In that case he would have been prepared to give his sanction, although he would have done so with a heavy heart. Now he knew that at any rate it would not be Mr. Slope, though he was perfectly at a loss to guess who could possibly have filled the place. For a moment he thought that the man might be Bertie Stanhope, and his very soul sank within him.

'Well, Nelly?'

'Oh, papa, promise to me that, for my sake, you will love him.'

'Come, Nelly, come; tell me who it is.'

'But will you love him, papa?'

'Dearest, I must love any one that you love.' Then she turned her face to his, and whispered into his ear the name of Mr. Arabin.

No man that she could have named could have more surprised or more delighted him. Had he looked round the world for a son-in-law to his taste, he could have selected no one whom he would have preferred to Mr. Arabin. He was a clergyman; he held a living in the neighbourhood; he was of a set to which all Mr. Harding's own partialities most closely adhered; he was the great friend of Dr. Grantly; and he was, moreover, a man of whom Mr. Harding knew nothing but what he approved. Nevertheless, his surprise was so great as to prevent the immediate expression of his joy. He had never thought of Mr. Arabin in connection with his daughter; he had never imagined that they had any feeling in common. He had feared that his daughter had been made hostile to clergymen of Mr. Arabin's stamp by her intolerance of the archdeacon's pretensions. Had he been put to wish, he might have wished for Mr. Arabin for a son-in-law; but had he been put to guess, the name would never have occurred to him.

'Mr. Arabin!' he exclaimed; 'impossible!'

'Oh, papa, for heaven's sake don't say anything against him! If you love me, don't say anything against him. Oh, papa, it's done, and mustn't be undone—oh, papa!'

Fickle Eleanor! where was the promise that she would make no choice for herself without her father's approval? She had chosen, and now demanded his acquiescence. 'Oh, papa, isn't he good? isn't he noble? isn't he religious, highminded, everything that a good man possibly can be?' and she clung to her father, beseeching him for his consent.

'My Nelly, my child, my own daughter! He is; he is noble and good and highminded; he is all that a woman can love and a man admire. He shall be my son, my own son. He shall be as close to my heart as you are. My Nelly, my child, my happy, happy child!'

We need not pursue the interview any further. By degrees they returned to the subject of the new promotion. Eleanor tried to prove to him, as the Grantlys had done, that his age could be no bar to his being a very excellent dean; but those arguments had now even less weight on him than before. He said little or nothing, but sat meditative. Every now and then he would kiss his daughter, and say 'yes,' or 'no,' or 'very true,' or 'well, my dear, I can't quite agree with you there,' but he could not be got to enter sharply into the question of 'to be, or not to be' dean of Barchester. Of her and her happiness, of Mr. Arabin and his virtues, he would talk as much as Eleanor desired; and, to tell the truth, that was not a little; but about the deanery he would now say nothing further. He had got a new idea into his head—Why should not Mr. Arabin be the new dean?

CHAPTER L

THE ARCHDEACON IS SATISFIED WITH THE STATE OF AFFAIRS

THE archdeacon, in his journey into Barchester, had been assured by Mr. Harding that all their prognostications about Mr. Slope and Eleanor were groundless. Mr. Harding, however, had found it very difficult to shake his son-in-law's faith in his own acuteness. The matter had, to Dr. Grantly, been so plainly corroborated by such patent evidence, borne out by such endless circumstances, that he at first refused to take as true the positive statement which Mr. Harding made to him of Eleanor's own disavowal of the impeachment. But at last he yielded in a qualified way. He brought himself to admit that he would at the present regard his past convictions as a mistake; but in doing this he so guarded himself, that if, at any future time, Eleanor should come forth to the world as Mrs. Slope, he might still be able to say: 'There, I told you so. Remember what you said and what I said; and remember also for coming years, that I was right in this matter,—as in all others.'

He carried, however, his concession so far as to bring himself to undertake to call at Eleanor's house, and he did call accordingly, while the father and daughter were yet in the middle of their conference. Mr. Harding had had so much to hear and to say that he had forgotten to advertise Eleanor of the honour that awaited her, and she heard her brother-in-law's voice in the hall, while she was quite unprepared to see him.

'There's the archdeacon,' she said, springing up.

'Yes, my dear. He told me to tell you that he would come and see you; but, to tell the truth, I had forgotten all about it.'

Eleanor fled away, regardless of all her father's entreaties. She could not now, in the first hours of her joy, bring herself to bear all the archdeacon's retractions, apologies, and congratulations. He would have so much to say, and would be so tedious in saying it; consequently, the archdeacon, when he was shown into the drawing-room, found no one there but Mr. Harding.

'You must excuse Eleanor,' said Mr. Harding.

'Is anything the matter?' asked the doctor, who at once anticipated that the whole truth about Mr. Slope had at last come out.

'Well, something is the matter. I wonder now whether you will be much surprised?'

The archdeacon saw by his father-in-law's manner that after all he had nothing to tell him about Mr. Slope. 'No,' said he, 'certainly not—nothing will ever surprise me again.' Very many men now-a-days, besides the archdeacon, adopt or affect to adopt the *nil admirari* doctrine; but nevertheless, to judge from their appearance, they are just as subject to sudden emotions as their grandfathers and grandmothers were before them.

'What do you think Mr. Arabin has done?'

'Mr. Arabin! It's nothing about that daughter of Stanhope's, I hope?'

'No, not that woman,' said Mr. Harding, enjoying his joke in his sleeve.

'Not that woman! Is he going to do anything about any woman? Why can't you speak out if you have anything to say? There is nothing I hate so much as these sort of mysteries.'

'There shall be no mystery with you, archdeacon; though of course, it must go no further at present.'

'Well.'

'Except Susan. You must promise me you'll tell no one else.'

'Nonsense!' exclaimed the archdeacon, who was

becoming angry in his suspense. ' You can't have any
secret about Mr. Arabin.'

' Only this—that he and Eleanor are engaged.'

It was quite clear to see, by the archdeacon's face, that
he did not believe a word of it. ' Mr. Arabin! It's
impossible ! '

' Eleanor, at any rate, has just now told me so.'

' It's impossible,' repeated the archdeacon.

' Well, I can't say I think it impossible. It certainly
took me by surprise; but that does not make it impossible.'

' She must be mistaken.'

Mr. Harding assured him that there was no mistake;
that he would find, on returning home, that Mr. Arabin
had been at Plumstead with the express object of making
the same declaration, that even Miss Thorne knew all
about it; and that, in fact, the thing was as clearly
settled as any such arrangement between a lady and a
gentleman could well be.

' Good heavens ! ' said the archdeacon, walking up
and down Eleanor's drawing-room. ' Good heavens !
Good heavens ! '

Now, these exclamations certainly betokened faith.
Mr. Harding properly gathered from it that, at last, Dr.
Grantly did believe the fact. The first utterance clearly
evinced a certain amount of distaste at the information
he had received; the second, simply indicated surprise;
in the tone of the third, Mr. Harding fancied that he could
catch a certain gleam of satisfaction.

The archdeacon had truly expressed the workings of
his mind. He could not but be disgusted to find how
utterly astray he had been in all his anticipations. Had
he only been lucky enough to have suggested this marriage
himself when he first brought Mr. Arabin into the country,
his character for judgment and wisdom would have
received an addition which would have classed him at
any rate next to Solomon. And why had he not done
so ? Might he not have foreseen that Mr. Arabin would
want a wife in his parsonage ? He had foreseen that
Eleanor would want a husband; but should he not also
have perceived that Mr. Arabin was a man much more
likely to attract her than Mr. Slope ? The archdeacon

found that he had been at fault, and of course could not immediately get over his discomfiture.

Then his surprise was intense. How sly this pair of young turtle doves had been with him. How egregiously they had hoaxed him. He had preached to Eleanor against her fancied attachment to Mr. Slope, at the very time that she was in love with his own protégé, Mr. Arabin; and had absolutely taken that same Mr. Arabin into his confidence with reference to his dread of Mr. Slope's alliance. It was very natural that the archdeacon should feel surprise.

But there was also great ground for satisfaction. Looking at the match by itself, it was the very thing to help the doctor out of his difficulties. In the first place, the assurance that he should never have Mr. Slope for his brother-in-law, was in itself a great comfort. Then Mr. Arabin was, of all men, the one with whom it would best suit him to be so intimately connected. But the crowning comfort was the blow which this marriage would give to Mr. Slope. He had now certainly lost his wife; rumour was beginning to whisper that he might possibly lose his position in the palace; and if Mr. Harding would only be true, the great danger of all would be surmounted. In such case it might be expected that Mr. Slope would own himself vanquished, and take himself altogether away from Barchester. And so the archdeacon would again be able to breathe pure air.

' Well, well,' said he. ' Good heavens ! good heavens ! ' and the tone of the fifth exclamation made Mr. Harding fully aware that content was reigning in the archdeacon's bosom.

And then slowly, gradually, and craftily Mr. Harding propounded his own new scheme. Why should not Mr. Arabin be the new dean ?

Slowly, gradually, and thoughtfully Dr. Grantly fell into his father-in-law's views. Much as he liked Mr. Arabin, sincere as was his admiration for that gentleman's ecclesiastical abilities, he would not have sanctioned a measure which would rob his father-in-law of his fairly-earned promotion, were it at all practicable to induce his father-in-law to accept the promotion which he had earned. But the archdeacon had, on a former occasion, received proof of the obstinacy with which Mr. Harding could adhere to his own views in opposition to the advice of all his friends. He knew tolerably well that nothing would induce the meek, mild man before him to take the high place offered to him, if he thought it wrong to do so. Knowing this, he also said to himself more than once: ' Why should not Mr. Arabin be Dean of Barchester ? ' It was at last arranged between them that they would together start to London by the earliest train on the following morning, making a little *détour* to Oxford on their journey. Dr. Gwynne's counsels, they imagined, might perhaps be of assistance to them.

These matters settled, the archdeacon hurried off, that he might return to Plumstead and prepare for his journey. The day was extremely fine, and he came into the city in an open gig. As he was driving up the High Street he encountered Mr. Slope at a crossing. Had he not pulled up rather sharply, he would have run over him. The two had never spoken to each other since they had met on a memorable occasion in the bishop's study. They did not speak now ; but they looked each other full in the face, and Mr. Slope's countenance was as impudent, as triumphant, as defiant as ever. Had Dr. Grantly not known to the contrary, he would have imagined that his enemy had won the deanship, the wife, and all the rich honours, for which he had been striving. As it was, he had lost everything that he had in the world, and had just received his *congé* from the bishop.

In leaving the town the archdeacon drove by the well-remembered entrance of Hiram's hospital. There, at the gate, was a large, untidy, farmer's wagon, laden with untidy-looking furniture ; and there, inspecting the arrival, was good Mrs. Quiverful—not dressed in her Sunday best—not very clean in her apparel—not graceful as to her bonnet and shawl ; or, indeed, with many feminine charms as to her whole appearance. She was busy at domestic work in her new house, and had just ventured out, expecting to see no one on the arrival of the family chattels. The archdeacon was down upon her before she knew where she was.

Her acquaintance with Dr. Grantly or his family was very slight indeed. The archdeacon, as a matter of course,

knew every clergyman in the archdeaconry, it may almost
be said in the diocese, and had some acquaintance, more
or less intimate, with their wives and families. With
Mr. Quiverful he had been concerned on various matters
of business ; but of Mrs. Q. he had seen very little. Now,
however, he was in too gracious a mood to pass her by
unnoticed. The Quiverfuls, one and all, had looked for
the bitterest hostility from Dr. Grantly ; they knew his
anxiety that Mr. Harding should return to his old home
at the hospital, and they did not know that a new home
had been offered to him at the deanery. Mrs. Quiverful
was therefore not a little surprised and not a little rejoiced
also, at the tone in which she was addressed.

' How do you do, Mrs. Quiverful ?—how do you do ?'
said he, stretching his left hand out of the gig, as he spoke
to her. ' I am very glad to see you employed in so pleasant
and useful a manner ; very glad indeed.'

Mrs. Quiverful thanked him, and shook hands with
him, and looked into his face suspiciously. She was not
sure whether the congratulations and kindness were or
were not ironical.

' Pray tell Mr. Quiverful from me,' he continued, ' that
I am rejoiced at his appointment. It's a comfortable
place, Mrs. Quiverful, and a comfortable house, and
I am very glad to see you in it. Good-bye—good-bye.'
And he drove on, leaving the lady well pleased and
astonished at his good-nature. On the whole things were
going well with the archdeacon, and he could afford to
be charitable to Mrs. Quiverful. He looked forth from
his gig smilingly on all the world, and forgave every one
in Barchester their sins, excepting only Mrs. Proudie and
Mr. Slope. Had he seen the bishop, he would have felt
inclined to pat even him kindly on the head.

He determined to go home by St. Ewold's. This would
take him some three miles out of his way ; but he felt
that he could not leave Plumstead comfortably without
saying one word of good fellowship to Mr. Arabin. When
he reached the parsonage the vicar was still out ; but,
from what he had heard, he did not doubt but that he
would meet him on the road between their two houses.
He was right in this, for about halfway home, at a narrow
turn, he came upon Mr. Arabin, who was on horseback.

'Well, well, well, well;' said the archdeacon, loudly, joyously, and with supreme good humour; 'well, well, well, well; so, after all, we have no further cause to fear Mr. Slope.'

'I hear from Mrs. Grantly that they have offered the deanery to Mr. Harding,' said the other.

'Mr. Slope has lost more than the deanery, I find, and then the archdeacon laughed jocosely. 'Come, come, Arabin, you have kept your secret well enough. I know all about it now.'

'I have had no secret, archdeacon,' said the other with a quiet smile. 'None at all—not for a day. It was only yesterday that I knew my own good fortune, and to-day I went over to Plumstead to ask your approval. From what Mrs. Grantly has said to me, I am led to hope that I shall have it.'

'With all my heart, with all my heart,' said the archdeacon cordially, holding his friend fast by the hand. 'It's just as I would have it. She is an excellent young woman; she will not come to you empty-handed; and I think she will make you a good wife. If she does her duty by you as her sister does by me, you'll be a happy man; that's all I can say.' And as he finished speaking, a tear might have been observed in each of the doctor's eyes.

Mr. Arabin warmly returned the archdeacon's grasp, but he said little. His heart was too full for speaking, and he could not express the gratitude which he felt. Dr. Grantly understood him as well as though he had spoken for an hour.

'And mind, Arabin,' said he, 'no one but myself shall tie the knot. We'll get Eleanor out to Plumstead, and it shall come off there. I'll make Susan stir herself, and we'll do it in style. I must be off to London to-morrow on special business. Harding goes with me. But I'll be back before your bride has got her wedding dress ready.' And so they parted.

On his journey home the archdeacon occupied his mind with preparations for the marriage festivities. He made a great resolve that he would atone to Eleanor for all the injury he had done her by the munificence of his future treatment. He would show her what was the difference in his eyes between a Slope and an Arabin. On one other thing also he decided with a firm mind : if the affair of the dean should not be settled in Mr. Arabin's favour, nothing should prevent him putting a new front and bow-window to the dining-room at St. Ewold's parsonage.

' So we're sold after all, Sue,' said he to his wife, accosting her with a kiss as soon as he entered his house. He did not call his wife Sue above twice or thrice in a year, and these occasions were great high days.

' Eleanor has had more sense than we gave her credit for,' said Mrs. Grantly.

And there was great content in Plumstead rectory that evening ; and Mrs. Grantly promised her husband that she would now open her heart, and take Mr. Arabin into it. Hitherto she had declined to do so.

CHAPTER LI

MR. SLOPE BIDS FAREWELL TO THE PALACE AND ITS INHABITANTS

WE must now take leave of Mr. Slope, and of the bishop also, and of Mrs. Proudie. These leave-takings in novels are as disagreeable as they are in real life ; not so sad, indeed, for they want the reality of sadness ; but quite as perplexing, and generally less satisfactory. What novelist, what Fielding, what Scott, what George Sand, or Sue, or Dumas, can impart an interest to the last chapter of his fictitious history ? Promises of two children and superhuman happiness are of no avail, nor assurance of extreme respectability carried to an age far exceeding that usually allotted to mortals. The sorrows of our heroes and heroines, they are your delight, oh public ! their sorrows, or their sins, or their absurdities ; not their virtues, good sense, and consequent rewards. When we begin to tint our final pages with *couleur de rose*, as in accordance with fixed rule we must do, we altogether extinguish our own powers of pleasing. When we become dull we offend your intellect ; and we must become dull or we should offend your taste. A late writer, wishing to sustain his interest to the last page, hung his hero at the end of the third volume. The consequence was, that no one would read his novel. And who can apportion out and dovetail his incidents, dialogues, characters, and descriptive morsels, so as to fit them all exactly into 439 pages, without either compressing them unnaturally, or extending them artificially at the end of his labour? Do I not myself know that I am at this moment in want of a dozen pages, and that I am sick with cudgelling my brains to find them? And then when everything is done, the kindest-hearted critic of them all invariably twits us with the incompetency and lameness of our conclusion. We have either become idle and neglected it, or tedious and over-laboured it. It is insipid or unnatural, over-strained or imbecile. It means nothing, or attempts too much. The last scene of all, as all last scenes we fear must be,

> Is second childishness, and mere oblivion,
> Sans teeth, sans eyes, sans taste, sans everything.

I can only say that if some critic, who thoroughly knows his work, and has laboured on it till experience has made him perfect, will write the last fifty pages of a novel in the way they should be written, I, for one, will in future do my best to copy the example. Guided by my own lights only, I confess that I despair of success.

For the last week or ten days, Mr. Slope had seen nothing of Mrs. Proudie, and very little of the bishop. He still lived in the palace, and still went through his usual routine work; but the confidential doings of the diocese had passed into other hands. He had seen this clearly, and marked it well; but it had not much disturbed him. He had indulged in other hopes till the bishop's affairs had become dull to him, and he was moreover aware that, as regarded the diocese, Mrs. Proudie had checkmated him. It has been explained, in the beginning of these pages, how three or four were contending together as to who, in fact, should be bishop of Barchester. Each of these had now admitted to himself (or boasted to herself) that Mrs. Proudie was victorious in the struggle. They had gone through a competitive examination of con- siderable severity, and she had come forth the winner, *facile princeps.* Mr. Slope had, for a moment, run her hard, but it was only for a moment. It had become, as it were, acknowledged that Hiram's hospital should be the testing point between them, and now Mr. Quiverful was already in the hospital, the proof of Mrs. Proudie's skill and courage.

All this did not break down Mr. Slope's spirit, because he had other hopes. But, alas, at last there came to him a note from his friend Sir Nicholas, informing him that the deanship was disposed of. Let us give Mr. Slope his due. He did not lie prostrate under this blow, or give himself up to vain lamentations; he did not henceforward despair of life, and call upon gods above and gods below to carry him off. He sat himself down in his chair, counted out what monies he had in hand for present purposes, and what others were coming in to him, bethought himself as to the best sphere for his future exertions, and at once wrote off a letter to a rich sugar-refiner's wife in Baker Street, who, as he well knew, was much given to the entertainment and encouragement of serious young evangelical clergymen. He was again, he said, 'upon the world, having found the air of a cathedral town, and the very nature of cathedral services, uncongenial to his spirit;' and then he sat awhile, making firm resolves as to his manner of parting from the bishop, and also as to his future conduct.

> At last he rose, and twitched his mantle blue (black),
> To-morrow to fresh woods and pastures new.

Having received a formal command to wait upon the bishop, he rose and proceeded to obey it. He rang the bell and desired the servant to inform his master that if it suited his lordship, he, Mr. Slope, was ready to wait upon him. The servant, who well understood that Mr. Slope was no longer in the ascendant, brought back a message, saying that 'his lordship desired that Mr. Slope would attend him immediately in his study.' Mr. Slope waited about ten minutes more to prove his independence, and then he went into the bishop's room. There, as he had expected, he found Mrs. Proudie, together with her husband.

'Hum, ha,—Mr. Slope, pray take a chair,' said the gentleman bishop.

' Pray be seated, Mr. Slope,' said the lady bishop.

' Thank ye, thank ye,' said Mr. Slope, and walking round to the fire, he threw himself into one of the arm-chairs that graced the hearth-rug.

' Mr. Slope,' said the bishop, ' it has become necessary that I should speak to you definitively on a matter that has for some time been pressing itself on my attention.'

' May I ask whether the subject is in any way connected with myself ? ' said Mr. Slope.

' It is so,—certainly,—yes, it certainly is connected with yourself, Mr. Slope.'

' Then, my lord, if I may be allowed to express a wish, I would prefer that no discussion on the subject should take place between us in the presence of a third person.'

' Don't alarm yourself, Mr. Slope,' said Mrs. Proudie, ' no discussion is at all necessary. The bishop merely intends to express his own wishes.'

' I merely intend, Mr. Slope, to express my own wishes,— no discussion will be at all necessary,' said the bishop, reiterating his wife's words.

' That is more, my lord, than we any of us can be sure of,' said Mr. Slope ; ' I cannot, however, force Mrs. Proudie to leave the room ; nor can I refuse to remain here if it be your lordship's wish that I should do so.'

' It is his lordship's wish, certainly,' said Mrs. Proudie.

' Mr. Slope,' began the bishop, in a solemn, serious voice, ' it grieves me to have to find fault. It grieves me much to have to find fault with a clergyman ; but especially so with a clergyman in your position.'

' Why, what have I done amiss, my lord ? ' demanded Mr. Slope, boldly.

' What have you done amiss, Mr. Slope ? ' said Mrs. Proudie, standing erect before the culprit, and raising that terrible forefinger. ' Do you dare to ask the bishop what you have done amiss ? does not your conscience——'

' Mrs. Proudie, pray let it be understood, once for all, that I will have no words with you.'

' Ah, sir, but you will have words,' said she ; ' you must have words. Why have you had so many words with that Signora Neroni ? Why have you disgraced yourself, you a clergyman too, by constantly consorting with such a woman as that,—with a married woman—with one altogether unfit for a clergyman's society ? '

' At any rate, I was introduced to her in your drawing-room,' retorted Mr. Slope.

' And shamefully you behaved there,' said Mrs. Proudie, ' most shamefully. I was wrong to allow you to remain in the house a day after what I then saw. I should have insisted on your instant dismissal.'

' I have yet to learn, Mrs. Proudie, that you have the power to insist either on my going from hence or on my staying here.'

' What ! ' said the lady ; ' I am not to have the privilege of saying who shall and who shall not frequent my own drawing-room ! I am not to save my servants and dependents from having their morals corrupted by improper conduct ! I am not to save my own daughters from impurity ! I will let you see, Mr. Slope, whether I have the power or whether I have not. You will have the goodness to understand that you no longer fill any situation about the bishop ; and as your room will be immediately wanted in the palace for another chaplain, I must ask you to provide yourself with apartments as soon as may be convenient to you.'

' My lord,' said Mr. Slope, appealing to the bishop, and so turning his back completely on the lady, ' will you permit me to ask that I may have from your own lips any decision that you may have come to on this matter ? '

' Certainly, Mr. Slope, certainly,' said the bishop ; ' that is but reasonable. Well, my decision is that you had better look for some other preferment. For the situation which you have lately held I do not think that you are well suited.'

' And what, my lord, has been my fault ? '

' That Signora Neroni is one fault,' said Mrs. Proudie ; ' and a very abominable fault she is ; very abominable and very disgraceful. Fie, Mr. Slope, fie ! You an evangelical clergyman indeed ! '

' My lord, I desire to know for what fault I am turned out of your lordship's house.'

' You hear what Mrs. Proudie says,' said the bishop.

' When I publish the history of this transaction, my lord, as I decidedly shall do in my own vindication, I presume

you will not wish me to state that you have discarded me
at your wife's bidding—because she has objected to my
being acquainted with another lady, the daughter of one
of the prebendaries of the chapter ? '

'You may publish what you please, sir,' said Mrs.
Proudie. 'But you will not be insane enough to publish
any of your doings in Barchester. Do you think I have
not heard of your kneelings at that creature's feet—that
is if she has any feet—and of your constant slobbering
over her hand ? I advise you to beware, Mr. Slope, of
what you do and say. Clergymen have been unfrocked
for less than what you have been guilty of.'

'My lord, if this goes on I shall be obliged to indict
this woman—Mrs. Proudie I mean—for defamation of
character.'

'I think, Mr. Slope, you had better now retire,' said
the bishop. 'I will enclose to you a cheque for any balance
that may be due to you ; and, under the present circumstances, it will of course be better for all parties that you
should leave the palace at the earliest possible moment.
I will allow you for your journey back to London, and
for your maintenance in Barchester for a week from this
date.'

'If, however, you wish to remain in this neighbourhood,'
said Mrs. Proudie, 'and will solemnly pledge yourself
never again to see that woman, and will promise also to
be more circumspect in your conduct, the bishop will
mention your name to Mr. Quiverful, who now wants
a curate at Puddingdale. The house is, I imagine, quite
sufficient for your requirements : and there will moreover
be a stipend of fifty pounds a year.'

'May God forgive you, madam, for the manner in
which you have treated me,' said Mr. Slope, looking at
her with a very heavenly look ; 'and remember this,
madam, that you yourself may still have a fall ; ' and he
looked at her with a very worldly look. 'As to the bishop,
I pity him ! ' And so saying, Mr. Slope left the room.
Thus ended the intimacy of the Bishop of Barchester
with his first confidential chaplain.

Mrs. Proudie was right in this ; namely, that Mr. Slope
was not insane enough to publish to the world any of his
doings in Barchester. He did not trouble his friend Mr.

Towers with any written statement of the iniquity of
Mrs. Proudie, or the imbecility of her husband. He was
aware that it would be wise in him to drop for the future
all allusions to his doings in the cathedral city. Soon
after the interview just recorded, he left Barchester,
shaking the dust off his feet as he entered the railway
carriage ; and he gave no longing lingering look after the
cathedral towers, as the train hurried him quickly out
of their sight.

It is well known that the family of the Slopes never
starve : they always fall on their feet like cats, and let
them fall where they will, they live on the fat of the land.
Our Mr. Slope did so. On his return to town he found
that the sugar-refiner had died, and that his widow was
inconsolable : or, in other words, in want of consolation.
Mr. Slope consoled her, and soon found himself settled
with much comfort in the house in Baker Street. He
possessed himself, also, before long, of a church in the
vicinity of the New Road, and became known to fame as
one of the most eloquent preachers and pious clergymen
in that part of the metropolis. There let us leave him.

Of the bishop and his wife very little further need be
said. From that time forth nothing material occurred
to interrupt the even course of their domestic harmony.
Very speedily, a further vacancy on the bench of bishops
gave to Dr. Proudie the seat in the House of Lords, which
he at first so anxiously longed for. But by this time he
had become a wiser man. He did certainly take his seat,
and occasionally registered a vote in favour of Government views on ecclesiastical matters. But he had
thoroughly learnt that his proper sphere of action lay in
close contiguity with Mrs. Proudie's wardrobe. He never
again aspired to disobey, or seemed even to wish for
autocratic diocesan authority. If ever he thought of
freedom, he did so, as men think of the millennium, as
of a good time which may be coming, but which nobody
expects to come in their day. Mrs. Proudie might be
said still to bloom, and was, at any rate, strong ; and
the bishop had no reason to apprehend that he would
be speedily visited with the sorrows of a widower's life.

He is still Bishop of Barchester. He has so graced
that throne, that the Government has been averse to

translate him, even to higher dignities. There may he
remain, under safe pupilage, till the new-fangled manners
of the age have discovered him to be superannuated, and
bestowed on him a pension. As for Mrs. Proudie, our
prayers for her are that she may live for ever.

CHAPTER LII

THE NEW DEAN TAKES POSSESSION OF THE DEANERY, AND THE NEW WARDEN OF THE HOSPITAL

MR. HARDING and the archdeacon together made their
way to Oxford, and there, by dint of cunning argument,
they induced the Master of Lazarus also to ask himself this
momentous question: ' Why should not Mr. Arabin be
Dean of Barchester ? ' He of course, for a while tried his
hand at persuading Mr. Harding that he was foolish, over-
scrupulous, self-willed, and weak-minded ; but he tried
in vain. If Mr. Harding would not give way to Dr.
Grantly, it was not likely he would give way to Dr.
Gwynne ; more especially now that so admirable a scheme
as that of inducting Mr. Arabin into the deanery had been
set on foot. When the master found that his eloquence was
vain, and heard also that Mr. Arabin was about to become
Mr. Harding's son-in-law, he confessed that he also would,
under such circumstances, be glad to see his old friend and
protégé, the fellow of his college, placed in the comfortable
position that was going a-begging.

' It might be the means, you know, Master, of keeping
Mr. Slope out,' said the archdeacon with grave caution.

' He has no more chance of it,' said the master, ' than
our college chaplain. I know more about it than that.'

Mrs. Grantly had been right in her surmise. It was the
Master of Lazarus who had been instrumental in representing in high places the claims which Mr. Harding had
upon the Government, and he now consented to use his
best endeavours towards getting the offer transferred to
Mr. Arabin. The three of them went on to London
together, and there they remained a week, to the great
disgust of Mrs. Grantly, and most probably also of Mrs.
Gwynne. The minister was out of town in one direction,

and his private secretary in another. The clerks who remained could do nothing in such a matter as this, and all was difficulty and confusion. The two doctors seemed to have plenty to do ; they bustled here and they bustled there, and complained at their club in the evenings that they had been driven off their legs ; but Mr. Harding had no occupation. Once or twice he suggested that he might perhaps return to Barchester. His request, however, was peremptorily refused, and he had nothing for it but to while away his time in Westminster Abbey.

At length an answer from the great man came. The Master of Lazarus had made his proposition through the Bishop of Belgravia. Now this bishop, though but newly gifted with his diocesan honours, was a man of much weight in the clerico-political world. He was, if not as pious, at any rate as wise as St. Paul, and had been with so much effect all things to all men, that though he was great among the dons of Oxford, he had been selected for the most favourite seat on the bench by a Whig Prime Minister. To him Dr. Gwynne had made known his wishes and his arguments, and the bishop had made them known to the Marquis of Kensington Gore. The marquis, who was Lord High Steward of the Pantry Board, and who by most men was supposed to hold the highest office out of the cabinet, trafficked much in affairs of this kind. He not only suggested the arrangement to the minister over a cup of coffee, standing on a drawing-room rug in Windsor Castle, but he also favourably mentioned Mr. Arabin's name in the ear of a distinguished person.

And so the matter was arranged. The answer of the great man came, and Mr. Arabin was made Dean of Barchester. The three clergymen who had come up to town on this important mission dined together with great glee on the day on which the news reached them. In a silent, decent, clerical manner, they toasted Mr. Arabin with full bumpers of claret. The satisfaction of all of them was supreme. The Master of Lazarus had been successful in his attempt, and success is dear to us all. The archdeacon had trampled upon Mr. Slope, and had lifted to high honours the young clergyman whom he had induced to quit the retirement and comfort of the university. So at least the archdeacon thought ; though, to speak

sooth, not he, but circumstances, had trampled on Mr.
Slope. But the satisfaction of Mr. Harding was, of all,
perhaps, the most complete. He laid aside his usual
melancholy manner, and brought forth little quiet jokes
from the inmost mirth of his heart; he poked his fun at
the archdeacon about Mr. Slope's marriage, and quizzed
him for his improper love for Mrs. Proudie. On the following day they all returned to Barchester.

It was arranged that Mr. Arabin should know nothing
of what had been done till he received the minister's letter
from the hands of his embryo father-in-law. In order that
no time might be lost, a message had been sent to him by
the preceding night's post, begging him to be at the
deanery at the hour that the train from London arrived.
There was nothing in this which surprised Mr. Arabin.
It had somehow got about through all Barchester that
Mr. Harding was the new dean, and all Barchester was
prepared to welcome him with pealing bells and full
hearts. Mr. Slope had certainly had a party; there had
certainly been those in Barchester who were prepared to
congratulate him on his promotion with assumed sincerity,
but even his own party was not broken-hearted by his
failure. The inhabitants of the city, even the high-souled
ecstatic young ladies of thirty-five, had begun to comprehend that their welfare, and the welfare of the place, was
connected in some mysterious manner with daily chants
and bi-weekly anthems. The expenditure of the palace had
not added much to the popularity of the bishop's side of
the question; and, on the whole, there was a strong
reaction. When it became known to all the world that
Mr. Harding was to be the new dean, all the world rejoiced
heartily.

Mr. Arabin, we have said, was not surprised at the
summons which called him to the deanery. He had not
as yet seen Mr. Harding since Eleanor had accepted him,
nor had he seen him since he had learnt his future father-
in-law's preferment. There was nothing more natural,
more necessary, than that they should meet each other at
the earliest possible moment. Mr. Arabin was waiting
in the deanery parlour when Mr. Harding and Dr. Grantly
were driven up from the station.

There was some excitement in the bosoms of them all,

as they met and shook hands; by far too much to enable either of them to begin his story and tell it in a proper equable style of narrative. Mr. Harding was some minutes quite dumbfounded, and Mr. Arabin could only talk in short, spasmodic sentences about his love and good fortune. He slipped in, as best he could, some sort of congratulation about the deanship, and then went on with his hopes and fears,—hopes that he might be received as a son, and fears that he hardly deserved such good fortune. Then he went back to the dean; it was the most thoroughly satisfactory appointment, he said, of which he had ever heard.

'But! but! but——' said Mr. Harding; and then failing to get any further, he looked imploringly at the archdeacon.

'The truth is, Arabin,' said the doctor, 'that, after all, you are not destined to be son-in-law to a dean. Nor am I either: more's the pity.'

Mr. Arabin looked at him for explanation. 'Is not Mr. Harding to be the new dean?'

'It appears not,' said the archdeacon. Mr. Arabin's face fell a little, and he looked from one to the other. It was plainly to be seen from them both that there was no cause of unhappiness in the matter, at least not of unhappiness to them; but there was as yet no elucidation of the mystery.

'Think how old I am,' said Mr. Harding, imploringly.

'Fiddlestick!' said the archdeacon.

'That's all very well, but it won't make a young man of me,' said Mr. Harding.

'And who is to be dean?' asked Mr. Arabin.

'Yes, that's the question,' said the archdeacon. 'Come, Mr. Precentor, since you obstinately refuse to be anything else, let us know who is to be the man. He has got the nomination in his pocket.'

With eyes brim full of tears, Mr. Harding pulled out the letter and handed it to his future son-in-law. He tried to make a little speech, but failed altogether. Having given up the document, he turned round to the wall, feigning to blow his nose, and then sat himself down on the old dean's dingy horse-hair sofa. And here we find it necessary to bring our account of the interview to an end.

Nor can we pretend to describe the rapture with which Mr. Harding was received by his daughter. She wept with grief and wept with joy; with grief that her father should, in his old age, still be without that rank and worldly position which, according to her ideas, he had so well earned; and with joy in that he, her darling father, should have bestowed on that other dear one the good things of which he himself would not open his hand to take possession. And here Mr. Harding again showed his weakness. In the *mêlée* of this exposal of their loves and reciprocal affection, he found himself unable to resist the entreaties of all parties that the lodgings in the High Street should be given up. Eleanor would not live in the deanery, she said, unless her father lived there also. Mr. Arabin would not be dean, unless Mr. Harding would be co-dean with him. The archdeacon declared that his father-in-law should not have his own way in everything, and Mrs. Grantly carried him off to Plumstead, that he might remain there till Mr. and Mrs. Arabin were in a state to receive him in their own mansion.

Pressed by such arguments as these, what could a weak old man do but yield?

But there was yet another task which it behoved Mr. Harding to do before he could allow himself to be at rest. Little has been said in these pages of the state of those remaining old men who had lived under his sway at the hospital. But not on this account must it be presumed that he had forgotten them, or that in their state of anarchy and in their want of due government he had omitted to visit them. He visited them constantly, and had latterly given them to understand that they would soon be required to subscribe their adherence to a new master. There were now but five of them, one of them having been but quite lately carried to his rest,—but five of the full number, which had hitherto been twelve, and which was now to be raised to twenty-four, including women. Of these old Bunce, who for many years had been the favourite of the late warden, was one; and Abel Handy, who had been the humble means of driving that warden from his home, was another.

Mr. Harding now resolved that he himself would introduce the new warden to the hospital. He felt that many circumstances might conspire to make the men receive Mr. Quiverful with aversion and disrespect; he felt also that Mr. Quiverful might himself feel some qualms of conscience if he entered the hospital with an idea that he did so in hostility to his predecessor. Mr. Harding therefore determined to walk in, arm in arm with Mr. Quiverful, and to ask from these men their respectful obedience to their new master.

On returning to Barchester, he found that Mr. Quiverful had not yet slept in the hospital house, or entered on his new duties. He accordingly made known to that gentleman his wishes, and his proposition was not rejected.

It was a bright clear morning, though in November, that Mr. Harding and Mr. Quiverful, arm in arm, walked through the hospital gate. It was one trait in our old friend's character that he did nothing with parade. He omitted, even in the more important doings of his life, that sort of parade by which most of us deem it necessary to grace our important doings. We have housewarmings, christenings, and gala days; we keep, if not our own birthdays, those of our children; we are apt to fuss ourselves if called upon to change our residences, and have, almost all of us, our little state occasions. Mr. Harding had no state occasions. When he left his old house, he went forth from it with the same quiet composure as though he were merely taking his daily walk; and now that he re-entered it with another warden under his wing, he did so with the same quiet step and calm demeanour. He was a little less upright than he had been five years, nay, it was now nearly six years ago; he walked perhaps a little slower; his footfall was perhaps a thought less firm; otherwise one might have said that he was merely returning with a friend under his arm.

This friendliness was everything to Mr. Quiverful. To him, even in his poverty, the thought that he was supplanting a brother clergyman so kind and courteous as Mr. Harding, had been very bitter. Under his circumstances it had been impossible for him to refuse the proffered boon; he could not reject the bread that was offered to his children, or refuse to ease the heavy burden that had so long oppressed that poor wife of his; nevertheless, it had been very grievous to him to think that in going to the hospital he might encounter the ill will of his brethren in the diocese. All this Mr. Harding had fully comprehended. It was for such feelings as these, for the nice comprehension of such motives, that his heart and intellect were peculiarly fitted. In most matters of worldly import the archdeacon set down his father-in-law as little better than a fool. And perhaps he was right. But in some other matters, equally important if they be rightly judged, Mr. Harding, had he been so minded, might with as much propriety have set down his son-in-law for a fool. Few men, however, are constituted as was Mr. Harding. He had that nice appreciation of the feelings of others which belongs of right exclusively to women.

Arm in arm they walked into the inner quadrangle of the building, and there the five old men met them. Mr. Harding shook hands with them all, and then Mr. Quiverful did the same. With Bunce Mr. Harding shook hands twice, and Mr. Quiverful was about to repeat the same ceremony, but the old man gave him no encouragement.

'I am very glad to know that at last you have a new warden,' said Mr. Harding in a very cheery voice.

'We be very old for any change,' said one of them; 'but we do suppose it be all for the best.'

'Certainly—certainly it is for the best,' said Mr. Harding. 'You will again have a clergyman of your own church under the same roof with you, and a very excellent clergyman you will have. It is a great satisfaction to me to know that so good a man is coming to take care of you, and that it is no stranger, but a friend of my own, who will allow me from time to time to come in and see you.'

'We be very thankful to your reverence,' said another of them.

'I need not tell you, my good friends,' said Mr. Quiverful, 'how extremely grateful I am to Mr. Harding for his kindness to me,—I must say his uncalled for, unexpected kindness.'

'He be always very kind,' said a third.

'What I can do to fill the void which he left here, I will do. For your sake and my own I will do so, and especially for his sake. But to you who have known him, I can never be the same well-loved friend and father that he has been.'

'No, sir, no,' said old Bunce, who hitherto had held his

peace; ' no one can be that. Not if the new bishop sent
a hangel to us out of heaven. We doesn't doubt you'll
do your best, sir, but you'll not be like the old master;
not to us old ones.'

' Fie, Bunce, fie ! how dare you talk in that way ? ' said
Mr. Harding ; but as he scolded the old man he still held
him by his arm, and pressed it with warm affection.

There was no getting up any enthusiasm in the matter.
How could five old men tottering away to their final
resting-place be enthusiastic on the reception of a stranger?
What could Mr. Quiverful be to them, or they to Mr.
Quiverful ? Had Mr. Harding indeed come back to them,
some last flicker of joyous light might have shone forth on
their aged cheeks ; but it was in vain to bid them rejoice
because Mr. Quiverful was about to move his fourteen
children from Puddingdale into the hospital house. In
reality they did no doubt receive advantage, spiritual as
well as corporal ; but this they could neither anticipate
nor acknowledge.

It was a dull affair enough, this introduction of Mr.
Quiverful ; but still it had its effect. The good which
Mr. Harding intended did not fall to the ground. All the
Barchester world, including the five old bedesmen, treated
Mr. Quiverful with the more respect, because Mr. Harding
had thus walked in arm in arm with him, on his first
entrance to his duties.

And here in their new abode we will leave Mr. and Mrs.
Quiverful and their fourteen children. May they enjoy
the good things which Providence has at length given to
them !

CHAPTER LIII

CONCLUSION

THE end of a novel, like the end of a children's dinner-
party, must be made up of sweetmeats and sugar-plums.
There is now nothing else to be told but the gala doings of
Mr. Arabin's marriage, nothing more to be described than
the wedding dresses, no further dialogue to be recorded
than that which took place between the archdeacon who
married them, and Mr. Arabin and Eleanor who were
married. ' Wilt thou have this woman to thy wedded wife,'
and ' Wilt thou have this man to thy wedded husband, to

live together according to God's ordinance ? ' Mr. Arabin
and Eleanor each answered, ' I will.' We have no doubt
that they will keep their promises ; the more especially
as the Signora Neroni had left Barchester before the
ceremony was performed.

Mrs. Bold had been somewhat more than two years
a widow before she was married to her second husband,
and little Johnnie was then able with due assistance to
walk on his own legs into the drawing-room to receive the
salutations of the assembled guests. Mr. Harding gave
away the bride, the archdeacon performed the service,
and the two Miss Grantlys, who were joined in their
labours by other young ladies of the neighbourhood,
performed the duties of bridesmaids with equal diligence
and grace. Mrs. Grantly superintended the breakfast
and bouquets, and Mary Bold distributed the cards and
cake. The archdeacon's three sons had also come home
for the occasion. The eldest was great with learning, being
regarded by all who knew him as a certain future double
first. The second, however, bore the palm on this occasion,
being resplendent in a new uniform. The third was just
entering the university, and was probably the proudest
of the three.

But the most remarkable feature in the whole occasion
was the excessive liberality of the archdeacon. He literally
made presents to everybody. As Mr. Arabin had already
moved out of the parsonage of St. Ewold's, that scheme
of elongating the dining-room was of course abandoned ;
but he would have refurnished the whole deanery had he
been allowed. He sent down a magnificent piano by
Erard, gave Mr. Arabin a cob which any dean in the land
might have been proud to bestride, and made a special
present to Eleanor of a new pony chair that had gained
a prize in the Exhibition. Nor did he even stay his hand
here ; he bought a set of cameos for his wife, and a sapphire
bracelet for Miss Bold ; showered pearls and workboxes
on his daughters, and to each of his sons he presented
a cheque for 20l. On Mr. Harding he bestowed a magnificent violoncello with all the new-fashioned arrangements
and expensive additions, which, on account of these
novelties, that gentleman could never use with satisfaction
to his audience or pleasure to himself.

Those who knew the archdeacon well, perfectly understood the cause of his extravagance. 'Twas thus that he sang his song of triumph over Mr. Slope. This was his pæan, his hymn of thanksgiving, his loud oration. He had girded himself with his sword, and gone forth to the war ; now he was returning from the field laden with the spoils of the foe. The cob and the cameos, the violoncello and the pianoforte, were all as it were trophies reft from the tent of his now conquered enemy.

The Arabins after their marriage went abroad for a couple of months, according to the custom in such matters now duly established, and then commenced their deanery life under good auspices. And nothing can be more pleasant than the present arrangement of ecclesiastical affairs in Barchester. The titular bishop never interfered, and Mrs. Proudie not often. Her sphere is more extended, more noble, and more suited to her ambition than that of a cathedral city. As long as she can do what she pleases with the diocese, she is willing to leave the dean and chapter to themselves. Mr. Slope tried his hand at subverting the old-established customs of the close, and from his failure she has learnt experience. The burly chancellor and the meagre little prebendary are not teased by any application respecting Sabbath-day schools, the dean is left to his own dominions, and the intercourse between Mrs. Proudie and Mrs. Arabin is confined to a yearly dinner given by each to the other. At these dinners Dr. Grantly will not take a part ; but he never fails to ask for and receive a full account of all that Mrs. Proudie either does or says.

His ecclesiastical authority has been greatly shorn since the palmy days in which he reigned supreme as mayor of the palace to his father, but nevertheless such authority as is now left to him he can enjoy without interference. He can walk down the High Street of Barchester without feeling that those who see him are comparing his claims with those of Mr. Slope. The intercourse between Plumstead and the deanery is of the most constant and familiar description. Since Eleanor has been married to a clergyman, and especially to a dignitary of the church, Mrs. Grantly has found many more points of sympathy with her sister ; and on a coming occasion, which is much looked forward to by all parties, she intends to spend a month or two at the deanery. She never thought of spending a month in Barchester when little Johnny Bold was born !

The two sisters do not quite agree on matters of church doctrine, though their differences are of the most amicable description. Mr. Arabin's church is two degrees higher than that of Mrs. Grantly. This may seem strange to those who will remember that Eleanor was once accused of partiality to Mr. Slope ; but it is no less the fact. She likes her husband's silken vest, she likes his adherence to the rubric, she specially likes the eloquent philosophy of his sermons, and she likes the red letters in her own prayer-book. It must not be presumed that she has a taste for candles, or that she is at all astray about the real presence ; but she has an inkling that way. She sent a handsome subscription towards certain very heavy ecclesiastical legal expenses which have lately been incurred in Bath, her name of course not appearing ; she assumes a smile of gentle ridicule when the Archbishop of Canterbury is named, and she has put up a memorial window in the cathedral.

Mrs. Grantly, who belongs to the high and dry church, the high church as it was some fifty years since, before tracts were written and young clergymen took upon themselves the highly meritorious duty of cleaning churches, rather laughs at her sister. She shrugs her shoulders, and tells Miss Thorne that she supposes Eleanor will have an oratory in the deanery before she has done. But she is not on that account a whit displeased. A few high church vagaries do not, she thinks, sit amiss on the shoulders of a young dean's wife. It shows at any rate that her heart is in the subject ; and it shows moreover that she is removed, wide as the poles asunder, from that cesspool of abomination in which it was once suspected that she would wallow and grovel. Anathema maranatha ! Let anything else be held as blessed, so that that be well cursed. Welcome kneelings and bowings, welcome matins and complines, welcome bell, book, and candle, so that Mr. Slope's dirty surplices and ceremonial Sabbaths be held in due execration !

If it be essentially and absolutely necessary to choose between the two, we are inclined to agree with Mrs.

Grantly that the bell, book, and candle are the lesser evil
of the two. Let it however be understood that no such
necessity is admitted in these pages.

Dr. Arabin (we suppose he must have become a doctor
when he became a dean) is more moderate and less outspoken on doctrinal points than his wife, as indeed in his
station it behoves him to be. He is a studious, thoughtful,
hard-working man. He lives constantly at the deanery,
and preaches nearly every Sunday. His time is spent in
sifting and editing old ecclesiastical literature, and in producing the same articles new. At Oxford he is generally
regarded as the most promising clerical ornament of the
age. He and his wife live together in perfect mutual
confidence. There is but one secret in her bosom which
he has not shared. He has never yet learned how Mr.
Slope had his ears boxed.

The Stanhopes soon found that Mr. Slope's power need
no longer operate to keep them from the delight of their
Italian villa. Before Eleanor's marriage they had all
migrated back to the shores of Como. They had not been
resettled long before the signora received from Mrs.
Arabin a very pretty though very short epistle, in which
she was informed of the fate of the writer. This letter
was answered by another, bright, charming, and witty,
as the signora's letters always were; and so ended the
friendship between Eleanor and the Stanhopes.

One word of Mr. Harding, and we have done.

He is still Precentor of Barchester, and still pastor of
the little church of St. Cuthbert's. In spite of what he has
so often said himself, he is not even yet an old man. He
does such duties as fall to his lot well and conscientiously,
and is thankful that he has never been tempted to assume
others for which he might be less fitted.

The Author now leaves him in the hands of his readers;
not as a hero, not as a man to be admired and talked of,
not as a man who should be toasted at public dinners and
spoken of with conventional absurdity as a perfect divine,
but as a good man without guile, believing humbly in the
religion which he has striven to teach, and guided by the
precepts which he has striven to learn.

THE END

BOOK 3

An Eye for an Eye

CHAPTER I

SCROOPE MANOR

SOME YEARS ago it matters not how many, the old Earl of Scroope lived at Scroope Manor in Dorsetshire. The house was an Elizabethan structure of some pretensions, but of no fame. It was not known to sight-seers, as are so many of the residences of our nobility and country gentlemen. No days in the week were appointed for visiting its glories, nor was the housekeeper supposed to have a good thing in perquisites from showing it. It was a large brick building facing on to the village street—facing the village, if the hall-door of a house be the main characteristic of its face; but with a front on to its own grounds from which opened the windows of the chief apartments. The village of Scroope consisted of a straggling street a mile in length, with the church and parsonage at one end, and the Manor-house almost at the other. But the church stood within the park; and on that side of the street, for more than half its length, the high, gloomy wall of the Earl's domain stretched along in face of the publicans, bakers, grocers, two butchers, and retired private residents whose almost contiguous houses made Scroope itself seem to be more than a village to strangers. Close to the Manor and again near to the church, some favoured few had been allowed to build houses and to cultivate small gardens taken, as it were, in notches out of the Manor grounds; but these tenements must have been built at a time in which landowners were very much less jealous than they are now of such encroachments from their humbler neighbours.

The park itself was large, and the appendages to it such as were fit for an Earl's establishment—but there was little about it that was attractive. The land lay flat, and the timber,

697

which was very plentiful, had not been made to group itself
in picturesque forms. There was the Manor wood, containing some five hundred acres, lying beyond the church and far
back from the road, intersected with so-called drives, which
were unfit for any wheels but those of timber waggons—and
round the whole park there was a broad belt of trees. Here
and there about the large enclosed spaces there stood solitary
oaks, in which the old Earl took pride; but at Scroope Manor
there was none of that finished landscape beauty of which the
owners of 'places' in England are so justly proud.

The house was large, and the rooms were grand and
spacious. There was an enormous hall into one corner of
which the front door opened. There was a vast library filled
with old books which no one ever touched,—huge volumes of
antiquated and now all but useless theology, and folio
editions of the least known classics,—such as men now never
read. Not a book had been added to it since the commencement of the century, and it may almost be said that no book
had been drawn from its shelves for real use during the same
period. There was a suite of rooms—salon with two with-
drawing rooms which now were never opened. The big dining-room was used occasionally, as, in accordance with the
traditions of the family, dinner was served there whenever
there were guests at the Manor. Guests, indeed, at Scroope
Manor were not very frequent—but Lady Scroope did
occasionally have a friend or two to stay with her; and at long
intervals the country clergymen and neighbouring squires
were asked, with their wives, to dinner. When the Earl and
his Countess were alone they used a small breakfast parlour,
and between this and the big dining-room there was the little
chamber in which the Countess usually lived. The Earl's own
room was at the back, or if the reader pleases, front of the
house, near the door leading into the street, and was, of all
rooms in the house, the gloomiest.

The atmosphere of the whole place was gloomy. There
were none of those charms of modern creation which now
make the mansions of the wealthy among us bright and

joyous. There was not a billiard table in the house. There
was no conservatory nearer than the large old-fashioned
greenhouse, which stood away by the kitchen garden and
which seemed to belong exclusively to the gardener. The
papers on the walls were dark and sombre. The mirrors were
small and lustreless. The carpets were old and dingy. The
windows did not open on to the terrace. The furniture was
hardly ancient, but yet antiquated and uncomfortable.
Throughout the house, and indeed throughout the estate,
there was sufficient evidence of wealth; and there certainly
was no evidence of parsimony; but at Scroope Manor money
seemed never to have produced luxury. The household was
very large. There was a butler, and a housekeeper, and
various footmen, and a cook with large wages, and maidens in
tribes to wait upon each other, and a colony of gardeners, and
a coachman, and a head-groom, and under-grooms. All these
lived well under the old Earl, and knew the value of their
privileges. There was much to get, and almost nothing to do.
A servant might live for ever at Scroope Manor,—if only sufficiently submissive to Mrs. Bunce the house-keeper. There
was certainly no parsimony at the Manor, but the luxurious
living of the household was confined to the servants' de-
partment.

To a stranger, and perhaps also to the inmates, the idea of
gloom about the place was greatly increased by the absence
of any garden or lawn near the house. Immediately in front
of the mansion, and between it and the park, there ran two
broad gravel terraces, one above another; and below these the
deer would come and browse. To the left of the house, at
nearly a quarter of a mile from it, there was a very large
garden indeed—flower-gardens, and kitchen-gardens, and
orchards; all ugly, and old-fashioned, but producing excellent crops in their kind. But they were away, and were not
seen. Cut flowers were occasionally brought into the house—
but the place was never filled with flowers as country houses
are filled with them now-a-days. No doubt had Lady Scroope
wished for more she might have had more.

Scroope itself, though a large village, stood a good deal out
of the world. Within the last year or two a railway has been
opened, with a Scroope Road Station, not above three miles
from the place; but in the old lord's time it was eleven miles
from its nearest station, at Dorchester, with which it had communication once a day by an omnibus. Unless a man had
business with Scroope nothing would take him there; and
very few people had business with Scroope. Now and then a
commercial traveller would visit the place with but faint
hopes as to trade. A post-office inspector once in twelve
months would call upon plethoric old Mrs. Applejohn, who
kept the small shop for stationery, and was known as the post-
mistress. The two sons of the vicar, Mr. Greenmarsh, would
pass backwards and forwards between their father's vicarage
and Malbro' school.* And occasionally the men and women of
Scroope would make a journey to their county town. But the
Earl was told that old Mrs. Brock of the Scroope Arms could
not keep the omnibus on the road unless he would subscribe
to aid it. Of course he subscribed. If he had been told by his
steward to subscribe to keep the cap on Mrs. Brock's head, he
would have done so. Twelve pounds a year his Lordship paid
towards the omnibus, and Scroope was not absolutely dissevered from the world.

The Earl himself was never seen out of his own domain,
except when he attended church. This he did twice every
Sunday in the year, the coachman driving him there in the
morning and the head-groom in the afternoon. Throughout
the household it was known to be the Earl's request to his
servants that they would attend divine service at least once
every Sunday. None were taken into service but they who
were or called themselves members of the Church Establishment. It is hardly probable that many dissenters threw away
the chance of such promotion on any frivolous pretext of
religion. Beyond this request, which, coming from the mouth
of Mrs. Bunce, became very imperative, the Earl hardly ever
interfered with his domestics. His own valet had attended
him for the last thirty years; but, beyond his valet and the

butler, he hardly knew the face of one of them. There was a
gamekeeper at Scroope Manor, with two under-gamekeepers;
and yet, for some years, no one, except the gamekeepers, had
ever shot over the lands. Some partridges and a few pheasants
were, however, sent into the house when Mrs. Bunce, moved
to wrath, would speak her mind on that subject.

The Earl of Scroope himself was a tall, thin man, something over seventy at the time of which I will now begin to
speak. His shoulders were much bent, but otherwise he
appeared to be younger than his age. His hair was nearly
white, but his eyes were still bright, and the handsome well-
cut features of his fine face were not reduced to shapeless-
ness by any of the ravages of time, as is so often the case with
men who are infirm as well as old. Were it not for the long
and heavy eyebrows, which gave something of severity to his
face, and for that painful stoop in his shoulders, he might
still have been accounted a handsome man. In youth he had
been a very handsome man, and had shone forth in the world,
popular, beloved and respected, with all the good things the
world could give. The first blow upon him was the death of
his wife. That hurt him sorely, but it did not quite crush him.
Then his only daughter died also, just as she became a bride.
High as the Lady Blanche Neville had stood herself, she had
married almost above her rank, and her father's heart had
been full of joy and pride. But she had perished childless,—
in child-birth, and again he was hurt almost to death. There
was still left to him a son—a youth indeed thoughtless, lavish,
and prone to evil pleasures. But thought would come with
the years; for almost any lavishness there were means sufficient; and evil pleasures might cease to entice. The young
Lord Neville was all that was left to the Earl, and for his heir
he paid debts and forgave injuries. The young man would
marry and all might be well. Then he found a bride for his
boy—with no wealth, but owning the best blood in the kingdom, beautiful, good, one who might be to him as another
daughter. His boy's answer was that he was already married!
He had chosen his wife from out of the streets,* and offered to

the Earl of Scroope as a child to replace the daughter who had gone, a wretched painted prostitute from France. After that Lord Scroope never again held up his head.

The father would not see his heir,—and never saw him again. As to what money might be needed, the lawyers in London were told to manage that. The Earl himself would give nothing and refuse nothing. When there were debts— debts for the second time, debts for the third time, the lawyers were instructed to do what in their own eyes seemed good to them. They might pay as long as they deemed it right to pay, but they might not name Lord Neville to his father.

While things were thus the Earl married again—the penniless daughter of a noble house—a woman not young, for she was forty when he married her, but more than twenty years his junior. It sufficed for him that she was noble, and as he believed good. Good to him she was—with a duty that was almost excessive. Religious she was, and self-denying; giving much and demanding little; keeping herself in the background, but possessing wonderful energy in the service of others. Whether she could in truth be called good the reader may say when he has finished this story.

Then, when the Earl had been married some three years to his second wife, the heir died. He died, and as far as Scroope Manor was concerned there was an end of him and of the creature he had called his wife. An annuity was purchased for her. That she should be entitled to call herself Lady Neville while she lived, was the sad necessity of the condition. It was understood by all who came near the Earl that no one was to mention her within his hearing. He was thankful that no heir had come from that most horrid union. The woman was never mentioned to him again, nor need she trouble us further in the telling of our chronicle.

But when Lord Neville died, it was necessary that the old man should think of his new heir. Alas; in that family, though there was much that was good and noble, there had ever been intestine feuds—causes of quarrel in which each party would be sure that he was right. They were a people who thought much of the church, who were good to the poor, who strove to be noble—but they could not forgive injuries. They could not forgive even when there were no injuries. The present Earl had quarrelled with his brother in early life—and had therefore quarrelled with all that had belonged to the brother. The brother was now gone, leaving two sons behind him—two young Nevilles, Fred and Jack, of whom Fred, the eldest, was now the heir. It was at last settled that Fred should be sent for to Scroope Manor. Fred came, being at that time a lieutenant in a cavalry regiment—a fine handsome youth of five and twenty, with the Neville eyes and Neville finely cut features. Kindly letters passed between the widowed mother and the present Lady Scroope; and it was decided at last, at his own request, that he should remain one year longer in the army, and then be installed as the eldest son at Scroope Manor. Again the lawyer was told to do what was proper in regard to money.

A few words more must be said of Lady Scroope, and then the preface to our story will be over. She too was an Earl's daughter, and had been much loved by our Earl's first wife. Lady Scroope had been the elder by ten years; but yet they had been dear friends, and Lady Mary Wycombe had passed many months of her early life amidst the gloom of the great rooms at Scroope Manor. She had thus known the Earl well before she consented to marry him. She had never possessed beauty—and hardly grace. She was strong featured, tall, with pride clearly written in her face. A reader of faces would have declared at once that she was proud of the blood which ran in her veins. She was very proud of her blood, and did in truth believe that noble birth was a greater gift than any wealth. She was thoroughly able to look down upon a parvenu millionaire—to look down upon such a one and not to pretend to despise him. When the Earl's letter came to her asking her to share his gloom, she was as poor as Charity —dependent on a poor brother who hated the burden of such claim. But she would have wedded no commoner, let his wealth and age have been as they might. She knew Lord

Scroope's age, and she knew the gloom of Scroope Manor; and she became his wife. To her of course was told the story of the heir's marriage, and she knew that she could expect no light, no joy in the old house from the scions of the rising family. But now all this was changed, and it might be that she could take the new heir to her heart.

CHAPTER II

FRED NEVILLE

WHEN FRED NEVILLE first came to the Manor, the old Earl trembled when called upon to receive him. Of the lad he had heard almost nothing—of his appearance literally nothing. It might be that his heir would be meanly visaged, a youth of whom he would have cause to be ashamed, one from whose countenance no sign of high blood would shine out; or, almost worse, he also might have that look, half of vanity, and half of vice, of which the father had gradually become aware in his own son, and which in him had degraded the Neville beauty. But Fred, to look at, was a gallant fellow—such a youth as women love to see about a house—well-made, active, quick, self-asserting, fair-haired, blue-eyed, short-lipped, with small whiskers, thinking but little of his own personal advantages, but thinking much of his own way. As far as the appearance of the young man went the Earl could not but be satisfied. And to him, at any rate in this, the beginning of their connexion, Fred Neville was modest and submissive.

'You are welcome to Scroope,' said the old man, receiving him with stately urbanity in the middle of the hall.

'I am so much obliged to you, uncle,' he said.

'You are come to me as a son, my boy—as a son. It will be your own fault if you are not a son to us in everything.'

Then in lieu of further words there shone a tear in each of the young man's eyes, much more eloquent to the Earl than could have been any words. He put his arm over his nephew's shoulders, and in this guise walked with him into the room in which Lady Scroope was awaiting them.

'Mary,' he said to his wife, 'here is our heir. Let him be a son to us.'

Then Lady Scroope took the young man in her arms and kissed him. Thus auspiciously was commenced this new connexion.

The arrival was in September, and the gamekeeper, with the under gamekeeper, had for the last month been told to be on his mettle. Young Mr. Neville was no doubt a sportsman. And the old groom had been warned that hunters might be wanted in the stables next winter. Mrs. Bunce was made to understand that liberties would probably be taken with the house, such as had not yet been perpetrated in her time —for the late heir had never made the Manor his home from the time of his leaving school. It was felt by all that great changes were to be effected—and it was felt also that the young man on whose behalf all this was to be permitted, could not but be elated by his position. Of such elation, however, there were not many signs. To his uncle, Fred Neville was, as has been said, modest and submissive; to his aunt he was gentle but not submissive. The rest of the household he treated civilly, but with none of that awe which was perhaps expected from him. As for shooting, he had come direct from his friend Carnaby's moor. Carnaby had forest as well as moor, and Fred thought but little of partridges—little of such old-fashioned partridge-shooting as was prepared for him at Scroope—after grouse and deer. As for hunting in Dorsetshire, if his uncle wished it—why in that case he would think of it. According to his ideas, Dorsetshire was not the best county in England for hunting. Last year his regiment had been at Bristol and he had ridden with the Duke's hounds.* This winter he was to be stationed in Ireland, and he had an idea that Irish hunting was good. If he found that his uncle made a point of it, he would bring his horses to Scroope for a month at Christmas. Thus he spoke to the head groom— and thus he spoke also to his aunt, who felt some surprise when he talked of Scotland*and his horses. She had thought that only men of large fortunes shot deer and kept studs— and perhaps conceived that the officers of the 20th Hussars*

were generally engaged in looking after the affairs of their
regiment, and in preparation for meeting the enemy.

Fred now remained a month at Scroope, and during that
time there was but little personal intercourse between him
and his uncle in spite of the affectionate greeting with which
their acquaintance had been commenced. The old man's
habits of life were so confirmed that he could not bring himself to alter them. Throughout the entire morning he would
sit in his own room alone. He would then be visited by his
steward, his groom, and his butler—and would think that
he gave his orders, submitting, however, in almost everything
to them. His wife would sometimes sit with him for half an
hour, holding his hand, in moments of tenderness unseen
and unsuspected by all the world around them. Sometimes
the clergyman of the parish would come to him, so that he
might know the wants of the people. He would have the
newspaper in his hands for a while, and would daily read the
Bible for an hour. Then he would slowly write some letter,
almost measuring every point which his pen made—thinking
that thus he was performing his duty as a man of business.
Few men perhaps did less—but what he did do was good;
and of self-indulgence there was surely none. Between such a
one and the young man who had now come to his house there
could be but little real connexion.

Between Fred Neville and Lady Scroope there arose a
much closer intimacy. A woman can get nearer to a young
man than can any old man—can learn more of his ways, and
better understand his wishes. From the very first there arose
between them a matter of difference, as to which there was
no quarrel, but very much of argument. In that argument
Lady Scroope was unable to prevail. She was very anxious
that the heir should at once abandon his profession and sell
out of the army. Of what use could it be to him now to run
after his regiment to Ireland, seeing that undoubtedly the
great duties of his life all centred at Scroope? There were
many discussions on the subject, but Fred would not give
way in regard to the next year. He would have this year, he

said, to himself—and after that he would come and settle himself at Scroope. Yes; no doubt he would marry as soon as he could find a fitting wife. Of course it would be right that he should marry. He fully understood the responsibilities of his position—so he said, in answer to his aunt's eager, scrutinising, beseeching questions. But as he had joined his regiment, he thought it would 'be good for him to remain with it one year longer. He particularly desired to see something of Ireland, and if he did not do so now, he would never have the opportunity. Lady Scroope, understanding well that he was pleading for a year of grace from the dullness of the Manor, explained to him that his uncle would by no means expect that he should remain always at Scroope. If he would marry, the old London house should be prepared for him and his bride. He might travel—not, however, going very far afield. He might get into Parliament; as to which, if such were his ambition, his uncle would give him every aid. He might have his friends at Scroope Manor—Carnaby and all the rest of them. Every allurement was offered to him. But he had commenced by claiming a year of grace, and to that claim he adhered.

Could his uncle have brought himself to make the request in person, at first, he might probably have succeeded; and had he succeeded, there would have been no story for us as to the fortunes of Scroope Manor. But the Earl was too proud and perhaps too diffident to make the attempt. From his wife he heard all that took place; and though he was grieved, he expressed no anger. He could not feel himself justified in expressing anger because his nephew chose to remain for yet a year attached to his profession.

'Who knows what may happen to him?' said the Countess.

'Ah, indeed! But we are all in the hands of the Almighty.' And the Earl bowed his head. Lady Scroope, fully recognizing the truth of her husband's pious ejaculation, neverthless thought that human care might advantageously be added to the divine interposition for which, as she well knew, her lord prayed fervently as soon as the words were out of his mouth.

'But it would be so great a thing if he could be settled.
Sophia Mellerby has promised to come here for a couple of
months in the winter. He could not possibly do better than
that.'

'The Mellerbys are very good people,' said the Earl. 'Her
grandmother, the duchess, is one of the very best women in
England. Her mother, Lady Sophia, is an excellent creature
—religious, and with the soundest principles. Mr. Mellerby,
as a commoner, stands as high as any man in England.'

'They have held the same property since the wars of the
roses. And then I suppose the money should count for something,' added the lady.

Lord Scroope would not admit the importance of the
money, but was quite willing to acknowledge that were his
heir to make Sophia Mellerby the future Lady Scroope he
would be content. But he could not interfere. He did not
think it wise to speak to young men on such a subject. He
thought that by doing so a young man might be rather
diverted from than attracted to the object in view. Nor would
he press his wishes upon his nephew as to next year. 'Were
I to ask it,' he said, 'and were he to refuse me, I should be
hurt. I am bound therefore to ask nothing that is unreasonable.'

Lady Scroope did not quite agree with her husband in this.
She thought that as every thing was to be done for the young
man; as money almost without stint was to be placed at his
command; as hunting, parliament, and a house in London
were offered to him—as the treatment due to a dear and only
son was shown to him, he ought to give something in return;
but she herself, could say no more than she had said, and
she knew already that in those few matters in which her
husband had a decided will, he was not to be turned from it.

It was arranged, therefore, that Fred Neville should join
his regiment at Limerick in October, and that he should
come home to Scroope for a fortnight or three weeks at
Christmas. Sophia Mellerby was to be Lady Scroope's guest
at that time, and at last it was decided that Mrs. Neville, who

had never been seen by the Earl, should be asked to come
and bring with her her younger son, John Neville, who had
been successful in obtaining a commission in the Engineers.
Other guests should be invited, and an attempt should be
made to remove the mantle of gloom from Scroope Manor—
with the sole object of ingratiating the heir.

Early in October Fred went to Limerick, and from thence
with a detached troop of his regiment he was sent to the
cavalry barracks at Ennis, the assize town of the neighbouring county Clare. This was at first held to be a misfortune by
him, as Limerick is in all respects a better town than Ennis,
and in county Limerick the hunting is far from being bad,
whereas Clare is hardly a country for a Nimrod. But a young
man, with money at command, need not regard distances;
and the Limerick balls and the Limerick coverts were found
to be equally within reach. From Ennis also he could attend
some of the Galway meets—and then with no other superior
than a captain hardly older than himself to interfere with his
movements, he could indulge in that wild district the spirit
of adventure which was strong within him. When young men
are anxious to indulge the spirit of adventure, they generally
do so by falling in love with young women of whom their
fathers and mothers would not approve. In these days a spirit
of adventure hardly goes further than this, unless it take a
young man to a German gambling table.*

When Fred left Scroope it was understood that he was to
correspond with his aunt. The Earl would have been utterly
lost had he attempted to write a letter to his nephew without
having something special to communicate to him. But Lady
Scroope was more facile with her pen, and it was rightly
thought that the heir would hardly bring himself to look
upon Scroope as his home, unless some link were maintained
between himself and the place. Lady Scroope therefore wrote
once a week—telling everything that there was to be told
of the horses, the game, and even of the tenants. She studied
her letters, endeavouring to make them light and agreeable
—such as a young man of large prospects would like to

receive from his own mother. He was 'Dearest Fred,' and in one of those earliest written she expressed a hope that should any trouble ever fall upon him he would come to her as to his dearest friend. Fred was not a bad correspondent, and answered about every other letter. His replies were short, but that was a matter of course. He was 'as jolly as a sandboy,' 'right as a trivet'; had had 'one or two very good things,' and thought that upon the whole he liked Ennis better than Limerick. 'Johnstone is such a deuced good fellow!' Johnstone was the captain of the 20th Hussars who happened to be stationed with him at Limerick. Lady Scroope did not quite like the epithet, but she knew that she had to learn to hear things to which she had hitherto not been accustomed.

This was all very well—but Lady Scroope, having a friend in Co. Clare, thought that she might receive tidings of the adopted one which would be useful, and with this object she opened a correspondence with Lady Mary Quin. Lady Mary Quin was a daughter of the Earl of Kilfenora, and was well acquainted with all County Clare. She was almost sure to hear of the doings of any officers stationed at Ennis, and would do so certainly in regard to an officer that was specially introduced to her. Fred Neville was invited to stay at Castle Quin as long as he pleased, and actually did pass one night under its roof. But, unfortunately for him, that spirit of adventure which he was determined to indulge led him into the neighbourhood of Castle Quin when it was far from his intention to interfere with the Earl or with Lady Mary, and thus led to the following letter which Lady Scroope received about the middle of December—just a week before Fred's return to the Manor.

QUIN CASTLE, ENNISTIMON,
14 December, 18——.

'MY DEAR LADY SCROOPE,

'Since I wrote to you before Mr. Neville has been here once, and we all liked him very much. My father was quite taken with him. He is always fond of the young officers, and is not the less inclined to be so of one who is so dear and near

to you. I wish he would have stayed longer, and hope that he
shall come again. We have not much to offer in the way of
amusement, but in January and February there is good snipe
shooting.

'I find that Mr. Neville is very fond of shooting—so much
so that before we knew anything of him except his name we
had heard that he had been on our coast after seals and sea
birds. We have very high cliffs near here—some people say
the highest in the world, and there is one called the Hag's
Head from which men get down and shoot sea-gulls. He has
been different times in our village of Liscannor, and I think
he has a boat there or at Lahinch. I believe he has already
killed ever so many seals.

'I tell you all this for a reason. I hope that it may come
to nothing, but I think that you ought to know. There is a
widow lady living not very far from Liscannor, but nearer up
to the cliffs. Her cottage is on papa's property, but I think she
holds it from somebody else. I don't like to say anything to
papa about it. Her name is Mrs. O'Hara, and she has a
daughter.'

When Lady Scroope had read so far, she almost let the
paper drop from her hand. Of course she knew what it all
meant. An Irish Miss O'Hara! And Fred Neville was spending his time in pursuit of this girl! Lady Scroope had known
what it would be when the young man was allowed to return
to his regiment in spite of the manifold duties which should
have bound him to Scroope Manor.

'I have seen this young lady,' continued Lady Mary, 'and
she is certainly very pretty. But nobody knows anything
about them; and I cannot even learn whether they belong
to the real O'Haras. I should think not, as they are Roman
Catholics. At any rate Miss O'Hara can hardly be a fitting
companion for Lord Scroope's heir. I believe they are ladies,
but I don't think that any one knows them here, except the
priest of Kilmacrenny. We never could make out quite why
they came here—only that Father Marty knows something
about them. He is the priest of Kilmacrenny. She is a very

pretty girl, and I never heard a word against her—but I don't know whether that does not make it worse, because a young man is so likely to get entangled.

'I daresay nothing shall come of it, and I'm sure I hope that nothing may. But I thought it best to tell you. *Pray* do not let him know that you have heard from me. Young men are so very particular about things, and I don't know what he might say of me if he knew that I had written home to you about his private affairs. All the same if I can be of any service to you, pray let me know. Excuse haste. And believe me to be,

Yours most sincerely,
MARY QUIN.'

A Roman Catholic—one whom no one knew but the priest —a girl who perhaps never had a father! All this was terrible to Lady Scroope. Roman Catholics—and especially Irish Roman Catholics—were people whom, as she thought, every one should fear in this world, and for whom everything was to be feared in the next. How would it be with the Earl if this heir also were to tell him some day that he was married? Would not his grey hairs be brought to the grave with a double load of sorrow? However, for the present she thought it better to say not a word to the Earl.

CHAPTER III

SOPHIE MELLERBY

LADY SCROOPE thought a great deal about her friend's communication, but at last made up her mind that she could do nothing till Fred should have returned. Indeed she hardly knew what she could do when he did come back. The more she considered it the greater seemed to her to be the difficulty of doing anything. How is a woman, how is even a mother, to caution a young man against the danger of becoming acquainted with a pretty girl? She could not mention Miss O'Hara's name without mentioning that of Lady Mary Quin in connexion with it. And when asked, as of course she would be asked, as to her own information what could she say? She had been told that he had made himself acquainted with a widow lady who had a pretty daughter, and that was all! When young men will run into such difficulties, it is, alas, so very difficult to interfere with them!

And yet the matter was of such importance as to justify almost any interference. A Roman Catholic Irish girl of whom nothing was known but that her mother was said to be a widow, was, in Lady Scroope's eyes, as formidable a danger as could come in the way of her husband's heir. Fred Neville was, she thought, with all his good qualities, exactly the man to fall in love with a wild Irish girl.* If Fred were to write home some day and say that he was about to marry such a bride—or, worse again, that he married her, the tidings would nearly kill the Earl. After all that had been endured, such a termination to the hopes of the family would be too cruel! And Lady Scroope could not but feel the injustice of it. Every thing was being done for this heir, for whom nothing need have been done. He was treated as a son, but

714

he was not a son. He was treated with exceptional favour as
a son. Everything was at his disposal. He might marry and
begin life at once with every want amply supplied, if he
would only marry such a woman as was fit to be a future
Countess of Scroope. Very little was required from him. He
was not expected to marry an heiress. An heiress indeed was
prepared for him, and would be there, ready for him at
Christmas—an heiress, beautiful, well-born, fit in every respect—religious too. But he was not to be asked to marry
Sophie Mellerby. He might choose for himself. There were
other well-born young women about the world—duchesses'
granddaughters in abundance! But it was imperative that he
should marry at least a lady, and at least a Protestant.

Lady Scroope felt very strongly that he should never have
been allowed to rejoin his regiment, when a home at Scroope
was offered to him. He was a free agent of course, and equally
of course the title and the property must ultimately be his.
But something of a bargain might have been made with him
when all the privileges of a son were offered to him. When
he was told that he might have all Scroope to himself—for it
amounted nearly to that; that he might hunt there and shoot
there and entertain his friends; that the family house in
London should be given up to him if he would marry properly; that an income almost without limit should be provided for him, surely it would not have been too much to
demand that as a matter of course he should leave the army!
But this had not been done; and now there was an Irish
Roman Catholic widow with a daughter, with sea-shooting
and a boat and high cliffs right in the young man's way!
Lady Scroope could not analyse it, but felt all the danger as
though it were by instinct. Partridge and pheasant shooting
on a gentleman's own grounds, and an occasional day's hunting with the hounds in his own county, were, in Lady
Scroope's estimation, becoming amusements for an English
gentleman. They did not interfere with the exercise of his
duties. She had by no means brought herself to like the yearly
raids into Scotland made latterly by sportsmen. But if Scotch

moors and forests were dangerous, what were Irish cliffs! Deer-stalking was bad in her imagination. She was almost sure that when men went up to Scotch forests they did not go to church on Sundays. But the idea of seal-shooting was much more horrible. And then there was that priest who was the only friend of the widow who had the daughter!

On the morning of the day in which Fred was to reach the Manor, Lady Scroope did speak to her husband. 'Don't you think, my dear, that something might be done to prevent Fred's returning to that horrid country?'

'What can we do?'

'I suppose he would wish to oblige you. You are being very good to him.'

'It is for the old to give, Mary, and for the young to accept. I do all for him because he is all to me; but what am I to him, that he should sacrifice any pleasure for me? He can break my heart. Were I even to quarrel with him, the worst I could do would be to send him to the money-lenders for a year or two.'

'But why should he care about his regiment now?'

'Because his regiment means liberty '

'And you won't ask him to give it up?'

'I think not. If I were to ask him I should expect him to yield; and then I should be disappointed were he to refuse. I do not wish him to think me a tyrant.'

This was the end of the conversation, for Lady Scroope did not as yet dare to speak to the Earl about the widow and her daughter. She must now try her skill and eloquence with the young man himself.

The young man arrived and was received with kindest greetings. Two horses had preceded him, so that he might find himself mounted as soon as he chose after his arrival, and two others were coming. This was all very well, but his aunt was a little hurt when he declared his purpose of going down to the stables just as she told him that Sophia Mellerby was in the house. He arrived on the 23rd at 4 p.m., and it had been declared that he was to hunt on the morrow. It was already dark, and surely he might have been content on the first evening of his arrival to abstain from the stables! Not a word had been said to Sophie Mellerby of Lady Scroope's future hopes. Lady Scroope and Lady Sophia would each have thought that it was wicked to do so. But the two women had been fussy, and Miss Mellerby must have been less discerning than are young ladies generally, had she not understood what was expected of her. Girls are undoubtedly better prepared to fall in love with men whom they had never seen, than are men with girls. It is a girl's great business in life to love and to be loved. Of some young men it may almost be said that it is their great business to avoid such a castastrophe. Such ought not to have been the case with Fred Neville now —but in such light he regarded it. He had already said to himself that Sophie Mellerby was to be pitched at his head. He knew no reason—none as yet—why he should not like Miss Mellerby well enough. But he was a little on his guard against her, and preferred seeing his horses first. Sophie, when according to custom, and indeed in this instance in accordance with special arrangement, she went into Lady Scroope's sitting-room for tea, was rather disappointed at not finding Mr. Neville there. She knew that he had visited his uncle immediately on his arrival, and having just come in from the park she had gone to her room to make some little preparation for the meeting. If it was written in Fate's book· that she was to be the next Lady Scroope, the meeting was important. Perhaps that writing in Fate's book might depend on the very adjustment which she was now making of her hair.

'He has gone to look at his horses,' said Lady Scroope, unable not to shew her disappointment by the tone of her voice.

'That is so natural,' said Sophie, who was more cunning. 'Young men almost idolize their horses. I should like to go and see Dandy whenever he arrives anywhere, only I don't dare!' Dandy was Miss Mellerby's own horse, and was accustomed to make journeys up and down between Mellerby and London.

'I don't think horses and guns and dogs should be too much thought of,' said Lady Scroope gravely. 'There is a tendency I think at present to give them an undue importance. When our amusements become more serious to us than our business, we must be going astray.'

'I suppose we always are going astray,' said Miss Mellerby.

Lady Scroope sighed and shook her head; but in shaking it she showed that she completely agreed with the opinion expressed by her guest.

As there were only two horses to be inspected, and as Fred Neville absolutely refused the groom's invitation to look at the old carriage horses belonging to the family, he was back in his aunt's room before Miss Mellerby had gone upstairs to dress for dinner. The introduction was made, and Fred did his best to make himself agreeable. He was such a man that no girl could, at the first sight of him, think herself injured by being asked to love him. She was a good girl, and would have consented to marry no man without feeling sure of his affections; but Fred Neville was bold and frank as well as handsome, and had plenty to say for himself. It might be that he was vicious, or ill-tempered, or selfish, and it would be necessary that she should know much of him before she would give herself into his keeping; but as far as the first sight went, and the first hearing, Sophie Mellerby's impressions were all in Fred's favour. It is no doubt a fact that with the very best of girls a man is placed in a very good light by being heir to a peerage and a large property.

'Do you hunt, Miss Mellerby?' he asked. She shook her head and looked grave, and then laughed. Among her people hunting was not thought to be a desirable accomplishment for young ladies. 'Almost all girls do hunt now,' said Fred.

'Do you think it is a nice amusement for young ladies?' asked the aunt in a severe tone.

'I don't see why not—that is if they know how to ride.'

'I know how to ride,' said Sophie Mellerby.

'Riding is all very well,' said Lady Scroope. 'I quite approve of it for girls. When I was young, everybody did not ride as they do now. Nevertheless it is very well, and is thought to be healthy. But as for hunting, Sophie, I'm sure your mamma would be very much distressed if you were to think of such a thing.'

'But dear Lady Scroope, I haven't thought of it, and I am not going to think of it—and if I thought of it ever so much, I shouldn't do it. Poor mamma would be frightened into fits —only that nobody at Mellerby could possibly be made to believe it, unless they saw me doing it.'

'Then there can be no reason why you shouldn't make the attempt,' said Fred. Upon which Lady Scroope pretended to look grave, and told him that he was very wicked. But let an old lady be ever so strict towards her own sex, she likes a little wickedness in a young man—if only he does not carry it to the extent of marrying the wrong sort of young woman.

Sophia Mellerby was a tall, graceful, well-formed girl, showing her high blood in every line of her face. On her mother's side she had come from the Ancrums, whose family, as everybody knows, is one of the oldest in England; and, as the Earl had said, the Mellerbys had been Mellerbys from the time of King John, and had been living on the same spot for at least four centuries. They were and always had been Mellerbys of Mellerby—the very name of the parish being the same as that of the family. If Sophia Mellerby did not show breeding, what girl could show it? She was fair, with a somewhat thin oval face, with dark eyes, and an almost perfect Grecian nose. Her mouth was small, and her chin delicately formed. And yet it can hardly be said that she was beautiful. Or, if beautiful, she was so in women's eyes rather than in those of men. She lacked colour and perhaps animation in her countenance. She had more character, indeed, than was told by her face, which is generally so true an index of the mind. Her education had been as good as England could afford, and her intellect had been sufficient to enable her to make use of it. But her chief charm in the eyes of many consisted in the fact, doubted by none, that she was every inch a lady. She was an only daughter, too—with an

only brother; and as the Ancrums were all rich, she would
have a very pretty fortune of her own. Fred Neville, who
had literally been nobody before his cousin had died, might
certainly do much worse than marry her.

And after a day or two they did seem to get on very well
together. He had reached Scroope on the 21st, and on the
23rd Mrs. Neville arrived with her youngest son Jack Neville.*
This was rather a trial to the Earl, as he had never yet seen
his brother's widow. He had heard when his brother married
that she was fast, fond of riding, and loud. She had been the
daughter of a Colonel Smith, with whom his brother, at that
time a Captain Neville, had formed acquaintance—and had
been a beauty very well known as such at Dublin and other
garrison towns. No real harm had ever been known of her,
but the old Earl had always felt that his brother had made an
unfortunate marriage. As at that time they had not been on
speaking terms, it had not signified much—but there had
been a prejudice at Scroope against the Captain's wife, which
by no means died out when the late Julia Smith became the
Captain's widow with two sons. Old reminiscences remain
very firm with old people—and Lord Scroope was still much
afraid of the fast, loud beauty. His principles told him that
he should not sever the mother from the son, and that as it
suited him to take the son for his own purposes, he should
also, to some extent, accept the mother also. But he dreaded
the affair. He dreaded Mrs. Neville; and he dreaded Jack,
who had been so named after his gallant grandfather, Colonel
Smith. When Mrs. Neville arrived, she was found to be so
subdued and tame that she could hardly open her mouth
before the old Earl. Her loudness, if she ever had been loud,
was certainly all gone—and her fastness, if ever she had been
fast, had been worn out of her. She was an old woman, with
the relics of great beauty, idolizing her two sons for whom
all her life had been a sacrifice, in weak health, and prepared,
if necessary, to sit in silent awe at the feet of the Earl who
had been so good to her boy.

'I don't know how to thank you for what you have done,' she said, in a low voice.

'No thanks are required,' said the Earl. 'He is the same to us as if he were our own.' Then she raised the old man's hand and kissed it—and the old man owned to himself that he had made a mistake.

As to Jack Neville——. But Jack Neville shall have another chapter opened on his behalf.

CHAPTER IV

JACK NEVILLE

JOHN IS a very respectable name—perhaps there is no name more respectable in the English language. Sir John, as the head of a family, is certainly as respectable as any name can be. For an old family coachman it beats all names. Mr. John Smith would be sure to have a larger balance at his banker's than Charles Smith or Orlando Smith—or perhaps than any other Smith whatever. The Rev. Frederic Walker might be a wet parson,* but the Rev. John Walker would assuredly be a good clergyman at all points, though perhaps a little dull in his sermons. Yet almost all Johns have been Jacks, and Jack, in point of respectibility, is the very reverse of John. How it is, or when it is, that the Jacks become re-Johned, and go back to the original and excellent name given to them by their godfathers and godmothers, nobody ever knows. Jack Neville, probably through some foolish fondness on his mother's part, had never been re-Johned—and consequently the Earl, when he made up his mind to receive his sister-in-law, was at first unwilling to invite his younger nephew. 'But he is in the Engineers,' said Lady Scroope. The argument had its weight, and Jack Neville was invited. But even that argument failed to obliterate the idea which had taken hold of the Earl's mind. There had never yet been a Jack among the Scroopes.

When Jack came he was found to be very unlike the Nevilles in appearance. In the first place he was dark, and in the next place he was ugly. He was a tall, well-made fellow, taller than his brother, and probably stronger; and he had very different eyes—very dark brown eyes, deeply set in his head, with large dark eyebrows. He wore his black hair very short, and had no beard whatever. His features were hard, and on one cheek he had a cicatrice, the remains of some misfortune that had happened to him in his boyhood. But in spite of his ugliness— for he was ugly, there was much about him in his gait and manner that claimed attention. Lord Scroope, the moment that he saw him, felt that he ought not to be called Jack. Indeed the Earl was almost afraid of him, and so after a time was the Countess.

'Jack ought to have been the eldest,' Fred had said to his aunt.

'Why should he have been the eldest?'

'Because he is so much the cleverest. I could never have got into the Engineers.'*

'That seems to be a reason why he should be the youngest,' said Lady Scroope.

Two or three other people arrived, and the house became much less dull than was its wont. Jack Neville occasionally rode his brother's horses, and the Earl was forced to acknowledge another mistake. The mother was very silent, but she was a lady. The young Engineer was not only a gentleman— but for his age a very well educated gentleman, and Lord Scroope was almost proud of his relatives. For the first week the affair between Fred Neville and Miss Mellerby really seemed to make progress. She was not a girl given to flirting —not prone to outward demonstrations of partiality for a young man; but she never withdrew herself from her intended husband, and Fred seemed quite willing to be attentive. Not a word was said to hurry the young people, and Lady Scroope's hopes were high. Of course no allusion had been made to those horrid Irish people, but it did not seem to Lady Scroope that the heir had left his heart behind him in Co. Clare.

Fred had told his aunt in one of his letters that he would stay three weeks at Scroope, but she had not supposed that he would limit himself exactly to that period. No absolute limit had been fixed for the visit of Mrs. Neville and her younger son, but it was taken for granted that they would not remain should Fred depart. As to Sophie Mellerby, her visit was elastic. She was there for a purpose, and might remain all the winter if the purpose could be so served. For the first fortnight Lady Scroope thought that the affair was progressing well. Fred hunted three days a week, and was occasionally away from home—going to dine with a regiment at Dorchester, and once making a dash up to London; but his manner to Miss Mellerby was very nice, and there could. be no doubt but that Sophie liked him. When, on a sudden, the heir said a word to his aunt which was almost equal to firing a pistol at her head. 'I think Master Jack is making it all square with Sophie Mellerby.'

If there was anything that Lady Scroope hated almost as much as improper marriages it was slang. She professed that she did not understand it; and in carrying out her profession always stopped the conversation to have any word explained to her which she thought had been used in an improper sense. The idea of a young man making it 'all square' with a young woman was repulsive, but the idea of this young man making it 'all square' with this young woman was so much more repulsive, and the misery to her was so intensely heightened by the unconcern displayed by the heir in so speaking of the girl with whom he ought to have been making it 'all square' himself, that she could hardly allow herself to be arrested by that stumbling block. 'Impossible!' she exclaimed—that is if you mean—if you mean—if you mean anything at all.'

'I do mean a good deal.'

'Then I don't believe a word of it. It's quite out of the question. It's impossible. I'm quite sure your brother understands his position as a gentleman too thoroughly to dream of such a thing.'

This was Greek to Fred Neville. Why his brother should not fall in love with a pretty girl, and why a pretty girl should not return the feeling, without any disgrace to his brother, Fred could not understand. His brother was a

Neville, and was moreover an uncommonly clever fellow. 'Why shouldn't he dream of it?'

'In the first place—. Well! I did think, Fred, that you yourself seemed to be—seemed to be taken with Miss Mellerby.'

'Who? I? Oh, dear no. She's a very nice girl and all that, and I like her amazingly. If she were Jack's wife, I never saw a girl I should so much like for a sister.'

'It's quite out of the question. I wonder that you can speak in such a way. What right can your brother have to think of such a girl as Miss Mellerby? He has no position—no means.'

'He is my brother,' said Fred, with a little touch of anger—already discounting his future earldom on his brother's behalf.

'Yes—he is your brother; but you don't suppose that Mr. Mellerby would give his daughter to an officer in the Engineers who has, as far as I know, no private means whatever.'

'He will have—when my mother dies. Of course I can't speak of doing anything for anybody at present. I may die before my uncle. Nothing is more likely. But then, if I do, Jack would be my uncle's heir.'

'I don't believe there's anything in it at all,' said Lady Scroope in great dudgeon.

'I dare say not. If there is, they haven't told me. It's not likely they would. But I thought I saw something coming up, and as it seemed to be the most natural thing in the world, I mentioned it. As for me—Miss Mellerby doesn't care a straw for me. You may be sure of that.'

'She would—if you'd ask her.'

'But I never shall ask her. What's the use of beating about the bush, aunt? I never shall ask her; and if I did, she wouldn't have me. If you want to make Sophie Mellerby your niece, Jack's your game.'

Lady Scroope was ineffably disgusted. To be told that 'Jack was her game' was in itself a terrible annoyance to her. But to be so told in reference to such a subject was painful in the extreme. Of course she could not make this young man marry as she wished. She had acknowledged to herself from the first that there could be no cause of anger against him should he not fall into the silken net which was spread for him. Lady Scroope was not an unreasonable woman, and understood well the power which young people have over old people. She knew that she couldn't quarrel with Fred Neville, even if she would. He was the heir, and in a very few years would be the owner of everything. In order to keep him straight, to save him from debts, to protect him from money-lenders, and to secure the family standing and property till he should have made things stable by having a wife and heir of his own, all manner of indulgence must be shown him. She quite understood that such a horse must be ridden with a very light hand. She must put up with slang from him, though she would resent it from any other human being. He must be allowed to smoke in his bed-room, to be late at dinner, to shirk morning prayers—making her only too happy if he would not shirk Sunday church also. Of course he must choose a bride for himself—only not a Roman Catholic wild Irish bride of whom nobody knew anything!

As to that other matter concerning Jack and Sophie Mellerby, she could not bring herself to believe it. She had certainly seen that they were good friends—as would have been quite fit had Fred been engaged to her; but she had not conceived the possibility of any mistake on such a subject. Surely Sophie herself knew better what she was about! How would she—she, Lady Scroope—answer it to Lady Sophia, if Sophie should go back to Mellerby from her house, engaged to a younger brother who had nothing but a commission in the Engineers? Sophie had been sent to Scroope on purpose to be fallen in love with by the heir; and how would it be with Lady Scroope if, in lieu of this, she should not only have been fallen in love with by the heir's younger brother, but have responded favourably to so base an affection?

That same afternoon Fred told his uncle that he was going

back to Ireland on the day but one following, thus curtailing his promised three weeks by two days.

'I am sorry that you are so much hurried, Fred,' said the old man.

'So am I, my lord—but Johnstone has to go to London on business, and I promised when I got leave that I wouldn't throw him over. You see—when one has a profession one must attend to it—more or less.'

'But you hardly need the profession.'

'Thank you, uncle—it is very kind of you to say so. And as you wish me to leave it, I will when the year is over. I have told the fellows that I shall stay till next October, and I shouldn't like to change now.' The Earl hadn't another word to say.

But on the day before Fred's departure there came a short note from Lady Mary Quin which made poor Lady Scroope more unhappy than ever. Tidings had reached her in a mysterious way that the O'Haras were eagerly expecting the return of Mr. Neville. Lady Mary thought that if Mr. Neville's quarters could be moved from Ennis, it would be very expedient for many reasons. She knew that enquiries had been made for him and that he was engaged to dine on a certain day with Father Marty the priest. Father Marty would no doubt go any lengths to serve his friends the O'Haras. Then Lady Mary was very anxious that not a word should be said to Mr. Neville which might lead him to suppose that reports respecting him were being sent from Quin Castle to Scroope.

The Countess in her agony thought it best to tell the whole story to the Earl. 'But what can I do?' said the old man. 'Young men will form these acquaintances.' His fears were evidently as yet less dark than those of his wife.

'It would be very bad if we were to hear that he was married to a girl of whom we only know that she is a Roman Catholic and friendless.'

The Earl's brow became very black. 'I don't think that he would treat me in that way.'

'Not meaning it, perhaps—but if he should become entangled and make a promise!'

Then the Earl did speak to his nephew. 'Fred,' he said, 'I have been thinking a great deal about you. I have little else to think of now. I should take it as a mark of affection from you if you would give up the army—at once.'

'And not join my regiment again at all?'

'It is absurd that you should do so in your present position. You should be here, and learn the circumstances of the property before it becomes your own. There can hardly be more than a year or two left for the lesson.'

The Earl's manner was very impressive. He looked into his nephew's face as he spoke, and stood with his hand upon the young man's shoulder. But Fred Neville was a Neville all over—and the Nevilles had always chosen to have their own way. He had not the power of intellect nor the finished manliness which his brother possessed; but he could be as obstinate as any Neville—as obstinate as his father had been, or his uncle. And in this matter he had arguments which his uncle could hardly answer on the spur of the moment. No doubt he could sell out in proper course,* but at the present moment he was as much bound by military law to return as would be any common soldier at the expiration of his furlough. He must go back. That at any rate was certain. And if his uncle did not much mind it, he would prefer to remain with his regiment till October.

Lord Scroope could not condescend to repeat his request, or even again to allude to it. His whole manner altered as he took his hand away from his nephew's shoulder. But still he was determined that there should be no quarrel. As yet there was no ground for quarrelling—and by any quarrel the injury to him would be much greater than any that could befall the heir. He stood for a moment and then he spoke again in a tone very different from that he had used before. 'I hope,' he said—and then he paused again; 'I hope you know how very much depends on your marrying in a manner suitable to your position.'

'Quite so—I think.'

'It is the one hope left to me to see you properly settled in life.'

'Marriage is a very serious thing, uncle. Suppose I were not to marry at all! Sometimes I think my brother is much more like marrying than I am.'

'You are bound to marry,' said the Earl solemnly. 'And you are specially bound by every duty to God and man to make no marriage that will be disgraceful to the position which you are called upon to fill.'

'At any rate I will not do that,' said Fred Neville proudly. From this the Earl took some comfort, and then the interview was over.

On the day appointed by himself Fred left the Manor, and his mother and brother went on the following day. But after he was gone, on that same afternoon, Jack Neville asked Sophie Mellerby to be his wife. She refused him—with all the courtesy she knew how to use, but also with all the certainty. And as soon as he had left the house she told Lady Scroope what had happened.

CHAPTER V

ARDKILL COTTAGE

THE CLIFFS of Moher in Co. Clare, on the western coast of Ireland, are not as well known to tourists as they should be. It may be doubted whether Lady Mary Quin was right when she called them the highest cliffs in the world, but they are undoubtedly very respectable cliffs, and run up some six hundred feet from the sea as nearly perpendicular as cliffs should be. They are beautifully coloured, streaked with yellow veins, and with great masses of dark red rock; and beneath them lies the broad and blue Atlantic. Lady Mary's exaggeration as to the comparative height is here acknowledged, but had she said that below them rolls the brightest bluest clearest water in the world she would not have been far wrong. To the south of these cliffs there runs inland a broad bay—Liscannor bay, on the sides of which are two little villages, Liscannor and Lahinch. At the latter, Fred Neville, since he had been quartered at Ennis, had kept a boat for the sake of shooting seals and exploring the coast—and generally carrying out his spirit of adventure. Not far from Liscannor was Castle Quin, the seat of the Earl of Kilfenora;* and some way up from Liscannor towards the cliffs, about two miles from the village, there is a cottage called Ardkill. Here lived Mrs. and Miss O'Hara.

It was the nearest house to the rocks, from which it was distant less than half a mile. The cottage, so called, was a low rambling long house, but one storey high—very unlike an English cottage. It stood in two narrow lengths, the one running at right angles to the other; and contained a large kitchen, two sitting rooms—of which one was never used—and four or five bed-rooms of which only three were furnished. The servant girl occupied one, and the two ladies the others. It was a blank place enough—and most unlike that sort of cottage which English ladies are supposed to inhabit, when they take to cottage life. There was no garden to it, beyond a small patch in which a few potatoes were planted. It was so near to the ocean, so exposed to winds from the Atlantic, that no shrubs would live there. Everything round it, even the herbage, was impregnated with salt, and told tales of the neighbouring waves. When the wind was from the west the air would be so laden with spray that one could not walk there without being wet. And yet the place was very healthy, and noted for the fineness of its air. Rising from the cottage, which itself stood high, was a steep hill running up to the top of the cliff, covered with that peculiar moss which the salt spray of the ocean produces. On this side the land was altogether open, but a few sheep were always grazing there when the wind was not so high as to drive them to some shelter. Behind the cottage there was an enclosed paddock which belonged to it, and in which Mrs. O'Hara kept her cow. Roaming free around the house, and sometimes in it, were a dozen hens and a noisy old cock which, with the cow, made up the total of the widow's live stock. About a half a mile from the cottage on the way to Liscannor there were half a dozen mud cabins which contained Mrs. O'Hara's nearest neighbours—and an old burying ground. Half a mile further on again was the priest's house, and then on to Liscannor there were a few other straggling cabins here and there along the road.

Up to the cottage indeed there could hardly be said to be more than a track, and beyond the cottage no more than a sheep path. The road coming out from Liscannor was a real road as far as the burying ground, but from thence onward it had degenerated. A car, or carriage if needed, might be brought up to the cottage door, for the ground was hard and the way was open. But no wheels ever travelled there now. The priest, when he would come, came on horseback, and there was a shed in which he could tie up his nag. He himself from time to time would send up a truss of hay for his nag's use, and would think himself cruelly used because the cow would find her way in and eat it. No other horse ever called at the widow's door. What slender stores were needed for her use, were all brought on the girls' backs from Liscannor. To the north of the cottage, along the cliff, there was no road for miles, nor was there house or habitation. Castle Quin, in which the noble but somewhat impoverished Quin family lived nearly throughout the year, was distant, inland, about three miles from the cottage. Lady Mary had said in her letter to her friend that Mrs. O'Hara was a lady—and as Mrs. O'Hara had no other neighbour, ranking with herself in that respect, so near her, and none other but the Protestant clergyman's wife within six miles of her, charity, one would have thought, might have induced some of the Quin family to notice her. But the Quins were Protestant, and Mrs. O'Hara was not only a Roman Catholic, but a Roman Catholic who had been brought into the parish by the priest. No evil certainly was known of her, but then nothing was known of her; and the Quins were a very cautious people where religion was called in question. In the days of the famine* Father Marty and the Earl and the Protestant vicar had worked together in the good cause—but those days were now gone by, and the strange intimacy had soon died away. The Earl when he met the priest would bow to him, and the two clergymen would bow to each other—but beyond such dumb salutation there was no intercourse between them. It had been held therefore to be impossible to take any notice of the priest's friends.

And what notice could have been taken of two ladies who came from nobody knew where, to live in that wild-out-of-the-way place, nobody knew why? They called themselves mother and daughter, and they called themselves O'Haras—but there was no evidence of the truth even of these assertions. They were left therefore in their solitude, and never saw the face of a friend across their door step except that of Father Marty.

In truth Mrs. O'Hara's life had been of a nature almost to

necessitate such solitude. With her story we have nothing to do here. For our purpose there is no need that her tale should be told. Suffice it to say that she had been deserted by her husband, and did not now know whether she was or was not a widow. This was in truth the only mystery attached to her. She herself was an Englishwoman, though a Catholic; but she had been left early an orphan, and had been brought up in a provincial town of France by her grandmother. There she had married a certain Captain O'Hara, she having some small means of her own sufficient to make her valuable in the eyes of an adventurer. At that time she was no more than eighteen, and had given her hand to the Captain in opposition to the wishes of her only guardian. What had been her life from that time to the period at which, under Father Marty's auspices, she became the inhabitant of Ardkill Cottage, no one knew but herself. She was then utterly dissevered from all friends and relatives, and appeared on the western coast of County Clare with her daughter, a perfect stranger to every one. Father Marty was an old man, now nearly seventy, and had been educated in France. There he had known Mrs. O'Hara's grandmother, and hence had arisen the friendship which had induced him to bring the lady into his parish. She came there with a daughter, then hardly more than a child. Between two and three years had passed since her coming, and the child was now a grown-up girl, nearly nineteen years old. Of her means little or nothing was known accurately, even to the priest. She had told him that she had saved enough out of the wreck on which to live with her girl after some very humble fashion, and she paid her way. There must have come some sudden crash, or she would hardly have taken her child from an expensive Parisian school to vegetate in such solitude as that she had chosen. And it was a solitude from which there seemed to be no chance of future escape. They had brought with them a piano and a few books, mostly French—and with these it seemed to have been intended that the two ladies should make their future lives endurable. Other resources except such as the scenery of the cliffs afforded them, they had none.

The author would wish to impress upon his readers, if it may be possible, some idea of the outward appearance and personal character of each of these two ladies, as his story can hardly be told successfully unless he do so. The elder, who was at this time still under forty years of age, would have been a very handsome woman had not troubles, suffering, and the contests of a rugged life, in which she had both endured and dared much, given to her face a look of hard combative resolution which was not feminine. She was rather below than above the average height—or at any rate looked to be so, as she was strongly made, with broad shoulders, and a waist that was perhaps not now as slender as when she first met Captain O'Hara. But her hair was still black—as dark at least as hair can be which is not in truth black at all but only darkly brown. Whatever might be its colour there was no tinge of grey upon it. It was glossy, silken, and long as when she was a girl. I do not think that she took pride in it. How could she take pride in personal beauty, when she was never seen by any man younger than Father Marty or the old peasant who brought turf to her door in creels on a donkey's back? But she wore it always without any cap, tied in a simple knot behind her head. Whether chignons had been invented then the author does not remember—but they certainly had not become common on the coast of County Clare, and the peasants about Liscannor thought Mrs. O'Hara's head of hair the finest they had ever seen. Had the ladies Quin of the Castle possessed such hair as that, they would not have been the ladies Quin to this day. Her eyes were lustrous, dark, and very large—beautiful eyes certainly; but they were eyes that you might fear. They had been softer perhaps in youth, before the spirit of the tiger had been roused in the woman's bosom by neglect and ill-usage. Her face was now bronzed by years and weather. Of her complexion she took no more care than did the neighbouring fishermen of theirs, and the winds and the salt water, and perhaps the working of her own mind, had told upon it, to make it rough and dark.

But yet there was a colour in her cheeks, as we often see in those of wandering gypsies, which would make a man stop to regard her who had eyes appreciative of beauty. Her nose was well formed—a heaven-made nose, and not a lump of flesh stuck on to the middle of her face as women's noses sometimes are—but it was somewhat short and broad at the nostrils, a nose that could imply much anger, and perhaps tenderness also. Her face below her nose was very short. Her mouth was large, but laden with expression. Her lips were full and her teeth perfect as pearls. Her chin was short and perhaps now converging to that size which we call a double chin, and marked by as broad a dimple as ever Venus made with her finger on the face of a woman.

She had ever been strong and active, and years in that retreat had told upon her not at all. She would still walk to Liscannor, and thence round, when the tide was low, beneath the cliffs, and up by a path which the boys had made from the foot through the rocks to the summit, though the distance was over ten miles, and the ascent was very steep. She would remain for hours on the rocks, looking down upon the sea, when the weather was almost at its roughest. When the winds were still, and the sun was setting across the ocean, and the tame waves were only just audible as they rippled on the stones below, she would sit there with her child, holding the girl's hand or just touching her arm, and would be content so to stay almost without a word; but when the winds blew, and the heavy spray came up in blinding volumes, and the white-headed sea-monsters were roaring in their fury against the rocks, she would be there alone with her hat in her hand, and her hair drenched. She would watch the gulls wheeling and floating beneath her, and would listen to their screams and try to read their voices. She would envy the birds as they seemed to be worked into madness by the winds which still were not strong enough to drive them from their purposes. To linger there among the rocks seemed to be the only delight left to her in life—except that intensive delight which a mother has in loving her child. She herself read but little, and never put a hand upon the piano. But she had a faculty of sitting and thinking, of brooding over her own past years and dreaming of her daughter's future life, which never deserted her. With her the days were doubtless very sad, but it cannot truly be said that they were dull or tedious.

And there was a sparkle of humour about her too, which would sometimes shine the brightest when there was no one by her to appreciate it. Her daughter would smile at her mother's sallies—but she did so simply in kindness. Kate did not share her mother's sense of humour—did not share it as yet. With the young the love of fun is gratified generally by grotesque movement. It is not till years are running on that the grotesqueness of words and ideas is appreciated. But Mrs. O'Hara would expend her art on the household drudge, or on old Barney Corcoran who came with the turf—though by neither of them was she very clearly understood. Now and again she would have a war of words with the priest, and that, I think, she liked. She was intensely combative, if ground for a combat arose; and would fight on any subject with any human being—except her daughter. And yet with the priest she never quarrelled; and though she was rarely beaten in her contests with him, she submitted to him in much. In matters touching her religion she submitted to him altogether.

Kate O'Hara was in face very like her mother—strangely like, for in much she was very different. But she had her mother's eyes—though hers were much softer in their lustre, as became her youth—and she had her mother's nose, but without that look of scorn which would come upon her mother's face when the nostrils were inflated. And in that peculiar shortness of the lower face she was the very echo of her mother. But the mouth was smaller, the lips less full, and the dimple less exaggerated. It was a fairer face to look upon —fairer, perhaps, than her mother's had ever been; but it was less expressive, and in it there was infinitely less capability for anger, and perhaps less capability for the agonising extremes of tenderness. But Kate was taller than her mother, and seemed by her mother's side to be slender. Nevertheless she was strong and healthy; and though she did not willingly join in those longer walks, or expose herself to the weather as did her mother, there was nothing feeble about her, nor was she averse to action. Life at Ardkill Cottage was dull, and therefore she also was dull. Had she been surrounded by friends, such as she had known in her halcyon school days at Paris, she would have been the gayest of the gay.

Her hair was dark as her mother's—even darker. Seen by the side of Miss O'Hara's, the mother's hair was certainly not black, but one could hardly think that hair could be blacker than the daughter's. But hers fell in curling clusters round her neck—such clusters as now one never sees. She would shake them in sport, and the room would seem to be full of her locks. But she used to say herself to her mother that there was already to be found a grey hair among them now and again, and she would at times show one, declaring that she would be an old woman before her mother was middle-aged.

Her life at Ardkill Cottage was certainly very dull. Memory did but little for her, and she hardly knew how to hope. She would read, till she had nearly learned all their books by heart, and would play such tunes as she knew by the hour together, till the poor instrument, subject to the sea air and away from any tuner's skill, was discordant with its limp strings. But still, with all this, her mind would become vacant and weary. 'Mother,' she would say, 'is it always to be like this?'

'Not always, Kate,' the mother once answered.

'And when will it be changed?'

'In a few days—in a few hours, Kate.'

'What do you mean, mother?'

'That eternity is coming, with all its glory and happiness. If it were not so, it would, indeed, be very bad.'

It may be doubted whether any human mind has been able to content itself with hopes of eternity, till distress in some shape has embittered life. The preachers preach very

well—well enough to leave many convictions on the minds
of men; but not well enough to leave that conviction. And
godly men live well—but we never see them living as though
such were their conviction. And were it so, who would strive
and moil in this world? When the heart has been broken, and
the spirit ground to the dust by misery, then—such is God's
mercy—eternity suffices to make life bearable. When Mrs.
O'Hara spoke to her daughter of eternity, there was but cold
comfort in the word. The girl wanted something here—
pleasures, companions, work, perhaps a lover. This had
happened before Lieutenant Neville of the 20th Hussars had
been seen in those parts.

And the mother herself, in speaking as she had spoken,
had, perhaps unintentionally, indulged in a sarcasm on life
which the daughter certainly had not been intended to
understand. 'Yes—it will always be like this for you, for you,
unfortunate one that you are. There is no other further look-
out in this life. You are one of the wretched to whom the
world offers nothing; and therefore—as, being human, you
must hope—build your hopes on eternity.' Had the words
been read clearly, that would have been their true meaning.
What could she do for her child? Bread and meat, with a
roof over her head, and raiment which sufficed for life such
as theirs, she could supply. The life would have been well
enough had it been their fate, and within their power, to
earn the bread and meat, the shelter and the raiment. But to
have it, and without work—to have that, and nothing more,
in absolute idleness, was such misery that there was no resource left but eternity!

And yet the mother when she looked at her daughter almost persuaded herself that it need not be so. The girl was
very lovely—so lovely that, were she but seen, men would
quarrel for her as to who should have her in his keeping. Such
beauty, such life, such capability for giving and receiving enjoyment could not have been intended to wither on a lone
cliff over the Atlantic! There must be fault somewhere. But
yet to live had been the first necessity; and life in cities,

among the haunts of men, had been impossible with such means as this woman possessed. When she had called her daughter to her, and had sought peace under the roof which her friend the priest had found for her, peace and a roof to shelter her had been the extent of her desires. To be at rest, and independent, with her child within her arms, had been all that the woman asked of the gods. For herself it sufficed. For herself she was able to acknowledge that the rest which she had at least obtained was infinitely preferable to the unrest of her past life. But she soon learned—as she had not expected to learn before she made the experiment—that that which was to her peace, was to her daughter life within a tomb. 'Mother, is it always to be like this?'

Had her child not carried the weight of good blood, had some small grocer or country farmer been her father, she might have come down to the neighbouring town of Ennistimon, and found a fitting mate there. Would it not have been better so? From that weight of good blood—or gift, if it please us to call it—what advantage would ever come to her girl? It cannot really be that all those who swarm in the world below the bar of gentlehood are less blessed, or intended to be less blessed, than the few who float in the higher air. As to real blessedness, does it not come from fitness to the outer life and a sense of duty that shall produce such fitness? Does anyone believe that the Countess has a greater share of happiness than the grocer's wife, or is less subject to the miseries which flesh inherits? But such matters cannot be changed by the will. This woman could not bid her daughter go and meet the butcher's son on equal terms, or seek her friends among the milliners of the neighbouring town. The burden had been imposed and must be borne, even though it isolated them from all the world.

'Mother, is it always to be like this?' Of course the mother knew what was needed. It was needed that the girl should go out into the world and pair, that she should find some shoulder on which she might lean, some arm that would be strong to surround her, the heart of some man and the work of some man to which she might devote herself. The girl, when she asked her question, did not know this—but the mother knew it. The mother looked at her child and said that of all living creatures her child was surely the loveliest. Was it not fit that she should go forth and be loved—that she should at any rate go forth and take her chance with others? But how should such going forth be managed? And then— were there not dangers, terrible dangers—dangers specially terrible to one so friendless as her child? Had not she herself been wrecked among the rocks, trusting herself to one who had been utterly unworthy—loving one who had been utterly unlovely? Men so often are as ravenous wolves, merciless, rapacious, without hearts, full of greed, full of lust, looking on female beauty as prey, regarding the love of woman and her very life as a toy! Were she higher in the world there might be safety. Were she lower there might be safety. But how could she send her girl forth into the world without sending her certainly among the wolves? And yet the piteous question was always sounding in her ears. 'Mother, is it always to be like this?'

Then Lieutenant Neville had appeared upon the scene, dressed in a sailor's jacket and trousers, with a sailor's cap upon his head, with a loose handkerchief round his neck and his hair blowing to the wind. In the eyes of Kate O'Hara he was an Apollo. In the eyes of any girl he must have seemed to be as good-looking a fellow as ever tied a sailor's knot. He had made acquaintance with Father Marty at Liscannor, and the priest had dined with him at Ennis. There had been a return visit, and the priest, perhaps innocently, had taken him up on the cliffs. There he had met the two ladies, and our hero had been introduced to Kate O'Hara.

CHAPTER VI

I'LL GO BAIL SHE LIKES IT

IT MIGHT be that the young man was a ravenous wolf, but his manners were not wolfish. Had Mrs. O'Hara been a princess, supreme in her own rights, young Neville could not have treated her or her daughter with more respect. At first Kate had wondered at him, but had said but little. She had listened to him, as he talked to her mother and the priest about the cliffs and the birds and the seals he had shot, and she had felt that it was this, something like this, that was needed to make life, so sweet that as yet there need be no longing, no thought, for eternity. It was not that all at once she loved him, but she felt that he was a thing to love. His very appearance on the cliff, and the power of thinking of him when he was gone, for a while banished all tedium from her life. 'Why should you shoot the poor gulls?' That was the first question she asked him; and she asked it hardly in tenderness to the birds, but because with the unconscious cunning of her sex she understood that tenderness in a woman is a charm in the eyes of a man.

'Only because it is so difficult to get at them,' said Fred. 'I believe there is no other reason—except that one must shoot something.'

'But why must you?' asked Mrs. O'Hara.

'To justify one's guns. A man takes to shooting as a matter of course. It's a kind of institution. There ain't any tigers, and so we shoot birds. And in this part of the world there ain't any pheasants, and so we shoot sea-gulls.'

'Excellently argued,' said the priest.

'Or rather one don't, for it's impossible to get at them. But I'll tell you what, Father Marty'—Neville had already

741

assumed the fashion of calling the priest by his familiar priestly name, as strangers do much more readily than they who belong to the country—'I'll tell you what, Father Marty —I've shot one of the finest seals I ever saw, and if Morony can get him at low water, I'll send the skin up to Mrs. O'Hara.'

'And send the oil to me,' said the priest. 'There's some use in shooting a seal. But you can do nothing with those birds— unless you get enough of their feathers to make a bed.'

This was in October, and before the end of November Fred Neville was, after a fashion, intimate at the cottage. He had never broken bread at Mrs. O'Hara's table; nor, to tell the truth, had any outspoken, clearly intelligible word of love been uttered by him to the girl. But he had been seen with them often enough, and the story had become sufficiently current at Liscannor to make Lady Mary Quin think that she was justified in sending her bad news to her friend Lady Scroope. This she did not do till Fred had been induced, with some difficulty, to pass a night at Castle Quin. Lady Mary had not scrupled to ask a question about Miss O'Hara, and had thought the answer very unsatisfactory. 'I don't know what makes them live there, I'm sure. I should have thought you would have known that,' replied Neville, in answer to her question.

'They are perfect mysteries to us,' said Lady Mary.

'I think that Miss O'Hara is the prettiest girl I ever saw in my life,' said Fred boldly, 'and I should say the handsomest woman, if it were not that there may be a question between her and her mother.'

'You are enthusiastic,' said Lady Mary Quin, and after that the letter to Scroope was written.

In the meantime the seal-skin was cured—not perhaps in the very best fashion, and was sent up to Miss O'Hara with Mr. Neville's compliments. The skin of a seal that has been shot by the man and not purchased is a present that any lady may receive from any gentleman. The most prudent mamma

that ever watched over the dovecote with Argus eyes, permitting no touch of gallantry to come near it, could hardly
insist that a seal-skin in the rough should be sent back to the
donor. Mrs. O'Hara was by no means that most prudent
mamma, and made, not only the seal-skin, but the donor also
welcome. Must it not be that by some chance advent such as
this that the change must be effected in her girl's life, should
any change ever be made? And her girl was good. Why
should she fear for her? The man had been brought there
by her only friend, the priest, and why should she fear him?
And yet she did fear; and though her face was never clouded
when her girl spoke of the newcomer, though she always
mentioned Lieutenant Neville's name as though she herself
liked the man, though she even was gracious to him when he
showed himself near the cottage—still there was a deep dread
upon her when her eyes rested upon him, when her thoughts
flew to him. Men are wolves to women, and utterly merciless
when feeding high their lust. 'Twas thus her own thoughts
shaped themselves, though she never uttered a syllable to
her daughter in disparagement of the man. This was the girl's
chance. Was she to rob her of it? And yet, of all her duties,
was not the duty of protecting her girl the highest and the
dearest that she owned? If the man meant well by her girl,
she would wash his feet with her hair, kiss the hem of his
garments, and love the spot on which she had first seen him
stand like a young sea-god. But if evil—if he meant evil to
her girl, if he should do evil to her Kate—then she knew that
there was so much of the tiger within her bosom as would
serve to rend him limb from limb. With such thoughts as
these she had hardly ever left them together. Nor had such
leaving together seemed to be desired by them. As for Kate
she certainly would have shunned it. She thought of Fred
Neville during all her waking moments, and dreamed of him
at night. His coming had certainly been to her as the coming
of a god. Though he did not appear on the cliffs above once
or twice a week, and had done so but for a few weeks, his
presence had altered the whole tenour of her life. She never

asked her mother now whether it was to be always like this. There was a freshness about her life which her mother understood at once. She was full of play, reading less than was her wont, but still with no sense of tedium. Of the man in his absence she spoke but seldom, and when his name was on her lips she would jest with it—as though the coming of a young embryo lord to shoot gulls on their coast was quite a joke. The seal-skin which he had given her was very dear to her, and she was at no pains to hide her liking; but of the man as a lover she had never seemed to think.

Nor did she think of him as a lover. It is not by such thinking that love grows. Nor did she ever tell herself that while he was there, coming on one day and telling them that his boat would be again there on another, life was blessed to her, and that, therefore, when he should have left them, her life would be accursed to her. She knew nothing of all this. But yet she thought of him, and dreamed of him, and her young head was full of little plans with every one of which he was connected.

And it may almost be said that Fred Neville was as innocent in the matter as was the girl. It is true, indeed, that men are merciless as wolves to women—that they become so, taught by circumstances and trained by years; but the young man who begins by meaning to be a wolf must be bad indeed. Fred Neville had no such meaning. On his behalf it must be acknowledged that he had no meaning whatever when he came again and again to Ardkill. Had he examined himself in the matter he would have declared that he liked the mother quite as well as the daughter. When Lady Mary Quin had thrown at him her very blunt arrow he had defended himself on that plea. Accident, and the spirit of adventure, had thrust these ladies in his path, and no doubt he liked them the better because they did not live as other people lived. Their solitude, the close vicinity of the ocean, the feeling that in meeting them none of the ordinary conventional usages of society were needed, the wildness and the strangeness of the scene, all had charms which he admitted to himself. And he knew that the girl was very lovely. Of course he said so to himself and to others. To take delight in beauty is assumed to be the nature of a young man, and this young man was not one to wish to differ from others in that respect. But when he went back to spend his Christmas at Scroope, he had never told even himself that he intended to be her lover.

'Good-bye, Mrs. O'Hara,' he said, a day or two before he left Ennis.

'So you're going?'

'Oh yes, I'm off. The orders from home are imperative. One has to cut one's lump of Christmas beef and also one's lump of Christmas pudding. It is our family religion, you know.'

'What a happiness to have a family to visit!'

'It's all very well, I suppose. I don't grumble. Only it's a bore going away, somehow.'

'You are coming back to Ennis?' asked Kate.

'Coming back—I should think so. Barney Morony wouldn't be quite so quiet if I was not coming back. I'm to dine with Father Marty at Liscannor on the 15th of January, to meet another priest from Milltown Malbay—the best fellow in the world he says.'

'That's Father Creech—not half such a good fellow, Mr. Neville, as Father Marty himself.'

'He couldn't be better. However, I shall be here then, and if I have any luck you shall have another skin of the same size by that time.' Then he shook hands with them both, and there was a feeling that the time would be blank till he should be again there in his sailor's jacket.

When the second week in January had come Mrs. O'Hara heard that the gallant young officer of the 20th was back in Ennis, and she well remembered that he had told her of his intention to dine with the priest. On the Sunday she saw Father Marty after mass, and managed to have a few words with him on the road while Kate returned to the cottage alone. 'So your friend Mr. Neville has come back to Ennis,' she said.

'I didn't know that he had come. He promised to dine with me on Thursday—only I think nothing of promises from these young fellows.'

'He told me he was to be with you.'

'More power to him. He'll be welcome. I'm getting to be a very ould man, Misthress O'Hara; but I'm not so ould but I like to have the young ones near me.'

'It is pleasant to see a bright face like his.'

'That's thrue for you, Misthress O'Hara. I like to see 'em bright and ganial. I don't know that I ever shot so much as a sparrow, meself, but I love to hear them talk of their shootings, and huntings, and the like of that. I've taken a fancy to that boy, and he might do pretty much as he plazes wid me.'

'And I too have taken a fancy to him, Father Marty.'

'Shure and how could you help it?'

'But he mustn't do as he pleases with me.' Father Marty looked up into her face as though he did not understand her. 'If I were alone, as you are, I could afford, like you, to indulge in the pleasure of a bright face. Only in that case he would not care to let me see it.'

'Bedad thin, Misthress O'Hara, I don't know a fairer face to look on in all Corcomroe than your own—that is when you're not in your tantrums, Misthress O'Hara.' The priest was a privileged person, and could say what he liked to his friend; and she understood that a priest might say without fault what would be very faulty if it came from any one else.

'I'm in earnest now, Father Marty. What shall we do if our darling Kate thinks of this young man more than is good for her?' Father Marty raised his hat and began to scratch his head. 'If you like to look at the fair face of a handsome lad——'

'I do thin, Misthress O'Hara.'

'Must not she like it also?'

'I'll go bail she likes it,' said the priest.

'And what will come next?'

'I'll tell you what it is, Misthress O'Hara. 'Would you want to keep her from even seeing a man at all?'

'God forbid.'

'It's not the way to make them happy, nor yet safe. If it's to be that way wid her, she'd better be a nun all out; and I'd be far from proposing that to your Kate.'

'She is hardly fit for so holy a life.'

'And why should she? I niver like seeing too many of 'em going that way, and them that are prittiest are the last I'd send there. But if not a nun, it stands to reason she must take chance with the rest of 'em. She's been too much shut up already. Let her keep her heart till he asks her for it; but if he does ask her, why shouldn't she be his wife? How many of them young officers take Irish wives home with 'em every year. Only for them, our beauties wouldn't have a chance.'

CHAPTER VII

FATHER MARTY'S HOSPITALITY

SUCH WAS the philosophy, or, perhaps, it may be better said such was the humanity of Father Marty! But in encouraging Mrs. O'Hara to receive this dangerous visitor he had by no means spoken without consideration. In one respect we must abandon Father Marty to the judgment and censure of fathers and mothers. The whole matter looked at from Lady Scroope's point of view was no doubt very injurious to the priest's character. He regarded a stranger among them, such as was Fred Neville, as fair spoil, as a Philistine to seize whom and capture him for life on behalf of any Irish girl would be a great triumph—a spoiling of the Egyptian to the accomplishment of which he would not hesitate to lend his priestly assistance, the end to be accomplished, of course, being marriage. For Lord Scroope and his family and his blood and his religious fanaticism he could entertain no compassion whatever. Father Marty was no great politician, and desired no rebellion against England.* Even in the days of O'Connell and repeal*he had been but lüke-warm. But justice for Ireland in the guise of wealthy English husbands for pretty Irish girls he desired with all his heart. He was true to his own faith, to the backbone, but he entertained no prejudice against a good looking Protestant youth when a fortunate marriage was in question. So little had been given to the Irish in these days, that they were bound to take what they could get. Lord Scroope and the Countess, had they known the priest's views on this matter, would have regarded him as an unscrupulous intriguing ruffian, prepared to destroy the happiness of a noble family by a wicked scheme. But his views of life, as judged from the other side, admitted of some excuse. As for a girl breaking her heart, he did not, perhaps, much believe in such a catastrophe. Of a sore heart a girl must run the chance—as also must a man. That young men do go about promising marriage and not keeping their promise, he knew well. None could know that better than he did, for he was the repository of half the love secrets in his parish. But all that was part of the evil coming from the fall of Adam, and must be endured till—till the Pope should have his own again, and be able to set all things right. In the meantime young women must do the best they could to keep their lovers—and should one lover break away, then must the deserted one use her experience towards getting a second. But how was a girl to have a lover at all, if she were never allowed to see a man? He had been bred a priest from his youth upwards, and knew nothing of love; but nevertheless it was a pain to him to see a young girl, good-looking, healthy, fit to be the mother of children, pine away, unsought for, uncoupled—as it would be a pain to see a fruit grow ripe upon the tree, and then fall and perish for want of plucking. His philosophy was perhaps at fault, and it may be that his humanity was unrefined. But he was human to the core—and, at any rate, unselfish. That there might be another danger was a fact that he looked full in the face. But what victory can be won without danger? And he thought that he knew this girl, who three times a year*would open her whole heart to him in confession. He was sure that she was not only inno-cent, but good. And of the man, too, he was prone to believe good—though who on such a question ever trusts a man's goodness? There might be danger and there must be dis-cretion; but surely it would not be wise, because evil was possible, that such a one as Kate O'Hara should be kept from all that intercourse without which a woman is only half a woman! He had considered it all, though the reader may perhaps think that as a minister of the gospel he had come to a strange conclusion. He himself, in his own defence, would have said that having served many years in the minis-try he had learned to know the nature of men and women.

Mrs. O'Hara said not a word to Kate of the doctrines which the priest had preached, but she found herself encouraged to mention their new friend's name to the girl. During Fred's absence hardly a word had been spoken concerning him in the cottage. Mrs. O'Hara had feared the subject, and Kate had thought of him much too often to allow his name to be on her tongue. But now as they sat after dinner over their peat fire the mother began the subject. 'Mr. Neville is to dine with Father Marty on Thursday.'

'Is he, mother?'

'Barney Morony was telling me that he was back at Ennis. Barney had to go in and see him about the boat.'

'He won't go boating such weather as this, mother?'

'It seems that he means it. The winds are not so high now as they were in October, and the men understand well when the sea will be high.'

'It is frightful to think of anybody being in one of those little boats now.' Kate ever since she had lived in these parts had seen the canoes from Liscannor and Lahinch about in the bay, summer and winter, and had never found anything dreadful in it before.

'I suppose he'll come up here again,' said the mother; but to this Kate made no answer. 'He is to sleep at Father Marty's I fancy, and he can hardly do that without paying us a visit.'

'The days are short and he'll want all his time for the boating,' said Kate with a little pout.

'He'll find half-an-hour, I don't doubt. Shall you be glad to see him, Kate?'

'I don't know, mother. One is glad almost to see anyone up here. It's as good as a treat when old Corcoran comes up with the turf.'

'But Mr. Neville is not like old Corcoran, Kate.'

'Not in the least, mother. I do like Mr. Neville better than Corcoran, because you see with Corcoran the excitement is very soon over. And Corcoran hasn't very much to say for himself.'

'And Mr. Neville has?'

'He says a great deal more to you than he does to me, mother.'

'I like him very much. I should like him very much indeed if there were no danger in his coming.'

'What danger?'

'That he should steal your heart away, my own, my darling, my child.' Then Kate, instead of answering, got up and threw herself at her mother's knees, and buried her face in her mother's lap, and Mrs. O'Hara knew that that act of larceny had already been perpetrated.

And how should it have been otherwise? But of such stealing it is always better that no mention should be made till the theft has been sanctified by free gift. Till the loss has been spoken of and acknowledged, it may in most cases be recovered. Had Neville never returned from Scroope, and his name never been mentioned by the mother to her daughter, it may be that Kate O'Hara would not have known that she had loved him. For a while she would have been sad. For a month or two, as she lay wakeful in her bed she would have thought of her dreams. But she would have thought of them as only dreams. She would have been sure that she could have loved him had any fair ending been possible for such love; but she would have assured herself that she had been on her guard, and that she was safe in spite of her dreams. But now the flame in her heart had been confessed and in some degree sanctioned, and she would foster it rather than quench it. Even should such a love be capable of no good fortune, would it not be better to have a few weeks of happy dreaming than a whole life that should be passionless? What could she do with her own heart there, living in solitude, with none but the sea gulls to look at her? Was it not infinitely better that she should give it away to such a young god as this than let it feed upon itself miserably? Yes, she would give it away—but might it not be that the young god would not take the gift?

On the third day after his arrival at Ennis, Neville was at Liscannor with the priest. He little dreamed that the fact of his dining and sleeping at Father Marty's house, would be known to the ladies at Castle Quin, and communicated from them to his aunt at Scroope Manor. Not that he would have been deterred from accepting the priest's hospitality or frightened into accepting that of the noble owner of the castle, had he known precisely all that would be written about it. He would not have altered his conduct in a matter in which he considered himself entitled to regulate it, in obedience to any remonstrances from Scroope Manor. Objections to the society of a Roman Catholic priest because of his religion he would have regarded as old-fashioned fanaticism. As for Earls and their daughters he would no doubt have enough of them in his future life, and this special Earl and his daughters had not fascinated him. He had chosen to come to Ireland with his regiment for this year instead of at once assuming the magnificence of his position in England, in order that he might indulge the spirit of adventure before he assumed the duties of life. And it seemed to him that in dining and sleeping at an Irish priest's house on the shores of the Atlantic, with the prospect of seal shooting and seeing a very pretty girl on the following morning, he was indulging that spirit properly. But Lady Mary Quin thought that he was misbehaving himself and taking to very bad courses. When she heard that he was to sleep at the priest's house, she was quite sure that he would visit Mrs. O'Hara on the next day.

The dinner at the priest's was very jovial. There was a bottle of sherry and there was a bottle of port, procured, chiefly for the sake of appearance, from a grocer's shop at Ennistimon—but the whiskey had come from Cork and had been in the priest's keeping for the last dozen years. He good-humouredly acknowledged that the wine was nothing, but expressed an opinion that Mr. Neville might find it difficult to beat the 'sperrits.' 'It's thrue for you, Father Marty,' said the rival priest from Milltown Malbay, 'and it's you that should know good sperrits from bad if ony man in Ireland does.'

' 'Deed thin,' replied the priest of Liscannor, 'barring the famine years, I've mixed two tumblers of punch for meself every day these forty years, and if it was all together it'd be about enough to give Mr. Neville a day's sale-shooting in his canoe.' Immediately after dinner Neville was invited to light his cigar, and everything was easy, comfortable, and to a certain degree adventurous. There were the two priests, and a young Mr. Finucane from Ennistimon—who however was not quite so much to Fred's taste as the elder men. Mr. Finucane wore various rings, and talked rather largely about his father's demesne. But the whole thing was new, and by no means dull. As Neville had not left Ennis till late in the day—after what he called a hard day's work in the warrior line—they did not sit down till past eight o'clock; nor did anyone talk of moving till past midnight. Fred certainly made for himself more than two glasses of punch, and he would have sworn that the priest had done so also. Father Marty, however, was said by those who knew him best to be very rigid in this matter, and to have the faculty of making his drink go a long way. Young Mr. Finucane took three or four —perhaps five or six—and then volunteered to join Fred Neville in a day's shooting under the rocks. But Fred had not been four years in a cavalry regiment without knowing how to protect himself in such a difficulty as this. 'The canoe will only hold myself and the man.' said Fred, with perfect simplicity. Mr. Finucane drew himself up haughtily and did not utter another word for the next five minutes. Nevertheless he took a most affectionate leave of the young officer when half an hour after midnight he was told by Father Marty that it was time for him to go home. Father Creech also took his leave, and then Fred and the priest of Liscannor were left sitting together over the embers of the turf fire. 'You'll be going up to see our friends at Ardkill tomorrow,' said the priest.

'Likely enough, Father Marty.'

'Of course you will. Sorrow a doubt of that.'* Then the priest paused.

'And why shouldn't I?' asked Neville.

'I'm not saying that you shouldn't, Mr. Neville. It wouldn't be civil nor yet nathural after knowing them as you have done. If you didn't go they'd be thinking there was a rason for your staying away, and that'd be worse than all. But, Mr. Neville——'

'Out with it, Father Marty.' Fred knew what was coming fairly well, and he also had thought a good deal upon the matter.

'Them two ladies, Mr. Neville, live up there all alone, with sorrow a human being in the world to protect them—barring myself.'

'Why should they want protection?'

'Just because they're lone women, and because one of them is very young and very beautiful.'

'They are both beautiful,' said Neville.

' 'Deed and they are—both of 'em. The mother can look afther herself, and after a fashion, too, she can look afther her daughter. 'I shouldn't like to be the man to come in her way when he'd once decaived her child. You're a young man, Mr. Neville.'

'That's my misfortune.'

'And one who stands very high in the world. They tell me you're to be a great lord some day.'

'Either that or a little one,' said Neville, laughing.

'Anyways you'll be a rich man with a handle to your name. To me, living here in this out of the way parish, a lord doesn't matter that.' And Father Marty gave a fillip with his fingers. 'The only lord that matters me is me bishop. But with them women yonder, the title and the money and all the grandeur goes a long way. It has been so since the world began. In riding a race against you they carry weight from the very awe which the name of an English Earl brings with it.'

'Why should they ride a race against me?'

'Why indeed—unless you ride a race against them! You wouldn't wish to injure that young thing as isn't yet out of her teens?'

'God forbid that I should injure her.'

'I don't think that you're the man to do it with your eyes
open, Mr. Neville. If you can't spake her fair in the way of
making her your wife, don't spake her fair at all. That's the
long and the short of it, Mr. Neville. You see what they are.
They're ladies, if there is a lady living in the Queen's dominions. That young thing is as beautiful as Habe,* as innocent
as a sleeping child, as soft as wax to take impression. What
armour has she got against such a one as you?'

'She shall not need armour.'

'If you're a gentleman, Mr. Neville—as I know you are—
you will not give her occasion to find out her own wakeness.
Well, if it isn't past one I'm a sinner. It's Friday morning and
I mus'n't ate a morsel myself, poor papist that I am! but I'll
get you a bit of cold mate and a drop of grog in a moment if
you'll take it.' Neville, however, refused the hospitable offer.

'Father Marty,' he said, speaking with a zeal which perhaps
owed something of its warmth to the punch, 'you shall find
that I am a gentleman.'

'I'm shure of it, my boy.'

'If I can do no good to your friend, at any rate I will do no
harm to her.'

'That is spoken like a Christian, Mr. Neville—which I take
to be a higher name even than gentleman.'

'There's my hand upon it,' said Fred, enthusiastically.
After that he went to bed.

On the following morning the priest was very jolly at
breakfast, and in speaking of the ladies at Ardkill made no
allusion whatever to the conversation of the previous evening. 'Ah no,' he said, when Neville proposed that they should
walk up together to the cottage before he went down to his
boat. 'What's the good of an ould man like me going bother-
ing? And, signs on, I'm going into Ennistimon to see Pat
O'Leary about the milk he's sending to our Union.* The thief
of the world—it's wathering it he is before he sends it. Nothing kills me, Mr. Neville, but when I hear of all them English

vices being brought over to this poor suffering innocent counthry.'

Neville had decided on the advice of Barney Morony, that he would on this morning go down southward along the coast to Drumdeirg rock, in the direction away from the Hag's Head and from Mrs. O'Hara's cottage; and he therefore postponed his expedition till after his visit. When Father Marty started to Ennistimon to look after that sinner O'Leary, Fred Neville, all alone, turned the other way to Ardkill.

CHAPTER VIII

I DIDN'T WANT YOU TO GO*

MRS. O'HARA had known that he would come, and Kate had known it; and, though it would be unfair to say that they were waiting for him, it is no more than true to say that they were ready for him. 'We are so glad to see you again,' said Mrs. O'Hara.'

'Not more glad than I am to find myself here once more.'

'So you dined and slept at Father Marty's last night. What will the grand people say at the Castle?'

'As I sha'n't hear what they say, it won't matter much! Life is not long enough, Mrs. O'Hara, for putting up with disagreeable people.'

'Was it pleasant last night?'

'Very pleasant. I don't think Father Creech is half as good as Father Marty, you know.'

'Oh no,' exclaimed Kate.

'But he's a jolly sort of fellow, too. And there was a Mr. Finucane there—a very grand fellow.'

'We know no one about here but the priests,' said Mrs. O'Hara, laughing. 'Anybody might think that the cottage was a little convent.'

'Then I oughtn't to come.'

'Well, no, I suppose not. Only foreigners are admitted to see convents sometimes. You're going after the poor seals again?'

'Barney says the tide is too high for the seals now. We're going to Drumdeirg.'

'What—to those little rocks?' asked Kate.

'Yes—to the rocks. I wish you'd both come with me.'

'I wouldn't go in one of these canoes all out there for the world,' said Kate.

'What can be the use of it?' asked Mrs. O'Hara.

'I've got to get the feathers for Father Marty's bed, you know. I haven't shot as many yet as would make a pillow for a cradle.'

'The poor innocent gulls!'

'The poor innocent chickens and ducks, if you come to that, Miss O'Hara.'

'But they're of use.'

'And so will Father Marty's feather bed be of use. Good-bye, Mrs. O'Hara. Good-bye, Miss O'Hara. I shall be down again next week, and we'll have that other seal.'

There was nothing in this. So far, at any rate, he had not broken his word to the priest. He had not spoken a word to Kate O'Hara, that might not and would not have been said had the priest been present. But how lovely she was; and what a thrill ran through his arm as he held her hand in his for a moment. Where should he find a girl like that in England with such colour, such eyes, such hair, such innocence —and then with so sweet a voice?

As he hurried down the hill to the beach at Coolroone, where Morony was to meet him with the boat, he could not keep himself from comparisons between Kate O'Hara and Sophie Mellerby. No doubt his comparisons were made very incorrectly—and unfairly; but they were all in favour of the girl who lived out of the world in solitude on the cliffs of Moher. And why should he not be free to seek a wife where he pleased? In such an affair as that—an affair of love in which the heart and the heart alone should be consulted, what right could any man have to dictate to him? Certain ideas occurred to him which his friends in England would have called wild, democratic, revolutionary and damnable, but which, owing perhaps to the Irish air and the Irish whiskey and the spirit of adventure fostered by the vicinity of rocks and ocean, appeared to him at the moment to be not only charming but reasonable also. No doubt he was born to high state and great rank, but nothing that his rank and state could give him was so sweet as his liberty. To be

free to choose for himself in all things, was the highest privilege of man. What pleasure could he have in a love which
should be selected for him by such a woman as his aunt?
Then he gave the reins to some confused notion of an Irish
bride, a wife who should be half a wife and half not*—whom
he would love and cherish tenderly but of whose existence
no English friend should be aware. How could he more
charmingly indulge his spirit of adventure than by some such
arrangement as this?

He knew that he had given a pledge to his uncle to contract no marriage that would be derogatory to his position.
He knew also that he had given a pledge to the priest that
he would do no harm to Kate O'Hara. He felt that he was
bound to keep each pledge. As for that sweet, darling girl,
would he not sooner lose his life than harm her? But he was
aware that an adventurous life was always a life of difficulties,
and that for such as live adventurous lives the duty of overcoming difficulties was of all duties the chief. Then he got
into his canoe, and, having succeeded in killing two gulls on
the Drumdeirg rocks, thought that for that day he had carried
out his purpose as a man of adventure very well.

During February and March he was often on the coast,
and hardly one visit did he make which was not followed by a
letter from Castle Quin to Scroope Manor. No direct accusation of any special fault was made against him in consequence. No charge was brought of an improper hankering
after any special female, because Lady Scroope found herself
bound in conscience not to commit her correspondent; but
very heavy injunctions were laid upon him as to his general
conduct, and he was eagerly entreated to remember his great
duty and to come home and settle himself in England. In the
meantime the ties which bound him to the coast of Clare
were becoming stronger and stronger every day. He had
ceased now to care much about seeing Father Marty, and
would come, when the tide was low, direct from Lahinch to
the strand beneath the cliffs, from whence there was a path
through the rocks up to Ardkill. And there he would remain

for hours—having his gun with him, but caring little for his gun. He told himself that he loved the rocks and the wildness of the scenery, and the noise of the ocean, and the whirring of the birds above and below him. It was certainly true that he loved Kate O'Hara.

'Neville, you must answer me a question,' said the mother to him one morning when they were out together, looking down upon the Atlantic when the wind had lulled after a gale.

'Ask it then,' said he.

'What is the meaning of all this? What is Kate to believe?'

'Of course she believes that I love her better than all the world besides—that she is more to me than all the world can give or take. I have told her at least, so often, that if she does not believe it she is little better than a Jew.'

'You must not joke with me now. If you knew what it was to have one child and only that you would not joke with me.'

'I am quite in earnest. I am not joking.'

'And what is to be the end of it?'

'The end of it! How can I say? My uncle is an old man—very old, very infirm, very good, very prejudiced, and broken-hearted because his own son, who died, married against his will.'

'You would not liken my Kate to such as that woman was?'

'Your Kate! She is my Kate as much as yours. Such a thought as that would be an injury to me as deep as to you. You know that to me my Kate, our Kate, is all excellence—as pure and good as she is bright and beautiful. As God is above us she shall be my wife—but I cannot take her to Scroope Manor as my wife while my uncle lives.'

'Why should anyone be ashamed of her at Scroope Manor?'

'Because they are fools. But I cannot cure them of their folly. My uncle thinks that I should marry one of my own class.'

'Class—what class? He is a gentleman, I presume, and she is a lady.'

'That is very true—so true that I myself shall act upon the

truth. But I will not make his last years wretched. He is a
Protestant, and you are Catholics.'

'What is that? Are not ever so many of your lords
Catholics? Were they not all Catholics before Protestants
were ever though of?'

'Mrs. O'Hara, I have told you that to me she is as high and
good and noble as though she were a Princess. And I have
told you that she shall be my wife. If that does not content
you, I cannot help it. It contents her. I owe much to her.'

'Indeed you do—everything.'

'But I owe much to him also. I do not think that you can
gain anything by quarrelling with me.'

She paused for a while before she answered him, looking
into his face the while with something of the ferocity of a tigress. So intent was her gaze that his eyes quailed beneath it.
'By the living God,' she said, 'if you injure my child I will
have the very blood from your heart.'

Nevertheless she allowed him to return alone to the house,
where she knew that he would find her girl. 'Kate,' he said,
going into the parlour in which she was sitting idle at the
window—'dear Kate.'

'Well, sir?'

'I'm off.'

'You are always—off, as you call it.'

'Well—yes. But I'm not on and off, as the saying is.'

'Why should you go away now?'

'Do you suppose a soldier has got nothing to do? You never
calculate, I think, that Ennis is about three-and-twenty miles
from here. Come, Kate, be nice with me before I go.'

'How can I be nice when you are going? I always think
when I see you go that you will never come back to me again.
I don't know why you should come back to such a place as
this?'

'Because, as it happens, the place holds what I love best in
all the world.' Then he lifted her from her chair, and put his
arm around her waist. 'Do you not know that I love you
better than all that the world holds?'

'How can I know it?

'Because I swear it to you.'

'I think that you like me—a little. Oh Fred, if you were to go and never come back I should die. Do you remember Mariana?*My life is dreary. He cometh not. She said, "I am aweary, aweary; I would that I were dead!" Do you remember that? What has mother been saying to you?'

'She was bidding me to do you no harm. It was not necessary. I would sooner pluck out my eye than hurt you. My uncle is an old man—a very old man. She cannot understand that it is better that we should wait than that I should have to think hereafter that I had killed him by my unkindness.'

'But he wants you to love some other girl.'

'He cannot make me do that. All the world cannot change my heart, Kate. If you cannot trust me for that, then you do not love me as I love you.'

'Oh, Fred, you know I love you. I do trust you. Of course I can wait, if I only know that you will come back to me. I only want to see you.' He was now leaning over her, and her cheek was pressed close to his. Though she was talking of Mariana, and pretending to fear future misery, all this was Elysium to her—the very joy of Paradise. She could sit and think of him now from morning to night, and never find the day an hour too long. She could remember the words in which he made his oaths to her, and cherish the sweet feeling of his arm round her body. To have her cheek close to his was godlike. And then when he would kiss her, though she would rebuke him, it was as though all heaven were in the embrace.

'And now good-bye. One kiss darling.'

'No.'

'Not a kiss when I am going?'

'I don't want you to go. Oh, Fred! Well—there. Good-bye, my own, own, own beloved one. You'll be here on Monday?'

'Yes—on Monday.'

'And be in the boat four hours, and here four minutes.

Don't I know you?' But he went without answering this last accusation.

'What shall we do, Kate, if he deceives us?' said the mother that evening.

'Die. But I'm sure he will not deceive us.'

Neville, as he made his way down to Liscannor, where his gig was waiting for him, did ask himself some serious questions about his adventure. What must be the end of it? And had he not been imprudent? It may be declared on his behalf that no idea of treachery to the girl ever crossed his mind. He loved her too thoroughly for that. He did love her—not perhaps as she loved him. He had many things in the world to occupy his mind, and she had but one. He was almost a god to her. She to him was simply the sweetest girl that he had ever as yet seen, and one who had that peculiar merit that she was all his own. No other man had ever pressed her hand, or drank her sweet breath. Was not such a love a thousand times sweeter than that of some girl who had been hurried from drawing-room to drawing-room, and perhaps from one vow of constancy to another for half-a-dozen years? The adventure was very sweet. But how was it to end? His uncle might live these ten years, and he had not the heart —nor yet the courage—to present her to his uncle as his bride.

When he reached Ennis that evening there was a despatch marked 'Immediate,' from his aunt Lady Scroope. 'Your uncle is very ill—dangerously ill, we fear. His great desire is to see you once again. Pray come without losing an hour.'

Early on the following morning he started for Dublin, but before he went to bed that night he not only wrote to Kate O'Hara, but enclosed the note from his aunt. He could understand that though the tidings of his uncle's danger was a shock to him there would be something in the tidings which would cause joy to the two inmates of Ardkill Cottage. When he sent that letter with his own, he was of course determined that he would marry Kate O'Hara as soon as he was a free man.

CHAPTER IX

FRED NEVILLE RETURNS TO SCROOPE.

THE SUDDENNESS of the demand made for the heir's presence at Scroope was perhaps not owing to the Earl's illness alone. The Earl, indeed, was ill—so ill that he thought himself that his end was very near; but his illness had been brought about chiefly by the misery to which he had been subjected by the last despatch from Castle Quin to the Countess. 'I am most unwilling,' she said, 'to make mischief or to give unnecessary pain to you or to Lord Scroope; but I think it my duty to let you know that the general opinion about here is that Mr. Neville shall make Miss O'Hara his wife—*if he has not done so already.* The most dangerous feature in the whole matter is that it is all managed by the priest of this parish, a most unscrupulous person, who would do anything —he is so daring. We have known him many, many years, and we know to what lengths he would go. The laws have been so altered in favour of the Roman Catholics, and against the Protestants, that a priest can do almost just what he likes.* I do not think that he would scruple for an instant to marry them if he thought it likely that his prey would escape from him. My own opinion is that there has been no marriage as yet, though I know that others think that there has been.' The expression of this opinion from 'others' which had reached Lady Mary's ears consisted of an assurance from her own Protestant lady's-maid that that wicked guzzling old Father Marty would marry the young couple as soon as look at them, and very likely had done so already. 'I cannot say,' continued Lady Mary, 'that I actually know anything against the character of Miss O'Hara. Of the mother we have very strange stories here. They live in a little cottage with one

maid-servant, almost upon the cliffs, and nobody knows anything about them except the priest. If he should be seduced*
into a marriage, nothing could be more unfortunate.' Lady
Mary probably intended to insinuate that were young Neville
prudently to get out of the adventure, simply leaving the girl
behind him blasted, ruined, and destroyed, the matter no
doubt would be bad, but in that case the great misfortune
would have been avoided. She could not quite say this in
plain words; but she felt, no doubt, that Lady Scroope would
understand her. Then Lady Mary went on to assure her
friend that though she and her father and sisters very greatly
regretted that Mr. Neville had not again given them the pleasure of seeing him at Castle Quin, no feeling of injury on that
score had induced her to write so strongly as she had done.
She had been prompted to do so, simply by her desire to prevent *a most ruinous alliance*.

Lady Scroope acknowledged entirely the truth of these last
words. Such an alliance would be most ruinous! But what
could she do? Were she to write to Fred and tell him all that
she heard—throwing to the winds Lady Mary's stupid injunctions respecting secrecy, as she would not have scrupled
to do could she have thus obtained her object—might it not
be quite possible that she would precipitate the calamity
which she desired so eagerly to avoid? Neither had she nor
had her husband any power over the young man, except such
as arose from his own good feeling. The Earl could not disinherit him—could not put a single acre beyond his reach.
Let him marry whom he might he must be Earl Scroope of
Scroope, and the woman so married must be the Countess of
Scroope. There was already a Lady Neville about the world
whose existence was a torture to them; and if this young man
chose also to marry a creature utterly beneath him and to
degrade the family, no effort on their part could prevent him.
But if, as seemed probable, he were yet free, and if he could
be got to come again among them, it might be that he still
had left some feelings on which they might work. No doubt
there was the Neville obstinacy about him; but he had

seemed to both of them to acknowledge the sanctity of his
family, and to appreciate to some degree the duty which he
owed to it.

The emergency was so great that she feared to act alone.
She told everything to her husband, shewing him Lady
Mary's letter, and the effect upon him was so great that it
made him ill. 'It will be better for me,' he said, 'to turn my
face to the wall and die before I know it.' He took to his bed,
and they of his household did think that he would die. He
hardly spoke except to his wife, and when alone with her did
not cease to moan over the destruction which had come upon
the house. 'If it could have only been the other brother,' said
Lady Scroope.

'There can be no change,' said the Earl. 'He must do as it
lists him*with the fortune and the name and honours of the
family.'

Then on one morning there was a worse bulletin than
heretofore given by the doctor, and Lady Scroope at once
sent off the letter which was to recall the nephew to his
uncle's bedside. The letter, as we have seen, was successful,
and Fred, who caused himself to be carried over from Dorchester to Scroope as fast as post-horses could be made to gallop, almost expected to be told on his arrival that his uncle
had departed to his rest. In the hall he encountered Mrs.
Bunce the housekeeper. 'We think my lord is a little better,'
said Mrs. Bunce almost in a whisper. 'My lord took a little
broth in the middle of the day, and we believe he has slept
since.' Then he passed on and found his aunt in the small
sitting-room. His uncle had rallied a little, she told him. She
was very affectionate in her manner, and thanked him warmly for his alacrity in coming. When he was told that his uncle
would postpone his visit till the next morning he almost began to think that he had been fussy in travelling so quickly.

That evening he dined alone with his aunt, and the conversation during dinner and as they sat for a few minutes
after dinner had reference solely to his uncle's health. But,
though they were alone on this evening, he was surprised to

find that Sophie Mellerby was again at Scroope. Lady Sophia
and Mr. Mellerby were up in London, but Sophie was not to
join them till May. As it happened, however, she was dining
at the parsonage this evening. She must have been in the
house when Neville arrived, but he had not seen her. 'Is she
going to live here?' he asked, almost irreverently, when he
was first told she was in the house. 'I wish she were,' said Lady
Scroope. 'I am childless, and she is as dear to me as a
daughter.' Then Fred apologized, and expressed himself as
quite willing that Sophie Mellerby should live and die at
Scroope.

The evening was dreadfully dull. It had seemed to him
that the house was darker, and gloomier, and more comfortless than ever. He had hurried over to see a dying man, and
now there was nothing for him to do but to kick his heels.
But before he went to bed his ennui was dissipated by a full
explanation of all his aunt's terrors. She crept down to him
at about nine, and having commenced her story by saying
that she had a matter of most vital importance on which to
speak to him, she told him in fact all that she had heard from
Lady Mary.

'She is a mischief-making gossiping old maid,' said Neville
angrily.

"Will you tell me that there is no truth in what she
writes?' asked Lady Scroope. But this was a question which
Fred Neville was not prepared to answer, and he sat silent.
'Fred, tell me the truth. Are you married?'

'No—I am not married.'

'I know that you will not condescend to an untruth.'

'If so, my word must be sufficient.'

But it was not sufficient. She longed to extract from him
some repeated and prolonged assurance which might bring
satisfaction to her own mind. 'I am glad, at any rate, to hear
that there is no truth in that suspicion.' To this he would not
condescend to reply but sat glowering at her as though in
wrath that any question should be asked him about his private concerns. 'You must feel, Fred, for your uncle in such a

matter. You must know how important this is to him. You have heard what he has already suffered; and you must know too that he has endeavoured to be very good to you.'

'I do know that he has—been very good to me.'

'Perhaps you are angry with me for interfering.' He would not deny that he was angry. 'I should not do so were it not that your uncle is ill and suffering.'

'You have asked me a question and I have answered it. I do not know what more you want of me.'

'Will you say that there is no truth in all this that Lady Mary says?'

'Lady Mary is an impertinent old maid.'

'If you were in your uncle's place, and if you had an heir as to whose character in the world you were anxious, you would not think anyone impertinent, who endeavoured for the sake of friendship, to save your name and family from a disreputable connexion.'

'I have made no disreputable connexion. I will not allow the word disreputable to be used in regard to any of my friends.'

'You do know people of the name of O'Hara?'

'Of course I do.'

'And there is a—young lady?'

'I may know a dozen young ladies as to whom I shall not choose to consult Lady Mary Quin.'

'You understand what I mean, Fred. Of course I do not wish to ask you anything about your general acquaintances. No doubt you meet many girls whom you admire, and I should be very foolish were I to make inquiries of you or of anybody else concerning them. I am the last person to be so injudicious. If you will tell me that there is not and never shall be any question of marriage between you and Miss O'Hara, I will not say another word.'

'I will not pledge myself to anything for the future.'

'You told your uncle you would never make a marriage that should be disgraceful to the position which you will be called upon to fill.'

'Nor will I.'

'But would not this marriage be disgraceful, even were the young lady ever so estimable? How are the old families of the country to be kept up, and the old blood maintained if young men, such as your are, will not remember something of all that is due to the name which they bear.'

'I do not know that I have forgotten anything.'

Then she paused before she could summon courage to ask him another question. 'You have made no promise of marriage to Miss O'Hara?' He sat dumb, but still looking at her with that angry frown. 'Surely your uncle has a right to expect that you will answer that question.'

'I am quite sure that for his sake it will be much better that no such questions shall be asked me.'

In point of fact he had answered the question. When he would not deny that such promise had been made, there could no longer be any doubt of the truth of what Lady Mary had written. Of course the whole truth had now been elicited. He was not married but he was engaged—engaged to a girl of whom he knew nothing, a Roman Catholic, Irish, fatherless, almost nameless—to one who had never been seen in good society, one of whom no description could be given, of whom no record could be made in the peerage that would not be altogether disgraceful, a girl of whom he was ashamed to speak before those to whom he owed duty and submission!

That there might be a way to escape the evil even yet Lady Scroope acknowledged to herself fully. Many men promise marriage but do not keep the promise they have made. This lady, who herself was really good—unselfish, affectionate, religious, actuated by a sense of duty in all that she did, whose life had been almost austerely moral, entertained an idea that young men, such as Fred Neville, very commonly made such promises with very little thought of keeping them. She did not expect young men to be governed by principles such as those to which young ladies are bound to submit themselves. She almost supposed that heaven had a different code of laws for men and women in her condition of life, and

that salvation was offered on very different terms to the two
sexes. The breach of any such promise as the heir of Scroope
could have made to such a girl as this Miss O'Hara would be
a perjury at which Jove might certainly be expected to laugh.
But in her catalogue there were sins for which no young
men could hope to be forgiven; and the sin of such a marriage as this would certainly be beyond pardon.

Of the injury which was to be done to Miss O'Hara, it
may be said with certainty that she thought not at all. In her
eyes it would be no injury, but simple justice—no more than
a proper punishment for intrigue and wicked ambition.
Without having seen the enemy to the family of Scroope, or
even having heard a word to her disparagement, she could
feel sure that the girl was bad—that these O'Haras were
vulgar and false impostors, persons against whom she could
put out all her strength without any prick of conscience.
Women in such mattters are always hard against women, and
especially hard against those whom they believe to belong to
a class below their own. Certainly no feeling of mercy would
induce her to hold her hand in this task of saving her husband's nephew from an ill-assorted marriage. Mercy to Miss
O'Hara! Lady Scroope had the name of being a very charitable woman. She gave away money. She visited the poor. She
had laboured hard to make the cottages on the estate clean
and comfortable. She denied herself many things that she
might give to others. But she would have no more mercy on
such a one as Miss O'Hara, than a farmer's labourer would
have on a rat!

There was nothing more now to be said to the heir—
nothing more for the present that could serve the purpose
which she had in hand. 'Your uncle is very ill,' she murmured.

'I was so sorry to hear it.'

'We hope now that he may recover. For the last two days
the doctor has told us that we may hope.'

'I am so glad to find that it is so.'

'I am sure you are. You will see him to-morrow after break-

fast. He is most anxious to see you. I think sometimes you
hardly reflect how much you are to him.'

'I don't know why you should say so.'

'You had better not speak to him to-morrow about this
affair—of the Irish young lady.'

'Certainly not—unless he speaks to me about it.'

'He is hardly strong enough yet. But no doubt he will do so
before you leave us. I hope it may be long before you do that.'

'It can't be very long, Aunt Mary.' To this she said nothing, but bade him good-night and he was left alone. It was
now past ten, and he supposed that Miss Mellerby had come
in and gone to her room. Why she should avoid him in this
way he could not understand. But as for Miss Mellerby herself, she was so little to him that he cared not at all whether
he did or did not see her. All his brightest thoughts were
away in County Clare, on the cliffs overlooking the Atlantic.
They might say what they liked to him, but he would never
be untrue to the girl whom he had left there. His aunt had
spoken of the 'affair of—the Irish young lady;' and he had
quite understood the sneer with which she had mentioned
Kate's nationality. Why should not an Irish girl be as good
as any English girl? Of one thing he was quite sure—that
there was much more of real life to be found on the cliffs of
Moher than in the gloomy chambers of Scroope Manor.

He got up from his seat feeling absolutely at a loss how to
employ himself. Of course he could go to bed, but how terribly dull must life be in a place in which he was obliged to
go to bed at ten o'clock because there was nothing to do. And
since he had been there his only occupation had been that
of listening to his aunt's sermons. He began to think that a
man might pay too dearly even for being the heir to Scroope.
After sitting awhile in the dark gloom created by a pair of
candles, he got up and wandered into the large unused
dining-room of the mansion. It was a chamber over forty
feet long, with dark flock paper and dark curtains, with dark
painted wainscoating below the paper and huge dark maho-
gany furniture. On the walls hung the portraits of the

Scroopes for many generations past, some in armour, some in their robes of state, ladies with stiff bodices and high head-dresses, not beauties by Lely or warriors and statesmen by Kneller,* but wooden, stiff, ungainly, hideous figures, by artists whose works had, unfortunately, been more enduring than their names. He was pacing up and down the room with a candle in his hand, trying to realize to himself what life at Scroope might be with a wife of his aunt's choosing, and his aunt to keep the house for them, when a door was opened at the end of the room, away from that by which he had entered, and with a soft noiseless step Miss Mellerby entered. She did not see him at first, as the light of her own candle was in her eyes, and she was startled when he spoke to her. His first idea was one of surprise that she should be wander-ing about the house alone at night. 'Oh, Mr. Neville,' she said, 'you quite took me by surprise. How do you do? I did not expect to meet you here.'

'Nor I you!'

'Since Lord Scroope has been so ill, Lady Scroope has been sleeping in the little room next to his, downstairs, and I have just come from her.'

'What do you think of my uncle's state?'

'He is better; but he is very weak.'

'You see him?'

'Oh yes, daily. He is so anxious to see you, Mr. Neville, and so much obliged to you for coming. I was sure that you would come.'

'Of course I came.'

'He wanted to see you this afternoon; but the doctor had expressly ordered that he should be kept quiet. Good-night. I am so very glad that you are here. I am sure that you will be good to him.'

Why should she be glad, and why should she be sure that he would be good to his uncle? Could it be that she also had been told the story of Kate O'Hara? Then, as no other occu-pation was possible to him, he took himself to bed.

CHAPTER X

FRED NEVILLE'S SCHEME.

ON THE next morning after breakfast Neville was taken into his uncle's chamber, but there was an understanding that there was to be no conversation on disagreeable subjects on this occasion. His aunt remained in the room while he was there, and the conversation was almost confined to the expression of thanks on the part of the Earl to his nephew for coming, and of hopes on the part of the nephew that his uncle might soon be well. One matter was mooted as to which no doubt much would be said before Neville could get away. 'I thought it better to make arrangements to stay a fortnight,' said Fred—as though a fortnight were a very long time indeed.

'A fortnight!' said the Earl.

'We won't talk of his going yet,' replied Lady Scroope.

'Supposing I had died, he could not have gone back in a fortnight,' said the Earl in a low moaning voice.

'My dear uncle, I hope that I may live to see you in your own place here at Scroope for many years to come.' The Earl shook his head, but nothing more was then said on that subject. Fred, however, had carried out his purpose. He had been determined to let them understand that he would not hold himself bound to remain long at Scroope Manor.

Then he wrote a letter to his own Kate. It was the first time he had addressed her in this fashion, and though he was somewhat of a gallant gay Lothario,* the writing of the letter was an excitement to him. If so, what must the receipt of it have been to Kate O'Hara! He had promised her that he would write to her, and from the moment that he was gone she was anxious to send in to the post-office at Ennistimon for

the treasure which the mail car might bring to her. When
she did get it, it was indeed a treasure. To a girl who really
loves, the first love letter is a thing as holy as the recollection
of the first kiss. 'May I see it, Kate?' said Mrs. O'Hara, as her
daughter sat poring over the scrap of paper by the window.

'Yes, mamma—if you please.' Then she paused a moment.
'But I think that I had rather you did not. Perhaps he did
not mean me to shew it.' The mother did not urge her request, but contented herself with coming up behind her child
and kissing her. The reader, however, shall have the privilege
which was denied to Mrs. O'Hara.

'DEAREST KATE,

'I got here all alive yesterday at four. I came on as fast
as ever I could travel, and hardly got a mouthful to eat after
I left Limerick. I never saw such beastliness as they have at
the stations. My uncle is much better—so much so that I
shan't remain here very long. I can't tell you any particular
news—except this, that that old cat down at Castle Quin—
the one with the crisp-curled wig—must have the nose of a
dog and the ears of a cat and the eyes of a bird, and she sends
word to Scroope of everything that she smells and hears and
sees. It makes not the slightest difference to me—nor to you
I should think. Only I hate such interference. The truth is
old maids have nothing else to do. If I were you I wouldn't
be an old maid.

'I can't quite say how long it will be before I am back at
Ardkill, but not a day longer than I can help. Address to
Scroope, Dorsetshire—that will be enough—to F. Neville,
Esq. Give my love to your mother—As for yourself, dear Kate,
if you care for my love, you may weigh mine for your own
dear self with your own weights and measures. Indeed you
have all my heart.

Your own F.N.'

'There is a young lady here whom it is intended that I
shall marry. She is the pink of propriety and really very

pretty—but you need not be a bit jealous. The joke is that my brother is furiously in love with her, and I fancy she would be just as much in love with him only that she's told not to—A thousand kisses.'

It was not much of a love letter, but there were a few words in which sufficed althogether for Kate's happiness. She was told that she had all his heart—and she believed it. She was told that she need not be jealous of the proper young lady, and she believed that too. He sent her a thousand kisses; and she, thinking that he might have kissed the paper, pressed it to her lips. At any rate his hand had rested on it. She would have been quite willing to show to her mother all these expressions of her lover's love; but she felt that it would not be fair to him to expose his allusions to the 'beastliness' at the stations. He might say what he liked to her; but she understood that she was not at liberty to show to others words which had been addressed to her in the freedom of perfect intimacy.

'Does he say anything of the old man?' asked Mrs. O'Hara.

'He says that his uncle is better.'

'Threatened folks live long. Does Neville tell you when he will be back?'

'Not exactly; but he says that he will not stay long. He does not like Scroope at all. I knew that. He always says that —that—.'

'Says what, dear?'

'When we are married he will go away somewhere—to Italy or Greece or somewhere. Scroope he says is so gloomy.'

'And where shall I go?'

'Oh mother—you shall be with us, always.'

'No dear, you must not dream of that. When you have him you will not want me.'

'Dear mother. I shall want you always.'

'He will not want me. We have no right to expect too much from him, Kate. That he shall make you his wife we have a right to expect. If he were false to you——'

'He is not false. Why should you think him false?'

'I do not think it; but if he were——! Never mind. If he be true to you, I will not burden him. If I can see you happy, Kate, I will bear all the rest.' That which she would have to bear would be utter solitude for life. She could look forward and see how black and tedious would be her days; but all that would be nothing to her if her child were lifted up on high.

It was now the beginning of April, which for sportsmen in England is of all seasons the most desperate. Hunting is over. There is literally nothing to shoot. And fishing—even if there were fishing in England worth a man's time—has not begun. A gentleman of enterprise driven very hard in this respect used to declare that there was no remedy for April but to go and fly hawks in Holland.* Fred Neville could not fly hawks at Scroope, and found that there was nothing for him to do. Miss Mellerby suggested—books. 'I like books better than anything,' said Fred. 'I always have a lot of novels down at our quarters. But a fellow can't be reading all day, and there isn't a novel in the house except Walter Scott's and a lot of old rubbish. Bye-the-by have you read "All isn't Gold that Glitters?"* Miss Mellerby had not read the tale named. 'That's what I call a good novel.'

Day passed after day and it seemed as though he was ex-pected to remain at Scroope without any definite purpose, and, worse still, without any fixed limit to his visit. At his aunt's instigation he rode about the property and asked questions as to the tenants. It was all to be his own, and in the course of nature must be his own very soon. There could not but be an interest for him in every cottage and every field. But yet there was present to him all the time a schoolboy feeling that he was doing a task; and the occupation was not pleasant to him because it was a task. The steward was with him as a kind of pedagogue, and continued to instruct him during the whole ride. This man only paid so much a year, and the rent ought to be so much more; but there were cir-cumstances. And 'My Lord' had been peculiarly good. This farm was supposed to be the best on the estate, and that other the worse. Oh yes, there were plenty of foxes. 'My Lord' had always insisted that the foxes should be preserved. Some of the hunting gentry no doubt had made complaints, but it was a great shame. Foxes had been seen, two or three at a time, the very day after the coverts had been drawn blank. As for game, a head of game could be got up very soon, as there was plenty of corn and the woods were large; but 'My Lord' had never cared for game. The farmers all shot the rabbits on their own land. Rents were paid to the day. There was never any mistake about that. Of course the land would require to be re-valued,* but 'My Lord' wouldn't hear of such a thing being done in his time. The Manor wood wanted thinning very badly. The wood had been a good deal neglected. 'My Lord' had never liked to hear the axe going. That was Grumby Green and the boundary of the estate in that direction. The next farm was college property,* and was rented five shillings an acre dearer than 'My Lord's' land. If Mr. Neville wished it the steward would show him the limit of the estate on the other side tomorrow. No doubt there was a plan of the estate. It was in 'My Lord's' own room, and would show every farm with its acreage and bounds. Fred thought that he would study this plan on the next day instead of riding about with the steward.

He could not escape from the feeling that he was being taught his lesson like a school-boy, and he did not like it. He longed for the freedom of his boat on the Irish coast, and longed for the devotedness of Kate O'Hara. He was sure that he loved her so thoroughly that life without her was not to be regarded as possible. But certain vague ideas very injurious to the Kate he so dearly loved crossed his brain. Under the constant teaching of his aunt he did recognize it as a fact that he owed a high duty to his family. For many days after that first night at Scroope not a word was said to him about Kate O'Hara. He saw his uncle daily—probably twice a day; but the Earl never alluded to his Irish love. Lady Scroope spoke constantly of the greatness of the position which the heir was called upon to fill and of all that was due to the honour of the family. Fred, as he heard her, would shake his head impatiently, but would acknowledge the truth of what she said. He was induced even to repeat the promise which he had made to his uncle, and to assure his aunt that he would do nothing to mar or lessen the dignity of the name of Neville. He did become, within his own mind, indoctrinated with the idea that he would injure the position of the earldom which was to be his were he to marry Kate O'Hara. Arguments which appeared to him to be absurd when treated with ridicule by Father Marty, and which in regard to his own conduct he had determined to treat as old women's tales, seemed to him at Scroope to be true and binding. The atmosphere of the place, the companionship of Miss Mellerby, the reverence with which he himself was treated by the domestics, the signs of high nobility which surrounded him on all sides, had their effect upon him. Noblesse oblige. He felt that it was so. Then there crossed his brain visions of a future life which were injurious to the girl he loved.

Let his brother Jack come and live at Scroope and marry Sophie Mellerby. As long as he lived Jack could not be the Earl, but in regard to money he would willingly make such arrangements as would enable his brother to maintain the dignity and state of the house. They would divide the income. And then he would so arrange his matters with Kate O'Hara that his brother's son should be heir to the Earldom. He had some glimmering of an idea that as Kate was a Roman Catholic a marriage ceremony might be contrived of which this would become the necessary result. There should be no deceit. Kate should know it all, and everything should be done to make her happy. He would live abroad, and would not call himself by his title. They would be Mr. and Mrs. Neville. As to the property that must of course hereafter go with the title, but in giving up so much to his brother, he could, of course, arrange as to the provision necessary for any children of his own. No doubt his Kate would like to be the Countess Scroope—would prefer that a future son of her own should be the future Earl. But as he was ready to abandon so much, surely she would be ready to abandon something. He must explain to her—and to her mother—that under no other circumstances could he marry her. He must tell her of pledges made to his uncle before he knew her, of the duty which he owed to his family, and of his own great dislike to the kind of life which would await him as acting head of the family. No doubt there would be scenes—and his heart quailed as he remembered certain glances which had flashed upon him from the eyes of Mrs. O'Hara. But was he not offering to give up everything for his love? His Kate should be his wife after some Roman Catholic fashion in some Roman Catholic country. Of course there would be difficulties—the least of which would not be those glances from the angry mother; but it would be his business to overcome difficulties. There were always difficulties in the way of any man who chose to leave the common grooves of life and to make a separate way for himself. There were always difficulties in the way of adventures. Dear Kate! He would never desert his Kate. But his Kate must do as much as this for him. Did he not intend that, whatever good things the world might have in store for him, his Kate should share them all?

His ideas were very hazy, and he knew himself that he was ignorant of the laws respecting marriage. It occurred to him, therefore, that he had better consult his brother, and confide everything to him. That Jack was wiser than he, he was always willing to allow; and although he did in some sort look down upon Jack as a plodding fellow, who shot no seals and cared nothing for adventure, still he felt it to be almost a pity that Jack should not be the future Earl. So he told his aunt that he proposed to ask his brother to come to Scroope for a day or two before he returned to Ireland. Had his aunt, or would his uncle have, any objection? Lady Scroope did not dare to object. She by no means wished that her younger nephew should again be brought within the influence of Miss Mellerby's charms; but it would not suit her purpose to give offence to the heir by refusing so reasonable request. He would have been off to join his brother at Woolwich* immediately. So the invitation was sent, and Jack Neville promised that he would come.

Fred knew nothing of the offer that had been made to Miss Mellerby, though he had been sharp enough to discern his brother's feelings. 'My brother is coming here tomorrow,' he said one morning to Miss Mellerby when they were alone together.

'So Lady Scroope has told me. I don't wonder that you should wish to see him.'

'I hope everybody will be glad to see him. Jack is just about the very best fellow in the world—and he's one of the cleverest too.'

'It is nice to hear one brother speak in that way of another.'

'I swear by Jack. He ought to have been the elder brother —that's the truth. Don't you like him?'

'Who—I. Oh, yes, indeed. What I saw of him I liked very much.'

'Isn't it a pity that he shouldn't have been the elder?'

'I can't say that, Mr. Neville.'

'No. It wouldn't be just civil to me. But I can say it. When we were here last winter I thought that my brother was—'

'Was what, Mr. Neville?'

'Was getting to be very fond of you. Perhaps I ought not to say so.'

'I don't think that much good is ever done by saying that kind of thing,' said Miss Mellerby gravely.

'It cannot at any rate do any harm in this case. I wish with all my heart that he was fond of you and you of him.'

'That is all nonsense. Indeed it is.'

'I am not saying it without an object. I don't see why you and I should not understand one another. If I tell you a secret will you keep it?'

'Do not tell me any secret that I must keep from Lady Scroope.'

'But that is just what you must do.'

'But then suppose I don't do it,' said Miss Mellerby

But Fred was determined to tell his secret. 'The truth is that both my uncle and my aunt want me to fall in love with you.'

'How very kind of them,' said she with a little forced laugh.

'I don't for a moment think that, had I tried it on ever so, I could have succeeded. I am not at all the sort of man to be conceited in that way. Wishing to do the best they could for me, they picked you out. It isn't that I don't think well of you as they do, but——'

'Really, Mr. Neville, this is the oddest conversation.'

'Quite true. It is odd. But the fact is you are here, and there is nobody else I can talk to. And I want you to know the exact truth. I'm engaged to—somebody else.'

'I ought to break my heart—oughtn't I?'

'I don't in the least mind your laughing at me. I should have minded it very much if I had asked you to marry me, and you had refused me.'

'You haven't given me the chance, you see.'

'I didn't mean. What was the good?'

'Certainly not, Mr. Neville, if you are engaged to someone else. I shouldn't like to be Number Two.'

'I'm in a peck of troubles—that's the truth. I would change places with my brother tomorrow if I could. I daresay you don't believe that, but I would. I will not vex my uncle if I can help it, but I certainly shall not throw over the girl who loves me. If it wasn't for the title, I'd give up Scroope to my brother tomorrow, and go and live in some place where I could get lots of shooting, and where I should never have to put on a white choker.'*

'You'll think better of all that.'

'Well!—I've just told you everything because I like to be on the square. I wish you knew Kate O'Hara. I'm sure you would not wonder that a fellow should love her. I had rather you didn't tell my aunt what I have told you; but if you choose to do so, I can't help it.'

CHAPTER XI

THE WISDOM OF JACK NEVILLE

NEVILLE HAD been forced to get his leave of absence renewed on the score of his uncle's health, and had promised to prolong his absence till the end of April. When doing so he had declared his intention of returning to Ennis in the beginning of May; but no agreement to that had as yet been expressed by his uncle or aunt. Towards the end of the month his brother came to Scroope, and up to that time not a word further had been said to him respecting Kate O'Hara.

He had received an answer from Kate to his letter, prepared in a fashion very different from that of his own. He had seated himself at a table and in compliance with the pledge given by him, had scrawled off his epistle as fast as he could write it. She had taken a whole morning to think of hers, and had recopied it after composing it, and had then read it with the utmost care, confessing to herself, almost with tears, that it was altogether unworthy of him to whom it was to be sent. It was the first love letter she had ever written—probably the first letter she had ever written to a man, except those short notes which she would occasionally scrawl to Father Marty in compliance with her mother's directions. The letter to Fred was as follows—

ARDKILL COTTAGE
10th April, 18—.

MY DEAREST FRED,

'I received your dear letter three or four days ago, and it made me so happy. We were sorry that you should have such an uncomfortable journey; but all that would be over and soon forgotten when you found yourself in your comfortable home and among your own friends. I am very glad to hear that your uncle is better. The thought of finding him so ill must have made your journey very sad. As he is so much better, I suppose you will come back soon to your poor little Kate.

'There is no news at all to send you from Liscannor. Father Marty was up here yesterday and says that your boat is all safe at Lahinch. He says that Barney Morony is an idle fellow, but as he has nothing to do he can't help being idle. You should come back and not let him be idle any more. I think the sea gulls know that you are away, because they are wheeling and screaming about louder and bolder than ever.

'Mother sends her best love. She is very well. We have had nothing to eat since you went because it has been Lent. So, if you had been here, you would not have been able to get a bit of luncheon. I dare say you have been a great deal better off at Scroope. Father Marty says that you Protestants will have to keep your Lent hereafter—eighty days at a time instead of forty; and that we Catholics will be allowed to eat just what we like, while you Protestants will have to look on at us. If so, I think I'll manage to give you a little bit.

'Do come back to your own Kate as soon as you can. I need not tell you that I love you better than all the world because you know it already. I am not a bit jealous of the proper young lady, and I hope that she will fall in love with your brother. Then some day we shall be sisters—shan't we? I should like to have a proper young lady for my sister so much. Only, perhaps she would despise me. Do come back soon. Everything is so dull while you are away! You would come back to your own Kate if you knew how great a joy it is to her when she sees you coming along the cliff.

'Dearest, dearest love, I am always your own, own
KATE O'HARA.'

Neville thought of showing Kate's letter to Miss Mellerby, but when he read it a second time he made up his mind that he would keep it to himself. The letter was all very well, and as regarded the expressions towards himself, just what it should be. But he felt that it was not such a letter as Miss Mellerby would have written herself, and he was a little ashamed of all that was said about the priest. Neither was he proud of the pretty, finished, French hand-writing, over every letter of which his love had taken so much pains. In truth, Kate O'Hara was better educated than himself, and perhaps knew as much as Sophie Mellerby. She could have written her letter quite as well in French as in English, and she did understand something of the formation of her sentences. Fred Neville had been at an excellent school, but it may be doubted whether he could have explained his own written language. Nevertheless he was a little ashamed of his Kate, and thought that Miss Mellerby might perceive her ignorance if he shewed her letter.

He had sent for his brother in order that he might explain his scheme and get his brother's advice—but he found it very difficult to explain his scheme to Jack Neville. Jack, indeed, from the very first would not allow that the scheme was in any way practicable. 'I don't quite understand, Fred, what you mean. You don't intend to deceive her by a false marriage?'

'Most assuredly not. I do not intend to deceive her at all.'

'You must make her your wife, or not make her your wife.'

'Undoubtedly she will be my wife. I am quite determined about that. She has my word—and over and above that, she is dearer to me than anything else.'

'If you marry her, her eldest son must of course be the heir to the title.'

'I am not at all so sure of that. All manner of queer things may be arranged by marriage with Roman Catholics.'

'Put that out of your head,' said Jack Neville. 'In the first place you would certainly find yourself in a mess, and in the next place the attempt itself would be dishonest. I daresay men have crept out of marriages because they have been illegal; but a man who arranges a marriage with the intention of creeping out of it is a scoundrel.'

'You needn't bully about it, Jack. You know very well that I don't mean to creep out of anything.'

'I am sure you don't. But as you ask me I must tell you what I think. You are in a sort of dilemma between this girl and Uncle Scroope.'

'I'm not in any dilemma at all.'

'You seem to think you have made some promise to him which will be broken if you marry her—and I suppose you certainly have made her a promise.'

'Which I certainly mean to keep,' said Fred.

'All right. Then you must break your promise to Uncle Scroope.'

'It was a sort of half and half promise. I could not bear to see him making himself unhappy about it.'

'Just so. I suppose Miss O'Hara can wait.'

Fred Neville scratched his head. 'Oh yes—she can wait. There's nothing to bind me to a day or a month. But my uncle may live for the next ten years now.'

'My advice to you is to let Miss O'Hara understand clearly that you will make no other engagement, but that you cannot marry her as long as your uncle lives. Of course I say this on the supposition that the affair cannot be broken off.'

'Certainly not,' said Fred with a decision that was magnanimous.

'I cannot think the engagement a fortunate one for you in your position. Like should marry like. I'm quite sure of that. You would wish your wife to be easily intimate with the sort of people among whom she would naturally be thrown as Lady Scroope—among the wives and daughters of other Earls and such like.'

'No; I shouldn't.'

'I don't see how she would be comfortable in any other way.'

'I should never live among other Earls, as you call them. I hate that kind of thing. I hate London. I should never live here.'

'What would you do?'

'I should have a yacht and live chiefly in that. I should go about a good deal, and get into all manner of queer places. I don't say but what I might spend a winter now and then in Leicestershire or Northamptonshire, for I am fond of hunting. But I should have no regular home. According to my scheme you should have this place—and sufficient of the income to maintain it of course.'

'That wouldn't do Fred,' said Jack, shaking his head—'though I know how generous you are.'

'Why wouldn't it do?'

'You are the heir, and you must take the duties with the privileges. You can have your yacht if you like a yacht—but you'll soon get tired of that kind of life. I take it that a yacht is a bad place for a nursery, and inconvenient for one's old boots. When a man has a home fixed for him by circumstances—as you will have—he gravitates towards it, let his own supposed predilections be what they may. Circumstances are stronger than predilections.'

'You're a philosopher.'

'I was always more sober than you, Fred.'

'I wish you had been the elder—on the condition of the younger brother having a tidy slice out of the property to make himself comfortable.'

'But I am not the elder, and you must take the position with all encumbrances. I see nothing for it but to ask Miss O'Hara to wait. If my uncle lives long the probability is that one or the other of you will change your minds and that the affair will never come off.'

When the younger and wiser brother gave this advice he did not think it all likely that Miss O'Hara would change her mind. Penniless young ladies don't often change their minds when they are engaged to the heirs of Earls. It was not at all probable that she should repent the bargain that she had made. But Jack Neville did think it very probable that his brother might do so—and, indeed, felt sure that he would do so if years were allowed to intervene. His residence in County Clare would not be perpetual, and with him in his

circumstances it might well be that the young lady, being out
of sight should be out of mind. Jack could not exactly declare
his opinion on this head. His brother at present was full of
his promise, full of his love, full of his honour. Nor would
Jack have absolutely counselled him to break his word to the
young lady. But he thought it probable that in the event of
delay poor Miss O'Hara might go to the wall—and he also
thought that for the general interests of the Scroope family
it would be better that she should do so.

'And what are you going to do yourself?' asked Fred.

'In respect of what?'

'In respect of Miss Mellerby?'

'In respect of Miss Mellerby I am not going to do anything,' said Jack as he walked away.

In all that the younger brother said to the elder as to poor
Kate he was no doubt wise and prudent; but in what he said
about himself he did not tell the truth. But then the question asked was one which a man is hardly bound to answer,
even to a brother. Jack Neville was much less likely to talk
about his love affairs than Fred, but not on that account less
likely to think about them. Shophie Mellerby had refused
him once, but young ladies have been known to marry gentlemen after refusing them more than once. He at any rate was
determined to persevere, having in himself and in his affairs
that silent faith of which the possessor is so often unconscious,
but which so generally leads to success. He found Miss
Mellerby to be very courteous to him if not gracious; and he
had the advantage of not being afraid of her. It did not strike
him that because she was the granddaughter of a duke, and
because he was a younger son, that therefore he ought not to
dare to look at her. He understood very well that she was
brought there that Fred might marry her—but Fred was intent on marrying someone else, and Sophie Mellerby was not
a girl to throw her heart away upon a man who did not want
it. He had come to Scroope for only three days, but, in spite
of some watchfulness on the part of the Countess, he found

his opportunity for speaking before he left the house. 'Miss Mellerby,' he said, 'I don't know whether I ought to thank Fortune or to upbraid her for having again brought me face to face with you.'

'I hope the evil is not so oppressive as to make you very loud in your upbraidings.'

'They shall not at any rate be heard. I don't know whether there was any spice of malice about my brother when he asked me to come here, and told me in the same letter that you were at Scroope.'

'He must have meant it for malice, I should think,' said the young lady, endeavouring, but not quite successfully, to imitate the manner of the man who loved her.

'Of course I came.'

'Not on my behalf, I hope, Mr. Neville.'

'Altogether on your behalf. Fred's need to see me was not very great, and, as my uncle had not asked me, and as my aunt, I fancy, does not altogether approve of me, I certainly should not have come—were it not that I might find it difficult to get any other opportunity of seeing you.'

'That is hardly fair to Lady Scroope, Mr. Neville.'

'Quite fair, I think. I did not come clandestinely. I am not ashamed of what I am doing—or of what I am going to do. I may be ashamed of this—that I should feel my chance of success to be so small. When I was here before I asked you to—allow me to love you. I now ask you again.'

'Allow you!' she said.

'Yes—allow me. I should be too bold were I to ask you to return my love at once. I only ask you to know that because I was repulsed once, I have not given up the pursuit.'

'Mr. Neville, I am sure that my father and mother would not permit it.'

'May I ask your father, Miss Mellerby?'

'Certainly not—with my permission.'

'Nevertheless you will not forget that I am suitor for your love?'

'I will make no promise of anything, Mr. Neville.' Then,

fearing that she had encouraged him, she spoke again. 'I think you ought to take my answer as final.'

'Miss Mellerby, I shall take no answer as final that is not favourable. Should I indeed hear that you were to be married to another man, that would be final; but that I shall not hear from your own lips. You will say goodbye to me,' and he offered her his hand.

She gave him her hand—and he raised it to his lips and kissed it, as men were wont to do in the olden days.

CHAPTER XII

FRED NEVILLE MAKES A PROMISE

FRED NEVILLE felt that he had not received from his brother the assistance or sympathy which he had required. He had intended to make a very generous offer—not indeed quite understanding how this offer could be carried out, but still of a nature that should, he thought, have bound his brother to his service. But Jack had simply answered him by sermons —by sermons and an assurance of the impracticability of his scheme. Nevertheless he was by no means sure that his scheme was impracticable. He was at least sure of this—that no human power could force him to adopt a mode of life that was distasteful to him. No one could make him marry Sophie Mellerby, or any other Sophie, and maintain a grand and gloomy house in Dorsetshire, spending his income, not in a manner congenial to him, but in keeping a large retinue of servants and taking what he called the 'heavy line' of an English nobleman. The property must be his own—or at any rate the life use of it. He swore to himself over and over again that nothing should induce him to impoverish the family or to leave the general affairs of the house of Scroope worse than he found them. Much less than half of that which he understood to be the income coming from the estates would suffice for him. But let his uncle or aunt—or his strait-laced methodical brother, say what they would to him, nothing should induce him to make himself a slave to an earldom.

But yet his mind was much confused and his contentment by no means complete. He knew that there must be a disagreeable scene between himself and his uncle before he returned to Ireland, and he knew also that his uncle could, if he so minded, stop his present very liberal allowance altogether. There had been a bargain, no doubt, that he should remain with his regiment for a year, and of that year six months were still unexpired. His uncle could not quarrel with him for going back to Ireland; but what answer should he make when his uncle asked him whether he were engaged to marry Miss O'Hara—as of course he would ask; and what reply should he make when his uncle would demand of him whether he thought such a marriage fit for a man in his position. He knew that it was not fit. He believed in the title, in the sanctity of the name, in the mysterious grandeur of the family. He did not think that an Earl of Scroope ought to marry a girl of whom nothing whatever was known. The pride of the position stuck to him—but it irked him to feel that the sacrifices necessary to support that pride should fall on his own shoulders.

One thing was impossible to him. He would not desert his Kate. But he wished to have his Kate, as a thing apart. If he could have given six months of each year to his Kate, living that yacht-life of which he had spoken, visiting those strange sunny places which his imagination had pictured to him, unshackled by conventionalities, beyond the sound of church bells, unimpeded by any considerations of family—and then have migrated for the other six months to his earldom and his estates, to his hunting and perhaps to Parliament, leaving his Kate behind him, that would have been perfect. And why not? In the days which must come so soon, he would be his own master. Who could impede his motions or gainsay his will? Then he remembered his Kate's mother, and the glances which would come from the mother's eyes. There might be difficulty even though Scroope were all his own.

He was not a villain—simply a self-indulgent spoiled young man who had realized to himself no idea of duty in life. He never once told himself that Kate should be his mistress. In all the pictures which he drew for himself of a future life everything was to be done for her happiness and for her gratification. His yacht should be made a floating bower for her delight. During those six months of the year which, and which only, the provoking circumstances of his position would enable him to devote to joy and love, her will should be his law. He did not think himself to be fickle. He would never want another Kate. He would leave her with sorrow. He would return to her with ecstasy. Everybody around him should treat her with the respect due to an empress. But it would be very expedient that she should be called Mrs. Neville instead of Lady Scroope. Could things not be so arranged for him—so arranged that he might make a promise to his uncle, and yet be true to his Kate without breaking his promise? That was his scheme. Jack said that his scheme was impracticable. But the difficulties in his way were not, he thought, so much those which Jack had propounded as the angry eyes of Kate O'Hara's mother.

At last the day was fixed for his departure. The Earl was already so much better as to be able to leave his bedroom. Twice or thrice a day Fred saw his uncle, and there was much said about the affairs of the estate. The heir had taken some trouble, had visited some of the tenants, and had striven to seem interested in the affairs of the property. The Earl could talk for ever about the estate, every field, every fence, almost every tree on which was familiar to him. That his tenants should be easy in their circumstances, a protestant, church-going, rent-paying, people, son following father, and daughters marrying as their mothers had married, unchanging, never sinking an inch in the social scale, or rising—this was the wish nearest to his heart. Fred was well disposed to talk about the tenants as long as Kate O'Hara was not mentioned. When the Earl would mournfully speak of his own coming death, as an event which could not now be far distant, Fred with fullest sincerity would promise that his wishes should be observed. No rents should be raised. The axe should be but sparingly used. It seemed to him strange that a man going into eternity should care about this tree or that—but as far as he was concerned the trees should stand while Nature supported them. No servant should be dismissed. The carriage horses should be allowed to die on the place. The old charities should be maintained. The parson of the parish should always be a welcome guest at the Manor. No promise was difficult for him to make so long as that one question were left untouched.

But when he spoke of the day of his departure as fixed—as being 'the day after tomorrow'—then he knew that the question must be touched. 'I am sorry—very sorry, that you must go,' said the Earl.

'You see a man can't leave the service at a moment's notice.'

'I think that we could have got over that, Fred.'

'Perhaps as regards the service we might, but the regiment would think ill of me. You see, so many things depend on a man's staying or going. The youngsters mayn't have their money ready.* I said I should remain till October.'

'I don't at all wish to act the tyrant to you.'

'I know that, uncle.'

Then there was a pause. 'I haven't spoken to you yet, Fred, on a matter which has caused me a great deal of uneasiness. When you first came I was not strong enough to allude to it, and I left it to your aunt.' Neville, knew well what was coming now, and was aware that he was moved in a manner that hardly became his manhood. 'Your aunt tells me that you have got into some trouble with a young lady in the west of Ireland.'

'No trouble, uncle, I hope.'

'Who is she?'

Then there was another pause, but he gave a direct answer to the question. 'She is a Miss O'Hara.'

'A Roman Catholic?'

'Yes.'

'A girl of whose family you know nothing?'

'I know that she lives with her mother.'

'In absolute obscurity—and poverty?'

'They are not rich,' said Fred.

'Do not suppose that I regard poverty as a fault. It is not necessary that you should marry a girl with any fortune.'

'I suppose not, Uncle Scroope.'

'But I understand that this young lady is quite beneath yourself in life. She lives with her mother-in a little cottage, without servants——'

'There is a servant.'

'You know what I mean, Fred. She does not live as ladies live. She is uneducated.'

'You are wrong there, my lord. She has been at an excellent school in France.'

'In France! Who was her father, and what?'

'I do not know what her father was—a Captain O'Hara, I believe.'

'And you would marry such a girl as that—a Roman Catholic; picked up on the Irish coast—one of whom nobody knows even her parentage or perhaps her real name? It would kill me, Fred.'

'I have not said that I mean to marry her.'

'But what do you mean? Would you ruin her—seduce her by false promises and then leave her? Do you tell me that in cold blood you look forward to such a deed as that?'

'Certainly not.'

'I hope not, my boy; I hope not that. Do not tell me that a heartless scoundrel is to take my name when I am gone.'

'I am not a heartless scoundrel,' said Fred Neville, jumping up from his seat.

'Then what is it that you mean? You have thought, have you not, of the duties of the high position to which you are called? You do not suppose that wealth is to be given to you, and a great name, and all the appanages and power of nobility, in order that you may eat more, and drink more, and lie softer than others. It is because some think so, and act upon such base thoughts, that the only hereditary peerage left in the world is in danger of encountering the ill will of the people. Are you willing to be known only as one of those who have disgraced their order?'

'I do not mean to disgrace it.'

'But you will disgrace it if you marry such a girl as that. If

she were fit to be your wife, would not the family of Lord
Kilfenora have known her?'

'I don't think much of their not knowing her, uncle.'

'Who does know her? Who can say that she is even what
she pretends to be? Did you not promise me that you would
make no such marriage?'

He was not strong to defend his Kate. Such defence would
have been in opposition to his own ideas, in antagonism
with the scheme which he had made for himself. He understood, almost as well as did his uncle, that Kate O'Hara ought
not to be made Countess of Scroope. He too thought that
were she to be presented to the world as the Countess of
Scroope, she would disgrace the title. And yet he would not
be a villain! And yet he would not give her up! He could
only fall back upon his scheme. Miss O'Hara is as good as
gold,' he said; 'but I acknowledge that she is not fit to be
mistress of this house.'

'Fred,' said the Earl, almost in a passion of affectionate
solicitude, 'do not go back to Ireland. We will arrange about
the regiment. No harm shall be done to anyone. My health
will be your excuse, and the lawyers shall arrange it all.'

'I must go back,' said Neville. Then the Earl fell back in
his chair and covered his face with his hands. 'I must go
back; but I will give you my honour as a gentleman to do
nothing that shall distress you.'

'You will not marry her?'

'No.'

'And, oh, Fred, as you value your own soul, do not injure
a poor girl so desolate as that. Tell her and tell her mother
the honest truth. If there be tears, will not that be better
than sorrow, and disgrace, and ruin?' Among evils there
must always be a choice; and the Earl thought that a broken
promise was the lightest of those evils to a choice among
which his nephew had subjected himself.

And so the interview was over, and there had been no
quarrel. Fred Neville had given the Earl a positive promise
that he would not marry Kate O'Hara—to whom he had

sworn a thousand times that she should be his wife. Such a promise, however—so he told himself—is never intended to prevail beyond the lifetime of the person to whom it is made. He had bound himself not to marry Kate O'Hara while his uncle lived, and that was all.

Or might it not be better to take his uncle's advice altogether and tell the truth—not to Kate, for that he could not do—but to Mrs. O'Hara or to Father Marty? As he thought of this he acknowledged to himself that the task of telling such a truth to Mrs. O'Hara would be almost beyond his strength. Could he not throw himself upon the priest's charity, and leave it all to him? Then he thought of his own Kate, and some feeling akin to genuine love told him that he could not part with the girl in such fashion as that. He would break his heart were he to lose his Kate. When he looked at it in that light it seemed to him that Kate was more to him than all the family of the Scroopes with all their glory. Dear, sweet, soft, innocent, beautiful Kate! His Kate who, as he knew well, worshipped the very ground on which he trod! It was not possible that he should separate himself from Kate O'Hara.

On his return to Ireland he turned that scheme of his over and over again in his head. Surely something might be done if the priest would stand his friend! What, if he were to tell the whole truth to the priest, and ask for such assistance as a priest might give him? But the one assurance to which he came during his journey was this—that when a man goes in for adventures, he requires a good deal of skill and some courage too to carry him through them.

AN EYE FOR AN EYE
VOLUME II

CHAPTER I

FROM BAD TO WORSE

AS HE was returning to Ennis, Neville was so far removed from
immediate distress as to be able to look forward without fear
to his meeting with the two ladies at Ardkill. He could as
yet take his Kate in his arms without any hard load upon his
heart, such as would be there if he knew that it was incumbent upon him at once to explain his difficulties. His uncle
was still living, but was old and still ill. He would naturally
make the most of the old man's age and infirmities. There
was every reason why they should wait, and no reason why
such waiting should bring reproaches upon his head. On the
night of his arrival at his quarters he despatched a note to
his Kate. 'Dearest love. Here I am again in the land of freedom and potatoes. I need not trouble you with writing about
home news, as I shall see you the day after tomorrow. All to-
morrow and Wednesday morning I must stick close to my
guns here. After one on Wednesday I shall be free. I will
drive over to Lahinch, and come round in the boat. I must
come back here the same night, but I suppose it will be the
next morning before I get to bed. I sha'n't mind that if I
get something for my pains. My love to your mother. Your
own, F.N.'

In accordance with this plan he did drive over to Lahinch.
He might have saved time by directing that his boat should
come across the bay to meet him at Liscannor, but he felt
that he would prefer not to meet Father Marty at present. It
might be that before long he would be driven to tell the
priest a good deal, and to ask for the priest's assistance; but
at present he was not anxious to see Father Marty. Barney
Morony was waiting for him at the stable where he put up

his horse, and went down with him to the beach. The ladies, according to Barney, were quite well and more winsome than ever. But—and this information was not given without much delay and great beating about the bush—there was a rumour about Liscannor that Captain O'Hara had 'turned up.' Fred was so startled at this that he could not refrain from showing his anxiety by the questions which he asked. Barney did not seem to think that the Captain had been at Ardkill or anywhere in the neighbourhood. At any rate he, Barney, had not seen him. He had just heard the rumour. 'Shure, Lieutenant, I wouldn't be telling yer honour a lie; and they do be saying that the Captain one time was as fine a man as a woman ever sot eyes on—and why not, seeing what kind the young lady is, God bless her!' If it were true that Kate's father had 'turned up' such an advent might very naturally alter Neville's plans. It would so change the position of things, as to relieve him in some degree from the force of his past promises.

Nevertheless when he saw Kate coming along the cliffs to meet him, the one thing more certain to him than all other things was that he would never abandon her. She had been watching for him almost from the hour at which he had said that he would leave Ennis, and, creeping up among the rocks, had seen his boat as it came round the point from Liscannor. She had first thought that she would climb down the path to meet him; but the tide was high and there was now no strip of strand below the cliffs; and Barney Morony would have been there to see and she resolved that it would be nicer to wait for him on the summit. 'Oh Fred, you have come back,' she said, throwing herself on his breast.

'Yes; I am back. Did you think I was going to desert you?'

'No; no. I knew you would not desert me. 'Oh, my darling!'

'Dear Kate—dearest Kate.'

'You have thought of me sometimes?'

'I have thought of you always—every hour.' And so he swore to her that she was was as much to him as he could possibly be to her. She hung on his arm as she went down to the cottage, and believed herself to be the happiest and most fortunate girl in Ireland. As yet no touch of the sorrows of love had fallen upon her.

He could not all at once ask her as to that rumour which Morony had mentioned to him. But he thought of it as he walked with his arm round her waist. Some question must be asked, but it might, perhaps, be better that he should ask it of the mother. Mrs. O'Hara was at the cottage and seemed almost as glad to see him as Kate had been. 'It is very pleasant to have you back again,' she said. 'Kate has been counting first the hours and then the minutes.'

'And so have you, mother.'

'Of course we want to hear all the news,' said Mrs. O'Hara. Then Neville, with the girl who was to be his wife, sitting close beside him on the sofa—almost within his embrace— told them how things were going at Scroope. His uncle was very weak—evidently failing; but still so much better as to justify the heir in coming away. He might perhaps live for another twelve months, but the doctors thought it hardly possible that he should last longer than that. Then the nephew went on to say that his uncle was the best and most generous man in the world—and the finest gentleman and the truest Christian. He told also of the tenants who were not to be harassed, and the servants who were not to be dismissed, and the horses that were to be allowed to die in their beds, and the trees that were not to be cut down.

'I wish I knew him,' said Kate. 'I wish I could have seen him once.'

'That can never be,' said Fred, sadly.

'No—of course not.'

Then Mrs. O'Hara asked a question. 'Has he ever heard of us?'

'Yes—he has heard of you.'

'From you?'

'No—not first from me. There are many reasons why I would not have mentioned your names could I have helped it. He has wished me to marry another girl—and especially a Protestant girl. That was impossible.'

'That must be impossible now, Fred,' said Kate, looking up into his face.

'Quite so, dearest; but why should I have vexed him, seeing that he is so good to me, and that he must be gone so soon?'

'Who had told him of us?' asked Mrs. O'Hara.

'That woman down there at Castle Quin.'

'Lady Mary?'

'Foul-tongued old maid that she is,' exclaimed Fred. 'She writes to my aunt by every post, I believe.'

'What evil can she say of us?'

'She does say evil. Never mind what. Such a woman always says evil of those of her sex who are good-looking.'

'There, mother—that's for you,' said Kate, laughing. 'I don't care what she says.'

'If she tells your aunt that we live in a small cottage, without servants, without society, with just the bare necessaries of life, she tells the truth of us.'

'That's just what she does say—and she goes on harping about religion. Never mind her. You can understand that my uncle should be old-fashioned. He is very old, and we must wait.'

'Waiting is so weary,' said Mrs. O'Hara.

'It is not weary for me at all,' said Kate.

Then he left them, without having said a word about the Captain. He found the Captain to be a subject very uncomfortable to mention, and thought as he was sitting there that it might perhaps be better to make his first enquiries of this priest. No one said a word to him about the Captain beyond what he had heard from his boatman.*For, as it happened, he did not see the priest till May was nearly past, and during all that time things were going from bad to worse. As regards any services which he rendered to the army at this period of his career, the excuses which he had made to his uncle were certainly not valid. Some pretence at positively necessary routine

duties it must be supposed that he made; but he spent more
of his time either on the sea, or among the cliffs with Kate,
or on the road going backwards and forwards, than he did
at his quarters. It was known that he was to leave the regiment and become a great man at home in October, and his
brother officers were kind to him. And it was known also, of
course, that there was a young lady down on the sea coast
beyond Ennistimon, and doubtless there were jokes on the
subject. But there was no one with him at Ennis having such
weight of fears or authority as might have served to help to
rescue him. During this time Lady Mary Quin still made her
reports, and his aunt's letters were full of cautions and entreaties. 'I am told,' said the Countess, in one of her now
detested epistles, 'that the young woman has a reprobate
father who has escaped from the galleys.' Oh, Fred, do not
break our hearts.' He had almost forgotten the Captain when
he received this further rumour which had circulated to him
round by Castle Quin and Scroope Manor.

It was all going from bad to worse. He was allowed by the
mother to be at the cottage as much as he pleased, and the
girl was allowed to wander with him when she would among
the cliffs. It was so, although Father Marty himself had more
than once cautioned Mrs. O'Hara that she was imprudent.
'What can I do?' she said. 'Have not you yourself taught
me to believe that he is true?'

'Just spake a word to Miss Kate herself.'

'What can I say to her now? She regards him as her
husband before God.'

'But he is not her husband in any way that would prevent
his taking another wife an' he plases. And, believe me,
Misthress O'Hara, them sort of young men like a girl a dale
better when there's a little "Stand off" about her.'

'It is too late to bid her to be indifferent to him now,
Father Marty.'

'I am not saying that Miss Kate is to lose her lover. I hope
I'll have the binding of 'em together myself, and I'll go bail

I'll do it fast enough. In the meanwhile let her keep herself to herself a little more.'

The advice was very good, but Mrs. O'Hara knew not how to make use of it. She could tell the young man that she would have his heart's blood if he deceived them, and she could look at him as though she meant to be as good as her word. She had courage enough for any great emergency. But now that the lover had been made free of the cottage she knew not how to debar him. She could not break her Kate's heart by expressing doubts to her. And were he to be told to stay away, would he not be lost to them forever? Of course he could desert them if he would, and then they must die.

It was going from bad to worse certainly; and not the less so because he was more than ever infatuated about the girl. When he had calculated whether it might be possible to desert her he had been at Scroope. He was in County Clare now, and he did not hesitate to tell himself that it was impossible. Whatever might happen, and to whomever he might be false —he would be true to her. He would at any rate be so true to her that he would not leave her. If he never made her his legal wife, his legal wife at all points, he would always treat her as his legal wife. When his uncle the Earl should die, when the time came in which he would be absolutely free as to his own motions, he would discover the way in which this might best be done. If it were true that his Kate's father was a convict escaped from the galleys, that surely would be an additional reason why she should not be made Countess of Scroope. Even Mrs. O'Hara herself must understand that. With Kate, with his own Kate, he thought that there would be no difficulty.

From bad to worse! Alas, alas; there came a day in which the pricelessness of the girl he loved sank to nothing, vanished away, and was as a thing utterly lost, even in his eyes. The poor unfortunate one—to whom beauty had been given, and grace, and softness—and beyond all these and finer than these, innocence as unsullied as the whiteness of the plumage on the breast of a dove; but to whom, alas, had not been given a protector strong enough to protect her softness, or guardian wise enough to guard her innocence! To her he was godlike, noble, excellent, all but holy. He was the man whom Fortune, more than kind, had sent to her to be the joy of her existence, the fountain of her life, the strong staff for her weakness. Not to believe in him would be the foulest treason! To lose him would be to die! To deny him would be to deny her God! She gave him all—and her pricelessness in his eyes was gone for ever.

He was sitting with her one day towards the end of May on the edge of the cliff, looking down upon the ocean and listening to the waves, when it occurred to him that he might as well ask her about her father. It was absurd he thought to stand upon any ceremony with her. He was very good to her, and intended to be always good to her, but it was essentially necessary to him to know the truth. He was not aware, perhaps, that he was becoming rougher with her than had been his wont. She certainly was not aware of it, though there was a touch of awe sometimes about her as she answered him. She was aware that she now shewed to him an absolute obedience in all things which had not been customary with her; but then it was so sweet to obey him; so happy a thing to have such a master! If he rebuked her, he did it with his arm round her waist, so that she could look into his face and smile as she promised that she would be good and follow his behests in all things. He had been telling her now of some fault in her dress, and she had been explaining that such faults would come when money was so scarce. Then he had offered her gifts. A gift she would of course take. She had already taken gifts which were the treasures of her heart. But he must not pay things for her till—till—. Then she again looked up into his face and smiled. 'You are not angry with me?' she said.

'Kate—I want to ask you a particular question.'

'What question?'

'You must not suppose, let the answer be what it may, that it can make any difference between you and me.'

'Oh—I hope not,' she replied trembling.

'It shall make none,' he answered with all a master's assurance and authority. 'Therefore you need not be afraid to answer me. Tidings have reached me on a matter as to which I ought to be informed.'

'What matter? Oh Fred, you do so frighten me. I'll tell you anything I know.'

'I have been told that—that your father—is alive.' He looked down upon her and could see that her face was red up to her very hair. 'Your mother once told me that she had never been certain of his death.'

'I used to think he was dead.'

'But now you think he is alive?'

'I think he is—but I do not know. I never saw my father so as to remember him; though I do remember that we used to be very unhappy when we were in Spain.'

'And what have you heard lately? Tell me the truth, you know.'

'Of course I shall tell you the truth, Fred. I think mother got a letter, but she did not shew it me. She said just a word, but nothing more. Father Marty will certainly know if she knows.'

'And you know nothing?'

'Nothing.'

'I think I must ask Farther Marty.'

'But will it matter to you?' Kate asked.

'At any rate it shall not matter to you,' he said, kissing her. And then again she was happy; though there had now crept across her heart the shadow of some sad foreboding, a fore-taste of sorrow that was not altogether bitter as sorrow is, but which taught her to cling closely to him when he was there and would fill her eyes with tears when she thought of him in his absence.

On this day he had not found Mrs. O'Hara at the cottage. She had gone down to Liscannor, Kate told him. He had sent his boat back to the strand near that village, round the point and into the bay, as it could not well lie under the rocks at high tide, and he now asked Kate to accompany him as he walked down. They would probably meet her mother on the road. Kate, as she tied on her hat, was only too happy to be his companion. 'I think,' he said, 'that I shall try and see Father Marty as I go back. If your mother has really heard anything about your father, she ought to have told me.'

'Don't be angry with mother, Fred.'

'I won't be angry with you, my darling,' said the master with masterful tenderness.

Although he had intimated his intention of calling on the priest that very afternoon, it may be doubted whether he was altogether gratified when he met the very man with Mrs. O'Hara close to the old burying ground. 'Ah, Mr. Neville,' said the priest, 'and how's it all wid you this many a day?'

'The top of the morning to you thin, Father Marty,' said Fred, trying to assume an Irish brogue. Nothing could be more friendly than the greeting. The old priest took off his hat to Kate, and made a low bow, as though he should say— to the future Countess of Scroope I owe a very especial respect. Mrs. O'Hara held her future son-in-law's hand for a moment, as though she might preserve him for her daughter by some show of affection on her own part. 'And now, Misthress O'Hara,' said the priest, 'as I've got a companion to go back wid me, I'm thinking I'll not go up the hill any further.' Then they parted, and Kate looked as though she were being robbed of her due because her lover could not give her one farewell kiss in the priest's presence.

CHAPTER II

IS SHE TO BE YOUR WIFE?

'IT'S QUITE a stranger you are, these days,' said the priest as soon as they had turned their backs upon the ladies.

'Well; yes. We haven't managed to meet since I came back —have we?'

'I've been pretty constant at home, too. But you like them cliffs up there, better than the village no doubt.'

'Metal more attractive, Father Marty,' said Fred laughing —'not meaning however any slight upon Liscannor or the Cork whisky.'

'The Cork whisky is always to the fore, Mr. Neville. And how did you lave matters with your noble uncle?'

Neville at the present moment was anxious rather to speak of Kate's ignoble father rather than of his own noble uncle. He had declared his intention of making inquiry of Father Marty, and he thought that he should do so with something of a high hand. He still had that scheme in his head, and he might perhaps be better prepared to discuss it with the priest if he could first make this friend of the O'Hara family understand how much he, Neville, was personally injured by this 'turning up' of a disreputable father. But, should he allow the priest at once to run away to Scroope and his noble uncle, the result of such conversation would simply be renewed promises on his part in reference to his future conduct to Kate O'Hara.

'Lord Scroope wasn't very well when I left him. By the bye, Father Marty, I've been particularly anxious to see you.'

' 'Deed thin I was aisy found, Mr. Neville.'

'What is this I hear about—Captain O'Hara?'

'What is it that you have heard, Mr. Neville?' Fred looked

into the priest's face and found that he, at least, did not blush. It may be that all power of blushing had departed from Father Marty.

'In the first place I hear that there is such a man.'

'Ony way there was once.'

'You think he's dead then?'

'I don't say that. It's a matter of—faith, thin, it's a matter of nigh twenty years since I saw the Captain. And when I did see him I didn't like him. I can tell you that, Mr. Neville.'

'I suppose not.'

'That lass up there was not born when I saw him. He was a handsome man too, and might have been a gentleman av' he would.'

'But he wasn't.'

'It's a hard thing to say what is a gentleman, Mr. Neville. I don't know a much harder thing. Them folk at Castle Quin now, wouldn't scruple to say that I'm no gentleman, just because I'm a Popish priest. I say that Captain O'Hara was no gentleman because he ill-treated a woman.' Father Marty as he said this stopped a moment on the road, turning round and looking Neville full in the face. Fred bore the look fairly well. Perhaps at the moment he did not understand its application. It may be that he still had a clear conscience in that matter, and thought that he was resolved to treat Kate O'Hara after a fashion that would in no way detract from his own character as a gentleman. 'As it was,' continued the priest, 'he was a low blag-guard.'

'He hadn't any money, I suppose?'

' 'Deed and I don't think he was iver throubled much in respect of money. But money doesn't matter, Mr. Neville.'

'Not in the least,' said Fred.

'Thim ladies up there are as poor as Job, but anybody that should say that they weren't ladies would just be shewing that he didn't know the difference. The Captain was well born, Mr. Neville, av' that makes ony odds.'

'Birth does go for something, Father Marty.'

'Thin let the Captain have the advantage. Them O'Haras

of Kildare weren't proud of him I'm thinking, but he was a
chip of that block; and some one belonging to him had seen
the errors of the family ways, in respect of making him a
Papist. 'Deed and I must say, Mr. Neville, when they send us
any offsets* from a Prothestant family it isn't the best that
they give us.'

'I suppose not, Father Marty.'

'We can make something of a bit of wood that won't take
ony shape at all, at all along wid them. But there wasn't
much to boast of along of the Captain.'

'But is he alive, Father Marty—or is he dead? I think I've
a right to be told.'

'I am glad to hear you ask it as a right, Mr. Neville. You
have a right if that young lady up there is to be your wife.'
Fred made no answer here, though the priest paused for a
moment, hoping that he would do so. But the question could
be asked again, and Father Marty went on to tell all that he
knew, and all that he had heard of Captain O'Hara. He was
alive. Mrs. O'Hara had received a letter purporting to be
from her husband, giving an address in London, and asking
for money. He, Father Marty, had seen the letter; and he
thought that there might perhaps be a doubt whether it was
written by the man of whom they were speaking. Mrs. O'Hara
had declared that if it were so written the handwriting was
much altered. But then in twelve years the writing of a man
who drank hard will change. It was twelve years since she
had last received a letter from him.

'And what do you believe?'

'I think he lives, and that he wrote it, Mr. Neville. I'll
tell you God's truth about it as I believe it, because as I
said before I think you are entitled to know the truth.'

'And what was done?'

'I sent off to London—to a friend I have.'

'And what did your friend say?'

'He says there is a man calling himself Captain O'Hara.'

'And is that all?'

'She got a second letter. She got it the very last day you

was down here. Pat Cleary took it up to her when you was
out wid Miss Kate.'

'He wants money, I suppose.'

'Just that, Mr. Neville.'

'It makes a difference—doesn't it?'

'How does it make a difference?'

'Well; it does. I wonder you don't see it. You must see it.'
From that moment Father Marty said in his heart that Kate
O'Hara had lost her husband. Not that he admitted for a
moment that Captain O'Hara's return, if he had returned,
would justify the lover in deserting the girl; but that he perceived that Neville had already allowed himself to entertain
the plea. The whole affair had in the priest's estimation been
full of peril; but then the prize to be won was very great!
From the first he had liked the young man, and had not
doubted—did not now doubt—but that once married he
would do justice to his wife. Even though Kate should fail
and should come out of the contest with a scorched heart—
and that he had thought more than probable—still the prize
was very high and the girl he thought was one who could survive such a blow. Latterly in that respect he had changed his
opinion. Kate had shewn herself to be capable of so deep a
passion that he was now sure that she would be more than
scorched should the fire be one to injure and not to cherish
her. But the man's promises had been so firm, so often reiterated, were so clearly written, that the priest had almost
dared to hope that the thing was assured. Now, alas, he perceived that the embryo English lord was already looking for
a means of escape, and already thought that he had found it
in this unfortunate return of the father. The whole extent of
the sorrow even the priest did not know. But he was determined to fight the battle to the very last. The man should
make the girl his wife, or he, Father Marty, parish priest of
Liscannor, would know the reason why. He was a man who
was wont to desire to know the reason why, as to matters
which he had taken in hand. But when he heard the words
which Neville spoke and marked the tone in which they

were uttered he felt that the young man was preparing for himself a way of escape.

'I don't see that it should make any difference,' he said shortly.

'If the man be disreputable—'

'The daughter is not therefore disreputable. Her position is not changed.'

'I have to think of my friends.'

'You should have thought of that before you declared yourself to her, Mr. Neville,' How true this was now, the young man knew better than the priest, but that, as yet, was his own secret. 'You do not mean to tell me that because the father is not all that he should be, she is therefore to be thrown over. That cannot be your idea of honour. Have you not promised that you would make her your wife?' The priest stopped for an answer, but the young man made him none. 'Of course you have promised her.'

'I suppose she has told you so.'

'To whom should she tell her story? To whom should she go for advice? But it was you who told me so, yourself.'

'Never.'

'Did you not swear to me that you would not injure her? And why should there have been any talk with you and me about her, but that I saw what was coming? When a young man like you chooses to spend his hours day after day and week after week with such a one as she is, with a beautiful young girl, a sweet innocent young lady, so sweet as to make even an ould priest like me feel that the very atmosphere she breathes is perfumed and hallowed, must it not mean one of two things—that he desires to make her his wife or else—or else something so vile that I will not name it in connection with Kate O'Hara? Then as her mother's friend, and as hers —as their only friend near them, I spoke out plainly to you, and you swore to me that you intended no harm to her.'

'I would not harm her for the world.'

'When you said that, you told me as plainly as you could spake that she should be your wife. With her own mouth

she never told me. Her mother has told me. Daily Mrs.
O'Hara has spoken to me of her hopes and fears. By the Lord
above whom I worship and by His Son in whom I rest all
my hopes, I would not stand in your shoes if you intend to
tell that woman that after all that has passed you mean to
desert her child.'

'Who has talked of deserting?' asked Neville angrily.

'Say that you will be true to her, that you will make her
your wife before God and man, and I will humbly ask your
pardon.'

'All that I say is that this Captain O'Hara's coming is a
nuisance.'

'If that be all, there is an end of it. It is a nuisance. Not
that I suppose he ever will come. If he persists she must
send him a little money. There shall be no difficulty about
that. She will never ask you to supply the means of keeping
her husband.'

'It isn't the money. I think you hardly understand my
position, Father Marty.' It seemed to Neville that if it was
ever his intention to open out his scheme to the priest, now
was his time for doing so. They had come to the cross roads
at which one way led down to the village and to Father
Marty's house, and the other to the spot on the beach where
the boat would be waiting. 'I can't very well go on to Liscannor,' said Neville.

'Give me your word before we part that you will keep
your promise to Miss O'Hara,' said the priest.

'If you will step on a few yards with me I will tell you
just how I am situated.' Then the priest assented, and they
both went on towards the beach, walking very slowly. 'If I
alone were concerned, I would give up everything for Miss
O'Hara. I am willing to give up everything as regards myself.
I love her so dearly that she is more to me than all the
honours and wealth that are to come to me when my uncle
dies.'

'What is to hinder but that you should have the girl you
love and your uncle's honours and wealth into the bargain?'

'That is just it.'

'By the life of me I don't see any difficulty. You're your own masther. The ould Earl can't disinherit you if he would.'

'But I am bound down.'

'How bound? Who can bind you?'

'I am bound not to make Miss O'Hara Countess of Scroope.'

'What binds you? You are bound by a hundred promises to make her your wife.'

'I have taken an oath that no Roman Catholic shall become Countess Scroope as my wife.'

'Then, Mr. Neville, let me tell you that you must break your oath.'

'Would you have me perjure myself?'

'Faith I would. Perjure yourself one way you certainly must, av' you've taken such an oath as that, for you've sworn many oaths that you would make this Catholic lady your wife. Not make a Roman Catholic Countess of Scroope! 'It's the impudence of some of you Prothestants that kills me entirely. As though we couldn't count Countesses against you and beat you by chalks! I ain't the man to call hard names, Mr. Neville; but if one of us is upstarts, it's aisy seeing which. Your uncle's an ould man, and I'm told nigh to his latter end. I'm not saying but what you should respect even his wakeness. But you'll not look me in the face and tell me that afther what's come and gone that young lady is to be cast on one side like a plucked rose, because an ould man has spoken a foolish word, or because a young man has made a wicked promise.'

They were now standing again, and Fred raised his hat and rubbed his forehead as he endeavoured to arrange the words in which he could best propose his scheme to the priest. He had not yet escaped from the idea that because Father Marty was a Roman Catholic priest, living in a village in the extreme west of Ireland, listening night and day to the roll of the Atlantic and drinking whisky punch, therefore

he would be found to be romantic, semi-barbarous, and perhaps more than semi-lawless in his views of life. Irish priests
have been made by chroniclers of Irish story to do marvellous things,* and Fred Neville thought that this priest, if
only the matter could be properly introduced, might be persuaded to do for him something romantic, something marvellous, perhaps something almost lawless. In truth it might
have been difficult to find a man more practical or
more honest than Mr. Marty. And then the difficulty of introducing the subject was very great. Neville stood with his
face a little averted, rubbing his forehead as he raised his
sailor's hat. 'If you could only read my heart,' he said, 'you'd
know that I am as true as steel.'

'I'd be loathe to doubt it, Mr. Neville.'

'I'd give up everything to call Kate my own.'

'But you need give up nothing, and yet have her all your
own.'

'You say that because you don't completely understand. It
may as well be taken for granted at once that she can never
be Countess of Scroope.'

'Taken for granted!' said the old man as the fire flashed
out of his eyes.

'Just listen to me for one moment. I will marry her to-
morrow, or at any time you may fix, if a marriage can be so
arranged that she shall never be more than Mrs. Neville.'

'And what would you be?'

'Mr. Neville.'

'And what would her son be?'

'Oh—just the same—when he grew up perhaps there
wouldn't be a son.'

'God forbid that there should on those terms. You intend
that your children and her children shall be—bastards. That's
about it, Mr. Neville.' The romance seemed to vanish when
the matter was submitted to him in this very prosaic manner.
'As to what you might choose to call yourself, that would be
nothing to me and not very much I should say, to her. I
believe a man needn't be a lord unless he likes to be a lord

—and needn't call his wife a countess. But, Mr. Neville, when you have married Miss O'Hara, and when your uncle shall have died, there can be no other Countess of Scroope, and her child must be the heir to your uncle's title.'

'All that I could give her except that, she should have.'

'But she must have that. She must be your wife before God and man, and her children must be the children of honour and not of disgrace.' Ah—if the priest had known it all!

'I would live abroad with her, and her mother should live with us.'

'You mean that you would take Kate as your misthress! And you make this as a proposal to me! Upon my word, Mr. Neville, I don't think that I quite understand what it is that you're maning to say to me. Is she to be your wife?'

'Yes,' said Neville, urged by the perturbation of his spirit to give a stronger assurance than he had intended.

'Then must her son if she have one be the future Earl of Scroope. He may be Protesthant—or what you will?'

'You don't understand me, Father Marty.'

'Faith, and that's thrue. But we are at the baich, Mr. Neville, and I've two miles along the coast to Liscannor.'

'Shall I make Barney take you round in the canoe?'

'I believe I may as well walk it. Good-bye, Mr. Neville. I'm glad at any rate to hear you say so distinctly that you are resolved at all hazards to make that dear girl your wife.' This he said, almost in a whisper, standing close to the boat, with his hand on Neville's shoulder. He paused a moment as though to give special strength to his words, and Neville did not dare or was not able to protest against the assertion. Father Marty himself was certainly not romantic in his manner of managing such an affair as this in which they were now both concerned.

Neville went back to Ennis much depressed, turning the matter over in his mind almost hopelessly. This was what had come from his adventures! No doubt he might marry the girl—postponing his marriage till after his uncle's death.

For aught he knew as yet that might still be possible. But were he to do so, he would disgrace his family, and disgrace himself by breaking the solemn promise he had made. And in such case he would be encumbered, and possibly be put beyond the pale of that sort of life which should be his as Earl of Scroope, by having Captain O'Hara as his father-in-law. He was aware now that he would be held by all his natural friends to have ruined himself by such a marriage.

On the other hand he could, no doubt, throw the girl over. They could not make him marry her though they could probably make him pay very dearly for not doing so. If he could only harden his heart sufficiently he could escape in that way. But he was not hard, and he did feel that so escaping, he would have a load on his breast which would make his life unendurable. Already he was beginning to hate the coast of Ireland, and to think that the gloom of Scroope Manor was preferable to it.

CHAPTER III

FRED NEVILLE RECEIVES A VISITOR AT ENNIS.

FOR SOMETHING over three weeks after his walk with the priest Neville saw neither of the two ladies of Ardkill. Letters were frequent between the cottage and the barracks at Ennis, but—so said Fred himself, military duties detained him with the troop. He explained that he had been absent a great deal, and that now Captain Johnson* was taking his share of ease. He was all alone at the barracks, and could not get away. There was some truth in this, created perhaps by the fact that as he didn't stir, Johnson could do so. Johnson was backwards and forwards, fishing at Castle Connel, and Neville was very exact in explaining that for the present he was obliged to give up all the delights of the coast. But the days were days of trial to him.

A short history of the life of Captain O'Hara was absolutely sent to him by the Countess of Scroope. The family lawyer, at the instance of the Earl—as she said, though probably her own interference had been more energetic than that of the Earl—had caused enquiries to be made. Captain O'Hara, the husband of the lady who was now living on the coast of County Clare, and who was undoubtedly the father of the Miss O'Hara whom Fred knew, had passed at least ten of the latter years of his life at the galleys in the south of France. He had been engaged in an extensive swindling transaction at Bordeaux, and had thence been transferred to Toulon, had there been maintained by France—and was now in London. The Countess in sending this interesting story to her nephew at Ennis, with ample documentary evidence, said that she was sure that he would not degrade his family utterly by thinking of allying himself with people who

were so thoroughly disreputable; but that, after all that was
passed, his uncle expected from him a renewed assurance on
the matter. He answered this in anger. He did not understand why the history of Captain O'Hara should have been
raked up. Captain O'Hara was nothing to him. He supposed
it had come from Castle Quin, and anything from Castle
Quin he disbelieved. He had given a promise once and he
didn't understand why he should be asked for any further
assurance. He thought it very hard that his life should be
made a burden to him by foul-mouthed rumours from
Castle Quin. That was the tenor of his letter to his aunt;
but even that letter sufficed to make it almost certain that
he could never marry the girl. He acknowledged that he had
bound himself not to do so. And then, in spite of all that he
said about the mendacity of Castle Quin, he did believe the
little history. And it was quite out of the question that he
should marry the daughter of a returned galley-slave. He did
not think that any jury in England would hold him to be
bound by such a promise. Of course he would do whatever he
could for his dear Kate; but, even after all that had passed,
he could not pollute himself by marriage with the child of so
vile a father. Poor Kate! Her sufferings would have been
occasioned not by him, but by her father.

In the meantime Kate's letters to him became more and
more frequent, more and more sad—filled ever with still increasing warmth of entreaty. At last they came by every post,
though he knew how difficult it must be for her to find daily
messengers into Ennistimon. Would he not come and see her?
He must come and see her. She was ill and would die unless
he came to her. He did not always answer these letters, but
he did write to her perhaps twice a week. He would come very
soon—as soon as Johnson had come back from his fishing.
She was not to fret herself. Of course he could not always be
at Ardkill. He too had things to trouble him. Then he told
her that he had received letters from home which caused him
very much trouble; and there was a something of sharpness

in his words, which brought from her a string of lamentations in which, however, the tears and wailings did not as yet take the form of reproaches. Then there came a short note from Mrs. O'Hara herself. 'I must beg that you will come to Ardkill at once. It is absolutely necessary for Kate's safety that you should do so.'

When he received this he thought that he would go on the morrow. When the morrow came he determined to postpone the journey for yet another day! The calls of duty are so much less imperious than those of pleasure! On that further day he still meant to go, as he sat about noon unbraced, only partly dressed in his room at the barracks. His friend Johnson was back in Ennis, and there was also a Cornet with the troop. He had no excuse whatever on the score of military duty for remaining at home on that day. But he sat idling his time, thinking of things. All the charm of the adventure was gone. He was sick of the canoe and of Barney Morony. He did not care a straw for the seals or wild gulls. The moaning of the ocean beneath the cliff was no longer pleasurable to him—and as to the moaning at their summit, to tell the truth, he was afraid of it. The long drive thither and back was tedious to him. He thought now more of the respectability of his family than of the beauty of Kate O'Hara.

But still he meant to go—certainly would go on this very day. He had desired that his gig should be ready, and had sent word to say that he might start at any moment. But still he sat in his dressing-gown at noon, unbraced, with a novel in his hand which he could not read, and a pipe by his side which he could not smoke. Close to him on the table lay that record of the life of Captain O'Hara, which his aunt had sent him, every word of which he had now examined for the third or fourth time. Of course he could not marry the girl. Mrs. O'Hara had deceived him. She could not but have known that her husband was a convict—and had kept the knowledge back from him in order that she might allure him to the marriage. Anything that money could do, he would do. Or, if they would consent, he would take the girl away with him to some sunny distant clime, in which adventures might still be sweet, and would then devote to her—some portion of his time. He had not yet ruined himself, but he would indeed ruin himself were he, the heir to the earldom of Scroope, to marry the daughter of a man who had been at the French galleys! He had just made up his mind that he would be firm in this resolution—when the door opened and Mrs. O'Hara entered his room. 'Mrs. O'Hara.'

She closed the door carefully behind her before she spoke, excluding the military servant who had wished to bar her entrance. 'Yes, sir; as you would not come to us I have been forced to come to you. I know it all. When will you make my child your wife?'

Yes. In the abjectness of her misery the poor girl had told her mother the story of her disgrace; or, rather, in her weakness had suffered her secret to fall from her lips. That terrible retribution was to come upon her which, when sin has been mutual, falls with so crushing a weight upon her who of the two sinners has ever been by far the less sinful. She, when she knew her doom, simply found herself bound by still stronger ties of love to him who had so cruelly injured her. She was his before; but now she was more than ever his. To have him near her, to give her orders that she might obey them, was the consolation that she coveted—the only consolation that could have availed anything to her. To lean against him, and to whisper to him, with face averted, with half-formed syllables, some fervent words that might convey to him a truth which might be almost a joy to her if he would make it so—was the one thing that could restore hope to her bosom. Let him come and be near to her, so that she might hide her face upon his breast. But he came not. He did not come, though, as best she knew how, she had thrown all her heart into her letters. Then her spirit sank within her, and she sickened, and as her mother knelt over her, she allowed her secret to fall from her.

Fred Neville's sitting-room at Ennis was not a chamber prepared for the reception of ladies. It was very rough, as are usually barrack rooms in outlying quarters in small towns in the west of Ireland—and it was also very untidy. The more prudent and orderly of mankind might hardly have understood why a young man, with prospects and present wealth such as belonged to Neville, should choose to spend a twelvemonth in such a room, contrary to the wishes of all his friends, when London was open to him, and the continent, and scores of the best appointed houses in England, and all the glories of ownership at Scroope. There were guns about, and whips, hardly half a dozen books, and a few papers. There were a couple of swords lying on a table that looked like a dresser. The room was not above half covered with its carpet, and though there were three large easy chairs, even they were torn and soiled. But all this had been compatible with adventures—and while the adventures were simply romantic and not a bit troublesome, the barracks at Ennis had been to him by far preferable to the gloomy grandeur of Scroope.

And now Mrs. O'Hara was there, telling him that she knew of all! Not for a moment did he remain ignorant of the meaning of her communication. And now the arguments to be used against him in reference to the marriage would be stronger than ever. A silly, painful smile came across his handsome face as he attempted to welcome her, and moved a chair for her accommodation. 'I am so sorry that you have had the trouble of coming over,' he said.

'That is nothing. When will you make my child your wife?' How was he to answer this? In the midst of his difficulties he had brought himself to one determination. He had resolved that under no pressure would be marry the daughter of O'Hara, the galley-slave. As far as that he had seen his way. Should he now at once speak of the galley-slave, and, with expressions of regret, decline the alliance on that reason? Having dishonoured this woman's daughter should he shelter himself behind the dishonour of her husband? That he meant to do so ultimately is true; but at the present moment such a task would have required a harder heart than his. She rose from her chair and stood close over him as she repeated her demand, 'When will you make my child your wife?'

'You do not want me to answer you at this moment?'

'Yes—at this moment. Why not answer me at once? She has told me all. Mr. Neville, you must think not only of her, but of your child also.'

'I hope not that,' he said.

'I tell you that it is so. Now answer me. 'When shall my Kate become your wife?'

He still knew that any such consummation as that was quite out of the question. The mother herself as she was now present to him, seemed to be a woman very different from the quiet, handsome, high-spirited, but low-voiced widow whom he had known, or thought that he had known, at Ardkill. Of her as she had there appeared to him he had not been ashamed to think as one who might at some future time be personally related to himself. He had recognized her as a lady whose outward trappings, poor though they might be, were suited to the seclusion in which she lived. But now, although it was only to Ennis that she had come from her nest among the rocks, she seemed to be unfitted for even so much intercourse with the world as that. And in the demand which she reiterated over him she hardly spoke as a lady would speak. Would not all they who were connected with him at home have a right to complain if he were to bring such a woman with him to England as the mother of his wife. 'I can't answer such a question as that on the spur of the moment,' he said.

'You will not dare to tell me that you mean to desert her?'

'Certainly not. I was coming over to Ardkill this very day. The trap is ordered. I hope Kate is well?'

'She is not well. How should she be well?'

'Why not? I didn't know. If there is anything that she wants that I can get for her, you have only to speak.'

In the utter contempt which Mrs. O'Hara now felt for the man she probably forgot that his immediate situation was one

in which it was nearly impossible that any man should conduct himself with dignity. Having brought himself to his
present pass by misconduct, he could discover no line of good
conduct now open to him. Moralists might tell him that let
the girl's parentage be what it might, he ought to marry her;
but he was stopped from that, not only by his oath, but by a
conviction that his highest duty required him to preserve
his family from degradation. And yet to a mother, with such
a demand on her lips as that now made by Mrs. O'Hara—
whose demand was backed by such circumstances—how was
it possible that he should tell the truth and plead the honour
of his family? His condition was so cruel that it was no
longer possible to him to be dignified or even true. The
mother again made her demand. 'There is one thing that you
must do for her before other things can be thought of. When
shall she become your wife?'

It was for a moment on his tongue to tell her that it could
not be so while his uncle lived—but to this he at once felt
that there were two objections, directly opposed to each
other, but each so strong as to make any such reply very
dangerous. It would imply a promise, which he certainly did
not intend to keep, of marrying the girl when his uncle
should be dead; and, although promising so much more than
he intended to perform, would raise the ungovernable wrath
of the woman before him. That he should now hesitate—
now, in her Kate's present condition—as to redeeming those
vows of marriage which he had made to her in her innocence,
would raise a fury in the mother's bosom which he feared to
encounter. He got up and walked about the room, while she
stood with her eyes fixed upon him, ever and anon reiterating
her demand. 'No day must now be lost. When will you make
my child your wife?'

At last he made a proposition to which she assented. The
tidings which she had brought him had come upon him very
suddenly. He was inexpressibly pained. Of course Kate, his
dearest Kate, was everything to him. Let him have that afternoon to think about it. On the morrow he would assuredly

visit Ardkill. The mother, full of fears, resolving that should he attempt to play her girl false and escape from her she would follow him to the end of the world, but feeling that at the present moment she could not constrain him, accepted his repeated promise as to the following day; and at last left him to himself.

CHAPTER IV

NEVILLE'S SUCCESS

NEVILLE SAT in his room alone, without moving, for a couple of hours after Mrs. O'Hara had left him. In what way should he escape from the misery and ruin what seemed to surround him? An idea did cross his mind that it would be better for him to fly and write the truth from the comparatively safe distance of his London club. But there would be a meanness in such conduct which would make it impossible that he should ever again hold up his head. The girl had trusted to him and by trusting to him had brought herself to this miserable pass. He could not desert her. It would be better that he should go and endure all the vials of their wrath than that. To her he would still be tenderly loving, if she would accept his love without the name which he could not give her. His whole life he would sacrifice to her. Every luxury which money could purchase he would lavish on her. He must go and make his offer. The vials of wrath which would doubtless be poured out upon his head would not come from her. In his heart of hearts he feared both the priest and the mother. But there are moments in which a man feels himself obliged to encounter all that he most fears—and the man who does not do so in such moments is a coward.

He quite made up his mind to start early on the following morning; but the intermediate hours were very sad and heavy, and his whole outlook into life was troublesome to him. How infinitely better would it have been for him had he allowed himself to be taught a twelve month since that his duty required him to give up the army at once! But he had made his bed, and now he must lie upon it. There was no escape from this journey to Ardkill. Even though he should be stunned by their wrath he must endure it.

He breakfasted early the next day, and got into his gig before nine. He must face the enemy, and the earlier that he did it the better. His difficulty now lay in arranging the proposition that he would make and the words that he should speak. Every difficulty would be smoothed and every danger dispelled if he would only say that he would marry the girl as quickly as the legal forms would allow. Father Marty, he knew, would see to all that, and the marriage might be done effectually. He had quite come to understand that Father Marty was practical rather than romantic. But there would be cowardice in this as mean as that other cowardice. He believed himself to be bound by his duty to his family.* Were he now to renew his promise of marriage, such renewal would be caused by fear and not by duty, and would be mean. They should tear him piecemeal rather than get from him such a promise. Then he thought of the Captain, and perceived that he must make all possible use of the Captain's character. Would anybody conceive that he, the heir of the Scroope family, was bound to marry the daughter of a convict returned from the galleys? And was it not true that such promise as he had made had been obtained under false pretences? Why had he not been told of the Captain's position when he first made himself intimate with the mother and daughter?

Instead of going as was his custom to Lahinch, and then rowing across the bay and round the point, he drove his gig to the village of Liscannor. He was sick of Barney Morony and the canoe, and never desired to see either of them again. He was sick indeed, of everything Irish, and thought that the whole island was a mistake. He drove, however, boldly through Liscannor and up to Father Marty's yard, and, not finding the priest at home, there left his horse and gig. He had determined that he would first go to the priest and boldly declare that nothing should induce him to marry the daughter of a convict. But Father Marty was not at home. The old woman who kept his house believed that he had gone into Ennistimon. He was away with his horse, and would not be back till dinner time. Then Neville, having seen his own nag taken from the gig, started on his walk up to Ardkill.

How ugly the country was to his eyes as he now saw it. Here and there stood a mud cabin, and the small, half-culti-vated fields, or rather patches of land, in which the thin oat crops were beginning to be green were surrounded by low loose ramshackle walls, which were little more than heaps of stone, so carelessly had they been built and so negligently preserved. A few cocks and ·hens with here and there a miserable, starved pig seemed to be the stock of the country. Not a tree, not a shrub, not a flower was there to be seen. The road was narrow, rough, and unused. The burial ground which he passed was the liveliest sign of humanity about the place. Then the country became still wilder, and there was no road. The oats also ceased, and the walls. But he could hear the melancholy moan of the waves, which he had once thought to be musical and had often sworn that he loved. Now the place with all its attributes was hideous to him, dis-tasteful, and abominable. At last the cottage was in view, and his heart sank very low. Poor Kate! He loved her dearly through it all. He endeavoured to take comfort by assuring himself that his heart was true to her. Not for worlds would he injure her—that is, not for worlds, had any worlds been exclusively his own. On account of the Scroope world—which was a world general rather than particular—no doubt he must injure her most horribly. But still she was his dear Kate, his own Kate, his Kate whom he would never desert.

When he came up to the cottage the little gate was open, and he knew that somebody was there besides the usual in-mates. His heart at once told him that it was the priest. His fate had brought him face to face with his two enemies at once! His breath almost left him, but he knew that he could not run away. However bitter might be the vials of wrath he must encounter them. So he knocked at the outer door and, after his custom walked into the passage. Then he knocked again at the door of the one sitting-room—the door which

hitherto he had always passed with the conviction that he
should bring delight—and for a moment there was no answer.
He heard no voice and he knocked again. The door was
opened for him, and as he entered he met Father Marty. But
he at once saw that there was another man in the room, seated
in an armchair near the window. Kate, his Kate, was not
there, but Mrs. O'Hara was standing at the head of the sofa,
far away from the window and close to the door. 'It is Mr.
Neville,' said the priest. 'It is as well that he should come in.'

'Mr. Neville,' said the man rising from his chair, 'I am informed that you are a suitor for the hand of my daughter.
Your prospects in life are sufficient, sir, and I give my consent.'

The man was a thing horrible to look at, tall, thin, cadaverous, ill-clothed, with his wretched and all but ragged over-
coat buttoned close up to his chin, with long straggling thin
grizzled hair, red-nosed, with a drunkard's eyes, and thin lips
drawn down at the corners of the mouth. This was Captain
O'Hara; and if any man ever looked like a convict returned
from work in chains, such was the appearance of this man.
This was the father of Fred's Kate—the man whom it was
expected that he, Frederic Neville, the future Earl of Scroope,
should take as his father-in-law! 'This is Captain O'Hara,'
said the priest. But even Father Marty, bold as he was, could
not assume the voice with which he had rebuked Neville as
he walked with him, now nearly a month ago, down to the
beach.

Neville did feel that the abomination of the man's appearance strengthened his position. He stood looking from one to
another, while Mrs. O'Hara remained silent in the corner.
'Perhaps,' said he, 'I had better not be here. I am intruding.'

'It is right that you should know it all,' said the priest. 'As
regards the young lady it cannot now alter your position. This
gentleman must be—arranged for.'

'Oh, certainly,' said the Captain. 'I must be——arranged
for, and that so soon as possible.' The man spoke with a
slightly foreign accent and in a tone, as Fred thought, which

savoured altogether of the galleys. 'You have done me the
honour, I am informed, to make my daughter all your own.
These estimable people assure me that you hasten to make
her your wife on the instant. I consent. The O'Haras, who
are of the very oldest blood in Europe, have always connected
themselves highly. Your uncle is a most excellent nobleman
whose hand I shall be proud to grasp.' As he thus spoke he
stalked across the room to Fred, intending at once to commence the work of grasping the Neville family.

'Get back,' said Fred, retreating to the door.

'Is it that you fail to believe that I am your bride's father?'

'I know not whose father you may be. Get back.'

'He is what he says he is,' said the priest. 'You should bear
with him for a while.'

'Where is Kate?' demanded Fred. It seemed as though, for
the moment, he were full of courage. He looked round at
Mrs. O'Hara, but nobody answered him. She was still standing with her eyes fixed upon the man, almost as though she
thought that she could dart out upon him and destroy him.
'Where is Kate?' he asked again. 'Is she well?'

'Well enough to hide herself from her old father,' said the
Captain, brushing a tear from his eye with the back of his
hand.

'You shall see her presently, Mr. Neville,' said the priest.

Then Neville whispered a word into the priest's ear. 'What
is it that the man wants?'

'You need not regard that,' said Father Marty.

'Mr. Marty,' said the Captain, 'you concern yourself too
closely in my affairs. I prefer to open my thoughts and desires
to my son-in-law. He has taken measures which give him a
right to interfere in the family. Ha, ha, ha.'

'If you talk like that I'll stab you to the heart,' said Mrs.
O'Hara, jumping forward. Then Fred Neville perceived that
the woman had a dagger in her hand which she had hitherto
concealed from him as she stood up against the wall behind
the head of the sofa. He learnt afterwards that the priest,
having heard in Liscannor of the man's arrival, had hurried

up to the cottage, reaching it almost at the same moment with the Captain. Kate had luckily at the moment been in her room and had not seen her father. She was still in her bed* and was ill—but during the scene that occurred afterwards she roused herself. But Mrs. O'Hara, even in the priest's presence, had at once seized the weapon from the drawer— showing that she was prepared even for murder, had murder been found necessary by her for her relief. The man had immediately asked as to the condition of his daughter, and the mother had learned that her child's secret was known to all Liscannor. The priest now laid his hand upon her and stopped her, but he did it in all gentleness. 'You'll have a fierce pig of a mother-in-law, Mr. Neville,' said the Captain, 'but your wife's father—you'll find him always gentle and open to reason. You were asking what I wanted.'

'Had I not better give him money?' suggested Neville.

'No,' said the priest shaking his head.

'Certainly,' said Captain O'Hara.

'If you will leave this place at once,' said Neville, 'and come to me to-morrow morning at the Ennis barracks, I will give you money.'

'Give him none,' said Mrs. O'Hara.

'My beloved is unreasonable. You would not be rid of me even were he to be so hard. I should not die. Have I not proved to you that I am one whom it is hard to destroy by privation. The family has been under a cloud. A day of sunshine has come with this gallant young nobleman. Let me partake the warmth. I will visit you, Mr. Neville, certainly— but what shall be the figure?'

'That will be as I shall find you then.'

'I will trust you. I will come. The journey hence to Ennis is long for one old as I am, and would be lightened by so small a trifle as—shall I say a banknote of the meanest value.' Upon this Neville handed him two banknotes for £1 each, and Captain O'Hara walked forth out of his wife's house.

'He will never leave you now,' said the priest.

'He cannot hurt me. I will arrange with some man of business to pay him a stipend as long as he never troubles our friend here. Though all the world should know it, will it not be better so?'

Great and terrible is the power of money. When this easy way out of their immediate difficulties had been made by the rich man, even Mrs. O'Hara with all her spirit was subdued for the moment, and the reproaches of the priest were silenced for that hour. The young man had seemed to behave well, had stood up as the friend of the suffering women, and had been at any rate ready with his money. 'And now,' he said, 'where is Kate?' Then Mrs. O'Hara took him by the hand and led him into the bedroom in which the poor girl had buried herself from her father's embrace. 'Is he gone?' she asked before even she would throw herself into her lover's arms.

'Neville has paid him money,' said the mother.

'Yes, he has gone,' said Fred; 'and I think—I think that he will trouble you no more.'

'Oh, Fred, oh, my darling, oh, my own one. At last, at last you have come to me. Why have you stayed away? You will not stay away again? Oh, Fred, you do love me? Say that you love me.'

'Better than all the world,' he said pressing her to his bosom.

He remained with her for a couple of hours, during which hardly a word was said to him about his marriage. So great had been the effect upon them all of the sudden presence of the Captain, and so excellent had been the service rendered them by the trust which the Captain had placed in the young man's wealth, that for this day both priest and mother were incapacitated from making their claim with the vigour and intensity of purpose which they would have shown had Captain O'Hara not presented himself at the cottage. The priest left them soon—but not till it had been arranged that Neville should go back to Ennis to prepare for his reception of the Captain, and return to the cottage on the day after that interview was over. He assumed on a sudden the practical views of a man of business. He would take care to have an Ennis attorney with him when speaking to the Captain, and would be quite prepared to go to the extent of two hundred a year for the Captain's life, if the Captain could be safely purchased for that money. 'A quarter of it would do,' said Mrs. O'Hara. The priest thought £2 a week would be ample. 'I'll be as good as my word,' said Fred. Kate sat looking into his face thinking that he was still a god.

'And you will certainly be here by noon on Sunday?' said Kate, clinging to him when he rose to go.

'Most certainly.'

'Dear, dear Fred.' And so he walked down the hill to the priest's house almost triumphantly. He thought himself fortunate in not finding the priest who had ridden off from Ardkill to some distant part of the parish—and then drove himself back to Ennis.

CHAPTER V

FRED NEVILLE IS AGAIN CALLED HOME TO SCROOPE

NEVILLE WAS intent upon business, and had not been back in Ennis from the cottage half an hour before he obtained an introduction to an attorney. He procured it through the sergeant-major of the troop. The sergeant-major was intimate with the innkeeper, and the innkeeper was able to say that Mr. Thaddeus Crowe was an honest, intelligent, and peculiarly successful lawyer. Before he sat down to dinner Fred Neville was closeted at the barracks with Mr. Crowe.

He began by explaining to Mr. Crowe who he was. This he did in order that the attorney might know that he had the means of carrying out his purpose. Mr. Crowe bowed, and assured his client that on that score he had no doubts whatever. Nevertheless Mr. Crowe's first resolve, when he heard of the earldom and of the golden prospects, was to be very careful not to pay any money out of his own pocket on behalf of the young officer, till he made himself quite sure that it would be returned to him with interest. As the interview progressed, however, Mr. Crowe began to see his way, and to understand that the golden prospects were not pleaded because the owner of them was himself short of cash. Mr. Crowe soon understood the whole story. He had heard of Captain O'Hara, and believed the man to be as thorough a blackguard as ever lived. When Neville told the attorney of the two ladies, and of the anxiety which he felt to screen them from the terrible annoyance of the Captain's visits, Mr. Crowe smiled, but made no remark. 'It will be enough for you to know that I am earnest about it,' said the future Earl, resenting even the smile. Mr. Crowe bowed, and asked his client to finish the story.

'The man is to be with me tomorrow, here, at twelve, and I wish you to be present. Mr. Crowe, my intention is to give him two hundred pounds a year as long as he lives.'

'Two hundred a year!' said the Ennis attorney, to whom such an annuity seemed to be exorbitant as the purchase-money for a returned convict.

'Yes—I have already mentioned that sum to his wife, though not to him.'

'I should reconsider it, Mr. Neville.'

'Thank you—but I have made up my mind. The payments will be made, of course, only on condition that he troubles neither of the ladies either personally or by letter. It might be provided that it shall be paid to him weekly in France, but will not be paid should he leave that country. You will think of all this, and will make suggestions tomorrow. I shall be glad to have the whole thing left in your hands, so that I need simply remit the cheques to you. Perhaps I shall have the pleasure of seeing you tomorrow at twelve.' Mr. Crowe promised to turn the matter over in his mind and to be present at the hour named. Neville carried himself very well through the interview, assuming with perfect ease the manners of the great and rich man who had only to give his orders with a certainty that they would be obeyed. Mr. Crowe, when he went out from the young man's presence, had no longer any doubt on his mind as to his client's pecuniary capability.

On the following day at twelve o'clock, Captain O'Hara, punctual to the minute, was at the barracks; and there also sitting in Neville's room, was the attorney. But Neville himself was not there, and the Captain immediately felt that he had been grossly imposed upon and swindled. 'And who may I have the honour of addressing, when I speak to you, sir?' demanded the Captain.

'I am a lawyer.'

'And Mr. Neville—my own son-in-law—has played me that trick!'

Mr. Crowe explained that no trick had been played, but

did so in language which was no doubt less courteous than would have been used had Mr. Neville been present. As, however, the cause of our hero's absence is more important to us than the Captain's prospects that must be first explained.

As soon as the attorney left him Neville had sat down to dinner with his two brother officers, but was not by any means an agreeable companion. When they attempted to joke with him as to the young lady on the cliffs, he showed very plainly that he did not like it; and when Cornet Simpkinson after dinner raised his glass to drink a health to Miss O'Hara, Neville told him that he was an impertinent ass. It was then somewhat past nine, and it did not seem probable that the evening would go off pleasantly. Cornet Simpkinson lit his cigar, and tried to wink at the Captain. Neville stretched out his legs and pretended to go to sleep. At this moment it was a matter of intense regret to him that he had ever seen the West of Ireland.

At a little before ten Captain Johnson retired, and the Cornet attempted an apology. He had not meant to say anything that Neville would not like. 'It doesn't signify, my dear boy; only as a rule, never mention women's names,' said Neville, speaking as though he were fully fitted by his experience to lay down the law on a matter so delicate. 'Perhaps one hadn't better,' said the Cornet—and then that little difficulty was over. Cornet Simpkinson however thought of it afterwards, and felt that that evening and that hour had been more important than any other evening or any other hour in his life.

At half-past ten, when Neville was beginning to think that he would take himself to bed, and was still cursing the evil star which had brought him to County Clare, there arose a clatter at the outside gate of the small barrack-yard. A man had posted all the way down from Limerick and desired to see Mr. Neville at once. The man had indeed come direct from Scroope—by rail from Dublin to Limerick, and thence without delay on to Ennis. The Earl of Scroope was dead, and

Frederic Neville was Earl of Scroope. The man brought a letter from Miss Mellerby, telling him the sad news and conjuring him in his aunt's name to come at once to the Manor. Of course he must start at once for the Manor. Of course he must attend as first mourner at his uncle's grave before he could assume his uncle's name and fortune.

In that the first hour of his greatness the shock to him was not so great but that he at once thought of the O'Haras. He would leave Ennis the following morning at six, so as to catch the day mail train out of Limerick for Dublin. That was a necessity; but though so very short a span of time was left to him, he must still make arrangements about the O'Haras. He had hardly heard the news half an hour before he himself was knocking at the door of Mr. Crowe the attorney. He was admitted, and Mr. Crowe descended to him in a pair of slippers and a very old dressing-gown. Mr. Crowe, as he held his tallow candle up to his client's face, looked as if he didn't like it. 'I know I must apologize,' said Neville, 'but I have this moment received news of my uncle's death.'

'The Earl?'

'Yes.'

'And I have now the honour of—speaking to the Earl of Scroope.'

'Never mind that. I must start for England almost immediately. I haven't above an hour or two. You must see that man, O'Hara, without me.'

'Certainly, my lord.'

'You shouldn't speak to me in that way yet,' said Neville angrily. 'You will be good enough to understand that the terms are fixed two hundred a year as long as he remains in France and never molests anyone either by his presence or by letter. Thank you. I shall be so much obliged to you! I shall be back here after the funeral, and will arrange about payments. Good-night.'

So it happened that Captain O'Hara had no opportunity on that occasion of seeing his proposed son-in-law. Mr. Crowe, fully crediting the power confided to him, did as he was

bidden. He was very harsh to the poor Captain; but in such
a condition a man can hardly expect that people should not
be harsh to him. The Captain endeavoured to hold up his
head, and to swagger, and to assume an air of pinchbeck
respectability. But the attorney would not permit it. He
required that the man should own himself to be penniless, a
scoundrel, only anxious to be bought; and the Captain at last
admitted the facts. The figure was the one thing important to
him—the figure and the nature of the assurance. Mr. Crowe
had made his calculations, and put the matter very plainly.
A certain number of francs—a hundred francs—would be
paid to him weekly at any town in France he might select—
which however would be forfeited by any letter written either
to Mrs. O'Hara, to Miss O'Hara, or to the Earl.

'The Earl!' ejaculated the Captain.

Mr. Crowe had been unable to refrain his tongue from the
delicious title, but now corrected himself. 'Nor Mr. Neville,
I mean. No one will be bound to give you a farthing, and any
letter asking for anything more will forfeit the allowance
altogether.' The Captain vainly endeavoured to make better
terms, and of course accepted those proposed to him. He
would live in Paris—dear Paris. He took five pounds for his
journey, and named an agent for the transmission of his
money.

And so Fred Neville was the Earl of Scroope. He had still
one other task to perform before he could make his journey
home. He had to send tidings in some shape to Ardkill of
what had happened. As he returned to the barracks from Mr.
Crowe's residence he thought wholly of this. That other
matter was now arranged. As one item of the cost of his adventure in County Clare he must pay two hundred a year
to that reprobate, the Captain, as long as the reprobate chose
to live—and must also pay Mr. Crowe's bill for his assistance.
This was a small matter to him as his wealth was now great,
and he was not a man by nature much prone to think of
money. Nevertheless it was a bad beginning of his life.
Though he had declared himself to be quite indifferent

on that head, he did feel that the arrangement was not altogether reputable—that it was one which he could not explain to his own man of business without annoyance, and which might perhaps give him future trouble. Now he must prepare his message for the ladies at Ardkill—especially to the lady whom on his last visit to the cottage he had found armed with a dagger for the reception of her husband. And as he returned back to the barracks it occurred to him that a messenger might be better than a letter. 'Simpkinson,' he said, going at once into the young man's bedroom, 'have you heard what has happened to me?' Simpkinson had heard all about it, and expressed himself as 'deucedly sorry' for the old man's death, but seemed to think that there might be consolation for that sorrow. 'I must go to Scroope immediately said Neville. 'I have explained it all to Johnson, and shall start almost at once. I shall first lie down and get an hour's sleep. I want you to do something for me.' Simpkinson was devoted. Simpkinson would do anything. 'I cut up a little rough just now when you mentioned Miss O'Hara's name.' Simpkinson declared that he did not mind it in the least, and would never pronounce the name again as long as he lived. 'But I want you to go and see her tomorrow,' said Neville. Then Simpkinson sat bolt upright in bed.

Of course the youthful warrior undertook the commission. What youthful warrior would not go any distance to see a beautiful young lady on a cliff, and what youthful warrior would not undertake any journey to oblige a brother officer who was an Earl? Full instructions were at once given to him. He had better ask to see Mrs. O'Hara—in describing whom Neville made no allusion to the dagger. He was told how to knock at the door, and send in word by the servant to say that he had called on behalf of Mr. Neville. He was to drive as far as Liscannor, and then get some boy to accompany him on foot as a guide. He would not perhaps mind walking two or three miles. Simpkinson declared that were it ten he would not mind it. He was then to tell Mrs. O'Hara—just the truth. He was to say that a messenger had come from Scroope announcing the death of the Earl, and that Neville had been obliged to start at once for England.

'But you will be back?' said Simpkinson.

Neville paused a moment. 'Yes, I shall be back, but don't say anything of that to either of the ladies.'

'Must I say I don't know? They'll be sure to ask, I should say.'

'Of course they'll ask. Just tell them that the whole thing has been arranged so quickly that nothing has been settled, but that they shall hear from me at once. You can say that you suppose I shall be back, but that I promised that I would write. Indeed that will be the exact truth, as I don't at all know what I may do. Be as civil to them as possible.'

'That's of course.'

'They are ladies, you know.'

'I supposed that.'

'Am I most desirous to do all in my power to oblige them. You can say that I have arranged that other matter satisfactorily.'

'That other matter?'

'They'll understand. The mother will at least, and you'd better say that to her. You'll go early.'

'I'll start at seven if you like.'

'Eight or nine will do. Thank you, Simpkinson. I'm so much obliged to you. I hope I shall see you over in England some day when things are a little settled.' With this Simpkinson was delighted—as he was also with the commission entrusted to him.

And so Fred Neville was the Earl of Scroope. Not that he owned even to himself that the title and all belonging to it were as yet in his own possession. Till the body of the old man should be placed in the family vault he would still be simply Fred Neville, a lieutenant in Her Majesty's 20th Hussars. As he travelled home to Scroope, to the old gloomy mansion which was now in truth not only his home, but his own house, to do just as he pleased with it, he had much to fill his mind. He was himself astonished to find with how great a weight his new dignities sat upon his shoulders, now that they were his own. But a few months since he had thought and even spoken of shifting them from himself to another so that he might lightly enjoy a portion of the wealth which would belong to him without burdening himself with the duties of his position. He would take his yacht, and the girl he loved, and live abroad, with no present record of the coronet which would have descended to him, and with no assumption of the title. But already that feeling had died away within him. A few words spoken to him by the priest and a few serious thoughts within his own bosom had sufficed to explain to him that he must be the Earl of Scroope. The family honours had come to him, and he must support them —either well or ill as his strength and principles might govern him. And he did understand that it was much to be a peer, an hereditary legislator, one who by the chance of his birth had a right to look for deferential respect even from his elders. It was much to be the lord of wide acres, the ruler of a large domain, the landlord of many tenants who would at any rate regard themselves as dependent on his goodness. It was much to be so placed that no consideration of money need be a bar to any wish—that the considerations which should bar his pleasures need be only those of dignity, character and propriety. His uncle had told him more than once how much a peer of England owed to his country and to his order—how such a one is bound by no ordinary bonds to a life of high resolves, and good endeavours. "Sans reproche" was the motto of his house, and was emblazoned on the wall of the hall that was now his own. If it might be possible to him he would live up to it and neither degrade his order nor betray his country.

But as he thought of all this, he thought also of Kate O'Hara. With what difficulties had he surrounded the commencement of this life which he purposed to lead! How was he to escape from the mess of trouble which he had prepared for himself by his adventures in Ireland. An idea floated across his mind that very many men who stand in their

natural manhood high in the world's esteem, have in their
early youth formed ties such as that which now bound him
to Kate O'Hara—that they have been silly as he had been,
and had then escaped from the effects of their folly without
grievous damage. But yet he did not see his mode of escape.
If money could do it for him he would make almost any
sacrifice. If wealth and luxury could make his Kate happy,
she should be happy as a Princess. But he did not believe
either of her or of her mother that any money would be
accepted as a sufficient atonement. And he hated himself for
suggesting to himself that it might be possible. The girl was
good, and had trusted him altogether. The mother was self-
denying, devoted, and high-spirited. He knew that money
would not suffice.

He need not return to Ireland unless he pleased. He could
send over some agent to arrange his affairs, and allow the two
women to break their hearts in their solitude upon the
cliffs. Were he to do so he did not believe that they would
follow him. They would write doubtless, but personally he
might, probably, be quit of them in this fashion. But in this
there would be a cowardice and a meanness which would
make it impossible that he should ever again respect himself.

And thus he again entered Scroope, the lord and owner of
all that he saw around him—with by no means a happy
heart or a light bosom.

CHAPTER VI

THE EARL OF SCROOPE IS IN TROUBLE

NOT A word was said to the young lord on his return home respecting the O'Haras till he himself had broached the subject. He found his brother Jack Neville at Scroope on his arrival, and Sophie Mellerby was still staying with his aunt. A day had been fixed for the funeral, but no one had ventured to make any other arrangement till the heir and owner should be there. He was received with solemn respect by the old servants who, as he observed, abstained from calling him by any name. They knew that it did not become them to transfer the former lord's title to the heir till all that remained of the former lord should be hidden from the world in the family vault; but they could not bring themselves to address a real Earl as Mr. Neville. His aunt was broken down by sorrow, but nevertheless, she treated him with a courtly deference. To her he was now the reigning sovereign among the Nevilles, and all Scroope and everything there was at his disposal. When he held her by the hand and spoke of her future life she only shook her head. 'I am an old woman, though not in years old as was my lord. But my life is done, and it matters not where I go.'

'Dear aunt, do not speak of going. Where can you be so well as here?' But she only shook her head again and wept afresh. Of course it would not be fitting that she should remain in the house of the young Earl who was only her nephew by marriage. Scroope Manor would now become a house of joy, would be filled with the young and light of heart; there would be feasting there and dancing; horses neighing before the doors, throngs of carriages, new furniture, bright draperies, and perhaps, alas, loud revellings. It would not be fit that such a one as she should be at Scroope now that her lord had left her.

The funeral was an affair not of pomp but of great moment in those parts. Two or three Nevilles from other counties came to the house, as did also sundry relatives bearing other names. Mr. Mellerby was there, and one or two of the late Earl's oldest friends; but the great gathering was made up of the Scroope tenants, not one of whom failed to see his late landlord laid in his grave. 'My Lord,' said an old man to Fred, one who was himself a peer and was the young lord's cousin though they two had never met before, 'My Lord,' said the old man, as soon as they had returned from the grave, 'you are called upon to succeed as good a man as ever it has been my lot to know. I loved him as a brother. I hope you will not lightly turn away from his example.' Fred made some promise which at the moment he certainly intended to perform.

On the next morning the will was read. There was nothing in it, nor could there have been anything in it, which might materially affect the interests of the heir. The late lord's widow was empowered to take away from Scroope anything that she desired. In regard to money she was provided for so amply that money did not matter to her. A whole year's income from the estates was left to the heir in advance, so that he might not be driven to any momentary difficulty in assuming the responsibilities of his station. A comparatively small sum was left to Jack Neville, and a special gem to Sophie Mellerby. There were bequests to all the servants, a thousand pounds to the vicar of the parish—which perhaps was the only legacy which astonished the legatee—and his affectionate love to every tenant on the estate. All the world acknowledged that it was as good a will as the Earl could have made. Then the last of the strangers left the house, and the Earl of Scroope was left to begin his reign and do his duty as best he might.

Jack had promised to remain with him for a few days, and Sophie Mellerby, who had altogether given up her London season, was to stay with the widow till something should be settled as to a future residence. 'If my aunt will only say that she will keep the house for a couple of years, she shall have it,' said Fred to the young lady—perhaps wishing to postpone for so long a time the embarrassment of the large domain; but to this Lady Scroope would not consent. If allowed she would remain till the end of July. By that time she would find herself a home.

'For the life of me, I don't know how to begin my life,' said the new peer to his brother as they were walking about the park together.

'Do not think about beginning it at all. You won't be angry, and will know what I mean, when I say that you should avoid thinking too much of your own position.'

'How am I to help thinking of it? It is so entirely changed from what it was.'

'No Fred—not entirely; nor as I hope, is it changed at all in those matters which are of most importance to you. A man's self, and his ideas of the manner in which he should rule himself, should be more to him than any outward accidents. Had that cousin of ours never died——'

'I almost wish he never had.'

'It would then have been your ambition to live as an honourable gentleman. To be that now should be more to you than to be an Earl and a man of fortune.'

'It's very easy to preach, Jack. You were always good at that. But here I am, and what am I to do? How am I to begin? Everybody says that I am to change nothing. The tenants will pay their rents, and Burnaby will look after things outside, and Mrs. Bunce will look after the things inside, and I may sit down and read a novel. When the gloom of my uncle's death has passed away, I suppose I shall buy a few more horses and perhaps begin to make a row about the pheasants. I don't know what else there is to do.'

'You'll find that there are duties.'

'I suppose I shall. Something is expected of me. I am to keep up the honour of the family; but it really seems to me that the best way of doing so would be to sit in my uncle's arm chair and go to sleep as he did.'

'As a first step in doing something you should get a wife for yourself. If once you had a settled home, things would arrange themselves round you very easily.'

'Ah, yes—a wife. You know, Jack, I told you about that girl in County Clare.'

'You must let nothing of that kind stand in your way.'

'Those are your ideas of high moral grandeur! Just now my own personal conduct was to be all in all to me, and the rank nothing. Now I am to desert a girl I love because I am an English peer.'

'What has passed between you and the young lady, of course I do not know.'

'I may as well tell you the whole truth,' said Fred. And he told it honestly—almost honestly. It is very hard for a man to tell a story truly against himself, but he intended to tell the whole truth. 'Now what must I do? Would you have me marry her?' Jack Neville paused for a long time. 'At any rate you can say yes, or no.'

'It is very hard to say yes, or no.'

'I can marry no one else. I can see my way so far. You had better tell Sophie Mellerby everything, and then a son of yours shall be the future Earl.'

'We are both of us young as yet, Fred, and need not think of that. If you do mean to marry Miss O'Hara you should lose not a day—not a day.'

'But what if I don't. You are always very ready with advice, but you have given me none as yet.'

'How can I advise you? I should have heard the very words in which you made your promise before I could dare to say whether it should be kept or broken. As a rule a man should keep his word.'

'Let the consequences be what they may?'

'A man should keep his word certainly. And I know no promise so solemn as that made to a woman when followed by conduct such as yours has been.'

'And what will people say then as to my conduct to the family? How will they look on me when I bring home the daughter of that scoundrel?'

'You should have thought of that before.'

'But I was not told. Do you not see that I was deceived there. Mrs. O'Hara clearly said that the man was dead. And she told me nothing of the galleys.'

'How could she tell you that?'

'But if she has deceived me, how can I be expected to keep my promise? I love the girl dearly. If I could change places with you, I would do so this very minute, and take her away with me, and she should certainly be my wife. If it were only myself, I would give up all to her. I would, by heaven. But I cannot sacrifice the family. As to solemn promises, did I not swear to my uncle that I would not disgrace the family by such a marriage? Almost the last word that I spoke to him was that. Am I to be untrue to him? There are times in which it seems impossible that a man should do right.'

'There are times in which a man may be too blind to see the right,' said Jack—sparing his brother in that he did not remind him that those dilemmas always come from original wrongdoing.

'I think I am resolved not to marry her,' said Fred.

'If I were in your place I think I should marry her,' said Jack—'but I will not speak with certainty even of myself.'

'I shall not. But I will be true to her all the same. You may be sure that I shall not marry at all.' Then he recurred to his old scheme. 'If I can find any mode of marrying her in some foreign country, so that her son and mine shall not be the legitimate heir to the title and estates, I would go there at once with her, though it were to the further end of the world. You can understand now what I mean when I say that I do not know how to begin.' Jack acknowledged that in that matter he did understand his brother. It is always hard for a man to commence any new duty when he knows that he has a millstone round his neck which will probably make that duty impracticable at last

He went on with his life at Scroope for a week after the funeral without resolving upon anything, or taking any steps towards solving the O'Hara difficulty. He did ride about among the tenants, and gave some trifling orders as to the house and stables. His brother was still with him, and Miss Mellerby remained at the Manor. But he knew that the thunder-cloud must break over his head before long, and at last the storm was commenced. The first drops fell upon him in the soft form of a letter from Kate O'Hara.

'DEAREST FRED,

I am not quite sure that I ought to address you like that; but I always shall unless you tell me not. We have been expecting a letter from you every day since you went. Your friend from Ennis came here and brought us the news of your uncle's death. We were very sorry; at least I was certainly. I liked to think of you a great deal better as my own Fred, than as a great lord. But you will still be my own Fred always; will you not?

Mother said at once that it was a matter of course that you should go to England; but your friend, whose name we never heard, said that you had sent him especially to promise that you would write quite immediately, and that you would come back very soon. I do not know what he will think of me, because I asked him whether he was quite, quite sure that you would come back. If he thinks that I love you better than my own soul, he only thinks the truth.

Pray—pray write at once. Mother is getting vexed because there is no letter. I am never vexed with my own darling love, but I do so long for a letter. If you knew how I felt, I do think you would write almost every day—if it were only just one short word. If you would say, "Dear Love," that would be enough. And pray come. Oh do, do, pray come! Cannot you think how I must long to see you! The gentleman who came here said that you would come, and I know

you will. But pray come soon. Think now, how you are all
the world to me. You are more than all the world to me.

'I am not ill as I was when you were here. But I never go
outside the door now. I never shall go outside the door again
till you come. I don't care now for going out upon the rocks.
I don't care even for the birds as you are not here to watch
them with me. I sit with the skin of the seal you gave me behind my head and I pretend to sleep. But though I am quite
still for hours I am not asleep, but thinking always of you.

We have neither seen or heard anything more of my father,
and Father Marty says that you have managed about that
very generously. You are always generous and good. I was so
wretched all that day, that I thought I should have died. You
will not think ill of your Kate, will you, because her father
is bad?

Pray write when you get this, and above all things let us
know when you will come to us.

Always, always, and always,

Your own

KATE.'

Two days after this, while the letter was still unanswered,
there came another from Mrs. O'Hara which was, if possible,
more grievous to him than that from her daughter.

'My Lord,' the letter began. When he read this he turned
from it with a sickening feeling of disgust. Of course the
woman knew that he was now Earl of Scroope; but it would
have been so desirable that there should have been no intercourse between her and him except under the name by
which she had hitherto known him. And then in the appel-
lation as she used it there seemed to be a determination to
reproach him which must, he knew, lead to great misery.

'MY LORD,

The messenger you sent to us brought us good news,
and told us that you were gone home to your own affairs. That
I suppose was right, but why have you not written to us before this? Why have you not told my poor girl that you will

come to her, and atone to her for the injury you have done in the only manner now possible? I cannot and do not believe that you intend to evade the solemn promises that you have made her, and allow her to remain here a ruined outcast, and the mother of your child. I have thought you to be both a gentleman and a christian, and I still think so. Most assuredly you would be neither were you disposed to leave her desolate, while you are in prosperity.

I call upon you, my lord, in the most solemn manner, with all the energy and anxiety of a mother—of one who will be of all women the most broken-hearted if you wrong her—to write at once and let me know when you will be here to keep your promise. For the sake of your own offspring I implore you not to delay.

We feel under deep obligations to you for what you did in respect of that unhappy man. We never for a moment doubted your generosity.

Yours, My Lord,
With warmest affection, if you will admit it,
C. O'HARA.

'P.S. I ask you to come at once and keep your word. Were you to think of breaking it, I would follow you through the world.'*

The young Earl, when he received this, was not at a loss for a moment to attribute the body of Mrs. O'Hara's letter to Father Marty's power of composition, and the postscript to the unaided effort of the lady herself. Take it as he might —as coming from Mrs. O'Hara or from the priest—he found the letter to be a great burden to him. He had not as yet answered the one received from Kate, as to the genuineness of which he had entertained no doubt. How should he answer such letters? Some answer must of course be sent, and must be the forerunner of his future conduct. But how should he write his letter when he had not as yet resolved what his conduct should be?

He did attempt to write a letter, not to either of the ladies, but to the priest, explaining that in the ordinary sense of the word he could not and would not marry Miss O'Hara, but that in any way short of that legitimate and usual mode of marriage, he would bind himself to her, and that when so bound he would be true to her for life. He would make any settlement that he, Father Marty, might think right either upon the mother or upon the daughter. But Countess of Scroope the daughter of that Captain O'Hara should not become through his means. Then he endeavoured to explain the obligation laid upon him by his uncle, and the excuse which he thought he could plead in not having been informed of Captain O'Hara's existence. But the letter when written seemed to him to be poor and mean, cringing and at the same time false. He told himself that it would not suffice. It was manifest to him that he must go back to County Clare, even though he should encounter Mrs. O'Hara, dagger in hand. What was any personal danger to himself in such an affair as this? And if he did not fear a woman's dagger, was he to fear a woman's tongue—or the tongue of a priest? So he tore the letter, and resolved that he would write and name a day on which he would appear at Ardkill. At any rate such a letter as that might be easily written, and might be made soft with words of love.

'DEAREST KATE,

I will be with you on the 15th or on the 16th at latest. You should remember that a man has a good deal to do and think of when he gets pitchforked into such a new phase of life as mine. Do not, however, think that I quarrel with you, my darling. That I will never do. My love to your mother.

Ever your own,
FRED.

I hate signing the other name.'

This letter was not only written but sent.

CHAPTER VII

SANS REPROCHE.

THREE or four days after writing his letter to Kate O'Hara, the Earl told his aunt that he must return to Ireland, and he named the day on which he would leave Scroope. 'I did not think that you would go back there,' she said. He could see by the look of her face and by the anxious glance of her eye that she had in her heart the fear of Kate O'Hara—as he had also.

'I must return. I came away at a moment's notice.'

'But you have written about leaving the regiment.'

'Yes—I have done that. In the peculiar circumstances I don't suppose they will want me to serve again. Indeed I've had a letter, just a private note, from one of the fellows at the Horse Guards explaining all that.'

'I don't see why you should go at all—indeed I do not.'

'What am I to do about my things? I owe some money. I've got three or four horses there. My very clothes are all about just as I left them when I came away.'

'Anybody can manage all that. Give the horses away.'

'I had rather not give away my horses,' he said laughing. 'The fact is I must go.' She could urge nothing more to him on that occasion. She did not then mention the existence of Kate O'Hara. But he knew well that she was thinking of the girl, and he knew also that the activity of Lady Mary Quin had not slackened. But his aunt, he thought, was more afraid of him now that he was the Earl than she had been when he was only the heir; and it might be that this feeling would save him from the mention of Kate O'Hara's name.

To some extent the dowager was afraid of her nephew. She knew at least that the young man was all-powerful and might act altogether as he listed. In whatever she might say she could not now be supported by the authority of the Lord of Scroope. He himself was lord of Scroope; and were he to tell her simply to hold her tongue and mind her own business she could only submit. But she was not the woman to allow any sense of fear, or any solicitude as to the respect due to herself, to stand in the way of the performance of a duty. It may be declared on her behalf that had it been in her nephew's power to order her head off in punishment for her interference, she would still have spoken had she conceived it to be right to speak.

But within her own bosom there had been dreadful conflicts as to that duty. Lady Mary Quin had by no means slackened her activity. Lady Mary Quin had learned the exact condition of Kate O'Hara, and had sent the news to her friend with greedy rapidity. And in sending it Lady Mary Quin entertained no slightest doubt as to the duty of the present Earl of Scroope. According to her thinking it could not be the duty of an Earl of Scroope in any circumstances to marry a Kate O'Hara. There are women, who in regard to such troubles as now existed at Ardkill cottage, always think that the woman should be punished as the sinner and that the man should be assisted to escape. The hardness of heart of such women—who in all other views of life are perhaps tender and soft-natured—is one of the marvels of our social system. It is as though a certain line were drawn to include all women—a line, but, alas, little more than a line— by overstepping which, or rather by being known to have overstepped it, a woman ceases to be a woman in the estimation of her own sex. That the existence of this feeling has strong effect in saving women from passing the line, none of us can doubt. That its general tendency may be good rather than evil, is possible. But the hardness necessary to preserve the rule, a hardness which must be exclusively feminine but which is seldom wanting, is a marvellous feature in the female character. Lady Mary Quin probably thought but little on the subject. The women in the cottage on the cliff, who were befriended by Father Marty, were to her dangerous scheming Roman Catholic adventurers. The proper triumph of Protestant virtue required that they should fail in their adventures. She had always known that there would be something disreputable heard of them sooner or later. When the wretched Captain came into the neighbourhood—and she soon heard of his coming—she was gratified by feeling that her convictions had been correct. When the sad tidings as to poor Kate reached her ears, she had 'known that it would be so.' That such a girl should be made Countess of Scroope in reward for her wickedness would be to her an event horrible, almost contrary to Divine Providence—a testimony that the Evil One was being allowed peculiar power at the moment, and would no doubt have been used in her own circles to show the ruin that had been brought upon the country by Catholic emancipation. She did not for a moment doubt that the present Earl should be encouraged to break any promises of marriage to the making of which he might have been allured.

But it was not so with Lady Scroope. She, indeed, came to the same conclusion as her friend, but she did so with much difficulty and after many inward struggles. She understood and valued the customs of the magic line. In her heart of hearts she approved of a different code of morals for men and women. That which merited instant, and as regarded this world, perpetual condemnation in a woman might in a man be very easily forgiven. A sigh, a shake of the head, and some small innocent stratagem that might lead to a happy marriage and settlement in life with increased income, would have been her treatment of such sin for the heirs of the great and wealthy. She knew that the world could not afford to ostracise the men—though happily it might condemn the women. Nevertheless, when she came to the single separated instance, though her heart melted with no ruth for the woman—in such cases the woman must be seen before the ruth is felt—though pity for Kate O'Hara did not influence her, she did acknowledge the sanctity of a gentleman's word. If, as Lady

Mary told her, and as she could so well believe, the present
Earl of Scroope had given to this girl a promise that he would
marry her, if he had bound himself by his pledged word, as
a nobleman and a gentleman, how could she bid him become
a perjured knave? Sans reproche!* Was he thus to begin to
live and to deserve the motto of his house by the conduct of
his life?

But then the evil that would be done was so great! She
did not for a moment doubt all that Lady Mary told her about
the girl. The worst of it had indeed been admitted. She was
a Roman Catholic, ill-born, ill-connected, damaged utterly
by a parent so low that nothing lower could possibly be raked
out of the world's gutters. And now the girl herself was—a
castaway. Such a marriage as that of which Lady Mary spoke
would not only injure the house of Scroope for the present
generation, but would tend to its final downfall. Would it
not be known throughout all England that the next Earl of
Scroope would be the grandson of a convict? Might there not
be questions as to the legitimacy of the assumed heir? She
herself knew of noble families which had been scattered,
confounded, and almost ruined by such imprudence. Hitherto the family of Scroope had been continued from generation
to generation without stain—almost without stain. It had
felt it to be a fortunate thing that the late heir had died because of the pollution of his wretched marriage. And now
must evil as bad befall it, worse evil perhaps, through the
folly of this young man? Must that proud motto be taken
down from its place in the hall from very shame? But the
evil had not been done yet, and it might be that her words
could save the house from ruin and disgrace.

She was a woman of whom it may be said that whatever
difficulty she might have in deciding a question she could
recognise the necessity of a decision and could abide by it
when she had made it. It was with great difficulty that she
could bring herself to think that an Earl of Scroope should
be false to a promise by which he had seduced a woman, but
she did succeed in bringing herself to such thought. Her very

heart bled within her as she acknowledged the necessity. A lie to her was abominable. A lie, to be told by herself, would have been hideous to her. A lie to be told by him, was worse. As virtue, what she called virtue, was the one thing indispensable to men. And yet she must tell him to lie, and having resolved so to tell him, must use all her intellect to defend the lie—and insist upon it.

He was determined to return to Ireland, and there was nothing that she could do to prevent his return. She could not bid him shun a danger simply because it was a danger. He was his own master, and were she to do so he would only laugh at her. Of authority with him she had none. If she spoke, he must listen. Her position would secure so much to her from courtesy—and were she to speak of the duty which he owed to his name and to the family he could hardly laugh. She therefore sent to him a message. Would he kindly go to her in her own room? Of course he attended to her wishes and went. 'You mean to leave us tomorrow, Fred,' she said. We all know the peculiar solemnity of a widow's dress—the look of self-sacrifice on the part of the woman which the dress creates; and have perhaps recognised the fact that if the woman be deterred by no necessities of economy in her toilet—as in such material circumstances the splendour is more perfect if splendour be the object—so also is the self-sacrifice more abject. And with this widow an appearance of melancholy solemnity, almost of woe, was natural to her. She was one whose life had ever been serious, solemn, and sad. Wealth and the outward pomp of circumstances had conferred upon her a certain dignity; and with that doubtless there had reached her some feeling of satisfaction. Religion too had given her comfort, and a routine of small duties had saved her from the wretchedness of ennui. But life with her had had no laughter, and had seldom smiled. Now in the first days of her widowhood she regarded her course as run, and looked upon herself as one who, in speaking almost, spoke from the tomb. All this had its effect upon the young lord. She did inspire him with a certain awe; and though her weeds gave her no authority, they did give her weight.

'Yes; I shall start tomorrow,' he replied.

'And you still mean to go to Ireland?'

'Yes—I must go to Ireland. I shan't stay there, you know.'

Then she paused a moment before she proceeded. 'Shall you see—that young woman when you are there?'

'I suppose I shall see her.'

'Pray do not think that I desire to interfere with your private affairs. I know well that I have no right to assume over you any of that affectionate authority which a mother might have—though in truth I love you as a son.'

'I would treat you just as I would my own mother.'

'No, Fred; that cannot be so. A mother would throw her arms round you and cling to you if she saw you going into danger. A mother would follow you, hoping that she might save you.'

'But there is no danger.'

'Ah, Fred, I fear there is.'

'What danger?'

'You are now the head of one of the oldest and the noblest families in this which in my heart I believe to be the least sinful among the sinful nations of the wicked world.'

'I don't quite know how that may be—I mean about the world. Of course I understand about the family.'

'But you love your country?'

'Oh yes. I don't think there's any place like England—to live in.'

'And England is what it is because there are still some left among us who are born to high rank and who know how to live up to the standard that is required of them. If ever there was such a man, your uncle was such a one.'

'I'm sure he was—just what he ought to have been.'

'Honourable, true, affectionate, self-denying, affable to all men, but ever conscious of his rank, giving much because much had been given to him, asserting his nobility for the benefit of those around him, proud of his order for the sake of his country, bearing his sorrows with the dignity of silence, a nobleman all over, living on to the end sans reproche! He was a man whom you may dare to imitate, though to follow him may be difficult.' She spoke not loudly, but clearly, looking him full in the face as she stood motionless before him.

'He was all that,' said Fred, almost overpowered by the sincere solemnity of his aunt's manner.

'Will you try to walk in his footsteps?'

'Two men can never be like one another in that way. I shall never be what he was. But I'll endeavour to get along as well as I can.'

'You will remember your order?'

'Yes, I will. I do remember it. Mind you, aunt, I am not glad that I belong to it. I think I do understand about it all, and will do my best. But Jack would have made a better Earl than I shall do. That's the truth.'

'The Lord God has placed you—and you must pray to Him that He will enable you to do your duty in that state of life to which it has pleased Him to call you. You are here and must bear his decree; and whether it be a privilege to enjoy, you must enjoy it, or a burden to bear, you must endure it.'

'It is so of course.'

'Knowing that, you must know also how incumbent it is upon you not to defile the stock from which you are sprung.'

'I suppose it has been defiled,' said Fred, who had been looking into the history of the family. 'The ninth Earl seems to have married nobody knows whom. And his son was my uncle's grandfather.'

This was a blow to Lady Scroope, but she bore it with dignity and courage. 'You would hardly wish it to be said that you had copied the only one of your ancestors who did amiss. The world was rougher then than it is now, and he of whom you speak was a soldier.'

'I'm a soldier too,' said the Earl.

'Oh, Fred, is it thus you answer me! He was a soldier in

rough times, when there were wars. I think he married when
he was with the army under Marlborough.'

'I have not seen anything of that kind, certainly.'

'Your country is at peace, and your place is here, among
your tenantry, at Scroope. You will promise me, Fred, that
you will not marry this girl in Ireland?'

'If I do, the fault will be all with that old maid at Castle
Quin.'

'Do not say that, Fred. It is impossible. Let her conduct
have been what it may, it cannot make that right in you
which would have been wrong, or that wrong which would
have been right.'

'She's a nasty meddlesome cat.'

'I will not talk about her. What good would it do? You
cannot at any rate be surprised at my extreme anxiety. You
did promise your uncle most solemnly that you would never
marry this young lady.'

'If I did, that ought to be enough.' He was now waxing
angry and his face was becoming red. He would bear a good
deal from his uncle's widow, but he felt his own power and
was not prepared to bear much more.

'Of course I cannot bind you. I know well how impotent
I am—how powerless to exercise control. But I think, Fred,
that for your uncle's sake you will not refuse to repeat your
promise to me if you intend to keep it. Why is it that I am
so anxious? It is for your sake, and for the sake of a name
which should be dearer to you than it is even to me.'

'I have no intention of marrying at all.'

'Do not say that.'

'I do say it. I do not want to keep either you or Jack in
the dark as to my future life. This young lady—of whom, by
the by, neither you nor Lady Mary Quin know anything,
shall not become Countess of Scroope. To that I have made
up my mind.'

'Thank God.'

'But as long as she lives I will make no woman Countess of
Scroope. Let Jack marry this girl that he is in love with. They

shall live here and have the house to themselves if they like it. He will look after the property and shall have whatever income old Mellerby thinks proper. I will keep the promise I made to my uncle—but the keeping of it will make it impossible for me to live here. I would prefer now that you should say no more on the subject.' Then he left her, quitting the room with some stateliness in his step, as though conscious that at such a moment as this it behoved him to assume his rank.

The dowager sat alone all that morning thinking of the thing she had done. She did now believe that he was positively resolved not to marry Kate O'Hara, and she belived also that she herself had fixed him in that resolution. In doing so had she or had she not committed a deadly sin? She knew almost with accuracy what had occurred on the coast of Clare. A young girl, innocent herself up to that moment, had been enticed to her ruin by words of love which had been hallowed in her ears by vows of marriage. Those vows which had possessed so deadly an efficacy, were now to be simply broken! The cruelty to her would be damnable, devilish— surely worthy of hell if any sin of man can be so called! And she, who could not divest herself of a certain pride taken in the austere morality of her own life, she who was now a widow anxious to devote her life solely to God, had persuaded the man to this sin, in order that her successor as Countess of Scroope might not be, in her opinion, unfitting for nobility! The young lord had promised her that he would be guilty of this sin, so damnable, so devilish, telling her as he did so, that as a consequence of his promise he must continue to live a life of wickedness! In the agony of her spirit she threw herself upon her knees and implored the Lord to pardon her and to guide her. But even while kneeling before the throne of heaven she could not drive the pride of birth out of her heart. That the young Earl might be saved from the damning sin and also from the polluting marriage—that was the prayer she prayed.

CHAPTER VIII

LOOSE ABOUT THE WORLD

THE COUNTESS was seen no more on that day—was no more seen at least by either of the two brothers. Miss Mellerby was with her now and again, but on each occasion only for a few minutes, and reported that Lady Scroope was ill and could not appear at dinner. She would, however, see her nephew before he started on the following morning.

Fred himself was much affected by the interview with his aunt. No doubt he had made a former promise to his uncle, similar to that which had now been extracted from him. No doubt he had himself resolved, after what he had thought to be mature consideration that he would not marry the girl, justifying to himself this decision by the deceit which he thought had been practised upon him in regard to Captain O'Hara. Nevertheless, he felt that by what had now occurred he was bound more strongly against the marriage than he had ever been bound before. His promise to his uncle might have been regarded as being obligatory only as long as his uncle lived. His own decision he would have been at liberty to change when he pleased to do so. But, though his aunt was almost nothing to him—was not in very truth his aunt, but only the widow of his uncle, there had been a solemnity about the engagement as he had now made it with her, which he felt to be definitely binding. He must go to Ardkill prepared to tell them absolutely the truth. He would make any arrangements they pleased as to their future joint lives, so long as it was an arrangement by which Kate should not become Countess of Scroope. He did not attempt to conceal from himself the dreadful nature of the task before him. He knew what would be the indignation of the priest. He could picture to himself the ferocity of the mother, defending her young as a lioness would her whelp. He could imagine that that dagger might again be brought from its hiding place. And, worse than all, he would see the girl prostrate in her woe, and appealing to his love and to his oaths, when the truth as to her future life should be revealed to her. But yet he did not think of shunning the task before him. He could not endure to live a coward in his own esteem.

He was unlike himself and very melancholy. 'It has been so good of you to remain here' he said to Sophie Mellerby. They had now become intimate and almost attached to each other as friends. If she had allowed a spark of hope to become bright within her heart in regard to the young Earl that had long since been quenched. She had acknowledged to herself that had it been possible in other respects they would not have suited each other—and now they were friends.

'I love your aunt dearly and have been very glad to be with her.'

'I wish you would learn to love somebody else dearly.'

'Perhaps I shall, some day—somebody else; though I don't at all know who it may be.'

'You know whom I mean.'

'I suppose I do.'

'And why not love him? Isn't he a good fellow?'

'One can't love all the good fellows, Lord Scroope.'

'You'll never find a better one than he is.'

'Did he commission you to speak for him?'

'You know he didn't. You know that he would be the last man in the world to do so?'

'I was surprised.'

'But I had a reason for speaking.'

'No doubt.'

'I don't suppose it will have any effect with you—but it is something you ought to know. If any man of my age can be supposed to have made up his mind on such a matter, you may believe that I have made up my mind that I will—never marry.'

'What nonsense, Lord Scroope.'

'Well—yes; perhaps it is. But I am so convinced of it myself that I shall ask my brother to come and live here—permanently—as master of the place. As he would have to leave
his regiment it would of course be necessary that his position
here should be settled—and it shall be settled.'

'I most sincerely hope that you will always live here yourself.'

'It won't suit me. Circumstances have made it impossible.
If he will not do so, nor my aunt, the house must be shut up.
I am most anxious that this should not be done. I shall implore him to remain here, and to be here exactly as I should
have been—had things with me not have been so very unfortunate. He will at any rate have a house to offer you
if——'

'Lord Scroope!'

'I know what you are going to say, Sophie.'

'I don't know that I am as yet disposed to marry for the
sake of a house to shelter me.'

'Of course you would say that; but still I think that I
have been right to tell you. I am sure you will believe my
assurance that Jack knows nothing of all this.'

That same evening he said nearly the same thing to his
brother, though in doing so he made no special allusion to
Sophie Mellerby. 'I know that there is a great deal that a
fellow should do, living in such a house as this, but I am
not the man to do it. It's a very good kind of life, if you
happen to be up to it. I am not but you are.'

'My dear Fred, you can't change the accidents of birth.'

'In a great measure I can; or at least we can do so between
us. You can't be Lord Scroope, but you can be master of
Scroope Manor.'

'No I can't—and, which is more, I won't. 'Don't think I
am uncivil.'

'You are uncivil, Jack.'

'At any rate I am not ungrateful. I only want you to understand thoroughly that such an arrangement is out of the

question. In no condition of life would I care to be the locum tenens for another man. You are now five or six and twenty. At thirty you may be a married man with an absolute need for your own house.'

'I would execute any deed.'

'So that I might be enabled to keep the owner of the property out of the only place that is fit for him! It is a power which I should not use, and do not wish to possess. Believe me, Fred, that a man is bound to submit himself to the circumstances by which he is surrounded, when it is clear that they are beneficial to the world at large. There must be an Earl of Scroope, and you at present are the man.'

They were sitting together out upon the terrace after dinner, and for a time there was silence. His brother's arguments were too strong for the young lord, and it was out of his power to deal with one so dogmatic. But he did not forget the last words that had been spoken. It may be that 'I shall not be the man very long,' he said at last.

'Any of us may die today or tomorrow,' said Jack.

'I have a kind of presentiment—not that I shall die, but that I shall never see Scroope again. It seems as though I were certainly leaving for ever a place that has always been distasteful to me.'

'I never believe anything of presentiments.'

'No; of course not. You're not that sort of fellow at all. But I am. I can't think of myself as living here with a dozen old fogies about the place all doing nothing, touching their hats, my-lording me at every turn, looking respectable, but as idle as pickpockets.'

'You'll have to do it.'

'Perhaps I shall, but I don't think it.' Then there was again silence for a time. 'The less said about it the better, but I know that I've got a very difficult job before me in Ireland.'

'I don't envy you, Fred—not that.'

'It is no use talking about it. It has got to be done, and the sooner done the better. What I shall do when it is done, I have not the most remote idea. Where I shall be living this day month I cannot guess. I can only say one thing certainly, and that is that I shall not come back here. There never was a fellow so loose about the world as I am.'

It was terrible that a young man who had it in his power to do so much good or so much evil should have had nothing to bind him to the better course! There was the motto of his house, and the promises which he had made to his uncle persuading him to that which was respectable and as he thought dull; and opposed to those influences there was an unconquerable feeling on his own part that he was altogether unfitted for the kind of life that was expected of him. Joined to this there was the fact of that unfortunate connection in Ireland from which he knew that it would be base to fly, and which, as it seemed to him, made any attempt at respectability impossible to him.

Early on the following morning, as he was preparing to start, his aunt again sent for him. She came out to him in the sitting-room adjoining her bedroom and there embraced him. Her eyes were red with weeping, and her face wan with care. 'Fred,' she said; 'dear Fred.'

'Goodbye, aunt. The last word I have to say is that I implore you not to leave Scroope as long as you are comfortable here.'

'You will come back?'

'I cannot say anything certain about that.'

She still had hold of him with both hands and was looking into his face with loving, frightened, wistful eyes. 'I know,' she said, 'that you will be thinking of what passed between us yesterday.'

'Certainly I shall remember it.'

'I have been praying for you, Fred; and now I tell you to look to your Father which is in Heaven for guidance, and not to take it from any poor frail sinful human being. Ask Him to keep your feet steady in the path, and your heart pure, and your thoughts free from wickedness. Oh, Fred, keep your mind and body clear before Him, and if you will kneel to Him for protection, He will show you a way through all difficulties.' It was thus that she intended to tell him that his promise to her, made on the previous day, was to count for nought, and that he was to marry the girl if by no other way he could release himself from vice. But she could not bring herself to declare to him in plain terms that he had better marry Kate O'Hara, and bring his new Countess to Scroope in order that she might be fitly received by her predecessor. It might be that the Lord would still show him a way out of the two evils.

But his brother was more clear of purpose with him, as they walked together out to the yard in which the young Earl was to get into his carriage. 'Upon the whole, Fred, if I were you I should marry that girl.' This he said quite abruptly. The young lord shook his head. 'It may be that I do not know all the circumstances. If they be as I have heard them from you, I should marry her. Goodbye. Let me hear from you, when you have settled as to going anywhere.'

'I shall be sure to write,' said Fred as he took the reins and seated him in the phaeton.

His brother's advice he understood plainly, and that of his aunt he thought that he understood. But he shook his head again as he told himself that he could not now be guided by either of them.

CHAPTER IX

AT LISCANNOR

THE YOUNG lord slept one night at Ennis, and on the third morning after his departure from Scroope, started in his gig for Liscannor and the cliffs of Moher. He took a servant with him and a change of clothes. And as he went his heart was very heavy. He could not live a coward in his own esteem. Were it not so how willingly would he have saved himself from the misery of this journey, and have sent to his Kate to bid her come to him in England! He feared the priest, and he feared his Kate's mother—not her dagger, but her eyes and scorching words. He altogether doubted his own powers to perform satisfactorily the task before him. He knew men who could do it. His brother Jack would do it, were it possible that his brother Jack should be in such a position. But for himself, he was conscious of a softness of heart, a feminine tenderness, which—to do him justice—he did not mistake for sincerity, that rendered him unfit for the task before him. The farther he journeyed from Scroope and the nearer that he found himself to the cliffs the stronger did the feeling grow within him, till it had become almost tragical in its dominion over him. But still he went on. It was incumbent on him to pay one more visit to the cliffs and he journeyed on.

At Limerick he did not even visit the barracks to see his late companions of the regiment. At Ennis he slept in his old room, and of course the two officers who were quartered there came to him. But they both declared when they left him that the Earl of Scroope and Fred Neville were very different persons, attributing the difference solely to the rank and wealth of the new peer. Poor Simpkinson had expected

long whispered confidential conversations respecting the
ladies of Ardkill; but the Earl had barely thanked him for
his journey; and the whispered confidence, which would have
been so delightful, was at once impossible. 'By Heaven,
there's nothing like rank to spoil a fellow. He was a good
fellow once.' So spoke Captain Johnson, as the two officers
retreated together from the Earl's room.

And the Earl also saw Mr. Crowe the attorney. Mr. Crowe
recognized at its full weight the importance of a man whom
he might now call 'My Lord' as often as he pleased, and as to
whose pecuniary position he had made some gratifying inquiries. A very few words sufficed. Captain O'Hara had taken
his departure, and the money would be paid regularly. Mr.
Crowe also noticed the stern silence of the man, but thought
that it was becoming in an Earl with so truly noble a property. Of the Castle Quin people who could hardly do more
than pay their way like country gentlefolk, and who were
mere Irish, Mr. Crowe did not think much.

Every hour that brought the lord nearer to Liscannor
added a weight to his bosom. As he drove his gig along the
bleak road to Ennistimon his heart was very heavy indeed.
At Maurice's mills,* the only resting-place on the road, it had
been his custom to give his horse a mouthful of water; but he
would not do so now though the poor beast would fain have
stopped there. He drove the animal on ruthlessly, himself
driven by a feeling of unrest which would not allow him to
pause. He hated the country now, and almost told himself
that he hated all whom it contained. How miserable was his
lot, that he should have bound himself in the opening of his
splendour, in the first days of a career that might have been
so splendid, to misfortune that was squalid and mean as this.
To him, to one placed by circumstances as he was placed, it
was squalid and mean. By a few soft words spoken to a poor
girl whom he had chanced to find among the rocks he had
so bound himself with vile manacles, had so crippled, hampered and fettered himself, that he was forced to renounce
all the glories of his station. Wealth almost unlimited was at

his command—and rank, and youth, and such personal gifts
of appearance and disposition as best serve to win general
love. He had talked to his brother of his unfitness for his
earldom; but he could have blazoned it forth at Scroope and
up in London, with the best of young lords, and have loved
well to do so. But this adventure, as he had been wont to call
it, had fallen upon him, and had broken him as it were in
pieces. Thousands a year he would have paid to be rid of his
adventure; but thousands a year, he knew well, were of no
avail. He might have sent over some English Mr. Crowe with
offers almost royal; but he had been able so to discern the
persons concerned as to know that royal offers, of which the
royalty would be simply money royalty, could be of no avail.
How would that woman have looked at any messenger who
had come to her with offers of money—and proposed to take
her child into some luxurious but disgraceful seclusion? And
in what language would Father Marty have expressed himself
on such a proposed arrangement? And so the Earl of Scroope
drove on with his heart falling ever lower and lower within
his bosom.

It had of course been necessary that he should form some
plan. He proposed to get rooms for one night at the little inn
at Ennistimon, to leave his gig there, and then to take one of
the country cars on to Liscannor. It would, he thought, be
best to see the priest first. Let him look at his task which way
he would, he found that every part of it was bad. An interview with Father Marty would be very bad, for he must declare his intentions in such a way that no doubt respecting
them must be left on the priest's mind. He would speak only
to three persons—but to all those three he must now tell the
certain truth. There were causes at work which made it impossible that Kate O'Hara should become Countess of
Scroope. They might tear him to pieces, but from that
decision he would not budge. Subject to that decision they
might do with him and with all that belonged to him almost
as they pleased. He would explain this first to the priest if
it should chance that he found the priest at home.

He left his gig and servant at Ennistimon and proceeded as he had intended along the road to Liscannor on an outside car. In the mid-distance about two miles out of the town he met Father Marty riding on the road. He had almost hoped—nay, he had hoped—that the priest might not be at home. But here was the lion in his path. 'Ah, my Lord,' said the priest in his sweetest tone of good humour—and his tones when he was so disposed were very sweet—'Ah, my Lord, this is a sight for sore eyes. They tould me you were to be here today or tomorrow, and I took it for granted therefore it'd be the day afther. But you're as good as the best of your word.' The Earl of Scroope got off the car, and holding the priest's hand, answered the kindly salutation. But he did so with a constrained air an with a solemnity which the priest also attributed to his newly-begotten rank. Fred Neville—as he had been a week or two since—was almost grovelling in the dust before the priest's eyes; but the priest for the moment thought that he was wrapping himself up in the sables and ermine of his nobility. However, he had come back—which was more perhaps than Father Marty had expected—and the best must be made of him with reference to poor Kate's future happiness. 'You're going on to Ardkill, I suppose, my Lord,' he said.

'Yes—certainly; but I intended to take the Liscannor road on purpose to see you. I shall leave the car at Liscannor and walk up. You could not return, I suppose?'

'Well—yes—I might.'

'If you could, Father Marty——'

'Oh, certainly.' The priest now saw that there was something more in the man's manner than lordly pride. As the Earl got again up on his car, the priest turned his horse, and the two travelled back through the village without further conversation. The priest's horse was given up to the boy in the yard, and he then led the way into the house. 'We are not much altered in our ways, are we, my Lord?' he said as he moved a bottle of whisky that stood on the sideboard. 'Shall I offer you lunch?'

'No, thank you, Father Marty—nothing, thank you.' Then he made a gasp and began. The bad hour had arrived, and it must be endured. 'I have come back, as you see, Father Marty. That was a matter of course.'

'Well, yes, my Lord. As things have gone it was a matter of course.'

'I am here. I came as soon as it was possible that I should come. Of course it was necessary that I should remain at home for some days after what has occurred at Scroope.'

'No doubt—no doubt. But you will not be angry with me for saying that after what has occurred here, your presence has been most anxiously expected. However here you are, and all may yet be well. As God's minister I ought perhaps to up-braid. But I am not given to much upbraiding, and I love that dear and innocent young face too well to desire anything now but that the owner of it should receive at your hands that which is due to her before God and man.'

He perceived that the priest knew it all. But how could he wonder at this when that which ought to have been her secret and his had become known even to Lady Mary Quin? And he understood well what the priest meant when he spoke of that which was due to Kate O'Hara before God and man; and he could perceive, or thought that he perceived, that the priest did not doubt of the coming marriage, now that he, the victim, was again back in the west of Ireland. And was he not the victim of a scheme? Had he not been allured on to make promises to the girl which he would not have made had the truth been told him as to her father? He would not even in his thoughts accuse Kate—his Kate—of being a parti-cipator in these schemes. But Mrs. O'Hara and the priest had certainly intrigued against him. He must remember that. In the terrible task which he was now compelled to begin he must build his defence chiefly upon that. Yes; he must begin his work, now upon the instant. With all his golden prospects—with all 'his golden honours already in his possession—he could wish himself dead rather than begin it. But he could not die and have done it. 'Father Marty,' he said, 'I cannot make Miss O'Hara Countess of Scroope.'

'Not make her Countess of Scroope! What will you make her then?'

'As to that, I am here to discuss it with you.'

'What is it you main, sir? Afther you have had your will of her, and polluted her sweet innocence, you will not make her your wife! You cannot look me in the face, Mr. Neville, and tell me that.'

There the priest was right. The young Earl could not look him in the face as he stammered out his explanation and proposal. The burly, strong old man stood perfectly still and silent as he, with hesitating and ill-arranged words, tried to gloze over and make endurable his past conduct and intentions as to the future. He still held some confused idea as to a form of marriage which should for all his life bind him to the woman, but which should give her no claim to the title, and her child no claim either to the title or the property. 'You should have told me of this Captain O'Hara,' he said, as with many half-formed sentences he completed his suggestions.

'And it's on me you are throwing the blame?'

'You should have told me, Father Marty.'

'By the great God above me, I did not believe that a man could be such a villain! As I look for glory I did not think it possible! I should have told you! Neither did I nor did Mistress O'Hara know or believe that the man was alive. And what has the man to do with it? Is she vile because he has been guilty? Is she other than you knew her to be when you first took her to your bosom, because of his sin?

'It does make a difference, Mr. Marty.'

'Afther what you have done it can make no difference. When you swore to her that she should be your wife, and conquered her by so swearing, was there any clause in your contract that you were not to be bound if you found aught displaising to you in her parentage?'

'I ought to have known it all.'

'You knew all that she knew—all that I knew. You knew all that her mother knew. No, Lord Scroope. It cannot be that you should be so unutterably a villain. You are your own masther. Unsay what you have said to me, and her ears shall never be wounded or her heart broken by a hint of it.'

'I cannot make her Countess of Scroope. You are a priest, and can use what words you please to me—but I cannot make her Countess of Scroope.'

'Faith—and there will be more than words used, my young lord. As to your plot of a counterfeit marriage——'

'I said nothing of a counterfeit marriage.'

'What was it you said, then? I say you did. You proposed to me—to me a priest of God's altar—a false counterfeit marriage, so that those two poor women, who you are afraid to face, might be cajoled and chaited and ruined.'

'I am going to face them instantly.'

'Then must your heart be made of very stone. Shall I tell you the consequences?' Then the priest paused awhile, and the young man bursting into tears, hid his face against the wall. 'I will tell you the consequences, Lord Scroope. They will die. The shame and sorrow which you have brought on them, will bring them to their graves—and so there will be an end of their troubles upon earth. But while I live there shall be no rest for the sole of your foot. I am ould, and may soon be below the sod, but I will lave it as a legacy behind me that your iniquity shall be proclaimed and made known in high places. While I live I will follow you, and when I am gone there shall be another to take the work. My curse shall rest on you—the curse of a man of God, and you shall be accursed. Now, if it suits you, you can go up to them at Ardkill and tell them your story. She is waiting to receive her lover. You can go to her, and stab her to the heart at once. Go, sir! Unless you can change all this and alter your heart even as you hear my words, you are unfit to find shelter beneath my roof.'

Having so spoken, waiting to see the effect of his indignation, the priest went out, and got upon his horse, and went

away upon his journey.* The young lord knew that he had
been insulted, was aware that words had been said to him
so severe that one man, in his rank of life, rarely utters them
to another; and he had stood the while with his face turned
to the wall speechless and sobbing! The priest had gone,
telling him to leave the house because his presence disgraced
it; and he had made no answer. Yet he was the Earl of
Scroope—the thirteenth Earl of Scroope—a man in his own
country full of honours. Why had he come there to be called
a villain? and why was the world so hard upon him that on
hearing himself so called he could only weep like a girl? Had
he done worse than other men? Was he not willing to make
any retribution for his fault—except by doing that which he
had been taught to think would be a greater fault? As he
left the house he tried to harden his heart against Kate
O'Hara. The priest had lied to him about her father. They
must have known that the man was alive. They had caught
him among them, and the priest's anger was a part
of the net with which they had intended to surround
him. The stake for which they had played had been
very great. To be Countess of Scroope was indeed a chance
worth some risk. Then, as he breasted the hill up towards
the burial ground, he tried to strengthen his courage by
realizing the magnitude of his own position. He bade himself
remember that he was among people who were his inferiors
in rank, education, wealth, manners, religion and nationality.
He had committed an error. Of course he had been in fault.
Did he wish to escape the consequences of his own misdoing?
Was not his presence there so soon after the assumption of
his family honours sufficient evidence of his generous admission of the claims to which he was subject? Had he not
offered to sacrifice himself as no other man would have done?
But they were still playing for the high stakes. They were determined that the girl should be Countess of Scroope. He was
determined that she should not be Countess of Scroope. He
was still willing to sacrifice himself, but his family honours
he would not pollute.

And then as he made his way past the burial ground and on towards the cliff there crept over him a feeling as to the girl very different from that reverential love which he had bestowed upon her when she was still pure. He remembered the poorness of her raiment, the meekness of her language, the small range of her ideas. The sweet soft coaxing loving smile, which had once been so dear to him, was infantine and ignoble. She was a plaything for an idle hour, not a woman to be taken out into the world with the high name of Countess of Scroope.

All this was the antagonism in his own heart against the indignant words which the priest had spoken to him. For a moment he was so overcome that he had burst into tears. But not on that account would he be beaten away from his decision. The priest had called him a villain and had threatened and cursed him! As to the villainy he had already made up his mind which way his duty lay. For the threats it did not become him to count them as anything. The curses were the result of the man's barbarous religion. He remembered that he was the Earl of Scroope, and so remembering summoned up his courage as he walked on to the cottage.

CHAPTER X

AT ARDKILL

SHARP EYES had watched for the young lord's approach. As he came near to the cottage the door was opened and Kate O'Hara rushed out to meet him. Though his mind was turned against her—was turned against her as hard and fast as all his false reasonings had been able to make it—he could not but accord to her the reception of a lover. She was in his arms and he could not but press her close to his bosom. Her face was held up to his, and of course he covered it with kisses. She murmured to him sweet warm words of passionate love, and he could not but answer with endearing names. 'I am your own—am I not?' she said as she still clung to him. 'All my own,' he whispered as he tightened his arm round her waist.

Then he asked after Mrs. O'Hara. 'Yes; mother is there. She will be almost as glad to see you as I am. Nobody can be quite so glad. Oh Fred—my darling Fred—am I still to call you Fred?'

'What else, my pet?'

'I was thinking whether I would call you—my Lord.'

'For heaven's sake do not.'

'No. You shall be Fred—my Fred; Fred to me, though all the world besides may call you grand names.' Then again she held up her face to him and pressed the hand that was round her waist closer to her girdle. To have him once more with her—this was to taste all the joys of heaven while she was still on earth.

They entered the sitting-room together and met Mrs. O'Hara close to the door. 'My Lord,' she said, 'you are very welcome back to us. Indeed we need you much. I will not upbraid you as you come to make atonement for your fault. If you will let me I will love you as a son.' As she spoke she held his right hand in both of hers, and then she lifted up her face and kissed his cheek.

He could not stay her words, nor could he refuse the kiss. And yet to him the kiss was as the kiss of Judas, and the words were false words, plotted words, pre-arranged, so that after hearing them there should be no escape for him. But he would escape. He resolved again, even then, that he would escape; but he could not answer her words at the moment. Though Mrs. O'Hara held him by the hand, Kate still hung to his other arm. He could not thrust her away from him. She still clung to him when he released his right hand, and almost lay upon his breast when he seated himself on the sofa. She looked into his eyes for tenderness, and he could not refrain himself from bestowing upon her the happiness. 'Oh, mother,' she said, 'he is so brown—but he is handsomer than ever.' But though he smiled on her, giving back into her eyes her own soft look of love, yet he must tell his tale.

He was still minded that she should have all but the one thing—all if she would take it. She could not be Countess of Scroope; but in any other respect he would pay what penalty might be required for his transgression. But in what words should he explain this to those two women? Mrs. O'Hara had called him by his title and had claimed him as her son. No doubt she had all the right to do so which promises made by himself could give her ... He had sworn that he would marry the girl, and in point of time had only limited his promise by the old Earl's life. The old Earl was dead, and he stood pledged to the immediate performance of his vow—doubly pledged if he were at all solicitous for the honour of his future bride. But in spite of all promises she should never be Countess of Scroope!

Some tinkling false-tongued phrase as to lover's oaths*had once passed across his memory and had then sufficed to give him a grain of comfort. There was no comfort to be found in it now. He began to tell himself, in spite of his manhood,

that it might have been better for him and for them that he
should have broken this matter to them by a well-chosen
messenger. But it was too late for that now. He had faced
the priest and had escaped from him with the degradation of
a few tears. Now he was in the presence of the lioness and
her young. The lioness had claimed him as denizen of the
forest; and, would he yield to her, she no doubt would be
very tender to him. But, as he was resolved not to yield, he
began to find that he had been wrong to enter her den. As
he looked at her, knowing that she was at this moment softened by false hopes, he could nevertheless see in her eye
the wrath of the wild animal. How was he to begin to make
his purpose known to them.

'And now you must tell us everything,' said Kate, still encircled by his arm.

'What must I tell you?'

'You will give up the regiment at once?'

'I have done so already.'

'But you must not give up Ardkill—must he, mother?'

'He may give it up when he takes you from it, Kate.'

'But he will take you too, mother?'

The lioness at any rate wanted nothing for herself. 'No,
love. I shall remain here among my rocks, and shall be happy
if I hear that you are happy.'

'But you won't part us altogether—will you, Fred?'

'No, love.'

'I knew he wouldn't. And mother may come to your grand
house and creep into some pretty little corner there, where
I can go and visit her, and tell her that she shall always be
my own, own darling mother.'

He felt that he must put a stop to this in some way, though
the doing of it would be very dreadful. Indeed in the doing
of it the whole of his task would consist. But still he shirked it
and used his wit in contriving an answer which might still
deceive without being false in words. 'I think,' said he, 'that
I shall never live at any grand house, as you call it.'

'Not live at Scroope?' asked Mrs. O'Hara.

'I think not. It will hardly suit me.'

'I shall not regret it,' said Kate. 'I care nothing for a grand house. I should only be afraid of it. I know it is dark and sombre, for you have said so. Oh, Fred, any place will be Paradise to me, if I am there with you.'

He felt that every moment of existence so continued was a renewed lie. She was lying in his arms, in her mother's presence, almost as his acknowledged wife. And she was speaking of her future home as being certainly his also. But what could he do? How could he begin to tell the truth? His home should be her home, if she would come to him—not as his wife. That idea of some half-valid morganatic marriage* had again been dissipated by the rough reproaches of the priest, and could only be used as a prelude to his viler proposal. And, though he loved the girl after his fashion, he desired to wound her by no such vile proposal. He did not wish to live a life of sin, if such life might be avoided.* If he made his proposal, it would be but for her sake; or rather that he might show her that he did not wish to cast her aside* It was by asserting to himself that for her sake he would relinquish his own rank, were that possible, that he attempted to relieve his own conscience. But in the meantime, she was in his arms talking about their joint future home! 'Where do you think of living?' asked Mrs. O'Hara in a tone which shewed plainly the anxiety with which she asked the question.

'Probably abroad,' he said.

'But mother may go with us?' The girl felt that the tension of his arm was relaxed, and she knew that all was not well with him. And if there was ought amiss with him, how much more must it be amiss with her? 'What is it, Fred?' she said. 'There is some secret. Will you not tell it to me?' Then she whispered into his ear words intended for him alone, though her mother heard them. 'If there be a secret you should tell it me now. Think how it is with me. Your words are life and death to me now.' He still held her with loosened arms, but did not answer her. He sat, looking out into the middle of the room with fixed eyes, and he felt that drops of perspiration were on his brow. And he knew that the other woman was glaring at him with the eyes of an injured lioness, though he did not dare to turn his own to her face. 'Fred, tell me; tell me.' And Kate rose up, with her knees upon the sofa, bending over him, gazing into his countenance and imploring him.

'There must be disappointment,' he said; and he did not know the sound of his own voice.

'What disappointment? Speak to me. What disappointment?'

'Disappointment!' shrieked the mother. 'How disappointment? There shall be no disappointment.' Rising from her chair, she hurried across the room, and took her girl from his arms. 'Lord Scroope, tell us what you mean. I say there shall be no disappointment. Sit away from him, Kate, till he has told us what it is.' Then they heard the sound of a horse's foot passing close to the window, and they all knew that it was the priest. 'There is Father Marty,' said Mrs. O'Hara. 'He shall make you tell it.'

'I have already told him.' Lord Scroope as he said this rose and moved towards the door; but he himself was almost unconscious of the movement. Some idea probably crossed his mind that he would meet the priest, but Mrs. O'Hara thought that he intended to escape from them.

She rushed between him and the door and held him with both her hands. 'No; no; you do not leave us in that way, though you were twice an Earl.'

'I am not thinking of leaving you.'

'Mother, you shall not hurt him; you shall not insult him,' said the girl. 'He does not mean to harm me. He is my own, and no one shall touch him.'

'Certainly I will not harm you. Here is Father Marty. Mrs. O'Hara you had better be tranquil. You should remember that you have heard nothing yet of what I would say to you.'

'Whose fault is that? Why do you not speak? Father Marty, what does he mean when he tells my girl that there

must be disappointment for her? Does he dare to tell me
that he hesitates to make her his wife?'

The priest took the mother by the hand and placed her
on the chair in which she usually sat. Then, almost without
a word, he led Kate from the room to her own chamber,
and bade her wait a minute till he should come back to her.
Then he returned to the sitting-room and at once addressed
himself to Lord Scroope. 'Have you dared,' he said, 'to tell
them what you hardly dared to tell to me?'

'He has dared to tell us nothing,' said Mrs. O'Hara.

'I do not wonder at it. I do not think that any man could
say to her that which he told me that he would do.'

'Mrs. O'Hara,' said the young lord, with some return of
courage now that the girl had left them, 'that which I told
Mr. Marty this morning, I will now tell to you. For your
daughter I will do anything that you and she and he may wish
—but one thing. I cannot make her Countess of Scroope.'

'You must make her your wife,' said the woman shouting
at him.

'I will do so to-morrow if a way can be found by which
she shall not become Countess of Scroope.'

'That is, he will marry her without making her his wife,'
said the priest. 'He will jump over a broomstick with her and
will ask me to help him—so that your feelings and hers may
be spared for a week or so. Mrs. O'Hara, he is a villain—a
vile, heartless, cowardly reprobate, so low in the scale of
humanity that I degrade myself by spaking to him. He calls
himself an English peer! Peer to what? Certainly to no one
worthy to be called a man!' So speaking, the priest addressed
himself to Mrs. O'Hara, but as he spoke his eyes were fixed
full on the face of the young lord.

'I will have his heart out of his body,' exclaimed Mrs.
O'Hara.

'Heart—he has no heart. You may touch his pocket—or
his pride, what he calls his pride, a damnable devilish in-
human vanity; or his name—that bugbear of a title by which
he trusts to cover his baseness; or his skin, for he is a coward.

Do you see his cheek now? But as for his heart—you cannot get at that.'

'I will get at his life,' said the woman.

'Mr. Marty, you allow yourself a liberty of speech which even your priesthood will not warrant.'

'Lay a hand upon me if you can. There is not blood enough about you to do it. Were it not that the poor child has been wake and too trusting, I would bid her spit on you rather than take you for a husband.' Then he paused, but only for a moment. 'Sir, you must marry her, and there must be an end of it. In no other way can you be allowed to live.'

'Would you murder me?'

'I would crush you like an insect beneath my nail. Murder you! Have you thought what murder is—that there are more ways of murder than one? Have you thought of the life of that young girl who now bears in her womb the fruit of your body? Would you murder her—because she loved you, and trusted you, and gave you all simply because you asked her; and then think of your own life? As the God of Heaven is above me, and sees me now, and the Saviour in whose blood I trust, I would lay down my life this instant, if I could save her from your heartlessness.' So saying he too turned away his face and wept like a child.

After this the priest was gentler in his manner to the young man, and it almost seemed as though the Earl was driven from his decision. He ceased, at any rate, to assert that Kate should never be Countess of Scroope, and allowed both the mother and Father Marty to fall into a state of doubt as to what his last resolve might be. It was decided that he should go down to Ennistimon and sleep upon it. On the morrow he would come up again, and in the meantime he would see Father Marty at the inn. There were many prayers addressed to him both by the mother and the priest, and such arguments used that he had been almost shaken. 'But you will come to-morrow?' said the mother, looking at the priest as she spoke.

'I will certainly come to-morrow.'

'No doubt he will come to-morrow,' said Father Marty—
who intended to imply that if Lord Scroope escaped out of
Ennistimon without his knowledge, he would be very much
surprised.

'Shall I not say a word to Kate?' the Earl asked as he was
going.

'Not till you are prepared to tell her that she shall be your
wife,' said the priest.

But this was a matter as to which Kate herself had a word
to say. When they were in the passage she came out from
her room, and again rushed into her lover's arms. 'Oh, Fred,
I will go with you anywhere if you will take me.'

'He is to come up to-morrow, Kate,' said her mother.

'He will be here early to-morrow, and everything shall be
settled then,' said the priest, trying to assume a happy and
contented tone.

'Dearest Kate, I will be here by noon,' said Lord Scroope,
returning the girl's caresses.

'And you will not desert me?'

'No, darling, no.' And then he went leaving the priest behind him at the cottage.

Father Marty was to be with him at the inn by eight, and
then the whole matter must be again discussed. He felt that
he had been very weak, that he had made no use—almost no
use at all—of the damning fact of the Captain's existence.
He had allowed the priest to talk him down in every argument, and had been actually awed by the girl's mother, and
yet he was determined that he would not yield. He felt more
strongly than ever, now that he had again seen Kate O'Hara,
that it would not be right that such a one as she should be
made Countess of Scroope. Not only would she disgrace the
place, but she would be unhappy in it, and would shame him.
After all the promises that he had made he could not, and he
would not, take her to Scroope as his wife. How could she
hold up her head before such women as Sophie Mellerby and
others like her? It would be known by all his friends

that he had been taken in and swindled by low people in the County Clare, and he would be regarded by all around him as one who had absolutely ruined himself. He had positively resolved that she should not be Countess of Scroope, and to that resolution he would adhere. The foul-mouthed priest had called him a coward, but he would be no coward. The mother had said that she would have his life. If there were danger in that respect he must encounter it. As he returned to Ennistimon he again determined that Kate O'Hara should never become Countess of Scroope.

For three hours Father Marty remained with him that night, but did not shake him. He had now become accustomed to the priest's wrath and could endure it. And he thought also that he could now endure the mother. The tears of the girl and her reproaches he still did fear.

'I will do anything that you can dictate short of that,' he said again to Father Marty.

'Anything but the one thing that you have sworn to do?'

'Anything but the one thing that I have sworn not to do.' For he had told the priest of the promises he had made both to his uncle and to his uncle's widow.

'Then,' said the priest, as he crammed his hat on his head, and shook the dust off his feet, 'if I were you I would not go to Ardkill to-morrow if I valued my life.' Nevertheless Father Marty slept at Ennistimon that night, and was prepared to bar the way if any attempt at escape were made.

CHAPTER XI

ON THE CLIFFS

NO ATTEMPT at escape was made. The Earl breakfasted by himself at about nine, and then lighting a cigar, roamed about for a while round the Inn, thinking of the work that was now before him. He saw nothing of Father Marty though he knew that the priest was still in Ennistimon. And he felt that he was watched. They might haved saved themselves that trouble, for he certainly had no intention of breaking his word to them. So he told himself, thinking as he did so, that people such as these could not understand that an Earl of Scroope would not be untrue to his word. And yet since he had been back in County Clare he had almost regretted that he had not broken his faith to them and remained in England. At half-past ten he started on a car, having promised to be at the cottage at noon, and he told his servant that he should certainly leave Ennistimon that day at three. The horse and gig were to be ready for him exactly at that hour.

On this occasion he did not go through Liscannor, but took the other road to the burial ground. There he left his car and slowly walked along the cliffs till he came to the path leading down from them to the cottage. In doing this he went somewhat out of his way, but he had time on his hands and he did not desire to be at the cottage before the hour he had named. It was a hot midsummer day, and there seemed to be hardly a ripple on the waves. The tide was full in, and he sat for a while looking down upon the blue waters. What an ass had he made himself, coming thither in quest of adventures! He began to see now the meaning of such idleness of purpose as that to which he had looked for pleasure and excitement. Even the ocean itself and the very rocks had lost their charm for him. It was all one blaze of blue light, the sky above and the water below, in which there was neither beauty nor variety. How poor had been the life he had chosen! He had spent hour after hour in a comfortless dirty boat, in company with a wretched ignorant creature, in order that he might shoot a few birds and possibly a seal. All the world had been open to him, and yet how miserable had been his ambition! And now he could see no way out of the ruin he had brought upon himself.

When the time had come he rose from his seat and took the path down to the cottage. At the corner of the little patch of garden ground attached to it he met Mrs. O'Hara. Her hat was on her head, and a light shawl was on her shoulders as though she had prepared herself for walking. He immediately asked after Kate. She told him that Kate was within and should see him presently. Would it not be better that they two should go up on the cliffs together, and then say what might be necessary for the mutual understanding of their purposes? 'There should be no talking of all this before Kate,' said Mrs. O'Hara.

'That is true.'

'You can imagine what she must feel if she is told to doubt. Lord Scroope, will you not say at once that there shall be no doubt? You must not ruin my child in return for her love!'

'If there must be ruin I would sooner bear it myself,' said he. And then they walked on without further speech till they had reached a point somewhat to the right, and higher than that on which he had sat before. It had ever been a favourite spot with her, and he had often sat there between the mother and daughter. It was almost the summit of the cliff, but there was yet a higher pitch which screened it from the north, so that the force of the wind was broken. The fall from it was almost precipitous to the ocean, so that the face of the rocks immediately below was not in view; but there was a curve here in the line of the shore, and a little bay in the coast, which exposed to view the whole side of the opposite cliff, so that the varying colours of the rocks might be seen. The two ladies had made a seat upon the turf, by moving the loose stones and levelling the earth around, so that they could sit securely on the very edge. Many many hours had Mrs. O'Hara passed upon the spot, both summer and winter, watching the sunset in the west, and listening to the screams of the birds. 'There are no gulls now,' she said as she seated herself—as though for a moment she had forgotten the great subject which filled her mind.

'No—they never show themselves in weather like this. They only come when the wind blows. I wonder where they go when the sun shines.'

'They are just the opposite to men and women who only come around you in fine weather. How hot it is!' and she threw her shawl back from her shoulders.

'Yes, indeed. I walked up from the burial ground and I found that it was very hot. Have you seen Father Marty this morning?'

'No. Have you?' she asked the question turning upon him very shortly.

'Not to-day. He was with me till late last night.'

'Well.' He did not answer her. He had nothing to say to her. In fact everything had been said yesterday. If she had questions to ask he would answer them. 'What did you settle last night? When he went from me an hour after you were gone, he said that it was impossible that you should mean to destroy her.'

'God forbid that I should destroy her.'

'He said that—that you were afraid of her father.'

'I am.'

'And of me.'

'No—not of you, Mrs. O'Hara.'

'Listen to me. He said that such a one as you cannot endure the presence of an uneducated and ill-mannered mother-in-law. Do not interrupt me, Lord Scroope. If you will marry her, my girl shall never see my face again; and I will cling to that man and will not leave him for a moment, so that he shall never put his foot near your door. Our name shall never be spoken in your hearing. She shall never even write to me if you think it better that we shall be so separated.'

'It is not that,' he said.

'What is it, then?'

'Oh, Mrs. O'Hara, you do not understand. You—you I could love dearly.'

'I would have you keep all your love for her.'

'I do love her. She is good enough for me. She is too good; and so are you. It is for the family, and not for myself.'

'How will she harm the family?'

'I swore to my uncle that I would not make her Countess of Scroope.'

'And have you not sworn to her again and again that she should be your wife? Do you think that she would have done for you what she has done, had you not so sworn? Lord Scroope, I cannot think that you really mean it.' She put both her hands softly upon his arm and looked up to him imploring his mercy.

He got up from his seat and roamed along the cliff, and she followed him, still imploring. Her tones were soft, and her words were the words of a suppliant. Would he not relent and save her child from wretchedness, from ruin and from death. 'I will keep her with me till I die,' he said.

'But not as your wife?'

'She shall have all attention from me—everything that a woman's heart can desire. 'You two shall never be separated.'

'But not as your wife?'

'I will live where she and you may please. She shall want nothing that my wife would possess.'

'But not as your wife?'

'Not as Countess of Scroope.'

You would have her as your mistress then?' As she asked this question the tone of her voice was altogether altered, and the threatening lion-look had returned to her eyes. They were now near the seat, confronted to each other; and the fury of her bosom, which for a while had been dominated by the tenderness of the love for her daughter, was again raging within her. Was it possible that he should be able to treat them thus—that he should break his word and go from them scathless, happy, joyous, with all the delights of the world before him, leaving them crushed into dust beneath his feet. She had been called upon from her youth upwards to bear injustice—but of all injustice surely this would be the worst. 'As your mistress,' she repeated—'and I her mother, am to stand by and see it, and know that my girl is dishonoured! Would your mother have borne that for your sister? How would it be if your sister were as that girl is now?

'I have no sister.'

'And therefore you are thus hard-hearted. She shall never be your harlot—never. I would myself sooner take from her the life I gave her. You have destroyed her, but she shall never be a thing so low as that.'

'I will marry her—in a foreign land.'

'And why not here? She is as good as you. Why should she not bear the name you are so proud of dinning into our ears? Why should she not be a Countess? Has she ever disgraced herself? If she is disgraced in your eyes you must be a Devil.'

'It's not that,' he said hoarsely.

'What is it? What has she done that she should be thus punished? Tell me, man, that she shall be your lawful wife.' As she said this she caught him roughly by the collar of his coat and shook him with her arm.

'It cannot be so,' said the Earl of Scroope.

'It cannot be so! But I say it shall—or—or—! What are you, that she should be in your hands like this? Say that she shall be your wife, or you shall never live to speak to another woman.' The peril of his position on the top of the cliff had not occurred to him—nor did it occur to him now. He had been there so often that the place gave him no sense of danger. Nor had that peril—as it was thought afterwards by those who most closely made inquiry on the matter—ever occurred to her. She had not brought him there that she might frighten him with that danger, or that she might avenge herself by the power which it gave her. But now the idea flashed across her maddened mind. 'Miscreant,' she said. And she bore him back to the very edge of the preci-pice.

'You'll have me over the cliff,' he exclaimed hardly even yet putting out his strength against her.

'And so I will, by the help of God. Now think of her! Now think of her! And as she spoke she pressed him backwards towards his fall. He had power enough to bend his knee, and to crouch beneath her grasp on to the loose crumbling soil of the margin of the rocks. He still held her by her cuff and it seemed for a moment as though she must go with him. But, on a sudden, she spurned him with her foot on the breast, the rag of cloth parted in his hand, and the poor wretch tumbled forth alone into eternity.

That was the end of Frederic Neville, Earl of Scroope, and the end, too, of all that poor girl's hopes in this world. When you stretch yourself on the edge of those cliffs and look down over the abyss on the sea below it seems as though the rocks were so absolutely perpendicular, that a stone dropped with an extended hand would fall amidst the waves. But in such measurement the eye deceives itself, for the rocks in truth slant down; and the young man, as he fell, struck them again and again; and at last it was a broken mangled corpse that reached the blue waters below.

Her Kate was at last avenged. The woman stood there in her solitude for some minutes thinking of the thing she had done. The man had injured her—sorely—and she had pun-ished him. He had richly deserved the death which he had received from her hands. In these minutes, as regarded him, there was no remorse. But how should she tell the news to her child? The blow which had thrust him over would, too probably, destroy other life than his. Would it not be better that her girl should so die? What could prolonged life give her that would be worth her having? As for herself—in these first moments of her awe she took no thought of her own danger. It did not occur to her that she might tell how the man had ventured too near the edge and had fallen by mischance. As regarded herself she was proud of the thing she had accomplished; but how should she tell her child that it was done?

She slowly took the path, not to the cottage, but down towards the burial ground and Liscannor, passing the car which was waiting in vain for the young lord. On she walked with rapid step, indifferent to the heat, still proud of what she had done—raging with a maddened pride. How little had they two asked of the world! And then this man had come to them and robbed them of all that little, had spoiled them ruthlessly, cheating them with lies, and then excusing himself by the grandeur of his blood! During that walk it was that she first repeated to herself the words that were ever afterwards on her tongue; An Eye for an Eye. Was not that justice? And, had she not taken the eye herself, would any Court in the world have given it to her? Yes—an eye for an eye! Death in return for ruin! One destruction for another! The punishment had been just. An eye for an eye! Let the Courts of the world now say what they pleased, they could not return to his earldom the man who had plundered and spoiled her child. He had sworn that he would not make her Kate Countess of Scroope! Nor should he make any other woman a Countess!

Rapidly she went down by the burying ground, and into the priest's house. Father Marty was there, and she stalked at once into his presence. 'Ha—Mrs. O'Hara! And where is Lord Scroope?'

'There,' she said, pointing out towards the ocean. 'Under the rocks!'

'He has fallen!'

'I thrust him down with my hands and with my feet.' As she said this, she used her hand and her foot as though she were now using her strength to push the man over the edge. 'Yes, I thrust him down, and he fell splashing into the waves.

I heard it as his body struck the water. He will shoot no more of the seagulls now.'

'You do not mean that you have murdered him?'

'You may call it murder if you please, Father Marty! An eye for an eye, Father Marty! It is justice, and I have done it. An Eye for an Eye!'

CHAPTER XII

CONCLUSION

THE STORY of the poor mad woman who still proclaims in her seclusion the justice of the deed which she did, has now been told. It may perhaps be well to collect the scattered ends of the threads of the tale for the benefit of readers who desire to know the whole of a history.

Mrs. O'Hara never returned to the cottage on the cliffs after the perpetration of the deed. On the unhappy priest devolved the duty of doing whatever must be done. The police at the neighbouring barracks were told that the young lord had perished by a fall from the cliffs, and by them search was made for the body. No real attempt was set on foot to screen the woman who had done the deed by any concealment of the facts. She herself was not alive to the necessity of making any such attempt. 'An eye for an eye!' she said to the head-constable when the man interrogated her. It soon became known to all Liscannor, to Ennistimon, to the ladies at Castle Quin, and to all the barony of Corcomroe that Mrs. O'Hara had thrust the Earl of Stroope over the cliffs of Moher, and that she was now detained at the house of Father Marty in the custody of a policeman. Before the day was over it was declared also that she was mad—and that her daughter was dying.

The deed which the woman had done and the death of the young lord were both terrible to Father Marty; but there was a duty thrown upon him more awful to his mind even than these. Kate O'Hara, when her mother appeared at the priest's house, had been alone at the cottage. By degrees Father Marty learned from the wretched woman something of the circumstances of that morning's work. Kate had not seen her lover that day, but had been left in the cottage while her mother went out to meet the man, and if possible to persuade him to do her child justice. The priest understood that she would be waiting for them or more probably searching for them on the cliffs. He got upon his horse and rode up the hill with a heavy heart. What should he tell her; and how should he tell it?

Before he reached the cottage she came running down the hillside to him. 'Father Marty, where is mother? Where is Mr. Neville? You know. I see that you know. Where are they?' He got off his horse and put his arm round her body and seated her beside himself on the rising bank by the wayside. 'Why don't you speak?' she said.

'I cannot speak,' he murmured. 'I cannot tell you.'

'Is he—dead?' He only buried his face in his hands. 'She has killed him! Mother—mother!' Then, with one loud long wailing shriek, she fell upon the ground.

Not for a month after that did she know anything of what happened around her. But yet it seemed that during that time her mind had not been altogether vacant, for when she awoke to self-consciousness, she knew at least that her lover was dead. She had been taken into Ennistimon and there, under the priest's care, had been tended with infinite solicitude; but almost with a hope on his part that nature might give way and that she might die. Overwhelmed as she was with sorrows past and to come would it not be better for her that she should go hence and be no more seen? But as Death cannot be barred from the door when he knocks at it, so neither can he be made to come as a guest when summoned. She still lived, though life had so little to offer to her.

But Mrs. O'Hara never saw her child again. With passionate entreaties she begged of the police that her girl might be brought to her, that she might be allowed if it were only to see her face or to touch her hand. Her entreaties to the priest, who was constant in his attendance upon her in the prison to which she was removed from his house, were piteous—almost heartbreaking. But the poor girl, though she was meek, silent, and almost apathetic in her tranquillity, could not even bear the mention of her mother's name. Her mother had destroyed the father of the child that was to be born to her, her lover, her hero, her god; and in her remembrance of the man who had betrayed her, she learned to execrate the mother who had sacrificed everything—her very reason—in avenging the wrongs of her child!

Mrs. O'Hara was taken away from the priest's house to the County Gaol, but was then in a condition of acknowledged insanity. That she had committed the murder no one who heard the story doubted, but of her guilt there was no evidence whatever beyond the random confession of a maniac. No detailed confession was ever made by her. 'An eye for an eye,' she would say when interrogated—Is not that justice? A tooth for a tooth!' Though she was for a while detained in prison it was impossible to prosecute her—even with a view to an acquittal on the ground of insanity; and while the question was under discussion among the lawyers, provision for her care and maintenance came from another source.

As also it did for the poor girl. For a while everything was done for her under the care of Father Marty—but there was another Earl of Scroope in the world, and as soon as the story was known to him and the circumstances had been made clear, he came forward to offer on behalf of the family whatever assistance might now avail them anything. As months rolled on the time of Kate O'Hara's further probation came, but Fate spared her the burden and despair of a living infant. It was at last thought better that she should go to her father and live in France with him, reprobate though the man was. The priest offered to find a home for her in his own house at Liscannor; but as he said himself, he was an old man, and one who when he went would leave no home behind him. And then it was felt that the close vicinity of the spot on which her lover had perished would produce a continued melancholy that might crush her spirits utterly. Captain O'Hara therefore was desired to come and fetch his child—and he did so, with many protestations of virtue for the future. If actual pecuniary comfort can conduce to virtue in such a man, a chance was given him. The Earl of Scroope was only too liberal in the settlement he made. But the settlement was on the daughter and not the father; and it is possible therefore that some gentle restraint may have served to keep him out of the deep abyss of wickedness.

The effects of the tragedy on the coast of Clare spread beyond Ireland, and drove another woman to the verge of insanity. When the Countess of Scroope heard the story, she shut herself up at Scroope and would see no one but her own servants. When the succeeding Earl came to the house which was now his own, she refused to admit him into her presence, and declined even a renewed visit from Miss Mellerby who at that time had returned to her father's roof. At last the clergyman of Scroope prevailed, and to him she unburdened her soul—acknowledging, with an energy that went perhaps beyond the truth, the sin of her own conduct in producing the catastrophe which had occurred. 'I knew that he had wronged her, and yet I bade him not to make her his wife.' That was the gist of her confession and she declared that the young man's blood would be on her hands till she died. A small cottage was prepared for her on the estate, and there she lived in absolute seclusion till death relieved her from her sorrows.

And she lived not only in seclusion, but in solitude almost to her death. It was not till four years after the occurrences which have been here related that John fourteenth Earl of Scroope brought a bride home to Scroope Manor. The reader need hardly be told that that bride was Sophie Mellerby. When the young Countess came to live at the Manor the old Countess admitted her visits and at last found some consolation in her friend's company. But it lasted not long, and then she was taken away and buried beside her lord in the chancel of the parish church.

When it was at last decided that the law should not interfere at all as to the personal custody of the poor maniac who had sacrificed everything to avenge her daughter, the Earl of

Scroope selected for her comfort the asylum in which she still continues to justify from morning to night, and, alas, often all the night long, the terrible deed of which she is ever thinking. 'An eye for an eye,' she says to the woman who watches her.

'Oh, yes, ma'am; certainly.'

'An eye for an eye, and a tooth for a tooth!* Is it not so? An eye for an eye!'

THE END

EXPLANATORY NOTES

xxxvii   *in the west of England*: in the manuscript, Trollope first wrote, then crossed out, 'Ireland'.

xxxviii   *who was its head*: the manuscript and first edition continue: 'Others there, who were cognisant of the conditions of the various patients, only knew that from quarter to quarter the charges for this poor lady's custody were defrayed by the Earl of Scroope.' This was removed in later editions presumably because the fact that there are three Earls of Scroope in the subsequent narrative might confuse the reader.

4   *Marlbro' school*: i.e. Marlborough College, in Wiltshire. The school was started in its modern form in 1843. (Trollope's spelling, incidentally, was normal in the nineteenth century.) Marlborough was originally set up for the sons of clergy, and in Trollope's day a large number of scholarships were reserved for them. The fact that Mr Greenmarsh's sons are evidently dayboys who walk to the school suggests that in describing the Scroope family and their estate, Trollope had the Seymours in mind (that noble family's old mansion formed the central building of the new school). See also note to p. 81.

5   *from out of the streets*: Trollope initially wrote, and crossed out, 'London streets' deciding almost immediately to make the abandoned woman French.

10   *the Duke's hounds*: the eighth Duke of Beaufort (1824–99) whose seat was Stoke Park, near Bristol. The Duke (who also served in the Hussars in his youth) presided over one of the country's most famous hunts and was, in Trollope's day, the greatest authority on the sport in England.

  when he talked of Scotland: Trollope originally wrote 'the moors' and crossed it out. What he meant was 'grouse moors' but evidently thought that 'Scotland', where Britain's best

ignorant, and it would have been cruelty to instruct her.

When Mr. Thorne saw the tear in her eye, he repented himself of his contemptuous expression. By him also it was recognised as a binding law that every whim of his sister was to be respected. He was not perhaps so firm in his observances to her, as she was in hers to him. But his intentions were equally good, and whenever he found that he had forgotten them it was matter of grief to him.

' My dear Monica,' said he, ' I beg your pardon ; I don't in the least mean to speak ill of the game. When I called it a rattletrap, I merely meant that it was so for a man of my age. You know you always forget that I an't a young man.'

' I am quite sure you are not an old man, Wilfred,' said she, accepting the apology in her heart, and smiling at him with the tear still on her cheek.

' If I was five-and-twenty, or thirty,' continued he, ' I should like nothing better than riding at the quintain all day.'

' But you are not too old to hunt or to shoot,' said she. ' If you can jump over a ditch and hedge I am sure you could turn the quintain round.'

' But when I ride over the hedges, my dear—and it isn't very often I do that—but when I do ride over the hedges there isn't any bag of flour coming after me. Think how I'd look taking the countess out to breakfast with the back of my head all covered with meal.'

Miss Thorne said nothing further. She didn't like the allusion to the countess. She couldn't be satisfied with the reflection that the sports of Ullathorne should be interfered with by the personal attentions necessary for a Lady De Courcy. But she saw that it was useless for her to push the matter further. It was conceded that Mr. Thorne was to be spared the quintain ; and Miss Thorne determined to trust wholly to a youthful knight of hers, an immense favourite, who, as she often declared, was a pattern to the young men of the age, and an excellent sample of an English yeoman.

This was Farmer Greenacre's eldest son ; who, to tell the truth, had from his earliest years taken the exact measure of Miss Thorne's foot. In his boyhood he had never failed to obtain from her, apples, pocket money, and forgiveness for his numerous trespasses; and now in his early manhood he got privileges and immunities which were equally valuable. He was allowed a day or two's shooting in September; he schooled the squire's horses; got slips of trees out of the orchard, and roots of flowers out of the garden; and had the fishing of the little river altogether in his own hands. He had undertaken to come mounted on a nag of his father's, and show the way at the quintain post. Whatever young Greenacre did the others would do after him. The juvenile Lookalofts might stand aloof, but the rest of the youth of Ullathorne would be sure to venture if Harry Greenacre showed the way. And so Miss Thorne made up her mind to dispense with the noble Johns and Georges, and trust, as her ancestors had done before her, to the thews and sinews of native Ullathorne growth.

At about nine the lower orders began to congregate in the paddock and park, under the surveillance of Mr. Plomacy and the head gardener and head groom, who were sworn in as his deputies, and were to assist him in keeping the peace and promoting the sports. Many of the younger inhabitants of the neighbourhood, thinking that they could not have too much of a good thing, had come at a very early hour, and the road between the house and the church had been thronged for some time before the gates were thrown open.

And then another difficulty of huge dimensions arose, a difficulty which Mr. Plomacy had indeed foreseen and for which he was in some sort provided. Some of those who wished to share Miss Thorne's hospitality were not so particular as they should have been as to the preliminary ceremony of an invitation. They doubtless conceived that they had been overlooked by accident; and instead of taking this in dudgeon, as their betters would have done, they good-naturedly put up with the slight, and showed that they did so by presenting themselves at the gate in their Sunday best.

Mr. Plomacy, however, well knew who were welcome and who were not. To some, even though uninvited, he allowed ingress. 'Don't be too particular, Plomacy,' his mistress had said ; ' especially with the children. If they live anywhere near, let them in.'

Acting on this hint, Mr. Plomacy did let in many an eager urchin, and a few tidily dressed girls with their swains, who in no way belonged to the property. But to the denizens of the city he was inexorable. Many a Barchester apprentice made his appearance there that day, and urged with piteous supplication that he had been working all the week in making saddles and boots for the use of Ullathorne, in compounding doses for the horses, or cutting up carcases for the kitchen. No such claim was allowed. Mr. Plomacy knew nothing about the city apprentices ; he was to admit the tenants and labourers on the estate ; Miss Thorne wasn't going to take in the whole city of Barchester ; and so on.

Nevertheless, before the day was half over, all this was found to be useless. Almost anybody who chose to come made his way into the park, and the care of the guardians was transferred to the tables on which the banquet was spread. Even here there was many an unauthorized claimant for a place, of whom it was impossible to get quit without more commotion than the place and food were worth.

CHAPTER XXXVI

ULLATHORNE SPORTS—ACT I

THE trouble in civilised life of entertaining company, as it is called too generally without much regard to strict veracity, is so great that it cannot but be matter of wonder that people are so fond of attempting it. It is difficult to ascertain what is the *quid pro quo*. If they who give such laborious parties, and who endure such toil and turmoil in the vain hope of giving them successfully, really enjoyed the parties given by others, the matter could be understood. A sense of justice would induce men and women to undergo, in behalf of others, those miseries which others had undergone in their behalf. But they all profess that going out is as great a bore as receiving ; and to look at them when they are out, one cannot but believe them.

Entertain! Who shall have sufficient self-assurance, who shall feel sufficient confidence in his own powers to dare to boast that he can entertain his company? A clown can sometimes, do so, and sometimes a dancer in short petticoats and stuffed pink legs; occasionally, perhaps, a singer. But beyond these, success in this art of entertaining is not often achieved. Young men and girls linking themselves kind with kind, pairing like birds in spring because nature wills it, they, after a simple fashion, do entertain each other. Few others even try.

Ladies, when they open their houses, modestly confessing, it may be presumed, their own incapacity, mainly trust to wax candles and upholstery. Gentlemen seem to rely on their white waistcoats. To these are added, for the delight of the more sensual, champagne and such good things of the table as fashion allows to be still considered as comestible. Even in this respect the world is deteriorating. All the good soups are now tabooed; and at the houses of one's accustomed friends, small barristers, doctors, government clerks, and such like, (for we cannot all of us always live as grandees, surrounded by an elysium of livery servants), one gets a cold potato handed to one as a sort of finale to one's slice of mutton. Alas! for those happy days when one could say to one's neighbourhood, ' Jones, shall I give you some mashed turnip?— may I trouble you for a little cabbage?' And then the pleasure of drinking wine with Mrs. Jones and Miss Smith; with all the Joneses and all the Smiths! These latter-day habits are certainly more economical.

Miss Thorne, however, boldly attempted to leave the modern beaten track, and made a positive effort to entertain her guests. Alas! she did so with but moderate success. They had all their own way of going, and would not go her way. She piped to them, but they would not dance. She offered to them good honest household cake, made of currants and flour and eggs and sweetmeat; but they would feed themselves on trashy wafers from the shop of the Barchester pastry-cook, on chalk and gum and adulterated sugar. Poor Miss Thorne! yours is not the first honest soul that has vainly striven to recall the glories of happy days gone by! If fashion suggests to a Lady De Courcy that when invited to a *déjeûner* at with a smile, but with an intense and overpowering gaze ; and then holding up her forefinger, and slightly shaking her head she said :—

'Whatever you do, my friend, do not mingle love and business. Either stick to your treasure and your city of wealth, or else follow your love like a true man. But never attempt both. If you do, you'll have to die with a broken heart as did poor Dido. Which is it to be with you, Mr. Slope, love or money ? '

Mr. Slope was not so ready with a pathetic answer as he usually was with touching episodes in his extempore sermons. He felt that he ought to say something pretty, something also that should remove the impression on the mind of his lady love. But he was rather put about how to do it.

'Love,' said he, ' true overpowering love, must be the strongest passion a man can feel ; it must control every other wish, and put aside every other pursuit. But with me love will never act in that way unless it be returned ; ' and he threw upon the signora a look of tenderness which was intended to make up for all the deficiencies of his speech.

'Take my advice,' said she. ' Never mind love. After all, what is it ? The dream of a few weeks. That is all its joy. The disappointment of a life is its Nemesis. Who was ever successful in true love ? Success in love argues that the love is false. True love is always despondent or tragical. Juliet loved, Haidee loved, Dido loved, and what came of it ? Troilus loved and ceased to be a man.'

'Troilus loved and was fooled,' said the more manly chaplain. ' A man may love and yet not be a Troilus. All women are not Cressids.'

'No ; all women are not Cressids. The falsehood is not always on the woman's side. Imogen was true, but how was she rewarded ? Her lord believed her to be the paramour of the first he who came near her in his absence. Desdemona was true and was smothered. Ophelia was true and went mad. There is no happiness in love, except at the end of an English novel. But in wealth, money, houses, lands, goods and chattels, in the good things of this world, yes, in them there is something tangible, something that can be retained and enjoyed.'

'Oh, no,' said Mr. Slope, feeling himself bound to enter some protest against so very unorthodox a doctrine, 'this world's wealth will make no one happy.'

'And what will make you happy—you—you?' said she, raising herself up, and speaking to him with energy across the table. 'From what source do you look for happiness? Do not say that you look for none? I shall not believe you. It is a search in which every human being spends an existence.'

'And the search is always in vain,' said Mr. Slope. 'We look for happiness on earth, while we ought to be content to hope for it in heaven.'

'Pshaw! you preach a doctrine which you know you don't believe. It is the way with you all. If you know that there is no earthly happiness, why do you long to be a bishop or a dean? Why do you want lands and income?'

'I have the natural ambition of a man,' said he.

'Of course you have, and the natural passions; and therefore I say that you don't believe the doctrine you preach. St. Paul was an enthusiast. He believed so that his ambition and passions did not war against his creed. So does the Eastern fanatic who passes half his life erect upon a pillar. As for me, I will believe in no belief that does not make itself manifest by outward signs. I will think no preaching sincere that is not recommended by the practice of the preacher.'

Mr. Slope was startled and horrified, but he felt that he could not answer. How could he stand up and preach the lessons of his Master, being there as he was, on the devil's business? He was a true believer, otherwise this would have been nothing to him. He had audacity for most things, but he had not audacity to make a plaything of the Lord's word. All this the signora understood, and felt much interest as she saw her cockchafer whirl round upon her pin.

'Your wit delights in such arguments,' said he, 'but your heart and your reason do not go along with them.'

'My heart!' said she; 'you quite mistake the principles of my composition if you imagine that there is such a thing about me.' After all, there was very little that was false in anything that the signora said. If Mr. Slope allowed himself to be deceived it was his own fault.

Nothing could have been more open than her declarations about herself.

The little writing table with her desk was still standing before her, a barrier, as it were, against the enemy. She was sitting as nearly upright as she ever did, and he had brought a chair close to the sofa, so that there was only the corner of the table between him and her. It so happened that as she spoke her hand lay upon the table, and as Mr. Slope answered her he put his hand upon hers.

'No heart!' said he. 'That is a heavy charge which you bring against yourself, and one of which I cannot find you guilty——'

She withdrew her hand, not quickly and angrily, as though insulted by his touch, but gently and slowly.

'You are in no condition to give a verdict on the matter,' said she, ' as you have not tried me. No; don't say that you intend doing so, for you know you have no intention of the kind ; nor indeed have I either. As for you, you will take your vows where they will result in something more substantial than the pursuit of such a ghostlike, ghastly love as mine——'

'Your love should be sufficient to satisfy the dream of a monarch,' said Mr. Slope, not quite clear as to the meaning of his words.

'Say an archbishop, Mr. Slope,' said she. Poor fellow ! she was very cruel to him. He went round again upon his cork on this allusion to his profession. He tried, however, to smile, and gently accused her of joking on a matter, which was, he said, to him of such vital moment.

'Why—what gulls do you men make of us,' she replied. 'How you fool us to the top of our bent ; and of all men you clergymen are the most fluent of your honeyed caressing words. Now look me in the face, Mr. Slope, boldly and openly.'

Mr. Slope did look at her with a languishing loving eye, and as he did so, he again put forth his hand to get hold of hers.

'I told you to look at me boldly, Mr. Slope ; but confine your boldness to your eyes.'

'Oh, Madeline !' he sighed.

'Well, my name is Madeline,' said she ; ' but none except my own family usually call me so. Now look me

in the face, Mr. Slope. Am I to understand that you say
you love me ? '

Mr. Slope never had said so. If he had come there with
any formed plan at all, his intention was to make love to
the lady without uttering any such declaration. It was,
however, quite impossible that he should now deny his
love. He had, therefore, nothing for it, but to go down
on his knees distractedly against the sofa, and swear that
he did love her with a love passing the love of man.

The signora received the assurance with very little
palpitation or appearance of surprise. ' And now answer
me another question,' said she ; ' when are you to be
married to my dear friend Eleanor Bold ? '

Poor Mr. Slope went round and round in mortal agony.
In such a condition as his it was really very hard for him
to know what answer to give. And yet no answer would
be his surest condemnation. He might as well at once
plead guilty to the charge brought against him.

' And why do you accuse me of such dissimulation ? '
said he.

' Dissimulation ! I said nothing of dissimulation. I
made no charge against you, and make none. Pray don't
defend yourself to me. You swear that you are devoted
to my beauty, and yet you are on the eve of matrimony
with another. I feel this to be rather a compliment. It
is to Mrs. Bold that you must defend yourself. That you
may find difficult ; unless, indeed, you can keep her in
the dark. You clergymen are cleverer than other men.'

' Signora, I have told you that I loved you, and now
you rail at me ? '

' Rail at you. God bless the man ; what would he
have ? Come, answer me this at your leisure,—not without
thinking now, but leisurely and with consideration,—
Are you not going to be married to Mrs. Bold ? '

' I am not,' said he. And as he said it, he almost hated,
with an exquisite hatred, the woman whom he could not
help loving with an exquisite love.

' But surely you are a worshipper of hers ? '

' I am not,' said Mr. Slope, to whom the word worshipper
was peculiarly distasteful. The signora had conceived
that it would be so.

' I wonder at that,' said she. ' Do you not admire her ?